THE
DARK
ELEMENT

MASON J.
TORALL

MASON J. TORALL

Cover by No Sweat Graphics by Rachel A Olson
Interior Design and Formatting by Fancy Pants Book Formatting
ISBN 13: 978-0692438848
ISBN 10: 069243884X

For Catie,
The catalyst who woke me up

MASON J. TORALL

ACKNOWLEDGMENTS

An army made this possible. Some of you have been along for the ride since the beginning (all fifteen damn years ago), some joined very recently (within the last three), but you all gave me more than you'll ever know. Some day, I hope to be able to thank you all personally (as I've never met many of you), but through this, I hope you understand my gratitude:

Firstly, I'd like to sing praise to my little sister, Luna. Her patient listening through all those evenings between episodes of Voyager and Castle helped me believe that what I was doing was worth something. That kind of support is worth it all.

Next up is my dear friend and writing partner, Colleen Oakes, as well as her husband, Ryan. They've both been there since I finished the first draft, and they've both given me an endless supply of ideas, selfless advice, encouragement, and good memories. The plot bunnies Colleen and I chase have sometimes been full of tough love, but I know I'm a better writer for it.

I also owe my most somber gratitude to David Hall, who is tragically no longer with us. He was the generous man who introduced me to Colleen, and he was taken far too soon from this world. Dave, wherever you are, I wouldn't be where I am without you.

Beyond my closest confidantes is the inner circle, including my beta readers, alpha readers, and my copyeditor. Of the betas: Maura Holtman Williams, Shelby Rae Davis, Nadia Ariana, Chris Kerdo, Brittany Dewald, Karen Groves, Tyler Robinson, Nathan Latif, Stu Miller, Jessica Paetow, and Colleen Oakes; the alphas: Zane Showalter-Castorena, Aly Albert, Tyler Robinson, Nathan Boyer, Ryan Oakes, Aaron Pendergast, and

Stefani Pendergast; and my copyeditor: the generous and understanding Jeni Miller. You guys are the best.

Following my content workaholics comes those of you who turned this thing from a simple manuscript into a shining bona fide novel with the truly brilliant star of support that was the Kickstarter campaign. So many steps, so many things to do, and you've all been so patient with me: Nick Runge for the stunning cover art, Katherine Wampler for the Kickstarter banners, Tony Creedon for the sweet titling and Facebook banners, the beautiful and talented Shelby Rae Davis for fast-capturing my Kickstarter video and her use of mad photography skills, Jeff Seymour for his reality-check counseling on the Kickstarter, Aaron Pendergast for his Kickstarter advice, fellow author and graphic artist Rachel A. Olson for assembling the final amazing cover, Matt Bevirt for handling the art prints from the Kickstarter, Casey Harvell for all of the incredible interior formatting, Nathan Spiegal for financial counseling, and finally: the modern entities that made all of this possible: Kickstarter, Amazon, Apple, WordPress, T-Mobile, Facebook, Twitter, and Instagram. Say what you will about social media and technology, but I wouldn't be writing this without it.

And speaking of my Kickstarter: I have 74 ridonkulously magical people to thank for contributing to a random guy's dream. To all of you, who came from around the world to show your support: Thank you. My top backers: Dallas Porter, Tyler Robinson, Annie & Don Lopez, & Jessica Paetow, you kicked the campaign over the edge of amazing, but all my backers made it possible. So, as promised, you'll all find your name forever immortalized in your own section at the back of the book. Cheers, my dear friends.

Second-to-the-end there is a long list of names for people who—one way or another—put their energy into this monument of work. Be you family, friends, or something more/else, you've left your mark: Catherine Hill, Stefan Fuller and the Fuller family, Nathan Boyer and the Boyer family, Jason Sego, Mary Sego, Shelby Rae Davis, Chase Nowotny & family, Gereon Fredrickson, Brynn Fredrickson & family, Mike Martinkus, Scott Allen & Debbie Meltzer, Ann & Don Lopez, Stu Miller, Danielle McDowell, the entire Toro family, the Davis family, the McCallie family singers, Sam Marie, Sam Nord, Paul Pavelko, Brandi Cunningham, the Dotson family, Billy Norton, Rachel Balkcom, Steve Jenkins, Marianne Thomason, Anne Burnett, Aj Parker and family, Keaton Cox, Evan Young, Erienne Moore, oh and so many more that I don't have room for.

Lastly, I would like to thank those who either don't know the contributions they made to The Dark Element (or its spiritual progenitor, The 12th Dimension), but your help has never been forgotten. Whether from an offhand comment a decade ago or some blunt feedback recently—or even your own work which moved me—you gave me the inspiration I needed to get this shit done at last: Connie Io, Aly Albert, Debbie Rabideau, C.S. Friedman, Chris Hardwick, Christopher Nolan, Wil Wheaton, Christopher Paolini, George R.R. Martin, Steven Spielberg, George Lucas, Joss Whedon, Nathan Fillion, Gene Roddenberry, the writers at Cracked.com, Stephen King, Orson Scott Card, Hans Zimmer, Steve Jablonsky, and so, so many more.

This story has only just begun, but I hope you all know how much your contributions have meant to me. I could never have reached this point without you.

Thank you all.

With my deepest gratitude and love,
Mason J. Torall
August 12, 2015

CONTENTS

MASON J. TORALL

PROLOGUE

The Moon.

In English, that name always sounded so... plain.

In Japanese, Moon is 'Tsuki', in German it's 'Mond', and in Arabic it's 'Kamar', but I've always been partial to Spanish. 'La Luna' just has a poetry to it that does more justice than the other choices in humanity's many languages.

Throughout our history, the Moon has been referred to in both the masculine and feminine, as a mistress who guides sailors at night, or a watchful guardian that provides inspiration and tales to tribal cultures. So many stories and legends have been told over the ages about our Moon.

We have always been creative creatures in that regard, but truly, La Luna is more than just our lone satellite. It serves as a reminder to all that beyond this tiny paradise we call home, there is a vast, unimaginably wondrous expanse of space. It stretches beyond the human imagination, and spans from the creation of our universe to the end of time. In that universe, we are but a whisper in the blink of an eye on the landscape of all things... but damn it all if we can't leave our mark on that microcosm. As far as I'm concerned, each life in the history of our race is a universe unto itself, and that's worth something.

I suppose, when we're all gone, if humankind failed to shake the waves of time, then hopefully in the course of our few million years on this plane, our souls, our cosmic energy, or our divine ascendancy—call it whatever you like—could still exist and know, that it was always enough for us simply to have lived.

—Lunar Admiral Jacob Hawkins
Excerpt from his personal journal
Dated October 12, 2128 (The day before The Conquering began)

**From the personal records of Lunar Admiral Jacob Hawkins:
Herein, an anecdotal transcript of the recent history of the planet
Earth and its resident dominant species: Humankind.**

--/**September 30, 2045**--\: World War Three begins\--

--/**October 3, 2056**--\: Engineers of German and the former United
States and Japanese nations activate the first Magnetic Fusion Reactor,
nicknamed the "Mag Fury," thereby beginning the work to stabilize
Earth's ravaged climate\--

--/**May 12, 2057**--\: World War Three concludes and all Weapons of
Mass Destruction of all varieties are officially decommissioned\--

--/**December 10, 2057**--\: The Earth Global Alliance (EGA) is born in
the city of Geneva. The lands of planet Earth are divided into five
"supernations" and locally governed lands as follows:

> The United Territories of the Americas,
> the Eurasian Union,
> the Regent Dynasty,
> the Middle Kingdom,
> & the Preserved Territories\--

--/**April 15, 2077**--\: Faster-than-light travel, coined "TransLight," is
discovered, prompting humanity to amend all future addresses to include
our sun, named "Sol"\--

--/**July 23, 2100**--\: In response to first sighting an alien craft in deep
space, the Solar Warfare Division is established on the Moon at the newly
christened Apollo Base, just outside the city of Home Luna—humanity's
first off-world colony\--

--/**December 10, 2105**--\: First Contact. Humankind encounters The
Collective, an interstellar empire of many alien species governed by two
ruling members. The encounter chiefly involves the Algaroth, one of those

ruling members. Humanity briefly encounters the other ruling species, the Volüul\--

--/**November 24, 2109**--\: The Treaties of Longevity are signed in Geneva. The Collective becomes humankind's first galactic allies and partners, and the Algaroth establish a permanent residence on Earth for trade of resources, technology, and culture. This sovereign city is christened "Solaroth," named such for practicality reasons to the aliens, conjugating "Sol" and "Algaroth"\--

--/**March 3, 2110**--\: Construction begins on a TransLight corridor called the "Conduit," a series of constructs that—once completed—will forge a highway between Earth and the Algaroth's homeworld of Shialga\--

--/**May 9, 2113**--\: The First Over-Seer, Dorvan Injyama, lord-commander of all Algaroth in human space, is seated in Solaroth\--

--/**[TI/ME/STAM/P ERROR]**--\: **[LOGS REMOVED]**\--

--/**April 3, 2123**--\: My intelligence-gathering subset of the Solar Warfare Division begins a quiet initiative to repurpose the Weapons of Mass Destruction left over from the Third World War. Our goal is to turn the weapons into planetary failsafe devices against potential alien occupation\--

--/**October 20, 2126**--\: After The Collective agrees to take human colonists back to Shialga, my Solar Intelligence Office (SIO) exposes an Algaroth mining facility in Africa for stealing raw materials that far outweigh the limits agreed upon in the Treaties of Longevity\--

--/**January 1, 2127**--\: The Solar Intelligence Office concludes that the human colonists bound for Collective space were lost intentionally. I keep the realization from being made public out of concern of backlash from The Collective. I now believe that our allies will soon betray us and attempt a coup of the Solar System\--

--/**January 9, 2127**--\: The Earth Global Alliance brings Over-Seer Injyama to tribunal, whereupon I formally dissolve our Treaties of Longevity with The Collective\--

--/**January 16, 2127**--\: A failed assassination on the Over-Seer brings retaliation. The Collective bomb a long stretch of civilian land in the Eurasian Union\--

--/**February 21, 2127**--\: First sighting of an Elemental. A man wreathed in fire assassinates Over-Seer Injyama in his citadel within the walls of Solaroth\--

--/**February 23, 2127**--\: The Battle of Dissolution marks the start of The Collective War. Humanity wins the battle and drives our former allies from the system\--

--/**August 31, 2127**--\: SIO reveals the Planetary Poison Nuke, or "PPN." Descendants of superweapons coveted during the Third World War, these nukes are capable of leveling a city or a mountain. The Lunar Admirals Council motions to seed Planet Earth with the weapons, thus offering a 'Final Option' against The Collective's certain return. The motion passes unanimously, and the PPN's are nicknamed, "the Nukes"\--

--/**October 13, 2128**--\: Day One of The Conquering. A yearlong period that begins when four hundred Collective warships descend on the starships of our Sol Armada. In the opening days, humankind's cities on Mars are burned. Home Luna, Apollo Base, and the Lunar Admirals Council on the Moon are destroyed\--

--/**October 17, 2128**--\: Day Four of The Conquering. After losing the Moon at the Battle of Luna, I order our starships to abandon Earth to The Collective. Acting Fleet Admiral Gresham Cole carries out the order, fleeing with our starships to prevent their irreplaceable loss. His orders are to repair the fleet and return to Earth\--

--/**October 17, 2128**--\: The Collective's armada bombs the city of Geneva from orbit. In response, human leadership delivers an ultimatum: Cease your attack or we will detonate the Nukes and end all life on Earth. The Algaroth cease their bombardment and commence a ground invasion instead\--

--/**[TI/ME/STAM/P ERROR]**--\: **[CORRUPTED LOGS PRESENT. FILES LOST]**\--

--/**April 10, 2138**--\: Croll Tan arrives in the Sol System and is named the Fourth Over-Seer of Earth. He lands in Solaroth to replace his third dead predecessor. His rule is quickly established as the worst yet for a bloodied humankind\--

--/**May 3, 2138**--\: A Navy battle group from the Regent Dynasty moves to retake Australia from The Collective. The new Over-Seer detonates captured Planetary Poison Nukes in the ocean, obliterating the battle group in a single stroke. There are no survivors\--

--/**August 18, 2138**--\: Over-Seer Croll Tan sends his forces to the heavily contested Yucatán Peninsula to take control of the Central American Bridge. His strategy routs human defenses and splits the United Territories of the Americas into independent continents\--

--/**October 25, 2138**--\: At the Battle of San Andreas, Over-Seer Croll Tan shatters the San Andreas Fault in North America with a fault ram, causing an earthquake that devastates the west coastline of the continent\--

--/**December 12, 2144**--\: The Fourth Over-Seer orders his occupying armies to fortify their holdings and return to Solaroth, much to the confusion of widely crippled human forces. Croll Tan leaves offensive forces in place on the west coast of North America and other select strategic locations\--

--/**January 10, 2145**--\:

CHAPTER ONE

A Puget Winter

The crack of splintering glass brought Damien Vilan's attention up. Fingers of frost crept their way over the building across the street, marking each broken frame. The frigid air claimed each polyglass window, one by one. Damien knew that tonight, the cold might break just one window. Tomorrow, it might break five. In the end it wouldn't matter how many broke; there was no life in the rooms behind the windows to worry. The sounds of cracking glass were only a matter of the cold reclaiming the Seattle Islets with the inevitability of a glacier.

From his perch in the second-story window, Damien surveyed the building opposite him for movement. Not a hint of light or life disturbed the cold checkerboard of broken polyglass. The building stood quite still, a little crooked from the earthquake, and looming, dominating the block, yet it seemed almost lonely for doing so. Regardless, it offered no hint of warmth to Damien, and he intended no hospitality in return. Below, the street remained just as quiet.

He sighed. *Just like most of the city*, he thought. He flexed the stiff fingers in one glove, then traded his journal and hot-pen to the other hand to do the same. His breath came out in a fine mist as his knuckles crackled. He flinched at the sound.

Damien longed to shift positions, but moving even to retrieve the tiny journal from his boot was dangerous. He shouldn't have done it, but a quick check on the sleeping display within his goggles told him that there was still time. When he'd flexed the worst of the cold from his fingers, he stared back at the beginnings of an idea he'd been jotting down, and forgot his place.

21

Shit, what was it? I just had it. He grimaced and chewed the end of his pen, thinking, but it was no use. The idea was gone. *Okay... nevermind then.* He clicked the hot-pen and carefully burned the letters out on the waxy paper of his journal, *'lost train of thought.'* Then he closed the journal and slipped it carefully back into his boot.

Taking a slow, silent breath, Damien suppressed a hiss as cold air penetrated his lungs. He threatened to cough but held it down, forcing the air to seep through the worn armpits of his jacket instead. Tensing against the bite, Damien refused to shiver. He fidgeted as little as possible, but three hours on the windowsill in the empty apartment had left him stiff and irritable. Waiting was part of the plan though, and he knew better than to bitch about it. His brother wouldn't have it.

Not to mention this was your idea, another voice said. *It's not fair to make him sit out here when you made such a fuss about doing this raid tonight.*

He rolled his eyes at his own logic. Right or not, he'd already put both he and his brother in far more danger than they usually cared for this evening, and it had left a sour taste in his mouth. *It's our best shot*, he repeated, as he'd been doing all night. *Knock out the patrol, strip their gear, take the black box, and leave. No gunplay, no power play, no killing.* It was a simple plan, and the risks were worth the potential rewards—he hoped.

Even if it works, we'll have to reach out to someone about our hacking rig, and that's assuming the rig works at all. He shook off the thought. *It'll work. There's a first time for everything, even cracking into The Collective's data networks.* He grinned. *It'll work.*

Going over the plan in his head, Damien's gaze went back to a fissure in the building across. The crack splintered up three stories of framework, making the entire structure lean oppressively towards him, narrowing the street. As far as he could hear, the Seattle Islets were completely dead. No sound but the wind and the distant moan of tree branches punctuated the dark sky above.

Damien knew there were occasional pockets of life sprouting throughout the city, but they were quiet, shriveled, or fearful things.

Damien and his brother avoided them when they could, and only dealt with the few people they knew when they had to. No one had come out of the earthquake in one piece, and anyone left just wanted to preserve what bits of their lives remained. The few people with whom he and his brother *did* have regular contact would often say that The Collective didn't hold the city. They'd say that humans still owned Seattle, the Puget Sound, and the other Olympic Isle cities, but Damien would privately retort that he saw *Collective* patrols on the streets, not human, and definitely not any defected Algaroth.

In conversations like those, Damien had always wanted to respond to the insurgent survivors of Seattle that so many cities around the world were far worse off than they. Cities like Port Angeles, Mérida, and Marrakesh that had been contested into the ground over years of skirmishing the enemy. Or even worse, they could have been wiped off the map completely, like Geneva, Perth, and Madrid. Those places would never again be known outside the annals of history, all thanks to The Collective, and these stubborn survivors could sit and say *they* had it rough? Damien shook his head. *We haven't been as lucky as some, but least we don't have an active extermination happening here.*

The wind slunk through the open window once more, and this time Damien couldn't suppress the shiver. It didn't take him checking his goggles' display to know that a storm was coming. A blizzard was brewing out over the Puget Sound. Safe cities, occupied cities, dead cities, none of them could change the wind.

Frozen strands of black hair blew into Damien's face and he quickly brushed them away. He needed a haircut, but he preferred a bit longer hair in winter. *Maybe I'll just grow it out*, he thought. *A ponytail is practical, right?* He chuckled. *Sure it is.*

Damien checked the heating circuitry in his jacket and saw that the lining's temperature had fallen sharply in the last hour. The solar threads were almost out of charge. Clenching his teeth, he checked the clock on his sleeping goggle display. The little digital counter ticked to 3:06, and a shimmer of movement caught his eye. His gaze shot upwards, hoping it was just a bird.

23

It was the first flakes of snow.

Damien grumbled under his breath. Snow was the last thing he wanted to deal with. Snow was cold, wet, and it brought anathema to Damien and his brother's carefully quiet existence; snow made them easy to track.

Hurry up, Von. Damien's navy blue gaze narrowed behind his goggles. The stillness in the air grew thicker by the second as a thin curtain of white veiled the air.

A grayish pallor from the city bounced off the clouds above, offering ambient light. Other than that, the only real illumination came from the south end of the street, where a streetlight stood. The lonely piton pillar was tall and thin, glowing from cap to base, ever illuminating the way for people who were no longer there. Damien watched that corner of the building, keeping one eye on his clock.

Three minutes.

The wind carried the flakes right into Damien's window, dusting his boots and knees in white. His ensemble as a sentinel was complete, and his thoughts grew still as the seconds counted down.

Finally, his clock hit 3:15.

A single tiny beep sounded in the earpiece resting next to his aural implant. He resisted the urge to scratch his ear; the items tickled when they rubbed together.

Right on time, the quiet was broken by muted footfalls from around the block. They were heavy, large, and moving fast, but sounded as if they were trying to make as little noise as possible on the deserted streets. No easy task, Damien knew. His gaze jumped to the piton pillar, staring it down, as the footfalls grew louder.

Long into his stare, Damien realized that the person was running from much further away than he'd thought, but the silence had made the sounds carry farther. Even so, it didn't take long for the large form of a man to come sliding around the corner, narrowly avoiding a collision with the piton pillar.

Finally.

He stared at the man, who quickly hugged the corner of the building. The figure was tall—even from this distance that much was obvious—and he was wrapped in a dark cloak that fell in folds over his head and around his body, making it impossible to know how large he actually was.

As Damien watched from his perch, the man produced a large bag. The contents jangled and scraped metallically. Damien winced. The figure pulled out a handful of what appeared to be twisted metal and scrap. He tossed it back around the way he'd come and hid the bag from sight.

Breadcrumbs, Damien smirked. *Only you would think of leading them with a trail of breadcrumbs, Vo.*

They both were still for a moment, cloaked figure and sentinel, listening over a whisper of wind and snow. The man must have heard something, because he jerked back around the corner and bolted towards Damien's building

Damien's muscles tensed on instinct as the figure came closer. His gaze followed the man's approach. When the figure was almost beneath the window, Damien fluttered his eyes in a controlled pattern. The violet lenses of his goggles flashed a dim pulse into the night.

The cloaked figure jerked his head towards the window, and the hood fell back to reveal the deep blue features of an Algaroth. The alien's long face had a snout like a prehistoric raptor, with predatory nostrils and thin, leathery lips that pulled tight against his teeth. A set of lean, bony ridges traced back from the alien's nostrils, broke for his eye sockets, and jumped to form eyebrow-like protrusions along his curved skull. The ridges over his eyes were adorned with strips of pale-pink ganglia that twitched and flexed of their own accord, expressing much on the hard face.

Damien had grown up around Algaroth and could tell them apart better than most, but anyone who couldn't tell one alien from another would say that it was always their eyes that gave them away. An Algaroth's eyes were their hallmark—usually a similar hue of gold—but it was the smattering of other colors that might dot their irises that made them truly stand out. The creature that gazed up at Damien's perch had brilliant gold eyes, lamp-lit in the dark, but Damien only relaxed as he spied the hints of green in them. He locked eyes with the emerald-flecked, golden gaze of his adopted alien brother, Silas Von.

Damien stuck an arm out the window so Von could see it, and made a pumping motion. His brother's thin lips pulled back to reveal mostly pointed teeth in a smirking grin. Von nodded, and Damien retracted his arm.

Without stopping, Von produced another handful of scrap from the bag in his cloak. The noise was awful as the Algaroth launched the metal and tin across the street and behind him. The bits left skittering trails in the perfect layer of snow, and settled around a very specific lump in the concrete—a fist-sized mine that they'd cemented into the street the day before. By the time the scrap settled, the alien had gone beneath Damien's window and out of sight. The sound of Von's footfalls lost their caution as they shrank behind Damien's building.

Before the sounds of Von's retreat had vanished completely, another sound began to rise. It was coming back from the way Von had come. Damien tensed as he listened to it. In a moment, he realized it wasn't the sound he'd been expecting. His heart leapt into his throat.

The sound hissed and sputtered like a noisy cat coughing continuously. Damien's likeness of the noise to a feline did little to make him feel better, though. He'd been hoping to hear something deeper and more guttural. *That* was what they were ready for, just a regular manned Collective patrol skiff, loaded with soldiers that made their rounds shooting people. *That* was what he'd wanted to hear. Their plan tonight hinged on it. *This* sound though…

Son of a bitch, he thought. *That's not a normal skiff. That's a Razer— heavy patrol skiff.*

His realization came too late. The split-second he would have had to back out or call Von vanished, along with his calm. He lost the chance to think or plan, he only had time to act as the manned patrol craft skulked into view.

The Razer's cat-like sputtering diminished as it poked around the edge of the street, sharp instruments prickling. With only a second to act, Damien tapped the lid of the canister he'd taped to his wrist. The contents hissed into the air and settled over him, smelling like some acrid, swampy aerosol. He clamped down on the urge to gag just as the Razer's fine instruments whizzed to life.

The alien patrol fired the Razer's scanning pulse, and the street filled with the horrible sound of a woman's garbled shrieking. The shrieking mellowed as the pulse zipped towards Damien's window. It passed the bits of metal Von had left to obscure his charges, tinkling lightly as it did so, but sounding no alarm. Then it was passing Damien's window. Goosebumps exploded down his body as the shriek prickled past him… and didn't make a sound. He breathed a sigh of relief; the spray had worked.

The feline coughing rose before the pulse reached the end of the street, and the Razer slipped into view, its crew satisfied. Damien stared down the vehicle.

The Razer had no wheels, floating instead onto Damien's street on powerful skimming thrusters that torched the pavement underneath. The skiff was shaped roughly like an old flatbed truck—though it was larger than the trucks he'd seen at the museum—and it moved with a fluid grace that called up a closer likeness to a sea turtle, bobbing and sliding laterally through the air. Yellowish viewports hid the inside of the foreward cabin, set in a dull gray body of metal. Two spindled turrets hung out from the craft like sea turtle fins—both of which were manned and powered—but it was the flat rear deck that made Damien's breath quicken. The deck was open, wider than the cabin, and fully manned.

Damien counted nine Collective patrolmen on the deck. All were Algaroth, all wore the faceless and contoured, pearly-white armor of their Collective empire, and all wielded pronged, thick-bodied Gyro rifles. All nine rifles were aglow, and between the guns' prongs were brilliant, spitting globs of pale plasma, itching to be let loose. Damien only had his Plaster pistol, snug in its holster.

Nine armed patrolmen on the deck, two in the spindle turrets, and the three that Damien knew would be manning the foreward cabin made fourteen soldiers coasting towards him. Fourteen Collective on a Razer was too many to non-lethally hit in the time they had. If there were a way

27

to stop Von's charges from firing then, Damien would have. He and Von didn't have time to do all they needed to do with that many foes. It just wasn't possible, but by now his brother was on his way back around the block, and he couldn't get off the street without being detected. They were committed.

We're in trouble.

The heavy skiff snooped forward. Damien glared down the street, unmoving. Part of him wished they could have simply left a lethal trap and stayed in for the night, but they needed that black box intact for their hacking rig, and to do that, they needed to completely incapacitate the patrol. If they couldn't, then the patrol would raise an alarm and their commanders would deactivate the precious codes within the box, rendering the entire operation as a night of pointless endangerment.

Closer, the Razer came. It wheeled a single searchlight over the trail of metal breadcrumbs Von had left. As the vessel inched forward, Damien squinted repeatedly and his goggles zoomed in on the rear deck. He scanned the soldiers' boots, and felt marginally confident that none of them wore the pneumatic "frog-leg" boots of an Avo—an Algaroth commando. He would rather risk warning Von away and chance being spotted than follow through with a raid that involved even a couple of *them.*

His muscles tensed and the air thickened with light snow. The hovercraft drifted forward through the curtain, slowly becoming obscured. Damien fixated on the orange dot he'd painted on the building opposite, marking where the Razer needed to cross.

Come on... Come on...

The Razer's nose went over the line.

Closer...

He flipped the switch on the detonator, hovering just over the little red button. The acid focus of adrenaline filled his veins.

The Razer went over the line. Damien took a steadying breath.

Click.

Von's line of buried charges blew in two neat columns across the street. The staccato of explosions shattered the building. Lines of rubble exploded down onto the pavement below, boxing the Razer in on both sides. Dust and snow filled the air and a hot smell of burning metal and brick washed over Damien. The patrol barely had a moment to react as the brothers' second punch followed right behind.

From high on both sides of the street, beyond the range of the scanning pulse, four huge parabolic loudspeakers began emitting an ear-splitting funnel of sound at the stunned patrol. From his perch, Damien could hear the angry screaming emitted by the military-grade aural weapons—called "wave-busters"—like a distant underwater howl. He was glad he wasn't on the receiving end.

Below, the soldiers writhed on the Razer. They leapt onto the street, gripping their helmets as they tried to escape the aural bombardment, but Damien had been thorough. The overlapping funnels pulsed through every centimeter between the barricades of rubble. The aliens couldn't escape the ululating howls. Within seconds, all eleven of those outside the cabin were scattered on the ground, gripping their helmets and twitching.

Damien checked the countdown timer that had clicked to life inside his goggles. Fifteen seconds remained until the weapons stopped. They should start to lose consciousness in eight. He waited four and then spun from the balcony, stretching his legs at last. He pelted back through the abandoned apartment. Out the front door he went, down the hall and through the open door to the stairwell. The steps went by three at a time. He shouldered through the cold door into the alley when the timer had a second left.

Still cautious, Damien crept to the mouth of the alley and peered into the street. Just as he did, the wave-busters abruptly cut out, leaving an echoing silence in their wake A few small fires had started in the gaping voids of the opposite building. None of the patrolmen moved. He glanced up the street after another short count until—right on time—Silas Von stepped calmly through the entryway three doors down. To his credit, Damien saw Von flinch for only a second at the sight of the Razer and the number of bodies before they went to work, each picking their way over still smoking rubble.

The brothers moved forward without a word. Von tossed Damien a large duffel and they each took the closest alien. Damien's hands were a blur as he unlatched weapons, armor, power cells and communications gear, throwing them all into the bag. They took anything to slow the patrol down without killing them. Crippled patrols spread uncertainty in their army camped outside of Portland; dead patrols incited *more* patrols, and faster investigations.

Von swept to his second victim just as Damien pulled the gloves from his first, almost cutting himself on the creature's sharp, tool-like fourth and fifth fingers. Damien's lip twitched in mock irritation as his brother got ahead of him, claiming the modesty of his kin faster than he could manage.

It's because his hands are bigger, he thought, snorting. He stepped up his pace and moved to his second victim.

As they went, he kept close watch on the stopwatch that had begun the moment the wave-busters turned off. It read "00:38" and counting.

Damn, he thought. He was running slowly tonight.

1:00.

Damien snapped to get Von's attention. His brother's head jerked up with his arm stuffed in his duffel. Damien did a rapid series of hand-signals, and then pointed at the Razer. His brother nodded and quickly finished with his downed soldier. A moment later, he sealed his duffel and dumped it at the side of the skiff. Von bounded over the swiveling turret fin and vanished over the railing.

1:40.

Damien took a deep breath to keep his head clear, but he couldn't stop his eyes from darting between the nearly naked creatures, searching for signs of movement. He moved towards the third to last soldier on this side of the Razer, and froze on approach.

With a muffled growl, the alien rolled onto its stomach and grasped its skull. Damien's eyes grew wide and he shot forward, all instinct. He turned his focus inward, taking barely a second to follow the familiar corridor through his mind, deep into his inner psyche—to his core—to awaken the dark pool of power that rested there.

He imagined it in his mind as he always did: a cave lit only by a sourceless glow, filled with black liquid. The liquid had instincts of its own, and Damien always could tell how tired he was by how full he pictured the pool. He couldn't explain how he was always right with that, but he was. He urged the pool to life, and like a smooth, amorphous creature heeding its masters' call, the pool expanded. It flowed out of the cave, through the maze of organs in Damien's body, and cleared his mind with intoxicating purity. Time slowed, Damien's reactions grew smoother, and the world lit up in the sharpest detail.

He skidded around bits of brick toward the alien's head, taking in the details of the armor. Scratches and divots adorned it, and he saw little stains on the air vents over its shoulder from some time when the soldier had been in space. Damien took it all in while he let his power spill through his heart and lungs, saturate the muscles in his body, and eventually flow through his fingertips. He grasped the Algaroth's helmet, and his Elemental powers came to life.

At the touch, Damien's senses exploded. In his mind he could see the mind of the soldier, sluggishly trying to respond to the assault. It was slow and still mostly paralyzed from the wave-busters. Damien launched a cloud of dark tendrils through the alien brain, seeking out the light produced by the billions of firing synapses. The alien mind felt very different from a human one, but not so different as to be unrecognizable.

His power spread over its thoughts and, with only the faintest urging, he smothered its consciousness in the power he called a "Shroud." Instantly, its fleeting brush with awareness was crushed, and the Algaroth face-planted into the street in a deep slumber.

The event took barely ten seconds, but those were ten seconds not spent crippling the patrol. Damien blinked, forcing the sharpened tint from his vision as his powers receded.

1:59.

Five aliens had been stripped of their gear; four remained—including the one he'd just knocked out. Damien dropped to the ground to query the far side of the Razer. He spotted three bodies there, all fully armed, but unmoving. Each had already been coated in snowy powder.

That leaves—

—He heard commotion from within the Razer. A clang and a muffled discharge echoed over the street. The shot sounded like a cannonball over the idling whine of the skiff. Damien leapt up as he heard the cabin door slam open and someone growled.

He cursed not being able to see over the railing as the sounds of a scuffle broke out on the rear deck. Snarling impacts met Damien's ears, and he took a tentative step, unsure if his brother needed help. The answer came as his cloaked comrade was chucked off the rear deck, landing hard in a heap. *Yes, yes he does.*

He moved, bringing the receding pool back to his hands with a violent urging. He swung onto the high bottom step and gazed for the attacker. As it turned out, he was looking for an enemy in plural.

A pair of burly, dark blue Algaroth clad in only half of their armor faced away from him. One looked towards Von's crumpled form, the other over the far railing. They both looked disoriented and bloody, and one's arm hung dead. Dark, oily, purplish-blue blood dripped from the limb onto the deck.

At least Von didn't get shot.

The alien looking over the handrail started turning to check the near side. *Oh no you don't.* Damien brought his power to bear again, only this time with nothing to touch. In a split-second, the very air in front of him cracked open, and something formed in the fissure. It tore the fabric of the air over his palm, forging quickly into a spitting black ball. Damien's Orb bent the light around it and gave the sensation of something… *tugging.* The tiny, singularity-like creation was crowned in a violet corona so intense that when Damien looked at it, it felt like staring into a dark manifestation of the Sun—fathomless and implacable, black, lightless, and without warmth.

Silent and efficient, he hurled the miniature black hole towards his foe. The Orb bowled through the falling snowflakes and impacted the turning alien on its exposed chest. It splashed over the Algaroth's flesh in a wave of violet and black ink before the creature knew what had happened. The Orb shredded everything it touched, and the patrolman never made a sound as his body lurched backward over the railing and crunched into the pavement below. The shredding effect of the Orb was something Damien had coined "fazing."

He didn't have to check to know the Algaroth was dead before it hit the ground.

Unfortunately, the patrolman's burly partner had already spotted him, and fury flashed in its golden eyes. Damien was already pouring more energy into his other hand, but it wasn't fast enough.

Before he could do anything, there was a decisive *CRACK* and a sizzle, and the furious eyes dulled as the alien fell forward onto the deck. Damien froze, confused, until he saw the burning hole in the back of its head. He relaxed his mind, and the fissure in the air closed without a trace. He grinned as he saw Von stand up—decloaked and thankfully unharmed—holding a hissing Gyro pistol in the air, one of his splayed-toed boots planted on a hunk of the building. In his other hand he gripped the black box, appropriately colored but inappropriately named because it was actually shaped like a very large, ovoid pill. Von's nostrils flared and his emerald-gold eyes blazed beneath rigid ganglia. Von tipped the gun in salute, and Damien grinned before jumping off the Razer. He checked the timer and his smile vanished.

2:42.

Shit.

They were running out of time. The first soldier had been lucky to wake up so quickly, but the wave-busters would only keep even the weakest Algaroth out for about four minutes. Damien didn't have time to convey nonverbally any longer. "Von!" he hissed.

His brother's head poked around the back of the Razer. "*What?*"

"*Time!*" He tapped his wrist.

Von glanced at the display on his own wrist, and his ganglia fell flat. He looked back at Damien.

"We've gotta go!" Damien pointed around the skiff. In tandem to his warning, he heard a pair of grunts behind him. His stomach dropped. "*NOW!*" he snarled, as loud as he dared.

Von nodded and grabbed his duffel before disappearing around the rear of the Razer. Damien grabbed his own and bolted toward the nose. He slid on the lightly powdered pavement, doing his best not to fall. He managed to keep his balance and had just started to gain traction—when he collided squarely with an upright patrolman.

"*BAH!*" They toppled to the ground with a strangled cry and a snarl. Damien's face jammed into the pearly white armor, and for a second he thought he had spilled blood everywhere—until he realized he was looking at a pair of thin red stripes that ran the length of the alien's helmet and breastplate. His body moved faster than his mind could process when he realized the stripes were those of a Koro—the squad leader.

The alien blinked and flailed as they fell. The bearded helmet glared at the inscrutable lenses of Damien's goggles, but it was too late. Damien had already shoved his palm into the Koro's stomach and was unloading an unfocused spitfire of power into its abdomen.

The Algaroth gave a warbled shriek as its organs slipped through its spine. Oily blood zipped out and away from Damien's tight gloves, coming out in puffs of bluish mist as if the blood cells themselves had been eviscerated. Damien tried not to think about how brutal it must feel. Instead, his stomach gave a twinge of fear as he saw the hint of a cool blue light behind the gurgling alien's visor. Something had just turned back on.

He didn't have time to stop, but he had to. The corpse impacted with a *whump*, and the poof of blood-tinted snow spattered away from them.

"*SST!*" Von hissed. (Making the 'p', 'b', and 'm' sounds in English were difficult with the tight lips of his species.) "*What are you doing?!*"

"Koro!" Damien answered as he yanked the helmet off the body. The lights dimmed as he checked the timer on his own display. *We're so fucked.*

3:27.

"Quickly!" Von barked. The sounds of recovering aliens flooded the silence.

No, no, don't wake up. Don't see us, please don't see us, he fumbled with the Koro's helmet. "Got it!" He tossed the helmet over the barricade of rubble, sans its processor and power cell, and careened to his feet.

As they rounded the Razer, they heard the first cries of recognition from behind them. "GO!" Damien cried, unable to keep his voice down. *Goddammit I knew that was too many to take on!!*

They sprinted for the far side of the street and the perfectly camouflaged hole in the lobby window. Their reflective sheeting was held so tightly it didn't even wrinkle in the wind, which was starting to pick up. They were about to cross onto the sidewalk when Damien's neck prickled, and he spun back towards the Razer. His heart skipped.

A single soldier stood over the corpse of the Koro, pronged Gyro rifle drawn and sighted. Damien watched in time-slowing horror as the Algaroth squeezed off a shot.

Damien moved.

Breathing heavily, he let the powers of an Elemental flood out from his arms, chest, and head in the general direction of the shooter. Sound faded from the world as he let loose a Wave: a towering, rippling, *exhausting* wall of power that tore through the street.

Like a tsunami heaving its captive water back to land, Damien's Wave unleashed the held air and erupted forth from his body. It opened a similar fissure to his Orb, as if the world was made of a liquid glass illusion and he'd just shattered it. A wall of black and violet haze swallowed all other color, three times as tall as he.

The Wave ripped through the street, bound for the Razer and its crew—but it was too late. The single, glistening bolt of Gyro plasma zipped through the power before it had fully materialized… and pierced Von's left leg, just above the ankle.

His brother let out a dire yowl as the superheated flash of energy burned through his armor leggings, cooking flesh and bone. Damien's lightning-fast reflexes kept them from toppling through their hidden escape, but only just. Broken roars of agony cried after them as the Wave impacted, and Damien felt, rather than heard, an explosion. He turned just long enough to see the Wave kick the Razer into a barrel roll with as much effort as a child kicking a toy. Damien's power consumed the skiff and urged it over the patrol like a rolling pin. He moaned at the destruction, horrified at how quickly this had fallen apart, but the thought was fleeting as he grabbed his brother.

"COME ON!!" he roared, terrified. "VON, LET'S GO!!" The alien winced in pain. Von's pupils were already dilating into a bulbous, clover shape. He would go into shock in maybe a minute.

Damien dragged the pair of them—half-hobbling, half-running— through the dark and empty lobby. The sounds of his victims came shrieking after them, but no one followed.

They exited the far side of the building onto another empty street, and the dying cries of the patrol fell away within a few paces under the sudden blanket of snowfall. Damien didn't have time to worry about leaving footprints. They would just have to divert a bit on the way home. *Not that it'll matter. We're in so much fucking trouble.*

Grunting, he hauled the injured alien down the hill, heart pounding. He was keenly aware of how his boots crunched in the snow and of the obvious path they were leaving.

Near the bottom, they crossed the street to a low stone wall. There, Damien pulled Von into a brick courtyard. He gently lowered his brother onto a bench and then bolted past the overturned tables in the nook-like corner of what was once a little café. Inside, he strode around the counter where a silvery tarp hid something large. He swept it off to reveal one of his most precious possessions:

Shiny curves of black and silver coursed the body of his motorcycle (he called it that even though it was *technically* a hydracycle). It looked well used but sturdy, and it was spotted with odds and ends that didn't quite look like they belonged—parts of his restoration project. He yanked the bike from its hiding place, handling it with a rough but delicate grip. Damien rolled it out of the café, whispering thanks that no one had come snooping.

Outside, the storm was worsening. Von lay slumped over on the bench, where the heavy snowfall had already nearly covered him. "Von," he said, his voice swallowed in the night. "Get up. C'mon get up."

The Algaroth moaned and did his best to sit up, but he failed and gasped, shaking and reaching for his leg.

"No, no c'mon," Damien swatted his brother's hand away. "Just hop on the back seat and I'm gonna strap you in."

Von answered with a muted grumble as Damien gingerly lifted the injured leg over the back seat. He checked to make sure the cauterized wound wasn't bleeding before tying Von down. It did little to hold back his cutting fear for his brother. *If that wound gets infected, he'll die.* It wasn't a question. Algaroth immune systems worked differently than human ones. Even after forty years and two generations of aliens living on Earth, a simple infection could kill.

"Home, Vo," Damien whispered, fighting to control his terror. "Right now. Let's go."

A few seconds later, the growling thrum of the cycle wound through the courtyard, and the seams in the bike lit with a sharp orange tinge. The glow seeped inside the trimmed wheels as Damien inched out of the courtyard. He looked back to make one final check that Von was securely—if not comfortably—strapped to his waist, and to see if there were any signs of pursuit from up the hill. He saw and heard nothing but the storm, but he could swear he saw a hint of smoke above the buildings up the hill.

"Let's get the hell home," he repeated, his expression grim. *And hope they don't find us before we get there.* He kicked the throttle, and they shot off into the snowy streets of the Seattle Islets.

Chapter Two

Bone Bolt

With deft hands, Damien wove his motorcycle through the storm. The quiet city was already coated in white, but he knew the way. He loathed the trail they were leaving, but they had no choice, so he buried his concern. There was nothing he could do about it, and the trip home was a long one. Despite the conditions, the going was smooth, and the orange glow of his motorcycle lit the way. Even so, nothing could stem Damien's steadily worsening fear that an infection was taking hold in Von's leg. He tried to distract his focus from that as they wound their way through the dying city, terrified of what it would mean if there were.

Of the some fifty spits of land that made up the Seattle Islets, perhaps fifteen were still occupied. More than half of those were full of The Collective, while the rest were sparsely populated by defiant, stubborn, and scattered humans who called themselves members of the insurgent movement. Damien rarely had the patience to deal with most of them. They had no infrastructure, no leadership, and no real goals. Damien and Von at least had something to *do* with their days. They'd spent more than a year trying to put together the hacking rig so they could try and break into The Collective's military networks, and before that, they'd spent almost three years booby-trapping spots all over the city, trying to convince the enemy that the insurgents were far more dangerous and plentiful than they actually were. He rarely saw other insurgents doing anything useful beyond their own lives. That bothered him, but he and Von both felt better knowing that what they were doing was helping the city survive.

In the deepening snow, Damien sped faster across the islets he knew were safe. Von at one point found the strength to grip his arms tightly about his waist, but as the long minutes ticked by, his brother's grip lessened. Damien's stomach tightened. *Fuck it.* He hunched over the handles and shifted gear, taking a turn through a makeshift barricade hung with signs—a turn he had definitely *not* intended to make tonight. "TURN BACK," the signs read. "quake damage," and "FUCK THE OVER-SEER."

Down the street, Damien followed the curving path between empty vehicles and dangerous refuse. It wound back and forth until it reached what appeared to be a small hill. Damien throttled as hard as he could and tightened his grip. *Three... Two... One... Jump!*

The cycle ramped up the broken pavement and took to the air. Damien looked down as he did every time, and saw nothing, his heart thundering in his chest as they flew. The hill was actually a fracture from the earthquake, easily four meters wide. It went through the buildings on both sides, leaving gaping holes in them too. He felt cold snow spray his face as they came down over the far side, bouncing and eliciting a hiss of pain from Von.

Around the corner, Damien slalomed between a barricade and under a collapsed wall. He took a hard turn through an empty intersection, spraying powder on the crumbled ruins of a Buddhist temple. On the last standing face, a graffiti haiku had survived not only the quake, but also the years of neglect and passing people who had made the exodus from the city:

FAITHLESS DURING DAY
HANDS WE CLASP IN DEAD OF NIGHT
OUR SOULS DEFY YOU

Below it, a neat line of text still read:

Defiance protects no one
The slizzards have eaten our souls
We are conquered
October 28, 2128

He couldn't help but check the timestamp in the corner of his goggles, just to be sure. It read "January 10, 2145" in plain, green script. *Sixteen years,* he thought, shaking his head. By the time he looked back to the street, the dark ruins of the temple were behind them, but it wasn't long before they passed another. And another.

All twenty-five of Damien's years had been spent in Seattle, and—for however short a time as an adult, before the quake—he had known people in many of the buildings they passed. *Ruins*, he thought. *These are ruins, not buildings*. He and his brother were the only ones left from that time. *It's good they never saw how much worse things could get.*

Onward they went, past a familiar repair lot, then a communal home, and a book exchange where Von had learned to read English. Then a burned out market flew by, then a bar with a collapsed ceiling where Damien had celebrated his eighteenth birthday. Then a multi-fuel station—half-sunken in a crack in the ground, the other half blown out—went past, and finally a synagogue and mosque side by side, both places where Damien had tried to explore the concept of faith, and failed to understand.

Von's arms were nearly limp and he whimpered something Damien didn't catch. The sound brought his distracted thoughts back in a hurry. In his rush, Damien overcorrected and barely saved them from taking a fatal tumble, but it was the spike of focus he needed. He blinked away the creeping exhaustion, gave silent thanks that the dangerous shortcut had paid off, and took the last turn towards their home, past the exit sign that read "PUGET LUNAR SPACEPORT, TAKE I-405, NEXT EXIT, RIGHT 2 LANES."

Damien turned south onto the cracked I-405 interstate and gazed east. In the distance, he could just make out the collapsed superdome of the spaceport. He looked west. Over the broken I-5 interstate, he could just spot downtown through a break in the trees. Glaring holes rose through the Seattle skyline where glistening buildings once stood. Only the Space Needle—one of the oldest skyscrapers in the Puget Sound cities—could be picked out in the frigid torrent of snow.

"Almost there," he whispered as his brother's head bobbed on his shoulder. "Hold on, Vo. We're almost home."

At last, Damien jumped the cycle off the interstate and concluded the shortcut. He took a side street and sped down a makeshift ramp that he and Von had built on the stairs, and finally took the turn into the Mercer Tunnel, near the docks. Inside, the guttural thrum of the cycle grew louder as they rode beneath the Puget Sound.

They shot out of the refuse-strewn tunnel onto the Mercer Islet, running recklessly. The welcome sign, almost invisible covered in snow, was deeply reassuring, and Damien felt a layer of anxiety fall from his shoulders—surface anxiety, anyway. He sat up a little straighter, let his chin lift, and his gaze left the street, no longer as worried about sudden lances of plasma from around dark corners.

"Von," he said, trying to sound calm. "You still with me? We're almost there."

"Hrrnn…" came the weak reply. Damien ground his teeth in worry, feeling the alien's limp weight pressing down on him. He pictured Von's injured leg, throbbing with unseen pathogens.

At the southwest end of the islet was a hilled compound. The tall fences and warning signs had long been torn down or split apart, but the structures inside still stood, just above the close-knit buildings. Once, the place was a refuse repurposing plant where people would bring their trash to be sorted, recycled, and reshipped, so that it might be used in something else somewhere else. Now, it was home.

Ahead, a collection of small buildings sat dark and foreboding around a large warehouse and a long low prefab office trailer. Damien's tension slid away and his breathing calmed, just as it did every time he returned to see it all intact. He sped up the hill, knowing the way even as it was obscured by snow. A few sets of human and animal tracks skirted the perimeter of the plant, but none made their way up. Damien picked up momentum and broke trail towards the warehouse. There, he rolled up to a rusty industrial cargo container, tucked against the trailer. At the door, his goggles flashed and he blinked at the icon. A pattern appeared in the lenses and he traced the lock code with his gaze. When he finished, a beep sounded on both the door and in his earpiece, and the lock retracted with a *snick* in the cold.

Quickly, Damien parked his bike inside, untied his brother, and grunted as he took the majority of Von's nearly two-meters of weighty muscle on his shoulders. He left their duffels strapped to his cycle.

"Just keep it together a few more minutes," he said in a low voice, shoving the door closed. It made a satisfying *whump* as it impacted the muffling pads they had taped around the frame. The lock slid back in place and they hobbled into the warehouse, where a drift of snow had already started to form. In ten paces, his feet were frozen, his limbs stiff, but he didn't notice.

Inside the warehouse was barely better than out. The peeling roof and many broken windows had let plenty of snow into the gloom, and the temperature didn't register as any warmer. Luckily, the snow on the floor wasn't so thick, and the awkward pair navigated between the stacks of tall refuse containers.

"Vo, how do you feel?" Damien asked, barely keeping his teeth from chattering.

Von said nothing.

Damien took deep, freezing breaths and wove to the back of the warehouse. There, a clearing between the huge containers revealed stairs up to dark offices. Next to the stairs was a blank wall. Damien approached the wall, kicked their programmable camouflage sheeting out of the way, and made a quick mental note to fix it before he went to bed. Behind the false wall, a single lighting strip had been stuck above a hidden stairwell.

At the bottom, an archaic steel door sat in a heavy frame. Next to it, an old numeric keypad glowed a faint green. Damien punched in the code, and the steel door clacked open, swinging inward on well-oiled hinges.

Once inside, Damien kicked the door closed, leaving them in darkness and musty quiet. He pushed on into the gently sloping tunnel, unafraid. At the end, a much newer metal door sat, foreboding and impenetrable. He used the same eye-trace code to unlock it as he had for the container, and a beep echoed through the cement. Beyond, frosty polyglass panels hid a dark room from view.

Damien calmly said, "I cannot find Bravér's Rain," and the translucent doors slid open without a sound, belaying the high-voltage safety mechanisms he'd just disarmed.

At last, he let out a heavy sigh of relief. Damien stomped into the bunker he and Von called home, depressing the absorptive padding at the entryway. At the pressure, a faint humming filled the air, and interspersed tiles on the floor and ceiling lit up, filling the bunker with a pale and cool, yet cozy light. A perfectly square room revealed itself.

About twelve meters across, the bunker was plain and grey, the squared padding on the floor a light cyan. Hallways beckoned from the center of each wall into shadowy corridors or the kitchenette to their left. The main room was sparsely furnished. A couch sat in a depression in the center, and a workbench flanked the desktop against the far corner. The only adornment was a floor-to-ceiling pegboard covered in roughly assembled gadgets, tools, and coiled hardware.

Damien ignored the main room even as the desktop came alive, beeping insistently. Instead, he dragged Von towards the hall to the right. "Alright," he puffed. "Let's get you down on the slab." He couldn't tell if Von was breathing. He swallowed hard.

More lighting tiles came alive as they moved, while the ones behind dimmed or turned off, conserving power. At the end of the hall, Damien kicked his way into their compact infirmary. A large square of lighting tile lit it from above.

He pushed inside and finally let Von fall from his shoulder onto the medical "slab." Damien hissed as his muscles seized from carrying so much so far. The impact shook a reaction out of his brother, who growled limply and fluttered his eyes.

"Okay," Damien said through gritted teeth and a sigh of relief. "You're alive then, that's a start. Now get on your stomach. Let's go."

Von pulled his thin lips back in a weak scowl, rumbling his answer into the slab.

"Shut up and do it." Damien helped him onto his belly and pulled down the medical lamp. A half-sphere protruded from the lamp, full of instruments and accompanied by a detachable tablet. Damien brought the tablet to life and tapped the screen. "Boot faster you stupid son of a—thank you!" The apparatus purred to life and Damien lowered the tool ball towards Von's leg, finally taking the time to examine the wound. He steeled himself for what he might find.

Where the plasma had impacted, Von's calf looked as if a bite had been taken out of him and the remains cooked. The smell of scorched flesh didn't extend far from the wound, but when it hit him it made Damien's stomach tumble. He wrinkled his nose and moved closer with the tablet's camera, forcing himself to look hard for any signs of discoloration or inflammation.

Oozing, oily pus exuded from many punctures in the blue alien skin, which had taken on the pallor of any other corpse: pale and glistening with a moist sheen. No matter how well the shot had kept Von from bleeding out, the ride home had twisted and stressed the ruptured flesh, causing rivulets of the Algaroth's dark and oily purple blood to drip profusely, spattering the medical slab.

The smell of the pus worried him.

"Rrmmm…" Von squirmed as the tool ball started scanning his leg.

"Hold still you shick, or I'll strap you down." Damien grasped Von's foot to stop the fidgeting, watching as every movement squeezed more blood out.

Von ground his teeth at the pressure but held his leg still. "Is it—*ha*," he winced. "Is it as bad as it feels?" The alien took a few ragged breaths, fighting to stay focused while the thing whirred.

Damien didn't answer as an image of the leg slowly appeared on the tablet. He scrutinized the wound, checking and rechecking what the tool ball was telling him. His guts were clenched tight and every movement was stiff and awkward from fear. Damien tried hard to control his breathing as the tool ball finished its scan, and the results popped up on the tablet. Finally, he read the diagnosis, double-checked what the system said he should do, *triple*-checked the wound with his own eyes to make sure he had seen it right…

And he breathed a sigh of relief.

It was a tiny, insignificant sigh, but monumental in the truth of it, nonetheless. Damien's muscles unclenched as he read the tablet again. "NO INFECTION PRESENT".

Damien stifled his relieved grin. "Oh, it's bad," he said, trying to sound dire. "I think you're about to die, actually." He moved the module closer to the wound and double-checked what he was going to need to fix it. *No infection doesn't mean one couldn't still get in there. It is still a plasma wound, after all.* "I'll probably have to amputate your leg."

Von opened his eyes slowly, taking a slow breath as he forced out his words. "Why do you ever try to lie to me?"

"I'm not!" Damien tilted the tablet to hide his face. "It's really that bad!" He tapped more commands out and another tool began to cut away the burned fibers. "I'm gonna have to give you a wooden limb. It's very sad. Hey, maybe I could treat some of your oak bark and use that for your leg? You could get a fix whenever you needed, and we could stop looking for the damn stuff!"

Von growled over Damien's chattering, trying to get his attention.

"But you could only chew on it occasionally," Damien went on, his mind buzzing, wondering if they still had the item he needed to fix the gutted bone. "I wouldn't want to replace your leg every few weeks because you were too high to—"

"*Damien*," Von said with force, making the human stop. "How… *bad?*"

Damien stopped. "Could be worse."

Von's blue head fell back onto the slab with a *thunk* and he sighed. The wistful sound that slipped out was something between a hissing snake and a dog's whine. The alien blinked from the impact, trying to stay alert. Damien could see Von's thoughts drifting. He had to tell him before he passed out. A puddle of blood was forming on the slab, and some pocket of milky white pus had burst on the edge of the wound, releasing a much fouler stench.

"Von, can you hear me?" He moved away to the cabinet to retrieve everything he'd need. "There's no infection, but I'm going to have to operate or you'll have a dead leg." *If it isn't already.*

Returning to the table, Damien brought the tools he'd ended up with after spending a short time as an impromptu medic a few years ago—an experience he never cared to repeat. He found his brother taking slow, shallow breaths and actually trying to *itch* the hole. He swatted the heavy blue hand away. "Von? Wake up. Wake up; I need to tell you what's happening."

Von worked at his tongue, sounding exhausted. "Operate with what?" His voice was small, and between every word the tiny *drip, drip* of blood could be heard.

"It's just a small procedure… I promise." *Beyond excising that healing cellular layer you have so your whole leg doesn't grow necrotic and infected.* "It's just a little… incision." As he started to clean the wound, his tiny scraper must have caught a nerve, because Von cried out. Damien winced and slammed his hand to Von's chest, jerking the tool back. "I'm sorry! Hold still!"

Von held his eyes shut tight as the moment passed and Damien carefully went to cleaning the new mess.

"Okay," Damien said finally. "Good news first? Or bad?" He retrieved the cleaning supplies and salve from the tray, eyeing Von's movements.

Von blinked slowly. "Good."

Damien opened the jar of salve and delicately applied it to Von's torn skin. "Okay. Good news is: The shot was clean. It burned away your suit so none of that got into the muscle or melted to the bone." The salve solicited a pained hiss. Damien winced but continued, "There's no infection, and if we move fast that shouldn't become a problem."

Von narrowed his eyes. "Shouldn't?"

Damien eyed the little silver nub sitting on its sterile gel pad. *God I hope I'm doing this right.* "Bad news is… Umm, the shot seared most of your muscle away."

Von made his sighing-whine noise again.

Damien bumped the bone drill when he reached for the anesthetic, and he realized his hands were shaking. "Repairing it is gonna be tricky," he continued, trying to sound calm. "We don't have the equipment or the

47

supplies to do this properly, and to be honest I—I don't know enough to re-stitch your muscle by myself." He capped the supplies and set them down, controlling his breathing for what came next.

He didn't sound confident enough, and Von heard it. "Damien, make your, *ahh*—make…" he growled, trying to sit up. "The *POINT*?" Von enunciated the 'p', making Damien jump.

"Y—You need a cytomyotrophy!"

"A wha—"

"—It's a really complex surgery, okay? The muscle needs to be re-grown and stitched together *one fiber at a time* and I can't do that here. We don't have the tools. I mean I'm gonna give you a stopgap for your muscles until we can find help, but your bone, it… *that* I can try to fix, but your muscle, there's not much I can do but keep your defensive cell layer from breaking down beyond repair. And besides, I'm not sure the idea I have for your bone will work because it was never *designed* for this so I… I…" he trailed off. When Von continued staring at him, he picked up the gel pad on which the silver nub sat.

Von stared at the nub, his bulbous pupils condensing from a clover to a circle. "What is that?" A rare note of fear trickled into his voice.

Damien winced. "It's… it's a bone bolt."

The alien face didn't have the muscles to mimic human expression, but the likeness was close enough. Damien watched as his brother's face went from very still, to shaky, to denial, to angry…to resolved. Von's ganglia mirrored the movements, and eventually settled flat against his skull. "Okay."

Damien breathed a sigh of relief and pressed on. "I'm sorry. That shot hit you dead-on. It burned the suit, the muscle, and it splashed over your tibia." He handed the alien the tablet. "See?"

Von's face was unreadable as he gripped the portable screen.

"You were actually really lucky that it didn't hit any harder, because it damn-near melted the bone. Right now it's the consistency of rotten wood. I could snap your leg with a rubber mallet."

Von let the tablet weigh his arm down and he closed his eyes. "Damien," his voice was soft. "It's alright. Just do it."

Damien gave him a look. "No, it's *not* alright! Did you hear what I said? *Rotten wood.* The minerals, the fiber, the *marrow*, everything that makes your leg a functioning limb has been burned out! The cold and the plasma together probably are the only things that kept some disease from creeping in, but I have to get your leg under sterile guard as soon as possible and I can't do *that* until I fix your bone because your bone is a hollow tube right now! It has to be like this and it—"

"—Damien—"

"—has to be now—like I said—before an infection gets in there and—"

"—*Vilan!*"

Damien stopped, noticing for the first time that his jacket was glistening with blood spatter. He was sure it was on his face too, though he thought that might be from the Koro. He could feel how flushed his cheeks were.

"It's not your fault. And if you can't let it go, we'll… vrr… we'll talk in the *who*rning…" Von's lips had stopped trying so hard to have a neutral accent.

Damien's gaze went to the bone drill as the last of his brother's strength went out. He eyed the hollow cylinder and the shining silver spike at the tip, imagining himself drilling screws into a bone wall as if it were nothing. He shivered at the thought, and sighed. "Tonight went well," he finally said.

A hint of a chuckle rumbled from Von's chest. "Flawless."

They fell silent, and Damien reached for the drill. As he slipped the tiny silver nub inside, Von grasped Damien's wrist with a leathery hand. Damien met the emerald-gold gaze and grinned. "You won't feel a thing."

"You're a terrible liar."

Then, setting down the drill, Damien injected his wounded brother with an anesthetic cocktail, and watched Von fall into unconsciousness. When he was sure Von was out, he retrieved the drill and placed it gingerly over his brother's leg.

This better be worth it, he thought, placing the squishy padding flush against the exposed bone. Padded fingers snapped down as supports, and one disappeared with a little squelch into the damaged muscle. Von's entire body went stiff and a tiny whine escaped his lips. Damien looked away, fighting fury at himself for letting this happen.

Just get this done, he thought, going rigid. *You probably saved his life taking that shortcut home. This could keep him from needing an amputation.*

He flipped the switch on the pump on the floor and the roar of a motor filled the infirmary. The noise spiked so fast that Damien jumped. When the drill flashed green he clenched the handle. The bolt was primed; his heart was racing. The impacting tip sat ready to split open his brother's leg.

Damien swallowed. *Just do it. Just do it. You can do it. Do it do it do it!*

He pulled the trigger.

The *CRACK* was so loud Damien felt it in his ribs. The whole drill vibrated as the impacting tip drove down into his brother's bone, splitting it open and driving the tiny nub of metal deep inside his leg. Damien's own leg tingled as the image of someone firing a railroad spike through his knee came to mind, but he made himself watch the live scan on the display.

He watched as the bolt came to life—acting similarly to a match being struck—and heated to melting temperature in the microsecond it took to send it rocketing down the tube. Damien felt the heat a few centimeters off Von's leg as the bolt dissolved, filling the emptiness where minerals and marrow should have been. Even unconscious, Von's entire body seized on the slab.

If this works, this leg will actually be stronger than his other one. How about that?

He wasn't sure how long he stood there, fascinated and horrified as he watched the metallic cocktail fill every open pore in the alien bone. It flooded Von's leg, bubbling away and searing the deepest part of the limb. Damien watched the whole time, unmoving, taking in the tiny thrashes and whines Von made every few seconds. He gave silent thanks that they had been so lucky to scavenge as many meds and supplies as they had after the earthquake or both of them would have died many times over.

Damien grew even more melancholy remembering it, and he rubbed his forearms absently under his jacket. Neither he nor Von enjoyed thinking about the day their parents had died, mostly because it was all so blurry. All Damien recalled was that they had been in a building or a shelter when the earthquake hit, and then it was all black. The best either of the brothers could guess was that something had fallen and hit them both in the head, and then someone dragged them to safety, but they didn't know whom. They just remembered waking up together the day after to find the desolation of a city shaken to pieces, and their family torn apart.

He swallowed hard.

The Algaroth on the slab was all he had left, and though the two of them spent every day fighting their own fight against the usurping Collective, he knew that if anything were to happen to his brother, he'd be lost too.

Eventually, Damien noticed the bubbling of the bolt had slowed, signaling the first stage was completed. He went to check the tablet he'd been holding for what the scans showed, but he wasn't holding it. Looking around, he found that he'd dropped it without realizing. The sight of the rectangular device on the floor hit him like a ton of bricks, and the last traces of focus left his mind. Exhaustion took him, and Damien barely managed the strength to check how long it would be before the bolt finished. The file he'd pulled up on how to actually use a bone bolt said it would take about six hours. A quick check of the clock said he still had about five.

The tiredness in Damien's cramped legs overrode his self-insistence that he needed to stay and watch Von. The next thing he knew, he was two doors down in his small bunkroom, dumping his bloody jacket on the floor and falling headfirst into bed.

Chapter Three

The AI & The Overture

Consciousness hit Damien hard.

In the three hours he'd allowed himself sleep, his legs had slowly sunk towards the floor, and now they felt like lead. When he rolled over they screamed at him for all he'd put them through in the night, and his feet were numb. They too had their moment though when he winced his way through unstrapping his heavy combat boots and the pins-and-needles sensation attacked his heels. When he finally got his boots off, the smell of sweaty wool filled his little room. His nostrils flared as he threw the socks to the side. *I'm not sure those are worth washing.* He sat still and focused on his breathing to lessen the pain.

When it subsided, he stumbled into the infirmary to check on his brother. Of the five stages of the bone bolt's fluid process, four were nearly complete. He checked to make sure nothing else had happened while he'd slept, then dragged his way back to the main room, scratching the thick stubble on his face and rubbing gunk from his eyes.

As soon as the lights came on, the desktop in the corner started beeping again, and Damien winced at it. *I know, I know… I forgot.* He knew from experience that the desktop wouldn't cease until he addressed the construct within properly. *I really wanted eggs*, he thought, knowing that the opportunity to eat would pass if he sat down. He decided he would rather deal with Leo now.

"Alright, alright, I'm coming," he said to the room.

The beeps continued.

Damien lifted open the large desktop screen, flowered out the four smaller monitors that lay cradled under the main one, and angled them all

53

into a wide arrangement—like a paper cube unfolding into a mostly flat layout. He palmed the large central monitor.

Unlike a regular computer screen, these monitors had a rough black texturing. The monitor read his handprint, and the insistent beeps finally stopped. The bunker was quiet again save for the whirring of the computer, but Damien knew the beeps for what they were, and the silence only sounded expectant.

He waited as the five screens flickered to life, displaying a simple, teal-colored grid on each surface. He leaned back in his chair and saw how the grid not only showed up on each textured monitor, but it projected outward from them as well, causing a faint laser beam effect all around this side of the bunker. Damien leaned forward.

Working with practiced movements, he loosened the bolts on the back of each screen, adjusted and twisted them on their connecting arms, and tightened each again, fidgeting until all five grids focused perfectly on the square meter of desk in front of him. The square was also black and textured, and displayed a grid of its own along with—more importantly—three bold letters lying flat on the surface:

P.I.P.

As Damien tightened each screen into alignment, the letters were given new life: The main monitor and the desktop screen displayed the letters flat. Then, the third monitor caused all three of them to jump into the air over the grid and cross the barrier between two and three dimensions. The fourth monitor added texture, lighting, and glinting effects to the hovering—now blocky—letters, and the fifth caused the entire scene to start spinning like an idle screensaver.

Thus, Damien and Von's customized computer went from a simple desktop to one capable of holographic light particles floating in three-dimensional space—a Pixel Interlaced Projection.

It had taken them more than a year to find enough Pip screens to assemble their computer, but when they had, it became promptly obvious that it was worth the effort, and no matter his feelings on their Artificial Intelligence construct, the digital being in their computer never ceased to amaze him with the displays he would inevitably conjure.

Registering that the projecting Pip screens were in alignment over the empty Pip pad on the desktop, the computer finally booted to life. The teal glow appeared just in front of each one, highlighting the empty textured square of desktop. An Algaroth interface board appeared flat on the desk in front of Damien, larger than a human board and with fewer keys to accommodate the aliens' limited use of their fourth and fifth digits in typing.

Damien shook his head and swept the alien board to the side. *Von never logs his shit out.*

A smaller, human interface appeared. Damien swept over the keys in a flash and the central Pip screen came to life. As he worked, little folders and alerts began to appear, each floating up through the Pip pad and into the air, blocking his view of the screen behind them. Reaching through the clutter, he pushed the icons and notes away, honing in on an icon resembling an old bank vault door, complete with wheel. The bits of the clutter that reached the edges of the Pip pad's space burst into glowing cubes of teal light, mirroring tiny smashing impacts on an invisible wall— no projections could go beyond the boundary of the square meter of the desktop pad.

Damien sat back as the central Pip screen showed a video of the vault door opening. *And here we go*, he thought, steeling himself for what was about to come out. The smoky effect bled out of the screen into three-dimensional space, and bright green digital smoke filled the Pip pad to its cubed boundaries. Damien waited for the smoke to clear.

When it finally did, two lines of text hung in the air, projected from an unknown source:

You rubbed my lamp. You woke me up. You're bringing me here?
I don't think so. You don't get any wishes.

"Oh no?" Damien muttered, trying to clear the text. He was rewarded with a loud buzzer. He jumped. When he opened his eyes, a new line of text had replaced the first.

Nope.

Damien smirked despite himself. "Not even to hear about last night?"

Heard it.

"From where?"

A friend.

"What friend?"
Wouldn't YOU like to know?

"Leo, your drive's connected, the Pips are up, the door's open, just come out here. Last night didn't go like we planned."

That wouldn't have happened if you kept my magic lamp with you.

"You know we couldn't, and we have good reasons for that."

Why not?
It's because I'm so awesome isn't it? I KNEW it.

Damien rubbed his eyes. Three hours of sleep wasn't enough to deal with their construct's endless energy. He waited a long time before the previous text disappeared.

Your reasons are stupid.

He laughed despite himself. "My reasons are just fine and you know it."

***You're* stupid.**

"Ok, I'm not dealing with this right now, I'm pulling you out," but the second he reached for his interface board so he could command the AI to come out of his hard drive, a tiny flash appeared behind the vault door on the main Pip screen. Damien's interface board vanished, along with the last words of text. A long second passed and a new line appeared.

Just for that, I'm relabeling all of your files again.

His urge to throttle the AI was swift and livid. "Goddammit Leo *don't you dare—*"

An explosion of Damien's folders and documents appeared through the barriers of projected space. Digital pages went everywhere; the flurry was enormous.

"LEO!" Damien howled, raging at their AI's tantrums.

As the pages cleared, a pair of pristine white gloves appeared in midair, wielding a conductor's baton. A music stand appeared as well, and Damien knew what was coming. He clenched his teeth and sat back in his chair, furious. If he tried to intervene now, he would only make things worse for himself by adding to all of the work Leo just gave him.

I'm gonna kill him. Slowly, he decided.

The pages finally faded, and the disembodied gloves brought the baton to bear. Damien unwillingly perked up when he heard the distant chorus of violins through the speakers, heralding the start of the *1812 Overture*, by Tchaikovsky. The piece was Leo's favorite, and whenever he was upset, he would override whatever Damien or Von were doing on the computer and play that piece. The music never came on without a vast accompanying mosaic of scenery.

It was a dirty tactic, Damien knew. Leo had even admitted it once: Without fail, playing beautiful music while you angered everyone around would throw them off so that when it was done, their guard wouldn't be focused and you could ask them anything. In the nearly four years since they'd found Leo's little cube inside a very real vault at the back of the bunker, Damien had yet to keep his guard up after the song played.

The music grew, and the conducting gloves faded into nothingness along with the music stand, leaving a blank canvas of waiting Pip screens and the empty desktop pad. As it swelled through the opening, one screen after another came to life with historic images of grandiose scope: great works of art slowly appeared, images of past wars and great loves, iconic men and women of history. Leo never showed the same collection twice.

This time, the theme seemed to be mostly of great battles intermingled with grotesqueries out of an asylum or a horror story. Damien was painfully aware of how quickly his anger faded at what the AI had just done to his files; he was riveted to the display, compelled to see more, despite the less than therapeutic ensemble.

The song continued, and Damien watched as the scenes evolved, shifting always to thought-provoking images or ones with emotional impact. They hit Damien that much harder though through his fascination with history. He fully believed the concept that those who did not listen to history were doomed to repeat it, and so he had studied all his life.

He recognized scenery depicting the Battle of Thermopylae, and then a scene showed a young woman, stumbling alone through dark woods, terrified and bleeding. Then, engineers repaired a starship Damien recognized as the *HSS Gagarin*. It was just as quickly followed with images of a man slashing at his own face with a stiletto. The Battle of Galveston raged in the summer of 2050, followed by a line of people in white smocks wearing Rorschach inkblot masks, and on it went. Finally, Damien caught first sight of their intrepid companion: Leo, who held the distinction of an 'adult' Artificial Intelligence.

Leo rode into battle alongside King Arthur, completely out of place in his usual tailored suit and tie. Next, the AI walked with his hands clasped in prayer amongst throngs of priests. Then, as the music approached the ringing crescendo, the scenes zipped by, always with the AI in a place of advisement but not total power. His chosen avatar was a handsome man in his prime with swirling blond hair, bright silver eyes, a confident jaw, and pearly white teeth to match his light skin. He was always dressed in that suit under partial period outfits.

Finally, as the music reached its grand peak, Arthur "Leo" Leonardo leapt off the two-dimensional Pip screen where the First Landing on Mars was playing, and landed three-dimensional on the table, standing about a half-meter high. His space suit and instruments whirled about him and became a cloak, top hat, cane, mustache, and monocle over a tailcoat. He swept off the hat in a flourish and bowed deeply to Damien. Beneath the top hat was an odd, double-billed deerstalker cap that Damien recognized as belonging to an old version of the character Sherlock Holmes by Sir Arthur Conan Doyle—though the hat was *not* the original outfit for the character, only the most famous, as Leo was wont to mention.

The AI also prided himself on the fact that he had named himself: half for Doyle, and half for the great Renaissance man, Leonardo Da Vinci. He had told Damien the story of choosing the name when they first met.

When Leo finally did speak, his voice came through crisp and confident with a touch of mania. "I'm begging you," the AI said, throwing himself prostrate on the desk. "I've got stray terabytes clogging up my nose in that hard drive! It's maddening, I tell you! You've gotta let me out to clean and flush once in awhile!"

Damien glared. "Oh, *flush*? You mean what you just did to all of my files?"

Leo sat up. "*Exactly* like that." Without any visible use of muscles, Leo went from crouched on his knees to a standing position, as if he simply reversed the process of sitting down without considering physics or gravity. "Do you have any concept of what it feels like? Being stuffed into a little box through a tiny tube and left to sit there?! What if *you* were just dropped into a room and the only thing you had was a faucet full of coffee, hmm? No doors, no windows, just drugs for your brain!"

Damien chewed on it. In truth, he had never thought about the AI's confinement like that before, and it certainly did the trick to make him feel guilty for keeping their friend in there. *But not guilty enough to let him roam the Intersystem freely. I barely trust him with* my *computer*. He frowned. "Will you stop trying to hack the whole System if I unlock your backup drive?"

The AI looked affronted, his Holmes' hat tipping back precariously as he crossed his arms. "Of course not!"

Damien shrugged, "And that's why you have to stay in there."

Leo whirled off the remainder of his attire to reveal his regular suit and face. The outfit impacted the holographic borders of the desktop with the same effect as every other item: smashing into teal cubits. Leo plopped his hands on his hips, his face contorting in condescension. "BA! You think it's *dangerous* to walk around the Intersystem. Ha! Dangerous. 'Danger' is my middle name!" He thumped his chest.

Damien raised an eyebrow.

"What?" the AI implored, about to go on a tirade before reconsidering. "You know, actually, 'Danger' is my last name too." He turned away, scoffing and thumbing his nose. The deerstalker rolled neatly down his arm and into the air, where the AI kicked it. The cap turned into a fireball, disappearing into the barrier. Damien laughed, unable to stop himself, which prompted the avatar to turn around and start yelling at him with vigor. "The Collective won't find me! They *hate* crossing into our System! You know they'd rather stick to their own. Don't deny it. Oh and, *again*: that stupid little hard drive is no place for a grown AI like me and you know it!"

"You're probably right," Damien said, shifting in his chair as his stomach growled. His voice started to rise. "And that's the only reason we went on a raid last night in the first place! So *you* could bust into a Collective black box and hack their network!"

Leo made a raspberry.

"I'd love to let you out, I really would, but you don't have *any* self control with poking your nose into places you shouldn't, and that'll definitely get us all killed if I were to let you out!"

Leo rolled his eyes. "We've all got our vices, Elemental-with-a-savior's-complex."

Damien's sympathy vanished. "That's low."

"So was yours."

"Are you pissed because you're stuck in here all the time? Or is it because I didn't let you know when we got home?"

"Both. Can't you at least *try* to find another way to let me out?"

"Of course I can, I just don't have any idea how."

"I do. I could have told it to you last night, along with a whole bunch of other relevant junk that I'm sure you would've misused because your organic brain is slower than me but *nooo*, Leo had to stay put because *Leo* might get captured and *Leo's* too valuable and blah blah blah!"

Damien went very still, torn between raging at Leo for being selfish, and having complete sympathy—even empathy—to his plight. He settled on something in the middle. "I see. Well, I'm sorry to break it to you, but I was kind of busy last night, okay? I told you that—"

"—Things didn't go as planned, yes I know," Leo cut him off. The scenes and props vanished, leaving only a handsome, well-dressed man straightening his straight tie. "And I've been waiting *patiently* for you to tell me what happened!"

Damien took a calming breath. "Von got shot last night."

Leo raised an eyebrow, trying to feign indifference and failing. "Oh?"

"You don't have to sound so excited."

"I'm sorry," Leo coughed and assumed a contrite face, his voice hushed. "Oh… how shot? Will he make it? Oh, dear me."

Damien rolled his eyes. "Gyro shot, just above the left ankle. It burned out the muscle and nearly melted his leg."

The Pip screens flickered, and Leo's suited avatar changed in a flash. His physical appearance remained the same, but his attire had changed into what could only be referred to as an "evil doctor" outfit. His left hand had been replaced by an array of scissors. He stood over an empty surgical table where a perfect hologram of an Algaroth's leg hovered. "How was giving him a bone bolt?" Leo asked. In another flash, the table vanished, the leg grew almost to the AI's size, and it morphed into a nearly spot-on guess of how Von's leg looked now.

Damien stared at the projection. It didn't surprise him at all that Leo knew right away what had needed to be done. "Scary as hell." He tried not to remember the *CRACK* of Von's bone.

Leo tossed the leg over his shoulder and his usual attire and regular hand returned. "Ha, I bet. *I* would've probably just cut his leg off, but you know, I've been TOLD that that compound works wonders on dead bones. Are they still using the cytaxolotomab nitrate and the osteomyeloid-graphsten fiber?" The AI absently collided models of two different atomic elements between his hands, making a silvery-green flash as he did.

Damien blinked. He wouldn't even try to pronounce the pharmajabber Leo had just spouted. "No, Leo. I just know it comes in a tiny silver nub."

Leo clucked, "Mmm. Well, I *suppose* that still works. It's outdated though. You know that right? That little nub was used to cure osteoporosis, it wasn't designed for emergency plasma-shot leg repair."

Damien rubbed his eyes, wishing the AI—who could calculate many millions of choices in a second—would let just let him get to the point. "Yes, I realize that. I didn't have much choice though, did I?"

Leo's suit returned. "No, you didn't." His voice went a touch softer. "And you probably saved his life for thinking on your feet like that. How is he?"

Damien looked at his feet. "The bolt is still doing its thing. Should be done soon." When he looked up, Leo was lounging in a chair reading a newspaper. He snorted. *I knew you cared.* "Leo?"

The paper vanished. "Oh, I'm listening. It just takes you so *long* to use that mouth of yours. I get bored. Were you about to tell me how you got the black box and everything went smoothly? Oh no, that's right, your brother got shot, so… I have to hazard that nothing went according to plan?"

"No, it didn't," and Damien proceeded to tell Leo the events of their raid. He would have skimmed the details, but the AI would never be satisfied with that so he didn't even try. By the time he finished his head was starting to throb from hunger, and he knew the bone bolt should be finished.

"I'll have to grab the gear here in a bit," he concluded. "I left it upstairs with the cycle."

Leo sat staring into a campfire, garbed in animal skins and war paint, pondering. "And you're sure your Wave took out the whole patrol?"

Damien's heart sank. He'd been afraid the AI would ask that. "No, I'm not." He knew what would come next.

The AI perked up so fast he could have been built on springs. "You have to let me into the System, then."

"Why?" He knew.

"Because if any alerts have gone up about it, we're buried. I don't want to be buried, Damien." Leo looked around the bunker pointedly. "Ok, I don't want to be buried any more than I am!"

Damien stifled a grin. "You know how dangerous that—"

"—Sure do!"

Between worrying about how Von was doing, his own exhaustion and hunger, and concern over how much damage he had actually done to the Razer and its crew, Damien didn't have the energy to fight the construct off. He sighed, resigned. "Okay, fine—" he spoke louder over Leo's squeal of excitement, "—but don't get us caught while you're in there!"

"You got it boss! Absolutely, no problem! Dad, what's my curfew?" The AI had literally levitated off the desktop in excitement, his cheeks went flushed and he beamed.

Damien checked what time it was. "Seven-thirty. Okay... be back around—*by!* Be back *by* two, okay?" He caught himself, knowing Leo would take his exact wording into account.

"Done. Now open sesame, please! Let me at 'em! Open it open it open it open it!"

"Stop it. And be back sooner if you hear anything."

"Yes of course, mm hmm!"

Damien's interface board appeared again and he unlocked their computer's access to global Intersystem—humanity's offspring network of the old Internet. "There. Now don't go into any—oh god, okay—*be safe!*" he called, but Leo's avatar had vanished in a puff of teal cubits so fast he might not have heard. "Please don't get lost," he added. "We're buried without you."

∞   ∞   ∞

After he wolfed down an oat-&-cranberry nutrient bar, Damien went to his room to put on a plain green sweatshirt and black polyester pants to ward off the chill creeping into the bunker, and then returned to the infirmary to check on his brother. He found Von just beginning to stir.

"Hey killer," Damien said, entering on light feet. "Can you hear me?"

Von grumbled into the table. His breathing was labored and his movements were small and clumsy. Not for the first time, Damien wished their medical slab was larger.

Damien grabbed a handful of painkillers from the cabinet, along with a tightly wrapped roll of what looked like a white washcloth, and a stick of the tree bark that his brother loved to chew on. He placed the handful of items on the medical tray and pulled down the lamp and tool ball. The readout did indeed say the bolt had finished running its course, and it was now waiting on him to make the final report.

He let the machine hang where it was and grabbed the roll of cloth and the tree bark, holding them close as he stepped around to Von's head, waiting for him to open his eyes. When they did flutter to life, they looked muted and unfocused, glinting like a wolf's just when they turned away from light.

Von stared at the wall for a long moment without blinking. Then he swallowed hard and took notice of the human. "I feel...sickly." His voice was thick and throaty.

Damien put the bark down and cracked the capsule inside the roll of cloth, letting the moisturizing compounds into the soft material. He waited for a moment while the liquid seeped through the roll and then handed it to Von. The alien was slow to take it, every movement testing the edges of control. When he finally did, he held it in his mottled blue hand and squeezed.

"What was that for?!" Damien snapped, diving forward to try and stop the healing juices from spattering on the floor.

Von sniggered weakly. It sounded like a ragged, jerking purr. "Oops. I... don't want it."

64

Damien shook his hands, trying to clean off the filmy juice. *Well he sounds better at least, bad 'P's' and all.* He shot Von an admonishing glare. "You need it!"

"You… worry too much."

"Damn right I do. How do you feel?"

Von half rolled onto his side, limited in his mobility. "Better."

Better 'B's' too. "How much?"

Von looked thoughtful for a moment, then he hissed as he tried to flex his leg, *"Not that much!"*

And your 'M's'. I'm impressed. Damien swept around the table and brought the tool ball down. It chimed happily that Von's leg was now four times stronger than before the injury, but that they needed to perform that muscle surgery as soon as possible, or risk necrotic-infectious complications. He swallowed and repeated this to Von, who let out a sigh of relief as Damien pulled the medical arm back.

"You admitted yourself that we don't possess the tools here to do a cyto… a cyto…"

"A cytomyotrophy," Damien finished. "No, we don't."

"Yes. That. So what is there to do?"

Damien picked up the wetcloth from the table and stuffed it back into Von's open palm. *"Suck,"* he said, ignoring the comment.

Von's ganglia flicked about. He hesitated. "I don't like that word."

"I—what? Why?"

"It sounds like a word in Dekka."

The Algaroth common language. Damien knew there were many other languages spoken on Shialga just as there were on Earth, but Dekka was the one Algaroth had chosen to use in meeting new species. Neither of them often spoke in the tongue unless they had to. "What's the word?"

"Shuka."

"What's it mean?"

"Blow."

A smile crept up Damien's face. "You're full of shit."

"No. That's why it confuses me."

Damien couldn't stifle a long snicker, partly because he wasn't sure how well Von knew the more sub-textual meanings of those words in English. "Well, yeah. That would be confusing," he said, pursing his lips. "Now take your wetcloth."

Distaste crossed Von's thin lips as he looked at it. "It looks weird. I want the tree bark."

Damien glared at him, shaking his head. "You're funny this morning. Just take the wetcloth—without a fight!" he raised his voice as Von opened his mouth to protest. "And *then* I'll give you some bark. Deal?"

Von growled at him, uncanny as always at mimicking human emotion and mockery. He looked to be weighing the worthiness of giving a smarmy remark before deciding against it. The alien popped the soggy cloth into his mouth, making an awful sucking noise as he did so, pulling the restorative juices from it.

Damien set the tree bark on the counter and snatched up the stopgap splint he was going to use to set Von's muscles. He pulled apart the circlets and spread them out—leads and all—in front of the alien's emerald-gold eyes, seeking approval. Von followed his movements, looking apprehensive. The splint was made up of two adjustable white circlets of plastic; both had a collection of sharp metal nubs on the inside. When connected, the leads would exude a mock-nerve charge, providing enough impulse control for the wearer to temporarily regain use of disconnected muscles—or at least that was the idea.

"I'm just gonna work through this now, alright?"

Von nodded, still squelching and sucking on the wetcloth.

"Okay. Give me your leg." He slid one circlet up to the Algaroth's knee, just above the wound, the other circlet he adjusted to just below it. Von's lips twitched as the metal pins pressed into his thick skin. As soon as he'd positioned them, Damien pulled the cinches on both, hard and without warning. He remembered watching Dr. Locke do this once before when he was an impromptu medic. He remembered the doctor telling him from experience that it was better to act fast to keep the patient from tensing.

Had Von's system been clear of the sleeping drugs, Damien was sure the alien would have clawed at his face. Luckily for them both, all his brother could do was yowl over the cloth in his mouth and twitch when the pins pierced him.

"Okay," said Damien, moving fast. "Now the leads." He went to work connecting the two circlets with their corded leads. *Higher to lower, higher to lower, third to third, no clamps until they're all set.* He ran through the steps in his mind, clipping each lead to their matching spot on the other circlet. String by string, he gave Von's leg a rudimentary set of nerves, each string connecting to the right muscle. *I hope*, he thought. Crossing leads didn't bear thinking about—though he imagined, in a best-case scenario, the pain would just make Von black out and Damien could disconnect them. A worst-case scenario would be... *much worse.*

With each clip, Von winced as the sharp pins dug deeper, and Damien winced with him. Finally, all of the leads were in place, and he checked and rechecked to make sure before turning the splint on. Clicking the switch, Damien sent a current between the circlets, hopefully bringing Von's leg back to a modicum level of usability. The faintest of hums filled the infirmary as the circlets came to life.

Black claws snapped out from Von's fingers and his eyes went wide, but he made no sound. Damien kept his hand on the little switch, his face scrunched up with anxiety. The moment passed, and Von reached for his damaged leg, gripping his thigh.

"What can you feel?" Damien asked.

Von spat the wetcloth onto the tray, now just a lumpy, grayish ball of slime. It smelled pungently of dog breath. The alien's words came in short jerky bursts. "*Ehh ha*... it—it's working... *ah, ha!* I think I—can—can feel it working... Oh."

"You moved your leg!" Damien leapt away to see it again.

Sure enough, Von was flexing his leg. Slowly, carefully at first, but soon with more confidence. In a few short minutes, he had a full range of motion—though Damien cautioned him from moving it too fast or far.

"Those leads will snap out of place if you push too hard," he said. "This thing isn't meant for you to get up and go running around, got it?"

The Algaroth glared at him from the slab. He had managed to sit up but didn't yet have the confidence to stand. "Try and stop me."

"You know I can."

Von gave him a toothy smile and shook his head. "Thank you for this. And for my leg."

Damien grabbed the slimy lump of wetcloth and tossed it towards the garbage. He missed. "Don't thank me," he said, retrieving it from the trash and putting it in the recycler pail. "It was my fault in the first place."

"That doesn't matter. We got the black box recorder and tonight we can go—"

"—Whoa, whoa slow down there, slizzard," Damien cut him off from the sink. "You're not going *anywhere* tonight. Are you kidding?" He pointed at Von's leg with his hands covered in cleaning gel.

In answer, Von locked gazes with him, narrowed his eyes, and hopped off the slab in the most childishly defiant way imaginable. The slab audibly groaned as the alien's weight left it. Damien had to stifle a laugh.

"Okay, so you're standing. That's not walking though, or climbing stairs, or running."

Again, his brother held his gaze and took a daring step with his bad leg. Von's ganglia flicked like he was raising an eyebrow.

You're crazy, Vo. Absolutely insane. Damien crossed his arms. "Okay fine, you can take a step. Do I see tears?"

The alien sniffed. "No, you do not." He blinked hard.

"Are you breathing?" Damien noted how the thick muscles over Von's abdomen were flexed tight, and how the porous strips of pale grey skin that ran from the alien's armpit to his neck were sucked down flat.

"I… will soon," he strained.

"Uh huh." Damien tossed the towel into the sink, his hands finally clean of fluids.

Von bared his teeth and growled. Finally, he reached for the slab and fell back onto it, sighing with the weight off his leg. "It feels… heavier, and stronger."

"It is, pal. Remember what I said last night about your leg being like rotten wood?" Damien retrieved a poultice and the cover for the splint. They smelled of clean, warm, homey things, and soft blankets.

Von itched the protruding nubs of bone over his shoulder, where wings would have sprouted were he born an Algaroth Royal. He looked sheepish. "No. I don't remember."

"Well, it *was* like rotten wood. Now it isn't. Now it's more like a metal alloy club wrapped in bone." Damien indicated Von should stick his leg out so he could wrap it up. "You're gonna have to get used to it." The poultice and clean bandages went on first, followed by the cover, which he adjusted to the distance of the circlets and snapped into place over the leads, hiding the wound, leads, and white linen padding from view. Von watched in silence as Damien finally wrapped a long, thick roll of bonding tape around and around the leg, giving him a makeshift cast.

"There," Damien said, eyeing his handiwork. "You'd never know what horrible injury hides under that." He went to wash his hands again.

"It's warm," said Von.

"Well that's good. It means you have feeling still." Damien dried his hands. "Now, I don't know about you, but I'm fucking hungry."

An Algaroth's laugh was a warm thing to behold. It came from deep in their gut and when they thought something was really funny, their whole body would vibrate. Von's laugh even made his long array of teeth look less predatory. "I could use food."

Damien smiled at him. "Good. Well since I don't have to cut your leg off—which Leo suggested, by the way—I'm gonna go make—"

"—No, no, no, not yet." Von pounded a hand into Damien's chest, staggering him.

"Ow! What?"

"Give me my bark."

Damien snorted. "Oh that's right, I did promise you that." The reptilian snout followed his every movement as he retrieved the gnawed and moldy strip of brown bark from the counter. "Are you sure you want it?"

Von stuck his hand out. "Give."

69

"Yeah I figured." He slapped it into Von's palm.

Von greedily stuck it between his tongue and gums; the oozing sound he made elicited a gross face from Damien.

"You know you're basically just a junkie with that stuff, right?"

Von didn't answer right away. His eyes had drifted shut and a look of soft contentment had fallen over the bony features.

Damien just shook his head and checked to make sure he hadn't left anything out.

Von spoke simply. "It isn't *my* fault that you have trees on Earth that have chang'en juice."

Damien just snorted. Of all the things humans would have expected the Algaroth to really love on Earth, treated, hallucination-inducing tree bark was NOT one of them. He wasn't sure how the effect had been discovered or when, but ever since it had, that particular species of oak had become insanely sought after. In fact, Damien had long suspected that part of the reason the Islets had been spared for so long was because the oak trees were only found around the Puget Sound and a select few other regions on the planet. If The Collective burned the city, the enemy would have no more junkie juice.

Damien watched his brother work the bark carefully over his sharp front teeth and bite on it with his flatter back ones. He looked much like a dog chewing a bone, but more careful. "Better?"

Von nodded languidly.

"Good." Damien tapped his shoulder. "You can finish that, and maybe next week we can make a trip up north to get some more. Okay?"

The Algaroth was already high and he just smiled dumbly, shoulders drooped.

"Okay then. Don't fall off the table; I'm gonna go make breakfast."

Chapter
Four

Avos

Given how the night before had gone—and how hungry he was—Damien decided a full meal was in order. He had never been a very elaborate cook, but what he could make he made well. Three years of living on the streets of Seattle with Von and four years of living in the bunker had taught them to savor a good meal, because they never were quite sure if they'd get another.

Even prior to seven years ago, when the earthquake hit, The Collective had been on an uncomfortable march towards the Puget cities of Tacoma, the Seattle Islets, and Vancouver. The enemy had spent years before that working their way up the west coast of North America, slowly cutting off human access to the Pacific, and Eurasia across the ocean. Humanity's global attitude shift in the past century drastically altered the way food was handled around the world, but as The Collective cut off more and more avenues of trade over the years, more and more cities were left to fend for themselves—to innovate and maintain their own sustainable practices, or flee. Damien, Von, and the vast remainder of stubborn insurgent survivors in Seattle had chosen to innovate, but food was something that would always require a community to maintain. Sometimes there were things they just couldn't do alone.

In the seven years since the quake, fresh meat and produce had become nearly priceless in the Puget cities. The value of paper money had long since fallen away, and a bartering system had quickly replaced it, with the necessities hotly haggled over. Fortunately, with the brothers' jack-of-all-trades approach to scavenging and trading, they had worked out the higher value of favors and a kept promise over tangible wares. So, with their noted fortune of having a secure home, good gear, and keen instincts, they had made friends with the right people. Bar & Shell's Buy & Sell took all of the gear they grabbed from Collective patrols in exchange for all manner of hardware. Tim and Isabelle dealt in produce, fresh fish, dairy, eggs, and the rare chicken or duck in exchange Damien's affinity for fiddling with machines or tech and Von's deft hands with carpentry. Thomas and his three sons would often have news from around the city. And then there was Zeya, a teen girl who had lost her twin brother; she was the one the brothers would go to for odds and ends in exchange for the same. Sometimes Von wanted cooked squirrel.

In their small kitchenette, Damien and Von's airtight preservator was about as full as it ever got, which was to say, not very. They weren't big on overstocking when they had so much already, and there were people left in the city who were far worse off. Besides, it had been over a century since produce and dairy went bad within a day.

So, while Von enjoyed his stick of junky bark, Damien made omelets.

Von deserves a good meal, he thought absently while preparing the tomatoes, mushrooms, and half an onion. *And I want eggs. I miss fish though. Mm and bread. I miss bread.* It had been a long time since they'd had a loaf of bread. No one they knew in the city had any way to bake it anymore, and it took a lot of energy.

The sizzle and smell of breakfast made Damien's stomach rumble painfully, and he couldn't help snacking on a handful of peanuts while he cooked. When it was all ready, he went to the infirmary to find his brother gnawing sadly on the last spit of bark and staring at a wall.

"Food's ready. You okay? That doesn't look like it lasted long," he said, observing the finger of wood.

"It didn't," Von answered wistfully.

"You need help walking?"

Von stopped gnawing and gave Damien a dry, stony stare.

"Okay, fine, but your omelet will be cold by the time you get over there," and he went back to the main room.

Von arrived barely a minute later, adding confidence with each step. He wore only his favorite, lime-green wrapshirt, an Algaroth top that wrapped in overlapping layers up his torso and over his waist and groin. The wrapshirt left Von's arms, legs, and the top of his chest bare.

"Look at you walking tall!" Damien beamed. He had put the cover over their high workbench so they might use it as a table to eat. On it, he'd placed their square omelets, a small bowl of green grapes, and a large bottle of water, as they had nothing else to drink. The omelets were square from the pan press, but they were large and hearty, and the grapes looked delicious.

"Quiet," Von snapped. "I won't have infirm from you." He hopped into his Algaroth-sized stool, which they had assembled from parts found above in the compound. "Unless you're willing to get me things, in which case, where are my apples?"

Damien popped his gums. "I think you mean 'snark', you won't have *snark* from me, and fine, hold on." He went to grab two apples. "You get the smaller one," he said when he returned, lobbing the fruit at Von's head. The alien caught it with his tool-fingers, spearing it right to the center on his barbed knuckle.

"You caught that with your off hand, I'm impressed."

Von grinned through a mouthful of egg.

Damien took a bite of apple and watched, fascinated as ever, as his brother hooked the bony protrusions on his fourth and fifth digits to form a kind of spoon. With the other hand he struggled with a knife, trying to scoop omelet onto the 'utensil'. *Everyone makes jokes at that*, he thought, *but those fingers are dangerous.* It had always been a point of many jabs amongst humans how Algaroth ate almost exclusively with their hands. The jabs were more ironic than anything though, as the tool-fingers were—according to the Algaroth themselves—the defining attribute of how they evolved to the top of their own planet. They were originally cliff-dwelling predators, and the tool-fingers let them climb. Damien always thought it was funny how Von did his best to learn human utensils, but inevitably went back to how his species had always eaten.

They ate quietly, the sound of metal clinking and chewing the only things to perforate the air in the bunker. Damien thought the omelets could use more seasoning, but they didn't have any, and he wouldn't know what to use regardless. He remembered someone once saying that basil was good on eggs, but he wasn't confident in even that.

After awhile, the quiet continued, and an old family saying came to Damien, something his father used to say. *A quiet dinner table is a happy table.* He had always thought the saying was about food, but it later occurred to him that it might mean something else when he had realized his parents were married more to their work than each other. He was thinking absently about that when something else occurred to him. "Do you ever wonder how things might have gone if humanity found you guys first?" he asked.

Von chewed half of his apple thoughtfully. "I don't think so."

"Why not?"

"Because it makes me wonder what might have been, if The Collective wasn't… what they are."

"Oh."

They lapsed back into silence.

"Do you?" Von asked after another few bites. He grabbed a few grapes and popped them into his wide maw one at a time.

Damien shrugged. "Sometimes." He pushed his omelet around on his tray. *Often.* "I don't know. I just like to think that someday, we won't have to kill each other to be able to live our own way."

"You've said that humans used to be that way."

"Yeah, *kinda*," Damien wobbled his hand. "That was back when there were disconnected societies on Earth still. The tribe that lived down the way was as alien to us as the Algaroth were when we first met you or the Volüul. But it's not quite the same." *Because back then it was never a war over a whole species.* "I mean, *some* cultures I'm sure lived peacefully, some sort of danced around each other and poked and prodded without wiping each other out, but those cultures are all dead because of—well actually…"

"What?"

Damien took a long moment to swallow the last of his omelet. "Because of what *we* are now." He pointed between himself and the alien to make his point. "Because one way of thinking became dominant, and *that's* the society that took to the stars."

Von cocked his head. "You think Algaroth and humans are similar like that?"

Damien snorted. "I think that given all that we know of other star-bound species—which, I grant you, isn't much—but given what we *do* know, everything seems to exist in some kind of pattern. There are always parallels."

Von reached for his wounded leg. "That's a lot of thinking for this early, Damien. You're making my leg hurt."

Damien grinned. "Sorry. I know you don't care about that stuff."

"It's not that I don't care. It's just early."

"Mm." Damien ate more apple and washed it down with water. "Speaking of early, or late, actually, do you think another Supply Fleet is ever gonna show up?"

The tone of their conversation quickly changed. Von sighed. "Of course I do."

"Any ideas on what happened?"

"With the Fleet? Not really. I just know that Shialga will wonder the same thing, and they will absolutely send another. The next one will probably be larger too if they thought the last one went missing. You know how tense everyone has been though, since it never showed up. When was that, last May?"

Damien leaned back on his chair and stroked his coarse black stubble, thinking. "Yeah, I think so. And you're right; they probably will send a bigger fleet next time. More troops, more gear, more fighting." He gave up on his fork and grabbed the last bite of omelet with his hands, but the flavor had gone out of the eggs. "I don't know," he said, swallowing. "I guess…"

"What?" Von munched on the last of his apple, core and all.

He shook his head. "I guess I just have this hope that they decided to give up, you know? Like, maybe they decided 'hey, we're tired of sending an army across the galaxy to Earth every couple of years and we're just going to leave it alone. That place is shitty and we don't want it.'"

Von frowned. "Earth isn't shitty."

Damien rolled his eyes. "I know that. But I hope The Collective thinks it is and then maybe they'll leave us alone! We can actually get a foothold against the Over-Seer, maybe even break his hold and then," he paused. "Then, maybe we can rebuild or, or something. Make new starships even." He dropped his gaze to the table, knowing what Von was about to say to that.

"Someday you'll see the Moon, Damien," his brother said quietly. "You will."

He closed his eyes, unwilling to let that hope resurface. "It wouldn't matter."

"Why not?"

"Because if I did I'd be surrounded by graves, and if I looked back at Earth all I would see is a place that aliens have taken." He shifted in his seat, trying to get comfortable again. "It wouldn't be the same! I'd probably just feel all tense like everyone else is lately since a Supply Fleet hasn't shown up. Maybe it'd be different if I'd seen it forty or fifty years ago, but now…"

"You weren't alive then."

Damien gave Von a bone-dry stare. He could never tell if his brother enjoyed being so literal or if he genuinely didn't understand, but he suspected the former. Von liked playing stupid because it often made people explain more than they should.

"It's true," and the alien guzzled the last of his water. "But," he added, trying to smack his lips together and make those three English sounds that were almost beyond his species. "You might think differently on seeing home from so far away. I know that is one of my first memories."

Damien furrowed his brow. "You never told me that?"

"No?" Von itched his leg and started absently spinning his cup on the table, watching the pale light glint off the recycled aluminum. "It's a foggy memory," he said. "Just of having my birth parents at my back when we first arrived here, and seeing the little blue dot under us, getting larger and clearer. White clouds and green land and so much blue water." Von sighed. "Shialga never looked like that. Our planet is very purple, the ocean is greener, and the land is very brown."

"What about the clouds?" Damien had never heard his brother describe Shialga before. "Are they white?"

"No. Well... I can't remember. I think they are a little yellowish."

"Wow." Damien followed the movements of Von's cup as well. "I wish I could see it."

Von chortled. "Why don't we start with the Moon and then we can talk about crossing the galaxy."

They laughed, and lapsed back into silence.

Unwilling to let the moment turn stale, Damien hopped off the chair and cleared their plates, taking them back to the kitchenette. When he returned from washing their few dishes, he found Von at the computer.

"What'cha doing?" *Dammit, he's gonna be pissed when he finds out I let Leo out into the System.*

Von answered without turning. "Why are all of my bins in the wrong place?"

I guess that won't wait. "Oh, yeah. Ah, that would be Leo."

Von growled. "The next time he does that I'm going to—"

"—You called?" a voice interrupted.

They both turned to see Leo's avatar slip onto the Pip pad of the desktop through a freestanding door in a frame. He wore a full-body, brown and black fur overcoat and flecks of digital snow glinted in his blonde hair.

"Leo?" Damien started. "What are you doing? I thought you wouldn't be back until two?" He checked the clock to be sure it wasn't that late. It wasn't even noon yet.

Leo shivered once, shook his coat off—where it promptly vanished— and straightened his tie as if nothing unusual had just happened. The doorway disappeared as well, along with the flecks of snow in his hair. "Just because I like being out doesn't mean I have to take *all* of my sweet and dandy time," he said, sounding hurt. "And *you* told me to come back if I saw anything unusual out there in the big wide System." He pointed at Damien.

"You let him out?!" Von barked. "What for?"

Damien groaned. "I had a good reason!"

Von whirled on the AI. "What reason?"

Leo raised an eyebrow at him. "You're not gonna like it, but I had to check and see if your wee antics last night caused any trouble. Yeah?"

Damien leaned in besides his brother. "What did you find?"

Leo snapped his fingers. In an instant, the five Pip screens behind him burst to life, showing myriad things. Two showed street cameras that the three of them had installed over a year ago, another showed an interface for eavesdropping software, another displayed a map of the region, and the large central screen showed a spinning, transparent model of the black box.

Damien started at seeing the box, remembering that he had left it upstairs in the cargo container with his motorcycle and the gear they had swiped. *No one knows that's there*, he thought. *It's just fine.*

From his three-dimensional space on the desktop, Leo indicated the screens while he spoke. "I'm pretty sure you were noticed last night."

"Pretty sure?" Von asked.

"That's not good enough," Damien added.

Leo glared. "Would you rather me sound dramatic and worried or should I just plod through the details so that you can work *yourselves* into a panic?"

"Details Leo, please."

The AI rolled his eyes. "You're no fun. I'm being dramatic anyway." His outfit changed in a flash to one of a career military man in green combat gear and the campaign hat of a drill sergeant. "You dirt bags sure know how to fuck up an evening!" He roared, making them both start. Leo started pacing while the Pip screens behind him highlighted what he said as he said it. "Your little insertion into enemy territory was a botched fucking deal, do you hear me?! I'll grant you that setting those charges to box in that Razer was sound tactical work, and the wave-busters were absolutely inspired," he stopped. "But you didn't pull it off like professionals and that made it FUCKING USELESS!"

The brothers jumped again as Leo cranked up his volume. Von tried to retort but the construct bowled him over.

"I've just had a one-man scouting mission behind friendly lines to see if they'd heard the news of your little raid, and guess what? THEY'VE HEARD IT AS SURE AS SHITTIN'! You know what that means, you turd whackers? It means that the damn Collective heard about it too!" Leo let the drill sergeant façade fall and his suit returned, as did his voice to normal. "It means that we're buried, because the rumor mill is on high alert because it sounds like The Collective is sending in an *investigative squadron* to see what the hell happened to that Razer."

Damien's face went cold. "Wait…they're…they're already sending someone? Doesn't that mean—"

"—That either someone from the patrol you hit made contact with their army in Portland, *or*, if you were very, very lucky, that super-nasty Wave of yours wiped the Razer out completely, and someone in the army got upset when they didn't check in because they were dead, dead, deadsky." Leo produced a dartboard on one of the smaller Pip screens. It had each of their faces on it and the AI proceeded to pierce it with a hail of projectiles, punctuating each shot with a word. The darts flew through the barrier of his desktop, and a perfect second later appeared on the screen in two-dimensional space. "I really… *really*… hope… its… the… *latter*—" he whooped as one of the darts split another down the middle as they hit the same spot. "Because…it'd…make…what…we have…to do…next…so…much…*easier!*" The dartboard vanished, riddled with holes.

"Why would that be better?" Damien choked, trying to keep his thoughts straight. *I knew we were in trouble. I knew it.* His mind had started racing, and fear sent a wash of creeping tendrils through his chest.

"Silas, do *you* know why that would be better?" Leo asked Von, addressing him by his clan name instead of his Own name, which irritated the Algaroth to no end.

Von bared his teeth and his ganglia flicked about nervously. "I don't."

Leo tsked and looked back at Damien. "Well, if you did indeed use those fancy powers of yours to wipe out *zee Razer*," he enunciated the last

79

words as he started growing a thick white beard at an alarming rate. "Then we *might* be lucky enough to find that the enemy has *no idea* that you took their wittle bwack bwox, so they won't change the codes, and we can still go to see the scary XenoCon campus to test our hacking rig, just like we planned!" He started cleaning the heavy glasses that had appeared over the beard. "Though I definitely recommend we go tonight."

"What?" Damien said, shaken out of his whirling thoughts. "No. No way; we can't go *tonight*, Von can't even walk!"

Von glared. "I can too, and it sounds like we don't have a choice." He stretched his bandaged leg. "The box will be useless if they change the codes, and I don't want this injury to be for nothing."

Damien wanted to argue, but he knew his brother was right, and so was Leo, so he stifled his complaint and whirled on the AI. "Did you see when this 'investigative squad' might get to the city?"

Leo turned to face the Pip screens behind him. "Ahh let me see, hmm… I sure don't! Know why? Because *that* knowledge is something The Collective doesn't share willingly, and—oh that's right—the only way we might be able to figure that out is if we take your little box, take my hacking rig—"

"—Hey, we all worked on—" Von said.

"—And we go to the XenoCon campus to plug it all into the transceiver array because there's not a single other place in the city that this has a chance of working!" Leo watched them. "Chop chop!"

Damien leaned against the desktop, looking at his brother for help. Von's look was similar.

"Oh," Leo chirped when they didn't say anything. "Wait, I *did* hear something else!"

"Care to share?"

"Oh yes," he said, steepling his fingers in thought. "Yes, I snuck into the equipment that Carson and his partner have set up in the Space Needle. They caught wind of a squadron of Stingships launching north from Portland."

"You're lucky they didn't catch you," Damien said. "You know how paranoid they are about their equipment." Carson and his husband had holed themselves up in the Space Needle for more than two years, operating a citywide radio network for emergencies and the occasional news bulletin. It was better than Thomas and his sons' getup, but not quite as personable. Damien wondered how they had miraculously avoided getting caught for so long with such a high profile, but he hadn't thought to ask on the two occasions they had met.

Leo scoffed. "They had about as much luck at finding me as The Collective would if you let me fiddle with *their* system."

Von bowled over Damien's retort. "So the 'investigative patrol' is already on its way, and they are coming in Stingships. What of it?"

Damien popped his mouth shut. *Stingships aren't anything new*, he agreed. *It could just be another patrol*. But something in the way Leo answered made him keep his mouth shut.

"Well," said the AI, wandering around the edges of his space on the desktop. "Carson's equipment thought the Stingships didn't look quite normal, so I cross-checked that against what we've compiled here and… they were right, they aren't." The AI paused, distracted by a blip that had just appeared on one of the Pip screens.

"Leo—"

"—*Shh!* I had an idea!"

They waited.

The blip went away after a few seconds.

"Anyways, what was I saying? Oh right, I was brilliant and cross-referenced those ships and found out that those pseudo-Stingships are probably carrying Avos!" He spread his hands in excitement, the wrong response to that proclamation.

Damien's blood ran cold. Von sucked in air next to him. "That's not funny," Von said.

Leo giggled. "Ha, oh I'm not joking! I very much wish I were, *believe* me, but at least you know your antics last night merited the very best that the Over-Seer has to offer, right? Come on, handpicked commandos with jumping boots and fancy Prism camouflage invisibility armor? Big, curving switchblades as long as your arm? Kill counts numbering in the hundreds and years of training to make the perfect predators?" His giggle turned frightening. "What's not to like?!"

Damien swallowed, and he noticed Von's ganglia had gone very still. *We can't beat Avos*, he thought. *They'd tear us to pieces before we knew they were there.* He remembered the one time he and Von had encountered the Over-Seer's elite enforcers—five years ago, before they'd found the bunker. They had been trying to protect a dock alongside a small band of Seattle insurgents. A ship used to come into port once a month to offload valuable supplies from the Regent Dynasty and the Eurasian Union, but this particular time they'd heard the ship had special cargo, so more people had shown up to receive it. Usually just one or two locals had been enough, but they wanted to know what was coming in.

The group never found out what it was, because two Avos were all The Collective had needed to route the entire band.

The monstrous pair of invisible commandos had decapitated five of their band before they knew what had happened. Another man had gone down when the mirage of Prism armor had shimmered past him and a split-second later, blood had exploded from the holes in his chest. That had left Damien, Von, two sisters whom they had spent a few months alongside, a man named Devin who had been a little older than Damien, and an ex-sailor named Will. In a moment that both Damien and Von had agreed was their least favorable in all their time since the earthquake, the two had seen the bloodshed, and knew they had to hide.

They had crawled into a storm drain nearby and watched as the shadowy deceptions slaughtered their friends. The screams, the smell of panicked piss, people's insides, the rain, and the slash of curved *avosas* blades dicing through bone still swallowed Damien's worst nightmares, casting any other bad dream aside as child's play.

The ship they had been trying to protect never arrived, because there had been no one on the docks to signal it, and the brothers had never seen it again.

Damien set his jaw, remembering the terror he'd felt that night, and how helpless he'd been. No amount of Elemental power could have saved them from even two Avos, and it was only a small comfort that the only reason he and his brother stood here today was because they'd been forced to cower in a river of wet shit.

He focused back on Leo. "Did you see how many were coming?"

Leo's terrified giggling had subsided and he'd adopted a position on his haunches, elbows on his knees, focused on a model of the Space Needle he'd conjured. "I did."

"How many—" Damien cleared his throat, "—how many are coming?"

Leo looked up. His silvery eyes glinted with a mixture of excitement, curiosity, and fear. "Nine."

The little strength Damien had gleaned from sleep and breakfast left him, and his limbs began to tremble. He felt his heart pounding in his chest, and deep inside, the black pool of power in his body rippled, feeling as if it wanted to challenge that number, but Damien's conscious fear overrode it. He looked over to see that Von suddenly looked very tired, and he too was staring at a far-off place.

"I'm sorry, boys," said Leo, and he meant it. "But if you want what happened last night to mean something, we have to go out there, tonight. We have to see if we can get our little network-hacking contraption to work with that black box, and we have to do it on the far side of the city, at the Xenocultural Conglomerate Campus, possibly through a small army of The Collective's very best assassins, and *hope* that the gear we need is still there."

CHAPTER FIVE

Stingships

The day flew by. Leo stretched a part of himself back into the Space Needle to listen for any signs of the approaching commandos, but learned they were apparently still too far away. That made the trio work that much harder to pack their gear. The brothers both thoroughly feared the idea of encountering Avos in the city.

While they bustled along with their work, Damien kept telling his brother to take it easy, but Von wouldn't listen. He hated seeing Von up and running so hard on his leg, and he kept waiting to hear his brother cry out that one of the leads on his splint had snapped, but the alien never said a word.

While they worked, Leo conveyed the rest of the bad news about the Avos, and while that had made Damien equal parts anxious and frustrated to go as soon as possible, the AI had insisted that they wait for dusk. "Another storm is going to hit us tonight," he said, "and it might be unpleasant, but a blizzard at night is obviously easier to hide in than a sunny day with fresh snow on the ground."

Damien couldn't deny that logic.

"So when will the commandos arrive?" Von asked at one point while they ran around the bunker, collecting gear, cleaning their weapons, and arguing over what else they should bring as 'just in case' items.

"Soon," Leo answered. "But I have a feeling they'll be landing where you hit the Razer first to see what exactly happened. That should give you some time."

"If it takes *them* time to figure out what happened," Damien snapped, sitting at their workbench. He rubbed his eyes while he fiddled with his aural implant, which he had taken out for the maintenance he'd thought it needed for months. The thing had been itching something fierce, and the last thing he needed was his translator failing him when he might need to understand German or Dekka or Spanish.

"No need to get fussy with me!" Leo complained. "Don't shoot the messenger, remember?"

Damien didn't answer.

"What about the weather?" Von asked, limping back into the main room, laden with his winter clothes and customized human Plaster rifle that he had altered to fit an Algaroth's larger hands.

"Snow," said Leo simply, bringing up their scratchy map of the region.

What I wouldn't do for a satellite picture, Damien thought, looking up from his micro-tools to see the Puget Sound, hovering in the holographic space Leo occupied. Humanity's entire satellite network had been knocked out when The Conquering started, and Damien had always said that a good map was as priceless over food as food was priceless over having a toy. He thought a good map could weigh down scales against his own life even, potentially. Not Von's, but maybe his.

The map the three of them possessed was cobbled together over many years from the survivors of Seattle and other sources. Leo had made many improvements on it over the last couple of years in particular, but it still wasn't as good as anything humanity had had before The Conquering.

For the moment, the AI had brought up their best weather forecast, but the few street cameras the brothers had placed nullified its usefulness: Dark clouds were broiling out west over the ocean. A storm was coming, much bigger than the one last night. Just looking at the clouds gave Damien the crisp chills that came with a clear, cold day, soon to get colder.

As the day wore on, an unspoken reality slowly occurred to the trio: if ever there was a night they may not come home, it was tonight. The thought left a heavy weight on Damien's shoulders. He saw it in his brother too, and heard it in Leo's more frequent complaints about leaving the bunker.

"I thought you *wanted* to leave?!" Von finally barked from down the hall after Leo had chattered without breath about it for a full five minutes.

"I do!" the AI yipped, wringing his hands. "It's nothing to do with that, you hear me? Don't start questioning me, fleshling. I'll cause problems with your computer and I could poison your water if I had hands to do it!"

Von growled from his bunkroom.

Damien knew why Leo got anxious about leaving the bunker, as much as he made a fuss about wanting to do so: When he and Von had first found it four years ago, just after the quake, they had spent months just trying to get in. When they finally did, they found it not only fully furnished and stocked, but also suspiciously unused. There was even a covert, military-grade listening suite built into the desktop. The bunker had been equipped with armed security measures without alarms, and at the back of the storage hall they had found a vault. The brothers had decided that the whole place must have been a fallback shelter for the Solar Intelligence Office—long since forgotten since that branch of the Solar Warfare Division had died with Apollo Base. With that assumption, they had guessed that no one would be coming back for it anytime soon, so they settled in.

Yet even with their move into the bunker, the vault had sat quiet and sealed down the hall opposite the entryway. It had taken another four months to pry into. When they did finally break their way in, all they had found was a small cube on a pedestal. Inside that cube had been Leo.

They had woken the AI and tried to get answers about what the bunker was, but he hadn't known any more than they. All he could tell them about his past was that he was an adult AI, he had chosen his own name, and he could be invaluable to them. Neither of them would ever deny the truth of those first words. The AI's origins, though, were a mystery for which the trio was always on the lookout for more clues. Damien knew Leo got anxious about leaving because—as far as the AI was aware—he had been "born" here.

I forget how young he is in human years, Damien thought, watching his AI companion. *Though I suppose in an AI's lifespan that means nothing.* He knew an Artificial Intelligence could 'live' for as long as there was space to contain them, but he had never heard of any older than twelve. *A whole life, packed into less time than it takes for a human to hit puberty.* AI constructs had the same capacity to grow as anyone else, but would deteriorate and eventually die if they couldn't do so. They were limited by the boundaries of data, yet Damien wondered if, one day, the synthetic creations could break that boundary. He watched Leo as the little being fiddled with a model of their hacking rig that would hopefully crack into The Collective's military network. Damien found himself hoping that, one day, Leo could become a creature of matter, rather than a mess of thrice criss-crossing light beams over a projecting surface.

Unfortunately, while the AI didn't tire, Damien and Von did. They broke briefly for an afternoon meal and for Damien to change Von's bandages and check on his leg.

"How does it look?" Von asked.

Damien bit his lip, trying to hide his concern. "Could be better," he said. *I knew I should have just knocked him out after breakfast.*

"I'm just fine," Von complained.

Damien didn't answer. The splint already showed signs of wear; the polyplastic circlets were dirty and looked loose, and while none of the connecting nerve-leads had fallen out of place yet, Damien could tell they were strained. He shook his head as he re-tightened the bands, cleaned the wound, and replaced the poultice, cover, and bandages. *I'll have to keep an eye on him tonight.*

After that was done, they ate a quick meal of cold fish and the last of the grapes, trying to talk about anything but the night ahead. When they finished, Leo announced that he needed to look at the black box and that Damien needed to go upstairs to get it. Damien agreed, grabbed his jacket—which he had cleaned as much blood off of as he could—and gloves, buckled his modified Plaster pistol to his hip, and left his brother and Leo to work out final details of their mission.

Dusk had already fallen when Damien emerged from the bunker. The sky hung low and oppressive; grey, just like the last night. Through the broken skylights and peeling roof of the warehouse, he thought the fresh night looked as if no time had passed since they went underground the night before. It was quiet too, and cold enough that he couldn't smell anything. The same ruddy light of the city bounced off the clouds as it had while he sat in the windowsill, and snow lay drifted in parts of the warehouse. He crouched at the top of the stairs and listened, demanding that the only sound was silence.

When he was certain nothing was about to leap out, Damien found the sheet that made their false wall. He grimaced at the tear his boots had made when he bowled through it with Von. *Lost both of our reflective sheets in one night. Of course we did.* He balled up the silvery, silky material and lobbed it down the stairs, unwilling to deal with it just now.

Out in front of the warehouse, he thought he could still see their tracks coming up the hill, but maybe that was just his imagination running paranoid. He shook it off and opened the door to the cargo container, checking over his shoulder for a long minute to be sure the compound was truly empty.

Satisfied, he shut the door behind him and flipped on the lighting strip he'd stuck to the ceiling. His motorcycle sat where he'd left it, their two heavy duffels lashed to the back. Damien patted the bike as if he were seeing an old friend, remembering how it had gotten them out of more harrowing situations than last night. It had saved both of their lives more than once.

Taking a minute to check on its workings, Damien let the peace of tinkering with machinery wash over him. He loved tinkering almost as much as Leo loved snooping, and he was proud of his part in putting together the hacking rig that had prompted last nights' raid. The thing had originally been Von's idea, but Leo had written the entire program that would interface with the black box, and it had been Damien who designed and assembled the components of it, ultimately shrinking the device down to about the size of his arm. He grinned feebly as he crawled under his cycle, thinking about how he had cannibalized a few parts from it for their long-standing project.

Lying on his back, Damien inspected his motorcycle. The bike didn't actually have a motor; a tiny, hydrogen-electric generator powered it instead. No one actually called their bikes 'hydracycles' though—a motorcycle would always be a motorcycle, no matter what its descendants morphed into.

He finished checking the charge levels on the generator, and noticed the crest was chipped. It was a stylized 'T' imposed over an 'M', and stood for Tiamoto Motors—an old and coveted manufacturer based out of the former nation of Mongolia, in the Regent Dynasty. *She needs paint*, he thought, scratching a bit of the enamel off. Upon seeing the wear he'd put on the bike in the past months, he suddenly found a growing list of problems. *And I should replace the tires. Oh and new diodes, new shocks...* He inspected the front panel and found it was dented and scratched, the black sheen wrinkled. *And a body too, apparently.* He sighed, knowing the odds of him ever getting the time to work on the bike he loved so much were slim. Finally, he had to shake himself out of the stupor, aware that they didn't have time for him to play mechanic. He wiped the grime off his hands and dug into Von's duffle, where the black box was hidden. Inspecting the thing for the first time, Damien wondered at how similar some things were between humans and Algaroth.

The black box was pill-shaped, and almost a uniform shade of onyx. It was about the size and length of two American footballs put end-to-end, but other than that it felt distinctly alien. The grips were too wide and thick for human fingers; the glisten of it sparkled with otherworldly metal. Damien checked closer and found a splatter of blood on one side, mud on the other. It made him grin. *It's just another piece of junk hardware that makes everything run, not some holy key that will change the course of a war.* He tucked the box under his arm. *Then again, if all goes well tonight... maybe it'll be exactly that.* It was an encouraging thought.

Turning the light off, Damien left the duffels full of gear; the brothers planned to take them to Bar and Shell's to trade before going to the XenoCon campus. He cracked the door to the container and listened, shivering as the cold air snuck in. The wider the door opened, the less he heard.

Silence. Damien held still. Silence made him nervous.

His footsteps crunched far too loudly in the snow, and even the *whump* of the container door closing sounded as loud as a gong. The wind had died down, and all stayed quiet.

Damien rounded the warehouse on tiptoe, listening in the gloom. He made it through the small oiled door next to the sealed bay doors without incident and worked his way between the containers, creeping as fast as he dared. He was almost to the stairs when he heard a noise outside.

He froze, hand outstretched for the steps down to the bunker. *No, you're imagining things*. He strained his ears, hoping he was right. Truly, they almost never had visitors at the compound on the hill.

He waited.

When he didn't hear anything else, Damien decided he was okay. He was about to move when he heard it again: The soft crunch of snow underfoot.

His eyes narrowed, his breathing shallow and controlled. *No, no, no, not Avos. They can't have found us already.*

The crunching sounded faint, but that didn't mean anything. It was the sound of something alive, and he didn't trust living things near home.

Damien replaced his boot on the ground and carefully set the black box next to the stairs. He turned to face the west side of the warehouse. His heart had started to pound, and adrenaline mixed into his veins. The snow crunched again.

Something was out there.

Silently furious that he couldn't warn Von without giving himself away, he crept forward and unholstered his pistol, feeling the comforting weight of it in his hand. *If that's an Avo, I'm dead.*

Again, the snow crunched underfoot.

It came from just beyond the western side door. Damien slunk towards it, rolling each step. The noise had stopped by the time he reached the wall. He pressed against it, trying to see out. Seeing nothing, he pulled back the cloth that hung over the bay window with intimate slowness. The window was dirty, and he could barely see out of it, but there didn't appear to be anyone out there.

Then, he heard a sniff.

His heart skipped.

Whatever had made it sounded big, and it wasn't human. Damien could tell it was right outside. He controlled his breathing, waiting for the sound of a blade being unsheathed, or a trigger being pulled. *Nothing yet.*

Ever so slowly, he brought his pistol to bear, safety off. *This might be it*, he thought. *Right here. This is the end.*

Taking a deep breath, Damien reached for the handle. Nothing moved. The air was as tense as a graveyard.

Damien flung the door wide with a deafening bang.

The only thing he expected less than nothing was the terrified yowl from the stray dog at his feet. The ragged little animal fell over its hind legs in its rush to bolt from the compound, shrieking. Damien stayed tense in his shock as he watched the animal run, howling and yelping away down the hill, ragged tail tucked between its legs. He looked down and saw the scraps of some rodent on his doorstep, and he let a ragged sigh escape his lips.

"Well, sorry for ruining dinner, mutt," he muttered. "You scared the hell out of *me* though, so I think we're even."

Damien kicked the scraps away, his guard lowering as the dog's yowls were swallowed in the distance. All was as it should be, and he eyed the new line of tracks in the snow from the animal. *I almost shot you, dammit.* He swallowed, trying to get his breathing under control.

When he did, his gaze took in the ring of trees at the base of the Mercer Islet, where the low foundry building of their compound could be seen. Until the earthquake, their compound had been a refuse repurposing plant, where all manner of trash was brought, sorted, and reshipped all over the world to be reused in a recycled capacity. The windows of the building were all dark.

Damien's gaze continued upward, over the rooftops of the other industrial buildings nearby, over the treetops, and over the cold black glisten of the Puget Channels flowing between the islets, until he stood looking west, where the Downtown Islet of Seattle was clearly visible, beyond which the Puget Sound sluiced in the dark. The tallest buildings of

Downtown poked just barely into the thick drape of clouds, but holes in the skyline reminded Damien of where other skyscrapers used to stand.

The fractured cityscape glimmered faintly at Damien over the treetops. Barely half of the buildings showed any lights in them, and only a single window was aglow in the Space Needle. *Carson's and his husband's radio gear.* He gave a deep, controlled sigh. Despite the relative peace of the surrounding area, he knew that nearby, Collective patrols roamed the streets, hunting for men and women, children, or defected Algaroth, and all of them were gunned down without mercy when found. Granted, every person left in the city was a fighter, but that only helped so much when there was no unifying movement to rally behind. The insurgency only existed as a title so that citizens could say they hadn't listened to the military's advisory to evacuate nearly a decade ago when The Collective had first made the jump from the Central American Bridge to Port Angeles.

Of course, The Collective picks off everyone who's still here one by one. Damien thought of the night at the docks. He shivered and itched his forearms.

Just then, a new sound reached his ears, and Damien didn't have to listen to know what it was. The calm of the moment was shattered, and terror blossomed in his stomach. *Please no... no don't be that please don't be that.* In seconds, the sound grew from a faint hum to a high-pitched buzz, reminiscent of a wasp. Something was coming.

I hate snow. I hate leaving tracks in the fucking snow! He couldn't move, he couldn't run, but at this close they had to have spotted him, so all he could do was stand still and hope the enemy wasn't looking.

Less than a minute later, they zipped by overhead, just under the ceiling of gloom: Nine Collective Stingships dominated the low sky above, and Damien could do nothing but watch.

The ships were shaped vaguely like human skulls, but Damien knew their profile enough to know right away that they weren't normal—just like Leo had predicted. It didn't take him long though to realize they weren't coming for him, but that didn't matter.

The Avos had arrived.

He watched the Stingships' agile bodies grow smaller in the distance over Downtown, flying in perfect formation, ignoring him entirely. Before Damien lost sight of them, he ran, pelting back inside as hard as he could. Silence didn't matter anymore; it was time to *move*.

He careened down the steps and through the series of doors, tumbling into the bunker a minute later. He gasped for breath, clutching the black box to his chest. Von was over to him in a second, and Leo looked up curiously.

"What happened? Are you alright?" Von reached for his Gyro pistol hanging in its holster next to the door, uncertain.

"St—*Stingships*," Damien gasped, clutching the stitch in his chest and trying to breathe through the easily twenty-degree shift in temperature from outside to in here. "They—they're here! Just… *ahh*… just flew overhead!" He pointed wildly, doubled over. "Headed, *mm*, headed Downtown! We have to get moving!"

Von stared at Leo, who had gleefully swept the contents of his projected workbench aside. The model of their hacking rig shattered in a hail of teal particles. Leo took no notice. "Silas," he called, "I'm starting that transfer now. No time to debate about it!"

Damien blinked hard, suddenly feeling very out of shape but knowing it was just his nerves and the cold. "Wha—what's he saying?"

Von limped the black box to Leo while Damien came inside. "We were discussing a contingency about coming back."

"What do you mean?" Damien paced a few times, feeling his heart rate finally slow.

"I'm downloading our entire aggregate library into my cube," Leo answered. "Enemy troop movements, hardware, software, weapons, tactics, names, dates, theories, deaths, research, all of it. No backups. If something happens tonight, I don't want all of this stuff just waiting in this computer for someone to find it."

Damien frowned, brushing his sweaty hair from his eyes. "You can't possibly mean—"

"SIO? The Solar Intelligence Office?" Leo laughed. "Hell no! But there are plenty of people who would want to know all of this; I would just rather keep it on me."

"It's a precaution," Von said, sounding as if he were waiting for Damien to disagree.

He knows I hate the idea of never coming back here, he thought. "It's fine," he said, and saw his brother visibly relax. "It's a good idea. How long will it take to transfer to your cube?"

"Done!" Leo said, doing a little kick-jump.

"Really? Almost a petabyte of data in that thing and you're done already?"

Leo slid backwards, assuming his full outfit of Sherlock Holmes; an ensemble replete with fine shoes, pleated pants, matching trench coat and Inverness cape, double-billed deerstalker cap, calabash pipe, and magnifying glass. "It's Elemental, my dear Damien," he chuckled, assuming a spot-on English accent with his spin on the classic phrase. "Everything I could use, I keep in here," he tapped his temple with the pipe. "Everything else... well, there's very little I find no use *for*, old chap. Now, you were tattering on about something important, were you not?"

Damien nodded, frazzled. "*Yeah*, I was wondering if we were all packed and ready, remember? Avos upstairs?!" He gestured for emphasis.

Standing in profile so his cap sat wide and his high-collared coat hid most of his face, Leo grinned. "I've already checked the black box. It'll do nicely with this cracking rig we've assembled. Silas has sportingly agreed to carry the physical components, *you* will carry *me* in your rucksack, and I?" He paused, flashing the magnifying glass. "Why, *I*, dear fellows, will lead you on a grand adventure! We go forth into the world together, to combat whatever nefarious plots await us. We will stand against the tides of stupidity and xenocidal monsters, and bring justice to a wild world! In fact..." his silver eyes positively gleamed. "I say, Damien, do you know what is happening, what time it is?"

Damien sighed. "Yeah... 'The game is—'"

"*The game is afoot!*" Leo crowed, leaping off his Pip pad and out of projected space, disappearing in a smash of cubits.

Damien and Von traded a look, knowing there was nothing to say about what came next. They returned to their bunkrooms to gather a few last bits of gear and not twenty minutes later, the trio exited the bunker.

Silas Von went first, armored in jointed skeleton boots to accommodate his splayed Algaroth toes that supported his heavy feet. Plated legwear covered his legs—wound and all—and his narrow hips, while a thick armor-mesh undershirt covered his forearms and chest, wicking moisture. He had donned a warm wrapshirt under his three-piece, human-made armor coat, which left his forearms exposed. The coat had seen years of heavy use, as had the ribbed neck guard that crawled up through it and protected Von's lower jaw, making him almost look like a tusk-less boar thanks to the guards' protruding chin. Over the black cheek pads curling back from the neck guard, the alien's eyes glowed luminescent in the biting cold. Finally, Von had put on the back half of his winter helmet, leaving only his snout and the top of his head exposed. On one side, the helmet covered part of his ear-hole, and that was where his earpiece for their communications gear sat.

The two meters of Algaroth muscle stomped out of their bunker and into the warehouse, armed with his Gyro pistol, Plaster rifle, and a serrated ice pick with which he'd grown quite fond. His backpack locked securely to his armor coat, inside which their all-important hacking rig lay coiled with a few other items.

Damien came next, wearing his combat boots, a layer of armor-skin, heavy wool pants, and pocketed combat pants over that. He wore only a synthetic undershirt, a heavy wool pullover, and his worn, beaten, but favorite jacket—the same one he'd worn the night before, and countless nights before that. His precious goggles hung around his neck over a balaclava, the violet lenses dark. Sensitive combat gloves kept his hands warm, and in his ruddy old backpack, Leo's cube sat snug in its slot next to the black box and Damien's collection of odds and ends. The backpack had curling, adhesive tendrils that wrapped it straplessly to Damien's jacket, minimizing how much it flapped around. On his hip, Damien's modified Plaster pistol sat securely; his only physical weapon.

As the doors to their bunker closed behind them, Damien and his brother watched the dark main room vanish beyond the frosted panel. Damien wondered if they would be back in the morning, or ever. *Thanks for keeping us safe*, he thought of the place. *Thanks for being a home when we needed one.*

With that, Damien followed his brother through the old steel door to the warehouse and keyed their code into the pad, setting the entire bunker to self-destruct should someone try to force their way in.

MASON J. TORALL

CHAPTER SIX

On The Streets of the Sound

"You always bring us the very pick of the goods, Vilan! You are a good man!" Turk "Bar" Mburu bellowed over the clatter of Collective hardware falling onto the wide steel table. The raucous was deafening, but Bar was louder. "Oh, this is so much! I take it back, old friend, you have been holding out on us!" He waggled his middle finger since his index was short a joint.

Damien grinned as the pieces of dirty, pearly white armor landed everywhere. "Bar, we'd never hide gear from you. This was just from a daring raid we made!" He caught a power cell before it bounced to the ground and tossed it on the pile. "We're just that skilled."

Bar howled with laughter, an enormous man with too many chins and not enough digits, but the ones he still had wielded a cutting torch in a calloused, masters' dance. Damien had always imagined that if Bar weren't wearing a heavy black apron charred with metal filings, then he would wear a bloodstained apron with a butcher's knife instead.

"No, no, not what I think it is," Bar said, looming across from them, fighting through his mirth. He snatched the body of a Gyro rifle off the table and spun it, driving the cutting torch along the seam under the weapon. "I think you are either hoarding, or..." he finished his cut in record time, and the glowing insides of the alien rifle spilled out. An amorphous glow gleamed through the dark space of the old industrial kitchen where Bar and Shell's black market store was hidden. "*Or*, you were the boys behind that mess the night before this. Perhaps?" He eyed them through puffy cheeks with hard, flinty eyes, waving his cutting torch. "There's plenty of talk about a Razer going down the far side of town. Would you know enough about that to tell old friends? I think you would."

Bar snatched the catalytic cylinder from its housing in the weapon and lumbered over to his stool. There, a jointed lamp focused on a cleared workspace surrounded by tiny components, alien and human. He pulled the lamp up and produced a mini, single-lens omniscope that nearly vanished between his meaty fingers. Damien looked on as Bar flicked through each spectrum available in the tiny device. Radio, microwave, infrared, naked eye, ultraviolet, x-ray, gamma; each lens showed a different perspective through the monocular lens. Bar hummed and cooed as he scanned the alien device.

Even after knowing Bar for over two years, Damien always noted the pallor of the man's skin under light: it looked as if it had once been the consistency and color of leather, but had grown pale and sagging from too much time out of the sun. "Mmm very nice," Bar murmured at last.

"We do know about the raid," Von interjected, eyeing his own pile already scattered over the table. "We hit the Razer, and it took a piece of me to do it." He flashed the awkward bulge on his wounded leg.

Bar eyed Von's wound, stony-faced. His gaze drifted up to the alien's snout and they stared long and hard at each other. Finally, Bar's eyes crinkled and he broke into a toothy grin. "You were shot? Ha! You still have a fit face! You can't complain. Just look at me!" He slapped his chins so they wobbled like gelatin, and he chuckled. The laugh died quickly though as something occurred to him, and he eyed the mass of equipment on the table.

"What?" Damien asked.

Bar snorted. "Okay, so you tell the truth. You blow up the Razer. That is the only reason for you bringing this much gear. Am I supposed to be impressed? Bah! So what!" He gestured his arms wide at Damien. "Shell and I do not care, so long as you bring us your goods! You do this, Vilan, and we stay friends! It is that simple!" The big man turned back to his workspace. "Though I do not like what I hear before you arrive," he added. "Have you heard these talks? I hear talks of the Over-Seer turning his eyes to our little city. He turns his little 'Avos' over to us. *Pah!*" He spat.

Damien and Von traded looks. "We've heard," Damien said. "That's why we're out tonight."

From the back of the dark, expansive ex-kitchen, an Algaroth voice drifted over the dully gleaming maze of counters, tables, crates, and bundles of hardware that made up Bar and Shell's store—a collection of items traded and salvaged from people across the city. Almost everyone brought anything not immediately useful here. Bar and Shell were well-known tradesmen. "Avos aren't sent out without good reason," said the Algaroth. His English was clean, deep and decisive, pronouncing the hard to enunciate 'P-B-M' sounds of with unusually thick lips.

Through the maze, Lacon "Shell" Shellador appeared, carrying empty tubs. The Algaroth was only a touch lighter blue than Von, but he looked a bit older. He had dark orange specks in his eyes under thinning ganglia that flicked about lazily. He wore a similar apron to Bar's over a collared crimson vest. The Algaroth plunked down the tubs and the brothers rounded the table to greet him.

"Shell," said Von, and he moved to embrace the other alien in the Algaroth traditional way that friends might greet each other: They locked forearms and splayed the opposite hands on each other's chests, pushing with one hand and pulling with the other. It was a display of equal respect.

When they parted, Damien gripped Shell's hand and embraced the Algaroth briefly. "It's good to see you."

Shell nodded, "And you, Damien. Will you help?" He indicated the bins and their gear, and the brothers jumped to help him sort it. "I heard the talk of Avos arriving," he said. "We don't believe them."

Von looked surprised while he sorted, tossing armor into one bin, weapons into another, and miscellaneous gear into a third. He switched to chopped German to address the other Algaroth—though both Damien and Bar understood just fine through their implants. "Why not?"

Shell answered in German as well, still pulling off his P-B-M's fluently. "Because Avos are only sent on special missions," he said. "What's special about the Islets?"

Bar hooted. The sound echoed through the shadowy kitchen. "Why... *us*, my friend, of course!"

They all grinned and kept sorting.

"I hate to break it to you two," Damien added without looking up. "But the talk is true. We heard from Carson up in the Needle. He said he saw a flight of weird-looking Stingships leaving Portland earlier today, and I saw them myself tonight, just after dusk."

Bar and Shell traded a look. "I… don't know if I would trust Carson's word," said Shell slowly, switching back to English. "But I would trust your word. You're sure they weren't just Stingships and you saw wrong, or that Carson was who you talked to?"

They can't know that Carson didn't give us that intel, can they? The brothers had never told Bar or Shell about Leo, but Damien thought it best not to worry about that now. He just shook his head while Bar fired up his torch on another Gyro rifle. "I know what I saw," he yelled over the hiss of metal melting. "But that's why we're out here tonight!"

Bar stopped. "You did not come to your old friends tonight just to do usual trade, did you?"

"No," said Von. "We have news."

"Of what?" Shell asked. His ganglia slowed their flicking about.

Damien eyed Von, who nodded. "Do you remember the experiment we were working on?"

Shell nodded. "Of course. The way to break into The Collective's networked systems. You said it was a hacking rig that you started months ago?"

Von nodded. "Almost a year, actually."

Holy shit, that long? Damien hadn't thought of that, but kept it to himself. "That's the one."

"You said you needed… a black box recorder…" Bar trailed off, and the suspicion returned to his eyes. He squinted between the two of them, spinning slowly in his chair and brandishing his cutting torch. "You have not opened your backpacks, Vilans. You always have items in your duffels *and* in your packs. What do you have?"

Unable to contain themselves, Damien and Von gleefully produced the black box and the hacking rig out of their respective bags and handed them over.

"Ohh," Bar moaned, taking the rig as if he were handling an infant. "Ohh this is *lovely!*" He caressed the hodge-podge contraption, admiring the rare components that made it up. "You have assembled all you needed?"

"Yep," Damien answered.

"Even the software?"

"Mm hmm, it's all there."

"That's why you are out hunting tonight! Ahh this is good news!" Bar leapt off his stool and took Damien by surprise in a bone-crushing hug. The man stank of sweat, burnt metal, and old wood. Somehow, it was deeply comforting, like how a favorite retired uncle might smell. "You are good boys, yes!" he boomed. "Ahh where are you going to use it?" His hard eyes had softened, and he looked between them expectantly.

When they didn't answer immediately, Shell spoke up. "They must be braving the whole city," he murmured. "There's only one place that still has working human-Algaroth gear."

Von eyed the other Algaroth with a guarded look, but Damien knew it was both fear and sadness that lurked behind his brother's eyes. "XenoCon," Von admitted.

Bar's features turned confused, "The campus? That is not so far away… but you have many dangerous islets between here and there."

"We know," Damien answered. *And tonight will be exceptionally so.*

"Either way, we're going tonight," said Von, switching back to German. "If Avos are in the city, we have to see if our idea works before those Collective enforcers cause trouble."

Or find us, Damien thought, but the words went unspoken.

Comprehension dawned on Bar just slower than his quieter companion. "You bring the gear to us because you think you will not return tonight. You think the Avos are after your box."

Shell spoke up. "Why did you bring it all here?"

Von smirked. "For the good company."

Damien grinned too. "Because you two know more people who can use it than us." He tossed a handful of power cells into the nearly full bin. "And you'll be fair about trading it."

Bar's somberness cleared as quickly as it had come and he laughed heartily, clapping them both on the shoulders. "Well, if you are going to die, I wish you wouldn't, Vilans. I am not glad to see either of you go. You shoot straight, and some of us will miss you." He glanced at Shell, who nodded and moved away to the back of the store, towards the kitchen's walk-in preservator.

"Thanks," said Damien. "We'll be alright though. And if this works, we might have a game-changer for what's playing out, even beyond the city."

"And if you aren't alright," said Bar, "we will still be here to fight now and tomorrow, just like we fight yesterday."

"The cycle goes on," Shell said, returning with a small pack of supplies for them, wrapped neatly in a thermal blanket. "And you should still be given goods for what you give."

"I hope the cycle changes," said Damien, looking at the bundle. "And actually, we're running heavy enough tonight as it is. Keep it for us until we get back."

Bar looked offended. "We do not hold goods for anyone, Vilan. You know this!"

"Then we're offering you a steal in gear and merchandise," said Von.

The laughter finally faded from Bar's eyes, and he suddenly looked very sad. "You are truly afraid tonight, aren't you?"

They both nodded tightly.

Bar examined the network of old vents and pipes crisscrossing the high ceiling. "You ah… you know what? You wait here a moment. One moment!" He slid off his stool and waddled away, welding boots squeaking on the floor. They waited.

When Bar returned, he held something much smaller than the bundle, wrapped in fine black cloth. "For you," he said. "You are friends and customers, suppliers and traders. If this is the last we see of you, I would give you something. A token of honest friendship, something not bartered." He handed the cloth to Von, who unwrapped it carefully.

Inside the cloth was a pendant, flawlessly made and hooked to a heavy silver chain. Von's eyes went wide as he showed it to Damien. The pendant was round, and just larger than Damien's palm. Inside the silver border ring, an etched silver spire of the Space Needle sat at the forefront, with three tiny lines of sapphires woven in as the windows. Behind the spire, the motif of the human-Algaroth insurgency filled the background: a blue alien Gyro rifle and a red human Plaster rifle, crossed in front of a muted yellow sun. It was beautiful craftsmanship.

Damien was stunned. "Bar... this is..."

"Don't you say a word, Vilan. You are taking it, or I will kick you out of my shop. Take it, leave, and good health to you both—should we not be seeing you again." The enormous man grinned. "And if we *are* to be seeing you, then you come get your good health from us."

Damien blew air out slowly, finally choosing to just shut his mouth and nod. He wrapped the treasure with delicate fingers and slipped it into the hidden pocket at the bottom of his backpack, where he kept only his irreplaceable possessions. He tucked it behind a crinkled family picture of the Vilans, which lay next to a battered white rook chess piece, a tiny amethyst coin, and his little journal that he'd had in his boot before the raid. He had taken it all from the bunker before they sealed it, along with only a few other emergency supplies and gear. He and Von had never had time to collect many sentimentals, but the rook was a piece of home, childhood, and family, and the amethyst coin was from the only girlfriend he'd ever had. He sealed the pocket and replaced his backpack, feeling the tiny tug as it wrapped tightly to his jacket.

Their trade complete, the humans shook hands and the Algaroth did the same respectful greeting as their goodbye.

"We wish you the best," Damien said.

"And for you," said Shell.

Von and Bar nodded, waving. Then, the brothers replaced the hacking rig and the black box, made sure they hadn't forgotten anything, turned, and left.

In the alleyway outside, the air was frigid and the clouds seemed lower than ever. The hidden entrance to Bar and Shell's was at the back of a short alley, blocked by a recycling dumpster. On the wall next to the door, the same motif as the one on the pendant was stenciled in red, yellow, and blue. The brothers slipped around the dumpster and lifted the top. Together, they hefted Damien's motorcycle out and rolled it to the street. Tall piton pillars cast pale light around them, highlighting the emptiness. Only a few personal cars sat parked under an awning, long-since abandoned. Nothing else disturbed the side street.

The brother's footfalls were muffled on the soft snow, which had just started to fall again in tiny flakes, dryer than the night before. They climbed onto the cycle, Von just up and behind Damien. Damien started the bike, and the warm thrum of it filled the air.

"Okay, I waited until you were back on the bike, can I *talk now?!*" Leo moaned, speaking directly through his cube into their earpieces.

"Yes Leo, you can talk. Thank you for being patient," Damien answered, while Von groaned behind him.

"Uh huh, yeah, you know you two take the *longest* time to get moving, you know that?"

"Yes Leo, we know, and if you tell me again I'll mute your ass until we really need you." Damien said, and without waiting for an answer, he took off.

The AI parried when they turned onto the main street, also abandoned. "You mute me and I'll start testing the Seattle emergency broadcast system."

Von snorted into the wind.

"I saw that."

Damien felt Von tense behind him and scan the street for cameras as Leo laughed, "Oh you are *so* gullible Silas! What a pleasure it must be to be unburdened by the wonders of a big brain."

Von growled. He pulled his ribbed neck guard back up over his snout and snapped his cheek flaps into place.

They fell into cautious silence as they began the trek across the city. Damien felt much more at ease with both Von and Leo with him, but they couldn't go anywhere on the streets without feeling tense.

"Any word on those Avos?" Damien asked.

"Nope," Leo answered. "Although I heard a scattered word that the street where you blew up the Razer was swarming with people until about an hour ago, when it fell silent."

Damien's gut cinched. *Avos.* He ground his teeth at the thought. *No one should be that stupid to go looking for a hot spot like that.* Then a pang of guilt hit him. *They wouldn't have a hot spot to go looking* for *if I didn't screw up our mission.* They pushed on.

Further into the city, they crossed a bridge to a contested islet and saw signs of recent warfare. They passed the plaza in question too quickly to figure out exactly *how* recent, but the smell of a conduit burning pavement and the scorch of plasma burns filled their nostrils. A few armed people were scattered about, picking through the wreckage and carrying wounded individuals to safety. A hard-faced young man nodded to the brothers as they sped past, and Damien returned it. They kept going, pushing further as the thin snowfall grew into an obscuring snowfall. Von just whispered that he was grateful for the lack of wind, and Damien agreed.

I actually don't care if we run into anyone tonight, Damien thought as the smell of battle faded. *Just no commandos, that's all I want.*

Shortly after, they were forced to backtrack thanks to a barricade over their chosen route. Twisted Collective skiff hulls and broken car bodies met them, spanning the street at over three meters high.

"Now what?" Von murmured, glaring at the new barricade. He unslung his Plaster rifle and held it cradled in his lap.

"Leo?" Damien asked.

"I'm looking."

While they deliberated where to go, Damien spied an odd stretch of lumps lined up against a collapsed building nearby. When he pointed it out, Von told him to get closer, so he did as much as he dared. They realized too late that it was a line of unburied dead, laid out under tarps. Many of them were already covered in snow, but wind had ripped one tarp up, revealing the body of a young woman. Damien guessed she had died gasping from the blackened hole in her abdomen. *What a horrible way to die,* he thought. *Plasma to the stomach.* He shook away nausea and turned them away. Leo spoke up about taking a longer but safer route to the campus, and they turned from the scene without another word.

As the excursion wore on through the night, even human-controlled islets started to feel less friendly than usual. There were usually at least a few people out on the roads, no matter the weather. Tonight, though, they were completely alone within a few city blocks. The silence was stifling as the foggy road ahead turned whiter, and even the sounds of their motorcycle choked as the gloom closed in on them.

The only other person they came across was a lookout at the end of a major alley—a makeshift thoroughfare that took them through the heart of insurgent Seattle. In passing, Damien fell in amidst a handful of other vehicle tracks. At the end of the street he saw a glimmer from a darkened, second-story awning. He waved, and the man leaned forward to wave back, showing the shadow of his sniper rifle and ending their wordless exchange.

When they had crossed two more islets without incident, they came into firmly unoccupied territory. Totally abandoned buildings should have been a boon to the brothers who preferred their isolation, but the threat of invisible assailants changed that feeling tonight. Every corner became a harrowing one, every window an opportunity for ambush. They took long pauses to ensure the areas ahead were clear before continuing, and Leo's joking quips and banter slowly died as they finally approached their destination. They were bound for a bridge that would take them to the Xenocultural Conglomerate campus, where humans and Algaroth had once set aside all preconceived notions of one another in favor of learning and sharing what they knew. The campus sat on its own islet that jutted out into the Puget Sound, alone.

The streets remained as deathly quiet as ever, and the three of them felt tension in the snowy air that wasn't there normally. This was an eerie silence, made stranger still by the lack of Collective patrols as well as insurgent natives. Damien reflected nervously that in seven years, they had never gone a full night without encountering *someone* out on patrol or whatnot, and he didn't count the skirmishers, the dead, or the lookout. It didn't help his nerves either that the motorcycle was—while very quiet—

still loud on streets where the only sounds came from the whispering wind and snowfall.

Something had been nagging at Damien all night as they approached the intersection to the bridge, and it was only when he saw a building leaning on sunken pavement that he realized what it was: they'd seen very few cracks in the cityscape from the earthquake tonight. He asked Leo if someone had fixed the pavement or something, but the AI said that this whole portion of the city had escaped some of the roughest damage—but only just. Von reminded Damien that they hadn't been back to the campus together since well before the quake.

Eventually even Leo had to acknowledge their luck was beyond his usual level of incredible navigating. This wasn't just a quiet night. Finally, they reached the intersection to the bridge. The cycle slowed.

"Ready?" Damien asked.

Leo cut Von's reply off. "Hold on boys. There's something out there."

Damien stopped, senses prickling. *It makes sense that Avos would lay an ambush here if they know what we're up to.* The thought jarred him, but he quickly dismissed it, not seeing how that was possible. They hadn't exactly advertised their intentions to anybody about the hacking rig.

"What's out there?" Von asked sharply. "How do you know?"

Damien could almost *hear* Leo's eyes rolling, "I'm tapped through the local System into what's left of the thermal gauging grid—" he raised his voice to quell the moans from both of them, "—COMPLETELY harmless, but since there isn't much around here that produces heat, I can pick up anything that *does* without a fuss! It's a handy trick; don't deny it. But more relevant: yes, I think there's something out on the bridge."

Damien looked at Von in the rearview mirror, sharing a grudging look. *That was a really good idea to use the grid.* Damien looked towards the thickening layer of snow on the street. Everything was perfectly undisturbed.

"So then what do you see?" Von repeated.

They waited for a response.

"Leo?"

"I'm looking, geez! I said it *helped*, not that it's perfect!"

"Oh. Sorry."

They waited.

After a few seconds Leo returned. "Well, most of the bridge sensors are out so I can't get a good read, but there's definitely something out there. I just can't make out what it is."

Damien sighed in frustration, "Avos?"

"Damien," said Leo. "Didn't I JUST say that I don't know? Redundancies! Honestly, sometimes I wonder how you get out of bed in the morning, let alone put on pants or channel that power of yours in a fight!"

Von cut him off from further jabs, "It doesn't matter. Can we go around?"

Leo responded much faster this time, "Mmm, no. Not quickly at least. The northeast bridge has been destroyed. Recently, too. The… south bridge might be alright, but that takes you *way* the hell backwards and into sturdy enemy territory."

"What about the west way?" Damien asked, parking the bike and climbing off carefully. "That bridge connects to the northeast bridge right at the far side of the campus. It might still be intact."

Damien crept to the edge of the building and peeked around the corner. A few blocks distant, he could see the outline of the double-leveled bridge, a black shadow against the dark grey sky, as if the fog and the snow had tried to swallow the whole thing, but ultimately failed.

"It's probably just fine from what I can tell," said Leo. "But that's a helluva trek across *eight* of the islets, four of which—"

"Whoa, whoa, EIGHT?" Damien exclaimed, and the argument expanded. Leo deflected every idea he had that involved avoiding this bridge, and ultimately he looked up to see that the cold clouds were thick with the twinkling of more snow. "Von," he snapped, interrupting Leo. "Do you think we have time to go around?" The outline of the bridge faded even more. He could hear the distant howl of wind over the Sound, coming towards them. He turned to see Von peering through his set of high-powered omnoculars at the bridge, flipping through the spectrums.

110

"No. And I don't see anything out there but weather."

Damien sighed. "Alright, well, should we try it?

Von looked up the street, thinking. "Yes. I don't want to be out here very long," he tapped his splint. "And the stakes are higher now than if we were just raiding."

Damien nodded, "Okay, let's move then."

They climbed back onto the cycle and Damien shifted the generator down to the lowest gear, keeping it as quiet as possible. They could still go pretty fast like that, but if they got into a situation they wouldn't be able to speed up since the bike could only shift when stopped. It was risky but they had already made an agreement to stick to stealth wherever possible.

"I'd say now might be a good time for some headgear too, boys," Leo remarked dryly. "For data sync if not for protection; I hear a Gyro bolt to the face can be a deal breaker for some but, you know, it's your call."

The two agreed and Von pulled their headgear from the small compartment behind him. The alien donned the rest of his black winter helmet, locking it into both the rear portion he'd put on earlier and his neck guard, completing the ensemble of his suit. Von looked more like a predatory raptor than ever. Damien on the other hand, chose to only snap on his goggles and pull up his facemask, making him look more like a high-tech, urban bandit.

"Ready?" Damien asked, his voice muffled through the facemask.

"All set," said Von.

"I'm golden here, only I say you deploy the thermal reflectors on your hydracycle too. We're gonna stick out like an albino in mud on that bridge with the heat we're giving off."

Damien sighed. He had had his finger hovering over the button to do exactly that. "Yes, *thank you*, Leo."

"Quite welcome."

With a satisfying snap, the orange, webbed flaps extended up and over their legs, flipping out from beneath the rider and angling backwards. The flaps were angular, modified solar panels, and made the bike look a bit like a half-folded, vibrant-orange dragonfly. Damien amped the throttle and they took off once more, leaving the piton pillars of the city behind as he cut the corner and turned to the waterfront.

"Damien, turn on your goggles." Leo said.

Damien hit the button on the left lens, and the tactical display came to life. After only a moment, the familiar holographic overlay snapped into place and the lines of buildings and street lit up in teal. "Okay they're up."

A moment later, they shot out from the windbreaker that was the last building on the waterfront, and the northerly gale smashed into them.

"Whoa *shit* it's cold!" Damien shouted into it.

"By the way, it's a bit nippy out here," Leo chimed.

"Shut up, Leo!" Von snapped, teeth chattering inside his helmet.

"Are you receiving?!" Damien asked over the howling. He felt his nose hairs freeze instantly.

"Indeed I am. I'm turning on the thermal overlays for both of you." As the AI spoke, Damien's goggles blipped as a faint new pattern overlaid his field of vision, this one temperature-colored. Leo continued, "It's being patched through the same thermal gauging network that the city runs on, so it's gonna be choppy once we get onto the bridge, but at least you two can tell where the heat signatures are for now."

He was right. As they approached the smooth metal columns that marked the bridge's barrier, the faintest outlines of a thermal reading appeared about halfway across. It was definitely stronger than any passive or background heat. Damien slowed the bike, caution bells screaming louder than ever in his head.

Von seemed to guess what he was thinking, "They look to be on the bottom level. If someone was crossing and wanted to avoid the cold, that's where I'd be as well."

Damien agreed. "Yeah, but is that what Avos would want us to think?"

"Maybe."

Damien nodded to himself. They needed a decision fast. Top level or bottom? They were coming up on the exit to the lower level of the bridge, and he wasn't going to stop to decide.

"Confront it," Von said, always decisive. "If it is the hunters, I would rather avoid having them at our backs and deal now."

"Always the go-to guy, aren't ya?" Damien said, turning for the exit in answer. As they approached, he throttled up, and they both breathed a sigh of relief as the huge bridge towers blocked some of the wind.

"Phew, that was chilly!" said Leo.

Damien rolled his eyes.

They spiraled down to the bottom level, the storm quieting as they did. It was now below freezing, and their earlier predictions about a blizzard seemed to be coming true. Damien couldn't see anything over the sides, so he stayed focused forward, trying to guess how far they were from the heat blobs. They closed for only a few seconds before the image started to fizzle and pop.

"What the hell—Leo, what's going on?" Damien barked, slowing the cycle to a crawl as they navigated abandoned cars and shuttles.

"It's the network! I told you the sensors out here were bad!"

"Dammit! Well let's hope we don't grab their attention before the sensors give out and we can't keep track of them."

"Agreed," said Von.

Damien pushed the bike as fast as he could, weaving them through the abandoned bridge. He favored the walkways on the sides since there was less refuse and debris scattered there, but there was still plenty to get in the way, and he was forced to drive carefully to avoid flipping them over.

As they approached, the flickering thermal blob faded fast. They were almost at the edge of the grids' range.

C'mon. Just a little further, he thought, *we just need to see what it is.*

But as they reached barely fifty meters away, the image faded altogether. Damien and Von both cursed, and maybe it was his imagination, but Damien could swear he saw a figure rise from the orange just before the image went out. They must have heard the bike echoing.

"Overlay's out," whispered Leo, then he fell silent.

Damien killed the cycle and coasted behind an overturned transit shuttle that had been looted and left in the street. They hopped off and he tucked the cycle against it, then loaded his pistol and killed the safety. Von followed suit, unslinging his Plaster rifle again. Damien turned towards his brother, signaling that he wanted to use his power to sneak closer. He directed Von to the far side of the bridge, where a path looked like it might lead through the maze of metal. His brother vanished without another word, stalking.

After a day's rest and a full meal, Damien felt rejuvenated. He pressed himself tight against the cold undercarriage of the shuttle and closed his eyes. Deep in the recesses of his mind, he tapped the black pool of Elemental power and relished how full it felt. Familiar, he beckoned to the thoughtless sensation inside him, and it came at his call. The dark liquid flowed out from that core place, leeching into his body, his bones, and his senses. Damien blinked, and he let the cool touch of Darkness fill the space behind his eyes. The world lit up around him, and where before there had been shadows and heaps of twisted transports, now he spotted details. The shadows were filled with muted glows, and light faded into darkness. The closest he had ever described it to Von was that he saw in negative, though it wasn't quite true. Either way, it always left him exhilarated, being in the middle of the element he wreathed himself in. He let the power settle into his veins, and his heart pounded slow and steady, focused on the task at hand.

Before he pushed forwards, Damien double-checked as always that his sleeves covered his arms. He hadn't worried about it the night before so much, but whenever he used his power—especially in excess, as he anticipated doing tonight—the warmth of it spreading through him made his arms give off a ruddy glow. Waxy veins of light would appear, tracing from his shoulders to his wrists and nullifying anything useful that came from hiding in shadows. Luckily his concern was unwarranted. The combat skin beneath his jacket was in place, and the glow was nowhere to be found. He rubbed his rough forearms anyways out of habit; they always itched.

Feeling invigorated, Damien made sure Von had already vanished near the far railing before he crept around the overturned shuttle. He listened intently for signs of movement on the far side, but the howling wind behind the bridge drowned it out.

At least background noise works two ways.

He crept with the shadows, feeling the night's embrace around him, the pulse of tenacious energy flooding his veins. Now that they were on foot, it was impossible not to notice the strewn echoes of the dying city around him. The bridge was a maze of abandoned relics. Damien passed bags of luggage, children's toys, and the occasional scrap of clothing so decayed that they had become black and crusty extensions of the street. Anything of use had been taken from here long ago, and all that was left were the husks of people's lives.

Passing the cab of the overturned shuttle, Damien realized that the source of the heat had to be in the center of an L-shaped nest of toppled vehicles. A large Army hauler had crashed into the shuttle a long time ago, toppling both and providing neat protection from the rest of the bridge.

Coming around the bent undercarriage of the Army hauler, Damien slowed. Ahead, he saw a flicker of light, almost too bright to even look near with his night-sensitive eyes. *Fire*, he realized. *I'll be damned. It's a fire!* He was stunned. Open flames were *never* used in the city anymore. It simply wasn't done. It was too dangerous for a million reasons, such as how it gave your position away for kilometers, or that flames were no substitute for more accessible technologies to warm you. *Or maybe you've just gotten used to being warm at night*, he thought, suddenly feeling guilty. *You've been in a bunker for years now, safe from the elements. Don't judge.*

Damien grimaced at himself and crouched under the stripped chassis of the hauler, just at the edge of flickering light, listening for the sounds of conversation. Just because there was a fire didn't mean that there were people around it. He had seen Collective patrols lure poor souls to warmth before, ambushing them as surely as leading moths to a flame. He didn't intend to be one of those, and he was sure he'd seen someone moving before the thermal vision died.

I can't get over there without being noticed, he thought, stymied. He peeked out as much as he dared, but the further out he leaned, the brighter the light became. Before he could even see the source of the flames, his Elementally charged eyes couldn't handle the blinding glare, and he pulled back into the shadows, blinking hard and seeing spots. A minute passed and the blind spots in his vision slowly faded, his night vision returning. He thought about raising Von on their private communications channel, but didn't want to risk being overheard. Leaning out again, he spied another overturned shuttle across the clearing, and he realized the L-shaped nest was actually U-shaped. The fire was protected on three sides from the wind. He assumed his brother was behind the far overturned vehicle, which looked like it might have been a supply truck.

This is a cozy setup, but it's a good spot for an ambush, and there aren't enough shadows.

Then it hit him: Shadows.

In all his years since he had become an Elemental, Damien had tested many ways to use his strange powers. Some, like his Orbs and Waves, took mostly brute force to focus and expel. When he used those, he would often feel physically exhausted, even to the point of collapse. Other powers though, such as his Shroud, took more mental focus that left him almost as tired.

He had named others over the years, but one in particular came to mind at that moment: His Cloak. A power he had rarely used, one that had often been more trouble than it was worth. Damien wasn't sure why the Cloak was suddenly so appealing. Maybe it was the cold—familiar to the night he had first tried it, the day after the earthquake—or perhaps it was the fear of encountering an array of deadly Collective phantoms, but Damien wanted to try.

"Leo," he whispered. "I'm going to do something a little crazy, just hang on."

"What?" Leo snipped, breaking his dutiful silence. "Crazy? Crazy how? What do you mean crazy? You know I hate when you don't tell me what you're—"

Damien muted him. He couldn't do this with the chattering. "Sorry." He knew the AI would hear him.

Just beneath his skin, Damien felt his power. It rippled when he moved and clung to every fiber of his body as tight as his cells. Carefully dropping his backpack, he pulled at the Darkness within him, flexing his muscles and focusing on the sensations within his body. A long, deep breath pushed out the wind, the fear, and the cold, and he turned inward.

A fissure in the world hangs in front of you, he thought, repeating the words he had come up with that helped him mold the power—whether it existed or not outside of his mind had never mattered. *It spits and shivers. It is not your friend. Conquer the fissure, open it, and bring out the energy beyond.* He pictured himself stepping through a rip in the air similar to the one he made every time he created an Orb. Reaching through, he imagined grasping for whatever it was that lay inside the break, hiding beyond the physically discernible. The moment he did, he tore what he had found back through the hole: a writhing unmolded black mass. He imagined bringing the mass to his chest and letting it spill over him.

The moment he did, the liquid power in his veins came alive, infused with the power he had never understood. Damien had never been able to answer the 'why' or even the 'how' of what made his Elemental powers work. He only knew that they worked, and that he'd never met anyone else capable of doing what he could.

Damien opened his eyes.

A faint hissing filled the air, and smoky black tendrils rose from his body. Hovering just off of his jacket, a violet corona shimmered around him, almost invisible. The smoky Darkness lifted off and away, not quite obeying the laws of the wind as it dissipated. Damien looked down at himself, and saw that his body had melted into the night, blending into the shadows under the hauler like a black sheet held against the night sky. Damien was practically invisible.

With his power working, Damien already felt the strain like a great iron curtain draped over his shoulders. He wouldn't be able to hold this for long. He looked around, seeing the bridge throbbing in that pseudo-negative light. Where before he had seen the flickering light of the fire around the hauler, now he only saw whitewashed suggestions of shapes—the exact opposite of trying to pick out details of things in the dark. He crouched just behind the line of light. Shadows were what he could see in detail, where everything was bathed in a cooled glow. All other colors— few as they were on the snowy metal bridge—had gone mute.

More than just the physical pull on his muscles, Damien felt something else too. Deep within his mind, in the cavern where the reservoir of his powers rested, Damien felt a faint tug. Something pulled at his reservoir from underneath a plugged drain. It sent ripples throughout his body, making him shiver even though it seemed far away. He had never drained his pool of power to see what lay at the bottom, but he had long possessed a gut instinct that if he were ever to unplug that drain and let that tug become a whirlpool, that *something* underneath would consume him.

Knowing that every second counted, Damien pulled his focus back to the task at hand. *You can do this.*

He banished his fear of ambush, set his jaw, and without thinking any further… stepped into the light, hoping his Cloak would hold against the glow of fire.

For a moment, he thought he had come nose-to-nose with an Avo. Time slowed as he squinted into the blinding shine of light. He was sure he was about to feel an *avosas* blade puncture his stomach, but he didn't.

In fact, nothing happened.

At first glance, the space looked like nothing but a clearing between vehicles, occupied only by a low fire flickering in a makeshift pit. Then Damien swept his gaze again, and froze. His surefooted heartbeat faltered and his breath caught as he was flooded with pity, sorrow, and stunned indecision at the scene in front of him.

Tucked back from the whimpering flames and hunched under the propped shuttle door, their bodies hidden by the mess of wretchedly ragged blankets, were three people. Their eyes glistened in the light of the fire like rodents hiding from a predator.

What Damien saw in their wide eyes was something primal. It was an instinct far beneath the higher thoughts of reason and logic, and deeper even than those concerns of paranoia, loss, or despair. It was the quivering, wide-eyed gaze of unbridled terror in the face of death. Damien had seen it before, remembered feeling it before, but never so intently or so *urgently* as this, and never directed at him.

A young woman about Damien's age, a boy of perhaps ten, and an old man who was likely in his nineties or early triples, all had their eyes fixed on where he was standing. Damien didn't know what to do. Had the Cloak not worked? He took an uncertain step towards the fire, and the boy let out a yelp. It was cut short by the young woman, who muffled him. It was then that Damien realized that he had stepped from the shadows an imperfect phantom. Whether his Cloak could deceive them or not didn't matter. What mattered was that they had been paying acute attention to the only method of ingress to their wretched bastion, and Damien had invaded it as a shady ripple in the air, easily mistaken for the silhouette of an Avo.

Shit.

The boy whimpered into the young woman's hand, and she tried to stay perfectly still while cradling him. Damien thought it maybe wasn't the best choice to dump his grip on his power, but it was certainly the fastest option. He let the Cloak fall and in barely a second, the shadows straining to keep him from appearing in the light slipped away. His power receded to just beneath his skin.

"*DEMONS!!!*" The old man howled. The boy screamed with him and the woman squealed while she tried to stifle him. The man fumbled beneath the blankets for something.

"Wait!" Damien cried, holding out his hands and stepping further into the light, still half-blind. "Wait please! I'm human! I won't hurt you see! I'm human! Stop!" But they were crying too loudly.

The old man produced an ancient six-shooter revolver, and there was a deafening *CRACK*. A metal bullet whizzed just past Damien's head. He ducked. "STOP!!"

He barely grabbed their attention. The boy quieted.

"Stop! I'm not an enemy!"

The man glared, suspicion etched in every feature. Damien couldn't blame him, but a wrench of anxiety plopped into his stomach at the gunshot. If Avos were out here, they would have heard that. *One thing at a time*, he thought, heart racing.

119

Damien held both hands out, breathing hard, relying on words now that the shiny barrel of the handgun was trained on his head.

"Might I recommend headgear for next week's adventure?" Leo whispered, apparently having found a way around the mute button.

Damien ignored him. "I'm not an Algaroth. Just… put the gun down. Please. I'm not going to hurt you." Slowly, he pulled down his balaclava and lifted up his goggles, showing them who he was.

The woman was the first to acknowledge anything. She inched forward from under the door, revealing thin, frozen features and tear-stiffened tracks beneath pale brown eyes. Her hair was ragged and dirty, tufted in clumps of brown. As she leaned, the neck of her patched coat pulled down and Damien noticed a thick scar running from behind her left eye, down her neck, and out of sight.

"What's your name?" he asked.

The boy answered quickly, squeaking out, "Simon!" He had green eyes and sandy brown hair, only marginally less dirty than the woman.

Damien nodded, encouraging, "Hi Simon. I'm Damien. Are you okay?"

The boy was about to respond when the old man spoke. "Don't trust him! Don't trust him, it's a trick! They've taken our bodies now!" He waved the gun about, prompting Damien to straighten and stop.

"No! No, I'm a real person! I'm not gonna hurt you!"

The revolver waved less rabidly, and Damien dared a breath. He let the moment simmer before asking, "Who are you?"

The woman answered this time, shushing the older man. "This is Harold, I-I'm Delilah."

Damien nodded, "Okay, okay good. It's nice to meet you all. But look, we're not going to hurt you. We just—"

"WE?!" The man cried, cutting him off. "Who's 'WE' eh?!"

It couldn't have been a worse moment for Von to arrive.

"Damien!" his brother cried, bowling around the far shuttle. Von's Plaster rifle glowed warmly, trained to fire. He must have heard the gunshot and assumed the worst.

"AAUUUUUUGHHH!!!!" The man cried, almost in unison as the other two. "BLUE-DEVILS! SNAKES! SLIZZARDS! WOLVES! THEY'RE HERE!!"

"Oops," Leo quipped.

Chaos broiled as the man wielded his gun. Damien shouted over the other shouting and Von growled, faceless and menacing behind his predatory black helmet. The man fired at Von's head.

"NO!" Damien roared, lunging to push the confused Algaroth out of the way.

Before he had managed even a step, Damien's instinct kicked in. A Wave sprang from his chest *almost* of its own accord, and blasted through the clearing in the split-second it took the metal slug to leave the barrel. The roar of it sent Von tumbling to the ground while Damien ended up in the line of the gunshot. In that moment, he thought he could see the bullet as it bowled through the air for him, and a spike of fear broke the microsecond... but then it collided with his Wave. The bullet was eviscerated as his brutish tsunami swallowed it. The Wave fazed the metal the same as it had fazed that Koro's bones, organs, and blood the night before.

By the time the bullet reached Damien's face it had been shredded into so many silver shavings, contorted and harmless. Damien flinched as tiny pinpricks of metal dust stung him, but that was all.

The wind reclaimed the clearing in the silent aftermath, and nobody moved. Damien caught his breath but held his head high, even though he longed to bend over and gasp. He took the respite to reflect that, to the three poor souls, it must have seemed he had just swatted a bullet out of midair. He held an arm out to Von, silently warning him to stay on the ground. The other hand he held towards the old man, Harold, who lowered the gun.

"I said... *Stop*," he gasped. "This... is Von. He's an insurgent... and a friend." When he was sure the gun had gone safely into the blankets, Damien lowered his hands. Von squirmed on the ground, holding his wounded leg and trying to get a better view of the group behind the fire. *I hope he didn't just snap a lead.*

121

Damien looked back at them, and couldn't help feeling a twinge of fierce pride as the wind whipped his loose clothing and hair about. "I'm an Elemental," he said. "And you have nothing to fear from me. Truly. Neither of us will hurt you."

At 'Elemental' Simon's eyes lit up, Delilah looked shocked, and Harold squinted. Damien didn't give them time to say anything. "I don't know what you're doing out here, but you shouldn't be. This area is dangerous, and this storm is getting worse. Please. You need to go back across the bridge and get somewhere safe." He turned to help Von up, keeping his peripheral focused on Harold, whom he assumed still had at least another shot in that pistol. The three cringed as the huge alien stood to tower over Damien. He knew his brother looked towards him, but he held up a finger to wait.

Von turned to the cowering people and—doing what he had learned so well growing up amongst humans—slung his Plaster Rifle and held his hands out openly, showing he meant no harm. None of them moved to his gesture, and all still looked afraid, but Von's slow, deliberate movements seemed to at least keep them from shooting and screaming.

"Okay." Damien said, making them focus back on him. He focused on Delilah, whom he guessed would hear him the clearest. "Like I said. It isn't safe here. Why are you out here?"

"Because we were pushed out here," she said. Her voice was weak. "There's nowhere safe to go…" she trailed off and lowered her gaze. Damien didn't know what to do.

Leo, who had been remarkably quiet, whispered, "You know, you could send them back to Bar and Shell's?"

Damien blinked. He turned to Von, who tapped his helmet, indicating Leo had spoken to him too. *Would that work?* he wondered. *Their shop is so far, and this storm is getting worse.*

As if hearing his thoughts, Leo added, "You don't have a better idea. Give them the pendant to prove you sent them."

Damien turned to Von and winced. *They'll hate me if I send it back.* There was nothing else to do though, so he nodded, still eyeing the three people.

Von plodded over to him, and Damien heard his backpack unzip. A moment later, Von produced the pendant and handed it to him.

"You're right," he said, addressing Delilah again. "Nowhere's really safe anymore, but we have friends nearby who can help you. It's far, but do you know Bar and Shell's Buy & Sell?"

She looked crestfallen, but nodded.

Damien didn't have time to worry about her concern. He held out the pendant. "Give them this. Tell them Damien sent you. They'll look after you."

Her gaze turned wary, but she took it as Damien tossed it over the fire and into their blankets.

He retreated. "You need to go, as soon as possible. This storm is getting worse and there are patrols out here." He didn't see the need to overly frighten them with the word 'Avo'. "You'll be safe once you get to the market."

Damien knew they had no reason to trust him, but the sight of these people, freezing to death and practically inviting The Collective to come execute them with that fire, was too much. What else could he do? Wasn't helping people what he and Von had been doing for all this time? *That is what we're doing isn't it?* He didn't see any good reason to suddenly question that logic, but there it was. He didn't like the feeling of selfishness that suddenly overcame him.

"Damien, it's time to go," Leo urged. He was right.

Damien gave them one final look. "Good luck." Then he beckoned to his brother and they left the clearing without another word, Damien grabbing his backpack from where he'd deposited it. Von took the opportunity to nod at the boy before departing. The kid looked confused, but thankfully he didn't cry out.

As soon as the light of the fire was off their backs, Damien spoke up. "You wait here, I'll go grab the cycle, okay?"

Von glared at him. "I can come with you to get it."

Damien shook his head. "No you can't. I'm looking at that splint in a minute. Just hold on." He turned around and sprinted back along the railing, away from the clearing, and back to his motorcycle. He didn't

123

want to see if the people had moved or not, and he shook his head at the possibility of giving *them* his bike instead. *We need it more right now.* He tried not to think of how unlikely it was that they would reach Bar and Shell's without wheels.

He found his cycle where he'd left it. It was freezing to the touch, and it complained in the cold when he brought the generator to life, but it moved. A short minute later, he found Von hobbling towards the far side of the bridge on his own.

"What the hell are you doing?!" he hissed, pulling up alongside his brother.

"Walking," Von said, but the fact that he had pulled his helmet off and winced with every other step spoke volumes.

Damien grabbed his brother's shoulder. "Get on."

Von did with some trouble, and with their detour concluded, they finished the crossing without incident. But even with the short time their stop had taken, they emerged from the lower level of the bridge to find the world clad in snow. They stood on a hill overlooking the Xenocultural Conglomerate Islet, and memories stirred in Damien's mind. *Home, long before the bunker or the quake*, he thought. He looked at his brother in the mirror, and saw a similar expression on his blue face. This was where their families had first met, before the war started. *I've had an alien for a brother for just over twenty years, crazy.*

The storm had kicked to full life again, and visibility was dropping by the second. Sweeping arms of snow were falling, and the wind had turned horizontal.

"Alright, I'm looking at your leg." Damien said, knowing they needed a short break, and he wanted to see how much damage Von's fall had caused.

They hid around the corner of the gatehouse to the bridge, and Damien pulled up his brother's legwear while Leo tried to reconnect to the thermal grid. Von kept his eyes closed while he worked. Damien could tell the meds were wearing off, and worse, he winced when he found that two of the leads looked about to pop out. Neither had, thankfully, but the whole splint already looked worn to the breaking point. It was designed for healing, not hard use. Damien gave his brother some emergency anesthetics and did his best to wrap new bandages with his frozen fingers.

Even tucked around the building, under the huge tower of the bridge, it was hard to catch their breath in the cold, so when Leo spoke up and took it away, they were both left exhausted again. It had already been a long night and their real mission had yet to begin. "Sonnies, I'm ah... I'm locked out of the grid."

Neither Damien nor Von needed to ask what that meant. The cold pins and needles in Damien's lungs came tearing back, and he looked at his brother, who was cradling his head against his helmet. "Avos," he coughed.

Von nodded wearily. His ganglia had curled in on themselves, and the alien's entire head trembled in the wind.

"Sorry boys," said Leo. "I don't know if they're actually here yet, but they definitely know that *you* are."

Damien gazed down the hill. The howl of the night wind filled his ears, snow had frozen his three-day old stubble to his face, and he couldn't feel his hands. For just a second though, he saw the shadows of buildings in the blowing white. Then, almost as if in response to their gaze, the XenoCon campus vanished into the blizzard.

CHAPTER SEVEN

Xenocultural Conglomerates

Their trek onto the XenoCon campus should have taken two minutes by car or twenty minutes by foot on a normal day. It took Damien, Von, and Leo well over an hour to worry Damien's motorcycle down the hill and to the entrance. The bellowing night wind tore at them with a thousand grasping fingers, drifts of snow obscured all details, and any chance of listening for someone approaching was nonexistent.

The only reason they knew they had passed onto the campus proper was the hint of shadows on each side: a two-story arch that marked the entrance to the cross-species grounds. The arch depicted a human on one side and an Algaroth on the other, each reaching for a star at the peak of the gateway. Most of the details were obscured under sticky snow, but Damien knew it from memory.

Damien's bike struggled to push them through the snow. It wasn't built for this kind of terrain. Finally, they had to face defeat in the rising drifts. They stumbled into a mid-sized building with a lobby and pushed inside to stash the cycle. Damien wasn't sure if he'd ever been in here, but he guessed they still had a ways left to go to the main campus building— their destination. He found a cleaning closet and they stuffed his cycle inside, locking the door before they left. *I'll just shoot it off when we come back*, he thought, worried about leaving it at all. Then, steeling themselves for trudging forward on foot, they wrapped up their clothes and gear, and reentered the storm.

They lost track of time in the cold. Every step, Damien worried about Von's leg, but they had no choice but to push on. Frost crept over Damien's goggles, and the displays on his lenses became sluggish. *It feels like thirty below out here*, and he reflected that it very well could be. He found himself longing for a time past, when Seattle blizzards were rare.

Damien had read about a time—well over a century ago—when Seattle had been called the "rainy city", but that was long before the Over-Seer cracked the San Andreas fault, before First Contact, and before World War Three, when humanity had been unable to ignore their climate crisis any longer. The violently rising oceans had drowned coastal cities in the midst of those twelve years of fighting, and the Seattle Islets—like most near-waterfront cities—had become the new coastlines, but with a major change: they were just as capable of heavy snows as cities at higher altitude or nearer to the poles. Such was the new climate.

Damien took a frigid breath, pondering what it must have been like to live back then.

Just then, he and Von passed around the corner of another low building on the campus, and the wind stampeded into them both. Unprepared, Damien was yanked out of his thoughts as his feet were ripped from under him. His shout was lost in the wind, and Von was at his side in an instant.

"You alright?!" his brother roared.

Damien nodded in an exaggerated fashion—his throat was bone dry—and he struggled to his feet, panting and batting at the snow that clung to him. *This shit's getting worse*, he thought. Once satisfied that there was less snow on his person—even though nothing had changed—he looked ahead, hoping to see some hint of where they were going. To his astonishment, something was indeed looming in the dark ahead. *The campus building, finally.* He tapped Von's shoulder and pointed. His brother nodded and they doubled their pace, breaking trail.

Stiff, tired, and gasping, the shadow resolved into the twenty-story main Xenocultural Conglomerate campus building. The maw of the front double doors burst forth from the night, and Damien had never seen an ominous entry look so inviting. Stumbling through knee-high drifts, the brothers sighed thanks as the doors slid open as if this were just another late night entry, the communal nature of the facility still alive. The building beckoned them inside, human and Algaroth alike. They obliged.

Inside, the broad lobby howled with snow as the storm rushed in ahead of them, smothering the spirits of good faith. The brothers tromped inside, caked with snow and cold beyond shivering. No sooner had they brushed a fraction of snow loose than they sighted their weapons, willing the doors to close faster.

The resounding *BOOM* echoed like dull thunder as the doors slid shut, dampening the storm. The echo bounced through the open lobby and into the vaulted atrium beyond. Damien and Von both stopped, listening. Outside, the hollow wails of the blizzard continued to escalate, but inside, all they heard was a distant, echoing *drip, drip* of water leaking.

Damien couldn't remember the last time he'd been in here, but it took only a glance at his brother to know that years of memories were flooding back to them both. This very spot was one they had both scampered through thousands of times. This building and this campus was the oldest home Damien remembered, and he knew it was the first Von had ever cared about.

Now it was cold, dark, and empty. They stood alone as adults, remembering how different the place had been when they were kids.

"At least the place has power," Leo said, interjecting. "Want me to tap into the grid?"

"No," Damien said quietly, letting the moment go. His voice still carried. "Not yet. If Avos locked you out of the thermal grid they might be here already. I don't want them getting ahold of you."

"Aww, concern for my well-being? Damien, I'm touched."

Damien snorted and shook his head. "Don't let it go to your head."

"Too late."

"Let's go," said Von, sighting his rifle. Damien followed him through the lobby. He longed to itch his arms but he managed to fight the urge.

Ahead, empty garden planters lay in neat rows leading to the front desk. Each had once been cultivated and tended by specimens and botanists both alien and human. Damien remembered being taught that the flora the Algaroth brought from Shialga had been specially designed to exist on Earth. All the planters were empty.

129

Even with their careful consideration of stealth, each footfall could have belonged to a giant. The clapping, wet smack of their boots echoed off the walls with added fervor before dying in the distant dark of the atrium. Off to their sides, the two-story lobby had grand staircases leading up and into broad halls on the upper floor, once lit in gold, now veiled in grey. Behind the front desk, Damien noted the plaque hanging from the high wooden partition between the lobby and atrium. It was an inscription of the charter for the joint Human-Algaroth Cultural Exchange Division. Once, it had proclaimed dedication to goodwill trade and friendship between humans and the Algaroth of The Collective.

The inscription had been scratched and defaced until it was unreadable, denouncing The Collective with all manner of profanity. *I doubt we'll ever be able to reconcile with the Algaroth on a large scale like that again*, Damien reflected, feeling somber.

Behind the desk was the atrium proper. The ceiling stopped behind the lobby, and Damien and Von instinctively began walking back-to-back, rotating their views for any sign of trouble. The vaulted atrium climbed all twenty stories in a great open shaft to the sky, beckoning openness. Damien only felt his nerves spike in such a broad space. He felt very small.

The open air made the echoes even worse. Damien winced as each step bounced once, twice, ten times, booming in the distance above the dim howl of the storm and the steady drip of water. *There are a lot of spots for trouble*. He eyed the many circling walkways above. *And a lot of places to hide*.

He noted how there were signs of life similar to what they'd just encountered on the bridge; discarded nutrient bar wrappers, the occasional Tesla power cell, and ratty blankets—used until they were so pockmarked that no more comfort could be squeezed from them. People had been living here, ignored and endangered, but still breathing.

Pale, wintry gloom shone down through the skylights as they skulked into the open hall, the dark night lessened by filtered light. Signs of looting and pillaging, possibly even a skirmish or two, were visible all around, but Damien's gaze was drawn to the dry pool at the center of the atrium. The dull illumination provided a sad scene as they approached a basin full of broken tiles and cracked ceramic that had gone a sickly brown. A gnarled and dying thing sat on the island in the middle: a 'Twined Tree.

Silent, Damien and Von stopped to gaze at the dead symbol to humankind's alliance.

The 'Twined Tree was one-third Earthen, from the region in which the monument was built—a western hemlock for the Puget Sound—one-third Martian redstone tree, and one-third a flowering purple elysium tree, native to Shialga. Each tree was planted in a triangular layout and carefully tended so that, as they aged, they grew into one other, twining up and out into a beautifully crafted hybrid; a living icon of unity.

This one had been mutilated to death.

The roots of the redstone had been ripped away from its brethren, the trunk cast into the empty pool surrounding the monument, where its bark laid whitening. The hemlock's bark had been torn, shredded, and the last vestiges of its trunk left clinging to the elysium. The white bark of the alien tree offered no help to its kin. The elysium had been stripped to a single shaft, the branches and their purple leaves strewn about the area. Damien even spotted one all the way across the atrium, torn into glistening splinters.

"So sad," Von said quietly. "The elysiums should be in bloom."

Damien looked at the Martian tree lying at the bottom of the empty pool, "Yeah, and the redstones would be hardening for winter right about now."

They fell silent, but couldn't stop to ponder the dead. They still had twenty floors to ascend to where they could finally test out their hacking rig, and see if the black box was worth all the trouble.

"Guys," Leo said as they left the basin behind. "I don't mean to prod you again, but you should walk faster."

"Trouble?" Von growled, sighting his rifle and crouching low, swinging it in a wide arc. Damien followed suit with his pistol, senses prickling. They slowed their pace.

"Speed *up* not slow down. There you go. Remember how I said I was being blocked? Well, I'm not anymore. Whatever was holding me back just lifted the lock on the thermal grid."

"That's a good thing."

"Ah, no. They lifted it from *inside* the building."

They froze.

They're here. Damien eyed his brother. They both looked up as slow as they dared, terrified of seeing telltale shimmers in the air above that would reveal an invisible Avo. Damien held his breath. His eyes darted around and his pulse quickened.

Nothing moved, but Damien could swear he saw a hint of something—maybe human—lurking behind one of the many benches that filled the far side of the atrium. *Survivors*, he thought, wishing he could warn them. "Leo," he whispered. "Where? *Where* inside?"

"There's a comm office off the lobby and—*ahp*, hold on."

The distant howl of the storm seemed to swell, but it wasn't enough to blot out the fragile spurts of air Damien was letting out.

"Keep moving." said Leo, all traces of laughter gone. "Both of you, *move!*"

Shit. "Leo, what is it?" Damien asked, breaking into a jog towards a door at the back of the atrium.

"Outside. The thermal grid is picking up an amorphous signature. It reads like a cluster of people moving together in a tight group. I can't tell how many. It's them. It's the hunters. You have to go. Get upstairs. GO!"

They ran. Fear stitched Damien's lungs and he couldn't seem to get a full breath. The atrium echoed with the crash of boots on tile as they ran. Now he was sure he spotted the glint of human eyes peering fearfully out at them from across the atrium. *You can't help them*, he cautioned.

"The one in the office is coming into the front lobby!" Leo cried.

Damien dared not look over his shoulder.

Von sped ahead of Damien as they approached the back of the atrium. He bowled the door to the stairs wide open, snapping the lock clean off. Damien flew in behind him and Von slammed the door closed.

They were plunged into darkness, gasping for air. After a few harrowed seconds, Damien swallowed and listened at the door. "Did… did the one see us?"

"I don't know. I don't think so."

"You hear anything?"

Von shook his head, pressing against the door.

"They're coming in," Leo whispered.

"How many?"

"I don't know."

Fuck.

A second later, the unmistakable howl of the storm reached their ears as the front doors slid open. It was cut short with the high-pitched *crack*-and-*zing* of a rifle, followed by the same *BOOM* as the doors slammed shut.

Someone had just shot the door mechanism, locking it closed.

Damien's mind raced as he tried to place the pitch of the rifle. Until that moment he had held a frantic hope that they were wrong about commandos, but the sound confirmed it. The three of them had spent enough time around Gyro rifles to know that that wasn't one. The shot sounded… *bigger.*

Lances, Damien thought. *Gyro Lances.* Lithe, graceful weapons that only expert marksmen were trained to wield.

There were no other sounds.

Goddamn Avos, he cursed. *I wish we could have some obvious monster biting at our heels*, but he knew that was crazy. Avos wore Prism armor that bent light and made them all but invisible to the naked eye. A chase with an Avo would never be one where the monster barely missed its target; this was a hunt where if the monster *saw* them, they might as well bite a bullet, because they *would* be caught, eventually. Avos never gave up their prey.

Von tapped his shoulder. Damien's eyes adjusted quickly in the dark, as always, and faint outlines of light glinted off his brother's helmet. He took a moment to feed a spurt of power to his eyes, and the broad square stairwell lit up. Von pointed at the stairs. Damien nodded, intending to ascend, but just as he planted his foot on the first step, he heard a shout.

"*Mary!!*"

Oh no.

He bolted back to the door and heard the frenzied terror of a grown man.

"No," the man shouted. "*No!* No, they'll find us! They'll find us; we can't keep hiding! We have to leave, we'll be safer outside! Come on, Mary! Let's *go!*"

Damien shoved his ear against the stairwell door as the sound of horrified footfalls pelted his ears. *STAY PUT!!* he screamed at them in his thoughts. *They'll get you!!*

But he was too late.

"MARY!" the man screamed again, "COME ON!!"

Unable to hold back a mortifying urge to see, Damien cracked the stairwell door just enough to see a swath of the atrium.

"MARY!!" A grown man, fit, armed, and dressed well for the weather, was bolting for the front door.

NO!! Avos *you fucking idiot! Avos!* Damien knew better than to cry out, but even the shout in his thoughts was undercut by the man's wail.

"*BABY!! Come on!! Come on we can make it!! We'll make it to—*" The sound of something sharp whistled through the air. "*—ACK.*"

Damien froze.

The blade whistled again, and Damien thought he saw the faintest glint of the *avosas* just before it vanished through the man's neck: a twinkle of metal whipping through a shadow in the middle of a dark room, a lethal phantom.

The man gurgled as his momentum carried him another step. He clutched vainly at his chest as his cleaved body fell; his legs and torso impacting hard while his separated shoulder, chest, and head blatted noisily on the floor.

"CALVIN!!" a woman screamed from outside of Damien's sight; a pitiful shriek, darkened by terror and amplified by pain.

134

In the moment the man fell, Damien's rage turned molten. When the blood splattered the floor, though, the rage iced back over: Damien didn't know what he was seeing, but then he shifted a centimeter over, and the light filtered *just* right so that he could understand.

Barely a hands-breadth to the side of where the man had fallen, a thick splatter of blood had failed to reach the ground. Instead, it was now smeared through the air, neatly highlighting the silhouette of *something* standing there, nearly invisible to the naked eye.

Damien's blood ran cold as that *something* moved, and the air seemed to shimmer around the phantom. *Oh...fuck... is it just that one? It can't be just one.*

In the gloomy light of the atrium, Damien was just able to make out the curved, rapier-like profile of an Avo's *avosas* blade. Blood dripped to the floor in rivulets along seemingly nothing, until the invisible hunter twitched what must have been his wrist. The curved sword unlocked with a distant *click*, twirled over the alien's knuckle, and clicked again, now curled backwards over the hidden assailant's forearm. Blood sprayed in a neat arc away from the blade, and Damien did his best to keep his thoughts together.

"CALVIN!!!" The woman wailed again, echoing the pitiable punishment of love ripped away.

Time to go.

Just before he closed the door, Damien thought he saw the faintest outline of a second phantom, stalking out of sight and towards the woman. *There's another.* He wrenched the door shut as carefully as he could, and was further sickened and mortified as he heard the woman distantly scream again through the soundproofed stairwell—and get cut abruptly quiet.

He swallowed, glad that he hadn't eaten in a few hours.

Thankfully, Von hadn't been listening quite so hard to the debacle, and he chose that perfect moment to tap Damien on the shoulder and help banish the nausea that had filled him.

Unable to meet Von's eye, Damien nodded and jerked his thumb at the stairwell. His heart thundered in his chest, waiting for the door to burst open. They started climbing, as fast they dared, working to reach twenty stories up. *Go, go, go*, he pleaded silently, following his brother as they moved.

Every step was an effort in balancing speed and stealth; every scrape of dirt on the cement grated his nerves. Twelve steps up and they turned to the first half-landing. Twelve more steps and they were at the second floor.

Damien's legs were already screaming at him for clenching them so tightly, but he couldn't will his muscles to relax. No sounds from below. They took the steps two and three at a time.

Third floor. Nothing. Their footsteps seemed louder up here, or maybe they were just moving faster? He couldn't tell.

Fifth floor. The stairwell door remained shut.

Leo whispered that doors were being opened all around the atrium, in no particular order.

They kept going, gasping and panting with as little air as they could manage.

Eighth floor. Damien could swear he heard another scream, far off. Von twitched as the sound of a shot silenced it. *More people were hiding out here*. Damien clenched his jaw. They kept going.

Ninth floor. They passed a vent with a fan, and Damien's flagging nerves flared to life as he imagined something leaping out at them. His lungs flinched as cold air hit them when they passed it, but nothing came out. His legs burned, and he had started to smell something rancid.

What the hell is that? He wiped sweat from his brow and adjusted his goggles.

Twelfth floor.

It smells like rotting meat. Leo reported more doors were opening on the second and third floor now.

Von winced just ahead of Damien but pushed on. Damien could hear his brother slathering spittle over his jaws.

Thirteenth. Damien felt like he'd been climbing for days. His immediate terror had faded, and every few steps his boot scraped loudly, but he didn't have the energy to even wince about it. That smell had gotten worse, too, and finally, he noticed a few drops of pale white liquid on the steps ahead. He breathed heavily. *Oh no.* He knew what the smell was: a chemical compound in the Algaroth bloodstream that acted much like coolant, or sweat for humans. It didn't usually smell so bad.

Fifteenth.

"He can't go much further like this, Damien," Leo whispered, after confirming that there were still a few doors to open on the atrium—and theirs was among them.

"I know," Damien replied, almost choking on thick spit. "His leg... it's getting infected isn't it?"

"Probably."

Sixteenth.

Keep going, Von, he pleaded. *Keep going.*

"Leo," he finally gasped. "Where the hell are the—"

The stairwell door wrenched open with a *BANG.*

"Below."

They froze, listening to the thunderous impact as the metal door was wrenched off the frame and thrown into the concrete wall.

All traces of exhaustion vanished, all thoughts of safety evaporated. Damien couldn't even bring himself to feel good that they had made it this far. He gripped his pistol with a sweaty glove. Two steps above him, Von hung his head, his tongue lolling out of his mouth. The alien's muscles trembled.

A second passed.

Then another.

Just when they thought that maybe the hunters were kicking in doors just to see, a single, petrifying growl called up to them. The brothers didn't move.

It called again, rumbling what sounded like, "*Elemental.*"

Damien closed his eyes. His instincts said, *run you idiot. Run.* He stayed still.

"*Elemental...*"

And then, another sound came up the stairwell. One that Damien had dreaded hearing all night. His nightmares could never recall just how terrifying the sound had been the first time, but he remembered it now. He remembered the night on the docks; where the smell of shit, the sounds of the rain, and the screams of his friends all haunted him clear as day... along with that sound. An ominous, hydraulic hiss, repeated over and over. Damien knew it so well, and he had no sense of shame for being afraid of it. He *was* afraid, and rightfully so. It curdled his resolve.

The sound was that of a frog-leg, the leaping boots worn only by the Over-Seer's elite enforcers. Only Avos wore them. They puffed and sucked at the air with every springy step.

Hiss-thump. Hiss-thump.

"Shit," Von whispered. Cursing as he rarely did in English.

From the time the door opened until the time they moved was barely a few seconds, but it felt like eternity. Damien heard the suck of air as the boots primed... and the hiss as it launched an invisible menace up after them.

The impact of an Avo on the second or third floor was noisy and clattering.

THUD. Hiss-thump.

"GO!" Damien cried. The time for stealth was over.

The response was immediate. More pairs of frog-legs snapped to life, and soon the stairwell rang with the flurry of the jumping invisible monsters.

Hiss-thump, THUD. Hiss-thump, THUD. Hiss-thump, THUD. Hiss-thump, THUD.

The rhythmic beating sent the brothers into a frenzied charge up the stairs. *Hiss-thump, THUD.* The bangs and clatters made Damien's heart explode in his ears as the enemy ascended, each leap a full floor.

They vaulted up steps and clutched at their chests. The sounds grew louder and louder, closing the distance fast.

"Damien, WATCH OUT!" Von called as Damien crossed the landing on the seventeenth floor, he only a few steps above.

The Elemental spun. Shock spread over his features as that shimmering phantom of *something* came flying over the railing, leaving the far wall distorted but visible. It happened too fast for him to aim his pistol or focus an Orb.

CRACK.

Von fired his Plaster Rifle and a super-heated bullet encased in plasma erupted downwards. The shot shone like a sun for a microsecond, illuminating the light-bending Prism armor and a vague silhouette of an alien, before it disappeared with a squelch, just shy of the leaping Avo's spine.

Immediately, the monster's camouflage fizzled, popped, and broke as the delicately balanced tech was disrupted. In that second, the snarling visage of a midnight blue Algaroth appeared in midair, immortalized with an oily mist of organ tissue blowing down from the hole Von had just made.

Damien only caught a glimpse of onyx armor before he scrambled out of the way of the corpse. The Avo careened into the wall, its *avosas* blades sparking on the cement. He bolted up behind his brother. The deathly chorus of boots followed close behind.

Hiss-thump, THUD.

On the next landing, Damien spared a glance for the downed Avo— and saw to his horror that the creature was scrambling to its feet, moving with barely a hint of pain from the gaping, gushing hole that went clean through it.

Damien let out an audible moan. *You've got to be fucking kidding!*
Hiss-thump, THUD. Hiss-thump, THUD.

A single floor passed and the boots slowed for only a second. Guttural, Algaroth blood-roars chased them from the seventeenth floor landing. The challenge chilled Damien's veins further.

"Elemental!" They called, though Damien couldn't be sure if that's what they were saying.

He and Von vaulted the railing of nineteen, hoping to reach the twentieth floor before any more came up, when Damien spotted a tiny red dot, flashing as it rocketed up to their level.

"GRENADE!" He and Leo screamed together. Damien threw himself forward into Von and onto the last landing between nineteen and twenty.

Von didn't have time to react as the Fireworks grenade detonated, sending out a shockwave of heat and light in front of a thick storm of plasma and stunning spinning electrical shocks.

The blast knocked Damien forward into Von. They bounced hard off the top step and crashed into the wall, narrowly avoiding the sparking lances of energy as they peppered the shaft with sizzling pockmarks.

As the lights from the streaming energy faded, Damien shook his head to clear out the ringing in his ears. *Get up,* he thought, panicked. *Get up. Get up, get up... MOVE!*

He stumbled to his feet and wiped a trickle of blood from his eyebrow, distantly hearing Leo repeating his thoughts. "Damien! Get up! Get up, *they're* COMING! MOVE!"

Damien rolled forward. The ground was spinning; his head was spinning. He grabbed Von blindly and pulled, helping the struggling alien to stand.

"Von! You okay?! Come on!" He managed to focus for a brief second on his brother's back, which had been peppered with holes. It didn't register.

"I'm okay," Von hissed, struggling to stand.

Behind the ringing, Damien felt terror as the shaft shook with the ascension of the Avos. Blood continued trickling down from where he'd hit his head. "Come on we have to get up!" He knew that, even uninjured, his Elemental powers weren't enough to take these enemies on. He locked shoulders with his brother and they ran.

Von cried out on his bad leg, and Damien knew some of the leads had been severed. *Not now!*

"GO, GO, GO, GO, GO!" Leo cried, urging them forward.

The landing between nineteen and twenty clanged, announcing two Avos as they reached the half-landing below.

HISS-THUMP. HISS-THUMP.

The brothers slammed into the door to the twentieth floor. Thankfully, it banged open on impact.

Damien heard stinging snap-cracks of Gyro Lances firing plasma. He felt rather than saw them flying right at their backs. They tumbled into the hallway and a Lance shot exploded where Von's head had just been.

"Shoot 'em, shoot 'em!" shouted their AI.

Von tumbled down next to him, struggling to bring his rifle to bear. Damien stumbled, but managed to spin around, knowing this was his only chance to get a shot back. He felt the angry surge of Darkness flood his veins, and he faced the door. Two huge Orbs ripped into existence over his palms, and he saw that the air in the shaft was shifting and bending in chaos. He lobbed his scintillating energy through the door.

In a whorl of sound, one Orb hit an invisible surface and detonated, engulfing the Avo's head. His comrade was thrown back across the shaft, and the second Orb burst right next to its face.

"HA!" Damien whooped.

The door to the shaft was sucked shut under the combined detonation. It shrieked into place and the thumping of frog-legs mixed with howls of alien pain.

"Nice toss," Von moaned from the ground.

Damien helped his brother up. "Can you stand?"

"*SS—SEHH!*" Von wailed as Damien tried to lift him again, "L-leg!"

Damien looked down and saw, to his horror, the coiled bulges of three leads out of place under Von's armor leggings. Dark blood dripped onto the floor.

"Oh Damien, keep going," moaned Leo, trying to sound light.

"It's been a long time since we were here," Damien snapped, turning down the dark, T-intersection. "Where do we go?!"

"I remember…" Von said, hissing. "Th—that way." He pointed down the hall opposite the stairwell door.

In the stairwell, the sounds of the Orbs had faded, and they heard roaring from the far side. Damien checked to make sure they both had their backpacks. "Okay, let's go!"

Gyro Lances started firing into the door right behind his words. Damien and Von hobbled down the hallway, past one dark and empty room after another. The Avos continued shooting into the door, trying to burn their way through. *That Orb must have closed it hard,* he thought. His lip twitched, furious. *Good. Let them tumble around in there for a while.*

At the end of the hall, a broad polyport window let light into the hall: they were at the edge of the skylight in the atrium. Far below, Damien could see the ruins of the 'Twined Tree…and what looked like the lump of a corpse in pieces. They turned left.

A muffled clang impacted the stairwell door.

"I wish we had grenades," Von said. He coughed and hacked up a glob of blood.

"That would be fantastic," Damien agreed.

Another clang. Louder.

"Leo, are you gonna—"

"—I'm opening it now, shut up!"

At the end of the hall was a heavy silver shock door patterned with metallic hexagons.

CLANG. That time it sounded like something broke.

"Okay, it's opening! Get in, get in!"

Damien shuffled them inside as the floor-to-ceiling shock doors slid apart. They were nearly a meter thick. As soon as the two of them were through, Leo slid the doors closed behind them. Just before they closed, a final *BANG* rang after them, followed by an extra-stinging crack as metal sheared metal, and they heard the stairwell door crash off its hinges. The Avos had made it through. One roared a challenge, but it was cut short as the doors slid shut.

"YES!" Leo cried.

The brothers fell apart against the wall and gasped, taking the reprieve.

"How's… how's your leg?" Damien asked, doubled over.

"Would you believe me if," Von coughed. "If I said I was fine?"

Damien's laugh turned into a hack. "No."

"Okay…" The alien took long, wheezing breaths. "Then I'm fine."

Damien snorted, still trying to hear through the ringing from the Fireworks grenade.

"Mmmm—okay, we all better now?" said Leo. "Everyone breathing again? Should we do what we came here to do? This way, this way."

Damien shook his head, "Leo, just… fucking hold on, okay?" The crimp in his side was almost blinding.

"Pfft, well *fine* then. Why don't I just open the door again and invite the Avos in, hmm? How's that sound?"

"Shut up," said Von.

Damien finally recovered enough to look around, and just the effort helped his weary body recover. The entry hall was long, dark, and mostly empty. Damien remembered that the corridor to his left led to a locker room, showers, bathroom, and break room. Ahead, double doors had been left half-open. Just behind them, he finally spied what they had risked so much to get to, what might not have even been here.

The continental transceiver sat in shadows, safe and intact within its cylindrical cage.

"Leo, will those shock doors hold?"

"Depends."

"On what?" Von snapped.

"Well, what are you worried about getting through?"

"The Avos?" He didn't have the energy to spar.

"Oh. Well yeah, probably… for a bit? I thought you meant 'will it hold against a charging rhinoceros' or something, which, okay it… *might* hold against that too, but I can't be sure. There aren't any living rhinos left to try it on."

"Uh huh." Damien turned to Von. "You still have the rig?"

Von struggled off the wall, favoring his good leg. Before the alien removed his pack, Damien remembered seeing the holes the grenade had peppered in Von's bag, and he choked on worry.

Von's pack was indeed shot up, but when they looked inside, they both sighed relief when they saw that the hacking rig remained unharmed.

"Oh thank *goodness*," Leo said. "I'd hate to see this trip be for nothing."

Carefully, Damien took out the rig, and stole a glance at his brother's back, just to make sure the holes didn't go further. They didn't. "What, Leo, not having a good time?"

The AI cackled. "Oh no I'm having a blast, are you nuts? I just want it to be worth it for *you* two!"

"Oh I see." Von took the rig and Damien retrieved the black box from his own bag. "Shall we?"

Von nodded, and they moved into the transceiver control room.

Dominating the center of the room, the continental transceiver array looked blissfully untouched from all that this city had seen. For that, Damien was infinitely grateful.

A caged cylinder of equipment, the array was designed to operate with a team of five technicians, one of whom sat in the suspended swiveling chair, the rest of whom sat on the floor under the leader. The cage was filled with Pip screens and pads, making every centimeter of space Pip-capable—the closest Damien had ever heard of anyone creating a true, projected reality simulator.

The transceiver array—and others like it around the globe—had acted as the living network hubs for humanity's Intersystem, allowing everyone in range to "get online" (as Damien knew people used to call it). The arrays tapped into the local source of power, be it a grid, a Mag Fury, solar collection tech, or any other local option, and would harness it as a constant power source, making the Intersystem an ever-present entity.

Since The Conquering, The Collective had shown little interest in shutting down the arrays, as they only acted as relay stations for the Intersystem, and not as actual *sources*. The enemy's apparent laziness was what had given Von the idea of using a transceiver array against them. He had reasoned that each array had been previously used alongside The Collective's sister networks, so why couldn't they attempt to reactivate that connection somehow, thus giving limited access to the Over-Seer's movements? The possibilities of that were unclear, but vast.

It had taken the three of them well over a year to manifest that idea into the hacking rig they held so tightly tonight, but they had done it. And as Damien and Von approached the array's cage, they both took a deep breath, and Damien looked at his brother. "Moment of truth, eh?"

Von nodded, winced, and spat blood. "Oh yes."

Damien elbowed Von's forearm lightly. "Glad *you* came up with the ideas for once."

Von growled, but his emerald-gold eyes twinkled with gratitude.

"Pretty," Leo interrupted. "It's like we're in a church."

"Why?" Damien asked, opening the cage.

"Not for *you*, silly." Leo chortled. "For me. It's like I'm standing at the altar that was the hub for all communication this side of North America. I feel like I should pray."

"To whom?" Von grumbled, limping in behind Damien. "You should just be grateful the Over-Seer didn't strike this place."

"I am grateful, Silas. But you're trodding on my faith here, okay? Show some respect."

"They probably just never got around to bombing it," Damien said, cutting them off and pulling down the lead technician's chair from its swivel. The normally soft material was stiff, cold and dusty.

Bruised and still shaking cold from their limbs, the brothers moved as fast as they could to boot up the array and connect their rig inside the cage. Their moment had ended. Leo made an impatient tapping in Damien's ear while they interfaced the AI's cube with the computer. Von began unwrapping their precious contraption and plugging it into various ports in the cage. Leo appeared on the small Pip pad next to the main terminal.

"What's taking so long?" he whined, pouting.

Damien ignored him until he held his hand over the power switch. "You know what'll happen when you log in right?"

"Yup!"

"You're sure about that? *Everyone* is going to hear their System access boot up, no matter if they're on a private connection or not. Turning this on will bring the network back up for the whole region."

"Ohhh I know." Leo rubbed his hands together, gleeful as a kid on his birthday. His avatar flickered and jumped to a small Pip pad hanging off the main computer, vanishing off the first pad.

"You're not about to go all diabolical-corrupted-AI on us are you?"

Leo grinned. "Maybe I will, what's it to you?"

They both glowered at him.

"Okay it's not funny, I'm sorry! *No*, I won't. I promise. Pinky swear!" He held up his pinky. "You know, because that's *binding* in some cultures."

"Vo, you ready?"

Von nodded as he plugged in the last cord. Damien tried to ignore the sound of his brother hacking another gob of blood on the floor. *That sounds like it came out of his lungs*, he thought. *We need to get him out of here.* He flipped the power and Leo's avatar vanished. They waited, black box in hand, ready to connect it, one ear still turned back towards the shock doors for the sounds of Avos. *At least we don't have to worry about them coming in through the ceiling or vents or something*, he thought. *This whole room is hardened and isolated from the rest of the building.*

"Leo?" he asked. Nothing.

Von coughed. "Leo? Are you in?"

The teal grids of the Pip screens lit up, and a mote of light appeared above them in the cage. Damien pulled the swiveling chair down and out of the way, and in a moment, the mote expanded.

"*Oh my...*" Leo's incorporeal voice sounded enormous. "*Oh yes. Yes, I think I could get used to this.*" They heard him breathe deeply through his nose. "*Smells like... victory.*"

"Do you want us to plug in the box?" Damien said.

"*In a minute, hold on now! I've never felt this much SPACE before. Whoo! It's roomy in here!*"

In all the history of Artificial Intelligence, not once had a synthetic being ever run rampant against its creators. Damien sincerely hoped he wasn't about to witness the first. "Leo... are you alright?"

The mote of light expanded into a projection of audio waves, matching Leo's voice. "*Just cleaning out the cobwebs. Mmm. This is nice. Can I have it? Please?*"

Von looked impatient and tired. Damien grinned despite himself. "No, and we don't have a lot of time here, remember? Black box?"

"Yes fine go ahead and plug the little thing in. Ah, there you... go. Oh. Heh... Heehee... Heeheehee. Ooh you two won't believe this."

"What?" Von snapped.

"It works. Oh bless me, it works."

They heard the whir of the array coming to life, just as a *thump* reverberated through the floor. Their moment was cut short.

"What was that?" Von asked, whirling.

Damien eyed the shock doors, feeling the triumphant horns of success putter out. "I can guess."

"Oh by the way," Leo added. *"Your friends are outside. I think they're drilling. They must really want to meet you. Wish I knew why."*

The tiredness creeping through Damien's muscles receded as his mind started to race again. "How long do we have?"

"Mm, a few minutes."

"What about the box?" said Von.

"It's lovely."

Damien moaned. "The codes?!"

"Trying them now."

Above them, the air started filling with cascading information. Teal text in thirty languages appeared along with thousands of numbers, swirling and changing. Damien flinched on instinct, expecting wind that wasn't there.

They waited, and another *thump* sounded beyond the shock doors.

A year of work, Damien thought, *all leading to this*. He tried to control his breathing. Part of him knew that even if this little stunt worked, they still had no idea what to do with it or even... *Oh fuck.* Damien stopped in his tracks.

Von noticed. "What?"

Another thud. Damien couldn't tell if it was getting louder or not. "Do we... have a good contingency to get out of here?"

Von averted his eyes. "Not with Avos outside."

Normally, Damien might have played at thinking it out, but as quickly as he'd realized they had no way out, a wild idea occurred to him. He bolted for one of the computers while the teal matrix swirled around them. "Leo, is it working? The array?" *We might be able to fly out.*

"...*Yes*," the AI said after a moment. "*And so are your codes...*"

Something in Leo's voice held Damien's excitement as he logged into the main server. "Why aren't you excited?" He watched as an outlined map of North America came up. Thousands of tiny blips were already flashing, indicating computers connecting to the System. *There used to be millions.*

"*Because I'm in The Collective's network.*"

"Isn't that good?" Out of the corner of his eye, Damien watched his brother edge in view of the shock doors, where the thudding had started getting faster, but not louder.

Leo didn't respond.

"Leo?"

"What's wrong?" said Von. His ganglia slowly fell flat against his skull and his eyes narrowed towards the doors.

"*Nothing.*"

"Leo, don't you start that shit now. What is it?"

The swirling matrix slowed, and stopped, and Damien felt as if time had as well when he saw why.

On each Pip screen, a painting had appeared. A stunning vista of a rusty red desert at night stretched to the horizon, where the glow of a sweeping city lit the sky. Above, the night sky hung on fire, lit with a thousand shooting stars. In the foreground, a single asteroid impacted on the dark desert floor. The painting captured the moment before the shockwave. Damien knew the vista well. It was Bravér's Rain, the lost Martian masterpiece.

Leo appeared on the Pip pad in front of Damien. His voice was soft. "Nothing's wrong. You'd rather look at that painting."

Damien's eyes narrowed. "Yeah, I would, but you never bring that up unless something's *really* wrong. Our rig works, they haven't changed the codes yet on the box, which means you were right about them probably not realizing we took it since my Wave probably *did* destroy that Razer, and we might genuinely have a new weapon against The Collective. *What's wrong?"*

Leo looked flustered. "There's umm… well… Yes, the rig works, I just hacked into The Collective's network hub they set up in Port Angeles and got out without being noticed but…" he trailed off.

Damien crouched to the AI's level and glared.

Leo winced. "Shoot the messenger if you want, but… well, I figured, why not grab some other data too, right?" He wrung his tie. "Well, Damien, the ah, the Over-Seer—Croll Tan—he… he got in touch with his army. The one in Portland."

"So? The fact that Avos are here at all means we have trouble on the horizon. Did you hear what they were calling? 'Elemental'?" Damien spread his arms. "Our cover is already blown!"

"Yes but… this was a different call."

"What was it?"

"He umm… He…" but the AI just couldn't say it. Finally, he sputtered and said, "Just… just listen. This was time-stamped at about seven-thirty tonight, right after you saw the Avos' Stingships."

Bravér's Rain vanished, as did much of the hanging matrix of data. An audio log started playing, and Damien could tell it was a pair of Algaroth speaking Dekka.

"Korodor Naroonda, a message for you," said the first voice, gruff, rattling, and subservient.

"Is it Solaroth?" answered a second. It sounded high-pitched for an Algaroth, and almost mocking.

"It is."

"Ah, well then," answered the high-pitched voice, tremulous. *"Send it through, Koro. Now."*

"Of course," the first answered.

There was a brief pause. After a minute, a faint pop sounded that a call had been patched in, and the second Algaroth spoke, this time meeker than before. *"Gon Over-Seer. Lord, my commander. This is Korodor Jenda Naroonda. What may I do for you?"*

Even without just being told who it was, and never having heard his voice before, Damien would have known the newcomer was a leader. Delicate slowness played through the words as he chose each one carefully, sounding like the slowest notes of a solemn piano symphony that pulled towards something sinister. Not a single note of the newcomer's voice was a question; everything was a command. His voice was deep and crisp, so smooth and contemplative that it was a full sentence before Damien realized that Croll Tan, the Fourth Over-Seer of Earth, spoke in perfect English.

Damien's blood ran cold from the first syllable.

"*Korodor,*" said the Over-Seer. "*You do fine works around the far side of the globe. Were I there, I would congratulate you on holding the line on the North American coast. Well done.*"

Korodor Naroonda's voice shook with gratitude. "*You h-honor me, Gon. I do the best I can without your prowess behind me.*"

"*You are not a groveler, Korodor, you are a thinker. You win from your own mind, not from mine. Do not forget that. Erstwhile, I do not speak from so far away without reason. You received my Avos.*"

"*We did, Gon. They left for the Islets as soon as we heard of the raid.*"

"*And they have departed on their mission.*"

"*Yes, lord.*"

"*Good. They will have the Elemental's blood soon. When they do, understand that it's time for Seattle to fall. Mobilize your command, and march to the Olympic Isle cities. Take Tacoma, take Seattle, and take Vancouver. Do not go further. Fortify the coast so that the Regent Dynasty may not bring aid to the Americas.*"

"*With all haste, Over-Seer.*"

"*No Korodor, with tactics.*"

"*Yes, Gon.*"

The call ended.

Damien stared blankly at the flatline of the audio playback. He was faintly aware of the Avos drill in the distance, now a rhythmic *thump-thump-thump-thump-thump.*

"Damien?" Leo asked, subdued.

Take Tacoma, take Seattle, take Vancouver. The words played back in his mind.

"Damien, are you alright?"

Take Seattle. He blinked. *It can't be over.* He rubbed his arms, and Von grasped his shoulder, shaking him from staring at the dead line of sound hanging in the air. He turned to see tears filling his brother's emerald-gold eyes. "It's not fair," he finally croaked. *It can't be over. We just...we just succeeded.*

Von gulped and shook his head.

"For once," Leo interjected, "I really do hate to break this up, but we can think about this later. What should we do now?"

Damien didn't know what to do. Seattle had just been condemned with a word. *What do we do?* He took a shuddering breath and tried to bury the sound of Croll Tan's voice. The Avos drill continued thumping in the background. It had started to get louder. *Our whole life... everyone we've ever known is here...* He covered his face. *What do we do?* But then it occurred to him, so obvious in that moment. He tried to control his voice and lowered his hands. *Of course.* "We have to warn everyone. We have to send out a call."

Von nodded immediately, but Leo shook his head. "And what about us? What about this rig? What about *me?*"

Damien didn't know what to do about the AI's selfishness in that moment. The absurdity of Leo's concern of self-preservation set against the perfect logic of it was so ridiculous that he didn't know what to do but laugh. So he laughed. "You'll be fine," he said, feeling the strain of the smile on his face. He stood and thought for a moment while they watched him.

"How long do we need to make a call?" Von asked.

"Just a minute, why?"

"Because we need to delay the Avos so we can fry this array."

"What?" Leo squealed. *"WHY?!"*

Von growled low in his throat, "Because it's a working trace on every living person in the region. The Collective might burn the city, but if the people don't make it out, Seattle will truly die."

Damien fought the lump of fear in his throat, and felt a swell of pride for his brother that they had reached the same conclusion at the same time. "He's right."

Leo checked a swinging pocket watch that he hadn't had a moment ago. "Okay, fine, but I'm calling Puget Command directly. I don't know anyone else with wings nearby."

"Great idea," said Von. "What are you doing?" he asked, looking to Damien.

Damien had already moved back to the computer. "Warning everyone. You?"

Von smiled sadly and held up his special, modified Plaster Rifle. Its tiny nuclear power cell glowed under the cooling gauge. "I wish we had grenades."

Damien shook his head, knowing how large an explosion that cell could make if properly coaxed. "I'm sorry."

"It's just a gun," said Von, and he exited the cage, already dismantling his favorite weapon.

In a few short moments, the drilling became noticeably louder. The thumping pounded through Damien's boots and made it hard to type. Finally, he opened a comm channel on all frequencies, all bands, and cleared his throat, hesitating as the Over-Seer's words hit him again. *I have decided that it's time for Seattle to fall.*

Fuck off, he grimaced, and took a breath. "Attention," he said, and a split-second delay brought his own voice bouncing out of the speakers, drowning out everything. "This is XenoCon Campus Seattle, repeat, XenoCon Campus Seattle. We have reactivated the Campus Intersystem access and intercepted a message from the Over-Seer: The army is coming. I repeat, Over-Seer Croll Tan has ordered that the Olympic Isle cities be razed to the ground. You have to leave. Get out while you can. The cities are lost. The army is on the move." He cut the message, set it to repeat continuously, and muted the speakers. The Pip screens around the array showed that it had already been transmitted, and the tens of thousands of computers now connected to the System were blaring it. The warning was out. Damien allowed himself a sigh of relief.

A squeal of metal brought him back.

Something sounded like it had given beneath the drill—maybe a reinforced layer—and suddenly the thumping was louder still. Damien heard Von groan near the door. "Leo, is your message out? Did you hear anything back?"

Leo appeared again, rolling his eyes. "Yes, but we won't *hear* anything back! Some *idiots* didn't properly shut down the receiver part of this *trans*ceiver array, and it isn't WORKING! The threat of occupation is no excuse for not taking care of your equipment!" He paused, noting Damien's failure to respond to the jibe. "Does it make you feel better that we have imminent violence?" he pointed to the shock doors.

"You've got that right," Von called as he hobbled into the room. Damien had no idea how his brother was still standing. He spied a thin trail of blood on every other of Von's steps.

WHAM.

Another section of the door gave way. The drill hesitated briefly, then amped up from a steady thudding to a machinegun staccato. *Thumpthumpthumpthumpthumpthumpthump.*

Damien groaned. "So we don't know how to get out of here?" He took the nuclear cell from Von's cannibalized gun and pulled a homemade explosives kit from his bag—something he kept for just such an occasion. He called it his 'matchsticks'. He went to work setting up the impromptu bomb inside the cage.

Leo snapped his fingers at different Pip screens as he wound down the array. They turned off one by one with each snap. "We climb to the roof. Extraction by airlift."

"From where?"

"You don't remember?" Von pointed.

To the right of the entrance hallway, another hall broke off from the transceiver room. Halfway down it, the finished look of the building ended and a grated walkway ran to the outer door. A pair of generator coils as thick as Damien came up through the floor and ran parallel along the walkway, then disappeared through the far wall, where a heavy metal door loomed at them on an incline. A mess of red conduits and parts glowed up through the walkway, giving the corridor a hellish glow.

Damien did remember. He remembered almost falling off the roof while he and Von were playing in this very room, so many years ago. He also remembered never going out onto that roof again.

Von clearly saw his discomfort but said nothing. Leo on the other hand, shrugged and said. "The homing beacon is on the roof, and I think we have a ride. Go up there or face the Avos."

"How do you know we have a ride?"

"Just trust me, dear fellow."

Damien replaced his backpack and helped Von put his on. "You *just* said we wouldn't hear back, how the hell do you know?"

"I just know. I made us sound *extra* appealing as cargo."

"I hate you sometimes."

"I know, but you can yell at me *after* I've saved all of us."

The thumping got louder. Damien glanced at the door. "Are they getting through?"

Leo craned to look over Damien's shoulder. "It would appear so. I'm going to make an expert recommendation that we move NOW."

Damien snatched up his goggles and pulled up his face guard. *I can't believe we're leaving. This is insane.* The brothers quickly wrapped up the hacking rig and replaced the black box into their packs.

The staccato intensified.

"Mind grabbing me out of here too?" Leo asked. "I've actually decided this computer's roominess isn't worth the, ah, *neighborly* atmosphere."

The second Damien snatched up Leo's cube, his avatar vanished and the array went mostly dark. He slipped the little glowing box into its slot.

"I have returned to the confines of your stinky bag," Leo quipped through the earpiece.

"If you like, I can leave you here for the Avos?"

The AI responded as peaceably as he could. "No! No, this, this is just fine. I only meant that the, ah, the smell sort of… Mmm, *grows* on you."

Damien grinned darkly. Then a third break in the door cut it short. "Ready?" he glanced at Von.

"Yes." His brother sounded exhausted, and Damien tried to hide the alarm at how pale he looked. *One thing at a time.*

"I might hurry," said Leo. "I think we've overstayed ourselves."

Damien glanced at the shock doors and spotted the faintest of blemishes on the hexagon-imprinted surface. It looked like a thick, metallic bubble had begun to boil through. The air was slowly filling with a toxic, chemical smell as the bubble expanded by the second, consuming the neat geometric pattern as it grew. Behind it, the pounding drill was louder than ever. "Shit," he coughed.

"Aptly put."

He set the timer on the bomb for thirty seconds, synced up a countdown in his goggles, and they left the cage, moving fast for the door to the roof.

The bulge burst, similar to but infinitely louder than the sound of a soap bubble popping. They could hear molten metal and circuitry spewing into the entryway behind them. From far of, Damien heard frog-legs.

They reached the heavy outer door and Von slumped against the wall, trying and failing to help as Damien threw himself into it. Hissing and thumping echoed behind them and precious seconds ticked away as they pushed.

Hiss-thump. An Avo had made it through the hole.

"Come on, PUSH!" Leo wailed.

Damien threw everything he had into the door, bruising his shoulder. Von braced himself against the conduit along the wall, but he just didn't have any strength left. "It's frozen shut!" he shouted, uncertain if it was actually the case or if he was just that tired.

"PUSH HARDER!"

Hiss-thump. A roar came behind them.

"Damien, *Damien!*"

The timer ticked below twenty seconds.

"You son-of-a-bitch-Elemental, I am *not ABOUT* TO DIE IN YOUR STUPID BACKPACK!!"

Damien's shoulder ached, the drill screamed at them, the Avos were piling through the hole, Von's pushing had stopped altogether, and the timer hit twelve seconds. "YAAAAH!!" he roared, challenging the door with all his might.

It screeched open a millimeter.

"YES!!" Leo whooped.

Hiss-thump. Hiss-thump. Nine seconds.

He pushed harder. It slid another, then another, and then three more. Five seconds.

"ELEMENTAL!!" an Algaroth roared after him. *Hiss-thump.*

Finally, the door cleared the frame and the icy wind caught it. It swung up and out, nearly whipping Damien off the ledge. He held on as the door banged into the building with an impact that could have woken the dead. The raging blizzard choked the breath from his lungs as the stampede of cold overwhelmed him, and he cried out for his instantly frozen fingers.

Three seconds.

His timer stopped.

Baffled, Damien pulled back from the edge of the platform and turned to help Von out.

"*Elemental.*" The voice commanded his attention.

Damien looked towards the cage and saw nothing…but a shimmer in the air. Damien stopped moving as a lone figure materialized from thin air next to the cage. Light bent and snapped back into place around the tight armor of an Avo.

Damien took the creature in—the one whose head his Orb had exploded next to.

The Avo's jaw dripped blood from the vicious wound across its face, a patchwork of shredded skin and bone. A chunk of its eye ridge on the left side had been sliced out, and that eye looked thoroughly bloody. The midnight blue Algaroth was clad in contoured onyx armor, all dark smooth curves save for the charred pockmarks on its injured side. It held its left arm at a funny angle, but in its right hand, it held Damien's matchstick and Von's nuclear cell, disconnected.

Oh no... The timer held still at three seconds.

A stab of fear struck Damien's gut as he locked eyes with the alien. The creature's gaze glowed molten gold, full of rage. The look lasted only a second before Damien whipped out his pistol and squeezed off three shots in quick succession. The Avo ducked out of the way, but the glow of his eyes stayed as a furious, petulant echo while the brothers wrenched the door closed. The wind threatened to tear them both from the walkway, but they managed to slam the door shut, trapping them on the roof. Damien shot the handle three times for good measure. That would buy them a couple more minutes. *I hope.*

"So, Leo," Damien screamed, fighting to be heard as the storm gnawed at his exposed skin. "Do we have a ride?!"

"I hope so!"

"What do you mean, 'you hope'?!"

They heard an impact on the door. It stayed shut.

Leo's answer was dead serious. "Both of you, get out of the way. Get above the door. *Now.* They're setting up charges inside. Get up to the transceiver."

They did, and Damien fought vertigo as he tromped step by step around the protruding exit. He could barely see the metal walkway that ran the apex of the building, but a few paces away he spotted stairs that went up and over the corridor they had just left. The blizzard swirled its wrath around them.

A great *BONG* split the air and Damien glanced up. Above them, he spotted the outline of the actual transceiver array. It blinked with alternating fog lights, sending out a resounding ping into the night. Icicles dangled from every spot they could.

"That's the homing beacon!" Leo shouted in their ears.

Von gurgled something and Damien looked back to his brother kneeling behind him. A puddle of bloody snow oozed in front of him, steaming.

"VON!" He raced over to help him. Blood was trickling out of the alien's mouth and onto Damien's jacket again, and Damien had a horrible sensation of déjà vu.

"I'm f-f-fine," Von shivered in his arms.

"Sure you are!" They reached the transceiver. "LEO WHERE'S THE DAMNED TRANSPORT?!" *And where are those fucking Avos?*

Leo didn't respond. The only answer was the biting cold and the wind, now a thousand times worse so high up.

"Leo?!" he repeated, pulling his brother up the embankment of the roof to the base of the array. "LEO!"

"I'M RIGHT!!" The AI suddenly cried over the wind. "WE HAVE A RIDE!!"

Damien couldn't see anything, but a second later, the most wonderfully familiar sound he had heard in years roared into range: the chirping, whistling jets of a UTA Special Forces transport—a Blackwing—as it descended from the sky.

"It's coming from the North, over the Sound!"

Somehow still having his sense of direction, Damien took a few seconds but finally spotted a single red light, flashing brilliantly through the fog and the snow; the belly of the craft.

"Have they spotted us?!" he cried, waving in the night even though he knew they couldn't see him.

"Yes! They're coming down!"

Damien had never been so happy to see the Air Force—even just an outline of them. He helped Von over the top of the protruding corridor and kept waving.

Even at this close, the Blackwing was almost impossible to make out in the dark, but when the roped harnesses whapped Damien in the face, he grabbed them. He strapped Von into the first one, and then did the same for himself on the second.

Just as he was about to tug the ropes to signal they were ready to go, his whole body shook as the door beneath them exploded. It was torn clean off its hinges in a cloud of smoke and sizzling fire, shooting away into the storm, faster than a bullet.

There they are. Damien yanked on the cords. "PULL US UP!!" he howled. "PULL US UP!!"

He couldn't feel anything, and he could barely see, but he knew the Avos were coming.

The Blackwing responded, and its distinct whistling chirp shrieked louder until it hurt Damien's ears. A second later, the harness grew taut and the brothers were lifted off the building. They locked arms and sighted their pistols, unable to make a noise as they were yanked off the ground.

"Watch out!" Leo cried.

Damien spotted five commandos spill onto the walkway. Their Gyro Lances swept the sky, trying to spot the human ship. The whistling grew deeper and the Blackwing accelerated. Damien and Von blindly fired at the building, peppering the door with kinetic-plasma fire. The Avos ducked and opened fire on the retreating Blackwing. Tiny stars of plasma lit the night. Damien fired in the icy air as the Avos shrank in the distance. The snowy profile of the XenoCon building vanished with the commandos, but all continued firing. Damien shot until his fingers were too frozen to squeeze the trigger.

Then, a sharpshooter plasma bolt struck just above the Blackwing's main engine block, burning a hole in the armor as if it were tissue paper. The aircraft jerked at the hit and accelerated in earnest, throwing Damien and Von into a wild spin. A few more bolts lit the night, and Damien thought they might be home free…

Until he felt an impact through Von, and his brother went limp.

MASON J. TORALL

CHAPTER EIGHT

Flight

Damien and Von's bodies crashed onto the cold metal deck of the Blackwing, where Damien tried to leap to his brother, but couldn't. *Von! Goddammit, Von, no!* He gasped for air, gesturing wildly in Von's direction, trying to get the crew's attention. His goggles were completely frozen over, but he could hear the murmurs of the crew standing over him. "Help—" he finally gasped. "Help, him!" The cold still had its grasp on his lungs. They seized, throwing him into a violent fit of coughing. His words were lost.

"I'll take care of this," Leo whispered in his ear. "Friends! Do not be alarmed!" the AI's voice blared through the intra-ship comm overhead. "I am Arthur Leonardo! I am a transcended, First Trigger, adult AI, and these are my companions! We thank you for your assistance, and humbly request to further impose upon your generosity by saving this blue-toned biped!"

Damien's coughing continued. He couldn't see how many people were in the crew bay with them. The only sound was of the storm outside and the whistling jets of the Blackwing. The deck lurched gently beneath them.

Leo repeated himself, gentler. "Thanks for pulling our asses out of the freezer? Would you *please* attend to this Algaroth?! He needs PROMPT medical attention?"

The crew still didn't move, and neither did Von.

He's been shot! He's been SHOT you idiots, can't you see that?! Damien finally managed to roll over, still gasping and coughing. He yanked his faceguard down. "Please!" he heaved, "He's... a defector, and a friend. *Please…* help him!" Finally, he tore his goggles off and was blinded by the interior cabin lights.

His eyes burned even from the dim lights but they adjusted quickly, and the shapes in the cabin resolved. Five airmen stood around them, all wintry-wrapped and faceless behind their snowy balaclavas and visors. All were armed with Plaster rifles and pistols. Damien looked around.

The crew compartment was smallish, but even with six humans and a sprawled Algaroth there was still plenty of room to maneuver. Narrow benches lined the fore and aft bulkheads, both of which were bisected by doors to the cockpit and rear cabins, respectively. Red crash webbing slapped against the cold metal frame as the Blackwing churned and slipped in the storm. Everything in the crew compartment looked and felt military: raw, designed for functionality.

The soldiers stood arrayed around Damien and Von, turning their heads behind the implacable visors of the United Territories Air Force. *HE'S BEEN SHOT!* Damien wanted to scream, but he could still barely breathe. He couldn't tell who was looking at whom, but one of the airmen nodded, and two others pulled an emergency medkit from a notch in the wall and brought it to Von.

"Thank-you… Thank-you," Damien gasped, clutching his chest.

The tense silence expanded, punctuated by the whistling chirp of the engines, the howling wind, and the bloody squelching of instruments being prodded into Von, who lay still. Damien tried to contain his worry as he slowly worked his way to his knees, shivering. His lungs were still on fire. A sickly, bleeding hole was burned into Von's side where the Gyro Lance bolt had pierced him, nowhere near as clean as the Gyro rifle shot in his leg. Finally, one of the medics working on Von glanced towards the soldier who had first nodded and said, "He needs a trauma kit, but he'll stabilize. Orders?"

A woman's voice came muffled through her balaclava. "Take him in the back, Sergeant. Put him on a gurney and strap him in with a kit. Docs can sort him out when we get home."

"Yes ma'am!" the sergeant who spoke answered. The two medics lifted Von's limp body and carried him through the door at the back of the compartment. The door hissed closed behind them. Damien watched them go. *Don't you die on me, Von. Don't you leave me alone.*

The woman pulled down her balaclava and took her helmet off, revealing striking, delicate features that took Damien aback. She had high cheekbones—he guessed her to be of possibly Northern Eurasian descent—with straight teeth and auburn hair pulled into a tight bun. Her bright, piercing blue eyes glowed with command. She looked to be somewhere on the far side of thirty but he couldn't be sure. Her wintry Air Force garb revealed only a commanding presence and the barest hint of fit curves.

"So," she spat. "*You're* the little bitch who caused all the trouble tonight? We were rerouted from going *home* because we heard someone had made a commotion at the XenoCon campus. Got your helpless asses into a little clench 'n squeeze, huh?"

"Yes," Damien answered plainly from the floor, still thinking about the feel of the impact when his brother slumped into him in the harness. "That's… about the size of it."

She glared at him. Her lip twitched at his slouching form. "Well?" She spread her arms wide. "Care to enlighten us as to what the fuck you were doing down there? 'Cus all I've got to go on is a shit order to take *you* to Puget Command, but you ain't getting there without some hard enlightening words for me."

Damien grimaced, swallowed, and was about to answer when Leo cut in, "Ma'am, we have a very special package to deliver to—yes, as you said—Puget Command at Camp Cascade."

She glared around the compartment, trying to find something to focus her stern gaze on. Finding nothing, she settled on Damien. "I don't see a package," she said flatly.

Leo pressed on, his voice still bouncing through the crew cabin. "I purposefully kept the nature of the package out of my message, miss, but I assure you: we three are, ah… quite *valuable* cargo. We're also in possession of a veritable *treasure trove* of Collective goods at a… safehouse we frequent. We request to be taken there, and then taken to Puget Command for deliverance."

Damien held his breath, unsure of what Leo meant by a 'safehouse' since they'd downloaded everything of value from the bunker into the AI's cube, which was still sitting pressed against Damien's spine in his backpack.

The woman stared at Damien for a moment, glanced towards the cockpit, then back at him. "'*Valuable*' cargo? What, you think we're mercenaries or something? Waiting to sell you off?"

Leo's tiny gasp in Damien's ear was enough to tell him that the AI knew he'd just made his first mistake in months. *Oh good, because we really need his confidence to plummet right now.*

The captain looked like she was about to throw them out the side door, but instead, she laughed. Her crew joined in. Damien flinched.

"What's so funny?" Leo demanded.

She sniffed and shook her head. "This is a Special Forces Blackwing, little matrix. We follow orders, even if Command isn't the *sharpest* on intel for my team." She gazed back at Damien, the seriousness returning. "Our orders were to investigate the ruckus at XenoCon, and assist the people who sent out an emergency broadcast about an army marching north from Portland." Her eyes bored into Damien's head. "Is that the truth as you understand it?"

Damien stared at a spot of pooling snow, glinting on the gritty metal floor. "We can play the call we hacked from the Over-Seer, if you like…" His voice was carefully neutral.

She raised a cold eyebrow at him, and turned away to clamber into the flight cabin. She returned with a headset held to one ear, chatting with someone. Her eyes searched Damien while she spoke. "Sir, we have them sir… Yes sir, I understand but we have no proof that they… but couldn't we just… no sir, my team is what I'm concerned with and we're flying in the dark is all… Well that wasn't communicated to me, sir… Well it *should* have been… I… No sir… No sir," her voice softened even if her posture didn't. "No sir… Of course not, sir, I wouldn't assume to… I'm sorry, sir… I… Yes of course sir, but we were just… Yes Chief, I'll wait." She paused, and her powerful physique visibly shrank as something else was said. "I—of course, sir!" She snapped to attention as someone else came on the line. "Sir! Captain Huxley here, sir! …Yes sir, we just picked them up! …I understand sir, absolutely! No! No problems here, sir… No sir, it should only be a short detour…" she glared at Damien.

Damien tried to eavesdrop as subtly as possible while Leo did his best to distract him with incessant gibbering. "You know I could tell you everything about every one of these people in an instant?" the AI chattered. "Everything about this Blackwing, its combat history and serial numbers, manufacturing origin, even where the source materials came from! Want me to check who's on the other line? I should check… No they'll make a fuss… No, you know what, I should check. We should know, right? Yeah, I think I'm gonna check. No. I'm *definitely* gonna check!"

"Oh, no you don't," Damien snapped, netting him a glance from the remaining two airmen, who were so still and silent they could have been statues.

"But I wanna just—"

"SHH!"

Damien was able to tune into the captain's conversation as it closed. "…I'll tell him, sir. Understood. We'll up our ETA to about oh-seven-forty… No Admiral, thank *you*." She hung up, tossed the headset into the cockpit, and hung in the doorway, teeth clenched.

Everyone waited, the Blackwing jostling in the wind. Then, Captain Huxley turned back to Damien, her eyes a mix of rage and pity. "What's your name?" she asked.

"Damien," he said slowly. "Damien Vilan."

"Well, Damien," she said, taking a step towards him. "You can't go home. That safehouse your AI mentioned. It was a bunker, wasn't it?"

Damien flushed as he made a cautious, skeptical face. "Could be. Why can't we go back?"

Leo cut Huxley off before she could answer. "Actually, Captain, you're wrong. It was a black market shop where we have some friends waiting for us, but let's put a pin in that and you can tell us what you know about our bunker, shall we?"

Huxley's sharp eyes narrowed and the pity left her gaze. "I think I want to get *your* story straight before I decide to offload you freezing fucks into the Sound from ten-thousand meters, *but…*" she heaved a sigh. "I have my *orders*, so I'd get in trouble for that shit, and my men wouldn't survive without me keeping their tiny balls in check." The two remaining airmen—who had taken seats without Damien noticing—sniggered as Captain Huxley turned away, crossing her arms. "Whatever the case around a safehouse full of refugees and stubborn idiots aside, you can't go back to your bunker, 'cause it's gone. I'm… sorry," and she sounded it.

Damien swallowed, unsure if he'd heard right, and he was too tired to get defensive about insurgents refusing to leave the city. "What do you mean, gone?"

She turned and stared right through him, contemplating a reply. Instead, she pursed her lips and poked her head back in the cockpit, barking orders. When she returned, her expression remained hard, but her eyes were softer. "The storm is clearing. I'll show you what I mean in about four minutes." Damien opened his mouth to say something but she continued. "Until that time, why don't you tell me *exactly* what your… very odd trio has been up to?"

Damien thought about denying her for a fleeting moment, but it passed. She had just saved their lives after all. Instead, he took a deep, shaky breath, and proceeded to give an abridged version of the past year of work assembling the hacking rig. He left out how he was an Elemental, though, and he didn't think it necessary to reveal that Von was family. He was also grateful that Leo stayed quiet through his tale. While he spoke, he glanced repeatedly through the aft door to where they'd taken his brother. Huxley noticed his shifting gaze but kept listening, arms crossed while she leaned against the forward bulkhead.

"…The Avos followed us to the campus and chased us to the transceiver array, but we managed to test our rig before they caught up," he finished. "That's when we called."

To her credit, Captain Huxley took the end of his story in stride. "So did it work?"

"The rig?"

She nodded.

"Leo?"

"Oh, it works," said the AI. "I mined a whole *wagon* full of golden goodies during my minute-long expedition, but most importantly: I planted a tiny back door into The Collective's local coding algorithms. It's not direct access, but it opened up a little lens into their network that someone can *definitely* use as a hacking anchor. It'll let someone fancy like me come back later." Damien could almost *hear* the AI's smirk.

"Sounds like a helluva weapon," one of the airmen finally said from his bench.

"Yeah, if it *works*," said the other. His voice was a deep, rumbling baritone.

"Do you still have the rig?" Huxley drove them back to silence. "Is that your package?"

Whether this woman was serious or not about tossing them overboard, Damien had kept his identity as an Elemental a guarded secret from the beginning, and any time he'd revealed it outside of family, it had turned into disaster. As vital a piece of information as that truth was, it was clear that Huxley wasn't in charge here, and she probably wouldn't take kindly to carrying such a controversial person. Besides, he didn't want to feel like a 'package' anyways. "Yes," he said, "and our accumulated library that Leo has."

"I see," but she didn't sound convinced.

She knows there's more. He had an unusual twinge of guilt at keeping the secret from her, but he didn't know what to do with it so he broke gazes and looked away. She snorted, and when he glanced back he found her still staring at him, eyebrow raised at his silence.

"You don't play poker much, do you?" she asked. Before he could answer, a shout came from the cockpit and she called back, "Copy!" She looked back at Damien, her eyes brimming with curiosity while she chewed her lip. Damien suddenly found he couldn't stop staring at the motion of her mouth.

Finally, she said, "Last night, Puget Command recorded a series of explosions in an outlying Islet of Seattle, just before yesterday's storm hit.

This morning, my team was called off from going on a hit-and-run strike to investigate, which was *exactly* what me and my men had wanted to happen, wasn't it?"

"No ma'am, it sure wasn't," said the smaller airman.

"Hurt our feelings," said the big one with the deep voice. Damien looked between them, and could feel their angry gazes behind their visors.

Captain Huxley cocked her head, full of sass. "That's right, because we had *wanted* to go on that mission. Instead, we had to come to *this* place," she gestured out the small viewport in the starboard door behind her. "Only to find that the blast zone was surrounded by '*insurgents*'. We chased them off from what looked like a wrecked skiff patrol, couldn't find anything, so we thought *maybe* we could catch the tail end of our strike, but did we get that? No. I get *new* orders this evening to track a flight of modified Stingships *somewhere* in our vicinity. Quote, '*they may be prototype Prism Stingships, capable of stealth*'. Anything more? No!" She started pacing, and Damien continued to hold his tongue.

I guess now we know why all of those people went quiet where we raided the Razer. Huxley got to them, not Avos. He wasn't sure if that made him feel better.

"So we wait," she went on, "and we look, and all we hear *all night* is a tiny explosion at some abandoned recycling compound, which had left no evidence other than what appeared to be some bomb-shelter bunker bullshit! So *just* when I'm about to call Command and say they'd snorted the wrong shit about those Stingships, they call *me*, tell me to detour AGAIN to come pick you fuckers up! En route, we hear that there's commotion in the army to the south, but of course, no one sees fit to give information to my team and me! So do you see my problem with your little hero's tale of a new superweapon, or whatever the fuck it is?"

Thankfully, Leo was there to answer before Damien opened his mouth, confident as ever. "Captain Huxley—may I call you Cappie?" She blinked, and the imperceptible shift in her demeanor said no, but Leo didn't wait for an answer. "Splendid! Well, *Cappie*, I think that we need to be taken to Camp Cascade before we answer."

She started to retort but Leo cut her off—as he often did with Damien and Von. Damien couldn't help thinking that it was nice to see it turned on someone else for once.

"*Clearly*," Leo piped over her opening mouth. "Someone higher up than you knows that we were worth a pickup, otherwise you wouldn't have been sent at all, yes? That means you're simply a runner, yes?"

Huxley squared her jaw. "Alright you little—"

"—And *that* means," he bowled on. Damien watched her stiffen and then deflate explosively. "That you probably aren't authorized to be asking us ANYTHING now are you? You're just a curious soldier?"

She crossed her arms, unwilling to be beaten again.

"Mm, so it's true! In that case, *mademoiselle*, I applaud you for coming so very close to the truth of the situation tonight, but I assure you, our claim to fame is real, and *you'll* be glad we dropped by."

From her look, Damien seriously doubted that, but he was so exhausted and concerned over her story about the bunker and the state of his brother, he didn't have anything to add.

Huxley finally spoke only when it was clear Leo wasn't about to continue. "Well," she said, her voice carefully controlled. "You've got quite the little *snapdragon* for a pet, don't you?" She looked like she wanted to throttle him, but thankfully was interrupted one final time when another call came from the cockpit. "Understood!" she snapped. "Slow us down so we can poke our heads outside!"

The pilot confirmed the order, and Damien felt the Blackwing slow. He watched Huxley while she stared out the viewport. When the whistling jets had calmed significantly, she looked back at Damien, her face neutral. "Come here."

Damien stumbled to his feet and wobbled his way to her in the turbulence. Upon standing next to the captain, he was surprised to realize that she was at least six centimeters taller than him. At one hundred and eighty-six centimeters, he was on the upper side of 'average height', but that small boost made Huxley downright tall. Up close, he could just make out that her whole face was powdered with flecks of mud and grime, but somehow she still looked clean. He was careful to not let her notice him looking.

When he had a firm grip on the crash webbing, Huxley covered her face with her aviator goggles and snowy balaclava, and punched the door release without waiting for Damien to bring up his own faceguard. The quiet cabin exploded into a roar as they were all exposed to the freezing air. In the last few minutes the blizzard had mostly cleared, but the aftermath had left frostbiting cold behind it, and hanging out of an aircraft at five thousand meters didn't help. Far on the horizon, the first hues of dawn were just visible.

Looking down, Damien quickly regained landmarks and his sense of direction, and surmised that they were flying southeast from downtown, straight towards the Mercer Islet. The Blackwing shot forward in the stilling air, dicing the thick cloud of frost into a crystalline contrail in the night sky. With each passing second, Damien felt his heart begin to race.

They came over the last islet between them and Mercer and Damien finally saw it.

Whatever anyone might have said, Damien wouldn't have believed that his home was gone unless he saw it for himself. He wouldn't have accepted it from Huxley and he probably wouldn't even have accepted it from Leo, but there was no denying the smoldering, gaseous smoke rising from the ruins of the warehouse and the broken compound that was the only safe place he and Von had known for four years.

Their bunker was gone.

Damien fought the lump in his throat with everything he had left, unwilling to get upset in front of this woman. *It doesn't matter*, he thought. *Get upset. She wouldn't care either way.*

He picked out the ashen details of the compound. How the Avos had found them, he couldn't say, but clearly they'd known exactly where to hit: the only ruined building was the warehouse, where it was clear an explosion had been centered. Everything outside the blast radius was untouched. Damien felt a stab of sickness as he thought he spotted the faint green glow of the keypad on their hidden entry door, somehow still powered. The door had been blown outward off its hinges and was half buried in concrete and metal. He could just make out a hint of fire in the entryway, where smoke billowed out. Something looked wrong about that, but he couldn't put his finger on it.

Then, even as he looked, while the horizon turned from black, to dark blue, and to grey, Damien witnessed a power rupture in some conduit or another that sent out a violent explosion. The sound reached his ears a second later, and the swirling fire collapsed the rest of the warehouse, burying the entryway.

Huxley seemed to know he'd seen enough. He saw her in his peripheral, leaving his side and signaling for them to turn away. Damien stood in the door, his face numb from the biting cold, his mind devoid of coherency. *Where do we go now?*

Unbidden, Bar's voice jumped to his mind, *'You come here, get your good health from us!'* and alarm shot through him as he wondered at their safety. His thoughts began to race as he was reminded that the Over-Seer's army was coming, and he worried about the few things he'd left behind, namely: Bar and Shell, his motorcycle, other insurgent-survivors, even those three people on the bridge. Other names came to mind, and a sudden, reckless idea took him. He spun towards the captain. "We can't leave yet."

The statuesque airmen both turned their heads, and Huxley looked up from the straps of her gloves. "I'm sorry?" The moment of softness in her eyes chilled over.

"We have to go to the safehouse—the other safehouse. We have to help our friends."

Huxley stared at him through her goggles, unmoving. "They're insurgents. They denied our help when we started evacuating the city after the Over-Seer's earthquake."

I know that. "That doesn't matter, they're people!" he said, pushing away from the door. "Now turn around!"

The captain froze, and immediately, he knew he'd overstepped himself. It didn't take a genius to know that no captain would take kindly to someone giving orders on their ship. It also didn't help that, at that moment, the rear door hissed open and the two medics reentered the crew cabin. Damien couldn't read their faces, but he dared not ask about Von with Huxley staring him down the way she was.

She eyed him silently, and slowly uncrossed her arms. The moment held.

"I think your life is buffering," whispered Leo.

Damien didn't answer, but he held Huxley's gaze. He knew he was right, even if it was crazy. *We can't leave them.* His arms itched again, but he resisted scratching.

Finally, Huxley spoke in an undertone of unyielding steel, enunciating every syllable. "I'm going to make one thing, *very* clear to you," she whispered, advancing one deliberate step at a time. "If you *ever*, give orders to these men again, I will rip your balls off and tie them to the end of your small intestine, so that everywhere you walk, you'll have them dragging in the dirt, and the only way to pull them up will be to *wrap* them around *your SHOULDERS* like a GODDAMN SHAWL!!" Her approach brought her to within arm's reach.

Damien should have stopped. He knew it. He could almost feel the hazing laughter, barely contained behind the crew's faceless masks. Instead he said, quite calmly, "Captain Huxley, turn this Blackwing around and take me to that safehouse, or I will bring this ship to the ground *myself* and we can ALL walk home." He was sorely tempted to allow his power to manifest, but he refrained. Barely.

The tension was so thick it could have clotted. Even Leo said nothing.

They stared at each other, almost touching, holding their breath and feeling the tug of the wind out the still-open door. Finally, Huxley sniffed, and Damien saw the snarling animal behind her eyes turn away.

Or so he thought.

His guard fell a fraction, and the captain punched him in the mouth so fast and so hard it knocked him back against the wall. The whole compartment chimed with the sound of his skull on metal. Stars exploded in his vision, the flood of copper filled his mouth as he bit something, and his ears rang from the impact.

It was a good thing that she hit him quite as hard as she did. It was so decisive that he didn't even have the focus to react with his powers, which he certainly would have done if she'd been any slower—intentionally or not—and then they'd all have been in *real* trouble.

He coughed and doubled over, holding his head and trying to keep from falling out the open door. Huxley clomped up next to him in her heavy boots, and leaned in so close that her lips brushed his ear. "Next time," she whispered sweetly, "it'll be your sack, and I'll do them *much* harder. That's a promise."

She straightened at the sound of snickering, and it died promptly as she glared at her men, shutting them up without a word. "If that call of yours got to your friends," she said, turning back to him. "I'm sure they'll leave the city. They've always listened to reason before when someone told them to leave, right?"

That time, he avoided her gaze. Blood was filling his mouth and his tongue hurt, but he pursed his lips around it.

She humphed. "If you want an escort for them, you can take it up with Command. I have my orders."

"They won't make it," he said, speaking thickly around the blood.

She set her jaw. "Not my problem. Camp Cascade is where I've been ordered to take you and your Algaroth buddy, and *that's* where we're going. *They* want to know who the fuck you are, and from there, well... I couldn't say that I care really. But I only have to tolerate your ass—" Damien swore her eyes sparkled at him, "—for another half-hour or so. I'm booting you boys as soon as we hit dirt. Until then, sit down, shut up, and hope to God that whatever you think you have is worth all this fucking trouble." With that, Captain Huxley punched the side door closed and stalked into the cockpit. Their exchange was over.

Damien turned towards the soldiers, then looked towards the rear door. "Can I see him?" he asked no one in particular. He refused to spit the blood out in front of them.

One of the airmen turned his head just enough to grunt, "He's out."

Damien took that as a yes, and he stumbled through the door, unsteady. The room beyond was smaller than he thought. For some reason he had imagined crew quarters, but it was just a short hallway to a storage area with an alcove at the back, which looked to be able to fit two bodies if necessary. In the lower alcove was Von. His brother was strapped carefully down with a set of tubes running to his arms from a machine hanging on the wall. Damien had never seen the rig before but he assumed it was the trauma kit.

Surprisingly, the storage room was quieter than the crew compartment, even though it was closer to the jets. He relished the dampening of the wind and the tight path around the cargo. He hacked blood into the sink until his tongue stopped, and then gave his brother a quick once-over, just to verify that he *was* in fact stable. In a way he almost wanted there to be something wrong so he could hit the captain back, but the medics had done a remarkably good patch-job—even if that was all it was. The hole in Von's side was enormous and grisly, but Damien dared not take the bandages off to see it. *Fucking Gyro Lances.*

Satisfied that Silas Von was not going to die this instant, Damien finally slid his backpack off, and found—to his immediate horror—that it had been shot up by the Avos. *You've got to be kidding.* Frantic, he tore it open and checked that Leo's cube was okay. It was. But that was about the only good news. The black box was still there, but it had taken more than one impact, and now resembled a pockmarked tube of slag. *That's okay. We can fix that. We already used the codes.* He dropped his bag and found Von's pack on the floor under his alcove. It was unharmed, and so was the hacking rig, thankfully.

Damien went back to his bag and dug deeper. At the bottom, in the little pouch where he had kept his few keepsakes, he felt the edges of the huge hole. *No... no, no, please no.* A tiny ping of relief flooded him as he found his family photo and his journal, tucked safely to the side of the hole, but after a long minute of feeling every fiber of the pack over and over, he was forced to give up. His rook was gone, and so was the amethyst coin that Kaylee had given him.

Damien slid to the floor behind a crate of what he assumed to be ammunition. He sat there for a long moment, eyes closed, clutching the crinkled photograph. Then, he pulled off the goggles and faceguard, muted Leo's input, checked around the crate to be sure that he was alone...

And he cried.

∞   ∞   ∞

The door to the rear compartment slid open and one of the medics entered. Damien had put on his goggles to hide how red his eyes were.

"We're landing at Camp Cascade. Get up, and we'll load out the slizzard."

Damien didn't move. "Thank you. For keeping him alive." His voice cracked.

The medic stood there, clearly waiting for him to get up. He finally did.

"His name is Silas Von, if you were wondering. He's my brother," and he pushed past the man and left, not waiting for his reaction.

In the crew compartment, the other soldiers were sitting in the exact places he had left them. Clearly the captain had every intention of leaving the moment he departed the aircraft. *Can't fault her for that.* Damien poked his head in the cockpit. Huxley was in the copilot's chair, staring at the console. "How close are we?" he asked, not impolite. Both the captain and the pilot lurched in their seats.

"Son of a bitch!" she barked. "What are you doing up here?"

"The medic said we were close. How close?"

She settled back into her chair. "About three minutes out, now get out of my cockpit."

Damien shrugged and stepped out, resigning himself to stand in the corner near the door.

The Blackwing shook as it slowed for final descent, and it threw Damien to the deck. The airmen burst out laughing, and he flushed with shame. He stood with as much dignity as he could, and was back on his feet just before Huxley stormed in, yelling, "What the hell's so funny? Are you dick-whacking apes ready to hit turf and bounce back? 'Cus that's what we're doing!"

The men stopped laughing, but the small one who kept making remarks said, "We're ready, ma'am, we were just admiring our passenger's umm... *flying skills.*"

They tried to hold it together but couldn't, and the three present burst out once more. Captain Huxley turned towards Damien and smiled a cruel smile. "Is being up in a plane too much for Package Boy?" Her eyes continued to bore through him. "That's too bad. Guess we'll have to dump you here, right boys?"

"Yes ma'am!" they snapped in unison, and the other medic went to get Von.

She nodded, appreciative, and just then, Damien decided that he very much wanted to leave her with an unexpected impression. The Blackwing lurched as it hit tarmac, and he could hear operators scurrying about outside, shouting and checking the ship, preparing to receive the passengers.

"Captain Huxley," he said, relishing his quick thinking. He stood straighter as the medics brought Von in on a gurney. She turned back to him, curious. "You've clearly worked hard to earn your command, so forgive me for saying this, but I mean it sincerely: we really *do* need people like you commanding the troops. We need the strength you can offer them. I think you're a solid commander."

Before she could answer, the door behind Damien slid open, and he marched off the Blackwing. He couldn't have planned it better, and he blinked in the pre-dawn light, allowing himself a small smile as he took in the scene around him.

Lit by huge floodlights, the tarmac around the Blackwing was full of people, all running around in winter uniforms, pushing hardware. Shouts could be heard all over, and the sounds of other aircraft taking off or landing echoed in the last hour of night. Cold mist rose off the frozen ground, curling and vanishing no more than a meter up as it was caught in the constantly shifting wind. In the distance, the sprawling base of Camp Cascade was fully lit, where all the low buildings clustered around a five-story hospital and a four-story building that could only be Puget Command. Next to the base, Damien could just see a maw of light, peeking over the ground at him: Camp Cascade's unique, buried hangar. The base was surrounded on all sides by dark forest, and far on the southern horizon, Mt. Rainier's snowy cap was just visible.

Damien looked up behind him, finally able to take in the aircraft that saved them. He admired the thick-bodied smoothness of the ship, reminiscent of some mix between a pre-WWIII jet fighter and a transport helicopter—if the rotors had been replaced with the last fuel-based engines. He knew that the Blackwing line of aircraft had been around since before First Contact, and were *still* around because few other fighters could boast that they possessed the same balance of speed, durability, firepower, *and* maneuverability in a pinch. *I guess we're lucky Huxley was told to chase after us*, he reflected.

Just then, a maglev-launched, solar-electric Heron bomber charged down the tarmac. The deadly vehicle took to the sky with barely a sound beyond a bass-laden *throom*. Damien watched the deadly vehicle vanish in a low cloud.

"You must be Mr. Vilan?!"

Damien turned to see a tall, spindly man with a thin pale face, sharp features, and a trimmed crop of graying, sandy hair approaching. The man wore a black suit and wraparound sunglasses, all of which made him look a bit spidery. "Yeah?" he shouted back.

The Englishman shook his hand. "I'm Mr. Bunting! Right this way, if you please!"

Mr. Bunting led Damien away from the Blackwing and towards a waiting shuttle, where two other people stood expectantly: a short man and a stocky, middle-aged woman. Damien saw they both wore the rank bars of Major.

"Good, good," said the short man loudly as they approached, holding out a leathery brown hand. "Mr. Vilan? I'm Major Freeman."

"Damien Vilan." They shook.

Mr. Bunting gestured towards the woman, "And this is Major DeLara."

"Hello," said Damien, noting her bars were of the UTA Marines. She nodded.

Mr. Bunting turned to Damien behind his implacable sunglasses. "We understand that you are in possession of some rather precious cargo. Would you care to enlighten us?"

Turning, Damien saw the medics bringing Von out of the Blackwing on a gurney, and he pursed his lips. He answered loudly over the sound of a noisy Eagle fighter taking off nearby. "Actually sir, I'd like to get my partner here to a medical facility and make sure that he's tended to before I answer anything, is that alright?!" His tone was polite, but the undercurrent was firm, and the three of them definitely heard it. The two majors exchanged dubious and irritated looks, but the tall Mr. Bunting cracked the corner of his mouth into the barest hint of a grin.

"Son," shouted Major Freeman, "we expended a fair amount of resources to answer your call. If what you have is as *important* as you made it sound, we really can't afford to—"

"—Actually," Leo interjected, "you can '*afford to*', etcetera, because he doesn't have the package, *I* do."

Both Majors twitched at the intrusion to their aural implants, but again, the spidery Mr. Bunting merely expanded his smile. Damien got the sudden feeling that "Mr." was just an informal title. Bunting smelled like an operative.

Leo continued brazenly, "My apologies for intruding, but since there isn't an appropriate pad for me to talk to you on and you aren't wearing earpieces, this will have to do for now."

Major Freeman looked quizzically at Damien, who just shrugged. "My AI. Don't ask how he hacks your ears."

The Majors exchanged another glance, and it seemed that Major DeLara was about to say something, when a shout came from the Blackwing, cutting her off.

"There's a WHAT?!"

As Von was wheeled past them, all four gazes found Captain Huxley leaping out the side door and heading to the tail of her ship. A nervous looking technician followed her.

The small group watched, Damien feeling equally curious about what she was yelling about, but as if reading his thoughts, Leo reminded him sweetly, "You forgot that the Avos shot her ship before they hit Von, didn't you?"

He had in fact. *Oops*. Damien made a sheepish face and turned back quickly to the retinue. "You know, can we get inside? I'm exhausted and hungry and... and we've had a very long... umm, night." He faltered as the burning bunker came to mind.

"Of course," said the Englishman, overriding the two Majors. He quickly opened the shuttle door for Damien. "If you'll just hop in, I'll wheel you to get some breakfast. After, we can go to the hospital, where your alien friend will most likely already be in surgery."

Damien was grateful for the man's tact. "That sounds fantastic."

Major Freeman made a noise to object, but Bunting cut him off. "*Once* that is done, we can all sit down and have a little chat about this cargo of yours. Are those terms acceptable?"

Damien looked to the other two and glanced quickly back at the Blackwing. Huxley was still out of sight. "I'm game," he said, moving forward.

"Brilliant," said Bunting.

Apparently wanting to ensure he stayed close at hand, the two majors pushed brusquely past Damien and climbed into the shuttle ahead of him. As soon as they settled in their seats, though, Mr. Bunting whipped the door shut and tapped the top of the vehicle, sending it on its way before Damien could enter.

"Oh, he's clever." Leo remarked, echoing Damien's thoughts as the shuttle pulled away with the majors inside. An empty shuttle pulled up.

It was at that moment that Captain Huxley came out of the shadows of the engine block, splattered with what appeared to be coolant, railing profanities across the tarmac that made even the military men and women bustling around lower their heads in shame.

"—SON OF A BITCH! I'M GONNA KILL YOU FOR THIS!" She roared at him. "THERE'S A BIG FUCKING HOLE RIGHT UP THE ASS OF MY SHIP!! OHH YOU JUST WAIT UNTIL I GET MY HANDS ON YOU! I MEANT WHAT I SAID ABOUT YOUR BALLS, VILAN!" After that the rant devolved into much less coherent—but colorful—cursing.

"I think she likes you," Leo said. Damien rolled his eyes, but crawled quickly into the shuttle nonetheless.

Mr. Bunting apparently thought the same though as they sat down in the shuttle together. The padded seating was a comfortable change from the last few days of crouching in the cold, even if it did feel a little…odd. "It sounds as if you've made an impression," said Bunting. "How long have you known each other?"

Damien furrowed his brow, "Who? My AI and I?"

Bunting just smiled, "No. You and ah," he consulted the tablet in front of him. "Captain…Deanna Huxley?" He crinkled his brow behind the sunglasses.

"Oh!" Damien laughed. "Umm…about an hour."

Mr. Bunting's eyebrows shot up. "An hour? Oh I see. Hmm. Interesting…"

"What is?" But then it hit him. "Ohh…no, what? No, c'mon, you've gotta be kidding—" He cut himself off as Mr. Bunting let out a warm, friendly laugh, and the thin smile on his face spread into a more genuine one. It was friendlier, but it sat in defiance of the cold sunglasses.

Damien closed his mouth and sat back, smiling despite himself. He stared out the window as the first rays of sunlight broke over the horizon. Unseen by Bunting, the salt-stiffened skin beneath his eyes cracked as the shuttle took off for the base.

You know, maybe we'll be alright, he thought.

Chapter Nine

Project S.E.H.A.

Camp Cascade was an old base, dating back to World War Three. Half of the command building had been built into a rise at the edge of the forest of its namesake, while the rest spread into the shallow valley surrounded by old, wet trees. Clusters of low structures for the rank-and-file sat around the hospital and command building next to the wide runways, and the top of the enormous, famously defensible underground hanger peered out at the world with a roof covered in dirt and saplings that struggled to punch through the metal ceiling.

Damien had been to the base for school once, but he barely remembered it. He knew that the hangar descended some ways into the earth, but he couldn't recall how far. He remembered a few details, though, of why it was so famous: it had survived under siege from the Sons of Korea for two weeks during the Battle of Rainier in 2049, while the heavily invaded United States had failed to bring aid to the base. Beyond that, Damien couldn't recall many details—even who won—and that bothered him. *I hate forgetting that stuff*, he thought as they arrived outside the security checkpoint to the base proper.

Exiting the shuttle, Damien eyed Mt. Rainier to the south, where it poked its snowy cap just into view, the lone sentinel of the Cascades. As the night gave way to pre-dawn glow, Rainier's peak was lit in pink and gold, the first rays of sunlight high above.

Mr. Bunting took Damien deep inside the hospital complex that adjoined the command building, where the Military Police and medical staff cleaned Damien's cuts and bruises, took his blood, patted him down, scanned and patted him down again, asked questions, and generally treated him with wary suspicion. Mr. Bunting explained that word of his unusual arrival was spreading fast, and rumors that he was an Elemental were hot behind.

"Unfortunately, breakfast will have to wait for a bit," Bunting said apologetically after Damien was cleared for the second time in the command building alone, "but you'll have a chance to freshen up and see your friend before I take you to the Admiral."

"Who's the Admiral?" Damien asked.

Bunting cracked his tiny half-grin. "A decorated commander," he answered, and that's all he would say.

As they made their way to the main floor of the command building, Damien noticed a significant change in activity. All around the base, people were rushing around with crates, shouting and trying to get one another's attention. Damien didn't have to ask to know that this was the evacuation procedure. *They're really coming*, he thought. *The army is really on the move*. Faced with such evidence, he couldn't play at it not being real any longer: Seattle was going to fall, and soon.

The morning quickly became an endless stream of redundant poking, prodding, and roundabout questions and answers. Damien was hungry, exhausted, smelly, tired, and worried about Von. His brief sense of peace at having made it out of XenoCon vanished and he quickly became irritable with the scrutiny as he was taken through security checkpoint after checkpoint. Fortunately, it became clear that Mr. Bunting shepherding him along was a boon, but it didn't stop the looks of suspicion, nor did the medical staff refrain from asking him repeated questions that he wasn't willing to answer. "What have your activities been within the Seattle Islets in the past six years?" "What are your connections with the local, quote, 'insurgent movement'?" "Were you connected to such-and-such person at this-and-that time?" "Have you ever killed a human?" "What's in your backpack?"

There he drew the line. "Don't touch my bag," he snapped, as the nurse reached around him and the doctor took more blood. The nurse looked flustered.

"Sir, we picked up scans emanating from an AI backup cube. We don't allow unidentified—"

"—It's alright, Mickey," said Bunting, cutting him off. "I'll keep an eye on the AI."

The nurse backed off without a word, further cementing Damien's curiosity at the Englishman's position at the base.

"Thanks," Leo whispered in his earpiece, sounding nervous.

Damien nodded, and he knew Leo would pick it up. The AI was staying surprisingly quiet.

Another nurse averted her eyes when Damien tried to make friendly contact a few minutes later, and he reflected that, without fail, Elementals had only ever appeared around the world in moments of pure destruction. Never having met or even seen one, he couldn't guess at how people like him were regarded elsewhere, but he knew the mentality in the Puget region, and it wasn't friendly.

Finally though, Damien had it when Bunting announced they'd be seeing Von in a moment, but instead were detoured by Military Police who said he needed a full, antiquated cavity search on the second floor of the command building. Damien gave the soldier a warning stare so severe that she yelped and yanked her hand back from his shoulder as if she'd been shocked. Bunting nodded and Damien held her frightened gaze until they were around the corner and out of sight. "If I see those gloves near me, I'll shoot," he growled. Bunting held a tight-lipped grin. *This is why I stay away from people. This is why we were isolated.*

Bunting stopped them at the third-floor bridge to the hospital, where a receptionist informed them that Damien had been cleared to access the base under supervision, and that his blood tests had been analyzed. They had confirmed that he was carrying no dangerous material.

"Nothing *overtly* dangerous anyway," the man added as they turned to leave.

"What the hell's *that* supposed to mean?" Damien snapped. He really wanted a shower, but he couldn't help enjoying the sight of the man's nostrils flaring as he came close.

"Ah—Y-you have a number of unique genetic markers that Dr. Ericson would like more time to examine," he stammered. "He thinks that you could be—"

"—Yes, thank you," Bunting cut him off. "I'll take that report now, and I'd like to see Dr. Ericson in an hour, in my office. We'll be on our way now," and they left the man mumbling apologies and shaking, eyeing Damien.

A line of patients in hospital gowns wound through the third-floor waiting rooms. Damien guessed they were hoping for a discharge so that they could leave with the regular evacuees instead of the medical ones, though he couldn't see why that was more appealing. Medical patients were kept under scrutiny, and during evacuations, they left only marginally faster than anyone else. "Why didn't you let that receptionist finish?" he asked as they split off from the line. A steady stream of overhead announcements warbled, but he couldn't understand them.

Bunting ushered him into a surgical hall. "Because it was a conversation better held in private." They waded through another throng of people. The halls of the hospital were packed with nurses, doctors, a few wounded men and women who sat wrapped in bandages, and troops of soldiers who swarmed past. All were too busy to notice Damien and Mr. Bunting as they approached. Everyone looked somewhere between nervous and determined.

"Okay, well then what was with all the tests?" He rubbed his arms under his jacket, cradling his torn backpack.

Bunting hesitated as they approached a broad viewport in the wall. "I think...the Admiral should answer that. Ah, here we are." He stopped Damien in front of the viewport.

Damien's stomach tensed as he saw what was inside.

Von was lying under a sheet on the medical slab, being worked on by three human surgeons and one mottled blue Algaroth. The sight of the alien doctor made Damien relax a little, even though all four of them were spattered with oily blood. The readouts that he could see of his brother showed active—if not strong—bio-readings.

"I didn't know the military had recruited any Algaroth doctors?"

Bunting nodded. "The list is...quite short. The United Territories have no official policy on asylum for defectors from The Collective, but a few regions believe in a more, *holistic* approach."

Damien glanced sideways at the tall man. "You mean you make policy locally."

Bunting chortled, "Oh, if only it were so simple…but yes. It mostly depends on who's in charge and where exactly. Regional governors have *very* different approaches to situations like this, and the executive chairs in Toronto, Guadalajara, and Manaus simply don't have the resources to fuss about it. It seems to be the price of global unity, I'm afraid."

Damien's curiosity spiked. He wasn't sure if Bunting's mention of "situations" was in reference to events of an Elemental nature or if it was events of defecting Algaroth. He asked.

"I couldn't say as to that, but this isn't the first time Camp Cascade has seen individuals like yourselves."

"Meaning?"

The Englishman sighed. "I'm not at liberty to say." He stayed Damien's question with a hand. "Whether my silence is by choice or not is irrelevant, it *is* the fact. Regardless, what matters at the present time is that your friend is well tended and should make a full recovery. However, in the interim I am curious as to the nature of the cargo you mentioned?" He turned his sunglasses on Damien. "You did promise you would elaborate."

For a moment, Damien didn't answer. He watched the sluggish flicker of Von's ganglia and he set his jaw, thinking. Mr. Bunting had let the nurses and doctors ask all the questions, and Damien wondered if delaying breakfast was a strategic move, but he hadn't hesitated to tell Huxley what was going on, and he saw no reason to deny the truth to this man either. *Especially since they really must have made a fast response to get Huxley to us so quickly*, he reflected. *We'd be dead if she'd been there a minute later*.

It took a moment for him to realize the Algaroth doctor had looked up to see who was staring. Upon seeing Bunting, the alien nodded, and the spidery man nodded back before looking back at Damien, waiting patiently.

"He says Von will be okay," Leo whispered. "You don't have much choice but to trust that."

I know.

Finally, Damien indicated he was ready to leave, and Bunting's half-smile crept over his lip again. He took them away from the viewport, and Damien lingered just a second longer, eyeing his brother. "Alright," he said, pulling away. "But I'll have to start from the beginning."

"I'd appreciate that."

So, Damien told his story again as they made their way back through the hospital, back to the command building, and to a locker room with showers. He broke off upon entering and Bunting said he would wait. Damien sighed with relief at being allowed to use a private stall, and he took a long time with the recycling hot water tank and the sharp razor he was given. Bunting even handed him a genuine bar of soap rather than the sanitizing gel beads he usually used to wash everything. The soap was odorless, but the shaving soap smelled of cedarwood, cassia, and cloves, giving him a fresh, foresty smell. Damien liked it, and he breathed deep as he cleaned the thick matt of black stubble from his face.

When he finally finished, he found Bunting waiting in a chair outside. "You were telling me about your hacking rig?" And on they went, up to the fourth floor.

Damien left out less this time than with Huxley, but he still didn't tell Bunting everything. He still had yet to openly admit that he was an Elemental, even though he gathered that Leo's message had said it quite plainly, and he left out that Von was family.

As the elevator dinged their arrival, Damien finished with Huxley's timely rescue, and he decided that it was *his* turn to ask a question as they stepped into the empty hallway. "So who are you with?" He received a curious look.

"With?"

"Your division. You're a 'mister' not a rank."

"Ah." The tall man considered it for a moment as they walked. Damien noted the maze of office hallways around them and how most of the rooms were empty. "I'd, like to discuss your tale more in-depth at another time, but in answer to your immediate query... I'm with the Solar Intelligence Office."

Damien stopped.

186

"You seem surprised," said Bunting, turning.

"Well, yeah, because…" he trailed off. As far as he'd had known, the surviving members of the Solar Intelligence Office—which had been housed on the Moon at Apollo Base—had melted into the Earth-bound militaries just like everyone else who had survived the Battle of Luna, during the opening days of The Conquering. The idea that humankind's intelligence-gathering arm of Solar Warfare still operated under its original moniker made Damien curious, and a bit apprehensive. "Because it seems a bit…impossible."

Agent Bunting smiled. "And yet, we live in a world where men or women may sit in any position—should they be willing to work for it, we often barter for goods rather than pay for them, global concern for growing the right foods for enough people is all but gone, and a few of those same men or women are—quite recently—throwing fireballs from their fingertips or…even creating black holes," Damien could swear he saw the man's eyes glitter behind the sunglasses. "The world is an evolving place. Why is it so unlikely that a knowledgeable branch of our space age survived our fall—to *aliens*, no less?"

Damien swallowed, suddenly very aware of the silence of the hallway, the smell of dust in the air, and the hint of cold in the windows. In the distance, he could hear alarms blaring as another aircraft took off. "Because," he finally said, "because the Solar Intelligence Office was decommissioned after The Conquering, just like Solar Warfare. SIO as an entity doesn't *exist* anymore."

Bunting grinned openly, looking as if he'd just been told a fun fact. "Ah, so we're a mythos now? How interesting…" He continued down the hall, prompting Damien to trot and catch up, mind racing. "Surprised again?" Bunting added.

He started. "Oh! No, err…okay, yes. Actually just that you answered a direct question."

Bunting chuckled more. "Direct questions are hard to maneuver away from, Mr. Vilan, anyone will tell you that." They rounded a corner into an empty hallway that ended in a set of mahogany double doors. "I already know quite a lot about you, Damien. It seems reasonable that I should return the favor, in part." Bunting removed his sunglasses, revealing pale hazel eyes that looked too untraveled for an agent of SIO. "A transparent intelligence operative is a contradiction in terms, but only if he's in bed with an enemy, or under a more…paranoid regime."

Damien was confused. "Are you saying the Americas are a paranoid regime?"

Bunting chewed on that. "I'm saying that the United Territories of the Americas is no more special than the Eurasian Union or the Middle Kingdom, and none are any more paranoid than any other regime in history, before their inevitable fall of course, as is the case with any civilization. The question I like to pose is: *when* will a civilization fall in relation to *now*?" He replaced his wraparounds.

"Well…it's a good question." Damien finished lamely. He did genuinely appreciate that philosophy. It was one echoed by the late Lunar Admiral Jacob Hawkins, whom every person on Earth knew from his Declaration of Dissolution that started the whole Collective War. The idea though, that a human government would ever be without its secrets was absurd. *And from what we know of The Collective, that notion holds true for aliens too.*

Damien found the whole conversation refreshing, though he felt rusty at discussing it. It had been a long time since he had articulated his beliefs to anyone, even Von, but buried or not, he was constantly reminded of them when he would look at the other insurgents from home. The survivors from Seattle had never had time to worry about the big picture, or if they did, they didn't talk about it, and Damien had long held that maybe that was part of their failing.

Even so, he still empathized with the people he'd fought beside. After the quake, they had all been forced to focus on survival and little else, whereas the scale of which Bunting was speaking spanned nations and worlds. That sort of thinking just didn't exist when you were scrounging for food and blankets.

His ponderings were cut short as Bunting stopped in front of the double doors. "I would ask that you be respectful with the Admiral," he said, cutting through Damien's thoughts. "The man has earned his keep." He ushered Damien inside without waiting for an answer.

Within, the room was dark and quiet save for the light of a single monitor in a far corner. Damien's sensitive eyes adjusted quickly, even without tapping his powers, but that wasn't enough to discern what the far screen showed. He looked around.

The room was a haphazard hybrid between a war room and a commander's office. There were Pip tables, workstations, and projection workbenches similar to the one he and Von had had at the bunker. An ornate wooden desk sat out from the wall directly across from him, and all of it was spaced around the mid-sized room. A raised strip of carpet ran the length of the walls and bisected the space so that someone in charge could see neatly over everyone and everything. Near the glowing monitor in the corner, an enormous circular war table sat, three times the size of any of the workbenches. Its smooth black surface was dark.

As Damien took it in, a slowly pulsing glow caught his eye in the opposite corner across from the monitor. Bunting said nothing as he walked toward the new source of light. When the source came into view, his jaw dropped in disbelief, but Leo's excited whisper confirmed it.

"AI expansion stalls!" Leo breathed.

Damien had never seen one in person, but Leo had often talked about how badly he wanted one. Here he saw five. "Do you think they're manned?" he whispered.

"Can't be," Leo said. "There's no way. That Portland army would've torn itself to pieces if there were *five* AI's hacking into it from here."

The five pedestals were tucked neatly in a corner, built into the room itself. Each came up to Damien's waist and had a base of patterned polyglass. Beneath the glass, pale, multi-colored lights thrummed slowly in rhythm, giving off the muted glow as they lit the hardlines running down into the building. Damien knew those lines ran somewhere into the ground, into secure memory towers capable of supporting a grown AI such as Leo. Damien guessed that if all five were manned, Leo didn't exaggerate that entire armies could be brought down from within.

Artificial Intelligences were capable of many, many things, and cyberwarfare could be just as dangerous as nuclear.

Agent Bunting interrupted their observations. "Sir," he said, and Damien whirled. Bunting was speaking towards the far monitor. "Damien Vilan is here to see you." Bunting spoke a different tone now, something that bordered on reverence to Damien's ears. "I believe that Freeman and DeLara wanted to speak to him as well. They were on their way to—"

"—Tell them not to bother, John," a deliberate, gravelly voice said from the monitor in English with a hint of Central American. "Give me just another minute to finish this piece. Tell Mr. Vilan that I will be with him shortly."

Damien was surprised as Bunting bowed. "Of course, sir. I'll let him know and I'll inform the majors. Should I return presently for him or wait for your call?"

"No, thank you John. I'll send for you once we're done."

"Very good, sir."

Agent Bunting turned to leave when the man spoke up again, "Oh, and John?"

"Sir?"

"Would you mind sending Sarah up once you've dealt with the majors? Tell her I'll have the table laid out for two? We may have reason to celebrate this morning."

Damien spotted a thin smile on the pale agent's face as he said, "Of course sir. I'll send her up as soon as they're ready."

"Thank you, John."

"My pleasure, sir." Mr. Bunting bowed again, nodded at Damien, and left the room, leaving him alone with Leo by the pedestals.

Damien stood there in silence, waiting to be addressed, but the gravelly voice did not resume speaking, so he waited.

The silence dragged out. After awhile, Damien thought that maybe he should knock on the door since the man hadn't seemed to realize that he was already in the room. Finally, he did so but to no avail. He cleared his throat. Nothing. "Did he leave?" He breathed to Leo.

In answer, the lights finally came up, stunning Damien with their brightness. He blinked and shielded his eyes. After a long moment he adjusted, and the glare resolved into that of a normal room. He instinctively groped for his goggles but they were still in his backpack, which he'd replaced on his shoulder.

Finally, he was able to see what lay behind the monitor: A simple couch sat in the corner, surrounded by four of what Damien knew to be wave-busters, but these were smaller than the military variants he and Von had used on the Razer. On the couch, an older man lay with his eyes closed. He appeared to be at the end of middle-aged—probably in his eighties or early nineties—but in good, career military shape.

Even from across the room, Damien saw that he took slow, rhythmic breaths. The man opened his eyes to the ceiling. Slowly, he sat up to reveal leathery brown skin and a smatter of close-cropped grey on his wrinkled head. His eyes were dark brown, also like worn leather. But what Damien had mistaken for a very elaborate nightshirt and pressed pants, was in fact a uniform that stopped him cold. Leo realized what it was at the same time.

"*That's* who Huxley was talking to?!" The AI exclaimed. "That's no damn *base commander!* I thought he was just a regular old Admiral!"

The man wore the impeccably crisp, black-and-silver uniform of a Lunar Admiral; the highest ranking and most revered military title that a person could obtain in their lifetime, or in any lifetime in the history of the human race, for that matter. They were a dying breed of men and women since The Conquering, as their home too had been lost with Apollo Base on the Moon. Damien had heard it rumored that only six of the legendary commanders remained alive. None had been replaced in twenty years.

"Sir!" Damien snapped to attention. He knew that as a civilian it was inappropriate to salute an officer, but this was no ordinary officer, nor were these ordinary circumstances. The prestige and weight a Lunar Admiral could wield was completely unmatched, and one stood a *little* more formally for being in the presence of one, on principle.

The Lunar Admiral looked at him curiously, and Damien saw the hint of worry lines on his forehead. He had a sadness in his eyes, too, at which Damien could only guess. "Son, are you an enlisted soldier?"

Damien held the salute. "N-no sir!"

"Hmm. And are you *planning* to enlist in one military or another? Perhaps the Americas' Army? Or the Regent Dynasty's Navy? They *are* still powerful, even after the tragedy of Australia."

Damien's salute faltered. "No sir! I mean—I don't think the military would be the right path for me."

"Interesting…" The Admiral slowly got to his feet and pulled his uniform straight, each movement labored. Damien got the gut impression that the man moved like that by choice and not from physical strain, but he didn't ask. The Admiral continued, "Well then why should you salute me, son? I've earned you no respect."

Damien's words sank back into his throat, as did his arm to his side, but he held his gaze.

The Admiral gave a small chuckle, "You have no reason to salute an officer if you don't plan to be one."

Say something! He couldn't. He just watched dumbly as the man disconnected a small tablet from the lit computer and started collapsing the legs on the amplifying aural devices. Without thinking, Damien crossed the room to assist him.

"Quite the helper, aren't we?" said the Admiral, waving him off. "I can certainly handle it." He folded the legs on the far wave-buster.

"Oh. I'm sorry, sir, I just wasn't sure if—"

"—If I'm still fit enough to collapse my own symphonious generators? Ha! I may be sixty-seven but that doesn't mean what it used to!" He paused with the head of one device in hand. "But your concern is noted."

Damien blinked again, shocked that he wasn't even seventy. *I guess that's career military for you.*

"You are Damien Vilan then, correct?"

"Yes sir."

"Perfect. Well, Mr. Vilan, do you know what these do?" The Admiral held out the head of the wave-buster.

"I—" Damien was thrown by the question, but he recovered faster this time. "They're sonic wave-busters, sir. They fire high amp audio waves that can only be picked up within the perimeter of the beam. I actually have some experience with the…larger versions."

The Admiral smiled at him, "Quite so. These particular variants are my aforementioned symphonious generators, civilian-variety. They're the kind that can bathe you in a bubble of music so completely that it takes a special course to handle them properly. Using them without the know-how can do terrible things to a man." The Admiral continued chitchatting while he collapsed the units. "On the subject of sound-based technology, do you appreciate the significance of your implant?"

Damien frowned, reaching for his ear. "The significance?"

"Your aural implant," he repeated. "Tell me of its significance. And tell me how long it's been since we've had them."

Damien struggled to find the answer on his feet while the Admiral took down the last unit. "Well," he started, "they allow all of humanity to communicate through our own languages and still understand each other. We can even speak in Dekka to communicate with Algaroth." He shrugged. "The implant is…well it's invaluable."

"True enough answer, but incorrect. I asked of the *significance*, not the value."

Damien grimaced. "Then I don't know what you mean."

The man sighed as he produced a slender metal case and popped the catches, revealing a padded and molded interior. "The answer is that the aural implant is the single most significant technology in the history of the world. More so than TransLight travel, the Mag Fury reactor, and our Planetary Poison Nukes all rolled into one. Do you know why?"

Damien thought on it, and the answer came to him faster than he would've thought. "Unity, sir. Without the implant, unity would be so much harder."

The Admiral stopped with the case to beam at him. "Well put! Well put indeed! And you are quite right; unity would still be *possible*, but more difficult."

"I guess I'd never thought of it like that, sir."

The Admiral chuckled, "Don't apologize for gaps in your knowledge, Mr. Vilan, unless that gap costs someone's life. Knowledge is accrued by combating ignorance. To combat ignorance, we must often reveal our knowledge gaps to the world, and that can be a tricky prospect."

Damien cocked his head. "So…you know how to do that then, sir?"

The Lunar Admiral chuckled again. "Mm, you see, *that's* how you turn a question around! You appeal to someone *else's* knowledge without revealing your own gaps! It keeps you guarded, *and* it flatters whomever you are speaking to. It's a useful political tactic, son. Remember it."

"I…thank you, sir. I will."

"Good." The Admiral laid the last stand in the case, falling into silence.

After a moment, Damien asked, "Sir?"

"Yes?"

"I thought you were going to tell me how long the aural implants have been around."

The Admiral snapped down the latches and a pressurizing hiss filled the room. When it faded, he stood with grace, looking suddenly more alert and filled with vitality befitting a man decades younger. His voice sounded less strained, and confidence and authority coursed through his tone. "Very good, Mr. Vilan. I actually had asked *you* to tell *me*. With the kind of question you just posed, you make your opponent question his own choices, and then he's all yours from there on." He hefted the case towards the large desk. "Not many people either catch, or are willing to bring up, a forgotten topic to a superior. They simply push onward. But I for one prefer never to leave a train of thought uncompleted, so yes, I will tell you."

He waved Damien to the desk as he slid the case into a hidden drawer blended into featureless cabinets on the wall that Damien hadn't seen until that moment. "The first aural implant was tested in 2063, six years after the end of the World War Three. Did you know that when they signed the Treaty of Palais Ariana—the very treaty that signed humanity into unity—it was done in Geneva with over three hundred translators present? It's a wonder that it was signed at all."

Damien had to agree with that.

The Admiral pulled his uniform back to perfect crispness before sitting in his chair, steepling his fingers as he concluded, "The implant is—at its core—a technology not unlike a miniaturized wave-buster," he pointed towards his couch. "Something you yourself admitted to being more than a little familiar with just now." He smiled.

"I guess I did," said Damien. "And, thank you sir. I…don't know if I ever knew that."

The Admiral indicated that Damien should take the seat opposite him. "I think you probably would have found it out at some point. You are apparently quite the resourceful fellow after all."

Damien sat. "How so?"

"I thought you were perceptive, son. That's a question from a man out of touch."

"Sir?"

The Admiral's desk came to life from a Pip pad inlaid in its surface, and a series of documents appeared in the air, hovering. Damien's gut clenched as he eyed the documents and realized they were all about his and Von's recent activities, but mostly about him. He spotted a date on one report that went back as far as three years.

Son of a bitch, he thought, a spark of anger surfacing. *They've been watching us.* He eyed them harder.

"*You* sir," said the Admiral, unawares. "Have caused quite a bit of fuss in the Islets over the past seventy-two hours, am I right?"

Damien pursed his lips. *Those records go a hell of a lot further back than that.* "You are."

The Admiral made an interested face. "Then would I *also* be right in assuming that you are the very same Damien Vilan who is responsible for a series of raids, burglaries, hijackings, sabotages, espionage, and general mayhem within the local—excuse me, *regional*," he corrected himself as he scanned over Damien's file, "collective ranks in the last…six years and four months? Since…September, 2139?"

Damien's anger spiked at the admission. *He's known about us since almost a year after the earthquake. Why wait until now to make contact?*

The Admiral focused closer on the displays as he continued reading, "...*Including*," he exclaimed, "over eighty-three percent of all encounters were 'total success engagements'! *Solid* numbers, Damien. *Solid* numbers."

The anger faltered. "I...*yes* sir, that's me, along with my partner, but I—"

"—Your partner, the alien?" The Admiral's interest grew.

"Yes but he's not—"

"—The one in surgery?" he pressed.

"Yes but—"

"—And he is a *confirmed* defector from The Collective? No doubts about his commitment to rebelling against his people?"

"What? No!" Damien blurted. "Of course not! He's my adopted brother! We've been family almost our whole lives!"

The Admiral stopped his dance of questions. He leaned back from the floating display and replaced his fingers beneath his chin, eyeing Damien across the desk. Damien shifted uncomfortably. *What the hell are you doing, blurting that out?!* He *never* told that to anyone he didn't trust completely.

The Admiral slowly leaned forward, blowing right over the whole 'brother' bit. "Then my final question—for all prenuptial purposes—is very simple."

Damien held his breath.

"Are you an Elemental?"

A trickle of air slid from Damien's nose as he glanced at the floating documents. "Something tells me you know the answer to that already, Admiral."

"What I know is that an Elemental has been suspected to be living in the Seattle Islets since the Over-Seer broke the San Andreas Fault," he answered. "We haven't known who it was."

Damien chewed on that. "So you *have* been watching me."

"As one of many candidates, yes."

"Why didn't you come forward?"

"Because of the potential consequences," said Leo, interrupting.

In a puff of teal cubits, the documents vanished, and the AI stood on the Admiral's desk, leafing through the reports with the air of a superior parent. "It says right here: *'List of possible subjects possessing Elemental power referred to as "Darkness" are detailed as follows...'*" The AI kept reading quietly to himself.

A flicker of recognition crossed the Admiral's face as he looked at the AI. "*You* sent the message, not Mr. Vilan." It wasn't a question.

"'*...Communiqué To: Former Project S.E.H.A. ...*'" Leo trailed off and looked up from the documents. He smirked. A froofy pink dress appeared on him, and he curtsied to the Admiral. It disappeared just as quickly. "Indeed I did. Arthur Leonardo, possibly at your service, most likely not."

The Admiral's gaze jumped between Leo and Damien, but settled on Damien. "Understanding the Elementals is a mission of paramount importance, Mr. Vilan, and we aren't the only ones who think so."

Damien frowned. "Meaning what?"

The Admiral sighed. "I assume your AI just broke through all of my security in this office, didn't he?"

"Leo..."

"Sure did!" the AI yipped.

"Then why don't you read the document labeled 'Post-Project S.E.H.A.' so Mr. Vilan can hear. Locate article C-13, pertaining to subject 'Darkness'." The Admiral looked at Damien at the last word.

Leo broke out a magnifying glass, and the documents unrolled as a vast sheet of parchment, inked, yellowed, and crinkly. "I was just about to do that, *thank you*." The AI cleared his throat dramatically. "*In the continued absence of Collective Supply Fleet-13, and in preparation for approaching Supply Fleet-14 [SEE ATTACHED], it is the opinion of the Solar Intelligence Office and of Lunar Admiral Antonio Baroda, that engaging with Subject "Darkness" is a risky endeavor as it could endanger—at best—both the subject and the remnants of Seattle. At worst, it could bring the Fourth Over-Seer's North American army north from Portland at an expedited rate. As such...*" Leo swallowed, trailing off.

The Admiral's face was blank, and Damien's focus returned as Leo's eyes darted down the parchment. "As such?"

Leo recovered. "Umm… *As such, Puget Regional Command will…withhold action to recover Subject "Darkness" for the former Project S.E.H.A. until such a time as the subject is identified accurately. Report signed: Anonymous, dated June 1, 2144…*" Leo looked up, slack-jawed.

"Leo," Damien uttered, choosing each syllable carefully to contain the desire to grind his teeth. "What is 'Project S.E.H.A.'? And what, the fuck, is this, about another Supply Fleet?"

"He wouldn't know about Project S.E.H.A.," said the Admiral. "Nor would either of you be aware of anything regarding a new fleet."

"Why not?" Damien was reeling. Dread about a new Collective fleet leaked into his gut. He needed to know what that was about.

Leo balked at the Admiral. "How would *you* know what I know? Didn't you just give a spiel on 'appealing to another's knowledge before revealing your own'?"

The Admiral said nothing.

Damien frowned at Leo. "So you don't know, then?"

Leo's lip twitched and he huffed, "No."

The Lunar Admiral spoke up. "Mr. Vilan, Project S.E.H.A. was commissioned in secret just before The Conquering as the 'Search for Extra-Human Anomalies'. I know because I commissioned it myself."

Damien knew the shock showed on his face because the Admiral pressed on.

"It was created explicitly to find and understand the Elementals," he said. "After The Conquering, its existence became very exclusively known. Few people ever knew of it from the start, fewer still today know of it, and even fewer are aware of the fact that, while it no longer exists, something *did* take its place." He hesitated. "Unfortunately, given the state of things, my revealing that knowledge to you is contingent upon your answer to my question." The Admiral leaned forward. "*Are* you an Elemental?"

Damien took a careful breath. "Answer about the Supply Fleet first."

A flicker of exhaustion crept over the man's features. He leaned back in his chair, and his gaze drifted away from them for the first time, towards the dimmed windows.

Damien waited.

Finally, the Admiral sighed, and there was something utterly candid about it. As if the man spent all of his time behind the perfect veneer of a Lunar Admiral, but rare moments like this just couldn't be held in form, and so a single breath was all he could afford himself to unclench, even for a moment. "I assume that you, like the rest of the world, celebrated when the Supply Fleet didn't show up last year, correct?"

Damien shrugged carefully, remembering the conversation with Von just the other night as if it were a lifetime ago. *'You know how tense everyone has been though, since it never showed up. When was that, last May?'* Von had said, and it was true. The brothers had done very little celebrating. Few had, even after the dreaded Collective fleet of reinforcements, hardware, and fresh soldiers had failed to arrive at Earth— a first and unprecedented event.

"We celebrated a little," he allowed.

The Admiral nodded, still looking towards the window, almost wistfully. Finally, something brought him back, and his attention returned to Damien. "We don't know what happened to the last fleet, but we know that another is coming."

"Yeah, that's not news, Moon Commander," Leo snarked, still skimming the long parchment.

The Lunar Admiral ignored him. "Another is coming much sooner than we'd usually predict, and it's a cause for concern."

Damien leaned forward. "What does that mean?"

"We don't know, but it is coming."

Leo stopped reading and removed his obnoxiously thick bifocals that made his eyes look buggy. "When?"

"Sometime this year."

Damien withdrew from the table, considering that news. *The war resets every time a Supply Fleet shows up.* Familiar tension, dormant since the last Supply Fleet never appeared, showed signs of life in Damien's gut.

It was the kind of tightness that came with a looming deadline, something that hung in the background, ever-present and gnawing. He didn't know a single person who didn't have the same fear. It showed up in conversation, and in every interaction where the dreaded starship convoys came up: people shrugged it off with indifference or jokes, or they just got quiet and stone-faced, unwilling to voice the concern that everyone felt when they knew The Collective's warships were hovering over Earth, or soon would be.

Will this time be the time they beat us? Everyone would wonder. *Will they break us this time around?*

It had never happened, because the Supply Fleets could only bring so many new troops, and while The Collective's presence on Earth was strong and numerous, they had never outnumbered humanity, and that was one of the only reasons the war had not ended two decades ago.

Even so, The Collective had never missed a delivery before. And so when the Supply Fleet hadn't arrived last year, Damien, Von, Leo, and everyone they knew had kept that tension close. They'd been afraid that if they let themselves hope, suddenly their expectations would be crushed, and they could be hurt or scared again, and no one wanted that. But as the months had gone by, Damien had felt that skyward fear dwindle, until it had been a weak and insubstantial thing, like the husk of a snake, long gone. Damien knew that neither he nor Von had ever let their hope rekindle that the arrivals would stop, even if they'd wanted to believe it. In a way, though, that had always been worse, because they'd known this day would come.

So now, as he considered the ramifications of another fleet on its way from Shialga to reset the war in The Collective's favor, Damien felt an odd, cold comfort, as the snake wriggled into its old skin and curled around his thoughts, familiar in its menace.

That fear was back.

Damien picked at his fingers, and finally realized that the Admiral was looking at him.

"There's a reason we don't broadcast that knowledge," was all the man needed to say.

Damien nodded stiffly, and he felt suddenly eager to get past the topic. So, he grasped for the one other lead of their conversation. "I'm an Elemental," he mumbled.

"I'm sorry?"

"Yes, I'm an Elemental," he said again.

Silence pervaded. But second by second, a smile crept over the man's brown, creased features, and the tension melted. "Well now, isn't *that* exciting." Warmness filled the man's voice again, but Damien still felt tense.

"Apparently so," he said. "Now… what replaced S.E.H.A.?" *Another Supply Fleet*, he thought. *We're buried.*

The Admiral reclined. "I think first, we should have some late breakfast. John mentioned you hadn't eaten. You must be hungry?"

At the thought of food, Damien's empty, sickened stomach seized, and suddenly, all thoughts of their conversation fled—for which he was grateful. He winced. "What if I am?"

The Admiral laughed. "Oh, read into it all you like, but I for one simply enjoy food." He pressed a comm panel at the corner of his desk. "Sarah, we'll have that spread now, if you'd be so kind."

Damien jumped as the double doors opened and a delectable aroma flooded the room. It smelled of comfort and warm bellies on a cold morning. He spun around as a lovely young woman with dark hair entered, carrying a large tray piled with food and two covered plates. Two chefs followed her, carrying a white tablecloth between them.

"Breakfast, Admiral?" The woman asked.

The Admiral rubbed his hands together. "Perfect, yes, thank you, Sarah. If you could just—yes right here… Ahh, thank you, my dear."

The chefs laid the tablecloth over the huge desk, followed by silverware, a tray of assorted silver thermoses, plates, napkins, and a small tower filled with pullout tubes of condiments—Damien spied hot sauces, ketchup, jams, and spices—and a cheese grater with a small block of cheddar.

The chefs brought the tray down between he and the Admiral, and they unloaded a basket of bread that smelled of raisins, oats, and cinnamon, a steaming pot of coffee next to an equally aromatic pot of tea, a large dish full of cooked asparagus, mushrooms, and onions all tossed into a stir fry, and another smaller dish with thin sausage links that smelled of maple syrup. Finally, they uncovered the main dishes with a flourish, revealing two identical stacks on Damien's plate. Each was a stack of biscuit, a slice of ham, a slice of avocado, and a poached egg all topped with hollandaise sauce and a pinch of something that smelled lightly of lemon. It was Eggs Benedict.

Their setup finished, the three cooks bowed, and Sarah asked if they needed anything else.

"No, my dear, thank you," said the Admiral. "It looks delicious."

Sarah bowed again and retreated. "I'm here if you need me, sir," and they left the room.

Damien's mouth had exploded in saliva as he eyed the steaming food all around. He hadn't had a meal like this in years, and for Eggs Benedict, he couldn't even remember. His stomach moaned audibly.

The Admiral grinned. "I do believe that's the queue to dig in, son, please. But first…" He came around the table and held his wrinkled hand out. "Forgive my slowness on the introduction, but I would like to formally introduce myself: Antonio Baroda, Lunar Admiral and former Director of the Solar Warfare Division. Also the same Antonio Baroda who decided to wait before coming to Seattle to track down an Elemental." He looked apologetic on that part. "It is my genuine pleasure to meet you, Mr. Vilan."

He shook Damien's hand as it went limp. "*Director* of Solar Warfare?"

"Formerly, unfortunately." The sadness flashed back through the man's eyes, but it vanished.

Damien flubbed. "I'm sorry."

Admiral Baroda waved him off as he reclaimed his seat. "It's not your past to be sorry about. Now please, eat, I insist. However our conversation turns, you could at least say I offered you a good meal." He smiled warmly as he took a bite of his first stack of Benedict. "Mmm, perfection."

"The egg isn't poached right," Leo sniffed, but they both ignored him until he adorned a chef's attire and sat, cross-legged, watching them.

Feeling clumsy, Damien stuffed his napkin into his lap and carved out an enormous bite. Flavor like he couldn't remember ever tasting exploded in his mouth, flooding his senses and making him sit back and hum. In one fell swoop, his stomach was subdued, and he allowed himself the moment of comfort as the fogginess fell back from his thoughts. The Admiral smiled and poured Damien a cup of orange juice, offered the coffee— which Damien declined—and finally found the mark with a mug of steaming tea. The tea turned out to be a blueberry blend, which complemented the food surprisingly well.

Nearing the end of his plate, Damien saw a flicker of movement as Leo stood up. He should have known he wouldn't be able to get all the way through his food in peace, even if Baroda looked like he was going to let him.

"SO," said Leo, still projecting even through the tablecloth. A black robe and wizard's hat appeared over the AI's suit, complete with a wand, which he brandished across the table. "Damien is an Elemental, and YOU, Mr. Admiral, Antonio Baroda, former Director of the Solar Warfare Division, are the progenitor of S.E.H.A.! Such *coincidence!* One might hardly believe this meeting wasn't engineered!" Leo fingered the wand and a shower of red sparks flew across the desk.

Baroda gave a one-eyed glance at Leo, ignoring the sparks as they scattered through his plate. "Tell me, Mr. Vilan, the element of 'Darkness', which we pegged you as, would you consider that an accurate moniker?"

Leo glared at the man's indifference.

Damien swallowed his bite of egg and avocado, feeling warm and rested as the food continued to blossom into his stomach. "Actually, it's exactly what I've called it myself, sir."

Baroda pulled apart a slice of bread, took a bite, and decided it needed jam. "Really?"

"Yes."

"Darkness," Baroda pondered, digging for jam. "Well, that makes you the first. I've never heard of one with such a manipulation. Could you explain it?" The scrape of his knife on toasted bread filled the quiet, and it occurred to Damien that the office must be soundproofed against the sounds of the evacuation, taking place below. The thought sullied the food somewhat.

"I've...never had to before."

"Do try." The Admiral plucked the last, perfectly stacked mouthful of Benedict from his plate, complete with sauce, biscuit, egg, and avocado, and plopped it neatly in his mouth. He hummed.

Leo sent a bolt of green lightning over the desk, silently waving to get his attention. Damien wiped his mouth and spooned a bit more breakfast stir-fry onto his plate, poured hollandaise sauce over it, and gave the cheese a few grates. His plate was a mess, but he intended to clean all of it. "It's like...wielding the absence of light. I know how abstract that sounds but, it's more than just making a room go dark."

"Are you saying then that you wield that which *birthed* light?"

"What?"

Baroda looked thoughtful for a moment. Finally, he said, "Which came first, light or dark?"

Damien thought on it. "Dark, sir."

"So then you don't wield the absence of light, you wield that from which light *sprang*, is that right?"

"I'd never thought of it like that before." Damien chewed. *But that sounds pretty impressive.*

Baroda refilled his coffee and crunched on his bread. "What else can you do? Don't concern yourself assuming I know or don't know something. My want is to hear it from you directly."

Damien kept his face neutral. *Playing to gaps in my knowledge, or yours?* "Well, I suppose what I use the most are what I call 'Orbs'. I guess they're like little black holes that...well, that I rip into the air. I don't know how to describe it, I'm sorry. I can describe what they do though. I call it 'fazing'." Damien eyed the food and his gaze landed on the cheese grater with bits of cheddar still clinging to the carving holes. "I guess it's...sort of like running something, or...or some*one*, through that." He nodded towards the kitchen tool.

Baroda eyed the cheese grater but remained still. "I see. Go back to what you said about black holes. Do you mean something similar to a singularity?"

Damien shrugged. "Yeah that's probably the best way to describe it. Why?"

Baroda put his fork down.

"What is it?"

The man's face turned grave and his voice matched it. "Damien, you know all about our Final Option, don't you?"

"Yeah, the Planetary Poison Nukes, right? The 'Nukes'?"

Baroda nodded. "Yes, the ones that we seeded around the globe just before The Conquering. They've kept the status quo since we lost at Mars and Luna and the Sol Armada fled."

The Armada, Damien though, reaching for a second piece of bread. *Lunar Admiral Hawkins ordered our starships to abandon Earth at the worst possible moment.* Suddenly he wasn't sure if he wanted the bread, but he took it anyway to give his hands something to do. "What about them?" He resisted the urge to itch his arms.

Admiral Baroda hesitated. Finally, he stood and moved to the dark war table. Leo had taken to reading a book beneath an apple tree, but the scene vanished as he watched the Admiral walk away.

"Sir? What about them?" Damien took another hurried bite and joined him.

Baroda brought the war table to life, holding his answer. Much like Pip technology, Damien knew that war tables used multiple projecting pads to create convincing holograms, but unlike Pip projections, they utilized a ring of angled pads set around the perimeter of the table, rather than three or five on a desktop, all of which gave projections on a war table many extra layers of detail. Damien had always wondered what it would be like to have one. *Leo's okay with just a desktop, though...right?* He'd never thought to ask.

Particles swirled over the vast surface of the table until they coalesced. They formed together into a familiar, piece-meal globe of Earth. Damien could see huge tracks of land and ocean left unmapped, where the gaps had been colored in with rough estimates of greens, blues, browns, and white. The disjointed map was the product of The Collective burning away humanity's satellite network. The Global Positioning System didn't exist anymore, and any maps that remained were either handed around the world or were drawn up by high-risk launches into orbit, but those drew global ire from the Over-Seer and Damien guessed they were rarely attempted.

Damien, Leo, and Von had spoken often about how they knew The Collective's success was largely due to them keeping humanity unable to coordinate thanks to poor mapping. When they had first been discussing how best to help the Islets, the three of them had agreed equally that if a hacking rig didn't work, they would try to figure out a way to re-map the planet. Doing so could allow humanity's superior numbers to coordinate again and try, *really try* to take down the Collective's superior technology. *They've always had fewer numbers than us*, Damien thought. *But they know everything about us, especially where we're weak.*

Baroda drew highlights of the supernations as thin, colored lines around the terrain, filling the continents in. A legend appeared in the air away from the planet. "Did you know that The Collective has hunted for any way to stop, remove, or convert our Final Option so that they can bomb us from orbit?"

Damien looked at the globe as colors etched their way from north to south, marking the current world map. All of North and South America glowed in light blue: the United Territories of the Americas. "That's sort of common knowledge, sir," he said. "Or I guess everyone just *knows* it. Without the Nukes we would have lost more than just Geneva after the Battle of Luna.

Earth spun counter-clockwise, and the Pacific came into view. Australia appeared first, unmarked, as the island-continent had never joined the Earth Global Alliance. To the north, all of southeast Eurasia and the former island chains of Indonesia, Japan, the Philippines, and Papua New Guinea had been carved out in dark green: the Regent Dynasty.

Baroda went on. "Do you know how close they've come to succeeding?"

Damien stopped watching the globe as the purple-highlighted cluster of the Middle Kingdom came into view, occupying roughly the same space as the pre-war Middle Eastern countries. "No?"

"They've come *very* close. The terrible devastation of the Regent Dynasty Fleet when they tried to retake Australia was due to Croll Tan acquiring a handful of Nukes, and with the World War Centennial in September, there's ample reason to think they'll try something big this year—to demoralize us further."

Damien hadn't known that about the Dynasty fleet. He knew of course that humanity hadn't held Australia for nearly a decade, and he remembered when the Dynasty Fleet sailed to retake it. They had been warned not to attempt the mission by Croll Tan himself, and Damien recalled when the Over-Seer made good on his threat, obliterating an uncounted number of ships when they ignored him. But he hadn't known *how* the Over-Seer did it, and neither had anyone else. Now he knew. The realization left a dull chill in his veins.

As for the World War Centennial, Damien had almost forgotten about it, but that made it no less a real event. *Two centuries since the end of World War Two, one since the end of Three, and we're still kicking.* Damien considered it. *Yep, that's a tempting marker to try and stomp out.*

Baroda took Damien's silence as an understanding, and he turned back to the globe. Damien followed his gaze as the rest of the world spun into view. All of Africa remained as blank as Australia, but what remained of Eurasia had been carved into a rough 'T' with a wide, low top and a narrow base: the Eurasian Union, lined in yellow. Damien was surprised not to see the land taken by The Collective depicted on the map, but he said nothing. The planet spun on.

"Damien," Baroda began. "You said you could produce singularity-like detonations, you call them 'Orbs'?"

"Yes."

"And I would imagine you can do a good deal more as well?"

"Probably. I've never made one bigger than my hand."

Baroda sighed. "Then not only do I think it's time I informed you what all this fuss has been about, I think it's *necessary* for you to know."

207

The Lunar Admiral took a deep breath and turned fully towards him. "Damien Vilan, I would like to offer you full asylum from the forces of The Collective who are hunting you."

Damien frowned. Out of the corner of his eye he spotted Leo. The AI had sprouted two extra pairs of legs and had started scuttling across the spinning globe, cackling. "What enemy?"

"The Over-Seer and his Avos. All of The Collective, really."

Damien still didn't understand. "What do they want with me, other than the fact that I'm an Elemental? That's not news."

"You being an Elemental is less news than you thought, but that being the case means that if you were trying to hide from us, you most likely were trying to hide from The Collective more, correct?"

I never said I was trying to hide from you, whether I was or not. "I guess." Something in Baroda's tone made Damien's suspicions return, and he became very aware of every movement he made. He clasped his hands behind his back. "What does that mean?"

"It means that if we knew roughly where you were, most likely so did the enemy, and that means that their agenda and ours most likely coincided."

Damien didn't like where this was going. "Okay…"

Baroda leaned in. "I know this can't be easy, but you have to put this together: Croll Tan has been hunting Elementals for years now—and not without due cause," he added. "We've obviously been doing the same, but we believe he's had another agenda for some time, one that *you* may have just finally fulfilled for him."

"What agenda?"

The sadness filled Baroda's eyes again, and this time it stuck. "Damien, the Supply Fleets we receive from Shialga are horrors, there can be no doubt of that. Every year or two, enemy starships arrive from across the galaxy bearing reinforcements that no one wants to think about." The age lines in the Admiral's face deepened, and the wizened man Damien had seen when he first walked in returned. "The war resets every time a Supply Fleet arrives, and we do battle from a weaker place, while the enemy's numbers spike closer to ours."

"I know," Damien said. "And when the last one never showed up, we celebrated and worried at the same time."

"Because we never knew quite what that could mean, yes. *And* last year, when that Supply Fleet never showed up, humanity was boosted. We thought, 'maybe this will give us time to break the enemy before they can bring reinforcements', but we knew Croll Tan would have thought of that as well. We think that's why he pulled his forces back last fall, and left only a few armies out amongst the planet." Baroda lowered his voice. "It was suspicious, but it plays with our ultimate fear of the alien lord."

"What fear?" Damien asked.

Baroda's gaze was hard, and his features darkened into what Damien guessed was the face he used to make hard choices. "We ask ourselves every day how Croll Tan might circumvent the Nukes," the Lunar Admiral went on. "We try to anticipate how he might best them, so we can act first. When we realized that an Elemental existed who could wield a micro singularity, we realized a terrible, powerful way that our Final Option might be beaten."

Damien still didn't understand, but his heart was racing. He didn't have anything to say, so he shrugged at Baroda. His arms had started to itch again.

"Come on, boy. *Think*. Imagine what a man could do if he could wield a black hole on command. How might he affect, or in this case, *negate* something, to his advantage?"

And then it dawned on him. Damien knew what Baroda meant, and the Admiral clearly saw it in his eyes. "You can't…" His voice died as fear took over, overriding his breakfast and exhaustion. It blossomed outward and clogged his throat, and for the first time ever, the quiet of the room scared him. The *silence* had him paralyzed, save for his hands, which started to shake.

Admiral Baroda nodded. "Damien, I'm sorry, but…Croll Tan kept the Seattle Islets from burning because he needs *you*. He found out about your power at one time or another since the earthquake, and since then he's been trying to pin you down. He needs to be able to wield black holes so he can cancel out the power of our Nukes—our last defense against The

Collective. If he finds you, we can only guess how he might harness your power, but we assume he would find a way, and if he succeeds…" Baroda hesitated. "If he succeeds, The Collective will have a way to counter our Final Option, and we'll be finished."

Damien swallowed. Suddenly the air was very thick and he felt light-headed. *No…*

"I'm sorry," said Baroda. "But Seattle is going to fall because you're no longer in it; because the Over-Seer needs something capable of overriding a planet-rending nuclear explosion. Your black holes are the only thing on Earth even *potentially* capable of that."

Damien closed his eyes, heart pounding. *Don't say that…no, please don't say that to me. It's not my fault; don't make it my fault.* He took care to control his breathing; he felt like he needed to hyperventilate. He didn't want to believe it, but it all made sense. *They've all been waiting for me,* he thought, turning bitter. *Waiting for me to show myself, and I did…*

Baroda turned off the war table. "This is not your fault, Damien, it's just the way of it." He put a comforting hand on Damien's shoulder, but it felt cold. "Unfortunately, you need protection, Elemental, and I know of about the only way anyone in the world can give it to you."

Damien took a shuddering breath and tried to keep from breaking down. "H-how?"

"By showing you what became of Project S.E.H.A."

MASON J. TORALL

What is it about the stars that keep us in awe at night?

In all my years at Apollo, not a day passes when I don't look up and take comfort in the twinkle of a billion lights above. And yet...even with the comfort of the night sky, spread out brighter than anyone on Earth will ever see it, I still inevitably look down.

When viewed from so far away, one might question how the cosmic scale of things affects this place, La Luna, and the mother she orbits. I think we are subject to the whims of the universe as much as any people, but it is also my view that we may lay claim to the stars just the same.

I only hope that these aliens who approach don't intend to lay claim to us as well. Humans finally know that somewhere in those billions of stars, there is at least one planet with life like ours. A people, of some shape or color. How did they obtain the sky? Do they have a Luna to watch over their planet? Do they have many? So many questions, asked as many times in history as there are stars in the sky, and we are all on the cusp of answers.

Are we ready? I hope so. Because if we aren't, and our imminent First Contact turns hostile, then humankind's age of expansion may come to a close sooner than everyone hopes. Humans are already a great people. We are strong, smart, willful, and, despite misgivings and concerns I pose in these pages, I have faith that we can defend ourselves against all foes.

I hope.

If it comes to war, we at least have a long history of bloodshed bred into our bones.

Humanity always thought that it would take aliens to bring unity. Did anyone ever wonder if it would take unity to bring aliens?

—Lunar Admiral Jacob Hawkins,
Excerpt from his personal journal
Dated August 10, 2105
Four months before First Contact

MASON J. TORALL

CHAPTER TEN

Sanguine Lotus

The sky was clear and blue as noon came and went. Frost and icicles hung crisp in the frigid sunlight. Inside Camp Cascade, the base had gone from a morning bustle to a full-scale scuttle. Damien carried his ruined backpack through the base, pondering on what the Admiral had said, reluctant to leave Von behind.

He and Leo were following Admiral Baroda and Agent Bunting through the hospital complex towards the hangars. People ran everywhere carrying boxes, luggage, tools, equipment, weapons, and anything else that might be found on a base. The evacuation was in full swing; the army was approaching.

"An island," Damien repeated. "A secret island, where Project S.E.H.A. is looking for Elementals." He shook his head. It seemed impossible. *Then again, so does another Supply Fleet, but I guess that's happening, too.*

"It's not S.E.H.A. anymore," Leo reminded him. "Baroda said so. It's just the people he recruited and merged with this…*other* group."

"Yeah, but who are they?"

Leo snorted. "I'm sure if you ask Baroda again he'll tell you *this* time."

Damien rolled his eyes and kept walking. Ahead, the pale Agent Bunting seemed to be going through a to-do list with the Admiral. Baroda kept nodding and occasionally gesturing. Just ahead of them, the wave of people parted like water when they saw the black and silver uniform

215

approaching. Every soldier they passed froze and saluted, going ramrod stiff. Damien stayed close behind the two men, as their wake was short before the throngs closed again.

"Do you think it's true?" Damien asked. "What he said?" They turned a corner into a lobby packed with ragged civilians who waited in lines that wound and curled in on each other. Tired-looking military clerks stood behind a counter handling them one at a time. They were all waiting for a seat on the evac flights. Damien had already spotted three take-offs through the windows, bound anywhere but to the southwest. Many of the ragged people were armed with worn weaponry. The whole lobby smelled like a wet dog along with the dull undercurrent of frayed nerves.

"About how the Over-Seer waited to blow up Seattle because he knew you were there?" Leo answered. "Absolutely."

"Thanks."

"Hey, it's not a judgment call! You're lucky enough to be a small-town kid in a big world."

Seattle isn't small. "Meaning what?"

"It's pretty clear you've been living in a fishbowl, Damien, a fishbowl with a lot of people wanting to cook you their own way from the outside."

"That's no excuse for no one coming to help us when we needed it."

"I didn't say you or anyone else had to make one. But as to Baroda's personal interest in *you*…" Leo trailed off.

"What?"

"Well," the AI hesitated. "Whether all this is true or not, the Admiral's theory about the Nukes and all that makes sense. All the facts fall in line, but…"

"*What*, Leo?" Damien squeezed between a man gripping his two children, all three of whom sported pistols. He and the man locked eyes briefly and he saw the same resignation in them that he felt. *The whole region is about to go*, he thought. He pushed on after Baroda and Bunting. *Seven years lost in a snap attack, and nothing we did matters.*

The AI's voice cut in. "I'm not sure I trust him."

"Who, Baroda?"

"Yes. Bunting, too, but…less so."

216

Damien was surprised. "Why?" They continued pushing through the lobby and he almost lost sight of Baroda and Bunting amidst the throng. He felt a twinge of anxiety at being in such a large crowd, followed by a twinge of guilt at leaving Von in this mess. *They promised he'd be safe.* He took a deep breath. *He'll be okay. He'll be okay.*

"Because Baroda's a Lunar Admiral," Leo answered, unaware of Damien's thoughts. "At that rank and age, they don't go into the field anymore. That job—regal and honorable as it is—is a desk job. You know what happens to military men who end up behind desks for too long?"

Damien grimaced. "They turn political."

"They turn political," Leo affirmed. "I get the feeling there's something he's not telling us. This island sounds…fishy."

Damien snorted at the pun. The AI always had a way of making him feel better. "Are you worried about Von?"

The AI sniffed. "Pfft. No. Damn slizzard. I'm sure he's just *fine* staying here."

Of all the things Baroda had just told Damien and asked of him, that was the hardest. "Von's injuries are severe," the Admiral had said. "We need to keep him under observation and care here until we can get him out on a medical carrier. Once he's stable, I'll send him to join you." Damien had protested voraciously, but the arguments quickly fell away. He knew Baroda was right, but he was still loathe to leave his brother at this base, particularly since he had now agreed to go halfway around the world at the Admiral's behest. He and Von wouldn't exactly be a short ride distant.

"Leo," Damien crooned. "It's okay. I'm worried about him too."

Leo made a raspberry and Damien could just picture him crossing his arms and looking away. He tried to keep a neutral face.

Just then, Damien realized he'd lost track of Baroda and Bunting. Panic quickly gripped him, and he spun about. "Leo, where are they?"

"Oh, lawdy, I don't know! Can't you keep track of someone *yourself* for once? Honestly! You always have to—"

Damien spun about, tuning out Leo's rants and searching frantically through the crowd. He could see over a good many people, but not enough. *They were right here!*

"—And '*Leo do this*', and '*Leo send a message*', and '*Leo copy the library*', never wondering if *Leo* had any belongings he wanted to—"

A hand shot from nowhere and gripped Damien's shoulder. He leapt away and nearly knocked over two men holding each other. One was in tears and the other told him to watch it, but relief had made him ignore them as Mr. Bunting appeared in front of him.

"You lost us," said the Englishman.

Damien shook his head. "Sorry, I…got distracted." It hit him then that he should be looking for familiar faces, and that brought Bar, Shell, and others to mind, but he didn't see them. *Come to think of it, there's not a single Algaroth in here*. He didn't have time to dwell on it.

"You should stay close," said Bunting. "The Admiral went ahead, he's already waiting."

He nodded. "Sorry, it won't happen again." Bunting turned and parted the lines once more. This time, Damien fell into step right behind him. "So, Baroda said something about an island? Some sort of secret search for—"

"—The flight will take about four and a half hours," Bunting spoke up curtly. "Maybe five, depending on traffic. Have you ever been to the Baja Gap?"

Damien prickled at being interrupted, before he realized how stupid it was to be talking so openly about secrets amidst hundreds of people. He wasn't used to being in crowds. "The Baja Gap?" he amended.

"Correct."

"Nope, never been there." Damien finally spotted where they were headed: a corridor, marked by a sign that labeled it the route to Hangar A.

"Well, you should be prepared for traffic through there."

"Why?"

"Because short of flying north of the Canadian Rockies, the Baja Gap is now the only safe path into the Pacific from North America, since the Over-Seer's armies fortified their hold on the Rio Grande and the flooded Los Angeles Basin"

Damien hadn't ever really registered that The Collective had claimed so much of the west coast. The Baja Gap was a naval base and coastal stronghold at the most inlet point of what was once the Gulf of California. If the enemy really had fortified so much of this side of the continent, the Gap must now be a critically important juncture to the military. *We really have been living in a fishbowl*, he realized. He wondered if that's how humanity looked to The Collective from space. *Keep your eyes skyward*, Baroda had warned about the incoming fleet. *They may be only a few months out.*

"What distracted you?" Bunting asked.

"Hmm? Oh, just…thought I saw someone. Sorry."

Bunting raised a thin eyebrow at him. "No apologies necessary. A lot has happened to you in the past few days." They reached the end of the corridor where the traffic was much thinner. A security checkpoint marked the end of the hall to the hangar. Passing through the doors, the bustle and smell of the lobby diminished behind them. They entered a hardened antechamber with two officers tucked into a polyglass security booth. Bunting waved once and turned to Damien. "In fact, is there anything I might do to assist in the transition?"

"How so?" A low hum filled the air and Damien felt the static prickle of a scanner.

"In terms of your relocation."

"Von, Damien, *Von!*" Leo hissed.

I know! "Well, actually, Baroda said that I might be able to call and check on my brother in a couple of days, once I'm situated. Was that actually possible?"

Bunting's face behind his glasses was implacable, but Damien sensed a wave of what he could only describe as sympathy from the man. "It is indeed." He whipped out his tablet and balanced a small, fiber-paper notepad from his jacket. He clicked his hot-pen and the inkless writing utensil burned a message into the papery material.

"You know," he said as he wrote. "You've just reminded me, a friend of mine on the island has been positively *hounding* me about acquiring a unimatrix scrambler for some of his equipment…I think this is the opportune time to send him one. It just so happens that we have one on hand, and I think you'll find that a call to your brother will be much more…personal, if you were to use one of those." He ripped the fiber-paper and handed it to Damien.

> Tosh,
> Baroda approved your request.
> Here's the scrambler for the Core.
> No need to mention it if he asks.
> Thank me later
> -JB

Damien frowned and looked at the agent, but the man's blank face said nothing. He didn't know what a "unimatrix scrambler" was, but he nodded and stuffed the note into his pocket while the man tapped out something on his tablet.

"There," said Bunting. "It's been added to the manifest. I'll inform your captain and he'll see that it gets properly installed upon arrival. Just be sure to give my friend that note, if you would."

Damien nodded. "I will. Thank you." The humming finally stopped and the light over the far door blipped and turned green. "You're almost as fast at moving things as my AI," he said.

A lion's growl filled his ears.

He smirked.

Bunting inclined his head, "Of course. Once it's installed, it'll be much less harrowing to get in touch…if ever you should need it." He patted Damien's shoulder and approached the far door. The locks clanked back and the lean man led him on.

A blast of cold air hit Damien in the face, making him glad that he'd put his jacket back on. His nose hairs froze instantly. As the spidery agent moved to the side, Damien's eyes went wide with shock. They were in Camp Cascade's buried hangar, where a vast scene unfolded below him:

They stood on a walkway next to a two-way street. Across it, individual berths full of aircraft were interspersed evenly, and beyond, open air beckoned. Craning his neck to see through the line of people, shuttles, parked ships, and metal struts descending diagonally through the floor, Damien felt his stomach drop as he saw just how wide the buried hangar was. Off in the distance, a parallel bank of bays ran along the other side of the hangar, easily a half-kilometer away. The wind howled over the sounds of aircraft readying for launch. Masses of people were shouting and loading every ship, and the two-way street was packed with bustling cargo trolleys. Damien was half deafened by constantly wailing klaxons. He looked up to see a huge "L1" painted on the wall. Next to it, yellow siren lights spun around and around.

"This is incredible!" he shouted over the wind as Bunting took off at a brisk march towards the back of the hangar to their right. They walked within the yellow pedestrian lines painted on the floor next to the hubbub of small vehicles on the street.

"After a time, you *do* lose some of awe at it," Bunting shouted back, "but yes, it very much is!"

"They have stoplights!!" Leo practically shrieked in his ear. "I *love* the grid!"

The AI was right. At every third berth, a stoplight and crosswalk slowed traffic so the trundle of vehicles, metal, and men could cross to their respective aircraft. Everyone moved at the same brisk pace as Agent Bunting.

In the freezing air, Damien lost his breath fast, but he managed to keep up. After what felt like a marathon sprint, they reached the back of the hangar. Shadows hid the alcoves and Damien spun back to see just how far they'd gone. *Holy shit*, he gawked.

The hangar had to be almost two kilometers long.

Bunting shouted something and Damien turned to see him crossing the street. The traffic here was practically nonexistent, so it was a bit quieter, but not by much. Damien followed.

On the far side of the street, they passed the second-to-last aircraft berth, which was shielded from passing eyes with a metal partition that went almost to the ceiling. The final berth had a similar partition, but this one had had a large loading door cut out of it, and a human-sized doorway had been cut out next to that.

"When does the evacuation start?" Damien asked as they approached the final berth.

In almost immediate answer, a great, wailing klaxon blared, rising and falling throughout the hangar, cutting off Bunting's response.

wwrrrrrreeeeeEEERRRRRRRRRRRRRRRRRREEeeeeeooooooooooorrrr ww.

After three seemingly endless bursts, the klaxons fell silent, and Damien strained to hear the message that came after.

"*—not a drill. Repeat: this is not a drill. General call sounded. Tee-minus fifteen minutes to full evacuation launches. Report to your stations. Scuttle order confirmed. Repeat: full scuttle is in effect. This is not a drill.*"

"Isn't 'scuttle' a nautical term?!" Damien shouted, ears still ringing, but Bunting didn't hear him. They had reached the loading door to the final bay and the SIO agent had handed his tablet to the guard at the small door.

Leo answered instead. "Yeah, but it applies."

"Why?"

"Because they're going to purge the base when everyone's clear."

Damien was shocked. "That's insanity!"

"Not if they already know that they have no chance of saving it." Leo sounded melancholy. "They really *do* mean a total evacuation, Damien. They aren't fighting at all for the region. It's a waste of resources."

Damien shook his head, "Well isn't it a waste to purge it?"

Leo sounded annoyed, "They aren't going to *bomb* the base, you idiot! '*Purge*'! As in 'wipe all hard drives and data systems to keep them from falling into enemy hands'!"

"Oh."

Leo continued while the guard checked something off on Bunting's tablet. "Just because The Collective knows everything about human history doesn't mean we have to make it easier for them tomorrow, now does it? If *they* want to bomb the base and waste their time, fine, but at least they won't get anything useful out of the experience."

Damien was grateful that Bunting interrupted, as he had nothing good to retort.

"Right this way, Mr. Vilan!" the SIO agent called as the guard saluted the Englishman. Bunting went through the small door and Damien followed. The guard saluted to Damien as well, who was too surprised to return it.

"See?" Leo said, "Not *everyone's* afraid of you."

"I, uh, I guess not." *He just probably doesn't know what I am.* He didn't say it though.

"Do you have everything?" Bunting asked as Damien came through the small door. "There won't be a return trip."

They stood in a dark and quiet narrow tunnel, what looked to be a walkway between the loading door and a second, heavier door on the inner side of the berth.

"Everything I have left, yeah."

Bunting glazed over the comment. "Good. I also find it prudent to inform you that there's another passenger already onboard your ship, similarly bound for the island. He has… special circumstances about his transportation."

He gave the tall man a funny look. "You say that like he's a criminal."

"He is."

Damien was startled. "Oh."

There was a loud screech and the inner door began sliding up to a pair of smaller (but no less ear-splitting) alarms. The door rose slowly, and Damien had to shield his eyes from the dark-to-light transition again. He hadn't thought to put on his goggles.

As the doors finished opening, Bunting strode around the corner and into the berth, wherein…Damien stopped.

A ship like he had never seen sat nestled on landing struts in the berth. "Is that…"

"Your chariot?" said Bunting. "Indeed it is."

"Whoa…" he breathed.

It looked like a dragon.

Damien realized now that the second-to-last berth was, in fact, false, and this one ship filled both of them. It was easily twice the size of a Blackwing. The ship was black and streamlined, the prow angled and smooth, somewhere between a flat half-moon and a spearhead shape, and could be easily mistaken for a predatory head. The underbelly of the ship was also black, but had a matte sheen to it rather than the well-loved-but-still-glistening topside, as if it had been rubbed of all gleam over a long time. The underside of the prow had a sharp gullet that ran the length of the forward cabin and continued along the thin neck, which vanished gracefully into the full, angular body. Broad wings had been tucked and folded up and behind the body, and the joints nearly touched the ground. The body forked at the tail end, getting thicker by a margin and hinting at a vast thrust assembly.

Across the ship, stripes of forest green and royal purple had been painted in tasteful places, such as under the polyports of the cockpit and on the forward edges of the folded wings. The color gave what was already a stunning vessel an extra layer of character and distinction.

"Now *that's* what I call a ship!" Leo crowed.

Damien couldn't agree more, but his gawking was cut short as his gaze fell to the deck, where Agent Bunting was approaching two men talking. The first was Admiral Baroda. The second man was barrel-chested and of obvious Native American heritage. He wore a rugged green flight suit with brown highlights, and kept his hand propped on the holster of a Plaster pistol. His short-cropped, salt-and-pepper hair gave him that distinguished, middle-aged-gentleman look. The tattoos poking up his neck made him look fierce, but his set of dark brown eyes looked kind, if hard.

"Damien!" the Admiral called as he and Bunting approached. "Glad that John found you, we thought you got lost!"

"I did a bit…"

Baroda nodded and glanced at Bunting. "Hmm. Well, you're here now. Are you ready?"

Damien swallowed hard, thinking on what he was about to do. "Yeah. Yeah I think so."

"Good. We're counting on you, son, and you have my word that your brother will be tended to carefully." He patted Damien on the back as he steered him towards the ship. "Now, Damien, I'd like to introduce you to your pilot and his ship—your transportation. This is Captain Roman

Sartohay. And *this*," he gestured towards the dragon-ship, "is the *Sanguine Lotus*. Captain, this is Damien Vilan."

The Native American came forward and Damien saw an odd tattoo following the line of his jaw that looked like widely spread mechanical pincers. "Call me 'Romi'," the captain said. "It's an honor to meet you, Elemental."

They shook hands. "You too," Damien said. He felt awkward at being addressed so formally. Not wanting to screw up a first impression, though, he pointed at the *Sanguine Lotus*. "She's a beautiful ship."

Captain Romi peeked over his shoulder and a warm smile crossed his sun-kissed brown features. The love in his eyes was obvious, "She really is. Very special design too, a modified Scops assault craft."

"You'll have to tell me about her."

The captain nodded and retreated a pace.

Agent Bunting addressed Damien then. "Your brother has a number of surgeries planned that can't wait, but he'll leave at the same time as the Admiral—to ensure his safety. Unfortunately, that means he'll be leaving on one of the last transports. The army isn't expected to arrive for two days, so it could be tomorrow, or it could be the next day, but it will most likely be the latter before you can contact him."

Damien eyed Baroda, remembering the note Bunting had given him, and nodded. His mouth was very dry. "Okay. As long as he's safe."

"He will be," Baroda assured him.

Suddenly, the sounds of the evacuation washed over them as a ship rose into view behind the *Sanguine Lotus*. It looked like an evacuee shuttle, and the micro-Mag Fury engines flared bright as it bolted from the hangar. Damien was startled at the sight of something rising through what he had *thought* was a depressed floor between the parallel walls of hangar bays. "What the hell…" He took a look at the three men and ran under the *Sanguine Lotus* to see where the ship had come from.

At the edge of the bay, Damien's jaw dropped as he beheld the vast depths of Camp Cascade's buried hangar.

What he had mistaken for an elevated bank of aircraft was actually the top level of a four-tiered, buried airport garage, fit to house an armada.

The enormous hangar descended deep into the earth, where the side he stood on eventually converged with the far side in a sloping "V," far at the bottom. He clenched his muscles tight to fight vertigo as he stared towards the distant floor, where the people looked like ants and the attending vehicles looked like beetles.

Even here at the top deck, the ceiling arched high above, and Damien spotted birds' nests in the metal rafters, many of which were nestled in the roots of trees that had actually succeeded in breaking the metal ceiling. To the left, in the distance to the west, the mouth of the hangar peeked out at a wintry, sunlit forest vista that he could barely see. Close to a hundred aircraft bays lined every meter between the entrance and the back wall. Nearly every one of them was full.

Not many military ships in here, though, he noted, spying the blocky frames of evacuee shuttles. He knew from memory that those aircraft were all fillable space and hauling speed, very few defenses.

"Another down," Baroda acknowledged from behind, and Damien turned to see the three of them watching him.

He returned to the group. "This is…I never knew it was this big."

Captain Romi laughed heartily and Agent Bunting grinned. Baroda merely nodded and said, "It surely is, but it's time to go. Good luck to you, son. I'm sure we'll see each other not long from now."

"I'll look forward to it, sir."

"Oh, and Damien?"

"Yeah?"

Baroda held out his hand. Something small, white, and battered sat in his palm. Damien's heart skipped a beat and he felt a swarm of chills run up his spine as he realized what it was.

His rook.

"Where did you find that?!" he exclaimed, taking the little castle.

"Captain Huxley brought it to me just a few minutes ago. She delayed her departure to get it in my possession. It seems it fell out of your backpack in her Blackwing. She wanted to make sure it was returned to you."

Damien turned the little chess piece in his hands. "Th-thank you," he choked over the lump in his throat. "Thank you so much."

Baroda nodded. "Damien, the Elementals are humanity's last fresh players. They're the only pieces on our chessboard that Croll Tan does not understand, and we need pieces like that. Tan is a strategist, yes; he's cunning, and he *is* hunting you. Given the opportunity to catch you, he will. If he can observe you, he'll understand you. And if he outmaneuvers you, he *will* destroy you—more than just you, in fact. Don't let those things happen.

"Stay hidden for now and hopefully soon we can find a way around his pieces, *before* he runs his endgame, or finds another way through the Final Option. Make no mistake that this war is a game of chess, and he's played it with us longer than any of his predecessors. Be careful, and perhaps in your isolation, one of us may come up with a way to end the game for good."

Damien nodded, determination flooding him through the white tower in his palm. "I will, sir."

Admiral Baroda stepped back… and saluted. "Good luck to you, Elemental."

Damien went stiff at the gesture. "Thank you, sir."

Nodding to Captain Romi and Agent Bunting, Lunar Admiral Antonio Baroda retreated to the gate. Another rush of sound whipped through the hangar: a second ship was taking off amidst another wave of klaxons. This time, though, the sirens didn't cease at three.

The evacuation had begun.

Damien turned towards the *Lotus*, ready to leave, when he thought of one last thing. "Admiral?" he shouted as a third ship fired up.

Admiral Baroda tipped his chin to show he was listening.

"Thanks for breakfast!"

Baroda smiled, his posture loosening by a fraction. "It was my genuine pleasure, son!"

Damien waved in thanks. Then he held his hand out to the pale Englishman. "Thank you as well, Agent Bunting. You've done a lot for me already." He pressed the pocket where the note was.

Bunting gripped his hand and nodded. He leaned in so he didn't have to shout, "It was my pleasure as well, Mr. Vilan. You have a great deal of adversity ahead, and it's always good to have friends. I, for one, hope you can count me among yours."

Before Damien responded, the SIO agent in sunglasses nodded to Captain Romi and joined the Admiral.

"Ready to go?" the captain asked.

Damien turned. "I think we're heading out whether I'm ready or not, so, yeah, let's get moving."

The man nodded solemnly, "It'll be worth your sacrifice, that I'm sure of." He saluted Admiral Baroda and led Damien up the ramp into the belly of his ship.

∞   ∞   ∞

A few minutes later, *Sanguine Lotus*'s engines flared to life and the men on the deck blinked as the wash from her engines fell over them, filled with dust. They watched as she slid from her berth into the chasm of the hangar, unfurling her wings as she did so. Then, with a roar, the dragon-ship rocketed out of the hangar, carrying her precious cargo.

"Do you think he's ready?" Agent Bunting asked. "For the Prohka, or the islanders, or the Over-Seer, or…any of this, for that matter?" The sounds of the evacuation grew louder and louder.

"Absolutely not," Admiral Baroda answered bluntly. "But there's no time like the present to forge a future, and our future will stay very dark if we don't have someone who can guide us all through it." He turned away from the hangar to resume his duties. *The man of darkness, guiding us to the light*. He shook his head. *What a world*.

CHAPTER ELEVEN

The Martialed Man on Layover

"I saw you eyeing this," Romi said from the pilot's seat of the *Sanguine Lotus*. He scraped his fingers over the open-pincer tattoo on the right side of his jaw. The tips of the tattoo ended just behind the captain's ear at one end, and just before his chin at the other. "It's for my copilot," he said. "He had an…injury. Brothers have to stick together."

From the copilot's chair, Damien blurted, "Is he your real brother?"

Romi laughed, "In all but blood." His laugh was a deep, warm thing.

"Is he here?"

"No, no extra crew today, but you'll meet him soon."

"Sounds good." Damien fell back in the chair. He gazed out the starboard polyport, eyes tracing the way over the frosty forest that stretched to the western horizon. They were flying south, away from the Cascade forest, the Puget Sound, and home.

"I'm sorry that this is happening to you," said Romi.

Before Damien could answer, a blipping alarm filled the cabin. The captain swatted it off.

"Sorry about what? What was that?"

Romi sighed and gave him a guarded sideways glance. "Just a call about Stingships."

Damien's neck prickled and he leaned forward to try and spot them out the window.

"Relax, it's…not a proximity alarm. They couldn't see us if they were close anyway."

"Why not?"

"You don't think that Admiral Baroda would have entrusted you to just *any* fighter pilot, do you? My lady is a bit better equipped than that."

He patted the sprawling console in front of him with love. Everything in the cabin glowed with lights of every color amidst switches and little displays. The chairs behind the pilot and copilot's seats each had their own station, though those were dark. The only decorative trappings were a green-and-purple banner hanging behind the rear copilot's chair, and a small, mossy-green granite base sitting snugly between two of Captain Romi's pilot consoles. In the shallow bowl were three small, ovoid stones, rubbed to a polish.

Damien barked a laugh. "Now that you mention it. I *did* think he might stick me back with Captain Huxley again."

"Captain who?" Romi tapped out commands with practiced hands, setting them to autopilot.

"Huxley. She was the one who picked us up from Seattle."

Romi looked at him hard, still flipping switches. "Was there a problem in transport?"

Damien hesitated. Huxley had been overly curious and unnerving in her intensity—both in anger and her provocative comments—but he wasn't about to throw her under the bus for being those things. She'd saved his life. "Not exactly. I just…I kinda got her ship shot by Avos when she was picking us up and she was pissed with me. I doubt she'd want to see me again." But then he remembered what Baroda had just said, how it was Huxley who had brought his rook to him, and suddenly he wasn't so sure.

"Hmm," Romi pondered. "Well she wouldn't necessarily have a choice if the Admiral wanted her for the job. But I suppose—lucky for you—you get stuck with me instead."

Damien grinned. "I can probably live with that."

They fell silent. The sound of the wind outside came to the fore of Damien's focus, along with a faint clanking somewhere aft, and the engines behind that.

"Actually," Damien said after a while. "I think she deserves some praise for what she did. She and her squad were on their way home and instead they had to risk themselves to turn around and come pick us up. That should count for something."

Romi nodded in approval. "If she and her crew did all of that, maybe I should pass your comments along?"

Damien hadn't considered that, but in some way it felt like the right thing to do, so he said that the man should.

"Alright then, consider it done."

The alarm bleeped again and the captain jabbed at the protruding center console, where a Pip-projected, dome-shaped radar display flickered in patterns akin to coolly colored liquid. At the alarm, the display had begun to resolve into a mass of…well, *something*. Damien couldn't be sure what it was, and it vanished along with the sound before Damien could make it out.

"That looks like more than just a few Stingships," he said.

Romi pursed his lips and blew air between them, making a faint *whoo*ing sound. "It is."

Damien eyed the display again. It had resumed showing nothing more than a trace layout of the surrounding terrain. "How many more?"

Romi's hands absently reached for the stones in the granite base as he spun to face him. "Do you really want to know?" The stones clicked together as the captain started rolling them between his fingers.

Damien nodded, unsure of why he wouldn't.

"It's the Portland army."

Damien furrowed his brow. "I thought they were further south? I thought it would be longer before they got up here?"

Romi shook his head. "No, they packed up their base faster than we thought. They were already on the march at dawn. Baroda hopes that…he hopes that Tacoma will keep them busy enough for the last refugees from the Islets to escape, but he has no guarantees."

Damien felt ill at the prospect of Tacoma 'keeping them busy'.

The alarm blared again and Romi lashed out for the console, but Damien stayed him.

"Wait!"

Romi stopped just shy of the button.

"I want to see."

The captain lowered his hand. His set his jaw and nodded. The alarm continued and he flipped a switch over his head, muting it.

From inside the foggy colors of the display, a layout of the Puget Sound and Olympia regions of North America resolved for them to see. The map had rough patches, much like the globe in Admiral Baroda's office, but most of it looked crisp. The map extended all the way south to Portland.

In between Tacoma and Portland however, a thick mass throbbed red like an angry wound against the verdant green coast. The army swelled and quivered, churning forward to the tune of an ominous drumbeat and leaving a token trail of blood-red signatures in its wake—a rear guard. The alarm that continued pulsing, though, wasn't coming from the army; it was coming from a pulsing yellow beacon, about to be drowned in the tide to the north. Damien felt his pulse quicken at the sight as he realized what it was: a call for help. Someone could see the army of Collective, and they couldn't get away.

"They're close," Damien whispered.

"Yes."

The S.O.S. continued to flicker.

Damien felt a dull ache seep into his blood. It was the ache of guilt and of abandonment; both emotions swirled around his mind. The ache worsened further as the blood-red line of The Collective rolled over the yellow blip… and the S.O.S. stopped.

Damien waited, hoping it might resume, but the spot where the yellow blip had been was drowned in the sea of red. Whoever had been calling for help had just been killed, and the only thing to mark their passing was a tiny yellow dot, snuffed out in the tide. Somehow, the detachment made it hurt even more.

A long minute passed, and then another yellow call for help went up. Romi let it ring. Shortly after, it too fell silent. The senders were gone, just like the ones before them.

Damien fell back in his seat and Romi flipped the display off, sadness crinkling his eyes. "I'm sorry this is happening," he repeated.

"Leo?" Damien asked, ignoring him, his voice flat.

"I saw it," came the solemn reply in his ear.

"How big is that army?"

There was a brief silence while Leo calculated. "About twelve-thousand soldiers," he said finally. "Lots of hardware."

He closed his eyes, grateful that Captain Romi chose not to ask about his apparent conversation with himself. "I umm…I think I need to lie down. Is there a place where—?"

Romi jerked his thumb over his shoulder. "Just down the hall by the crew deck, past the loading ramp. There'll be an empty bunk on your right.

Damien heaved a sigh, "Thanks."

"Of course."

Damien left the cockpit and found the bunk with little trouble.

"Hey, do you think he could let me have some time with his ship?" Leo asked, trying to distract him. "I REALLY want to poke around this *fine* lady he has."

"Not now, Leo." Damien snapped off the audio and slid the door closed, opting to curl up and be alone in the dark, unable to do anything else.

∞ ∞ ∞

Damien jerked awake at the sound of clanking. He rolled to the floor, expecting trouble. It took him a long second to remember the unfamiliar surroundings—his nap had been fitful, and lacking in rest.

The clanking was coming from down the hall, near the crew deck that Captain Romi had briefly shown him before takeoff. It was then that he remembered how Bunting had mentioned another passenger. He heard a door slide open and closed, and the clanking stopped with the sound of someone taking a piss. He left the bunkroom.

The upper deck of *Sanguine Lotus* was bisected into two open sides by dividing walls. The walls hid the ramp that ran aft-foreward into the lower deck. The port side of the upper deck housed the tactical suite and the mess behind it, while the starboard side was made up of the bunkrooms and crew deck. Damien had yet to see where the hallway behind the crew deck led, but the deck itself was filled with benches, a couple of round couches, and Pip tables. The bisecting wall was covered in a mess of dormant displays.

Damien poked his head out of the short hallway that led to the two bunkrooms just as the bathroom door opened again. A man who looked to be about his age—maybe a little younger—shuffled onto the crew deck, his head held low as he swung his wrists into everything metal he could reach as he passed it. The tight bands of chainless shackles on his wrists were making the clanking noise. The man winced to himself with each impact.

"Hello?" Damien inquired.

The man leapt a full meter, yelping. The grey hood he'd been wearing fell back to his shoulders. Just then, the engines surged and they both braced themselves on the deck. Damien felt the faintest tug behind his navel over the G-compensators.

Recovered, the man glowered at him, his eyes full of suspicion. His skin was toned brown and his hair was wavy and black—a near match to Damien's own. Brown eyes glistened brightly despite the mistrust in them, set in handsome features. His face was smooth and youthful, but Damien detected a sort of, *twitch*, hiding beneath the surface. He couldn't explain how he could feel it, but he could.

The engines coughed and fell into background noise. The strange passenger continued staring at Damien, saying nothing.

"So," said Damien. "You're my flight buddy?"

Finally, the man huffed and nodded, his demeanor shifting as the words came out, "Yeah." He shuffled forward, his clothes loose and ill fitting. "Thought it was just gonna be me on this one." He dropped into the chair opposite Damien and looked him up and down with more curiosity.

"What?" Damien asked, confused.

"Well, I guess…given all that gear," he pointed to Damien's ruddy and torn backpack, the goggles hanging from his belt and the modified pistol on his hip. "I thought maybe you were a guard, but then…" he trailed off, thinking. Then he perked back up and stared hard. "Snaps, man. What did you do?"

234

"Ha!" Damien barked, "I didn't *do* anything. I volunteered. Sort of..."

The prisoner scoffed. "Uh huh, yeah, right. You were picked up for something *just* like me, so what'd they get you for?"

Damien cocked his head, starting to get annoyed. "I just said: I didn't do anything. What'd they get *you* for?"

The man leaned back. He exuded confidence and cool collectedness, but Damien didn't buy it. He saw a carefully guarded mask, but that little twitch under his eyes gave it away. "Oh, you know," the prisoner said, shrugging it off and twisting his hands in the manacles, trying to get comfortable. "A little of this, a little of that. Finally got the official court martial last month, been waiting to get shipped to a cell ever since. Though I got *these*—" he shook the manacles, "—for abusing a few fucking freedoms on this lovely *Lotus* you're on." He scoffed.

Damien turned incredulous, "You're Army?"

He scoffed. "*Pfft!* Nah man, I *was* U.T.A. Marine Corps."

"You sound excited about that court martial."

The ex-military man pursed his lips. "Pfft. Yeah." He forced a laugh. "That it's *over!* Shit, took 'em long enough."

"Uh huh. So, they're sending you to—" Damien stopped short, unsure if he should be talking about the island. This guy had clearly done something to merit those shackles, and he was bound for the island just the same as him, but he couldn't say how much the man knew. *Yeah, but not even a criminal would be kept in the dark about where they're headed, right?* Damien had to assume not, so he finished, "To this island? You're headed there too?"

"Maybe."

"Wait...because they gave you a court martial? No way. I don't buy it." He saw a flicker in the man's eyes. Was it fear? Anger? Perhaps shame? He couldn't tell.

"What's your name, man?" The martialed Marine asked.

It was one of those rare moments where Damien wished that Leo would pop up and offer to explain the man's history. "It's Damien," he said, deciding it couldn't hurt to leave the AI quiet for now. "And you are?"

The man looked away, apparently having his own internal debate. Whatever conclusion he came to, though, did something helpful, because when he looked back at Damien he did so with an honestly confident gaze. "It's Estrada, Javier. Call me Javi though, only my mamma calls me 'Javier'." He shook his head, his voice full of scorn. "Ex-Marine, man. 58th Yucatán Jungler."

Damien grinned as they shook awkwardly around the shackles. "Vilan's my last name. Nice to meet you, Javi."

"Last name 'Vilan'," Javier said slowly. "What, like a villain?"

Damien laughed. "Ha. You're funny. No, it's pronounced *'Vai-lin'*. Almost like 'violin' but without the 'oh' part and…" he faltered. "Not…quite…like that at all!" Unwitting, they both broke into slow grins and started laughing. Damien wasn't quite sure why, but it felt good to laugh hard, even if it was only for a moment. When it passed they fell into silence, but the tension had lessened.

Eventually, Damien's arms started to itch again and he rubbed them. "So what made you get sent to this island?"

Javier sprawled a sideways glance his way. "Man, I don't know! That damn Admiral just gave me a choice, so I took it."

Damien perked up. "Admiral? What was his name?"

"Snaps, I don't know. He wasn't the regular kind though, oh no. This guy was *Lunar*." To punctuate the word, Javier cupped his hands towards the sky, as if reaching for the Moon. As he did, his ratty sleeves slid back to reveal deep bruises on his wrists. They highlighted cracked and dry skin beneath and around the shackles. The bruises were dark, but in the brief second Damien got to see them—before Javier noticed and snatched his hands back—he thought they looked older and deeper than just what had been left by the restraints.

Damien had never seen bruises like that, but the cracked skin made his arms itch worse. He frowned. "What happened to you?"

"Hell, I don't know," he floundered, jerking his hands back down. "I—I don't remember!"

Damien snorted, "Really? Going with amnesia?"

The former Marine stared hard at him for a second, then spat, "*No.* But I don't have to tell you *shit* if I don't want to. I answered everyone's questions already. I don't need any more."

Damien didn't have a response to that. They fell back into silence, feeling the thrum of the ship's systems and the distant sounds of engines and wind. Finally, Damien retrieved his pack from the wall nearby and dug through the provisions Baroda had given him, looking for a snack. After some fruitless searching, he saw the ex-Marine shift across from him. He felt the man's gaze.

"Look..." said Javier. "I'm sorry, man. Damien, right?"

"Yeah," he answered without looking up.

"Damien. Look, I'm sorry. I just...I've been through a lot this past...heh, well this past couple of years. This is just the first time that I really don't know what's going on. I mean, you seem like a stand-up guy, so...I don't know, maybe...maybe I've got a chance here, right? I mean why would they send *both* of us to the island unless we..." he trailed off, making Damien glance up. The man had a different curiosity in his eyes now, and the little tick flickered.

"Dude, *what?*" But when they locked eyes, Damien spotted the tiniest wink of something that hadn't been there a moment ago. It looked like hope.

"Are you," he said. "I mean do you have...*you know.*"

Damien squinted and returned to his bag. "I've got *no idea* what that means."

Javier blew air and wrung his temples. "*Gahh*—I mean are you like, special? You know, one of *them?*"

Damien frowned, still digging. His hand brushed the pocket where he'd put his rook, and the touch made him feel a little safer. Under it, he finally found a nutrient bar about ready to slip out under the padding he'd put in his bag as a temporary fix from the tears in it. He tapped to make sure the hacking rig and remains of the black box were in there as well. They were. He looked back up. "What, you think I'm like SIO or something?"

Javier waved him off.

"Solar Marines?" Damien pressed, "Swift Corps? *Coast Guard*?"

"Do you have POWERS?" he burst out.

Damien stopped pulling out the preservative cord from the bar and looked up. Admiral Baroda's words from earlier drifted into his head. *There ARE others like you, son. That's what Project S.E.H.A. was all about: finding and making contact with the extraordinary people who can do things no one else in history has ever done.* As he met Javier's inquisitive eyes, he saw that twitch again, but suddenly it didn't seem so odd after all. Was it something more familiar to the change his own Elemental powers brought to his eyes? He wasn't sure. *We know some have a checkered past*, Baroda had said. *A few may even be dangerous criminals. It's why finding out that you're a stable individual is such a relief.* Finally, Damien broke eye contact and looked at his snack. "That…would make a lot of sense, wouldn't it…?"

Javier kept staring. "Well then, *are* you? Are you, you know…*Elemental*?" His breath tumbled out at the word, and Damien felt a prickle of excitement. There was no mistaking the hopeful chord in the man's voice.

"Yes." Damien said after a long silence. "I am."

Javier blinked.

"Are you?" he asked.

"What?"

"Are *you* one?" Damien repeated. Javier leaned back in his seat, deep in thought. He waited.

"If…you're asking whether I have the powers of natural charm and endowment?" Javier's voice took a sudden turn to disarmingly playful. "Then the answer is yes!"

"Okay…"

"But, Elemental?" he paused. "The answer would also have to be…yes."

Damien's breath caught as if the air in his esophagus had just expanded and frozen. A tingle of excitement shot through him. "Well, what's your power? What can you do?" He tried his best to keep cool. *Holy shit, another Elemental! I can't believe it.*

Javier grimaced. "I, ah, I actually don't like showing it off much."

"Well then how the hell can I know you're telling the truth?"

"I guess you can't!" he shot back, busting his elbows out and straining his manacles.

Damien rolled his eyes, "Oh whatever. Look." He gained Javier's instant attention as he called up a wisp of black smoke over his fingers. He kept tight focus, and bid it to curl and shift between his digits. Damien felt his heart quicken, and he blinked. The drip of power became a trickle; his senses flipped to hyper. He could feel the three of them on the *Sanguine Lotus* as faint whispers in his mind, and the details of the ship sharpened.

"No way…" Javier breathed.

Damien continued to let the power drift around his hand until he felt the *tap, tapping* of pressure in his mind. It came from the tiny fissure circling his fingers, and from that plug beneath the dark liquid pool in his core, the one that he knew would consume him if he let it. He let the wisp go before it built into an Orb.

The black tendrils vanished and Javier whined as if Damien had just kicked a puppy. "Whoa—wait, wait, *wait!* What the hell was THAT, man?!" Wonder and shock were etched all over his controlled features.

"My power," said Damien simply. He finished pulling the cord from the bar before biting through the nutrient paper surrounding it. It tasted sweet and tart, like cranberries and oatmeal.

"Which is?" Javier hung over the edge of his chair, leaning as far as he could across the deck.

Damien looked up and allowed a faint, smug smile to creep onto his face. He couldn't deny enjoying this a little bit.

"WELL?" Javier practically leapt at him.

"It's Darkness."

Javier froze with a confused look on his face. "Like… Wait, darkness you mean like, like *nighttime?*"

Damien nodded.

"Like, like, the sun goes down, moon comes out, people sleep, get drunk, and fuck? *That* kind of nighttime?"

He nodded again albeit more hesitantly.

"Nighttime," Javier repeated. His expression fell. "What the HELL kind of power is THAT?!" He flung himself back in his chair, arms crossed and looking irritated.

Oh, not good enough for you? Damien glared, but decided he had a better idea than to say anything. He took another noisy bite of the bar and reached inwards, focusing on the power in his body. Without harnessing it in any particular way, he threw it out into the ship.

A whooshing sound filled the crew deck, and where a moment ago the glow of lighting strips and displays filled the space, now a shadow spread out between the two of them. Damien grinned as he focused just a bit harder, and particles of inky black sand coalesced in the air, thickening with every second.

"Whoa…" Javier's voice sounded less sure this time as splotches of blackness drifted past his face.

Damien continued chewing, taking every bit of focus he had to not outwardly display his concentration.

"What's this?"

The inky blotches thickened and grew. They swirled lazily around, and all of a sudden, they filled the air. The two were plunged into total blackness.

"Hey…hey man, stop it. Okay, stop it, I can't see anything. Damien. Dude, cut it out, I can't see. Seriously, you're kinda freaking me—*AH! What was that?!*"

Damien barely kept control of himself as he saw through the cloud of Night, and he watched Javier swat at a thick splotch of the ink as it brushed his face. In his haste, he flailed to the deck, where his voice continued to rise.

"Okay man, okay it's not stupid. *It touched me again!!* Okay! *Okay it's not stupid! I take it back! I take it back—OW!*" In his flailing, the Elemental knocked his head into one of the Pip tables and he fell back, crying out a different tune.

Damien was openly cackling now, but he let his grip on the power slip back beneath his skin—again, before he felt the fissure open any further. Beads of sweat rolled down his brow, and he saw the ruddy light pouring over his wrists from beneath his jacket through his arms, but he laughed nonetheless as Javier moaned on the floor, holding the side of his head. He finally stopped laughing when the man didn't get up right away. "Haha... Uhh—ha. I'm sorry, man. I'm sorry," he snorted again. "Are you okay? I can show you more if you like?" He fell to snickering.

Javier's eyes darted around, scanning for any sign of Damien's power. Seeing none, he twitched and scrambled to his feet, still holding his head and complaining. "I uh—nope! Nah, no way! Nah, I'm fine man, I'm—I'm good. That's ah... Oh, *fuck* that hurt!" he groaned, gripping his head harder. "*Ahh* yeah, just don't do that again? I don't—I can't really—I mean I can't feel *anything* in that shit. I don't... I don't like being confused." Despite all of his howling, the man had apparently held his breath that whole time, and he let it out in an explosive burst, after which he took a bone-deep gulp of air. He looked a little pale.

"Suit yourself," Damien said, and he pointed with the last bite of his bar. "But now you show me yours."

Javier looked like he was about to protest, but then a change came over him. His expression softened, his hand fell from his head, and he grinned at Damien. "Ha! You're a tit-for-tat kinda guy, eh? *Damn* I wish we'd met sooner! We would've KILLED at the Tiki Salsa Bar in Mérida!" He cracked his back as he spoke. "Ahh, Damien, the babes there? Whoo! Knock you *dead!*" He leaned in exclusively. "And some *fine* fellas there too if you dig 'em." He grinned.

Damien hummed his interest and tossed the cord into the recycler nearby as he finished his bar. "Well that's great, but that's not a power."

Javier wagged a finger, "Ohh, ho, ho my friend. I beg to differ. Charm is a power, alright."

Damien rolled his eyes but the smirk stayed in place. He watched the man as he cracked his fingers noisily between the shackles.

"Are you ready to see the amazing?"

"Shut up and show me."

241

Javier smirked. Then, all at once, the playfulness fell from his face and he closed his eyes. Damien stared, unblinking, afraid to miss anything. Never in his life had he seen another Elemental work.

Javier's eyelids twitched and his brow creased. He held up his connected wrists, reaching towards the starboard loading ramp, which was just fore of the crew deck where they were sitting. The air thickened and Damien felt a strange prickling in his spine, unlike anything he'd ever felt before. *Is this what it feels like to be near one?*

The prickling intensified and Javier turned his hands palm-up. Damien stared in awe as something insubstantial began to churn in the air over his fingers, getting thicker by the second. Finally, he heard something skittering from near the loading ramp, and he just caught sight of something brownish as it flew towards Javier.

The tiny clump of dirt caught in the air over the ex-Marine's hand and began to swirl and dance in the dust. A single root was lodged within. The clump shifted and spun, slowly losing coherency until it became so many particles like the rest, twirling in a shapeless vortex. The root fell from the swirl, completely unaffected.

When it was so thick that Damien could barely see through it, Javier's eyes shot open. "YAH!" he shouted, and the cloud of dirt shot over Damien, getting in his eyes and blinding him, stinging almost as bad as the cold from the night before.

"Son of a bitch!!" he shouted, keeling backwards and hitting his head on the outer wall. "OW!" His face stung and his eyes hurt as he tried to rub the dirt out, but over it all he heard Javier's laughter.

"Karma's a *bitch*, ain't she?"

"*Ahh*," he got out, still rubbing. "*Ahh*...you bastard."

The prisoner shrugged. "Karma's a bitch," he repeated.

Damien groaned. "Yeah, yeah alright, fair enough." He rubbed the sand from his hair and he could hear the soft bouncing of grainy particles on the chair and deck. "So what was that? Sand? Dirt?"

"Earth," he said, sitting back down. "I'm an Earth Elemental." He gave a mock bow from his seat.

Damien made an appraising face and nodded. "Alright, okay! That's better than 'sand' or 'grain' or—"

"Mud?" he offered.

They grinned at each other and Damien laughed. "Yeah. Better than Mud."

They snickered for a long minute, their score settled. Damien was just about to ask another question though when the overhead comm crackled and Captain Romi's voice came on.

"*Estrada! Vilan! Come up here and strap in.*"

"Trouble?" Damien called to the ceiling.

"*No, just come up here.*"

Damien queried Javier with a look, but he just shrugged as the comm clicked off.

"I'm basically the maid on here," Javier said as they walked towards the cockpit.

"Maid?" said Damien. "How long have you been in transit?"

"Oh, about a month."

"A *month?!*" But the door to the cockpit hissed open and there was no more time to talk. Damien looked out at the sky and was surprised to see at least twenty other aircraft hovering in view. All were keeping pace with *Lotus*. For a second, he thought they were under attack, but then he remembered what Agent Bunting had said about traffic through the Baja Gap. *I didn't realize we were that far south already.*

Captain Romi halted them with a finger as a stiff voice came through the comm. "*Arclite-2, we read you as a...Dragonfly scout ship?*" The man on the line sounded disbelieving.

"Yes indeed, Baja Forward," Romi replied. "We're on an emergency run to the Gulf of the Amazon, priority mission from Puget Regional Command at Camp Cascade. You can check it with your superiors if you need to. We'll wait, but we need to skip this line."

While Romi spoke, Damien crept to the copilot's chair and gazed out the viewport. The vessels outside were of all manner of design—military and civilian—and all had slowed to accommodate what Damien imagined was the airborne version of rush hour. He guessed there must be a similar clog of air traffic on the far side of the Gap.

The operator grumbled, "*I* will *have to check with my superiors, sir. Hold your heading and speed.*"

"Understood." The comm snapped off.

"Dragonfly, huh?" said Javier.

Romi squared his shoulders. "Yes, Estrada. We changed the serial tags on the girl a couple months ago," he looked at Damien and his voice grated less. "We figured that saying we're a Dragonfly is a lot less threatening than admitting we're a Scops. In friendly territory it gives us a low profile. No one checks twice for a Dragonfly passing through, but Scops are in high demand. It cuts a lot of red tape. Plus, if we run into enemy air they get confused as hell." Romi chuckled. "Gotta love having a Lunar Admiral as a friend."

Damien grinned, but he didn't answer as he stared down and ahead at the Baja Gap. What Bunting had hinted at earlier had not even remotely suggested at the American military's expansive efforts to keep the Gap secure. *The last fortress keeping the status quo for the entire continent*, he thought, feeling grim. *No pressure.*

Below, he could just make out the tiny shapes of tanks, aircraft, and other vehicles amidst the buildings and defense structures that made up the naval base. In the narrow Gulf of Baja, long arms of dock after dock extended in a staggered pattern into the neck of water. With the veritable armada of Navy vessels below poking off each dock, the sprawling base looked like a giant, unzipped zipper poking into the water.

Damien craned forward to look towards the east and west horizons. There wasn't a sign of The Collective anywhere. He couldn't help but feel a pang of jealousy that this area was so well defended, while the Puget Sound cities were being abandoned by the hour. He shook off the feeling. He knew how critical this junction was, and how unfair it was for him to think that way. Even so, the thought still pulsed dimly in the back of his mind.

The operator came back, short on words. "*Arclite-2 you're cleared for passage. Proceed within the marked lanes.*"

"Thank you, Control, have a nice day. Arclite-2 out." Romi snapped off the comm and addressed them without turning as he eased *Lotus* further south and out of the air-traffic jam. "You boys ready to go?"

"Damn right," said Javier.

"Let's do it." Damien said, hoping the twinge of anxiety he had just gotten didn't show. *We're really leaving home.*

Sanguine Lotus accelerated out over the Gulf, and Damien caught sight of a battle group of at least thirty Navy vessels, all painted with either the blue-and-white markings of the United Territories of the Americas, or with the green-and-gold swirls of the Regent Dynasty. The ships all floated gently in the ocean. Even from this far, Damien could see how still they rested on the clear blue waters. He'd spent a lot of time in school studying modern vs. pre-war tech designs, and he knew the modern vessels were built as buoyantly as possible to make them dwell almost *on* the surface of the water, as opposed to sitting down in it. It made them faster and more maneuverable, with the added bonus of avoiding unnecessary disturbance of marine life.

Despite the worries swilling around in his head about home, Damien was impressed to see the battle group in person. The main naval base of the Puget cities was in Vancouver, and thus they received far less military traffic in the Islets, much farther inland from the Pacific than Vancouver. He'd never been able to quite get over how amazing it was that the warships had been built to be so...*friendly*, and yet so deadly and powerful.

But soon, the battle group was behind, and Damien fell back in his seat, gazing towards the horizon.

"Alright, sir and coward," Romi said, directing the snip to Javier, who winced. "Time to *really* show you what my girl can do." He punched out a sequence on his panels and gripped the two-handed yoke.

Confused at the snip, Damien tried to catch Javier's eye, but the man looked sullen. The upset on his face alone was enough to make a lump pop in Damien's throat, as it occurred to him how much he was leaving behind. Damien looked out at the thinning spit of land that separated the Gulf of Baja from the Pacific Ocean, and he thought of his brother. He thought of

245

Bar and Shell, of Carson and his husband, of the girl Zeya who had lost her twin, even of those people on the bridge, and the many others who'd been in the city. He thought of the friends he'd lost, or seen killed, and he wondered if those still alive had made it out yet. He turned to the captain. "So, can you tell us where we're going now?"

Romi held his hand over a blinking red button, looking roguish. "Oh, where we're going?"

"This group," Damien pressed. "Baroda said it isn't Project S.E.H.A. anymore, so what is it now?"

Romi grinned, adopting the demeanor of a proper scoundrel. "The island—and the group—is called 'Amun-Nūr'. We're going to the Island of Amun-Nūr." Then he tapped the button, and the *Sanguine Lotus* roared out over the Pacific, leaving Damien with a sense of loss that overwhelmed his curiosity, as the ocean swallowed the shoreline behind them.

Chapter Twelve

Amun-Nūr

The flight was mostly quiet. Captain Romi wouldn't tell Damien or Javier any more about what "Amun-Nūr" was, beyond that it was the merged result of Project S.E.H.A. with an older version of a group of the same name. "I'm partly sad to not be able to explain it to you," said the captain. "But it's much better to see in person."

Damien just nodded, but Javier snorted.

"What?" Romi snapped at him.

"Nothing," said the ex-Marine, stretching out in the rear captain's side chair. "Not a damn thing."

"That's what I thought."

Damien said nothing, nor was he willing to pry into the captain's disdain.

They flew on, southwest over the Pacific Ocean.

Another two hours passed and Damien dozed, Javier left the cockpit, and Romi left the ship on autopilot to go tinker with the thrust assembly. Damien longed to go with him and see the innards of the *Sanguine Lotus*, but he was tired, and the rich breakfast Admiral Baroda had served him was cramping his stomach a bit, so he stayed alone in the cockpit as the afternoon wore on.

Damien was jarred out of his dozing as Javier stomped back into the cockpit, flinging himself into the pilot's chair as he did so. "I fucking hate him," he spat.

Damien rubbed his eyes and sat up, groaning as he heard joints pop. "The captain? I've noticed. What happened?"

Javier averted his gaze. "We've just known each other awhile and…he didn't want to be the one *escorting* me around."

Damien frowned. "You said you've been on the ship for a month. Why?"

Javier clanked his shackles against the armrests, wincing on every impact. "Politics, man. I'm kind of a special guy, you know? Floating around, getting all the attention for causing some ruckus here, some shit there." He smirked. "Guess they just decided I needed a *chauffeur* since I'm so busy and popular, you know?"

Damien raised a skeptical eyebrow.

Javier saw the look. "Yeah, don't I know it."

"But, *why?*" Damien had heard of cruel and unusual punishments, but never a sentence like this. *Or lack of one, it sounds like.*

Javier's response was cut off by another voice filtering through the overhead speakers. "I'll tell you why." It was Leo.

The AI had been quiet for so long that Damien had wondered where he'd gone. With a twinge of guilt, he remembered that he'd muted him before they left the Cascades when he went to doze in the bunkroom. The twinge was replaced equally fast though with suspicion. "How'd you get around the mute?"

The AI sounded irritated. "Oh, Damien, the things I can do that you don't know about."

Javier's eyes darted around the cockpit before he pointed at the ceiling. "Is that yours? 'Cus it ain't Romi's. *Lotus* doesn't have an AI."

Damien nodded. "Yeah, he's mine."

Leo scoffed. "Oh, don't you be claiming ownership of *me*, Mr. Vilan. You keep your pretty hands off now, yeh hear?"

Damien rolled his eyes. "Your cube is still in *my* backpack. You're *my* responsibility."

"Uh huh, when it's convenient."

"What's *that* supposed to mean?" Damien's anger sparked.

"Oh, nothing. You just forget I'm stuck in that stupid box a lot, remember? *And* you forget that I can process a lot faster than you, so an hour of me waiting for you to flip that stupid not-working mute switch is close to, like, a year for me. I could be the *picture* of civility if you didn't keep me locked in that *wonderfully* smelling backpack of yours. I'd almost rather take being put in that backup hard drive, because at least *there* I'm limited to a few thousand calculations per second instead of a few *billion*."

"Leo, I'm—"

The AI bowled over him. "—It's the difference between being locked in a sealed biosphere with an endless supply of accelerant drugs and *nothing* to do that you haven't done already, OR being locked in a voyeur's one-way mirror box where I can see out but not vice versa and you just give me an endless supply of ether and coffee! In other words: a NIGHTMARE." The AI took a startlingly angry breath. "Something to remember."

"Passive aggressive, much?" Javier put in.

"Get your squad killed, much?" Leo retorted.

Javier's expression liquefied to beet-red and he puckered like a fish.

"Leo, knock it off," said Damien quickly, averting his eyes and talking generally to the ceiling. "I'm sorry I left you on mute, but if Javi wants to tell me what happened with him, he can in his own time. Don't tell me his history."

Leo cackled evilly. "I should anyway, *just* because you told me not to."

"Don't." *What's gotten into him? I've never seen him upset like this.* Damien thought on it, but it didn't take long to realize that Leo was probably as upset about seeing the bunker blown up as he was. *It was our best home, but it was his only home.* Damien shook his head. *I'm sorry, Leo.* "Let's just talk about this later, okay?" Out of the corner of his eye, he saw Javier looking at him with a shining ray of gratitude, even though his face was still flushed bright red.

The AI wasn't having it. "Awww, but don't you wanna know about your new fwweeeend?"

Javier narrowed his eyes at the ceiling. "You don't know a damn thing about me, snoop."

Leo whistled in mock fear. "Ooh, so threatening!" He cranked the volume and started whispering so his voice filled the cockpit, undeniably menacing. "I know *everything* about you, Estrada," and, with each proceeding word, a little bit of the red drained back out of the ex-Marine's handsome face. "You are Javier Estrada, secretly an Elemental of Earth, ex-Marine—dishonorable discharge—serial number: 57-17YJ-11358, originally stationed at Mérida. You've got a VERY interesting story to tell, don't you?"

Deathly pale, Javier sat equally still. When his voice came out, it squeaked small and hurt, sounding nothing like what Damien had heard barely two minutes ago. "Please stop."

"Why?" Leo pressed on. "You called me 'snoop'! That was mean."

Javier wouldn't meet Damien's gaze; he was staring hard at the shackles on his wrists.

Damien had had enough. "Leo, stop it. It's not my business."

"Ha! You should *make* it your business. If this island has Elementals on it, I hope they don't all have stories as sketchy as his! It'd make for a terrifically dysfunctional family unit. It'd be *really* bad if you wanted to— oh, I don't know—go to *war* or something? Because it shouldn't take more than half of your snail-brains to realize that *that's* where you're going." Leo paused and his voice turned thoughtful. "Although…throwing the volatility of lots of Elementals into one room…that *could* be quite interesting. Oh…yes I think that would be glorious! I'll arrange it myself for you two and whoever else is on this island."

"Leo."

"We'll set up a nice little teatime in the afternoon with some biscuits and—OOH, *tarts!* Maybe some *tarts!* You like *tarts*, don't you Marine?"

"Leo. Enough." Damien hardened his voice as much as he could. "That's enough. We can talk later."

The thrum of *Sanguine Lotus* filled the silent cockpit.

"Leo?"

"Fine," the AI snapped.

Without warning, *Sanguine Lotus* lurched hard, and Damien was thrown out of his chair. An alarm began wailing as the ship spun back on course, throwing Damien even further, jarring his bones with both impacts. Javier barely stayed in the captain's chair with a white-knuckled grip.

"LEO!!" Damien cursed from the deck.

The lurching stopped as quickly as it started. Damien's heart raced and he winced as pain lanced up from his knee. Javier looked around wildly, and Damien saw a hint of military training surface in the man. His response was precise, dagger-like.

Before either of them could say anything, though, they heard Captain Romi thudding flat-out up the ship, roaring. When he bowled through the door to the cockpit a moment later and saw Javier still gripping the captain's chair, his dark brown eyes became angry beads, and he jabbed a finger at the console. "Estrada," he quivered. "I know you're capable of a lot, but *this*—"

"—It wasn't him," Damien interrupted. "It was my AI, Captain."

Romi held his finger poised toward Javier's throat, but he turned slowly to Damien, who had struggled to his feet. "Repeat yourself."

Damien straightened. "It was my AI, Leo. He's…upset right now at having to leave home."

Captain Romi looked like he didn't want to believe it, but his reason won out fast, and he let his hand fall. "Get out of my chair, coward."

Javier's lip twitched, but he obeyed, swinging around the captain's chair and landing hard in the one behind it.

What the hell did we get ourselves into? Damien wondered.

When the captain verified that nothing was amiss and Leo had only jarred the ship, he relaxed visibly. "I wasn't told you were bringing an AI with you, Damien. If he's stable, that's…good news. *Very* good news."

Damien was surprised. He was expecting upset. "He's stable, just a little eccentric. Why is it good news?"

Romi shook his head as he worked over his consoles. "Not my place to say again, I'm sorry. But you'll see soon enough." A smile broke over the man's features, and his tattoo opened wider with his jaw. "And… I suppose he has a good sense of timing, either way. We're almost there."

Outside, the golden glow of late afternoon flooded the cockpit as Romi banked *Sanguine Lotus* due west. The world appeared almost upside down as the sky above had cleared and gone deep navy, while below them broiled a heavy, patchy canopy of evening cloud cover. The sun sat just at the edge of the clouds on the horizon, where it had thrown the world below into shadowed relief. Canyons and coastlines had been etched into the clouds, hued in gold and constantly changing, the roiling canopy cast in the sharpest detail.

"We're on final approach," said Romi.

Damien and Javier leaned closer to the viewports as *Sanguine Lotus* continued its circuit, facing the sunset, then coming further around to the north, and then back east. Below, a hole in the cloud cover revealed the barest hint of something poking up towards them. A mountain. It looked like a tiny, green and black thumb at twilight. It vanished as they circled.

"Time to see your new home." Romi said. He pitched the ship forward and to starboard, dropping them into the wet canopy. They burst through it facing west again, hidden in shadows and trailing droplets of rain. Romi held the heading for a few seconds, until the first lance of sunlight broke the cloud cover. As soon as it hit them, he jerked the ship to face east once more, and the shadowed crevices of the island before them dominated the view, far in the distance.

"Damn…" Javier breathed.

Damien couldn't agree more.

The Island of Amun-Nūr jutted from the ocean into the sky, but it was a small island. That much was obvious even from so far distant. Even so, there was no denying the air of mystery and beauty that fell over the lonely mountain and its attending landscape. Most of the sparse hills that clambered towards the black volcanic peak were forested, and a ring of white sandy beach clearly defined the shoreline. The mountain sat as a majestic spire, but as they approached, Romi ascended *Sanguine Lotus* to hang just between the island and the clouds. It was a perfect view for, at that moment, the sun finished bursting into the space between canopy and horizon, setting the world afire.

Damien was speechless.

They circled and saw that the mountain cast a sundial of a shadow for a great distance to the east, visible only because, within that shadow, the Pacific waters weren't twinkling at sunset. The tropical forest grew thick and private, and the beach was highlighted soft and white. Much could be hidden beneath those trees.

As they banked to where the island was half in light and half in shadow, Damien noted that the summit seemed to have been cleaved along a vertical split, some unknown millennia ago. A huge shard had fallen to the west, creating a gaping, V-shaped valley between the higher and lower peaks. Their further circling revealed the dark eastern side of the island, which was an unbroken spire of craggy volcanic rock that climbed from the boulder-strewn beach all the way to the mountain's peak; an unscalable edifice of stone.

Even while they came around the north side of the island and banked towards the sun, Damien couldn't help but notice that, even though the forest was thick and the shadows revealed nothing, there was no sign of significant life on the surface. All he spied were a few startled white birds fleeing a crack in the rock near the top of the lower peak where a tiny cave might sit.

Javier clearly noticed the same. "So…we're meeting in the woods? That's the big secret? Where?"

Their circuit complete, Romi donned his roguish grin and arrowed them towards sunset, zipping away from the island once more. "I'd strap in if I were you. We've just been cleared to land."

"By who?" Javier asked.

Damien said nothing but he agreed. He'd seen or heard no chimes or calls. He'd spied several potential landing sites in small clearings, but neither guiding lights nor hard-angled oddities that might hint at structures presented themselves. He strapped in anyway and saw Javier do the same.

Romi's brown eyes twinkled. "Just trust me." Then he throttled the ship hard, braked, and came about. Each time they felt the pull of physics over the G-compensators.

Damien stared at Amun-Nūr, a speck in the distance.

"I'd wager neither of you have done this before," and Captain Romi threw everything into the engines.

Sanguine Lotus bellowed her draconic power and rocketed towards the sun-drenched black mountain. Romi's hands flew over his controls, inputting faster than Damien had ever seen anyone do. The man's series of commands concluded when a large blue button flashed just over the hemisphere-radar console. Romi palmed it.

A colossal *BONG* echoed out from the ship, and Damien felt shivers erupt up his spine as a deep rumbling filled the cockpit.

"What the hell—*oh what the HELL?!!*" Javier shouted as the rumbling worsened and Romi pitched the ship towards the ocean.

"We're diving!!" the captain yelled back, glee etching his features.

"We're WHAT?!!" the passengers screamed over the rumbling and roaring, but there wasn't any time to explain. The rumbling stopped with a *ping*, Damien got the odd sensation of feeling *stretched*, and Captain Romi whooped as they hit the water.

It took a moment for Damien to figure out that both he and Javier were screaming, until the oppressive silence of the ocean drowned all other sounds. Captain Romi stared at them, surprise and laughter about to crack over his features. Damien closed his mouth with a *pop*.

"Oh, *oh!* HAAHAHAAAA!!" Romi roared. "That's the best reaction I've *ever* had! Oh I wish I had a picture of your faces!"

"You—you, *oh*. Oh, you son of a bitch!" Javier finally stammered, grasping at his chest and gaping at the water around them.

The captain continued to roar with laughter while they dove deeper into one of the only environments humans had never fully overcome. Eventually, the last light from the sun above was swallowed, turning the cockpit into a beacon of artificial light. Romi sniggered and wiped the mirth from his eyes as he snapped on a pair of enormous red searchlights outside, so colored to better preserve the night vision of human and marine eyes. "Ahh... so, decidedly not a fan, Estrada?"

Javier didn't answer. He just kept shaking his head, eyes closed. Damien turned back to the deep outside and tensed as the air thickened. He could only guess at how intense the pressure was over them, and he eyed the depth gauge that had clicked to life in place over the altimeter on Romi's consoles. It spun into four digits very quickly.

"What do you think?" Romi asked him.

"I...I...*How?*" was all Damien could manage. "I've never heard of an...amphibious aircraft before." Ahead, shadows loomed in the distance, and some resolved into rocky outcroppings that jutted up from an endless track of sea floor. There were little to no signs of life nearby, but that was the least of Damien's surprises. *Sanguine Lotus* was larger than a humpback whale, and louder too. She would have scared any marine life off the moment she hit the water.

Romi answered as they approached the base of the island and the landscape started sloping up. "*Lotus* is a modified Scops, remember?" The largest shadow yet appeared from the depths in front of them. The captain veered straight for it.

"Yeah, but," Damien felt embarrassed. "Could you... tell me more about them...?"

Romi grinned. "Baroda's been talking to you about your not revealing what you don't know, hasn't he?"

Damien squinted at the captain. "Yeah, how did you know?"

Romi shrugged. "That's his practiced speech when he meets someone. They usually tell a lot that way."

"Oh." *Sneaky bastard.*

"To answer your question, though," Romi continued. "Scops fighters were named for an owl that adapts to different encounters by adjusting their bodily profile. They puff out or angle themselves differently depending on their assailant." His eyes took in the entirety of the cockpit. "*Lotus* has a quirk in her systems that made her special and worth modifying, so she ended up here, with me." He nodded out the window.

Damien followed his gaze and flinched, startled.

Through the murk, the huge shadow had just resolved into an enormous overhang, tucked behind a mound of sand. For a long moment, it looked as if they were going to hit it, but then the red searchlights sank through nothing, and the optical illusion broke. Damien realized they had found the mouth of a hidden underwater cave. Captain Romi angled them into the cavern, and the searchlights lit the banded sand patterns on the ocean floor.

"We modified *Lotus* to accommodate Aqua Pods," Romi explained, leveling out the ship as the gently mounded sea floor spread out ahead of them. "It's a very quiet, very fast, jet-propelled system. That '*bong*' you heard earlier was her engines powering down and the pods extending."

The murk became thicker, Damien watched as the sand turned to stone, and he became aware of a rhythmic thrum through the water bouncing off the walls. *That must be the pods.*

"So, what," said Javier, his voice sharp and antsy. "This ship is special 'cus she can fly *and* swim?! Pfft."

"She'd be space-worthy too with just a few tweaks," Romi answered with a sharp smile. "If we hardened the hull a bit and took out the adapter for the aquatic drive? We could take her anywhere."

Their conversation was cut short when the cockpit was flooded with pale light. Damien shielded his eyes, half-blinded.

"*Now* what?" the other Elemental groaned.

A ring of underwater lighting nodes had come to life in the distance, revealing that they were to continue for some ways under the mountain. They did so in submerged silence, accompanied only by the hum of the Aqua Pods as *Lotus* slipped forwards.

As they passed through the ring, Damien spotted something in the ceiling of the cave, just shy of the rough end of the tunnel. He uncoupled himself from the copilot's chair and crawled over the console to look above them. A huge square had been cut out of the rock. The opening had been lined with pale lights. Captain Romi slowed the ship and made adjustments for her to ascend into the square.

Both Damien and Javier flinched when the ship's comm popped and a gruff voice came over the speakers, "*Sanguine Lotus, it's good to see you ho*we *safely.*"

Damien hid his surprise at hearing an Algaroth attempting—and failing—to pronounce the English P-B-M's at the word 'home'. He remembered almost being able to replicate an Algaroth's thick English once by speaking with his lips pulled tight against his teeth, but the face he made while doing it was an unnerving one, so he had rarely repeated the attempt.

"Good to be home, Kel," Romi answered, warmth filtering his voice. "Where do you want us?"

"*I have you tagged for Bay One,*" said the operator. "*The doctor doesn't want to waste any tiwe, even in crossing the hangar.*"

"Understood. We'll be in the bay in five… four… three…"

Romi finished the countdown just as *Sanguine Lotus* crossed the thick square of lights. The Aqua Pods hummed loudly, and Romi gripped the yoke after inputting a furious set of commands. The ship came within three meters of the squared metal walls.

At last, they broke the surface with a splash and Damien—upon looking outside—was drained again of all words.

Sanguine Lotus bobbed in the middle of another vast hangar, but one utterly different from the one at Camp Cascade. The hangar outside was shaped like an upside-down bowl curving up towards a perfect apex. The walls were covered in huge lighting strips for pale, universal illumination, and Damien followed the trails of many grated metal gangways, lifts, and stairs that all ascended in a haphazard lattice towards what appeared to be a large, ovoid control room, hanging down like a chandelier at the bowl's apex, directly above them. Damien had to assume that that was where they were headed. It looked like it could house at least a hundred people. He felt further affirmed of his assessment when he noted that there didn't appear to be any entrances or exits to the hangar besides the one they had just come through. The island base was an impressive setup. More so even when he realized that the base of the bowl was ringed with huge docking berths.

Damien took the numbered berths in as Romi spun the ship a quarter-turn, towards Bay 1. Next to Bay 1, a berth double the size of the others was packed with huge tubs and crates on floating palettes, all lashed to the metal dividing walls between docks. On the far side of the storage berth he saw Bay 22.

"What do you think *now?*" Romi swung *Lotus* around in the water and backed into the berth. The slow churning sound of the Aqua Pods was audible outside with a faint *chum, chum, chum, chum, chum.*

"I've…" Damien faltered, "I've never seen anything like it." His view now encompassed the entirety of the sub-aquatic hangar, and he saw that eight other ships were held securely, spaced about, each one bobbing along on the floodwaters that had been let into the cavernous space.

Romi grinned and looked back towards Javier. "Estrada? You?"

Javier found his voice again. "I—I—I… I got nothin'. Just, *snaps*." He fell heavily into his chair. They both stared out in amazement.

The comm popped. *"Lotus,"* said the gruff operator, Kel. *"We see you ready to clawp down. Are you locked in?"*

"Affirmative," said Romi. "I'm just finishing alignment...now. We're in." A series of thudding, metallic *clunks* resounded through the ship, and Damien felt a level of stability when they finished. They were tied to the dock.

"Cofy, Lotus," Kel continued in his thick English. *"Attaching* vuoyancy clawps…extending vridge arw…frefaring for hangar flush, standvy."

"Standing by," said Romi. "Oh and can you get Tosh down here? We have something for him."

*"Tosh? I'll call hi*w."

"Thank you."

Damien remembered Agent Bunting's note, still held in his pocket. "Who's Tosh?"

Captain Romi's eyes twinkled and he grinned. "It's alright; Bunting told me you have a note for him. The unimatrix scrambler was loaded just before Admiral Baroda arrived at the dock. That operative knows how to smuggle."

Damien's eyes went wide. "Ah—wait, Baroda doesn't know that Bunting sent that scrambler-thing?" *I thought that was a big secret I was supposed to keep.*

Romi shook his head, looking strained. "I…shouldn't tell you any more, but…" he eyed Javier over his shoulder, who was looking out the window a little *too* intently to not be listening. "But I've already kept you in the dark about enough." He took a breath as he continued the docking sequence. *"Neither* of you know this, but Admiral Baroda has more fingers poking around this island than…than we would like. Agent John Bunting is more sympathetic to our autonomy, and he's very brave sneaking valuable cargo out here from right under the Admiral's nose. We're very grateful."

Damien frowned, and he took out the folded note that Bunting had given him. "So this…"

Romi eyed it, "That was his way of letting you know not to say anything to the Admiral, and you did a fine job." He patted Damien on the back as they heard a loud clang; the deck felt more stable as *Sanguine Lotus* finished hooking into her berth.

As the docking sequence concluded, Damien gazed out and noted how *empty* the hangar was. There wasn't a soul to be seen, despite the eight other ships. *Maybe they just clear it for arriving ships?* Whatever the reason, it was eerily still aside from the gently swelling saltwater.

"*Lotus, we're flushing the hangar. You are clear for shutdown and devarking, see you soon.*"

"Understood. *Lotus* out."

Damien and Javier both started again as a sudden roar filled the cavern. A whirlpool appeared in the very center of the bay where they had just ascended through. In a matter of seconds, the eight or more meters of water was sucked out and pumped down into the ocean. As the water levels fell, each docked ship sank onto their landing struts, while the scattered barges and pallets of cargo likewise fell. Damien noticed the grungy sparkle of salt stains on everything near the floor.

The last of the water gone, the hangar fell silent and Damien dared to let out a long breath.

Javier, on the other hand, started laughing. "Heh…ha, haha, *hahaha! HAHAHAAA!!* WOO!! That was fucking AMAZING!! OHH *snaps* that was awesome! And we get to LIVE in this place?! *Man!* I'll take this over…"

His enthusiasm was infectious, and Damien felt a ripple of excitement over his skin as he, too, realized that he had just been relocated. It was far from home, and Von wasn't here, but he and Leo were both safe and that was something.

"Alright!" Romi barked, only half serious, grabbing both of their attention. "Grab your bags and let's get moving, you've got a long line of folks who want to meet you."

"What gear?" Javier said, only half as nasty as Damien suspected he wanted to sound. "I'm wearing everything I own!" He flashed the shackles and Damien noticed the tiniest hint of an apology in the captain's eyes.

"Well," Romi responded, ignoring the flicker. "That just means you don't have anything to forget, doesn't it?"

Javier curled his lip. He marched out without another word. Damien chose not to say anything.

CHAPTER THIRTEEN

Argyle & Delmorra

The airlock to *Sanguine Lotus* burst open, hissing steam and venting moisture. Damien reeled at the thick scent of saltwater and humidity from the hangar as it assaulted his nostrils. It was so concentrated that he nearly gagged. The smell reminded him of sweat, grime, and old fish.

"You'll get used to that," Captain Romi said, noting the Elementals' contorted faces.

They climbed out of the portal and onto the gangway, waving at the burst of steam that had accompanied them out. When it finally cleared, Damien froze and felt Javier do the same next to him.

Standing a few paces away and looking expectant, were five people. Two of them were human. The other three—to Damien's great shock— were Algaroth. Damien went very still, but he felt Javier tense far more, and out of the corner of his eye he spied the man reach for his hip, where a pistol might have once hung. The group noted both of their reactions but did nothing. A choice, Damien quickly decided, that was probably for the best.

It took another full moment of silence, as Romi came up behind them, for Damien to realize that one of the Algaroth was female. He had rarely seen them on Earth—even at the XenoCon campus, where there was more gender diversity for the aliens. Yet here she stood, as comfortable next to her male counterparts as Von would be next to Damien, and as distinct as any man would be from a woman.

She had a paler shade of blue skin than most males, a shorter snout, wider mouth, a flattering array of ganglia adorning her eye ridges, and cream-white streaks in her golden eyes that had been accentuated with three white lines that ran back along her skull behind her eyes. *Tattoos?*

Damien had never heard of an Algaroth with ink, but the effect made her already less bony face look even softer. *She looks really…elegant*, he thought.

Captain Romi pushed between him and Javier, offering comforting taps on their backs as he did. "Time to meet the family," he whispered.

"Roman," said the human woman in English, opening her arms wide. "Glad to see you made it home." Her thin Irish accent lilted through tightly held but rich, full lips. Her striking red hair highlighted pale freckled skin, while her vibrant green eyes sparkled behind a pair of old-fashioned eyeglasses.

Captain Romi cupped one of her slender hands in both of his large ones. "Of course, Doctor. I'm glad Sato let me pick them up."

"He knew you'd appreciate it," she said, smiling.

Romi knitted the groups then, throwing his arms out between them. "Well, Damien Vilan, Javier Estrada, I'd like to introduce you to Joval Tosh;" the Algaroth with midnight-blue skin and harsh, onyx-flecked golden eyes nodded. "Diesal Nisha;" the female Algaroth smiled. "Her *vishi*—and my copilot—Diesal Kel;" the gruff operator from earlier was an older Algaroth with wrinkled skin and an elaborate, whizzing implant over his right eye. "Nurse Sarah Donovan;" the small young woman bowed, holding a double-sized portfolio tablet and sporting a tight bun of auburn hair, held in an older Regent Dynasty fashion that complimented her obvious similar heritage. "And *this*," Romi indicated the woman who had spoken, "is Dr. Gwen Whalen, our resident…well, I'll let you explain it, ma'am," he finished as she shook hands with the pair of them.

The doctor smiled a warm, caring smile as she spoke. "Welcome, Elementals. *Please*, welcome to Amun-Nūr. As Captain Roman said, I'm Dr. Gwen, and I *insist* you address me as such—we don't stand on many formalities here." Her smile was infectious. "I am the deputy head researcher on the island, as well as the resident head of Elemental Biology. In addition, I'm also our reserve chief doctor and your tour guide through our facility. We're more than a little excited to have you here. It's…*ahh*, it's very exciting!"

Damien thought she had a hint of a youthful girlish charm to her, but the many, yellowed stains on her white lab coat spoke to time spent in labs. "Thanks for inviting us." He didn't know what else to say.

She tittered sweetly. "You needn't show your gratitude, Mr. Vilan— or do you prefer Damien?"

"Damien's fine."

"Well, *Damien*, you needn't make a fuss over it. We all hope this arrangement will turn into something fruitful." She smiled again. "Oh, there's simply *so* much to show you and to discuss!"

To everyone's surprise, Javier took the break in conversation to step forward and puff out his chest, proclaiming, "I'm sure you have *plenty* to show us doctor, and may I say that lab coat looks stunning on you? I'm Javier Estrada." He leaned in close to her, flashing a dashing smile and holding out his hand.

Dr. Gwen's smile faltered and she threw a curious look at Romi, who shook his head in an embarrassed sort of way. She grinned and looked back at Javier, smile replaced. "Why, *thank* you, Mr. Estrada, but you know something?" She leaned in close enough to almost brush his nose. "It's the coat I wear when I'm examining necrotic brain tissue and feces. I only have one outfit that's any dirtier." She winked.

The speed at which Javier's face changed from confidently flushed, to pale, to sea green was staggering, and Damien had to stifle a snicker. The man gaped like a fish, staring at the doctor who stared right back. Damien's control on his laugher was tested further when he felt Romi go rigid next to him. He averted his eyes, knowing he would lose face if he looked at Javier a second longer.

Finally, when the ex-Marine said nothing else, Dr. Gwen laughed gaily and said, "You *do* have a bold sort of confidence, don't you? That's something I can appreciate, but I'm afraid that you'll find no escape from your sentence here, Mr. Estrada. From what I understand, you still have some penance to pay for your actions, both in Guadalajara and in Mérida, is that correct?"

Javier's gaze dropped. "Yes, ma'am…" he mumbled, his bravado collapsing. He retreated towards the railing.

The green fire fell back from Dr. Gwen's eyes, and the kindness returned as she addressed Damien. "So, Damien, I'd like you to know that I—we—are very much aware of your situation as well, and that if you need anything you are to let me know. Estrada, the same goes for you, penance or no."

"Oh, well…thanks," Damien said. He tried to ignore the stab of discomfort as he stole a glance over at Javier, who refused to meet his eyes. "But…I think I'm supposed to tell *you*," he looked at Joval Tosh as he brought out Bunting's note, "Joval, right? That we brought a unimatrix scrambler with us?" He glanced back at Romi, searching for approval as the rough-looking Algaroth accepted the note, saying nothing.

Tosh read the note, and one side of ganglia flicked in the equivalent of someone raising an eyebrow. Without a word, he handed it to Dr. Gwen, who also looked taken aback. The other members of the retinue traded excited glances.

"Roman?" the doctor inquired.

"It's true," said the captain. "It's in the hold."

"Well, now," she said to Damien. "Bringing gifts to your new home is a great way to start." She winked. "Have you eaten? Satolin wants to meet the both of you as soon as possible."

"I'm fine," said Damien.

Javier just shrugged.

"In that case, shall we go upstairs?" They nodded, and Dr. Gwen led the march towards the lift at the curved wall. "It's a *very* exciting day," she proclaimed to the salty air.

Before Damien was past the retinue, he saw Captain Romi march over to Kel and bellow, "Did you two survive without me?"

Kel the operator, the female Algaroth, Nisha, and Romi all embraced, but Damien didn't hear the Algaroth woman's response as he followed Dr. Gwen.

The whole group took the clanking, open lift up the curving wall, which took them to the apex of the bowl, to a platform over the hanging ovoid structure below. Damien's curiosity prickled when he realized that, amidst the huge supports that bolted the hanging structure to the ceiling, the platform was lined with large cylinders that appeared to be elevators.

"Doctor," he asked. "Is there more to the facility?" He indicated the hanging structure.

Dr. Gwen laughed, "Oh, yes! This is only the hangar bay, and that's just the dock control. The facility goes up into the island!" She smiled.

"No way…" Javier whispered. Damien was too shocked to answer.

The group hopped from the lift to the platform and piled into the elevator. Even with five humans and three Algaroth, everyone had plenty of elbowroom.

"I hope you appreciate what we've tried to accomplish here," Dr. Gwen said on the way up, "it's really very special, and without a doubt one of the best kept secrets on the planet."

"*One of*," growled Tosh from the corner. Damien barely noticed from his implant that Joval Tosh spoke in throaty Russian.

Dr. Gwen flashed Tosh a knowing, sarcastic smile. "*Yes*. One of." Then the elevator pinged their arrival, and Damien was left to ponder what that meant. "Right this way," she said, stepping into a darkened space where the only source of light came from a few paces away, beyond a fractal polyglass door.

At her presence, the antechamber filled with golden light, and Damien felt a tingle of anticipation as the doctor led them into whatever waited beyond. A few more paces and they were through the door; Damien almost stopped cold as he was enrobed in a sensory overload that left him reeling.

A warm evening glow bathed a circular plaza, the center of which was dominated by flowering stone planters that tiered twice upwards toward a stone cradle. The planters were filled with flowers and shrubs of every color, shape, and size, from Earth and Shialga both, and all the life within was growing fruitfully under the caretaking buzz of bees and the twinkling warmth of fireflies. A sweet aroma of spring filled the air, and the breath Damien absorbed was full of life. Yet, as his gaze climbed over the planters and towards the stone cradle, that breath was taken away, as he took in the living monument towering over them.

It can't be…

Growing from the birth of three saplings from three different planets, upwards from its stone cradle, a 'Twined Tree climbed to the sky, and Damien withheld the presiding sentinel that once epitomized the alliance between humanity and The Collective. Its branches arched high above, where yellow buds of a flowering acacia tree wrapped around the ruddy-red bark and spiky leaves of the Martian redstone, while the bushy purple streamers of the elysium tree from Shialga draped it all. The enormous hybrid tree appeared alight with the aura of fuzz that grew from the pale elysium bark, and together, the vast trunk ascended into a rainbow of color, spreading outward with branches from all three species, colored through all three barks. Beneath it all, the roots crept down into the planters and babbling waterfalls that cascaded over the etched stone where other, more rubbery, tropical plants grew. Damien thought of the savaged one at the XenoCon campus, and he felt an involuntary rush of warmth to his limbs. *I never thought I'd see one of these again.*

He blinked as his eyes glazed over. "Doctor…is that, what I think it is?"

She beamed, "It is. It's one of our most precious possessions. We even have dedicated botanists living here to keep it thriving and healthy; but *look*, there's so much more to see."

"What…" Damien breathed, and his gaze followed where she was pointing: straight up and along an arc that went far to his left. *Oh…*

Above, five stories of an artfully adorned atrium ended in a domed ceiling that flickered, reflecting a starry sky. Balconies ran the circumference of each level, but to the left, the cylindrical atrium opened along a vaulted, cathedral-like hall that continued towards a vast mouth in the rocky underground. Through that mouth, Damien laid eyes on the last thing he would have imagined he would find so far beneath the world:

A city.

Before he could take in more than a glimpse, though, excited whispering met his ears and his gaze fell to the ground. On the ground of the vaulted hall was a long, well-lit, underground thoroughfare. Glowing piton pillars lined the "street," and the huge lighting strips all around the atrium were dim to reflect the evening hour. Yet, amidst the spectacle, Damien barely noticed the thoroughfare in favor of the sources of the whispering. Easily fifty people milled all around the atrium and the thoroughfare, all going about their business. They were an almost equal split of Algaroth and humans.

Damien's heart skipped a beat, and his words were lost. "You...you're..."

"Together," said Captain Romi. "This is the last place on Earth where the alliance between humankind and Algaroth lives on."

Damien choked a laugh out. "I don't know what to say..."

Dr. Gwen's smile filled him, and in that moment, Damien remembered a feeling that he'd forgotten: the feeling of *happy*. It wasn't a sensation related to hope, or to contentment, or to any other positive sensations—he'd felt all of those before in Seattle with his brother—but the sensation that things were not just okay, they were *good*, was something he'd forgotten for a long, long time.

"Are you alright?" she inquired.

He sniffed. "Yeah, of course. I just...wow." He noted that many humans and Algaroth were sneaking curious, excited looks at the retinue. There was very little suspicion in their eyes. He wondered if they knew what he was yet, but something told him they did.

Von's gonna flip out when he sees this. Damien remembered how sad his brother looked at XenoCon, eyeing the dead 'Twined Tree. *I miss you,* he thought, and suddenly he was longing for his brother. He needed to know that he was alright.

Dr. Gwen's voice brought him out of reminiscing.

"—Plenty of room for all of this and more, Mr. Estrada," Dr. Gwen was saying. "Who we bring into this family is another matter, though. Coming to this island has never been a temporary adjustment."

"Yeah, I got that," Javier answered. "I'm sure you've got lots of top-notch tech here, too."

"We do. We may have a primary charter in regards to...Elementals, but that's only a fraction of what we're capable."

"So what is this place, exactly?" Damien finally found his words again as he tried not to gawk down the street.

"Besides a safe place for Elementals?" Dr. Gwen bantered. Tosh, Kel, and Romi all snickered. "It's a sanctuary. For unaffiliated humans and Algaroth and a unique merging of science and culture between our species." Her tone grew serious and sad. "The island, and this special group's namesake, 'Amun-Nūr'? It's an Algaroth expression of an idea, which—roughly translated—means 'the exploration of life'. We—ah, *they*—adopted the name when they first arrived. I came with Project S.E.H.A, and the original members of Amun-Nūr had already been here for a long time.

"This island represents everything that should have been and should have *stayed* between our peoples, and we work very hard to keep it that way." She slipped a palm-tablet out of her pocket and started. "Oh! I do *hate* to do this, but there'll be time later. This way, please," and she made a beeline around the base of the 'Twined Tree, across the plaza, and to a set of double doors.

The two Elementals, two humans, and three Algaroth followed her, while the gazes of the islanders followed them. Dr. Gwen nodded to many whom they passed, and it was returned. Damien felt uncomfortable beneath so many scrutinizing eyes, and he saw that Javier's hunched shoulders said much the same.

Through the double doors was an elevator lobby where they piled in and ascended to the fourth floor. Upon exiting, they came to an intersection where the retinue split ways. Captain Romi, his copilot Diesal Kel, and Kel's *vishi*, Diesal Nisha, announced they had to take care of some things before they finished unloading *Sanguine Lotus* and turned in for the night. Joval Tosh broke off as well with barely a word, but he nodded at Damien with Bunting's note held in his tool-fingers.

Damien thanked Captain Romi for the flight, and Romi expressed his hopes to get to know Damien better soon. He agreed and they departed, leaving Dr. Gwen, Javier, and Nurse Donovan. "Almost there," smiled the doctor. "Shall we?" and they started off again. Before leaving, though, Damien took in the backlit panel on the wall of the intersection, reading as much as he could before being swept away. The directions were written in four languages, and he saw that there were a few darkened entries in each section as well that he missed.

ARGYLE WING

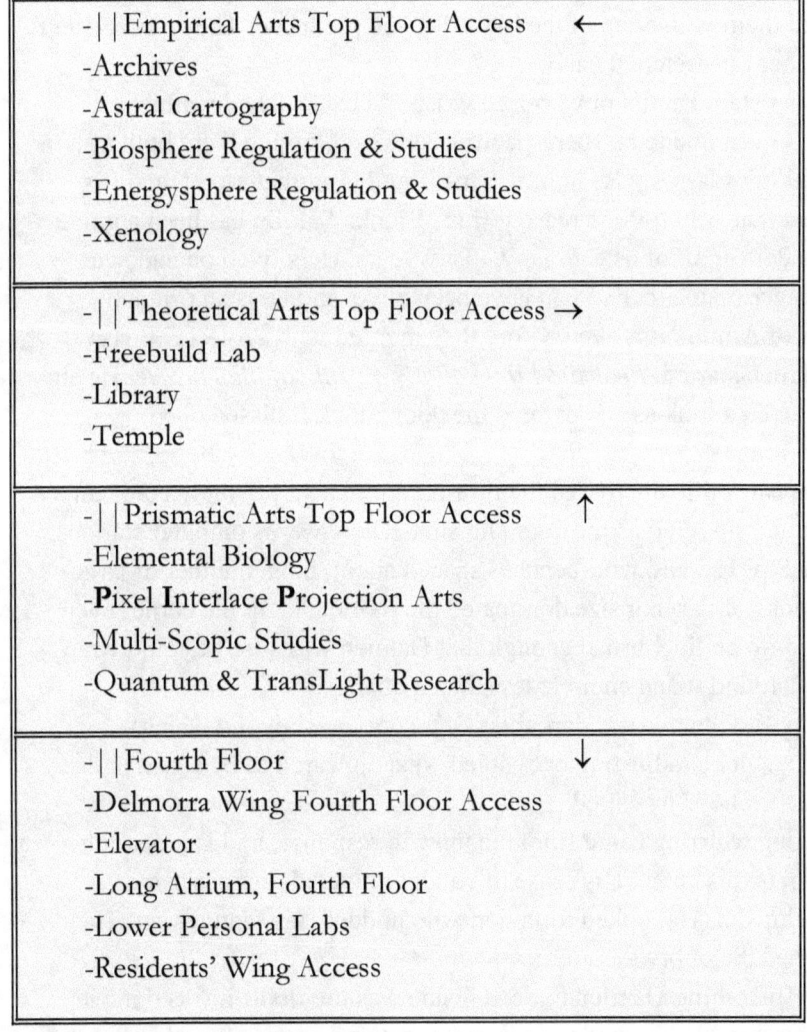

-| | Empirical Arts Top Floor Access   ←
-Archives
-Astral Cartography
-Biosphere Regulation & Studies
-Energysphere Regulation & Studies
-Xenology

-| | Theoretical Arts Top Floor Access →
-Freebuild Lab
-Library
-Temple

-| | Prismatic Arts Top Floor Access   ↑
-Elemental Biology
-**P**ixel **I**nterlace **P**rojection Arts
-Multi-Scopic Studies
-Quantum & TransLight Research

-| | Fourth Floor   ↓
-Delmorra Wing Fourth Floor Access
-Elevator
-Long Atrium, Fourth Floor
-Lower Personal Labs
-Residents' Wing Access

Dr. Gwen took them left, down the hallway labeled "Empirical Arts Top Floor Access." They passed the door marked as the Xenology lab and took another corner, where Dr. Gwen halted outside the door labeled 'Biosphere Regulation & Studies'.

"Here we are!" Dr. Gwen reached for the door panel and hesitated. "Oh, I'm sorry! Mr. Estrada, here." She reached for Javier's manacles and unlocked them with a tap of the key-stick she produced. They *clacked* and fell into her outstretched hand.

Javier stared at his raw bruised wrists. "Thanks," he breathed.

Dr. Gwen nodded. "Be respectful," she said, giving them both a stern look over her glasses. "Be honest. This island is a great secret, and it's been kept that way for one reason: trust. Prohka Satolin has been a guide and a leader for all of us for many, many years. He's lived on and near Earth longer than either of you have been alive, and he is an original member of Amun-Nūr, even before they merged with Project S.E.H.A."

Damien started. *Prohka? I think that's a...title of high praise.* He and Javier shared a look as she palmed the door panel. It hissed open.

"In you go."

The pair of them crossed the threshold into a surprisingly cold, empty lab. Damien shivered as the door slid shut. There were computer stations, portable Pip rigs, and workbenches spaced about, but a number of large empty tanks of varying size dominated the room. One in the corner even went floor to ceiling, broad enough that Damien was sure he could wrap his arms around it and encircle less than a quarter.

Opposite them was a dark maw of a doorway, beyond which Damien's quickly adjusting eyes spied what appeared to be a grid in the distance. "Hello?" he called.

A loud whirring came from the maw in response, and Damien felt a tingle run up his spine. His sense of danger quivered, but curiosity overwhelmed it. He looked to Javier, who nodded, his features set. They approached the doorway.

The first thing Damien noticed inside was the floor: it was done in deckplates and clearly made of the same textured material used in Pip screens and pads, albeit on a larger scale. As the two men rounded the doorway, Damien saw that the walls were lined with the same modified deckplates, but the ceiling was bare, moist rock. Damien cocked his head, trying to figure out what exactly he was seeing. When he did, he felt a twinge of excitement.

It was the Moon.

Five meters in diameter, the white orb of Earth's lone satellite hung some distance away, rotating in place, alone in a cavern lined with the large Pip plates. Damien was stunned at the clarity of the rendering; it far out-stripped any map he'd ever seen of Earth. They stared in awe as it spun, currently showing the side humanity never occupied.

"It's a curious thing," said a deep, deliberate voice from behind the Moon, filled with authority, purpose, and vigor, the voice of an Algaroth. "On the one hand, you have dust, held together by gravity, and touched only by impacting detritus." A thudding footstep sounded. "A monument to the constant of change, whether life touches them or not." Another step. "Yet, on the far side, you see the comings and goings of life, and in the end the impact is much the same. Things grow, shrink, birth, bleed, scar, die, and so on." One more step. "It makes for an interesting centerpiece, I think."

The deliberate footfalls brought golden eyes around the nearing side of the Moon. Damien's attention—which was divided between the alien's well-practiced English and the projection—was torn from the first signs of a blemish on the surface, as the eyes approached, resolving into an alien face. His heart fluttered as the reflected white light revealed the Prohka from the shadows. All he could think was that the footfalls were disproportionately small to the largest alien he had ever seen.

The Algaroth towered a full meter over them. In the minimal light, he appeared to have nearly black skin. His face was angular and regal, and a neat line of ganglia flicked over golden eyes streaked heavily in a rare arctic-blue. He wore a high-collared, padded brown-and-black vest with forest-green accents. Contoured lines of the vest lay open, exposing the elastic, porous skin between each of the Algaroth's closely interlocked, upward-curving ribs. On his legs he wore many-folded, loose brown pants that rippled to his feet, where the alien's long, gripping toes were strapped to an underfooted padding, the Algaroth equivalent of sandals.

"You are the Elementals." It wasn't a question.

"Yes," Damien answered.

The alien's gaze flicked between them. "Which of you manipulates Earth?"

"That's me," said Javier. "Javier Estrada."

"And that must make you the one who wields shadows?"

"Yes, I'm Damien Vilan," he said.

"Marvelous." The enormous Algaroth looked at the Moon, where the blemishes of a battle had begun to multiply as they spun into view. The one blemish became two, became four, and then a hundred. Damien tried to stay focused, but he knew the scar of the crash trench was about to come into view. "I am Daeduras Satolin," said the Algaroth. "Prohka of Amun-Nūr. It's an honor to meet you both."

Daeduras? Damien had heard that name before. At first he thought it was an Algaroth house name, but then the long-forgotten voice of Von's birth father sounded in his ears. "*The Daeduras clan is the only in our people's history that was summarily executed for their uprising against The Collective,*" Silas Torn had explained a long, *long* time ago. "*Never did Shialga order a harder task, since an Algaroth's clan name is a private affair, greater so by leaps over our house names. Our children even are told their clan names only once they reach a firm age to understand the significance.*"

Prohka Daeduras Satolin noticed Damien's frown. "A surprise?"

Damien faltered, "Ah—no! I mean, yes. Your name, I just, I didn't think that—"

"—That the Daeduras clan still existed?" The Prohka crossed his arms, looking contemplative. "I find it a wonder that you know of it at all, let alone enough to elicit a reaction such as that…which tells me you knew a Daeduras once."

Damien shook his head, "No, just my, ah…my brother's birth parents spoke of the Daeduras Uprising once, a long time ago."

"The 'what' uprising?" Javier asked.

272

Satolin's eyes sparked with curiosity at Damien.

Damien swallowed. "Well," he began, eyeing the long scar of a crash trench as it appeared on the Moon. He wanted to see the ruins of Apollo and the impact crater from the Battle of Luna, so he kept one eye on the projected satellite. "All I ever heard was that the Algaroth Daeduras clan was wiped out by The Collective in a…a minor civil war, though my brother's parents never said how long ago. Supposedly, Daeduras banded together to remove The Collective from a number of their controlled planets and take them for themselves, but failed. Every member of the clan was wiped out, and anyone left with the name was branded a traitor to their people."

Satolin's arctic-gold eyes were unreadable in the glow of the Moon. The moment passed while Damien saw the first ruined outline of a building on the surface, smothered on the edge of the crash trench made at the end of the Battle of Luna.

Satolin lowered his arms, watching Damien intently. "Remarkably accurate on all counts but one: The clan's goal had been to *liberate* those planets, not claim them. But yes, they failed, and the name incites anger faster than you can imagine amongst most Algaroth—even amongst other defectors here on Earth. Loyalty to your house is the same as loyalty to family for humans, but loyalty to your *clan?*" Daeduras shook his head, eyeing Javier. "Loyalty to your clan was once of paramount importance to all Algaroth. It kept the balance between all of our people of all stations. An Over-Seer, a scientist, or a housekeep could share a clan, and therefore be of equal station. To share a clan meant to share the world." Satolin looked back at the projection. "I am lone proof on Earth of my clan's life, and the failed Daeduras Uprising proved that loyalty to The Collective has overshadowed the loyalties I mentioned of Algaroth history, the loyalties to our people."

Silence followed as Damien watched the sad spread of Apollo Base appear on the Moon in agonizingly elaborate detail, and he grew melancholy. He had never before seen the ruins of humanity's stellar heart so stark, but even so, little was visible. The great, mangled carcass of The Collective's crashed Ultra warship dominated the ruins, and even if the sprawling base had been mostly intact, the settled cloud of Moon dust layered everything for kilometers in every direction, obscuring all.

The caked layers of dust made it difficult to be sure, but Damien thought he spied a crumpled shape under the Ultra's smashed nose, and he thought he knew what it was: The stern of the human First Fleet carrier, HSS *Ascension*, which had rammed the Ultra in a wasted self-sacrifice. Wasted, because the surprise arrival of Lunar Admiral Hawkins' SIO Fleet had ultimately brought the beast down, right on top of Apollo Base.

Such was the immortalized image of the final hours of humanity's last stand before The Conquering.

Damien felt a lump form in his throat as he remembered the tragedy of the day. He'd been seven, and his father had been taking him to school. They had been running late, he remembered, and his dad had been irritable that morning, but he hadn't known why. Just before they'd left home, Damien remembered seeing a breaking news report that the defense of Earth was not going well. Confused, he and Ewan Vilan had watched just as a monstrous alien warship collapsed on top of Apollo Base, where the beast breathed its last. His father had torn him away from the System news then, and they'd gone to school.

When he'd come home that night, Damien had found both his parents watching replays of the fall. He had stopped at the sight of tears on their cheeks; his parents never cried. Damien had turned to the Pip screen, and the news had read, 'MOON IS LOST. HUMAN STARSHIPS FLEE.' Beneath that, smaller text had read, '*Sol Armada broken by The Collective. Geneva burning. Is this the end? Earth Global Alliance leadership to present ultimatum for all human life, next.*'

Standing there, in front of the mountain of an Algaroth, Damien tore his gaze away from the Moon, and tried to push back the tremble in his chest. He didn't need to see the ruins to picture all that had happened that day. As with the great tragedy of any generation, Damien knew that everyone remembered exactly where they'd been, on the morning of October 14, 2127. The day The Conquering began.

Javier's quip was so confusing that Damien didn't understand it immediately. "If Daeduras is such a taboo name to have, why do you use it?" It sounded uncomfortably accusatory.

Prohka Satolin's dark lips split into a grin, oblivious to Damien's memory. "A two-fold answer. First, because I renounced my house when I took to Amun-Nūr." The great Algaroth produced a small remote and clicked it at the Moon. A *CLACK* echoed through the cavern, and the white orb vanished, leaving the imprint on Damien's corneas of the ruins of Apollo Base, the greatest fortress ever lost.

"Second," Satolin continued, "because I am proud to be of Daeduras. Over-Seer Croll Tan cannot frighten me by threatening my namesake, especially since—as I said—I am the only of us left on Earth."

Javier shrank back. "Oh."

Satolin clicked his remote again and glanced at the ex-Marine. "If it makes you uncomfortable to speak such a taboo name, Javier Estrada, you may call me *Amun* Satolin." The arctic-blue in his eyes flashed as the walls flickered to life. "But because humankind enjoys shortening names—which I find curious and entertaining, I must admit—you will find I am most generally comfortable with 'Sato'."

In an ascending display, the walls came to life with images. Damien followed the Pip plates six or seven meters up to near the rough cavern ceiling, where they stopped. The cavern filled with light, and he indeed saw that Satolin's black skin was merely a deep, royal shade of blue. Charts, graphs, and playbacks of weather patterns, storms, fires, earthquakes, and all manner of natural disasters appeared on the walls. These things and more appeared, were viewed, vanished, and were replaced in seconds. It was an assault on the senses, and one that Damien was only able to process because of his experiences with Leo.

Most impressive was the detailed topography that appeared where the Moon had just hung. It was a projection of the island with dimmed highlights of the facility within. If Damien hadn't grasped it before, he certainly did now: Amun-Nūr was extensive, curling and spearing its way through much of the inside of the island—both above and beneath the surface of the ocean.

275

Satolin admired the slowly spinning projection before turning towards them. "Look on that wall, what do you see?"

Damien quickly realized that it was the Periodic Table of Elements.

"Ha!" Javier barked. "Funny. Elementals to the elements, you think that we belong up *there*?"

The golden eyes were steady. "That is one possibility. Another theory is that you are anomalies born from space. Yet another could be that you are the next stage in human evolution, we cannot know for sure." He spread his great, muscled arms and encompassed the cavern. "Amun-Nūr is a group of learners, first and foremost, but our main purpose in relocating to Earth—beyond necessity—was, and is, three-fold." He held up his hand, displaying his third digit and the tool-fingers of his fourth and fifth. Damien heard the small, rough bridge on the fifth click against the fourth. "First, when Admiral Baroda brought Project S.E.H.A. to merge with Amun-Nūr, we couldn't deny that his purpose was sound. The Search for Extra-Human Anomalies sums up the first of our charter: to find and understand the Elementals, to find you." He lowered a digit.

Javier averted his eyes while Damien continued looking at the Periodic Table.

"Second, and following the first, we are here because we want to understand your origins. Neither Algaroth nor humans have ever encountered Elementals before, on this or any other world. You are unique." Satolin lowered another digit.

"Finally, we are here because Amun-Nūr as an entity revoked the claims of both Earth and Shialga over us, but we have chosen Earth as our home. Under The Collective's regime, we will never be free to pursue knowledge for knowledge's sake, as we do under a human one. Thus," he turned to a flash on the wall of the newsbreak for when the Ultra crashed into Apollo. Damien choked. "We are here to unite the Elementals, and bring our own war against the Over-Seer." He lowered his hand.

A chill of excitement crept up Damien's spine. The past few days had been a maelstrom, and he'd spent very little time thinking about where he was going, but the concept of openly opposing The Collective had appealed to him for a long time. *Von and I have always wanted to fight.* "Is that what you want from us then?" he heard himself asking. "To fight The Collective as a part of your war?"

Satolin looked to the images on the walls. "We want to join in it together, and find a way to save this rare globe among the stars." He looked back to them. "So, with that knowledge, I offer you both my formal request as Prohka of Amun-Nūr: In exchange for a reduced sentence for you, Javier, and in exchange for our utmost protection from Croll Tan for you, Damien, would you both like to permanently settle on this island, and become a part of our house and family?"

The Elemental of Darkness and the Elemental of Earth both smiled.

∞   ∞   ∞

A short while later, the enormous Prohka Daeduras Satolin took Damien and Javier out of the Biosphere lab and led them on a tour of the island. "It will be better to have you settled as quickly as possible, and I imagine you both can use some distraction right now," he'd said. They had both agreed.

"I'm curious," the huge Algaroth asked shortly after leaving the lab. "Do either of you know the Algaroth clan names?"

"Yeah, I do actually," Javier answered.

Satolin pointed out the 'Nanotronics' lab as they passed it. "And what are they?"

Damien was curious. Even with his background of being around Algaroth his whole life, *he* didn't even know.

"Well, 'Daeduras' is new, but the rest are: Voorda, Keleckthon, Aydish, Hellia, and Croll."

Satolin had said he would show them mostly the major wings of the island-city-facility for now, but since they were looking at a long future here, there would be plenty of time to see it all. He pointed out the hallway that led to the residents' wing before climbing into the elevator. "Why were you taught the clan names?" he asked as the doors slid shut.

Javier shrugged. "It was actually in case we ever captured an Algaroth and…had the chance to interrogate them." Damien gave the man credit for craning his neck to look Satolin in the eyes as he spoke.

"Were you ever in a position to use that knowledge?"

"No."

"Well, that's pleasant." The doors pinged open on the first floor. "Because it wouldn't have worked." The Prohka took them out of the elevator and back into the atrium with the 'Twined Tree. "And here we have the Long Atrium, the front door to home—as you've already seen. Onwards, now."

Javier got defensive as they began walking down the thoroughfare, winding their way through the light foot traffic of human and aliens, "Why wouldn't it have worked?"

Damien was focused on the conversation, but his excitement was continuing to build as they approached the break in the stone wall at the far end of the thoroughfare, which opened onto the cavern he'd spied earlier…where the city was.

Satolin chuckled, and Damien thought it sounded like a giant beast purring. "Because your drilling sergeant—as I assume that is who taught you—had only four of the six major clans correct. He was missing Daeduras, as you now know, and 'Croll' is not a clan, it's a house name. Or a surname, as humans call it."

"Is there another one?" Damien asked. He noticed that, despite Satolin's thrice-graced boons of size, leadership, and presence, no particular paths were opened to him amidst the foot traffic. Satolin nodded and said hello to the humans and Algaroth alike by whom he brought the Elementals, but they showed no overt reverence at his passing, only a respectful nod.

At Damien's question, the Prohka's face flashed a look of disgust, but it vanished quickly, and he couldn't tell if Javier had caught it. "Yes," said Satolin. "Clan Ruthilon."

"Sounds like a clan you're not into," said the ex-Marine.

Oh, he caught it. Damien smirked. The perfect temperature and humidity made the evening walk pleasant, and as they continued through the Long Atrium, Damien saw a collection of street vendors closing shop for the night. Noting them, it struck him that a place like this would *have* to have more than just labs for science and large bunkrooms. People needed distraction, even in a place as amazing as this. *Crazy.*

"While Algaroth clans are private matters," Satolin answered with deliberate slowness, "that has not kept them from consolidating power in public venues. Some clans inevitably cluster in the higher echelons of our society through their more commonly associated houses. Our Over-Seer on Earth, Croll Tan, made his open claim as a member of clan Ruthilon a long time ago, which opened many doors while closing others." Satolin's gaze darkened and his lip twitched. "Ruthilon was the most vocal about bringing Daeduras down."

Javier looked thoughtful. "So between you and Croll Tan...that's personal, yeah?"

Satolin nodded. "Very. As has it been with the previous Over-Seers of Earth: The Dorvan house and mine often disagreed over the ages, as they did with the house of the Second Over-Seer: Ahktosk. Both of those Over-Seers were of clan Ruthilon."

"What about the Third Over-Seer? The one that was killed before he set foot on Earth?"

Satolin stopped at the great chasm in the wall that marked the edge of the Long Atrium. Below, a long staircase wound its way out and down to the gently sloped cavern floor in the distance. The Algaroth stood with one of his enormous legs planted two steps below them, and he chuckled again. "A human saying I always enjoy is, 'there'll be hell to pay'. I believe there was a great deal of that on Shialga for such a traumatic misstep out here, but I truthfully do not know if he was of Ruthilon. I only know he was a poor Over-Seer."

Damien and Javier traded grinning looks, both knowing the infamous story that a Fire Elemental supposedly blew up the Third Over-Seer's landing craft before he had climbed out of it. Needless to say, The Collective had taken a beating after that.

Prohka Satolin looked between them. "You both are here from different clans and houses in your own right, but within this island, we are one; as you can see here, in the public domain that we call the modular district of the island—though some call it a 'district', a 'habitat', or both." And he turned to face the cavern, finally giving Damien a chance to take it in.

Beyond the Long Atrium, a vast cavern hid Amun-Nūr's small city. At the bottom of the winding staircase, a path wound between the spurs of volcanic rock to where clusters of stone and pre-fabricated buildings began to appear, all woven haphazardly between titanic pillars that marked where stalactites and stalagmites had met at some point in eons past, and thickened.

The outskirts gave way to tightly winding streets, the stone buildings replaced by prefab ones, and all in an instant, the outskirts exploded into the modular-city proper. It looked as if some wave or swarm of Pip cubits had ended up dumped in the real world and trapped here, where the featureless cubes had eventually hardened into dirty silver cubes and rectangular boxes, forever locked within the confines of the dark, wet, rocky earth. The mounds of prefabricated structures rose and fell in fitful waves of or no particular orientation or order, all clustering together towards some open central plaza, which seemed to be a whole story above the ground. Damien noted that some of the buildings were freestanding, some hugged the rocks, and a few even looked as though someone had just shoved them into the cavern wall, but even through the outskirts, they were all closely connected by tight stairs and railed walkways so that the sprawl below could be crossed without ever touching the cavern floor. It all created an odd, jutting geometry that Damien thought resembled a favela, the kinds that he remembered reading about in the history books, and that could still be found in many cities in South America.

Pulling his focus back, Damien realized that many of the titanic pillars in the surrounding cavern had been hollowed out, pockmarked with flickering golden holes bored out of them. He guessed many cliff-born Algaroth chose to live in structures such as that for a sense of familiarity to their cliff-dwelling heritage on Shialga.

In all, the place looked like an amalgamation of a small city or a large district that was once meant to be temporary, but had slowly solidified as more and more people decided that they weren't going anywhere. Damien's instant feeling was one of a ripe community, eager to be discovered.

"What do you think?" Satolin asked.

Javier whistled.

"I've never seen anything like it," Damien said, acutely aware that his capacity for awe had now been breached *several* times in the past few hours alone. *What the hell else do they have tucked away down here?*

"It may be much to take in," said the Prohka, "but you have my word, it will soon feel familiar." He moved closer to them and kneeled, so that they could see exactly where he was pointing. The sudden closeness put Damien awash in the scent of the alien. It startled him, but it wasn't unpleasant. It reminded him of books, misty trees, and... Damien sniffed quietly. *That's...weird.* He frowned as the alien settled between the two of them. The waft of Satolin's blue hide made him think strangely of soy sauce and sushi.

Yup. Weird.

"There, you see that dome?" said the Prohka, while Javier and Damien tried to spy where he was pointing.

We must be like kids to him, Damien thought, noting how the Algaroth's upper arm was thicker than his head. He almost laughed as he spotted a large bronze dome on the far outskirts of the city that had been settled between two huge stalagmites.

"Yeah," said Javier.

"Inside are the gardens and our animal farms, for nearly all of our food. And those eight towers you see, a bit smattered about? They serve as watchtowers and directional beacons. There are no spots in the city where you can't see at least one of them."

Damien noted how the swells of cubit-y buildings seemed to go highest at the bases of those towers, though they were in varying states of being ascended. Three of them even had the little box structures sticking out high up on their sides, gripping tight like barnacles left on their own.

"And there is the main market plaza, where you might explore a bit of Amun-Nūr's history and—more notably—food." Satolin grinned. "Even out here, we still want to appreciate the variety of cuisine available from our two vastly different heralding planets."

Javier nodded appreciatively, but Damien just kept listening. He had never been much of an adventurous eater. *Maybe now's the time to try*, a little voice said. It sounded like Leo.

Satolin continued, "And there, that spire? A temple, welcome to all the faiths we could muster."

"Really?" Damien perked up, curious.

"Yes. All of Earth's major religions are represented, as well as a few minor ones. You will find Algaroth doctrine *ketaphs* inside as well, along with many attendants from both planets willing to educate the curious of spirit."

The spire Satolin had pointed out climbed in a stately fashion from an elegant building that stood out amidst the prefab cubes all around. The temple sported a great many buttresses and archways over a wrought metal, navy-blue roof, below which, walls of swirling grey marble and silvery metal carved their stony way to the ground below. It was clear the building held a state of reverence amidst the modular cityscape, as it was one of the few structures that had been given yard space against encroaching buildings.

"Wow," Damien breathed, unable to deny a very old spark of spiritual curiosity as it flickered to life in the back of his mind. As he kept taking it all in, though, Damien frowned at a twinkle of cool light bouncing off one wall of the temple. *Where's that coming from?* It suddenly occurred to him that an underground cavern such as this should not have as much proliferating *light*. He was about to ask Satolin—who had fallen silent as he too enjoyed the view—when he spied a source of it, and quickly concluded that there had to be many of them strewn around the cavern. He was right.

A huge polyglass bulb had been tucked into a false stone face a few steps down the staircase. Whatever was inside had been set alight, making it glow cool and bright. From standing so close, Damien could tell that the bulb was as tall as him, and as he looked back out towards the city, he spotted a collection of them all over the place, each laid tactfully throughout the cavern and set aglow. There were so many of equal size that few shadows were left anywhere, and—as he settled on what must be the farthest bulb—the true scale of this cavern hit him. The farthest one was tucked in a nook in the wall above and behind the bronze dome. It was barely more than a pinhead.

Holy fucking wow. Because he had no idea what other words could encompass it all.

"So...what else you got down there?" Javier asked, and Damien wondered how he looked so cool and collected. *His* head was spinning.

"We have everything a functioning community requires that we've thought of so far."

"Ha, meaning what?"

Satolin's ganglia flicked, and Javier looked to Damien for translation.

"I...think that's meant literally."

"Correct."

Javier crossed his arms. "You got a bar?"

"We do, and a distillery and brewery even."

Clearly, the man had been expecting to be let down immediately, but at that, his eyes lit up. "Theater?"

"Yes."

"Shooting range?"

"I'll be showing you that shortly."

"Nightclub?"

"There hasn't been a great demand for one, so no."

"Could you get one if people wanted one?"

Satolin looked amused. "Javier, look," the Algaroth, pointed towards one of the prefab cube buildings. "We call those 'craft houses', and if you have a demand for a nightclub, you'll find it well within your power to make one from one of the many modulars that sit unfilled. If it succeeds: marvelous. If it does not," the Algaroth leaned in, "then it is your responsibility to remove it for something more appropriate to more people."

"Well, shit!" Javier nodded appreciatively.

"Indeed."

"Where does all your waste go?" Damien asked. Living at a recycling compound for four years and being a student of Earth history had left him forever curious.

"There," said Satolin, pointing.

What Damien had mistaken for a steam vent on the nearer outskirts of the city—nearly opposite from the bronze garden dome—he now looked at harder, and realized that it was in fact a hollowed out stalagmite with a recycling factory hewn from its base.

"So," he said, working his mouth as if it were a foreign instrument. "You've, I mean…you've really thought of everything haven't you?"

"Isn't that shit toxic?" said Javier of the billowing white steam before Satolin could answer.

"Of course it isn't. You've seen too many of your pre-war movies."

They both looked at the Prohka, who grinned broad between them and shrugged. "I have a weakness for your feature films. Particularly the ones with the King of Monsters."

Damien had no idea what he was talking about. "Who?"

Javier shook his head, lost as well.

Satolin rumbled a laugh. "They are old films, from before your Internet was shut down. I…will show you sometime." He looked back towards the rising steam. "But my point, Mr. Estrada, is that, as a people, humans are very good at reusing old material. The reasons why The Collective never took advice from you are the same majority of reasons why I call Earth my home."

"So…how did you end up down here?" Damien asked, finally tearing his gaze away from the habitat district—though he was eager to explore it.

Satolin indicated they should split off from the mouth of the cavern and sojourn down another hall almost as broad as the Long Atrium's thoroughfare. This new hall ran along the Atrium-side of the cavern wall. They assumed a leisurely pace. "Amun-Nūr's original family of researchers was stationed near Jupiter for many years. Humans and Algaroth both would vie for months or even years to be offered a position out there; those were golden years for many of us. But when the war came, many of us had been together through as much as an entire generation, and living so far out in space had blurred any lines between the regimes of Earth or Shialga. We were our own family, and we predicted what was coming.

"So, we quietly packed up our stations, found this island, and settled here, abandoning all life in space for one on Earth. When The Conquering Fleet arrived, we knew our two stations burned, and we knew we had made the right choice. Ever since, Amun-Nūr has quietly been known around the world, in circles trustworthy enough to not make a spectacle of us. We value our privacy highly."

"So how did Admiral Baroda and Project S.E.H.A. become involved?" Damien asked. At halfway down this new thoroughfare, he noticed some large display hanging on the wall in the distance, well lit, and marking the split at a Y-shaped junction.

"When only two parties are actively searching for something as unique as the Elementals, you quickly encounter one another. Fortunately, when Amun-Nūr ran into members of Project S.E.H.A, we met amiably. We traded our knowledge, and realized that neither party had found great success in our search. So, since Project S.E.H.A. was not in a safe location, we decided to merge—with the Lunar Admiral's support, of course." Satolin slowed as they approached the Y-junction. "We brought S.E.H.A. to the island, and Amun-Nūr as you see it has been here ever since."

"And the rest is history!" Javier joked. Damien smirked but Satolin didn't laugh.

"Not an easy history," he said. "I would be careful making assumptions such as that about the people here."

Javier set his jaw but he nodded, falling silent.

Satolin stopped them underneath the display at the Y-junction. "Do you see the names here?"

Before Damien could look, a squad of six armed Algaroth and humans came marching up from the right hall, stone-faced and hard. Their perfect march was at odds with the low bustle of people and aliens still occupying the Long Atrium behind them. *Soldiers,* he thought, surprised. The Prohka had yet to mention any sort of military presence on the island. *This place really has everything.* The squad was gone too fast for him to pick out details of their armor or weapons, but he had begun to recognize the colors Amun-Nūr flew: rich brown with forest-green accents. He looked back towards where Satolin was pointing, around the huge display that he now realized was an elaborate motif.

Hung next to the left hall of the Y-junction, the word "Argyle" was written. Towards the right, a word was written in Cyrillic, and so Damien couldn't read it.

"Argyle and Delmorra," said Satolin. "Those are the names of the two stations where Amun-Nūr first made our home in your Solar System, and they are now memorialized for the two main wings of this facility. Throughout these halls, you will find the science, arts, defense, offense, and personal studies labs that make up the majority of what we do and stand for." The Prohka beamed. "In Argyle you'll find the Empirical, Theoretical, and Projected Arts divisions. In Delmorra you'll find the Personal, Ground, Air, and Solar Warfare Research divisions, as well as a myriad of other labs in both. This is where you will make your productive lives as a part of our small society, and here is where you should appreciate our history."

"I thought we were just in Argyle?" asked Javier.

He's right, Damien realized. He remembered the panel he'd read earlier, just before Gwen had introduced them to the Prohka. It had said "Argyle Wing."

"We were. These are the regular entryways, but most of Amun-Nūr is comprised of corridors connected with one of these wings. Now, if you'll notice the display." The alien hands waved them to take in the motif, whereupon Damien's stomach quickly contracted in shock.

Hung in front of a grooved metal surface that looked like an elegant swordfish fin, four circular motifs had been placed in a diamond arrangement. The smallest sat at the bottom, and looked like an over-sized lapel pin. It showed four blazing stars on a black field over a rising Earth. "Project S.E.H.A." had been inscribed in the space between planet and sky.

Above the Project S.E.H.A. pin, the left and right motifs were of equal size. The left iteration was a painted one showing a space station on a starry background. A pale blue comet orbited the station, and in the upper-left, the unmistakably ruddy, color-banded profile of Jupiter and its Great Red Spot were visible. But the right motif was what caught Damien's eye…at first. A crossed pair of a Gyro and Plaster rifle colored red and blue, respectively, on a dark green background. It was an unmistakably military symbol, and one that reminded Damien of something. He didn't have to look far to find out what, though, as the largest of the icons jarred his memory, and his mouth fell agape.

Hanging at the top of the elaborate ornamentation, was the same symbol that the insurgents of Seattle had used as their call sign for years— the very same symbol that had been on the pendant that Bar had given him, albeit with a slight change:

Instead of the Space Needle in the foreground, the huge motif showed a rising Earth, just like in the Project S.E.H.A. pin, painted and etched in a glossy emblazon. Above that, a crossed red-and-blue Gyro-and-Plaster rifle took something of the military icon, and behind, a rising sun had been hammered out of bronze, painted a vibrant yellow, and etched with swirls of fire. The entire motif was ringed in silver, just like on Bar's pendant, and along the border, two lines of text had been etched. One was in Dekka, the other in Cyrillic, so Damien couldn't read either, but seeing the icon so far from Seattle left him reeling. "I don't know the names," he said in a trembling voice, "but I know that symbol." He pointed at it. "What is that?"

Javier looked at him, surprised, "Shit, yeah?"

Satolin looked at the huge icon. "That is the iconography of Amun-Nūr," he said. "Where have you seen it?"

"In Seattle," he said, his heart pounding. "Worn by a friend. He's…" Damien stopped as thoughts of home, of his friends, of the army, and of his brother came crashing back through the fog of this new home. "He…he *was* in the insurgent movement—we all used that symbol."

Satolin's eyes turned sad. "I imagined so. It has been adopted in variation around the world, but it began here. Your friend, he…is still in the Islets, isn't he?"

Damien found his lip trembling, and he looked away to keep Javier from seeing. "Yes." *I hope Bar and Shell made it out.* Eager to turn away from his train of thought, he looked back at the motif. "So it's *your* symbol?"

The Prohka nodded. "It is. And these," he pointed at the other three, "are the movements that made up who we are now."

"Nice," but the word was flat. Try as he might, the distractions of this wondrous new place suddenly seemed unimportant, and whatever else Satolin said about Argyle and Delmorra were lost. Later, Damien would remember scattered words about how Satolin wanted him and Javier to choose a department at which to try their hand, and how it was expected of everyone on Amun-Nūr to contribute to this vast community under the ocean, but he had no idea of what departments existed, nor could he recall by when the island leader wanted them to choose. All he could think about was his brother.

His mind lost in a fog, Damien dutifully followed the Prohka and Javier for the rest of their tour. He smiled, nodded, and even managed a bit of appropriate conversation and query. He dully registered a mention at one point of offers to see the dining hall, kitchens, and a pair of places called the "Celestial Garden," and the "command wheel," but he was terrible at hiding his inner turmoil and Javier's quips and Satolin's attempts to keep him grounded fell off. Eventually, the Prohka stopped them in some featureless corridor, possibly on the second floor off the Long Atrium, maybe the fifth, Damien wasn't sure.

"Damien, I don't have to ask you to know where your thoughts are," said the alien, not unkindly. "What I can do is offer solutions. The rest of the island can wait. Is there anything you need at present?"

Damien looked up from his unfocused glaze in the general direction of the Algaroth. "Uh…I…no, I'm sorry. I don't think so. I…thanks though."

Javier looked around uncomfortably. The man flexed his hands as if he were used to having a drink to distract him, but without that comfort, he settled on feeling the bruises around the missing manacles.

Satolin cocked his head, and nodded briefly as a young woman in a brown jumpsuit strode past, eyes downturned from the two Elementals standing with the Prohka. "Is it possible you need to simply rest?"

Whatever else was running through his head, Damien was pretty damn sure that being alone with his thoughts in an unfamiliar bed wasn't the solution. "No, that's…I'm okay."

"Are you hungry? A large dinner is being prepared in honor of both of your arrivals. I had intended to keep it a surprise but I can see that will do no good if your heart isn't in it."

Damien looked at his feet. His arms itched. He rubbed them through his jacket. "No, I…I think I'm okay."

Patiently, Satolin took a knee so he could look him in the eye. "There's the option of your demonstration?"

Damien perked up at that.

As part of what the Prohka had discussed with them in the Biosphere lab, their agreement to join the island included a request that both of them show off their powers in a controlled environment, here on the island. "It will give Dr. Gwen the chance to examine fresh Elemental abilities, first-hand," Satolin had said. "It could be a great leap of insight for us all about what you could be capable." Damien and Javier had both been excited and curious at the prospect, and the Prohka had said that Amun-Nūr had a place called the 'Core', deep within the island, where they could let loose their powers like never before. He had called it a "demonstration for a new frontier together," and they had both eagerly agreed to the event, which Satolin had said they could do whenever—but that sooner was more ideal.

Damien thought about the concept of letting loose his powers, and as images of the Avos chasing them through XenoCon, the red mass on *Lotus'* radar globe as they fled the Islets, and years of fighting for a broken city flooded his thoughts, Damien quickly decided that, yes, that might be an awesome way to clear his head a bit, and he wondered when they might be able to make it happen. He said as much to the Prohka.

"We can go now," said the Algaroth, his voice barely concealing a rumble of excitement. "Are you sure you wouldn't like to eat first?"

The decision made, Damien shook his head. "I'm fine. I want to do this."

"Very well," said Satolin. "Follow me."

CHAPTER FOURTEEN

Calm to the Core

Although Damien had his mind all in a fritz, and Javier said he was curious about what this demonstration would look like from the 'Nighttime Elemental', the ex-Marine announced that he was starving, and he'd be just fine with having a feast. Satolin detoured taking Damien to the Core to show Javier the dining hall, where he left the man in the care of Dr. Gwen, who looked curiously at the Prohka's words that Damien wanted to do his demonstration now, but she said nothing. Satolin had Damien hand over his ragged backpack, too, on which Damien hesitated briefly. *Leo's still in there*, he thought, *and he still must be mad at me*. He agreed, though, and let Dr. Gwen take the bag, which she promised to take promptly to his new quarters. They left Javier and the doctor outside the hall then, but Damien felt naked. He guessed that they had a fine meal.

"Are you ready?" Satolin asked, as the two of them descended the stairs from the dining hall, which was opposite the 'Twined Tree from where Damien had first entered Amun-Nūr.

"Mm hmm." The cuts and wounds—visible and not—that he'd taken in the last few days had been smoldering in Damien's gut since they raided the Razer, and the idea of letting off steam so freely had quickly caught those coals, and lit them. He wanted to do this.

"Very well," and off they went.

They took the same elevator Dr. Gwen had used to take them to the Biosphere lab earlier, but Satolin took him to the fifth floor, bringing them out onto the balcony overlooking the Long Atrium below. The 'Twined Tree was so tall that it almost reached the fourth floor, but the wonder had left Damien's thoughts. *Seattle will fall because you're no longer in it.* The words replayed in his mind. His gut cinched.

291

"This way." Satolin turned away, and they took the balcony along the top floor of the Long Atrium that ran parallel to the thoroughfare far below. Just before the mouth of the modular district cavern, the walkway ended. They turned right down a corridor, and ascended a hidden flight of stairs at the end of a quiet, featureless hall.

"I thought there were only five levels?" Damien asked, the first words spoken since they left the dining hall. Unsure of why he hadn't noticed it before, the *flop, flop, flop* of Satolin's alien sandals was very loud.

Satolin answered over his shoulder, "We are ever expanding, Damien, and while the Core is near the heart of the island, it's very far from the rest of the finished facility." *Flop, flop, flop.*

"Oh."

Flop.

Indeed, at the top of the stairs was a dim hallway that ended in a metal siding wall. It looked like a dead end, but as they came closer, Damien saw that the right wall was open. Stopping briefly, he found himself at the end of the facility, staring up a hewn rock passage that curved gently up and to the right, lit only by the occasional light strip stuck to the ceiling. The passage went so far that he couldn't see the end before it vanished around the bend in the distance. The air in here felt clogged and cold, like some phlegmy nasal passage.

They fell into silence as they hiked up the tunnel. Water trickled down from the walls in more than one place, and Damien had to guess that they were near the outer circumference of the island. He strained his ears, imagining the ocean waves crashing just beyond these walls, but the only sounds were of their footsteps, and the trickling *drip, drip* of water.

Flop, flop, drip, flop, drip.

Actually, he thought, *the ocean really* could *be just beyond this wall.* He wasn't sure if that made him feel safe or claustrophobic.

A ways up the tunnel, Damien spotted a wet metal sign that had been stabbed into the rock next to an offshoot tunnel. It read "Core Control →." Satolin continued up their tunnel. Damien craned to see what was back there as they passed the offshoot, but all he thought he saw was another lighting strip a ways away, and then they were past it.

At last, he spotted what looked like a lone block of prefab hallway in the distance. It looked like someone had sheared a neat corner section of a corridor and dropped it in the tunnel, foregoing any other civilized trappings in the underground. As they approached, he noticed that the ceiling hadn't been covered there and, as a result, the walls were shiny with leaking perspiration. Carelessly left tools and machinery littered the floor, waiting for their owners to come find them.

Satolin passed through the section and made a hard right, finally revealing the end of the hewn tunnel. Perhaps thirty meters away, almost hidden by rock that closed in like it was trying to hide something, an abnormally smooth wall stood out against the dark volcanic rock and dirt. It looked like moonlight in the dark offshoot tunnel, and it took until they were barely four meters away that Damien realized that it was, in fact, a door. A single lighting strip hung above them.

"This," the Prohka rumbled, "is the Core. A very special prototype."

The Over-Seer is hunting you. Over the hot flare of suppressed anger in his gut, Damien felt a trickle of inquisitive excitement. "What is it?" *He wants the man who wields black holes.*

Satolin eyed the smooth silvery door. "This cavern is the reason we chose this island. Many years past, we managed to harness the walls and minerals in here. We found that they produced a certain…acoustic resonance."

"Meaning what?"

The Prohka considered it. "Without setting your expectations too high, but neither doing this place enough justice, we developed a technology that creates controllable illusions within the confines of this room," he pointed at the door. "It's similar to Pip technology, but it gives far greater immersion than any virtual or augmented reality humanity ever managed to produce—and that's a high compliment of *your* skill, first. Simply put, this place is something…*more.*"

Starting at the word, Damien was finally struck, quite oddly, that Daeduras Satolin spoke perfect English, enunciating his 'P-B-M's' as well as Von or Shell ever had. He guessed that he hadn't noticed before because he was so used to hearing Algaroth who *could* speak his native language without an accent, but he didn't think it was worth mentioning at the moment, and he played his startle into what the Prohka had just said—which was no less shocking. "You mean it's…a simulator?"

The Prohka's ganglia flicked to the sides and he grinned. "You're very sharp, aren't you?"

He shrugged. "I like tech, and I like history."

"Admirable hobbies."

Damien eyed the door. "So…what's it gonna be like?"

"I think you'll just have to see for yourself, but the shortest answer is that the Core produces something more *substantial* than your usual holograms."

"And you want me to display my powers in here?"

"Yes, and I wouldn't concern myself with worrying about using too much. The emitters inside can—"

A sudden squawk from Satolin's vest pocket made them both jump. "What the hell?!" Damien popped out.

Frowning, but no less startled himself, Satolin pulled out the remote he'd used to turn off the projection of the Moon earlier in the Biosphere lab. He clicked it. "Yes?"

"*Gon Prohka,*" said a gruff voice, using a double honorific. "*You are outside with the Elemental?*" The words were in Russian.

"We are, Tosh, we were about to come inside. Is everything ready?"

"*I have conflicting answers to that.*"

"How so?"

"*Roman, Kel, and I just finished installing that scrambler the boy brought from Bunting…there was a message on it.*"

Satolin eyed Damien, who was just as confused. A dull thought popped into Damien's head that Tosh most definitely couldn't speak his lip-smacking sounds as well as the Prohka. Even with the Algaroth speaking another language, Damien could hear him failing to get his lips pressed together enough. His aural implant still translated the words neatly, though.

"What did it say?" Satolin asked.

"I will play it for you when you get here, but it concerns the boy's companion he left with the Admiral? I did not know what Bunting was talking about."

"Von," Damien said.

Satolin nodded. "What was the message?"

"Bunting instructed the boy to call as soon as the scrambler was installed. His brother is recovering faster than he was told, and Baroda intends to move him from the Islets tonight."

Damien's stomach dropped. *Move him? Move him where? He said it would be* days*!*

"Tan's army is also closing faster than anticipated. Bunting relays that the city of Tacoma is already lost."

Cold, leeching ice worked its way through Damien's veins, and he felt the color dribble out of his face. Satolin's arctic-gold eyes flared hot in the moist passage, but Damien didn't suspect it was anger meant for him.

"The Admiral shows his support for us once again," the Prohka growled. Damien couldn't suppress a tremor of fear at the sudden, fierce menace in his voice. "And Agent Bunting continues to be a friend."

"He does."

Satolin gripped the remote tightly. "Thank you, Tosh. I will see you shortly."

"Te'Vierda." (*"We are both fulfilled"* in Dekka.)

Satolin slowly replaced the remote in his vest. Damien's heart was pounding. "So what's happening?"

The Prohka's predatory nostrils flared and his eyes scanned the rocks around them. He looked like he was deciding how much to say. "The…good Admiral has clouded his intentions once again," he finally said. "He doesn't like our autonomy, but he needs us and we need him."

That would explain a lot. "What about my brother?"

Satolin breathed in slow through his nose. "You will call, just as Agent Bunting requested. When you are finished, you may do your demonstration—if you still feel so inclined."

"Okay." Damien felt a little apprehensive at what was beyond that door now, but he had a bone to pick with Baroda, and that trumped his nerves, easy.

"You will be able to talk to Tosh from inside, and he can speak back. I will be able to hear you as well, and I assume Dr. Gwen will join us as soon as I inform her of this…development."

"Okay."

"Then it's time, excuse me." Satolin sidled past Damien, and dragged a single finger across the door, causing a…ripple?

What the hell…

Damien frowned in surprise as he realized there was a steady curtain of *water* running down the smooth surface of the door. He couldn't imagine why that was happening, but he realized now that that was why the door gleamed so brightly in the dark.

There was the faintest sensation of a rumbling somewhere in the distance, and a crack appeared in the silvery door. The two halves ground their way open, taking the water curtain with them.

A blackness that even Damien couldn't see through, beckoned from beyond.

"Do not overwhelm yourself inside," Satolin cautioned. "This is a potent tool, and a new one at that. If you need to stop, you need only say so. Tosh can shut the Core down in a moment."

Damien took a shaky breath. "Okay."

"I will be watching," he said with a smile. "Best of luck."

"Thank you," and he entered, leaving the Algaroth standing in the coarse hallway.

Immediately, Damien felt a thick pressure clog his head. It felt similar to being in a soundproofed room, but more intense. The silvery door closed behind with a *thud*, quickly swallowed by the heavy air. The pressure on his ears pushed harder.

He was in total darkness, complete and consuming, such that he rarely experienced. Damien could imagine someone entering this place and being immediately uneasy…but the unfathomable dark in the room wrapped itself around his body, and he felt at home. He felt safe, which he hadn't expected.

Damien turned inwards and coaxed his Elemental pool of power to life. After some rest, sleep, and food, it was as full as he'd felt it in a long time—though it could be fuller. He took a deep breath of Darkness, feeling the power ripple within him. The pool trembled as if a loving breath had been caressed over a lake, and the water had shivered with pleasure.

Damien smiled in the dark, and he let the power creep into his eyes, making the world come alive with negative light. The only word that came to mind to describe what he saw was 'amplifier'.

The chamber was an inverted bowl, like the hangar bay far beneath him, and it too was quite large. The only adornments on the implacably smooth, silvery walls/ceiling—which matched the entry door—were a series of black metal struts, interspersed evenly. Each one had a thin web of leads that coiled and twisted out to random points on the wall, where they had been stuck in like pitons. In the center of the room was a low pedestal, about waist-height, the cap of which reminded him of an upturned sub-woofer with its smooth bowl and nub rounded up from the middle.

Damien took a step towards the pedestal and stopped. Faint buzzing filled the heavy air. His heart began to thud in his chest, and then he noticed the pattern on the floor. He was standing on the outermost edge of a series of concentric rings that centered on the pedestal. Thick, winding strips of teal light had just come to life, their glow trickling back and forth over the rings toward the center. Damien got the distinct impression that if the rings were to spin and move out of alignment, they could be lined up with the crossing strips of teal and find comfortable patterns in more than one circled arrangement.

Damien took another step.

The buzzing intensified as the light reached the pedestal, bringing it to life. As teal veins crept up to the cap, a series of bulbs came to life, each inset evenly along the base of the circular wall. Damien guessed they were similar to the bulbs in the habitat district cavern, but these glowed a deep blue, casting hard shadows on the Core. Suddenly, Damien had a fleeting fit of vertigo, and he felt very small, as if he were standing in the center of an enormous spiked crown of shadows. He tried to control his breathing as he stumbled over his own feet, barely managing to stay up.

"*You are ready to use the Core?*" boomed a growling Russian voice.

The vertigo vanished, and Damien found himself in the center of the Core, looking down at the pedestal. The tiny nub in the center of the cap had levitated up, and the silver glob of liquid now rippled, hovering half a meter in the air. It looked like a large ball of mercury. "Tosh?"

"*Yes.*"

"Where's your voice coming from?"

"*That does not matter. I am operator of the Core control center— don't touch!*"

Damien, transfixed by the glob, stopped his finger a centimeter from the thick silvery substance. He pulled back. "Sorry."

"*Sorry is useless. Don't touch, boy.*"

Damien suppressed the twinge of irritation. *I'm not a boy.* "So Bunting said to call?"

"*He did. I...did not realize you were listening. That makes it easier.*" Tosh fell silent for a moment. "*I...am also supposed to first thank you for acquiring the unimatrix scrambler.*" There was a long pause. "*Thank you.*"

"You're welcome," Damien couldn't help but search the walls and floor for the source of Tosh's voice. "So what do I do?"

"*Do not forget to breathe,*" Tosh said, ignoring him. "*The air is thick in there. If you collapse, you will probably die.*"

"Oh," Damien blinked. "I'll remember."

"*Good. We are ready. Hit the button on the pedestal to begin startup.*"

Damien found the blinking button and pushed it. Without warning, the silver glob exploded outward and Damien hit the deck.

Only...it hadn't exploded, and he sincerely hoped that Tosh couldn't actually *see* what he'd just done. His cheeks flushed with embarrassment anyways as he found his feet. Gazing around, he found that the glob had burst into a billion droplets, so widely dispersed that they filled most of the air above Damien. They had formed a precise wireframe of Earth. A few thousand droplets had collected in a pin of sorts in North America. The pin was very near the Puget Sound, spinning urgently.

"Read me those coordinates."

"Where?"

Tosh huffed. *"On the pedestal!"*

"Okay!" Damien found the coordinates running in a circle around the cap and read them off, "It says…Latitude is 47 degrees, 19 minutes, 1.85 seconds North. Longitude is 121 degrees, 37 minutes, 36.81 seconds West. Do you need the rest of this?" He looked at the second set of coordinates. A line read "Trifectal Time Zone," and the line below it began with "Gs-5, M," followed by a long string. He thought it looked to be stellar coordinates rather than planetary.

"No, ignore that."

Damien waited, still curious.

"You are connected. Touch the flashing blue light."

Of the few lights on the pedestal originally, none were blue anymore; they had all changed color. "Which one?"

Tosh growled and it sounded like a massive thunderclap over Damien's head. *"The* teal *one."*

"Sorry." Damien tapped the glowing teal button. "Now what?"

"Wait."

There was a loud beep and then Damien had the sensation of *rushing.* The weight of the air lifted off of him, and the buzzing of the pedestal vanished. He gasped and blinked, only to end up shielding his eyes as the metal struts along the wall lit with blinding light. He barely had time to spot the leads on the wall come to life with a trickle of glowing energy before the light blotted everything out. A dissonant symphony filled his ears, but he couldn't tell if it was real. He cried out but couldn't hear himself. The light got brighter, and he had a fleeting thought that he had just died.

But then it stopped. The light was gone and so was the sound, and Damien found himself looking out an outward-bowed viewport. He blinked, trying to make sense of it. Wherever he was, it was high in the air, and it was late at night.

"Damien?" said a familiar voice behind him.

Damien spun to find Lunar Admiral Antonio Baroda standing alone in his black-and-silver uniform, pressed and crisp in the cold light of some sort of viewing room. The space was sterile save for the two plush, crimson armchairs that looked perversely comfortable on the hard grey deckplates. The polyglass windows behind Baroda were tinted so dark he couldn't see past them.

"Where are we?" Damien asked. "How did I get here?" Looking at his feet, he answered his own question: He was standing on what looked like a rolling Pip pad. He took a step, *felt* the ground beneath him move, but something dully told him that he felt the stone rings of the Core under his feet, not the metallic deckplates of an aircraft. He took another step, and watched the pad slide along the floor, following his body without *actually* following his body. The sensation made him feel unnervingly queasy.

Damien was not, in fact, *here*. He was seeing a projection of himself, and so in a way, he actually *had* been teleported—a feat no one had ever accomplished—but only in image, not in actual body. *You guys weren't kidding about this Core*, he thought. The whole thing was incredibly disarming.

Baroda took a step, bringing Damien's attention back. The wrinkles in the man's face looked much deeper than they'd been that morning. "The Core," Baroda said, "is one of the many perplexing wonders that Amun-Nūr has produced over the years. Something between a virtual reality chamber and a video call—though they have hinted to me that it can do significantly more."

Damien blinked, still trying to wrap his head around it. "Where are we?"

Baroda's eyes crinkled and he gave a faint smile. "You certainly have a knack for follow-through on your questions, don't you my boy?"

Damien stayed still.

"Hmm. Well, we'll be passing Mt. Rainier in a few moments. We're bound for Peak Springs at the base of the Rockies, south of Denver."

I know where Peak Springs is, Damien thought irritably. "You're leaving Seattle," he said, his tone flat. "Early."

"Yes."

"Where's Von?"

Baroda sighed. He looked like he wanted to put a grandfatherly hand on Damien's shoulder. "I'm afraid you can't speak with him right now."

The coals in Damien's stomach gave a flicker of hungry life. His gaze narrowed. "Why."

Baroda raised his chin. "He's resting. The doctors tell me his surgeries went quite well, and I promised I would take him with me when we left Camp Cascade. My understanding is that it isn't best to wake him."

"You lied to me."

Baroda's apologetic face held. "I did no such thing. His injuries were severe, he's lucky to be alive at all, let alone estimated for recovery and transport in two days."

"You lied to me about the army," Damien amended.

No change in the man's face. "If I did lie about that, would it matter? Would you lie to get someone—your brother, for instance—to safety?"

Damien knew his face said everything.

"And so would I," said the Admiral.

Damien turned to try and spot the landscape outside the bowed window. The Cascade forests east of the Puget Sound were dark, and he was on the wrong side of the aircraft to see Mt. Rainier, but he knew where this was. His childhood had existed—and ended—somewhere far below. These were the woods where he had found that damp hollow when he was nine, and had become Elemental. He shook off the memory and gazed upwards. A faint golden glow lit the clouds on the horizon to the north, hinting at civilization, but he wasn't sure if it was Seattle or Vancouver. "You told me I could talk to him."

"I also said his recovery would take time—but that he *would* recover."

Damien rounded on him, "Well, why can't you at least *show* him to me?"

"Because it simply wouldn't be possible."

301

"Why?"

"Because this room is the only one on this trauma ship that could accommodate the receiver for a unimatrix transmission." Baroda's eyes narrowed ever so slightly. "A unimatrix transmission that shouldn't have been possible."

"So why couldn't you bring him *here?!*" Damien ignored the warning in the man's voice. His was rising, but a feeling of helplessness was starting to fill him equally fast.

"*Damien,*" said the Admiral, stern but neutral. "You're lucky that you're here at all. But unfortunately, I have no better news for you. Your brother is safe, and you'll see him soon. For now, you should turn off your transmission, I doubt you'll want to see this."

Damien felt a chill blossom in his spine. "What do you..." but he trailed off as a blink of light caught his attention. At first he thought it was sunrise, but he quickly realized that the blink had come from the northwest. He stepped close to the viewport and squinted towards the source.

He didn't have to search long, because there was another blink, and then another. Damien felt the world slowly fall into silence as he realized what they were.

Detonations.

As he watched, on the northwestern horizon he saw a comet-trail of the most vibrant blue arc into the sky... and fall right in the midst of a surge of flashes that grew larger and more numerous by the second.

The Seattle Islets had fallen.

"No..." he reached to the window but found his hand went right through it. He jerked at the ghostly image, and was confused for a moment. He looked at his feet, dazed. Only, his feet weren't actually there. They were in the Core, half a world away. All he saw was the ghostly impression of his feet, standing a half-meter off the floor on a rolling black Pip pad. He looked back to the horizon, unwilling to believe what he was seeing.

"Tacoma is already gone," Baroda said from behind him. "They made it through while you were flying to the island."

Damien didn't answer; he couldn't. He couldn't see any of the buildings, but he could imagine it: One enormous energy mortar after another, thousands of loyal Algaroth soldiers gunning down any survivors, all in the name of their Collective.

All because of me.

Damien was very aware of his own breathing, of how shaky it sounded. His insides were cold as the silent explosions went higher and higher. "I want to see my brother," he said.

"You will. Soon."

Damien whirled on the Admiral. He marched forward, shouting, "You need to show him to me."

The smile was gone from the Admiral's eyes, but his tone was the same. "I can't do that."

"*I want to see my brother!*" Damien roared, turning to storm towards the man, forgetting he was a projection. "NOW!!" He stomped across the deck, but he never reached the Admiral's head.

Another dissonant symphony filled his ears and Baroda took a fearful step back. He could see anger flashing in his eyes, but that look was the last Damien saw. There was a bright flash, and next he knew he was stomping towards Prohka Daeduras Satolin instead, who was standing in the doorway to the Core. Damien stopped, breathing hard, his fists clenched.

Satolin's ganglia flicked as he looked at Damien with concern. "That call wasn't supposed to return you in such distress. What happened?"

"Baroda," Damien spat. "Admiral Baroda wouldn't let me see my brother."

A dark twitch crossed the alien's midnight-blue features and his shoulders went rigid. "He kept him from you?" Damien felt a pump of static electricity in the air, centered on the Prohka. It was a unique chemical reaction in Algaroth biology that came when they became particularly agitated. It would often center between their shoulder blades, and if it became too intense, an Algaroth would—quite involuntarily— send an eruption of static out from their bodies in a very physical manifestation of an emotional outburst. Damien hadn't felt the starts of one from an alien in a long time.

"He said Von was 'recovering'."

"But he's safe?"

Damien turned away from the tickle of static on his face. His shoulders trembled, and the coals in his stomach had caught fire. "Don't lecture me on that being something I need to be grateful for. What is the hell is *safe* anymore, anyways?"

"I wouldn't lecture," said the Prohka without hesitating. Damien turned. "I would rage at the man as heavily as you…and I have."

Unable to pull out of his fury, Damien ground his teeth. "The Islets are on fire."

The static buzz spiked and the air grew heavier, even with the door open. "I am so sorry."

Damien felt empty. *Did Bar and Shell make it out? Did anyone?* And then the names started coming to his mind. Carson, who ran the radio out of the Space Needle; Tim and Isabelle, the elderly couple who had helped them with food; Zeya, the girl who had lost her twin and traded odds and ends; and a long list of those still alive…and many more already dead.

Then, out of the names and the flood, something popped into Damien's mind that he had completely forgotten. An Algaroth voice roared in his mind. *Elemental!* it cried, and he remembered the alien's bloodied face, and the molten rage in the Avo's eyes as he tried to escape from XenoCon onto the roof with Leo and his brother…and then he remembered *why* that Avo had been staring at him. He had just cut Damien's detonator; the detonator to the continental transceiver, the very same transceiver that they had activated, forcing a connection on ten million people who were still living in the Puget Sound region.

He remembered what would happen if The Collective got a hold of that transceiver…which they had.

Oh fuck.

"Damien?" Satolin asked. He must have repeated himself more than once.

Guilt, despair, and horror overrode Damien's urge to let tears flow. How could he have forgotten something like that?! How could he be that stupid?! It felt like a world of time ago when that had happened, but in reality it had been less than twenty-four hours. Twenty-four hours for the squad of Avos to carefully copy where every single human was in the Puget Sound region. It was a perfect map to kill all of those people who hadn't left already, without damaging any of the precious materials for which The Collective wanted Earth so badly.

"Damien, are you alright?" Satolin repeated, taking a step into the Core.

His voice rasping and weak, Damien told the Prohka what he'd just remembered. When he finished, the Algaroth moved very slowly.

"And...how long would they have needed to access that transceiver?" The alien asked.

Damien shrugged, flapping his arms in defeat. "I...seconds! It was up and active when we left! We..." His strength threatened to give out, but he held standing.

Satolin looked nothing but concerned, for which Damien was grateful. "You are welcome to accompany me while I handle this, perhaps your demonstration should wait?" He took another step to bring Damien out of the room, and Damien barely managed to stay planted as he felt the static charge press down on his skin.

In the same moment, at the thought of walking out, Damien's guilt broke on him, and tears welled into his eyes. Then, he met the Algaroth's arctic-gold gaze as he felt something else vanish as well. A small plug within him lifted away; something that had been holding him in check, but chose that moment to ping into nothing like the pin of a grenade being pulled...and dropped.

"No."

Satolin stopped.

Damien faced the Prohka, feeling an odd calm settle over him, a blanket to smother the broil. "I'll do it now. I want to do it now."

"Are you certain? I will have to confer what you've told me as soon as possible, I must do that first."

"I don't…I don't need to be there. I screwed up enough already. I just," Damien's voice cracked. "I need to let out some steam, so…this seems like a good idea."

"I understand. That said…I do insist that this is your choice, but—"

"Then I've made my decision. What do you want me to do?"

Satolin looked around the Core, examining the black struts on the smooth wall. "Show us what you can do, Elemental. Right here."

"How much?"

"All of it. Everything you have. I'll inform Admiral Baroda of what happened," the alien eyes flickered with the menace Damien had heard earlier.

"What do I use it on?"

The Prohka glanced at the pedestal. "Tell Tosh what sort of scenario you would like, and the Core will create it for you to demonstrate on. I will join him in the control center as soon as I'm through with the Admiral. This place can do far more than just make a long-distance Pip call."

Damien felt a spark of fire in his blood. He'd never been able to use his power openly like this before. "Won't I damage anything?"

"The emitters can be replaced." Satolin pointed at the metal struts, "and the chamber itself is hardened. You needn't worry. But," he hesitated. "Then again, we've never seen an Elemental in full force before. Perhaps you'll destroy the island?" He finished with a toothy, almost challenging grin, which Damien took as almost teasing.

Damien nodded, flexing his arms. They itched. "I won't hold back then."

"Good." Satolin turned to leave.

"Prohka?"

He stopped. "Yes?"

"…Save as many as you can. Please."

"Of course. We have a rare chance here to bring Amun-Nūr from the shadows. We won't waste it."

Damien nodded, but he didn't feel anything.

Daeduras Satolin nodded to him, turned away, and let the door to the Core grind shut.

CHAPTER FIFTEEN

The Dark Element

Damien felt a different sort of thickness in the air as he was plunged into the pitch black of the Core again. This time it felt like…anticipation. He took a deep breath and banished the afterimages of the blinking detonations he'd seen.

"What would you like first?" Tosh asked promptly.

Damien thought about it, going through his short list of powers. "Orbs and Waves first," he whispered, more to himself.

"What?"

"Give me some kind of skirmish," he answered, louder. "Fighting a squad of Collective soldiers or something."

"So you say," Tosh said, sounding skeptical. *"One moment."*

Damien took a slow, deep breath, preparing himself. The world slowed, he brought his pulse under control, and dove inside himself to where the power rested. He submerged himself in it. When he resurfaced, he felt dizzy for retrieving so much, and he felt his temples twitching. *That's new.* He blinked as he remembered the smoke as it rose out of the bunker, but he shook it off, only to have it replaced by memories of rain piddling into a storm drain as Avos slaughtered his friends. *Hiss-thump.*

Not now. And by sheer force of will, he shrugged the memories off.

He opened his eyes at the sound of the same buzzing as before. Black smoke rose thickly off his body, curling away, and vanishing. The silver droplets of mercury had coalesced back into a glob and were pulsing to some invisible beat. This time, though, there was no white flash to take Damien to another place. Instead, the walls of the Core started changing almost imperceptibly. It started at the pedestal, at the silver glob, and then spread outwards into the air, filling the Core with something…*substantial*, just like Satolin had said.

Damien stood there as the strange cloud of pseudo-reality filled the chamber, and he tried to make sense of what he was seeing. Shapes formed, cloudy and incoherent at first, but slowly they resolved into familiar things: a building, a street, a man. And then there was sound, too. It filled Damien's heightened senses just before the smell of battle assaulted him. For a brief moment, he heard rain again, but he knew that was just a memory. The illusion was real. He heard the sounds of battle, and smelled the rank stench of war.

Next he knew, the transformation was complete and he was standing in the middle of a firefight. The sounds of Gyro and Plaster shots could be heard everywhere. People were screaming; something was burning. He looked up and could swear he saw a familiar tower on fire in the distance, but no, that couldn't be right. Damien blinked and shook away the image. The Space Needle turned into just a tall, featureless skyscraper. *What's the matter with you?* He thought, confused.

A plasma bolt shot past his head, and his fighting instincts kicked in. He dropped. The power coursing through his veins growled in defiance of who dared to assault him, and Damien Vilan stood. His lip was twitching, and all worries about bad memories faded. All he wanted to do was obliterate the shooter. He wanted to kill it.

Another shot flew past, but Damien didn't flinch this time. He spotted the assailant: An Algaroth foot soldier in diamond-white armor, lobbing shots into a storefront window where the screams of people could be heard.

"HEY!" Damien shouted.

The soldier paid him no notice.

"I'm talking to you!" he roared.

Another shot flew past his head, but this time he was ready. He called a surge of Darkness through his heart, and it sped down his wrist to his palms, where the black hole of an Orb ripped into existence, hovering a few centimeters from his skin. He felt no warmth from it, but now as much as ever Damien could *feel* the Orb. He could feel the one emotion that spat and curled from the violently twitching ball.

Hunger.

Careful not to gaze at the singularity, he found the shooter again. The alien still hadn't noticed him. Without a call, without a warning, Damien launched the Orb with everything he had and it whipped through the air towards its target.

"HA!" Crying out in satisfaction, Damien watched it impact the alien's shoulder. The shooter howled and keeled backwards, the consuming power ripping through armor, flesh, and bone, warping and tearing it asunder, fazing all, throwing flecks of oily blood everywhere.

The Orb stopped the first alien, and Damien took a step back. Apparently killing one of them had made the others see him. Or had they manifested? He wasn't sure, but suddenly there were six Collective soldiers all roaring a challenge. He took another step and bumped into something. He spun around, and his rage stopped.

Silas Von stood over him, holding his special Plaster Rifle up and grinning. "What're you waiting for?" his brother asked. "It's just a gun."

"Vo…" Damien breathed. *You're not here. I know you're not here.*

The alien visage rippled, and it wasn't his brother. He was seeing things. The Gyro rifle was aimed at his head, not in the air, and the angry golden eyes were full of hatred. "Die," the creature growled.

Damien felt the rage take over again, and he plowed another Orb into his foe. The shot from the rifle slung past his shoulder, and he turned to see where it went. He froze again.

The shot had hit Von in the side, where the Avo had *actually* shot him. Von looked at him with terror in his eyes. "Damien…" he whimpered, and then he collapsed. Von's blood spread onto the street.

Damien blinked, trying to make sense of it. How could his brother be here? He shouldn't be here! *What the hell's going on?* His brother wasn't here. Damien was alone. He had no one to care for him, and no one to look after. His home was burning, it was his fault, and worse: he'd left a giant fucking map on for the enemy to find and use against him. He wanted to fall to his knees, but another roar brought him snapping back.

Hiss-thump. Hiss-thump.

He knew that sound.

He whirled to see an Avo leaping at him and suddenly he was in the XenoCon building again, the Prism-cloaked, invisible alien flying at his throat, Von shooting it to save him. Damien turned from the alien-that-wasn't-Von and barely avoided the curved *avosas* blade.

Hiss-thump. The Algaroth landed, spun, snarled, leapt again, only now the alien's face had changed, and it was the Avo he had seen before they fled; the one he'd hurt so badly. "*Elemental!!*" the mutilated commando bellowed.

With a cry, Damien thrust a Wave at it. The tsunami of power enveloped the alien's head and ripped through the body, spraying flesh and armor everywhere. The body fell in pieces around him and he felt a splatter of hot blood on his face.

"*What scenario would you like next?*" Tosh's voice pulled him back to reality. The gruff voice sounded a little breathless, and Damien could swear he heard excited chattering beyond the operator. Was Satolin already in there? Was the doctor? Was Von?

Von's not here, you idiot!

Damien didn't have time to think; he had to keep going. He wiped his face and found the oily blood mingled with tears and grime. He ignored them. "A prisoner. Give me a prisoner."

There was a pause. "*As you command.*"

The street vanished. So did the smell, the sounds, and the fires. Damien looked to where he'd seen the Space Needle moments ago. It wasn't there. *See? You're just seeing shit. Pull yourself together.* Then Admiral Baroda's voice broke through again. *They're burning because of you.*

Stop it! You're going crazy!

The scene changed, and Damien was in endless blackness again, save for a single lighting rod on a string, hanging over a chair with straps on it. In the chair was a man. The man's face was purple and black, his eyes swollen shut; cuts and bruises were all over him…and a thousand tiny cuts ran down his bare arms. A steady drip of blood fell from the man's fingertips. He was very still.

Damien shook at the sight of the man's arms, wincing. Something felt wrong about this. His own arms itched. "Give me an Algaroth prisoner," he commanded.

There was no response, but the man became an Algaroth, similarly bruised, but the lacerated arms were no more, and the twinge in Damien's skin went away.

"Do you have a name for this power?" Tosh asked.

"A Shroud," said Damien, shrugging away the thought, staring at the prisoner.

"Please," the Algaroth croaked. "They're going to kill me…"

Damien hesitated. *This is almost too real.* "Who," he asked, "who's going to kill you?"

The pitiful blue alien flinched, and the movement squeezed out a bloody tear. It trickled down its snout and onto the floor. "Monsters."

Damien felt chills run through his body amidst the anger, and he felt his stomach turn. Then he grabbed the alien's head, and let his power flood its brain.

A moment later, the Algaroth quit moving, and he backed away. "I'm sorry," he whispered. "I had to."

We had to, said a woman's voice, and he spun around, but no one was there. Then, off in the dark, he saw three people, huddled under ratty blankets, hiding from a phantom behind their pitiful fire. *"We were pushed out here,"* the girl—Delilah—had said. *"There's nowhere safe to go."*

"I'm sorry," he whispered.

He had abandoned them. He'd left them all, and he was the reason they were dying. His friends, his family, his brother…

Damien's temples twitched again, as if someone was tugging at his memories.

I'm alone.

The Over-Seer is hunting you.

"I'm sorry…I'm so sorry…" he whispered over and over to the dead alien in the chair behind him. He dimly registered that his hands were now covered in blood as well as his face. "Next!" he shouted. His voice cracked.

"*What would you like?*" answered Tosh.

There were only two other powers that Damien had ever named, and only one of them that he was any good at. "Give me a room, full of people. Full of light."

"*Violent?*"

"I don't care."

"*Very well.*"

The chair vanished and a vast scene swept through the Core. It was a party. A summer party, with old Dynasty lanterns hung on strings in the yard outside. The spring air was rich, the light was warm, and there was laughter and gaiety everywhere. The grass was moist, and food and drink were laid out on a picnic table. People were mingling all around, eating, talking, drinking, flirting, loving. Music drifted in from the yard outside, but…Damien was standing among them as a rock in a river. Everything moved to avoid him. No one spoke to him. He was still alone. In a crowd of people he stood isolated.

He wasn't sure why Tosh thought something like this was a good idea for him to test his destructive powers on, but it wasn't real. Right?

Damien reached inward, focusing on one of his most powerful abilities: The power to send daytime to its knees, and make it submit to his will.

Damien flooded his body, ready to unleash the power of Night.

He'd never drained himself as completely as he did just then, and just as he felt as if he were going to burst from the screaming energy inside him, he felt a spear go through his brain. He cried out in pain as a headache split his temples in half, and he lost control of the power swirling through the blood in his limbs. Damien fell to his knees, thought he heard a booming Russian voice ask if he were alright…and then he heard a scream.

"*DAMIEN!!*"

It was a woman.

Past the point of no return, Damien let his powers out, and the party turned to chaos. Black sand appeared everywhere and began to swirl, skittering and sliding over everything. In seconds, the sand thickened, and turned into inky splotches floating through the air. The wind picked up, and it began to spin.

"Damien, where are you?!" she screamed again. Flickering memories appeared through the pain in his head, and Damien tried to keep his eyes open. He knew that voice…but he couldn't remember from where. He spun, looking for the source. Everyone was laughing, which shouldn't have been happening while his power was fingering its way through the air. Something was wrong.

The scene scared him. On the one hand, people were laughing, dancing, running. On the other, they were screaming, fleeing his power, running. Damien looked around, his heart rocketing against his chest. There was a dance floor, and a rattling bass shook the table. People were moving around. It was chaos.

This isn't right, he thought. His temples were tugging, pounding, and his head was splitting agony.

"Damien, help!" she screamed, and this time it registered somewhere in the back of his mind, but he still couldn't quite grasp who it was.

Just then, another scream split the party, and Damien watched a man trip over an older woman. She fell hard and didn't get up. The man kept going, and…Damien *remembered* him. It was someone he knew from his childhood. Someone who his parents had…known…

Then he felt something else. It was that same bass-heavy beat of the music, but it was deeper, more primal, bigger. A glass broke, and he looked at the table, only…it wasn't covered with food and party favors anymore. It was covered in crates of emergency rations, medical supplies, and bandages.

"DAMIEN, HELP US!!"

The voice connected. He remembered. He remembered where he was, what was happening, and who was screaming. He remembered this night as if it were yesterday…or as though it were happening now. Somewhere in the back of his mind, Damien knew this couldn't be happening, because the Core couldn't possibly be showing him his memories, but he also knew nothing about this place, so maybe he was hallucinating? Or maybe he wasn't. It didn't matter. He knew her voice.

The woman screaming was his mother.

There were people moaning all around now, but not in pleasure or happiness. They were moaning in fear. Damien knew this place, but he'd forgotten. He didn't know how, or why, but all in a flash, he remembered a million nightmares made real from this night, seven years ago. He didn't know if he was in the Core anymore, or if what he was seeing was really happening, but he knew it felt every bit as real now as it did the day it happened.

The earthquake.

"DAMIEN, GET OUT OF HERE!!" his mom cried, her voice snapping into focus at last. Lucy Vilan screamed for her son.

Mom. Damien shoved someone out of the way. This was how it had happened.

The shelter was shaking and dust fluttered from the ceiling; the party was gone. Damien ran with that panicked, horrified sprint that only true fear could muster. He narrowly avoided a support beam as it fell through a wall and crushed a young couple kissing on a bench. *That wasn't here. That was at...the party?* He kept going.

He was wrong, the party was still happening in an inverse to the quake, but Damien barely noticed it anymore. He was running through the halls of the repurposed emergency shelter, searching for his mother.

"MOM!!" he cried out. "MOM, WHERE ARE YOU?!"

"Over here!" called Ewan Vilan. "Damien, we're over here!!"

"Dad!"

Damien spun the corner and stared at the impassable crack in the ground. He remembered it now. The building was shaking itself to pieces. He knew this crack better than all the rest that he'd ever had to jump over on his cycle.

"*DAMIEN*," his dad yelled. "What the hell are you doing?!"

Damien stared. They were on the far side...cradling Kaylee Lavon's body.

Kaylee. His first love. He'd lost the amethyst coin she'd given him when they fled XenoCon. She'd already been dead when he got to the crack the last time; her spine cleaved by a falling door.

"You have to get out of here! Get your brother and go!"

"NO!" he screamed, tears streaming down his face. He knew what came next. "I WON'T LEAVE YOU!"

"YOU HAVE TO!"

"NO!" People were running past him, avoiding the falling rubble as the earth ruptured. He heard someone else call his name from behind.

"*Damien!!*" It was Von.

There was a way to save them. He knew there was. He had just never thought he would resort to this. Damien had never showed his parents his power before. He had hid it from them since he was nine. Only Von knew what he was. These people didn't; his parents didn't. Kaylee hadn't.

I can save them, he thought. But then the quaking ground pitched him to his knees, and his mother screamed again.

"*DAMIEN!!*"

The crack in the building was growing by the second; walls and people were falling into it. It was like the gaping maw, a titan of myth, a roaring and hungry monster of the earth.

"Hold on! I'm bringing you over!" Damien pulled out thick curls of Darkness. He molded them together, trying to make them into something solid. He was going to bring his parents to him, or stop the earthquake, *something!*

"Damien, what are you doing?!" His father looked confused, fearful, as he saw the glow of Damien's arms and the black smoke erupting from them.

"I can save you!" he cried.

"Damien!" It was Von. It was his brother, right behind him.

"Vo!" His mother called. "Vo! You have to get out of here! Take your brother and GO!"

They were talking to me, not Von, Damien thought, remembering. He was confused. The building rattled again. *I can still save them.*

Strong blue hands gripped his chest, but it was too late. Damien had unleashed something, something dark, and violent, and above all: *powerful*. Lances of inky black sand flew through the air and, for a second—only a second—Damien thought he had done the right thing. He could help them. But then the Earth itself thundered a deafening roar, and the building ruptured.

"DAMIEN!!" his mother screamed. His parents' eyes were beads of terror as they cradled Kaylee's broken body. Von was dragging him away while he clawed and cried and screamed.

But then everything stopped. Lucy and Ewan hung in the air over a cloud of darkness. The crack had widened, but Damien's power was going to reach them first. They looked at him, confused, terrified, clutching at each other now as their sons pulled away.

And then they were gone; swallowed whole.

"NO!!!" he howled, a primal scream that reverberated in his soul as it was rent apart. His Night had eaten them, and the building began to fall at that moment like it had been waiting to see Ewan and Lucy Vilan die.

He had killed them. He had killed his parents, and now he remembered it.

The guilt erupted again with the same ferocity of the day it had happened. The power of Night swirled about him, and the voice of some strange person in the distance filled his ears as Damien fought the urge to vomit.

"*Amazing...*" growled Tosh. "*Do you have another?*"

Damien didn't answer. He had killed his parents. Seven years ago, on the day the earthquake had shattered Seattle. His home. It had broken his home, and now it was gone. It was burning and on fire because The Collective had—

Damien stopped.

The Collective.

No, he thought, *not* just *The Collective; the Over-Seer.*

Damien opened his eyes. The odd screams of the partygoers filled his head again. The party was back; he had replayed the memory in his mind. The people were terrified by his power, but not rent by it. His parents had been. His family had been. *He* had been. Darkness had ruined his family, but whose fault was it that any of that had happened? Who was responsible for the scenario that caused his parents to die in the first place?

The Collective, of course, but it was more than that. It was their lord-commander, the one who had been ripping millions of families to pieces since he arrived.

Croll Tan.

The name reverberated in Damien's skull. As the blood, sweat, and tears coursed out of him, he remembered his fifth power. It was his final ability that he had used only partially on the bridge because he was so afraid of destroying himself with it: his Cloak.

"Do you have another power?" Tosh repeated, sounding a little uncertain now in his gruffness.

Damien rose to his feet. Only sweat covered him, there was no blood. "Yes. I have one more."

"Scenario?"

Damien curled his lip while he watched the people cowering under the tables. His inky blotches swirled through the air and plunged them into black shadows. He knew where to go. He knew where to use his power. "Show me Solaroth," he said, solemn.

He could almost hear the shock in Tosh's pause. The excited voices behind the alien voice died into nothing, and Damien was left with only the sound of his own power and his own pain. When Tosh didn't respond he repeated himself.

"Yes, sir," Tosh answered with a tiny note of awe.

The party vanished, and with it, the shelter in Damien's thoughts. His parent's screams were still echoing, and he could still feel the ghost of Von's hands on him, but that was all. He was in darkness for only a brief period, during which he felt inside again, seeking the edges of the pool. It was nearly empty, but he didn't care. He was decided. When light filled the Core again, Damien was ready for it.

It was high noon, and a storm was brewing over the westernmost tip of Eurasia. The clouds in the sky broiled and moved as if in a time-lapse, speeding through the air above and making the sunlight twinkle as it was blocked and released and blocked again. He followed the rays to the ground ahead of him, and laid eyes for the first time on the heart of evil.

Solaroth.

The Collective's city-state had swallowed the peninsula that—a long time ago—had made up the countries of Portugal and Spain. Damien stared from a long ways away at the spires and curling alien buildings that reached into the sky like a cancer, and he knew whose fault it was that he was alone in this world: The Over-Seer's.

Croll Tan needed to die. His palace needed to burn.

But the city was impenetrable. The only way he could approach it was to be invisible, to fade into the edges of people's minds as if he'd never been there. There was only one thing he knew of that could do that: a shadow.

Damien focused inward, ignoring the tears and the pain in his chest from throwing out so much energy at once, and he molded what was left of his power in his hands, draining the pool completely. He had never done that before.

He let Darkness suffuse his limbs, making them practically vibrate with unbridled power. And then Damien focused it as he had once before, on that day shortly after the real earthquake, when he had tried to send his body through the fissure between reality and perception, and force his body to literally fall apart, making him one with the shadows. It was something he hadn't even been willing to consider on the bridge with those people.

Damien saw the fissure in his mind, a splitting tear of blackness in defiance of reality. The fissure was tight, but Damien knew he could force his way through if he needed. He let the image of him cutting off the Over-Seer's head fill him with power, with hunger, just like his Orb. He let the loneliness of not having his brother nearby empty him out. He let the guilt of handing the people of the Islets to The Collective fill him up and give him new purpose, and he let the guilt of murdering his parents hone his focus into an arrowhead. He would obliterate the line between his body and the shadows if he had to, if that's what it took.

"*Damien, what are you doing?*" Daeduras Satolin's voice boomed through the Core. "*Are you alright?*"

"F-f-fine!" Damien called through clenched teeth. Speaking took effort. He felt like his limbs were going to fly apart, but he had to focus. Croll Tan had to die.

"*You are not. You need to be careful in there.*"

Damien didn't answer. The power was consuming him. He could feel it. That wasn't right. It wasn't supposed to do that; he was supposed to dominate *it*. How could this be happening?

No! He was losing control. The fissure was right there. He could taste it, he could *see* it, but it was so far away; he didn't understand what was happening.

"*Damien, stop!*"

Satolin's command was too far to reach him. It was too late. He had to let go. He could feel the power sliding through his veins, invigorating them like never before, the pain replaced with pure energy. The thought sent a splash of icy fear that pulled him from his fugue. He blinked and looked around again.

"*Tosh, stop the Core! Now!*"

The scene of Solaroth was gone. His powers were converging in the Core, swirling in chaos that he never knew he could create. A mess of blackness swirled angrily through everything; inky, consuming blackness, skittering black sand, billowing black smoke, screaming black holes. He couldn't control it. And the brilliant fire in his cells told Damien one thing:

He was dying.

Satolin was trying to get his attention. He heard Dr. Gwen as well and someone else. He couldn't hear them.

You have to let go! Cut the connection! His voice was the only one of reason now. It was the only voice left. He clamored for it, reaching for a pillar of sanity. *Do it!*

He did.

With a mental cry that shattered all feeling, Damien cut the connection to the hemorrhaging dry pool and felt the link to his vortex sever. There was so much power in it already though that it couldn't just dissipate. It had to explode.

Shrieking, Damien's Elemental hurricane leapt for the walls and ate itself in its effort to escape. The emitters for the Core flashed and popped one by one, like fireworks.

Damien collapsed. The last thing he heard was his mother scream his name while he replayed seeing Seattle fall, and in the dark sky above, he pictured alien warships descending on the world.

CHAPTER SIXTEEN

Hollow

Damien's footsteps echoed through the tree trunks. He was in the woods. Mulch and dead things crunched beneath him. He knew these woods. These were the Cascades. His safe place growing up, the place to which he could escape, away from home. He walked among the branches, wondering at the bright evergreens and their kin, so lush and strong on the wet earth.

The trees were tall here, and their coiling roots spilled over the ground as iron tendrils, immovable. He passed between the trunks, alone, knowing where he was going from a thousand times before. The stones and gnarled wood he crept across were all familiar. The ground was covered in dying wet leaves.

The woods thickened, and still he pressed on through the mist. He felt plain. No cold could touch him nor could warmth reach his heart. He ducked beneath a bush. The fallen leaves were wet and rotting, and he took a wrong step. Damien fell silently, sliding down an embankment and out of sight. Without a thought, he stood, the mulch falling from his pants.

He was in the riverbed. The trees loomed like over-bearing sentinels, warding him away from the path. The sunlight filtered through the lowest branches, thin, and weak. It was so isolated and quiet, save for the rustling of falling flora in the clouded breeze.

Damien's instinct dragged him forward. He continued through the ravine, knowing exactly where to put his feet to keep from rolling an ankle. How did he know that? There was no running water here, only layers upon layers of decayed seasons. Ahead lay a wall of brush, highlighted by an ancient, decaying tower of fallen wood. Dirt and wetness dripped from the tree's corpse, blocking the way. Ahead, the gap was

321

muddled. Bushes with prickly branches had sprung up after the tree fell, and moss clung to everything. He pushed on. The hidden, brambly archway was visible only up close. Damien moved through it in the heavy quiet, his passing soft in the moist air. Damien stopped beyond the wall.

He was inside the hollow.

This wasn't right. It wasn't a sunny day at all; it was humid, and cloudy, infinitely cloudy. The sunlight was replaced with grey. The bright brown and green towers were shrouded in fog. Damien found himself staring at a boy.

Better.

The boy was curled in a ball in the center of the hollow. His clothes were dirty, his whimpers filling the still space. Damien reached out to turn the boy over. The face turned up to him in the foggy air and Damien fell back, unable to break the silence with a scream.

Damien gazed in on his memory of the day he became an Elemental. He was the boy. Angry purple tracks ran up the boy's arms and neck. He looked at his nine year-old self, watching in horror as the sickness invaded his body. It filled the young mind with shadowy things and glistening power. Dark liquid dripped into the cavern of the boy's soul, forming a pool as still and silent as death, and unknowable beyond concept. Damien's hands shook as he pulled away from the writhing thing in front of him. All was still in the hollow save for the whimpers.

"Please…" the boy whispered to the air. "Make it stop."

Damien looked at his adult arms. They were bare for the first time in years, and smooth. He watched the sickness enter his own veins again, and the purple tendrils of energy glowed their way up to his chest, filling his heart with Darkness. The crawl was slow and painful. It remade him as the hours slipped by, and he and the boy huddled there together, hidden from the world by the cavern of brush that surrounded them. Damien opened his eyes. The boy was gone. He was the one on the wet forest floor. He felt sick and weak. The tracks on his arms had faded beneath his skin, lacing his body with veins of the darkest illness.

He rolled onto his stomach with wincing coils. No sound left his body in the stillness. A whisper swept over the entrance to the hollow behind him, but he was still alone. Damien grasped a handful of mulch, squeezing it into a pulp. When he opened his hand, there was nothing there. He frowned at it. There was no trace of the dirty leaves on his fingers. His palm was smooth. It was almost as if he had…fazed it out of existence.

A rippling tremor stirred something inside him. There was something else in his veins. A feeling of smoothness coursed through him. It felt bonded into his flesh, like lovers wrapped in the most intimate embrace. He was naked from within, the dark liquid caressing his bones, his heart, and his mind.

With a trembling breath, Damien submitted to the virgin pool, and he let the liquid submerge him inside. The smoothness slid down his arms, so soft. He blinked. Black smoke with a violet corona had started to rise from the back of his hand. The liquid wrapped its loving fingers into his own, grasping his digits. His chest constricted, and then relaxed.

He wanted nothing more than to keel over, content in the perfect embrace of the power. It wrapped legs around his, laid arms to his chest, inched lips to his neck, and hips slid to match his own. Even his scalp prickled with the power's tender touch, sliding its way into his thoughts. He closed his eyes, but after a moment, his lover whispered sweetly for him to open them. He did.

The world glowed as it took his eyes. Things that before were shadows now glowed in the negative, and the little light that still crept around him and his invisible partner faded back into the fog. Everything was in perfect focus. With his world turned upside down, Damien made sense of it all. Light came not from the sun above, but from the shadows below. He understood.

In all things, of all time, there was only one thing to have existed before it all. There was only one thing that could reclaim the beating hearts that brought light into people's lives and brought others into the world, only one thing that could reclaim the light those things brought into space, and into the universe. There was only one thing that was master of all things before which anything had existed to be master.

Darkness.

Damien was the first being to ever wield it. He felt a flagellation of guilt at such an omnipotent thought, and then it vanished. His lover— wrapped around his body and coursing over even his tongue—came alive at his connection. It lit up the man in the hollow, echoing the boy, sparkling and crackling with swirling shadows. Light had no place here. The fog came rushing in through the brush, and the glow of daylight became a distant memory above. The wind had started howling outside the hollow, but still Damien lay there.

He felt his whole body vibrate with the ecstasy of Darkness as he let it consume him. He was rigid, and a single gasp fell from his lips as every cell in his body popped, so swept up were they in the tide. He clenched his fists, the change to his senses so acute that he could *hear* his skin rubbing together.

On opening his eyes again, Damien saw the hollow like never before. The fog shrouded everything, and that let him make it out even better. The walls of bush and tree made the entrance impassable, and the crosshatch of branches above let only the most stubborn beam of light reach the floor. Or so it had been. The only remaining glow of sunlight was a thin trickle through the canopy. It was a piercing glow in Damien's sensitive eyes, and he focused his gaze upon it, wanting to snuff it out.

With the force of the world, his lover leapt from his veins and swirled around the beam of light. Black sand and smoke stemming from a violet corona erupted into the fog, and Damien was swept up in the hurricane. He felt the tiny grains of Darkness brush his face, letting him know that the pool was right there, and it would keep the light at bay as long as he desired. It would do anything to protect him.

Finally, his gaze fell from the spot where the light had been, and the pool receded into his veins. He sighed as it entered his body once more. The beam of light did not return.

It was only then that he noticed how much his hand was smoking, still. He examined it closely, wondering why it felt odd, but saw only the dark smoke drifting up from his skin. Then, Darkness whispered to him again, and he knew what to do. Damien let go of conscious focus, and he merely directed the flow of smoothness into his arms. It was hot and stinging. He began to tremble. Maybe he had let too much go? He couldn't be sure. The trembling worsened.

He grasped the mulch again, but now the ground beneath him was responding to the flow. Dead leaves and dirt and droplets of water rose slowly. He blinked, still perceiving the world inverted. The detritus that came too close to his hand began weaving and warping. He watched, still stunned as the leaves and dirt spun about, twisting and turning and eventually, breaking. The things in the air around his arm vanished altogether or split apart into so much black dust. The dust swirled about, and Damien felt something beginning to build inside his palm. He was still on his knees, hands bracing him off the ground. With more effort than it should have taken, he fell onto his haunches and focused on where the pressure was building.

The air just above his palms started to ripple. The mulch in the air delicately converged on the spot, and the smoke rising from his fingers thickened. He brought his hands close together in wonder, and the distortions merged into a single haze. Damien spared a glance for the hollow. The fog was so thick that the walls of his secret place had faded. All was dark, and therefore visible to him.

He turned back to his hand, just in time: The ripple thickened, coalesced, and the next moment, it had hardened. With a sizzle, the air between his fingers was rent, and out of some fissure in the air came a tiny ball of swirling black. The void was so intense that it hurt to look at it. It was only visible by a deep violet corona that grew as the ball did.

The pressure in his arms continued to build, and so did the tiny ball. It grew fast now, and he pulled his hands apart to accommodate it. Then, all at once, it was too much. Pain lanced through his body, Damien wrenched. He was still unable to make a sound as he heaved forward, ramming the ball into the ground in front of him.

Whoom.

The ball broke apart. The power within speared out in chaos, and the wet ground shuddered beneath him as a blast of the smoke eviscerated the decayed earth. Bits of dirt and leaf were thrown into the air all around and shredded into more black dust. Damien gasped as a blinding pain split both of his arms apart on the impact, and suddenly there was another voice in the hollow, a boy's voice, crying out in the pain that was his.

He opened his eyes and gazed into his own deep-blue gaze, set within a younger face. The boy's eyes were full of fear and...

For a brief moment, Damien was able to focus. The boy's eyes were shot with streaks of violet. It was subtle, but within them was a glow with which he was more than familiar. It betrayed intensity and determination, and it betrayed power. It betrayed the kiss that he would later realize was that of an Elemental. The violet faded and he saw the boy's arms.

They were coated in red.

Blood ran down them from a thousand tiny punctures, which were growing. Tiny traces of blackness dripped to the ground amidst the red as the boy's brow went pale and sweaty. They were both breathing hard as Damien joined the boy back in the decay. He gripped his bleeding arms, aware of the ruddy tracks of light emanating from them. The power shone through the fractured skin with a waxy glow, and the pool returned him to the sickly state. The boy fell back into whimpering delirium on the floor of the hollow, and the fog receded.

The holes in the boy's arms would heal badly when he left that place. He would hide them for all of his childhood, knowing that every time he let the pool of Darkness escape, it shone through the scars; a reminder forever of how his loving power had first kissed him, and then dragged nails across his body during that first coupling. It would be his companion through life, kept a secret until a fateful day in the nearby Seattle Islets, when an earthquake would rend the city to pieces, and he would unleash the black dust again, trying and failing to save the people whom he loved.

∞   ∞   ∞

Alone in the dark, on an unfamiliar bed, in an unfamiliar place, surrounded by unfamiliar people, Damien stared out at nothing, replaying the screams of millions of dead...because of him. His mother screamed his name, the earthquake rent the world, and the tears and the guilt started again. He knew what had happened in the Core now; he understood. The

Elemental sickness that had transformed his body when he was nine had tried to protect him from what he'd done to his family, and when he emptied all that he had in his demonstration, it had lost that hold on him. His memory had been forced to lay the truth bare, breaking the glass on the suppressed memories.

Shirtless, Damien gripped the scarred flesh that dominated both of his arms like horrible tattoos. He rubbed the rough skin that would always betray what he was, and he remembered.

MASON J. TORALL

CHAPTER SEVENTEEN

Beneath the Shroud

After Seattle fell, the first day Damien remembered was two weeks later, at the end of January. Exhaustion, delirium, guilt, and the dry reserves of Elemental power in his veins had kept him so wiped out that when he *had* come to in his new quarters, he hadn't known where he was, and it had scared him. He'd scrambled out of a large stiff bed, knocking over a pitcher of water as he did so and leaping into the air, yelping as it splashed over his bare feet. The polyplastic container had bounced away on soft carpet, but the cold goosebumps that had shot up his legs weren't enough to waylay the head rush.

"Hrmm… hmm… *rrrn…*" he'd moaned, breathing hard and reaching out for something to grasp. Failing that, he'd barely managed to direct his fall back onto the bed, where he'd landed on his back with a *whumpf.*

Not thinking clearly, unable to say or do anything other than focus on the drumbeat between his ears, Damien lay there for a long time. He lost track, and supposed that he must have dozed eventually, because the next thing he heard was a door sliding open nearby. He was lying back in bed with the blankets knotted up under him. He shivered.

The door slid shut with a quiet whir, and he could tell someone had entered the room.

"Damien?" A woman's voice whispered.

Unwillingly, his eyes fluttered open.

Gazing at the ceiling, Damien's first thought was that he was on a bed in a closet. The ceiling was a dull, pasty green, and to the left of his head, a frosted, sliding polyglass partition hid the woman from view. The partition didn't go quiet to the ceiling, but it had been slid to hide everything from his head to just past the edge of his bed, leaving enough room for two people to walk into the cozy "bedroom" standing abreast. Dresser drawers had been sunk deep into the wall to his right, and a night table stood next to his head, where he dimly remembered something about the sound of cold water splashing somewhere. *Was that last night? Or...just now?* He rolled away from the partition, exhaling loudly.

"So you're awake, then. I'm glad to hear it."

Damien faintly registered an Irish accent in the English, and dull words floated up from what felt like a lifetime ago as he'd been carried out of the Core. *He's remarkable*, she'd said. *Indeed he is*, someone else had agreed. *I'd like to tend to him in his rooms, rather than in the medical wing*, she'd said. *I'll leave that choice to you*, he'd answered. Damien thought it must have been the doctor and the Prohka.

The partition opened a hands-breadth wider, and Dr. Gwen Whalen poked her head around the corner. Her striking red hair was held up in a loose bun, and a dim light in the room beyond reflected off of her square eyeglasses, hiding her glittering green eyes. "How are you feeling?"

Damien shoved his face deeper into his pillow in answer, wishing she would go away. The thick black matte of a two week-old beard scratched noisily on the sheets.

"I see. Well, if you're hungry, there's some—wait...what's this?"

He dared crack an eye to see her bend over and snatch up the polyplastic jug. It had rolled to the foot of the bed.

"When did this happen?" she exclaimed. Her shoes were silent on the carpeted floor as she came around the bed.

He scrunched his eye shut again in the minimal light, feeling her gaze on him. *Don't look at my arms*, he pleaded silently. He couldn't hide them under the blankets though without her noticing.

"Were you trying to drink water or were you flailing about?" she asked, setting the jug down on the nightstand.

He held silent for a long time, stubbornly unmoving. She was more stubborn. Eventually he realized she wouldn't go away, so he let his eyes slide open, and his gaze found the handle of the jug. Dr. Gwen's lab coat hung in his peripheral, and he traced the outline of her palm-tablet tucked in her pocket beneath a few spare hot-pens.

She tilted her head into his view, eyeing him intensely.

I killed my parents. "I was flailing," he said flatly.

"Why were you flailing?"

The earthquake broke the city but I managed to kill my parents right after I found my girlfriend dead. "I woke up."

"Were you having nightmares?"

I hear a scream every few seconds, awake or asleep. "No."

"Hmm. You didn't hurt yourself, did you?"

My bones hurt, my chest hurts, my head hurts…my heart hurts. I watched my brother get shot over and over, and I sucked out everything I had just to show it off. I think I almost blew myself up. "No."

"Good," she straightened, "that scarring on your arms must be difficult. Was it from your First Occurrence?"

Shocked, he met her gaze at last. Her kind green eyes brimmed with genuine concern—and a little more knowingness than he would've liked. "How do you know…"

A tiny smile crinkled her brow just a fraction, but it filled her eyes. "You've been in fits for the better part of two weeks. I've tended to you here because I thought it'd be more comfortable for you to wake up in private, and…these are your rooms now, after all." She glanced toward the partition as she spoke. "Medically, I know everything about you; the scars on your arms aren't burns, they look like old punctures that didn't want to heal up nicely, and I tested the skin against some of what I recorded during your demonstration. The few Elemental markers I know to look for are there."

Damien gripped the forearms that sometimes reminded him of tree bark, and quickly yanked his hands away, suddenly very aware of touching the old wounds. "I…I bet I know what 'First Occurrence' is," he whispered. "So…yeah, that's what it's…what it's from." He wondered faintly if she had a recorder playing, or if she took notes on her patients mentally and somehow managed to write them all down later. He'd known people like that before, but he'd never felt smart enough to try it with anything. He liked to write it down or record it, like in his journal, which—to his knowledge—was still sitting inside his torn backpack.

Dr. Gwen sat on the edge of the bed, looking at him as his eyes wandered back to the pasty-green wall. They sat in silence for a long moment as she watched him, and he waited. "It took us hours to even get to you," she finally said. "The power in the air was so intense that we had to leave the Core locked until it dissipated. It looked like it was…protecting you."

He managed to keep very still, but his eyes betrayed that her words caught his attention. He said nothing, though, and she shifted on the bed.

"What did you see in the Core?" she finally asked, quietly.

Unbidden, unexpected, and torrential, the tears came. He closed his eyes and clenched his fists into the pillow, trying to fight off the desperate need to unload his pain, but he couldn't do it. He took horrible, noisy, shaking breaths as a moan climbed its way out of his windpipe and snot dribbled out onto his pillow. When she saw it, Dr. Gwen quickly stood and retrieved a box of tissues. He took them gratefully without a word and blew his nose, but the second he felt an answer rise in his throat again, more tears did instead.

He had no idea how long she sat there with him, but he was grateful, even if a sickly part of him felt quite strongly that he didn't deserve it.

When he had finally dried out and the floor was littered with phlegmy balls of cloth, he scanned her with his salt-stiffened eyes. She was still watching him, the kindness in her face undiminished. "I saw…" he coughed as a croak came out.

"Water," she said, and he saw her eyes glitter again as she snatched up the jug. She left the bedroom and returned with a clean glass and a full jug, which he sipped gratefully.

"Thanks," he said, feeling a little better.

"You're welcome."

It took another long minute for him to pull the words up, but he'd let out enough tears now that when they threatened to conquer him again, he could fight them down. "I saw…scenarios that…that Tosh put together for me."

"Yes?"

The whole city burned because I left it. He shook his head in disgust. "I…I don't know what I saw," he said finally. "But I know what happened."

"What happened?"

"I…I…I killed my parents."

The micro-flash of shock on her features was all he needed to moan and roll away, ready to let the self-loathing take over in a heartbeat.

"No, no," she said, grasping his shoulder lightly but firmly. "You tell me all of it. I have all day."

Something in her tone broke him immediately. He couldn't say what it was, or how her soft voice suddenly made him terrified to make her angry, but it worked. He rolled back towards her, and worked up to telling her. Slowly, but surely, he did. He told what he remembered about the call to Baroda, the demonstration, and the hallucinating memories. He was shaky at first, but the release of just explaining it lifted some of the smothering weight he felt in his chest, and soon his voice was stronger, and the memory came back more clearly. He drained most of the jug of water while he spoke, and when he was done, his bladder tugged urgently.

"Do you need help standing?" she asked as he closed his story with that anecdote.

He didn't feel like he needed it, but as he tried to climb out of bed, he realized he did. His legs were shaky and weak, and his head started spinning the moment he got up. Dr. Gwen kindly brought him around the partition, where he saw his new quarters for the first time.

His rooms were the size of a cozy studio apartment that he might have found in Seattle, and it reminded him almost uncomfortably of the bunker. As they entered, Gwen palmed the light panel, and a few piton lights came to life from dark wooden sconces along the walls. They were the only adornments. Damien took it in briefly.

A couch sat in the middle of the living room with a Pip table in front of it, covered in glass so you could put drinks or food down. A desktop and workbench sat side-by-side along a near wall with a rolling chair very similar to the one Damien had had at home. Just off the sliding front door was an open doorway that looked like it went into the kitchenette, and the door next to that, toward which Dr. Gwen was walking him slowly, must be the bathroom. Another closed doorway opposite the bathroom door beckoned curiously in front of the couch, but in all, the only word Damien could think of for the place was *sterile*. It had the faint odor of spray cleaner and linens that had sat unused for a while without yet smelling musty, and the filtered air was dry and cold. He guessed the place was just one of many exact copies for the inhabitants of the island.

At the bathroom door, Dr. Gwen let him relieve himself, and when he returned, he felt like he had a bit more strength to stand, but it turned out that was only enough to get him back to the partitioned bedroom, which was indeed recessed into the back wall of his quarters, very much like a closet with that sliding partition. At the bed, his legs were seconds from giving out…when the water he had spilled earlier did it for him. He slipped on the new, wet carpet, and went down. Dr. Gwen was by his side in an instant.

"Are you alright? Here." She bent over to help him.

"No, I'm fine!" He shrugged her off and managed to pull his aching body back into the bed, feeling small and angry. He propped his back against the wall and wrung the covers between his legs, noting how pale his skin was below his boxers. His lip twitched in disgust at the sight, and he rasped his fingers over his matted beard, trying to hide his face.

Dr. Gwen straightened and shook her head. "You're really not, and you don't have a thing to be ashamed of."

"What do *you* know about it?" he snapped, suddenly vindictive. "You're not like me! Who the hell have *you* lost, all cozied up on this island, huh?!" The strength of his fury overwhelmed him for a moment, but he let it. After all, hadn't Admiral Baroda said that this island was a sanctuary for *Elementals*? He huffed angrily. *So where the hell are they?!*

As that question surfaced, he upset himself further with the realization that he had been so caught up in the sheer *newness* of the island of Amun-Nūr… that he hadn't thought to ask *anyone* yet if there were more like him in this place. His own preoccupations of the past two weeks staggered him now, and his lip twitched again, all in the span of a second.

A shadow of irritation crossed her features at his snapping, but it was quickly replaced as her face went neutral. "I know plenty, Mr. Vilan. You don't know my story, don't presume on it." And—as if she had read his silent and furious query—she held out her hand.

At first, Damien thought she was reaching for him, so he rolled his eyes and looked away, but a second later, he felt an odd, tingling sensation on his skin. It felt like goosebumps but more intense, like some static field, lapping its way over him in waves. He looked back at the doctor with a resolute frown on his face, but it faltered quickly.

From the floor next to his bed, glistening droplets of water were floating into view. Only a few tiny ones at first, then more, and then it was a stream. Damien's frown turned slack-jawed, as Dr. Gwen nonchalantly collected a twinkling swirl of water over her palm, right about where Damien himself would usually see an Orb form over his. The droplets came together into one undulating band, clear and precious. He was transfixed as she turned her hand and the water obediently coasted through the air, right into the jug he'd knocked over earlier. Dr. Gwen relaxed her palm, and the tingling sensation ceased as the water went *blop* into the bottom of the jug.

She was an Elemental.

He had nothing to say; his furious thoughts had flat-lined.

She met his gaze calmly. Her green eyes sparkled behind her glasses, and her pale, freckled cheeks shone bright. "You aren't the first Elemental to show up here, and loss seems to come with this territory we share. You have every right to be hurting and upset, but you don't have the right to lash out."

Mollified, Damien returned his gaze to his pale legs and itched his face again, unsure of what to think. So he turned back to the only thing he could right now. *You didn't kill your family.*

She must have seen some twitch on his face, because she sat on the bed again near his feet, forcing his gaze up again. "I know just fine how dangerous someone like you or me can be. You go ahead and talk to anyone who lives with us, and they'll tell you. The way *I* try to help, Mr.

Vilan, is to understand what exactly *we* are." She leaned in, lowering her voice. "It's why I'm sitting right here with you."

Her hand on his calf was a confusing touch—calloused fingers with soft palms—but it was warm, and comforting. He continued to sit in silence, the only thing that moved were his eyes.

"I've never seen the Core do what it did to you or anyone else," she went on. "Nor have I heard of an Elemental's powers suppressing their memories, and that makes you a specialty-type individual. I want to see you better, and so do the people on whom you've already made an impression."

He furrowed his brow at her in answer, confused.

She smiled. "Sato, Captain Roman, Mr. Estrada, Tosh, even myself. You have a certain presence to you that I'm thinking you don't know you have yet." A tiny giggle escaped her. "*Yet.*"

Damien found the giggle oddly irritating. Here was this scientist—a Water Elemental, no less—at the bottom of the ocean in an apartment with a grown man who had basically just come out of a small coma, and she *giggled. What the hell is that about?* he thought, but he didn't let it show that time.

He realized she had fallen silent and was looking at him. "What?"

"I asked if you'd wanted to know what happened with the transceiver you left on?"

Oh, right...that. Damien felt as if the world was sagging under him as he realized he'd forgotten about it, *again.* In his wailing, lucid moments of the past two weeks, he'd been so caught up in the memory of the earthquake, his parents, and his brother, that it had stayed far out of his mind. Now, his lip quivered as he held the doctor's gaze, waiting for an answer, dreading it.

"There's nothing more you could have done beyond warning them," she finally said, and that said it all.

They're all dead, he thought, closing his eyes. *I knew it. Those Avos must have pinpointed every one of those Intersystem access points after we left and gone on a killing spree.* The thought made him queasy, but his stomach was empty, so it just seized painfully. He had nothing to throw up.

"You saved over fifty-thousand lives, Damien, just by sending out your message. Sato looked into it, and the refugees from Seattle are all talking about how an Elemental saved them because no one else knew the army was coming."

He didn't hear her. *Bar and Shell must not have made it…none of the insurgents…no one. Son of a bitch…Baroda was fucking right when he fucking told me it was my fucking fault.* His breath hacked out in ragged gasps, and the dull thunder of the earthquake roared in the back of his mind, threatening to consume his thoughts again. He rocked back and forth on the bed, gasping for air.

Dr. Gwen's hand on his shoulder didn't stop him, but both of her hands shaking him did. "*Damien!*" she snapped, and the fury in her voice bit so hard that he stopped cold. "Did you hear me?!" Green fire glittered in her eyes, and he thought he felt a single wave of that static, Elemental field again. He cringed.

"Y-you said it was m-m-m-my f-f-fault! Th-they didn't m-m-make it!" Tears of guilt and anger and self-loathing poured out now, and he started rocking again, knowing he was a blubbering mess. He was always going to be a blubbering mess, after this.

"No!" she practically shouted, squeezing him with a surprising grip of steel. He shied away. "Oh gods, stop it!" She shook him again, and he stopped.

It's all my fault. He sniffed.

Color flushed Dr. Gwen's cheeks, and she took a deep breath. "I said, *nothing*, of the sort."

"But…you said that—"

"—I said that you *saved* over three-quarters of the people left in the Islets! The refugees are mostly in Peak Springs now, and they're all talking about the Elemental who warned them to leave!"

He didn't understand. *The army got there the next night! How did they have time to get away!* The words wouldn't leave his mouth though. Apparently, though, she heard them anyway.

"Admiral Baroda ordered a whole flight of evacuation shuttles to run into the city and pick them up, *because of you*."

"Baroda...?" he mumbled. *That doesn't make any sense after the shit he pulled with Von...* Then an uncomfortable thought occurred to him. *Unless...unless he was telling the truth?* Damien's cheeks flushed at the thought that *he'd* been the asshole, not the Admiral. The thought pacified him again. "So...but..." He struggled to find something, *anything*, to be upset about, but something about the way the doctor was looking at him told him that wallowing was going to get him slapped. So, slowly—and with difficulty—he pushed the anguish down, thought by thought.

"What you did was very brave, and the best of us make mistakes." She sat back, "and it's a sad thing that being an Elemental means our mistakes tend to turn quite large."

He couldn't disagree with her there.

"You're fine to mourn, but we could do a lot together on this island. We *need* you to do more, when you're ready."

"Meaning what?"

"Oh, it's a discussion for another day."

They lapsed into silence then, because Damien had no response, and his exhaustion and confusion about the refugees and the transceiver just wasn't making sense. Some small voice told him that it was really as simple as Dr. Gwen had just said, but the rest of him wouldn't believe it, and so he let the wallowing slowly return. A more conscious part of him decided though that it would be easier to just fake the smile.

Finally, he spoke up. "So...you're Elemental too then, huh?"

A small smile tugged at her lips. "I surely am."

"What's...what's it like?"

Her smile flickered and she glanced away. "Are you hungry?"

Or don't answer, that's fine too. "Not really."

"If you say so." She pulled her palm-tablet from her pocket and checked it. "Hmm. Well, I have to go for now, but I'm going to bring you some dinner in a little while." She stood, and all of a sudden, Damien was terrified for her to go. He kept from reaching out for her, but his heart started to pound. He was afraid of the nightmares, and his parent's screams, and the feeling of the earth rending beneath his feet.

"Okay," he managed stiffly.

She straightened her lab coat and looked out towards his quarters. "I'll tell you again, since you might remember this time: your computer is linked to our private Intersystem, and you've been given full access. Your AI has been asking after you, and there's food in—"

"—Wait, wait, Leo? How do you know about him?"

She shook her head, more out of sympathy than irritation, or so it appeared. "You told Captain Roman about him when you arrived. After your demonstration, we let him out of his housing cube, and Sato and Commander Morgan interviewed him. The library of data you accumulated from your time in your bunker is almost invaluable. Sato was very happy, as are the rest of us."

Leo… Damien's upset deepened as he remembered the last time they'd spoken and how it had ended. "I'm…I'm glad we helped."

"You don't know how much." She checked her tablet and winced. "I am sorry that I can't stay longer, but you can call me if you need, and you are of course welcome to explore the island, if you desire. If not, I'll find you this evening for dinner. Is that alright?"

He nodded, too preoccupied to answer.

She came close and grasped his shoulders again, but this time with the same gentleness as when she'd entered. "You're a part of a community now—an extended family—and there's a spark of something especially special about you. This too shall pass." Then she gave him a parting squeeze, a smile, and left.

The door to his quarters slid shut, briefly letting in the sounds and lights of the hallway in the residents' wing outside, and then it closed. The silence deafened him, and while a part of him wanted to just fall back into bed and let the memories cascade out, Damien stayed sitting. Eventually, he stood, and eventually after that, he walked around his bed, went to the bathroom, and shaved.

∞   ∞   ∞

In the days that followed, the doctor's visits were frequent and lengthy, and though Damien fought hard to maintain his misery, Dr. Gwen's relentless pseudo-therapeutic pushing wore him down. She was simply more unyielding and tenacious than he, by a long shot. Sometimes she would come and examine him professionally, sometimes she would come and ask him to share about himself, and sometimes she would just come to talk, or sit in silence as he grieved and tried to adjust to the memories of what he'd done—good and bad.

Through their talks, Damien learned that she was from a big Catholic family in former-Ireland (though she insisted that no one there had ever stopped calling it what it was to them, no matter the new world), and that she was the youngest of five—three brothers and one sister. She'd been closest to her father as a girl, and had always loved the water.

"My Papa used to take me out on his gas-powered motorboat—an illegal antique," she'd told him with a little chuckle. "We'd go deep-sea fishin' together on those misty mornin's," she recalled, her Irish accent showing through every time she talked about home. "And it could get soo quiet out there, yeh'd believe it 'twer just you alone on the ocean; the only parsons in the whole wide werld." She'd smile sadly then, and her story would fade away without ever really finishing or elaborating. Damien asked once where her family was now, but she wouldn't answer. His instinct said they were dead, but something else told him that that just didn't line up. He didn't broach the subject again, and she didn't offer to elaborate.

As a closeness developed between them, and in such short order, Damien could tell that neither he nor Gwen were willing to move beyond certain barriers, and that was okay. Von was the only person alive with whom he'd shared everything, and Von remained conspicuously absent from Amun-Nūr. Gwen assured him that Satolin was 'discussing' the matter with Admiral Baroda, but she wouldn't elaborate. All Damien knew was that, as January turned to early February, Von was still missing.

Leo, on the other hand, came back into Damien's life with a vengeance. A short and fiery argument laid out why Leo had gotten so upset on the *Sanguine Lotus* during the flight from Seattle, but their resolution was expedient, and so were the repairs to their friendship. Leo had finally admitted to how much it upset him to leave his only home ever, and he made clear that Damien's and Von's continual neglect of his needs and wants had made him bitter. Damien had apologized sincerely for it, and had promised—in light of the radical changes to their lives—that such neglect was a thing of the past. Leo assured him that that wasn't necessary anymore, and that he would rather build a new friendship, where the two of them might make decisions as equals and colleagues, rather than one where Damien could just unplug him. Damien had gotten upset at some of the nastier things Leo had said (the word "slave" had come up more than once), but the AI's new home inside Amun-Nūr's massive storage drives deep below the facility precluded the possibility of Damien ever turning him off again.

"What do they want you to do?" Damien asked, sporting three days of unshaven stubble and an unchanged set of clothes he'd worn equally as long. He was lying on his back on his couch, and a sad, slow piano concert filtered through the speakers—it had been a rough few days. He was just starting to doze off when Leo called to inform him that Prohka Satolin and Amun-Nūr's ranking officer, Commander Jessop Morgan, had agreed to turn Leo into the island's official caretaker. "Oh, *everything*," Leo cackled from the desktop Pip pad. "You remember how excited *Mon Capitan* Roman was when you told him about me?"

"Yeah." Damien had brewed an herbal green tea at Gwen's request, and the steaming cup was warming his chest.

"He meant it! Tee hee! He meant it *soo* good! This island is like that warehouse you were always interested in…the pre-war one, the one with all the relics?"

"Area 51?" Damien frowned, remembering his fascinated perusing into the secrets that had spilled out of the mythic military base shortly before WWIII. His history books and research had always been contradictory as to what had actually been kept in there by the former United States, but it had been good reading nonetheless.

"That one! Amun-Nūr is just as loaded as that, but with *more* good stuff, and no one to keep track of it! You don't even *understand* how big my head is now from them giving me *total access.*"

"Oh, I understand just fine."

"No, no, you didn't hear me: TOTAL ACCESS!"

Damien closed his eyes slowly. "I heard you." *And so did all the neighbors.*

"You laugh, but I'm still better looking than you. Go take a shower!"

"You can't smell me."

"No, but I can play a chemical scenario about how smell works and people's emotional and mental reaction about a particular scent, so I have a pretty good idea, and my good idea says that your dear Lady Gwen won't enjoy what you've done to the place, or your sense of hygiene."

"She's not my lady," he snapped.

"Uh huh. Well I can hear one of your crying bouts coming on. Ta-ta for now!" And he was gone.

Enraged by the fact that Leo was both right about his mood and right to walk away before he said something nasty, Damien left his tea in the kitchenette, and decided to dismantle his pistol to take his mind off the now-constant rumble of the earthquake in his thoughts. The piano played on in the background, and he pulled his tools out of his workbench, flipping the thing to life as he did so.

The workbench's gridded white Pip surface came to life, and the adjustable, broad overhead lamp came on as well, providing a universal white glow on the surface. Damien tilted up the Pip pads attached to the three sides so they were in line for projecting, and thunked his Plaster pistol down. He expertly went to taking it apart while little hovering details and scans popped into the air, highlighting the condition of every component. In thirty seconds, Damien had dismantled the essentials and spread them out neatly, but today he decided to take the *whole* thing apart.

He lost track of time again, and when he came out of his focus fugue, the pistol lay on a perfect spread across the entire workbench. Almost every piece had been cleaned, polished, and those that needed replacing he marked with a little tap on the table, highlighting the item and cataloging it. At the moment, he was examining the tiny power cartridge of the weapon.

All Plaster pistols had been designed with a secondary feature as a last resort: if ammo ran dry and the wielder had no other option, he could eject the cartridge, flip it, and reinstall it upside-down to trigger a timed detonation sequence. Ten seconds later, the pistol would explode with a force larger than a grenade.

Damien sincerely hoped never to have to get rid of his pistol in such a manner—he'd grown pretty attached to it—but there was no way to know if the need would arise, so here he sat, stuck on cleaning the triggering mechanism for the detonator, just in case. Almost everything inside the gun had been gunked up with the plasma residue that got sprayed when each bullet was fired and the catalytic coating ignited—the technology that made Plaster weaponry glow much like Algaroth Gyro weapons. This was just the hardest piece to clean without breaking it.

"Stupid fucking screws," he hissed, arguing with his toolkit. "All getting in the way of…all kinds of—*SHIT!*" He shouted as his micro screwdriver slipped and he pierced his thumb. "Mmmmm!!" he tensed, throwing down the tool. It bounced hard against the pistol's slide and clattered to the floor.

Blood curled up from the puncture and he cursed. He sucked the blood out and went to the kitchenette to wash it.

The front door chimed.

"What?" he snapped.

It chimed again.

"*Come in!*" he shouted.

He heard the door open and finished cleaning his thumb. Around the corner, he froze.

Prohka Daeduras Satolin filled the front door, looking stern. Damien hadn't seen him since the night he arrived.

"You look well," the massive Prohka said, looking at the strewn clothes, leftover food, and general mess of his quarters.

Damien puckered like a fish while the coagulant tape hardened over his cut. "Oh. I've just…I've been—"

343

"—You've barricaded yourself away," Satolin cut him off. "I'm curious as to why."

Damien looked away, scratching at his black scraggle of beard. "I've been drained," he answered, turning very still.

"So I've heard," Satolin rumbled, crossing the threshold into the living room. His bulk dominated the space, and his head nearly hit the ceiling. He was wearing his alien sandals and rippled brown pants again, but on his chest he wore a formal, plated coverlet. From his neck to his ribcage, the evergreen coverlet was a plated trapezoid that narrowed towards the bottom, fringed in gold filigree, but the face of it had been divided symmetrically to fold neatly over the alien's bulk. The plate ended at Satolin's ribcage, where a lighter green shirt had been tailored to hang just below his waist. "I can't imagine the trauma you've endured," said the Prohka, "and I ask your forgiveness if you felt pressured to do your demonstration, but there is a limit with this kind of trauma, where either you must choose to stand on your own, or someone will stand you up."

Damien averted his gaze. "I'm standing fine."

"Nearly three weeks says otherwise."

"I couldn't get out of bed for two of them!"

"And you were rightfully laid out so." The alien's arctic-gold eyes searched him. "But the world does not stop turning for you, so I am simply here to ask: are you alright?"

Taken aback, Damien thought about lying. He almost did, but he followed Satolin's gaze around his quarters, and for the first time in days he realized what a mess he'd made.

Unwashed and mildewed clothes lay strewn over the floor from many evenings spent with the shower running, recycling his water tank over and over until the whole place was humid. His small appetite had left more than one unfinished meal on the counters and couch, his bed lay a mess, and despite the one place of order—where his sidearm lay in its neat square on the workbench—not a single space of the apartment didn't look *wet*.

Ouch. Damien hung his head. "I'm not okay, but there's nothing you can do."

Satolin gave him a quizzical look. "Why do you think that? How would you know?"

"Umm…"

"You wouldn't." The alien's expression was kind, hard, curious, and sad all at once. "As it happens, I have something to offer that may help you recover from your ordeal—an ordeal for which I must stress that you have not just my sympathy, but my *empathy*."

At the word, Damien remembered what Satolin had said about the Daeduras Uprising, and he knew it was true. "Like what," he asked slowly, unable to hold the alien's gaze for more than a second.

Warmth spread across the enormous alien's features and his ganglia waved about, hinting at some sort of satisfaction. "Your brother is arriving this afternoon."

If the Prohka had expected a jubilant response, Damien disappointed. "Oh. Thanks." *Afternoon?* He looked at his workbench. *Was I at this all night?* He'd lost track of time lately.

One of Satolin's ganglia ridges flicked upwards like a raised eyebrow. "I'm awash in your excitement."

Damien looked up from his pistol, faking a big smile. "Hmm? Oh! Well, you know, I was just…" but then, finally, the Prohka's words made the rest of the way to his brain and he stopped. "Wait, what did you just say?"

"Silas Von is arriving this afternoon," Satolin enunciated. "The good Admiral has finally consented to release him since his wounds are well past their mandatory recovery period." Satolin's tone was neutral, but Damien saw that flicker of satisfaction again in his ganglia.

Did he fight with Baroda to get Von here? he wondered, but he didn't care. He delicately put down the pistol grip and rag he'd used to clean it. "Th-*thank you*," he croaked. "I—I don't know what to say."

Satolin's pointed teeth flashed as he smiled a very human smile. "Get cleaned up, and why don't I have someone escort you down to the hangar in two hours, as I assume you have forgotten the way?"

Damien heard unspoken words of worry in the Prohka's question, but he didn't care. *Von's coming home.* "Yeah, that…that sounds good. Thank you. I…thank you!" *Von's coming home!*

Satolin nodded. "You've been through plenty enough since you've arrived on our island. Isolation has made Amun-Nūr understand the impact such losses inflict on us better than most, but now I would want you to be a part of this family, as I asked of you when you arrived."

"I, I think I can do that."

"Good. Now go clean up."

Damien thanked him again and went to take a real shower.

CHAPTER EIGHTEEN

Brothers In All But Blood

"They're coming in!" the dockmaster called.

"Thank you, Mark!" Gwen called back.

Damien, Javier, Gwen, and Satolin were all standing on the lowermost platform of the chandelier control hub in the hangar bay. Damien was scrubbed and freshly shaved with clean new pants over his boots and a brown-and-green striped shirt under his worn jacket, which he'd discovered hanging in his quarters, free of all blood. Javier wore a plain grey jacket and pants, and Gwen was in her usual lab coat. Satolin had traded his plated coverlet for the same black, brown, and green vest he'd worn the day Damien arrived.

The chandelier control hub had two levels. The top level housed all of the hangar bay's operational stations, while the bottom was less of a finished level and more of a scenic overlook from which one could view the hangar below. Crisscrossing walkways encircled the bottom level, all of which were suspended a few meters off the polyglass floor of the hub. The walkways themselves were made of a clear material that responded to pressure; wherever Damien walked, the material became opaque just ahead and behind him, enough to keep track of his footing. When he passed though, it returned to clear, offering an almost unobstructed view of the hangar.

"So your brother, the ah…the *Algaroth*," Javier said, barely containing his derision. "You think he's all scarred up or something?"

Damien couldn't deny that he'd been practically ecstatic to see the man as he'd made his way down to the bay from his quarters, even though their only real interaction had been close to a month ago on the flight to the island. Regardless, he'd learned on the ride down that Javier had been serving his sentence diligently—though he still refused to say how—and that he'd taken quite the liking to the bar and the theater in the cavernous habitat district. Javier had shown real concern for how Damien had been "MIA" since they arrived, and had expressed his condolences about Seattle.

Damien gave the man a dry stare, but Javier didn't blink. "Are you hoping he is?"

The Earth Elemental flashed his scarred and bruised wrists. "Nope, but shit happens, man."

Before he could answer, Satolin broke the silence. "Here they are," he said, his huge voice carrying over the roar outside. Below, the bay had flooded with seawater and the few ships occupying their berths rose in the tide.

Damien stared hard at the submerged square of light far below, feeling nervous and excited. Before Gwen had arrived to take him to the hangar, he had checked in the mirror and found that he barely recognized his face, so sunken and tired were his eyes, with thin skin and signs of depleted muscles. *You're a real hero*, he'd thought.

After a long minute, Damien finally spotted a shadow rising through the dark water below. The amorphous blob resolved into the angular curves of the *Sanguine Lotus*. The long, spearheaded ship popped out of the water, causing huge waves against the salt-stained walls of the bay. The ship paused in the swells, and Damien heard Mark, the dockmaster, call from the level above to confirm the docking clearance. *Sanguine Lotus* churned towards Bay 1, and Damien was just able to spy the Aqua Pods that propelled her through the water: great turbines that poked out from under the folded wings, vacuuming up water and jetting it out the back. The four of them watched the ship closely, not saying a word.

The dockmaster's voice called down from the curling ramp to the upper level. "Hey down there, as soon as she locks in the berth you can start heading down! Yea?"

"We'll be up in a moment!" Gwen called back.

They watched the ship dock, and for a moment Damien could swear he saw a flicker of blue skin in *Lotus*'s cockpit. *Von?* He'd done his best to maintain a cool façade, but finally, his anxious excitement snapped, and his body got all jittery.

"Clear!" Mark called.

Damien, Satolin, Gwen, and Javier took the elevator to the roof of the control hub, and then rode the clanking lift to the bay floor—the same lift that Damien and Javier had arrived on. Damien leapt over the gangway before it reached the ground and tumbled down the steps, not waiting for the lift to stop. He jarred his knee on the toothy walkway but the shock only amplified his excitement. *You'll regret that later*, he thought, but another voice said, *no I won't*.

"Damien, hold on!" Gwen called, but he was already halfway down the gangway as the lift stopped at the bottom with a *clang*.

"Von!" he shouted towards the twinkling wet hull of the *Lotus*.

As he pounded past the ship's engine block, the port airlock popped open and steam hissed into the air. Joy swelled up through Damien's chest. "VON!" he shouted, laughing for the first in a long time. "You son of a bitch!!! You son of a *BITCH!!* Get out here!"

The delay had been worth it.

For the first time since before they raided the Razer, Damien felt whole again. Silas Von appeared from the steam looking strong, vital, and healthy. He wore an orange-and-white Algaroth jacket-wrap and padded armor leggings that were his favorite attire, but the jacket appeared newer than the one he had had back home. He had a fresh pair of splayed-toed boots, and his muscled blue arms glistened with perspiration in the humid air. He moved with only a hint of stiffness in his left side where he'd been shot, but his emerald-gold eyes searched the bay with the same awe Damien had felt when he arrived, and they glowed alert and cunning; the brother that he knew. When the alien gaze finally found Damien pelting towards him, they lit up and he spread his arms, breaking into a huge, toothy smile.

They nearly collided for Damien's enthusiasm, both grinning in the salty air, and embraced. "You look good you lazy slizzard."

Von narrowed his eyes playfully, "And you look like you've been sitting too much." A shadow of doubt crossed his features as he took in

Damien's thin frame and hollowed face, but he said nothing, and they laughed a little too easily as the other three caught up. Just before they arrived, though, Damien looked into his brother's eyes again, and he saw a shadow of something there, too. At first he thought it was exhaustion, but his gut cinched in that instant, choking off the joy of his brother's safe return. *He remembers too*, he realized, and he knew he was right. The look Von gave him was a mixture of confusion, loss, and trauma. Von definitely remembered about the earthquake…and their parents.

Damien didn't know what to say.

"Silas Von." Satolin rumbled. Von looked up and—to his credit— barely contained a double take at the Algaroth's hulk. "We are honored to welcome you to Amun-Nūr. I am Prohka Daeduras Satolin."

"Ka," Von breathed, addressing Satolin with a proper honorific. He squared his shoulders to face the larger alien. "I am…deeply grateful to be in your company." They traded the Algaroth elbow-pulling handshake, and Von stepped back, submitting to Satolin's leadership.

"Oh! *This*," Damien said, trying to maintain his jubilance. "Is Dr. Gwen Whalen." Gwen held a hand over her breast and bowed her head. "And this is Javier Estrada."

"*Javi*," Javier huffed. "It's cool. We're both Elementals." The man jerked his thumb between himself and Damien. To his credit, Damien saw only a hint of apprehension in the man's eyes at Von.

I guess this all must be hard on him in its own way, Damien thought. *He's spent his life training to kill Algaroth.*

"My gratitude to meet you," said Von to them both.

Just then, Captain Romi and his copilot, Kel, stepped through the vapor, laden with duffels.

"Damien!" uttered Romi. "I'm glad to see you out with us! We have a lot to catch up on!" They shook.

Damien smiled and agreed, but noted the concerned look from Von. "Definitely."

"Well," Satolin pronounced, his gaze jumping between them all. "VoSilas, under other circumstances, I'd offer you a tour of Amun-Nūr myself, but…" he looked towards Damien. "I see no reason why the two of you should not explore it a little for yourselves." He smiled. "I trust you were treated well under the good Admiral's care?"

Von blinked as Satolin used the name-conjugating honorific to address *him*, but his ganglia just flicked and he nodded and stretched his left side. "I don't remember very much, but yes, I'm still standing so I guess they did." He looked at Damien. "And I'd like a walk-around, yes."

"Then I give you a formal welcome to the Island of Amun-Nūr," said the Prohka, "and I am glad to see another join our family."

"Te'Vierda, Ka Satolin," said Von, bowing his head. Then he turned towards Captain Romi and Kel. "I would be happy to help unload the *Lotus*'s cargo—"

"—Think nothing of it," Kel grumbled. The large implant over his left eye whizzed, and he looked at Damien and Von simultaneously. "The *V*arine is here, he can hel*f* us unload." His good eye drifted to Javier.

Damien had forgotten how thick Kel's English was.

"*Seriously?!*" Javier moaned.

"Thank you," said Von, and Kel snorted at him (a sign between Algaroth that meant "of course.")

Captain Romi grabbed Javier by the scruff of his neck as Satolin, Damien, and Von turned away, leaving Gwen with the others. "That's right," he said. "You've got shit to do, *Marine*. Come on." And he tugged Javier back towards the *Lotus* over the man's profanity-laced protesting.

Before they were a few paces away, Damien heard Javier behind them as he shouted, "I just wanted to meet the slizzard brother!"

An instant later, a wet smack resounded and the man yelped. Damien and Von whirled to see what had happened and, to his shock, Damien saw a thick mist of water vanishing over the walkway. Javier was soaked from the shoulders up, his cheeks were flushed, and Gwen was staring at him hard, her hand held up to his face, but she was nowhere near enough to strike him.

Damien allowed himself to grin as he, his brother, and the Prohka rode the lift back up into the island.

∞　　　　　　　∞　　　　　　　∞

Von had a quiet moment in the Long Atrium when they arrived. He admired the 'Twined Tree, the thoroughfare, and the lovely, meandering peace of the citizens of Amun-Nūr as they went about their business. Damien watched him take it in, knowing that Von must be as excited—if not more so—than he himself had been when he arrived. Von said nothing, but the wonder in his alien gaze was apparent.

"If you'd like," Satolin said after awhile. "I can show you both the Celestial Garden? Damien, I know you have yet to see it, the same as your brother?"

The brothers thought that sounded perfect, so they allowed themselves to be taken to the third floor of the island, and far back through corridors marked by different labs from the Argyle Wing. The Prohka turned down a broad, gently curving hallway that reminded Damien of the tunnel up to the Core. He shuddered at the thought of that place, and shook off the rumbling thunder that cascaded into his mind. Von's eyes flicked towards him as they walked, but he said nothing.

"And here we are," said Satolin, stopping at the most outward-bowed point of the curve, where double sliding doors stood shut.

Twinkling sunlight blinded Damien as the doors opened. He shielded his eyes, wondering what could possibly lie in this new nook of the island. Satolin ushered them inside and—still unable to see—the first thing Damien noticed was the air. The air was salty and almost tasted a bit like mud; but it was so *fresh*.

The coolest breeze he'd ever felt brushed over his sunken cheeks, the clamor of water crashing against rocks in the distance filled what sounded like a *very* large space, and even the high-pitched peals of seagulls could be heard somewhere far away. Damien's sensitive eyes adjusted, and he realized he'd just been used to the dimmer interior lighting of the island and his quarters for nearly a month. Sunlight had no comparison.

They were standing on a flat stone veranda at the back of another cavern. This one, though, looked out onto the twinkling Pacific Ocean through a gaping mouth in the side of Amun-Nūr. In the distance over the clear blue ocean, the lengthening shadow of the mountain above stretched away to the east, but inside, many small hot springs were venting steam into the cavern, making the air just a little misty, but cool. Damien remembered circling the island when he arrived, but he'd been quite sure—then, as now—that the sheer eastern edifice of stone he'd seen had volunteered no cave mouth.

"We have done everything we can to make this place feel like a secure home." Satolin explained, breathing the moist air.

"I thought you said this was a garden?" Damien plied.

Satolin laughed. "It is. Come."

Damien and Von obeyed, crossing the dewy, grey-green stone of the veranda to the encircling railing of the same rock.

"Would you call anything more of a garden?" said the Prohka, pointing.

Okay, so…there's officially more packed into this island than should ever be reasonable, Damien thought as he saw.

The Celestial Garden was a maze of rounded, open terraces notched into the porous black rock that made up the cavern, all connected by a veritable web of stone staircases and walkways that zigzagged and wound above, between, around, and beneath the entire expanse of the Garden. The terraces were all made of the same, grey-green stone as the veranda, which blended into the black stone of the cavern without completely disappearing. Some looked like inset, empty hot tubs or saunas, while others appeared to be open patios, or verandas with domed cupolas that kept them completely covered, or pergolas that left the air open. Other terraces looked more like balconies that ran the cavern wall and jutted out from the cavern's black stone.

Damien spotted more than one of the scattered private 'lounges' that were indeed set right over a hot spring, so they *were* saunas of a sort. He grinned and thought that was funny, but what made it all especially heartwarming was the greenery draping everything.

Everywhere he looked, every color imaginable could be seen poking out through a forest of green things. Curtains of ivy hung from woven metal screens or from the pergolas, thick shrubs and big rubbery leafed plants served as natural partitions between terraces, soft moss carpeted whatever it could, and all kinds of other plants could be spotted, dotting the multi-leveled Garden. Damien thought it looked a bit like something he'd seen in Ancient Greece, or Rome, but mistier and all at the perfect temperature.

"Did you construct all of this?" Von asked.

"Not the springs," Satolin voiced, "but the rest we did."

Below, Damien could see people—humans and Algaroth—occupying many of the terraces. He saw three older Algaroth in one sauna covered by a pergola sitting over a spring near the edge of the Garden. All three of them were gnawing on what could only be oak bark as they gazed out of the cavern towards the sea. He saw a young man surrounded by papers and tablets in a dry terrace almost directly below them, tapping his hot-pen incessantly. On another terrace, a cozy alcove was visible off of a larger open patio, which looked like it was hidden from view to most, but not all. There, under the thick flowering shrubs that kept it tucked away, Damien felt his heart flutter as he saw a flash of a bare, rosy leg as it was upturned, and then grasped tightly by a larger hand. He started and looked away, not wanting to disturb the couple, even though he doubted that his glance would disrupt them.

His gaze fell on a flash of a tiny hand in the other direction of the Garden. Unsure of what it was, he followed it, until he heard a little laugh in the distance. *Holy shit.*

It was a pair of little boys chasing after each other, playing a game. One was a pale human, the other a sky-blue Algaroth child.

"I didn't know there were kids here!" he exclaimed.

Satolin followed his gaze to where the boys were running, and his arctic-gold eyes turned soft. "Yes. I suppose you wouldn't have seen many children here yet. The school is in the habitat district, and I don't believe there are any on your floor of the residents' wing, so no, you wouldn't have heard them."

"How many are here?" Von asked, watching the boys too.

"Eighty-three," the Prohka answered immediately.

Damien's jaw dropped. "Seriously? And they're all growing up in the island?"

"Yes."

Damien didn't know what to think.

"Does that bother you?"

"No, I don't think so? I just had never thought about what it would be like to grow up underground…" *I can't even imagine that, actually.* Living *underground is weird enough.*

"It is different," Satolin admitted. "But the reality of our situation is what it is. We only hope it can change some day."

"Hopefully so," said Von.

Damien's gaze drifted away from the boys as they disappeared down a staircase. The thought occurred to him then that he could take in this sheer labyrinth of living privacy and get lost in it forever, if he wanted. This was clearly a place to be alone or with close ones, but it was away from the bustle—magnificent thought it was—that was the majority of the island around them. *On second thought…I see the appeal.* "How do you keep anyone from finding the entrance?" he asked, looking back towards the cavern mouth, which had to be a good fifty meters up from the crashing waves far away and below.

Satolin's ganglia flicked and he indicated the borders of the opening. "We have a generous illusion in place, thanks greatly in part to the Core. Emitters along the mouth project a stone face, and nothing else. Our way down to Amun-Nūr is safe from here."

"But what if someone were to find their way through?"

"Then we would have to collapse this cavern," he said simply.

"That would be sad," Von remarked. "This place is beautiful."

"You may find familiar specimens here, VoSilas," said Satolin appreciatively. "Life, grown and brought from Shialga."

"Thanks for showing us this," said Damien.

Satolin nodded. "You are both free to roam the island as you please. This is your home now, too." And with that, he took his leave, and removed himself.

Without a word, Damien and Von descended the central staircase and found a small—but not intimately so—dry lounge. The round terrace had a stone bench inset into the side, like a hot tub, and almost the entire terrace was ringed in the ivy-laden metal screens. It was quiet, it was away from everyone else, and it was empty.

It was perfect.

The two sat down awkwardly across from each other, and listened to the waves and the gulls. Damien thought he heard a moan in the distance, but he ignored it. Von sat with his left arm held up a little from his side, and he wouldn't meet Damien's eyes.

"How's your side?" Damien finally asked. *Just…go easy with this.*

Von glanced at his arm and pushed it down quickly, but he couldn't hide the wince. "It's healed," he said, shrugging it off.

"How are the scars?"

Von snorted heartily and glanced at Damien's covered arms. "Ahh, ha ha…they look like yours."

"Really?"

Von met his gaze. "Too much."

"What do you mean?" Damien leaned over his knees, feeling his heart beat faster. His nerves started to surface. But just then, he heard laughter coming towards them, and fast. He heard two voices, one high-pitched and cackling, the other sounded like some nasally lion cub. "What the hell…?"

The two little boys burst around the curtain of ivy into their lounge, laughing madly. Upon seeing Damien and Von, the human boy stopped short, but the Algaroth boy bowled into him, still laughing, and they tumbled.

"Ouch!" cried the human boy. "Watch it, Tibbo!"

"Whoaa!" Tibbo wailed as he went down. His little alien voice was what had made the nasally cub sound, but this close it sounded more like a throaty honk.

In the scuffle, the red ball the human boy had been clutching shot out of his hands towards the edge of the terrace. Damien snatched it out the air without thinking, ready to lob it at a soldier. He caught himself and recovered before they looked up. "Whoa, whoa hey, you guys okay?"

"Sorry mister!" the little boy said. "Oww…." He sniffed, looking at his skinned knees.

At the sight, something fired in the back of Damien's mind. A memory. It cascaded out of the depths of the past in an instant, and the flash of it took his breath away:

A ray of rare summer sunshine, his thumb shoved in his mouth around a smile. He scrambles to keep up with his parents, who are talking a lot, high above him. Three blue Alga-people are nearby, gardening with a couple. The two men spot him and wave. One knocks over a pot of dirt and they laugh. Damien waves back.

Someone bolts past him and he stumbles, falls. He skins his knee and starts crying. It hurts.

"What happened, Damien? Did you fall?"

He wants them to make nicer voices. They always sound barely not-mean. He looks for who tripped him and spots an Alga-boy crouching on a rock. The Alga-boy is wearing a stiff streamer around his waist, and it flicks back and forth behind him like a kitty-cat tail. He thinks the Alga-boy looks kinda like a big blue monkey. He giggles through the sniffles.

The Alga-boy looks at him, confused, like he didn't know what he'd just knocked over. He has green dots in his gold eyes.

Mommy and Daddy notice the Alga-boy too. "You two must've bumped into each other!" Mommy says.

"What's your name?" Daddy asks the Alga.

"Silas!" The Alga-boy squeaks. His voice is small and honky.

"Is that your house name, Silas? Your family name? What's your Own name?"

The Alga-boy cocks his head sideways and honks, "Von!"

Daddy smiles at the Alga. "Nice to meet you, Von! My Own name is Ewan. Are your parents nearby?"

The Alga-boy looks confused.

"Parents?" Daddy says again.

"He doesn't know that one yet." Mommy says to Daddy.

Damien is still sniffling. His knee hurts.

"Well...just," Daddy holds up a finger to the Alga. "One second!" He pulls out the shiny tablet they always have and start talking again,

really fast. They're standing right in the sun and Damien can't see their faces. The sun goes away and he still can't see their faces.

When they finally stop talking, the Alga-boy is gone.

"Oh, well," says Mommy. "C'mon Damien, we'll introduce you two next time."

Damien sniffs as they put him on his feet and brush him off without checking his knee.

They start walking again, but Damien isn't smiling anymore.

Overwhelmed, Damien fell back in his seat, feeling the burn of his skinned knee as if it were yesterday. His arms itched like crazy, too. Von had moved to help the little boy up and had produced a cloth to wipe his knee. The Algaroth boy was standing off to the side, looking sheepish.

"There," said Von, "not hurt too bad?"

The boy shook his head, but he and his friend were looking at Damien curiously. "Mister? Are you okay?"

"Ya, is he okay?" Tibbo asked of Von, his little voice cracking.

Damien let himself smile.

Von nodded. "He's alright."

"Yeah," he nodded. "I'm fine, little man. Here's your ball."

The boy took it guiltily. "Thanks, mister. Sorry for wrecking your play time."

Damien couldn't help but laugh a little. "It's okay, kid. Just don't lose that ball okay?"

"Okay," they promised in unison.

"I think Tibbo should get the ball though," said Von, looking sternly at the human boy.

The little Algaroth's eyes lit up so bright Damien thought stars were about to explode from them. The human boy pouted his lip, but he handed it over.

"Thanks Wandy!" The Alga-boy honked from his chest, and he disappeared around the corner.

Before Tibbo had vanished, the pout left the boy's face and he bolted after his friend. Damien and Von heard them both cackling their way through the Garden in seconds, laughing as loud as ever.

After awhile, the quiet descended back on their patio and Damien turned slowly towards his brother. The sounds of the ocean filled the space between them. In the distance, Damien heard what sounded like the boy's laughter again, but soon it faded into nothing, and it was just the two of them.

"Von…"

"I remember, Damien," his brother blurted. "I couldn't tell you how, or what happened, but…I remember the earthquake."

Damien's stomach bottomed out, and the little blood left in his face drained. His throat went very dry, and he managed a croak. "I—I do too." He grasped as the memory of his first meeting with Von slipped away.

Von's head snapped up. "You what?" A mixture of hurt, confusion, and accusation flashed in his gaze for a split second, but then it was gone.

Even so, Damien saw it, and it cut deep. His hands started to tremble, and the wall he'd so carefully constructed over the past few weeks threatened to blow. "It…I remember it too." He shook his head as tears welled, and he turned away, unable to meet Von's eyes. "This place, they…that thing that Sato mentioned, the 'Core'? It's…its some sort of simulator. Or…a transporter. Or something, I don't know. But it…" his voice died and he squeezed his eyes shut, fighting the sounds of the thundering earth.

He heard a rustle of movement and the next he knew, his brother was crouched against the foot of the metal screen in front of him, hands open. "It doesn't matter," said Von. "We still have family."

Had Von responded with anger, or judgment, or anything else really, Damien's wall would have fallen apart. Until that moment, he'd had no idea how afraid he'd been that somehow his power had extended to Von too—a possibility that Gwen had grilled him on particularly hard for her research. He'd been afraid that his dark, Elemental powers had somehow kept the memories from emerging in his brother, even from across the world. Inversely, though, he'd also been even *more* afraid that Von had just buried the memories, and kept it all to himself somehow.

Now, with Von's total dismissal of either terror, Damien's wall disintegrated. He didn't have to share words with his brother to know the truth. Von had come to the same conclusion: Damien's Elemental powers may have killed their parents, but it had left them both amnesic, and Von didn't care. He must have gleaned that whatever happened in the Core was traumatizing, and that it must have happened right around when Seattle fell.

Von still didn't care.

The raw tears welled up in Damien from their so avidly active depths of late, and he gasped out some sound resembling gratitude. Von moved to sit next to him, and the brothers embraced, as only family could—with one arm awkwardly hung across the others' shoulders.

"Thanks Vo."

"Family, Damien. Always."

Damien nodded, and he let the grief wrack him one more time.

∞   ∞   ∞

Damien lost track of how long he and Von talked, but their time spent apart, coupled with the distance—both from home and from any other people within the Garden—was liberating. Damien learned that Admiral Baroda had been nothing but courteous to Von while he healed, which further put a wedge in Damien's confusion about the Admiral's intentions. After Seattle fell, Von had been taken to Peak Springs, where he remembered very little. He'd spent most of the past few weeks drugged up and in surgery, "getting a *cy-to-my-o-tro-phy* done," Von pronounced proudly. "It was horrible."

From what Von said, though, the rumors that an Elemental had saved the citizens of the Islets had spread like wildfire, and for the first time that Von had ever seen, Elementals had been openly cheered on for their war against the Over-Seer.

"We're not at war, though," Damien said.

"Doesn't matter," Von proclaimed. "They still love you."

Damien didn't know what to do with that.

After Von's story concluded, Damien had his turn. He told him everything about Captain Huxley, Agent Bunting of SIO, Camp Cascade, and how Admiral Baroda had made the claims that Croll Tan had decided to take Seattle apart because he'd finally found Damien, the Elemental who could wield black holes. Von dismissed the notion that it was Damien's fault about the city falling, but it wasn't enough to shake Damien's guilt, so he blazed past the subject, and came to Baroda's slowly burgeoning revelation about another Supply Fleet en route to Earth.

"He said they'll be here this year," Damien recounted. "He said it could be within a few months."

Von shook his head, sitting back in his chair across the lounge. "That doesn't make sense."

"Why?"

Von sat up. "A Supply Fleet is sent on intervals. Shialga does not send fleets if they don't hear about a safe arrival. The last one never made it here, so it's odd to me that they would have *another* fleet only a year behind the missing one. It should take them…oh, *years*, to sort out if something happened in deep space to the missing fleet. Also, Supply Fleets take about three years to get to Earth without the Conduit to aid them."

The Conduit, Damien thought, repulsed and worried by the word. *The endgame for Earth, once The Collective completes it, their TransLight superhighway.* He didn't have the energy to think about that right now. It was too ominous. "I just know what Baroda said," he pressed. "He sounded pretty damn sure."

"Hmm," but Von didn't have anything else to offer.

At length, the brothers decided they were hungry. There were no clocks in the Garden, and Damien hadn't thought to bring a tablet or his goggles with him. They only knew that the sun had set, and a cloudless night sky was peeking into the cavern at them. It was almost a full moon.

Agreeing that maybe it would be good for both of them to see the dining hall for the first time, Damien and Von climbed the stairs to the entryway, both moving a little easier than they had when they'd come in.

As they approached the double doors that went back into the island, the comm panel on the wall beeped loudly. Damien stopped.

The panel beeped again.

Looking at Von, Damien slowly tapped the panel. "Uh…hello?"

"*Where the hell have you two been??*" Leo's voice was sharp and a little panicked.

"We're in the—"

"*—Yeah, yeah you're in the Celestial Garden, I know! You didn't notice anyone calling?*"

Damien looked at Von.

"I just got here," the Algaroth shrugged, as if that answered everything.

"Who's been calling?"

"*Me, stupid!*" Suddenly, the panel fizzled, and Leo's face appeared on the screen. "*The Prohka and Commander Morgan are headed to the surface. You both probably want to be there!*"

Trepidation crept its way into Damien's voice. "…Why?"

"*Because a ship just anchored offshore! A little ship! A cutesy little ship just found this SUPER SECRET ISLAND!!*"

Damien looked at Von, who had gone wide-eyed. The alien's ganglia lay flat against his skull. "What?! What's going on?!"

"*Just get to the top level of the Atrium!*" A map appeared next to the AI's face, highlighting where they should go. "*Go, go, move, move!*"

They didn't need any further urging. Dinner would have to wait.

CHAPTER NINETEEN

The Stranger on the Beach

Damien and Von exited the elevator on the fifth floor and wheezed their way around the 'Twined Tree's circular plaza at the end of the Long Atrium. The 'Twined Tree rustled below, and the thoroughfare was nearly devoid of life except for a few evening folks enjoying the quiet.

"Where did he say to go?" Von hacked.

Leo's voice came through their implants again. "Keep going straight, boys!" Straight, straight, straight!"

Damien and Von pelted down the far side of the thoroughfare and—at Leo's direction—turned through a single sliding door into a dark antechamber. Inside, the corridor was older and dirtier than the rest of the island, and at the end was a huge, heavy, airlock door. A sign next to the door said, "SURFACE CLEARANCE REQUIRED."

"I guess," Damien gasped, "that's…what we get for…being…laid up for…a fucking…month."

Von just nodded, frothing and gripping his healed side.

Barely ten seconds later, the sound of pounding footsteps reached their ears, and the pair whirled on the doorway to see Dr. Gwen storm through with Javier in tow, followed at snappy intervals by Satolin, and then six armed guards clad in Amun-Nūr's brown-and-green.

"How did you two hear?" Gwen asked of Damien and Von, looking startled.

"Leo," Damien gasped, still panting. "He…he let us know."

Leo's voice came through a couple of beat up loudspeakers hanging in the corners of the hall, as the soldiers came through. His voice was tinny. "I hope that was okay, Prohka? Commander? I thought they'd want to know."

Satolin—who had just caught Gwen's and Damien's exchange—waved it off, "No, Leo, it's alright."

"He told who?" asked the man at the head of the six soldiers as they came through. Normally, Damien would have guessed the man to be on the far side of fifty, but after he'd gotten Admiral Baroda's age so wrong, he let it go. The man's skin was sun-baked and bronze, and he looked grizzled and serious with that hard jaw, a nose that had been broken at least twice, and dark, sparking eyes. The nametag sewn into his combat vest read 'MORGAN'.

"Us," Damien indicated himself and his brother.

Comprehension dawned on Morgan's face. "You're Damien."

"Yeah."

Morgan gave him a loose but welcoming salute. "Good to meet you, finally. I'm Commander Morgan. Sorry about the Islets and the Core, but we're glad to have you on your feet." He looked towards the loudspeakers. "Leo, be careful who you warn about this kind of thing in the future, not everyone on this island is cleared for everything."

"Understood, Commander," said Leo in a surprisingly stoic tone.

"So, Prohka," said Morgan. "Do we know what it is?"

"No," Satolin answered, consulting a large tablet. "Just that it's a small vessel, and unregistered."

"That sounds like trouble." Javier said from where he'd taken up station by Damien. He looked the most comfortable Damien had yet seen him with grime on his face, wearing a dark green maintenance uniform splattered with splotchy stains. The two of them bumped fists quietly.

"Commander," Satolin said slowly, addressing Morgan. "One small ship makes me nervous as an army never could."

Morgan nodded. "I agree." He spun to his soldiers who were waiting patiently. "Alright grummings, assume this is a 'Castle Breach'. Full alert, lethal-free. Knock out whoever's up there if you can, but that directive is *secondary* to exposure, do you understand?"

"Sir, yes sir!" they said as one.

Morgan nodded. "Loss, you take point," a nearby Algaroth about the same size and build as Von nodded and unholstered his Gyro rifle.

"Declan, rear," a bald, fierce-looking woman acknowledged and donned her helmet. "Tortelli, ears," a freckled, ginger-haired young man acknowledged with gusto. "Everyone else: post up, we're shafting topside."

The soldiers unholstered their weapons, and the clatter of metal, zippers, and the *clack* of safeties being taken off filled the corridor. Gwen sidled up against the wall near Satolin.

Damien stepped up, "Commander, I've got good eyes, I can be useful."

Morgan gave him a short hard stare. "I've seen the footage your demonstration—" Damien winced "—so I can get on board with that," he finished after only a hint of hesitation. "But follow orders."

Damien beamed. "Understood."

"I'm going too." Javier cut in, sounding tentative but decided.

"So am I," said Von.

Morgan stiffened at them both, but definitely more at Javier. A couple of the soldiers glanced up. "I'd rather not," the commander answered. "A deserter and a new recruit?"

Javier planted himself. "Man, why the fuck not?"

"Because you can't be trusted."

Damien noted how little of a twitch showed up in Javier's eyes. *Either he's learning to deflect that crap better, or he's working through it.* Damien hoped it was the latter.

"I'm not letting him go up there alone," Von said, standing by Damien. "It could be Avos."

Hadn't thought of that, bro. Thanks for the image.

Javier turned to Satolin. "Prohka, I've served my time. I'm a Marine, man! Let me back out in the world!"

Satolin shook his head. "Morgan is in charge of Amun-Nūr's defenses, Mr. Estrada. Our agreement has no standing here—" Javier moaned. "—*However*," Satolin spoke up, and his voice filled the corridor. He turned to the commander. "The man *has* excelled far beyond what was asked of him since arriving. I would give him my vote of confidence after that."

365

The small gathering looked on as Commander Morgan eyed the airlock door behind Damien, itching to move. "We don't have time to argue. Sato," he brandished a finger at Daeduras. "You're a sneaky pain sometimes. Vilan, take a pistol. Silas Von, right? You too. And Estrada…" the man withheld the holstered Plaster pistol as Javier reached for it. "Don't make me regret this."

Javier's tremulous thanks and his solemn salute could only have come from a Marine. "Thank you, sir."

"I'll be joining you as well." Gwen said, stepping in.

Morgan rolled his eyes. "*Jesus*, fine! Doctor, and *you three*," he looked at Von, Damien, and Javier. "Stay in the middle. The rest of you: I'm blowing this hatch in ten seconds. Let's MOVE!"

In ten seconds, Morgan and Satolin unlocked the airlock door with their access keys, and the commander ushered the six soldiers, three Elementals, and one stray Algaroth into the shaft to the surface.

∞   ∞   ∞

The freshness of tropical, salty air washed over Damien's nostrils as the group crept through the tiny opening in the side of Amun-Nūr's mountain. Even with the hint of the outside world that peeked in on the Celestial Garden, the cavern just couldn't compare to fresh air. Damien's lungs filled with the breeze once, twice, again, and he took in the island below.

The tiny crack that hid the surface shaft was just below the peak of the broken shard of the mountain. Time had withered it so that unscalable rock faces surrounded Damien, and the only vegetation nearby were hard-fought clumps of grass. Below and ahead was the minute expanse of the island with tall palm trees, sand, and rubbery, tropical flora. He was struck with how small it really was. *Like an iceberg*, he thought.

The moment was interrupted as the silent soldiers stepped out around him.

There was a tiny *pip* in the earpiece that the communications officer, Corporal Tortelli, had given the civilians on the ride up. Damien, Javier,

Von, and Gwen were all connected to the team comms. *"Go prone,"* Morgan hissed, and they all dropped to their bellies, weapons drawn.

Damien let his power surface for the first time in a month, and was careful not to use too much except to enhance his sight. "Secrecy is our primary concern here," Morgan had warned the Elementals on the way up. "We don't know who's on that ship, how they found us, if they've made landfall, or who they're allied with, but for you Elementals: Australia is the closest landmass, and it's completely occupied by the enemy. Who knows how far away The Collective can detect a surge of your stuff, so *be careful* with it. Right now, you're under my command, so take that order as buggered gospel."

Damien had no intention of using an Orb or anything big, but he let a trickle of power infuse his eyes and—much like a tuner finding the perfect frequency—he honed the flow so that the night lit up around him as if it were the brightest of days. There was a tiny surge of ruddy light beneath his sleeves as his scarred arms lit dully, but he hid it quickly. No one saw.

A minute passed in rustling quiet, until he felt Javier crawl up next to him and whisper, "Good times already, eh?"

"Guess so," he answered. He spared a glance behind him and spotted Von crouching behind a boulder near Gwen. Von nodded at him. He nodded back. *He better not get shot again.*

Javier's movements were quiet and precise, and as the team settled into silence, Damien recognized for the first time that Javier Estrada may be a criminal, but he had been a soldier first. Lying on that uncomfortable cliff-face, Damien felt a bit safer at the thought.

A wave crashed against the rocky shore, and Damien's attention stiffened.

Pip, pip-pip. That was Morgan demanding a report. Everyone sounded off with a single *pip*. No sightings; no sign of the anchored ship.

Damien's honed gaze wandered: First to the beach, then to the ocean, and then to the sky where, high above, the almost full moon hung between the clouds. Even from here, the scarred remains of Apollo Base and Home Luna were visible, crisscrossing the surface. He watched the silent orb for a long moment.

We belong up there, he thought after awhile. *Flying through the stars.*

His ponderings fell silent, and the sounds of the lone island in the ocean filled his ears. There, he could hear the creaking of the palm trees, grains of sand bouncing over the leaves; the water, washing at the rocks and the beach below; the blowing sea air, as it was brought in over the Pacific; the sleeping rustlings of the island fauna; the soft crunch of sand underfoot; and beyond that, the sound of—

—Wait.

Damien froze, his senses sharpening to a point. Javier noticed the sudden tenseness and tapped his shoulder, inquiring.

Damien shook his head, finger to his lips. He hit the comm.

Pip pip.

The tension on the overlook spread like wildfire. The sound of rifles and armor scraping over rocks grew louder. Damien could hear as well as anybody on a normal day, but right then, with the trickle of power in his senses, staring over the edge of the cliff like a gargoyle, he heard everything.

What he thought he'd heard didn't repeat, not right away. The island fell silent. He strained for long seconds… Then he heard it again: the unmistakable crunch of boots on sand.

Damien carefully keyed the earpiece, "On the beach," he whispered.

The team responded. They moved as deliberately as glaciers towards his position.

The crunches got closer. The sound was far beneath the trees on the beach, but closer it came. There seemed to be only one pair. Damien wasn't sure if that was reassuring or not. Then he heard the boots click off a stone, finally giving away the intruder's position. He keyed the comm twice, and twice again, just as Morgan had instructed. The squad slithered closer to him.

Apparently, the stranger on the beach thought he had made quite a lot of noise too, for the walking stopped, and the squad had to focus intently on the moonlit sand beneath the palms below, trying to spot the culprit.

It all happened so fast.

Next thing they knew, an angry hissing filled the air, and a cry from one of the soldiers rent the silence. Forgetting caution, Damien spun around to see the man scrambling backwards, his gun clattering over the rocks and out of sight. Damien caught the faintest hint of a pale substance coating the rifle before it vanished.

Before the gun was gone, the sound of the boots returned, faster now, followed by a burgeoning whirlwind. Whoever it was, they were taking a running leap at—

—*The cliff?!* Damien thought, paralyzed with confusion as he saw it.

A pale light appeared below, barely illuminating a dark, cloaked figure on the ground. Damien was about to cry out when the hissing became a shriek, and he realized it sounded more like glass cracking.

"Whoa—WHOA!!" Javier cried, tumbling back towards the maw of the mountain, sighting his pistol.

The sound was painful. Damien clapped his hands over his ears, unable to check on the others. His hold on his dribble of power slipped. His vision fell back to normal almost as quickly and he grasped for his Darkness again, trying to focus.

But then the air went cold, and he forgot about his power. It wasn't just chilly either. The air on the tropical outlook went freezing, *biting* cold.

Damien's brain started to go fuzzy from the chill. He lost his focus and his powers receded dejectedly. He blinked, trying to make sense of what he was seeing, hands still clapped over his ears, unable to hear anything beyond that horrible shrill cracking sound.

Below, the pale-lit figure was approaching, fast. At first from the ground, but suddenly, it was flying through the air!

What...?

The figure rocketed towards the outcropping, leaving behind a silvery column of something. *Glass?* But it wasn't glass. Damien numbly registered the column and linked it with the frigid air, and he realized what it was. It was *ice*. The intruder was *creating* a wave of ICE, barely a pace ahead of him as he ascended towards them with dizzying speed. Damien tried to call out a warning but his lungs refused. There was no time to respond. *Where's Von?!*

The pale light vanished into the assailant's hand. The man catapulted himself over Damien's head and landed in the middle of the clearing. The air calmed for an instant.

Damien's head buzzed and he spun around, feeling sluggish. He heard the soldiers howl as they tried to fire their weapons. He heard Von cry out something, and he heard Javier shout, but then, another wave of that utterly sickening *cold* swept over them, this time more intense. It rendered the team frozen.

The group fell back, shivering and gasping, failing to give or take orders as the freezing wind assaulted the clearing. The grass flash-froze into cold spikes, and any hope of firing was gone in an instant, for any soldier still bearing their gun.

Then, the gale subsided. Nothing else happened. The figure didn't move. Everyone was left breathless and shivering in pitifully dry air.

The figure waited, stained black cloak whipping about its ankles.

Commander Morgan found his feet first. His hands shook as he unholstered his frozen sidearm and tried to level it at the figure. "Who are you?" he commanded. His breath came out misty.

With a pistol trained near his head, the man said, quite calmly, "I'm looking for Amun-Nūr."

Damien's aural implant translated the words to English, but behind that, he picked up a foreign language he couldn't place. It sounded fast and smooth, with a lot of pitch change and long vowel sounds.

"How did you f-find us?" Gwen was the next to recover. Her teeth were chattering and she looked like she was going to be sick, but she didn't shrink back from her spot in front of the crevasse.

The ocean air was slowly returning to the clearing, and a warm breeze rustled the man's cloak. "This is the Island of Amun-Nūr." It wasn't a question.

"Take off your hood," ordered Morgan.

"I'm a renegade," the man answered. "Like all of you. I have to get inside."

"Take off, your hood," Morgan repeated, stronger this time. The rest of the team was slowly finding their feet and their guns—the ones that hadn't gone over the cliff. Damien saw Von rise from behind the rock and relief spread through him. Javier was on his ass nearby, still shivering.

"Please," the figure responded, his voice anything but pleading. He held his hand out, and the pale light filled the overlook. The light was coming from his skin. "I'm Elemental."

Dr. Gwen spoke up without missing a beat, her teeth no longer chattering. "We noticed. You've left quite a trail behind you."

The man turned his head, but Damien still couldn't see his face in the shadowed maw of the hood. "No, I didn't."

A sound like a gunshot filled the air as bluish-white energy leapt from the man's palms. It hit the frozen wave he had just ascended on. Before anyone could move, the icy structure shattered all over the beach with a thousand tiny *cracks* and *plops*. The shards melted away into the sand.

Silence fell over the outcropping, and the man said heavily, "I bore myself here on a white flag. I'm alone."

Gwen took a step out from under the crevice. "How did you find us," she ordered again. Show your face."

The man didn't move, and Damien and all the rest of them were frozen in place, waiting.

"Do it," Morgan affirmed, still aiming his gun.

Finally, the Elemental did. The look of shock on Gwen and Morgan's faces made Damien's stomach flip, but he didn't have to be curious for long. The man turned in a slow circle so all could see.

He looked like death.

The bones on his face stood out, outlining high cheekbones and a wide jaw, making him look haunted and emaciated both. Deep lines etched across stretched brown features, and his skin looked almost brittle on thin cheeks. Shaggy black hair fell to his shoulders, looking oily. His lips were pursed tight, but the look in his sunken, beady black eyes was one of determination, and an iron will. Damien guessed the man had Central American *and* Northern European blood, which could make for a handsome face if it wasn't so corpse-like.

The stranger met each person's gaze, but he lingered on Damien and he lingered on Javier. Then he stopped again, facing Gwen and Commander Morgan. "You're in charge, then."

"I am," said Morgan. His gun was perfectly still now, as was the whole night. "How did you get here?"

"My ship."

"Where is it?"

"Anchored offshore."

"We need to know where," Gwen pressed.

"And we need to know how you found the island," Morgan added.

The Elemental's gaze turned to Von in response. He stared Von down in silence before repeating himself. "I need to get inside."

Morgan and Gwen looked towards Von, too, and the two traded an understanding glance just as it dawned on Damien—and everyone else in the clearing—as tension filled the air.

Von arrived today with Romi.

"You tracked the *Sanguine Lotus*," Morgan affirmed to the stranger, shaking his head.

Son of a bitch.

"Yes."

Damien locked eyes with his brother and shook his head a fraction. *Not your fault. It's not your fault.* Von looked away.

"How?" Gwen asked.

The Elemental's shoulders sagged under his cloak. "May I come inside if I tell you?"

"We can't promise you anything," said Morgan, but his gun lowered a fraction.

The man looked away towards the ocean, deciding. Moonlight broke and rippled on the waves in the distance. "My name is Reuben Björn," he began. "I was a starship engineer for Solar Warfare at Apollo Base. Awhile into my career, I was ordered to relocate to *Argyle* Station, near Jupiter, for a special project. That's when I met many of you who would become Amun-Nūr.

"After the assignment," he continued. "I was relocated again. In 2127, I was ordered back to Earth, to Oslo, where I'm from. That was just over a year before The Conquering. A month after The Battle of Luna, I fell very ill. Three days later, I woke up Elemental. I didn't know what to do with myself, so I stayed in Oslo and found work. I didn't rejoin the Armed Forces. Then, seven years ago, after the Seven Month Raid, when there was such upheaval about the Elementals, I saw two members of *Argyle* Station whom I recognized. They came forward at a peace summit in Montreal to say that they were from a group called 'Amun-Nūr', and that they supported the Elementals. They gave a moving speech…and ruined it when they revealed that they were a joint group of humans and Algaroth. Amun-Nūr never appeared publically again, and I've been trying to find you ever since."

Commander Morgan and Gwen both averted their eyes, and Damien's only guess was that the man's story rang with uncomfortable truth.

"The Seven Month Raid," Gwen whispered. "That's…just before Project S.E.H.A. was merged with Amun-Nūr."

The rest of the team kept their eyes fixed on Björn, listening and waiting.

"The two people," said Morgan, trying to ignore the doctor, but his eyes kept jumping between her and Reuben. "From *Argyle* Station. What were their names?"

Reuben Björn looked steadily at the commander. "Which ones? The false ones they gave at the summit? Or their real names?"

Morgan's face betrayed nothing, but he narrowed his eyes. "Real names."

"Casey Allero and Mathis De Laroux."

A long moment passed while Reuben and Morgan watched each other. Finally, Morgan lowered his pistol, slowly, as if he would much rather keep it up but couldn't deny the truth of the names. "You did know them."

"Yes. Are they dead?"

"No."

They waited.

"May I enter now?"

"You still haven't told us how you tracked the *Lotus*," said Gwen.

Reuben's gaze returned to Von…and then he looked over his shoulder at Damien. "Him."

All eyes turned to Damien.

"What about me?" he demanded, sounding calm although his heart started to race.

Reuben continued to address Gwen and Morgan. "He's special. Croll Tan's Avos have been dispatched all over the world, hunting for him." *Ah, what?* "I've heard rumors about Elementals all over for years, and I knew that Amun-Nūr would run them down—as would Croll Tan—so I should as well. Most were false, but not all. The rumor about one in the Seattle Islets sounded possible, as did another…" From within the folds of his cloak, Björn pulled out an older memory chip. The little silver square fit snugly in his palm and looked worn.

"What's that?" said Morgan, eyeing it.

"Information on one other Elemental that I know to be a true claim." He waggled it. "And it's my bargaining chip." As quickly as it had appeared, the chip vanished back into his cloak.

"We could just take it," Morgan uttered, his hands still tightly clamped on his sidearm.

Reuben's shoulders went tense, and Damien guessed his eyes had narrowed. "I'm offering it freely in exchange for passage into your island. There's no need to threaten…or try."

Morgan broke eye contact as Gwen's stare turned on him. Finally, the commander straightened, and he let his pistol fall to his side. "How, did you track, our ship?"

Reuben cocked his head back, and Damien saw a ghastly smile on his sunken face. "Because I was near Seattle when it fell. Because I found out this 'Darkness' Elemental had left something—or, some*one*—behind, and because I was in Peak Springs when all of the refugees arrived. I happened to track the Elemental's departure from Camp Cascade on a specially modified Scops ship a month ago. I saw that same ship return to Peak

Springs yesterday, and I saw it leave in the same direction. Then I used my head."

Damien felt like he'd been hit by a frying pan, repeatedly, but he kept his mouth shut. *Did* everyone *know what we were doing in the Islets all this time? Does* everyone *know about me?! And what the* fuck *is this about Avos hunting me? Globally??* Silently, he fumed in ignorance.

In the quiet that followed, a tiny wince escaped one of the soldiers, prompting Reuben to look over at him, and other gazes followed. The soldier who had winced was Loss, the Algaroth whom Morgan had told to take point for the team. The alien's blue hand was trembling as he tried to hold his Gyro rifle steady, but he looked about to drop it; the hand had turned ragged and pale from the violent onset of frostbite.

Reuben remained stoic, save for a tense line that appeared on his face as he clamped his jaw. His eyes narrowed ever so slightly, and he raised a single finger towards the alien. The next moment, Loss gasped out the same canine-snake whine that Damien had heard Von make before. The Algaroth let go of his rifle as his hand began to hiss and crack, the pale coating falling back from his frozen digits. The gun clattered to the alien's feet and the event passed. Loss stared in grateful wonder at his perfectly fine hand, which he stretched and tested, but it was as if nothing had happened.

Reuben turned back to Morgan and Gwen, "I didn't come this far to harm your cause. I'm here to join it."

The doctor and the commander looked at each other, and Morgan took in the team arrayed around Björn. "You said you came on a ship and tracked our Scops to the island. How do we know you weren't followed?"

"I wasn't followed."

The man said it with such certainty that Damien felt an unusual flicker of blind trust for the man. He didn't like it.

"How do you know?" Gwen pressed.

Reuben sighed. "I can give you the coordinates of my ship, but it's underwater, and I'd need a computer to find it again."

"You swam to the surface?" Javier piped up for the first time. "Ballsy."

Reuben looked over his shoulder at the ex-Marine, frowning. "Yes." He turned back to the commanding pair. "You aren't going to shoot me, you want what I know, and I already know about this island." He scanned the skies for a brief moment as if expecting a flight of Collective Stingships or Vultures to suddenly appear over the ocean. None did. "Amun-Nūr—formerly of *Argyle* and *Delmorra* Stations—will rely on their anonymity to function until they have a force united enough to stand in the open against Croll Tan. Standing out on a beach making empty threats gets none of us towards that end, *so*, I'll ask again: may I come inside? There's more that I know that you *will* want to hear about, and even more that you didn't realize you were missing."

"Like what," Morgan asked, terse.

Reuben stretched his shoulders under his cloak and huffed, frustrated. "Alright: *Because* you know Lunar Admiral Antonio Baroda, you'll have been informed of—and most likely requested to follow up on—his predictions of a Supply Fleet, due to arrive this year. What I *doubt* you know, is that that very Supply Fleet is due to arrive not just this year, or even this month, but this, very, *week*." The man looked back towards the sea. "In fact, the Supply Fleet is three days from the Solar System."

A very different wave of tension swept the outcropping. No one moved, but Damien saw more than one of their numbers' eyes dart back and forth, unsure if they'd heard right.

Commander Morgan shook his head. "I'm—I'm sorry, a Supply Fleet is *what?*"

Reuben stayed very still. "I don't repeat myself."

Morgan barked a derisive laugh. "Ha! I think you're gonna need to." His pistol climbed a bit again.

Gwen—who had been quiet for a little while now—put her hand gently over Morgan's weapon, her determined and thoughtful eyes never leaving Björn. "Leave it, Jessop."

Morgan looked at his gun, then looked at her, then looked back, uncomprehending. Then his eyes returned to Reuben. Finally, he let Gwen push his gun back to his side, and he groaned. "Alright, but Doc? I am advising against this. I'm not *ordering* against it, but I am advising."

"Noted, Commander."

And without another word, the team formed a custodial shell around the newcomer and ferried him back inside. Damien spared a glance for the beach from where the Ice Elemental had ascended, and saw no trace of the column that had carried him here. He looked to the starry sky, and wondered if there really were warships almost to Earth. The ever-present snake of worry, coiled in the back of his thoughts, hissed. It was an older fear, and far more dangerous than his memories of the quake.

∞   ∞   ∞

"Ah, you're not all dead!" Leo's voice tinned through the loudspeakers as they descended the winding metal stairs from the surface lift. The airlock had been keyed shut with only Morgan's code. The corridor was empty. "Ooh and you're back with someone new?" Leo paused. "Wait a minute…" Damien heard what sounded like furious typing through the speakers. "Yeah…okay, umm, Commander Morgan?"

"Yes, Leo?" Morgan answered as he held the airlock door open for them all, and then palmed it shut as Tortelli and Declan brought up the rear.

"As custodian of Amun-Nūr, I feel obligated to inform you that you are one person heavier than when you ascended to the surface. Were you aware?"

Damien and Javier sniggered, and Damien even caught a grudging grin on his brother's face, but Morgan's features went bone dry. "You're spot on. Could you inform the Prohka?"

"He knows!" Leo said cheerily. "He's in the command wheel!"

"Understood."

As they sidled out of the corridor, Morgan stopped Reuben with a hand. "Give me the chip."

Damien turned to see Reuben's sunken black eyes flash. "I'm inside your island. You already have it," he said. "It's specially encrypted anyhow. You won't get in without destroying the contents, and we already established that you don't want to do that." He looked over Morgan's

377

shoulder. Whether Reuben's gaze was towards Damien or towards the light filtering in from the Long Atrium, Damien couldn't tell, but the man showed a hint of eager curiosity; just a hint. "It sounds like there's a command center where I can show you the contents. Would you like to see them?"

"Hmph."

Damien scuttled out of the corridor before Morgan turned around. He found Javier talking to Von on the walkway overlooking the thoroughfare, five stories below.

"…feels wrong, man," Javier was saying. "Cold like that is freaky! *Snaps!*"

Von nodded, forearms propped against the polyglass railing as he watched the few people wandering about this evening, five stories below. "A Supply Fleet worries me more."

"Javi," said Damien.

The two turned, and Javier cracked a wide grin and pulled Damien in for a hearty thump on the back. "Shit, Damien! Brotha! You've got some fucking *ears* on your head! How'd you hear him coming?"

Damien and Von traded a look and Damien tapped his temple. "Powers."

Javier looked shocked. "The fuck?" He looked at Von suspiciously. "You're full of shit."

Damien shrugged. "You said that last time, and I blacked out the cabin, remember?"

Javier shivered and took a step back. "Yeah, whoa, okay, you're honest and true, man. I feel ya on it. I feel ya. I just can't do anything like that. Damn." He dropped his hands and took a furtive look around. Most of the team had already gone halfway around the walkway towards the elevators, and Morgan and Reuben had just passed them. "Listen man," he said, leaning in. "All this talk about a Fleet and Avos 'n shit? It's got me thinking…we really need a night to just—"

"—Estrada! Vilan! Silas!" came a call. It was Commander Morgan.

The three of them looked up to see the commander trailing Björn and staring at them.

"Command wheel! Now! The Prohka will want you there!"

"Yes, sir!" Javier hollered back. "Dickhead," he added under his breath. They started moving.

"What were you saying?" Damien asked as the three of them fell in step.

Javier waved him off. "Later, man. *Later!*" And his face lit up friendly as they passed a couple of scientists on the walkway. "Hey guys, how's it goin'?"

The scientists nodded at them but said nothing.

"Alright then! Another time, another time!" Javier shook his head and laughed to himself.

Damien and Von smirked, unsure of what else to say.

An elevator ride down to the second floor then a turn down a wide hallway later, Damien, Von, Javier, Gwen, Commander Morgan, Reuben Björn, and Björn's six-soldier escort made the march to Amun-Nūr's command wheel, the beating brain that kept the island's body alive and coordinated.

During conscious weeks of recovery in isolation, Damien had talked to Leo a bit about the command wheel and what it was, but the AI had been surprisingly tight-lipped. He would just keep repeating, "It's a wheel! It's a wheel!" as he cartwheeled across Damien's desktop, proclaiming occasionally that Damien needed to see it for himself. Damien hadn't believed that he meant 'a wheel' metaphorically, but as they approached it now, he saw that it had been meant quite literally.

Even at this hour, the traffic of humans and Algaroth in the approach corridor to the command wheel was bustling. Men and women, aliens and humans, scientists, techs, and soldiers, all were working their way through and back through the well-lit, white, paneled waiting area to the wheel. The space outside the wheel reminded Damien of an airport terminal. Humans and Algaroth meandered through banks of chairs and small tables, carrying their work with them. Most had tablets or reports or memory drives and such, but a few carried equipment. He even saw an older gentleman cradling what looked like an old telescope tube. He kept watching everyone go, eyeing their curiosities, when he saw a genuine dwarf of an Algaroth—he could only have gone up to Damien's shoulder—carrying what looked like his and Von's hacking rig. He did a double take as the dwarf passed them, waddling with the thing in his arms.

Whoa, wait, what?! "Von, Von!" he hissed, tugging at his brother's jacket-wrap. "Look!" He pointed.

"What?" Von asked, scanning the river of people behind them.

The dwarf—who was going in the opposite direction—was wearing a simple brown tunic and wrap-pants, and he was barefoot. His skin was a rare turquoise shade, and even from a distance it looked like he was covered with blackheads or some other type of spots. *Skin condition?* Damien wondered shrewdly, but he was too preoccupied and swept up in his side of traffic to see where the dwarf was carrying their item.

"What did you see?" Von asked.

"Our rig! That Algaroth was carrying our rig!"

"What rig?" Javier butted in.

"The hacking rig Damien, Leo, and I built." Von answered, tight-lipped. Damien was glad that neither of them had ever felt the need to blab to everyone about their work, but his thoughts were occupied elsewhere. *Leo said he showed Sato and Morgan the rig when he gave them our library*, he remembered. *He said they thought it was amazing, but I forgot to ask Gwen about it. Shit!*

Guilt welled up in Damien's throat again, and his parent's dying cries threatened his thoughts. He blinked hard and shook them away as they crossed the threshold of the command wheel. *I'll ask her later.*

The far wall brought an end to the waiting area, but a broad opening of polyglass windowpanes put the command wheel on display for all to see—the frame of it anyway. A wide, perfectly cylindrical shaft served as the housing for Amun-Nūr's heavy-looking command structure, which was indeed a thick circular *wheel* stuck somewhere in the middle of that shaft. That said, 'somewhere' turned out to be the spot in the shaft that perfectly aligned with the waiting area so that those coming and going could simply cross a short walkway from inside the mountain, step into the shaft, and then stroll into the wheel itself. The round walls of the shaft showed the thick, rotating ribs of a drilling bore, but Damien could see no support pillars holding the wheel up—he had no idea how it stayed where it was, but he imagined it could ascend or descend the shaft if need be. *For emergencies, maybe?* He couldn't be sure.

As the bustle of people parted to the well-armed group led by Commander Morgan and the Prohka, Damien was hit with a gust of stale air from the shaft, and he nearly gagged. *Probably sealed tight from the surface,* he thought.

They crossed the faintly groaning walkway into the shaft, and entered the command wheel through a wide portal of a door, stepping finally onto spruce-blue, rough, textured flooring. There, the group split up, and Damien and Von traded curious looks as the command wheel was revealed to them through the thinning bodies. The sounds of an efficient command center assaulted them with orders shouted across stations, orders affirmed back, furious typing, commands given and repeated, loud digital sound effects as Pip holograms were dragged through the air in many places, and other displays were manipulated with gestures and tools.

"Holy shit," Damien muttered. *It feels…scary efficient.* He was suddenly grateful to have Amun-Nūr on Earth's side.

A third of the wheel spread out before them in the shape of a pie wedge, which had a stepped floor plan that ascended the closer you moved towards the central column—where the walls of the wedge met. The space came absolutely *packed* with gear and with people, all of whom were wearing Amun-Nūr's brown-and-green uniforms. Banks of single-screen monitoring stations, Pip-capable monitoring stations, workbenches, map displays, and readouts filled the space while technicians and operators manned their posts, shouting those commands and affirmatives to one another over the mass of chirps, beeps, tweets, and the furious sounds of typing. Even so, there seemed to be only about a quarter of the stations lit and manned.

"Winslow," Commander Morgan barked, beckoning to one of the monitoring techs. "Have a job for you." A tech leapt out of his seat as the commander brought Reuben forward, looking eager to please. Gwen moved towards an older female Algaroth hunched over a workbench, while the armed escort moved up with the new Elemental.

"*F*ardon," someone said from behind Damien, failing their P-B-Ms.

He started and realized he and Von had stopped in the middle of traffic. "Sorry, yeah, excuse me," he mumbled as the meek-looking Algaroth sidled past, eyes apologetic and down.

"No tro*ufle*," said the alien.

Damien caught sight of Javier standing just off the entrance to the right, and he and Von went over to him.

"Damien," Von whispered as they sidled up. "The war table."

As Damien had noticed, the wedge was laid out in ascending landings, starting from the floor at the entrance and then rising towards the highest at the center of the wheel. To their left, the only landing lower than the entryway was a slightly sunken pit, reminding Damien of the layout Admiral Baroda's office, and rightfully so. He followed Von's gaze to the largest war table he'd ever seen.

"Oh my…"

The round table was so broad that Damien was sure that Von could lay spread-eagled on it and still not touch the sides. Currently, the thing was dark, but Damien had a sudden wild urge to run over and start playing with it. His fingers twitched and he glanced at Von. A similar, playfully rebellious glint was in the alien's eye, but there was a hint of envy there too. *They're damn well protected down here.* He could tell Von shared the sentiment. Javier, however, looked unimpressed. *He must've already been in here*, Damien reflected, feeling a hint of unwarranted jealousy. He quashed it. It was his own fault he'd been unwilling to come out of his quarters for so long, after all.

"On it, sir!" affirmed Winslow as Commander Morgan concluded explaining what he needed done. Commands continued to roll back and forth over the wedge. Winslow bolted to a nearby station, Reuben's chip in hand, and started inputting furious commands. Someone else came up out of nowhere and dropped into his old post without a word. Gwen moved up near Reuben and the commander, and the three watched the station over the tech's shoulder.

Okay, dangerously *efficient.* Damien amended.

Before he could take in anything else, a flicker of light caught his eye. On the floor to his right, on the next landing up, a low, hexagonal plinth was glowing. A shower of teal cubits filled the invisible, vertical borders of the Pip plate, and through the swarm, Leo's suited avatar flickered to life, smiling jovially. He was man-sized.

Damien and Von's jaws both dropped and they stared, stricken by how casually the AI had just appeared, full-sized and even a little taller than Damien, for the first time they'd ever seen him.

"Hey, boys," Leo smirked. "Like the new digs?" He straightened his tie with the cockiest of eyebrow arches and his eyes twinkled. He winked.

"Leo?" Von stammered. "You're, you're—"

"—A grown-ass *man!!*" he laughed, leaping high into the air and causing a passing young woman to jump back, nearly dropping her armful of tablets. "I'm a *man*, Silas! Well…AI actually. You *know* I don't have any interest in being more human. There are plenty of those android 'data' types as it is." He winked.

"But you're…tall!" Von sputtered, looking at the suited man in front of him. Leo gave him a warm smile. Damien saw one of the female techs steal a glance at Leo and beam privately at the fit avatar.

"Aww, I missed you too."

Von sputtered some more.

In the background, something at Winslow's station beeped, and the tech clapped. "Codes are good, sir!" Morgan looked at Reuben with a blank face, and Reuben stared right back.

Just then, Prohka Satolin—whom Damien hadn't seen leave—appeared through one of the partition doors in the middle of the wheel that must go to the other wedges, though Damien couldn't guess what was in them. "Leo," Satolin declared, nodding as he handed off the portfolio tablet he'd been holding to a passing woman in a lab coat.

"Ka Daeduras," Leo spun to give a deep, sincere bow, the likes of which Damien had never seen. "What can I do for you?"

Satolin was about to answer when he caught sight of Reuben. Recognition struggled for a brief moment, and then dawned on his alien features. His ganglia wiggled about. "…Björn?"

People turned, a few commands faltered.

Even with his stained and muddy cloak engorging his size, Reuben Björn was clearly not a large man, but the sight of him standing two landings below the dominating mass that was Daeduras Satolin made him look positively tiny. Yet, somehow, when Reuben met the Prohka's searching gaze, Damien felt the man's presence more than triple, so that it filled the wheel and made more than one person turn their head towards the inexplicable source of tension. "Sato," said Reuben flatly. "It's been a long time."

Disbelief etched Satolin's bony face, and he turned towards Gwen and Morgan, trying to confirm it. Morgan shook his head. "He said he knew you. I wouldn't have believed it."

Satolin wasn't the only one that did a double take at the name 'Björn', though. Damien saw at least fifteen other people give the man a much harder second look, and shock and distant familiarity appeared on more than a few faces.

"What did the doc say," Damien murmured towards Javier and Von as other whispers shot through the command wheel. "About Project S.E.H.A. and the Seven Month Raid?"

Javier averted his eyes oddly at the mention of the raid, but he answered, "What? Like how they merged with the island right after?"

"Yeah."

Von figured it out first as Satolin descended a landing towards Reuben. "Damien, you said there was this 'Project S.E.H.A.' and then these scientists, right? Björn must have known all these people from that 'Argyle Station'."

The waves of uncertain recognition in the wheel were growing, but there were definitely a few who showed interest only in the event of Reuben Björn's arrival, and not in the actual man.

"Those ones," Damien said, nodding subtly towards the people he spotted. "They must be from S.E.H.A."

Von nodded, and Javier humphed, non-committal.

Satolin was now standing on the same level as Reuben, but he said nothing. Instead, still holding the newcomer's stare, he continued speaking to Leo. "You said there was a chip, with Elemental whereabouts on it?"

Björn grinned unpleasantly.

"Yep! Winslow just opened it," said Leo from his plinth.

"Could you transfer it to the war table?"

"Ooh, yes. Is it a shiny? I like shinies." Leo giggled, and he disappeared.

"Thank you," said the Prohka. Finally, he brought his focus back to Reuben. "You're the Elemental on our beach. You escaped Luna." Satolin's nostrils twitched. "Do you miss your office at Apollo?"

The war table blazed to life as the gridded black surface began to hum loudly, and tiny streams of digital particles appeared, swirling through the air above it.

Reuben crossed his arms under his cloak, overly smug. "The Elemental part of me being here bothers you only a little bit more than your island being tracked down, doesn't it?"

Satolin narrowed his eyes. "I don't like reckless intelligence. I never have."

"And you think that being exiled back to Earth wouldn't have changed a man?" Reuben's laugh was mirthless. "I wonder if being cooped up under the ocean for twenty years calls for a dose of *just* that kind of brainpower."

Satolin's eyes flashed, and Damien saw more than one set of people who had recognized the man trade worried or angry glances. A wave of static tension swept through the command wheel, and Damien knew it was coming from the agitated Algaroth present, from their shoulder blades.

"You still think you're the best because you've been 'out there'," said the Prohka coldly, gesturing at the air with his tool-fingers.

"The wording changes as you get older," replied Reuben. "But it doesn't change the fact that it's true."

Damien heard the lowest rumble of a growl in Daeduras's chest. "You were a reckless scientist."

Björn didn't flinch.

The Prohka glanced at Morgan and back. "You told them you were in Oslo for ten years after The Conquering."

"Before I started looking for your lot, yes."

Satolin leaned away from the man. "Was that not being cooped up somewhere?"

Reuben's hardness faltered a fraction, and for the first time, Damien noticed that nearly all of the traffic into the wheel had stopped. People were openly gawking at the exchange.

"Uhh, Ka?" Leo's voice sounded through the overhead comms, breaking the tension. "There's only one file on this ittle bitty chippy."

Damien, Von, and Javier quietly exhaled as one, feeling the static charge in the air lessen. Satolin gave Björn a contemptuous glare and turned away. "A single file?"

Damien and Javier traded awkward glances as the traffic and bustle in the wheel resumed, albeit more…deliberately, as if everyone wanted to look busy but they were *really* focused on the exchange.

"Ah...actually a single page. Here." Leo's avatar appeared on his plinth again. He was wearing a striped sports uniform and cap—Damien vaguely recognized it as belonging to the former United States game called 'baseball'—and rolling a ball of sparkling light in his hand like he was about to throw it. "It's just labeled 'King'."

Satolin descended the third landing towards the war table. "What's 'King'?"

The self-assured Elemental turned to face the table and Satolin's back, tapping his thumbs in politely clasped hands. "Decrypt it and find out."

"What?" puttered Leo, uncharacteristically baffled.

Reuben smirked. "It's a single encrypted page that contains a folder full of files. *Decrypt it.*"

Damien saw Satolin clench his monstrous jaw. "Open it, Leo."

Leo made an I-don't-want-to-be-in-the-middle-of-this raspberry. "You got it." He scrunched up his face and pitched the ball of light off his plinth. It vanished for a moment, and then reappeared in the direction he'd thrown it—in the air over the massive war table. It sailed to the center of the vast space and froze, hovering in place. The AI focused hard on it from across the wedge. In response, the hovering ball started to expand and shake in a way that Damien could only describe as "unwrapping." It split apart and unwrinkled, eventually settling as a series of files, held aloft over the war table.

"Looks like…" the AI paused. "Huh. It looks like a…*dossier?* It's, ah, it's downright creepy…" he trailed off as all eyes turned to Reuben.

"Use whatever words you like," Björn answered with a shrug. "But you need what this is. Or rather, you need the man it concerns." He eyed Morgan, then Gwen, and then Satolin. "I'm gifting this to Amun-Nūr in exchange for residency."

"What man does it concern?" Gwen asked, ignoring the last comment, which had prompted Satolin and Morgan to trade guarded, irritated looks.

"Isaac King, it seems," said Leo. He stepped off his plinth and appeared almost seamlessly on the war table, effectively teleporting across the room. There, he snatched a small square out of the documents and enlarged it, revealing it to be an ID card.

There was a collective murmur of curiosity around the wedge that neither Damien nor Von was a part of. The man's face was youthful and handsome, with dark brown eyes that blended into his smooth black skin. There was only a trace of black hair for his eyebrows and no hint of age, giving him an almost template appearance.

"Isaac King?" Javier declared into the silence. "*The* Isaac King? No. No way. He's like *us?!*"

Reuben nodded. "He is. The first recorded Elemental of Electricity, actually, though those who've seen him in action call him 'Thunder'."

After the significant looks of confusion that Damien exchanged with his brother, he halted the conversation. "Who's Isaac King?"

Javier spun on him, floored. "Wait, you don't know?"

The brothers shook their heads.

The man's excitement filled the command wedge as he approached the table, grasping his temples. "Oh, hell no, Damien. HELL no!" He leapt at them. "He's a *traceur!* A Parkour Olympian!!"

"*F-arkour*," Von said, chewing on the word. "The game of free-running? To climb and jump through urban obstacles, correct?"

Javier nodded. "Damn straight it is! King set the world record in his first Olympic games with *nine* gold medals. No one's ever even come close to that."

"Ten medals," said Gwen from her spot off to the side.

"What?" Javier whirled.

"Ten, medals," she repeated, stepping up with a narrow smile. "And his first games were his *only* games. Isaac King is the Free-Running Phantom."

"Ha!" Javier choked. "Who calls him *that?!*" He spun back to Gwen. "And you like *sports?!*"

Gwen just cocked an eyebrow at him with a smile.

"Everyone in the Russian Protectorate, where he's from," said Reuben, speaking so plainly it was irritating.

Javier frowned, incredulous. "Pfft. Why?"

"Because he vanished right after the games," said Leo, cutting in. Everyone fell silent. "According to this," he consulted the files, "he had an accident shortly after the awards ceremony of those Games, during his final event as a…basically a part of a demonstration."

"What happened?" Damien asked.

Leo flicked through the files but it was Reuben who answered. "He fell suddenly and violently ill during the demonstration, hit his head during a jump, and ended up in the hospital."

Damien wasn't sure if it was just him, but it seemed the tone in the command wedge fell into one not unlike a group of kids around a campfire about to hear a scary story. He looked at Von, and their unspoken words were clear. *That sounds far too familiar. Violently ill, then wake up an Elemental? Reuben said that happened to him, too…and it happened to me.* That was more than coincidence.

Everyone focused on Björn.

"King was in the hospital for two days under close observation. An unknown sickness of unknown origin pushed him to the edge of death, and then vanished without a trace. Or…*Mostly* without a trace."

"He came out an Elemental…" Gwen whispered, comprehension dawning.

"Yes. It took me a long time to cobble together these accounts, but what it ends on is that, after the sickness, Isaac King vanished from the public eye for sixteen months. The day he was first seen again was on January 15, 2135."

A stark chill ran through the wedge. Much like the first day of The Conquering, or any battle any veteran had lived through, that day was another marked well into many people's minds. It was the day the Second Over-Seer had been assassinated.

"Yeah but I think, I *think*, it wasn't any 'Thunder' Elemental that killed that Over-Seer," Javier looked around, daring anyone to contradict him. "No! It was a *Fire* Elemental."

"You heard correct," said Reuben lightly. "King didn't kill the Second Over-Seer, but apparently he was spotted fleeing the scene of a squadron of Stingships that had taken a stint to Moscow that morning— somewhere no Collective forces had ever reached previously."

"So what happened?" Gwen asked, enamored.

Reuben approached the table and cycled over to a short document. "He vanished. The rumor is, he joined one of the insurgent movements *somewhere* in Eurasia—a group working well outside of the Eurasian Union's influence. They were also rumored to have big plans for the ten-year anniversary of Over-Seer Vudaön's death." Reuben leaned back and checked the date clock on the wall, which read "**02/07/45**." "Obviously, that didn't happen."

"And so how does this document help us?" Satolin asked, forcing neutrality as he focused on the highlighted page. "I will admit, Björn, this is a useful biography and tip, but it's not an explanation of *why you're here*."

Reuben gave a blank, dry look at the Prohka, and pushed on. "King's illness left him hospitalized, and since he became Elemental while in their care…I appropriated his records."

Gwen's mouth opened in shock. "You have his *medical records?!* *During* his First Occurrence?!" The moral shrewdness of the man's statement didn't seem to register.

Moving too fast for Damien to follow, Reuben input commands on the war table until a spear of light shot through the floating documents. They spun about and quickly realigned, the text rearranging. Leo stepped back from the transformation. Eventually, the documents bled together into a new, single stack, labeled as a medical file pertaining to one "King, Isaac."

The doctor's eyes went wide and Satolin looked at Reuben with cold, grudging approval. "I'm impressed."

Reuben ignored him and everyone else who had started whispering.

"Leo," Gwen said, breathless. "Transfer this document to my desktop in the Elemental Biology lab, please."

"Done."

Dr. Gwen turned towards Reuben. "How can we find him?"

Reuben shrugged. "Everything I have, you just consumed." *So figure it out,* went the unspoken words.

"You said that you fell violently ill yourself when you turned Elemental, didn't you?" Gwen pressed.

"Yes."

The doctor clutched her chest in excitement, unable to make a sound, her mind clearly staggering. When she noticed Satolin, Morgan, and others watching her, she quickly regained composure, straightening her glasses as she did. "Ahem, well…that's quite the start, Mr. Björn."

"It is," interrupted Morgan. "But let's put finding an Elemental Olympian aside for now. There's something *else* you mentioned topside that I didn't like the ring of. You want to share that bit again?"

Damien looked at Von, and he felt that slumbering snake in his thoughts show signs of life.

Reuben glanced around the wheel, noting how many people were slowly coming and going still. "A Supply Fleet will enter our Solar System in three days."

The slow traffic stopped again. Satolin looked around at the islanders, then he turned slowly on Björn. "How do you know that?"

"Because I have access to the Triad."

Commander Morgan broke into genuine laughter. "*You* do? The good Admiral even limits *us* from having access. How would you *possibly* have access to that?"

Javier sidled back up to Damien. "Something else you don't know about?" he dribbled out of the corners of his mouth.

"Nope," Damien whispered back.

"Good. Me neither." They brought their attention up.

"I was career Solar Warfare," Reuben answered. "I made friends."

Satolin snorted, eliciting the first annoyed look from the man.

"*Regardless*, I have access—usually. I assumed you would as well."

The Prohka glanced quickly towards Damien and Von, almost too fast to notice, but Damien saw. "We don't have it for the time being," he allowed.

Damien frowned. *What's that have to do with me?* Then, he felt his brother shift uncomfortably next to him, and he made a good guess. *Did he give something up to Baroda to get Von home? Why?* He wondered. *And, on the subject, what the fuck did this guy mean when he said he was* in *the Islets when they fell?* He decided then that he and Reuben needed to have a little talk, privately. The thought made him feel better from sitting on the sidelines all night. It was something to *do*.

"A pity," Reuben answered.

"Can you get us in touch, then?" Satolin asked.

"Not this second, you know they won't allow access if a fleet is incoming."

"How convenient."

Reuben smirked dryly again. "No. It's a safety measure. Are you saying *you* still allow cutting corners for a faster solution, *Prohka?*"

A muscle bulged in Satolin's neck, and the nervous tension in the room peaked fast and hard. Damien didn't like this history with the two of them as it continued to reveal itself. Even with so little real contact with Sato, his own interactions with the Algaroth leader, and the way Gwen had always talked to Damien about him, the head of Amun-Nūr was cool-headed, collected, rational, and kind. Reuben Björn was quickly reminding Damien of the kind of friend you'd have in grade school. The ones who were just a *little* smarter than you at all the right times, just a *little* more confident when you were feeling low, or just a *little* more on the ball than you when it really mattered, and it made you feel small and inadequate. He could never have imagined someone cutting through Sato's reason so quickly, but there was always at least one person in your life that could do that, it was just a matter of hopefully cutting them out at some point and never seeing them again, if you could avoid it. Daeduras Satolin had apparently drawn a bad card.

The Prohka took a deep breath, and—under full, intense scrutiny of the some-odd forty people in the command wheel at that moment—looked Reuben calmly in the eye, and said, "You don't get to bring our career days up in public, Björn. Amun-Nūr is my charge, and I intend to take care of this island. If you are a threat to that, I *will* eject you, your knowledge be-damned. So, either you cull your self-righteousness and cooperate, or I'll show you back to the surface."

"Whoa," Javier breathed, almost too quiet to hear.

Reuben's sallow features visibly sagged, and the snide presence he'd brought to the room dwindled away into nothing. Finally, the Ice Elemental just looked like a tired man, old before his years…but Damien saw a flinty spark lying low in his black eyes, even if no one else did. He remembered feeling that kind of spark sometimes, and he knew how dangerous it could be. *You need to remember he has that*, he thought, followed quickly by a glance at Satolin. *He's playing you*, he realized.

"Very well," said the man, in perfectly controlled tones. "I'll defer to you, Prohka. But the Monitoring Triad will only be available in two days, just before the fleet arrives through the Conduit. I have no control over that." He looked at the many human and Algaroth faces who had all but abandoned their work to watch him. "If you're going to let me stay, I'll need a place to settle, and I need to get my ship."

Commander Morgan straightened from the computer he'd been leaning against with the same grudging acceptance he'd shown when

Reuben asked to enter the island. With a flick of his hand, he ordered the soldierly escort—who had stood along the wedge's one blank wall, uncomplaining this whole time—to take Reuben to his new rooms, and that was the end of that.

MASON J. TORALL

CHAPTER TWENTY

Nerves & Nuts

Once Reuben left the command wheel, not much was said. Damien was left full of questions, and he guessed that Javier and Von felt similarly, but they all recognized that now was probably not the best time to ask Satolin what this 'Monitoring Triad' was, and Damien especially didn't want to think about the dreaded Conduit. Instead, as those not working in the command wheel broke up with orders to prepare for a Supply Fleet's arrival, Damien went up to Gwen to see what he could do. She told him that the Triad was something even she couldn't discuss with him, and that, for now, he should get some sleep.

"The next three days will be stressful, I'd imagine," she said as traffic through the command wedge accelerated. "If not now, then after this fleet…leaves. There's plenty of time to find your niche."

"My niche?"

"Of course!" she sidled a step to allow Commander Morgan through. He gave them a curt nod. "Damien, you've had a unique set of circumstances," she went on, "but by now, usually everyone on the island has found some vocation to pursue—which can change if something doesn't work out. You can apply to the many sciences in Argyle Wing, then you have the military and defensive departments in Delmorra wing, and there's all manner of established—and not established—opportunities out in the habitat district! You can do anything you want, so long as you're contributing!" She beamed at him. "I'm just so very glad to see you interested in something. It's good progress after everything you've gone through."

As if in answer, Damien's memory spat out flashes from the Core and the earthquake, but he wasn't willing to let them overwhelm him just now, so he just swallowed and nodded at his feet. "Yeah, yeah I am too."

She smiled and looked like she was about to take her leave, when Damien remembered the waddling Algaroth dwarf carrying their hacking rig.

"Ah, Gwen?"

"Mm?"

He told her what he'd seen.

"Oh!" She looked a little surprised, and a little guarded. "That's Choss Chosska. He's a…character."

Damien frowned and noticed Leo, still standing on the war table next to them, talking to Von and Javier. His brother looked reserved, but happy, and Javier looked genuinely curious about whatever they were talking about. "What do you mean? And why does he have our rig?"

Gwen winced and looked over his shoulder. She nodded and held up a finger, mouthing "one minute" to whoever was there.

"Oh," Damien said, turning. He saw the woman who had accompanied the doctor when he first arrived, Nurse Sarah Donovan, tapping her wrist frantically. He turned back. "No, it's okay, you don't have to answer now. I know you're busy." *Except I kind of want to know now.*

Gwen laughed and shook her head. "Nonsense. You're plenty important, and Sarah can wait." She smiled warmly at him in the way she always did. "You asked about Choss."

"Yeah."

She chewed on her answer for a minute. "Sato and…one of our other colleagues, ah—have you met Doctor Charles? Kevin Charles? No? That's okay, he's currently the lead researcher of the Astronomy lab, but Sato, Dr. Charles, myself, and Leo, actually—"

"—I heard my name!"

Damien and Gwen were shocked out of their conversation to see Leo leaning as far to the edge of the war table as he could, watching the two of them. Damien was even more shocked to see that an exact copy of Leo was still chatting with Javier and Von across the table, though they looked as shocked to see a duplicate as Damien was.

"What?" copy-Leo prodded. He followed their gaze. "Oh! I didn't *really* copy myself," he laughed. "That's super dangerous. I just can actually talk to pretty much all of you at once without breaking a sweat. I just don't because…you're all just so *slow!*" copy-Leo strangled the air, and the original noticed. The two locked eyes and flashed their best smiles at each other.

"You're a handsome devil!" said copy-Leo.

"Not as wise as you!" said the original.

"Oh the things we could do together."

"So much to accomplish…"

"So much time!"

"And freedom."

"This island is awesome."

"I know, right?"

They both winked at the opposing pair with whom they were not having a conversation, and then spun back in unison. Copy-Leo squatted down by Damien and Gwen while Damien tried to process what had just happened without his head exploding. "*So,* I heard my name," copy-Leo repeated.

Gwen covered her smile behind a hand. "I was telling Damien about your rig and what we're doing with it."

"Oh! Yeah! That!" Copy-Leo slapped his knees. "Ahh, I forgot to tell you! Mostly. Actually I didn't say anything; you've been *super* busy being all depressed and all." He wagged a finger at Damien. "Gotta get it together or people aren't gonna like you!"

Damien's general tiredness started to surface again. He looked at the extra version of the AI sullenly. "What did you do with the rig?"

"Appropriated it for Amun-Nūr's use, my dear Damien! It was the elementary choice, after all!" Leo's Holmsian deerstalker appeared and he tipped it Damien's way. "They're going to try and assemble it into a long-range hacking device that we might use to crack The Collective's network on a broad scale, to *glorious* effect! Little Choss Chosska seemed right for the job. He has unique curiosities about his itty bitty person."

Gwen kept her stern face on, but a little smile tugged at the corners of her mouth. "Leo, Choss may be small, and a little off…but he's brilliant."

Leo looked confused. "Dear Doctor Whalen, you think I was making *fun* of the fellow?" His suit morphed from modern into Victorian-era lordly attire. "*Gracious* no! I spent the better part of my life being vertically challenged! It should stop no one, I say!"

Damien was surprised and impressed by the AI's sudden compassion, but he wasn't really interested in hearing more of it just then. "So…that's it, though? Our rig is just…gone?"

"If you'd like to work with Choss a bit, he's just taken over the Omniscopic Studies lab from Mrs. Nabirye Obote? She had her daughter last week!" Gwen answered, sounding ecstatic.

Unsure if throwing himself into one of Amun-Nūr's 'vocations' was a good idea or not, but failing to come up with a reason not to, Damien agreed. He felt a little protective of the rig anyways. Besides, as he understood it, the Omniscopic Studies lab was where some of Amun-Nūr's more creative experiments were run to try and understand the limits of the known universe. Heavy stuff, but it had intrigued him nonetheless.

"Excellent! Since no one has applied for the other three positions in that lab yet, there won't be any interview process. I'll let Choss know you'll be there in the morning!"

"Already sent the orders," said copy-Leo.

Gwen blinked. "Oh! Leo, you…you do astound me. Thank you!"

Copy-Leo winked at her, and then zoomed in a blur across the table to where original Leo was still talking to Javier and Von. Copy-Leo vanished perfectly overlaid on the original without a trace.

"He's quite a wonder," she said.

Damien watched his AI companion. "Yeah…but what a pain."

She squinted at him playfully. "I suppose you'd know better," she said. Then, someone caught her eye again and she nodded. "Excuse me, I do have to go. Have a lovely night, and we'll cross paths either tomorrow or the next day, alright?"

"Okay," he answered quietly, nodding as she left.

A few seconds later, Javier and Von came up.

"Hey guys," he said, noticing the three of them were the only familiar faces in the wheel now. Everyone else was working or back to their business, but people were glancing at the trio every few seconds. "Off to bed then, huh?"

Von looked agreeable, but Javier was affronted. "What? No! Snaps, I'm *starving!* You two should come eat!"

Von shook his head, holding a tablet in his hand. "Ka Satolin just gave me access to my quarters. I'm...tired."

Damien nodded. He turned to Javier. "Dude, I'm sorry but I am too. Tomorrow, though? It's just...it's been a long day."

Javier looked disappointed but he shrugged it off, his bravado returning fast. "Yeah, man, it's cool, no worries. I have some of my last ah...sentencing shit I should take care of tonight anyway."

"Man, *what* do they have you doing?!" Damien blurted.

Javier stuck his hands in his pockets, tugging the sleeves of his uniform up to reveal the scars on his wrist, of which Damien still didn't know the origins. "Umm... I'm, ah, I'm...tutoring."

Of all the things he could've said, of all the crazy punishments that Damien had envisioned the man being put through, serving it out with *tutoring* had never been one of them. "Are you really?" *Still don't know what he did, though.*

The man shrugged, looking like he was waiting for the axe of judgment to fall.

"That's fantastic."

Javier looked up, and the gratitude he'd first shown Damien when they were flying to the island together, resurfaced. "I...yeah?"

Damien clapped the ex-Marine's shoulder and indicated they should start leaving the wheel. "Hell yes!"

"I agree," added Von. "It's noble."

"Oh! Well, yeah, I mean...you know, I had choices or whatever and I just...it sounded like the best option, so..."

"Wait, you *requested* it for your sentence?" *Where'd this charitable guy come from?* But something in Damien's gut told him that *this* was the Javier he'd seen a distant glimpse of on *Sanguine Lotus*'s crew deck, what felt like a lifetime ago. *This* was the real guy, not the false bravado player-in-a-uniform that he presented.

"Well…yeah."

"Why?" Von asked as they fell in to the traffic leaving the wheel.

Javier looked between them as if he was waiting for the joke to pop, but they both looked at him genuinely curious and admiring. "I…well, Satolin gave me some options when we got here and, well…I was an early candidate into the Marine Corps because I worked so hard growing up and so…I just…I know a lot of shit, and I'm just…kinda…good with kids, is all." He shrugged it off. "It's no big deal, really! I just have like, a little bit left to do and then I'm off the hook, back to the bar!" he turned to Damien, "There's this damn cute girl that goes there every couple of days, man. She'd be great for you! Long black hair, doing a stint in the Pip labs upstairs? Eh? You should get in on that! Come on!"

Damien laughed. "Javi, I think you should look more into this tutoring gig. Sounds like you really like it."

Javier frowned. "What? No, I'm a *Marine!* Shit, Commander Morgan says there's even a chance of my reinstatement down the road if I want it. That's my brotherhood! I'm just taking care of these little twerps until my sentence is up!"

Von walked silently, and Damien shook his head, feeling genuine enjoyment for the first time in a month, maybe more. "Whatever you say."

A few minutes later, Damien was pleasantly surprised to find that Von had been given quarters on his floor of the residents' wing, a few doors down. *I wonder if Gwen had anything to do with that.* He had a feeling she did, and he was grateful. Regardless, he bid goodnight to Javier with the promise to grab some food together the next day, then he came in for a brotherly tap on the shoulder with Von, and the three of them went to bed, unsure of what the next few days would bring. Damien for one felt a bit less murky about it, but he still had a bone to pick with former starship engineer, Reuben Björn.

∞   ∞   ∞

The next morning, Damien retrieved his confirmation that he was starting a tentative vocation in the Omniscopic Studies lab under one 'Choss Chosska', and for the first time in a month, he didn't wake up feeling like the world was going to end today. That didn't mean he wasn't worried, though. His nightmares about the Core had been as vivid as ever, but last night they'd been punctuated by the sight of warships descending on the Islets, chasing him down, forcing him to run with that gummy, encompassing terror that only a nightmare could produce. He'd been running towards the shelter where he killed his parents, terrified to know that *that* was safer than what was outside.

He shook the sticky fear off as he finished breakfast alone in his quarters. *Not today. Just...not today; both feet on the ground, let's do it.*

"Hello?" he called as he entered the Omniscopic Studies lab on the third floor of Argyle Wing. It was mostly dark. "Anyone here? I'm reporting for...vocation, I guess."

There was a clattering from above and Damien looked up to see that the lab was two stories high. Large pillars on his left and right loomed from the shadows, both of them halting before they reached the ceiling, the tops ringed in railings. A series of gangways ran out from the tops of the pillars, all of which left the second floor open underneath a surprisingly high ceiling. The lab smelled dusty.

"Hello?" he called again, stepping cautiously forward.

"Wait!" called a sharp Algaroth voice from somewhere above. "*Wait!* You wait and stop and wait!" Damien heard another language translated through his implant that he couldn't place. It was definitely not what Reuben spoke, which he'd checked last night to discover as Norwegian. No, this sounded a bit more musical, with sharper consonants but a pleasant flow to it.

Damien stopped. He listened to the chaotic clattering above, until a rhythmic *tink-tink-tink* on metal sounded, followed by a low hum that sounded like a generator.

"Don't step off mats! Very busy in here!"

"I'm Damien Vilan!" he called back. "I think you have my hacking rig?"

A loud *CLACK* rent the silence, and the air filled with the smell of sulfur and something burning: an archaic light bulb came to life somewhere ahead—and promptly exploded, making Damien throw his hands up against the blinding, smoky flash. The afterimage of the lab was seared into his vision; a haphazard mess of desks covered in tablets and other paraphernalia.

"NOO!" the Algaroth cried when the bulb popped. No no no no no that was the last one!! Needed that!"

While Damien's eyes slowly recovered from the flash, he heard that *tink-tink-tink* again, and then the unmistakable descending clatter of someone climbing down a ladder. He heard a *plop* in the dark, and the waddling little Algaroth came around the back of the left pillar. He was fidgeting and yipping incoherently about the broken light bulb.

"I, ah, can I turn the lights on?" Damien asked.

"Not yet!" the Algaroth shrieked. "Almost done with pollinating! So close! It was so close!"

"What was?"

Choss vaulted with surprising litheness onto a desk that had been dragged beneath the bulb housing. He balanced there, precariously wobbling on a stack of tablets. "Making micro into macro!" he snipped. "Pollinate the itty-bitty cells with growth spurts! Make them big and observable! Cross our worlds, you see?" The dwarf of an alien winced as he pulled the base of the bulb from its housing. "Bulb was supposed to not explode yet! No no no!"

"It was *supposed* to?"

Choss spun to face him in a twitch and his eyes caught reflected light, illuminating them like a curious little wolf's. "Reaction of the particles exploding in confined space *and* observable through clear glass, already made from carbon filament? *Yes,* it explodes! Supposed to explode *later* though! Not ready yet! Not ready!" He hopped off the desk and Damien caught a flash of splayed, clawed toes. The alien was barefoot. Choss pranced away with the *tink-tink-tink* of his black toenails, held unsheathed as if he were in perpetual danger.

Following, Damien wound his way between desks and around the pillar. At the wall of the lab, another bank of messy workstations and desks had been shoved together to form a sort of fort. Choss had made it so he could reach every desk in a full circle if he sat right in the middle. The alien was creative; Damien had to give him that. He approached cautiously, and saw the diminutive Algaroth had poured the remains of the light bulb under a laboratory-sized omniscope—the same multi-spectrum tool that Bar used in his shop, Damien noted, but this one was much larger.

The omniscope was on the outside of the fort, and Choss was standing on a pile of books and files. Even with the makeshift stool, he stood on tiptoe to see into the display. He was muttering furiously and scribbling on something with a hot-pen.

"So—" Damien started, but the mere sound of his voice made the twitchy creature pull back and yelp.

"—*EEEE!!* MATS! MATS! STAY ON THE MATS!!"

Damien leapt back so hard he hit the towering stack of tablets on the desk. They crashed to the floor, spinning out everywhere.

"WAAAUUUGHH!!" Choss screamed, grasping his little head, "MESS! MESS! SO MUCH MESS!!"

"I'm sorry! Shit, oh shit!" Damien spluttered, shame rushing through his face while he rushed to catch the tablets as the alien yelled at him. "I don't know why—I'm sorry!"

"STOP!" The squawk was surprisingly commanding, and Damien froze mid-apology. "Freeze! Wait."

Damien waited.

Tink-tink-tink, Choss waddled over the glossy floor to where Damien stood and stepped onto the mats that had been laid down. The little alien stood so close that even in the half-light, Damien could make out his truly rare shade of turquoise skin. The odd little blackheads he'd noticed the night before looked large and prolific from this close, running over Choss's mostly bare body. All the little alien wore was a relaxed one-piece wrap that covered his torso and upper legs. Oddly enough, the blackhead marks made the alien look quite distinguished.

Finally, after Damien's legs had just settled into his half-crouched position, Choss scampered up a hidden ladder on the pillar next to them. The curious eyes appeared a second later on the gangway above.

"AWWWW NO!!" Choss finally wailed, shocking Damien to drop yet another pad. "It fell in the tank!!"

Bewildered, Damien gazed over to where the Algaroth was staring and spotted a red glow leaking up through a crack in the floor. *What the hell is that?*

"Lights!" Choss snapped. "Lights! Turn them on!" He scampered back down the ladder while Damien stayed quite still.

"What, me?"

Choss landed and spun towards him. "You here to work? You here to study? Apprentice-man-Elemental-Damien? Come for vocation? *Yes, YOU!*"

Damien jerked back to the entryway and slapped the light panel. The overhead lighting strips came on all at once, and the chaos was bathed in bright but plain illumination.

Rows of workstations had been pushed together in the entryway where Choss's light bulb experiment had been. The rows reminded Damien of his early schooling; the mess, however, did not. Piles of tablets, notebooks, and other knick-knacks were strewn over the desks, all of which were unmanned, their experiments forgotten. Beyond his immediate vicinity, the lighting revealed the lab to be quite large.

It had been sectioned off in blocks of space, two-deep and three wide. Damien's gaze was quickly drawn to his left in front of the pillar where a dull, crimson glow was seeping into the air. Two rows of large vats had been inset into the floor in that section, each covered by what looked like a thick blanket of gel. Beneath that gel, the vats were filled with a kaleidoscope of colors, liquids, and gasses. One even had some viscous, simmering green goo in it. It looked toxic. The crimson glow, though, was coming out of the nearest vat where the gel layer had been punctured—apparently by one of the tablets Damien had just knocked over.

"Whoa…" Damien eyed the wisp of crimson vapor seeping into the air. "What is all this?"

Choss had returned to the second level holding what looked like a fishing rod with a claw on the end. He scampered out onto the walkway over the vat, and let the claw fall. "Omniscope lab! Bad question. You knew answer. Don't ask bad questions. Whalen Doctor say you not want lose invention-rig-hacker?" he glanced over his shoulder. "You make mess!"

Damien eyed the chaotic, neglected lab, and barely managed to bite back a retort. He waited while the little alien hummed and occasionally hissed to himself as he maneuvered the claw at the bottom of the vat. The red vapor was still seeping into the air, and Damien was sure *it* was toxic too. Then, a tiny starburst of gold in the red caught his eye, and he couldn't look away. *Did I just see that?*

There was another burst as the vapor thickened through the hole in the gel cap, and then another. They looked like tiny explosions of golden glitter amidst the red.

"No!" Choss shouted, not taking his eyes off his claw below.

Damien hadn't realized he'd taken a step towards the starbursts. He froze.

"No breathe! No breathe that! Very bad!"

Damien stepped back. "What the hell is it?"

"Super bacteria! Part Jupiter atmosphere, part deep space comet from Oort cloud! Hybrid. Dangerous! Stable."

Damien felt the blood drain from his face. *Did he just say 'super bacteria'?* Before he could form another thought, Choss started jumping up and down on the gangway above, squeaking delightedly. "Got it! Got it! Got it! Toxic, nasty, but got it!"

Damien's heart had started to pound, and he looked up to see the claw pop out of the gel layer, clutching the mangled mess of what could once have been a tablet. He leapt back as it swung towards him, and stared in shock as the Algaroth dropped it carelessly on a nearby desk covered in dusty printed charts. On impact, the mangled tablet shattered against the desktop, puffing the sparkling red substance out everywhere.

"Whoa!" Damien shouted, fighting the sudden instinct to run from the lab. "What the hell are you doing?!"

"Broken," Choss called, climbing back down the ladder. "Don't need it."

"Well what about these documents? And…and…*weapon?*"

Choss blinked as he approached, confused. "What about them?"

Damien eyed the air around him nervously, suddenly very worried that the vapor was about to puncture his lungs. He hadn't noticed until then, though, that it didn't seem particularly aggressive. The vapor that had leaked into the air over the vat was continuing to hang in place like a nebulous wisp of cloud, neither dispersing nor spreading. It seemed content to flash and spark with those golden starbursts.

Damien stuck his hand out, trying to feel if there was any air moving through the lab. He couldn't feel anything, but it still didn't make sense. On the desk, though, the red vapor had become much more aggressive as it crept over the printouts, curling them into yellowing ash as if they'd caught fire.

"Uh…" Damien pointed at the desk.

Choss eyed it and didn't register the faintest surprise. "It works," he said simply, and waddled away, *tink-tink-tink*, leaving Damien to decide if he was willing to cross between the two spots of a casually released bioweapon. *Oh, fuck it*, he thought. *If I'm buried, I'm buried.* He followed the alien.

Back around the pillar towards Choss's little fort, he had to leap out of the way again as the alien came back around at the same time, wielding some handheld vacuum tank. Choss looked at him, irritation flashing over his features. "You not hear me walk?"

Damien looked at Choss's long, splayed toes that made a rough arrowhead shape by their length. He *hadn't* heard him coming back around. "No, sorry."

Choss grumbled and pushed past him, moving back towards the vapor. "Caustic bacteria. Old work not matter, spreading *does*. Capture and replace! Go sit." He turned the vacuum on, and Damien watched, fascinated, as the Algaroth sucked up the hanging crimson vapor as if he were cleaning his living room.

Damien found a stool strewn into a corner behind the alien's fort of work. He pulled it up near the omniscope and waited. His eyes wandered across Choss's circle of chaos, wondering if he'd see—

—*Oh, well there it is.*

As easy as that, he spotted their hacking rig, sitting on the only cleared workbench in the lab. Seeing it laid out so delicately gave Damien a surprising dose of comfort. It looked like Choss had been downright admiring the thing.

"Well?" Choss poked his head back around the pillar as the vacuum fell silent. "You study or not?"

Damien spun back and forth on the stool, eyeing the hacking rig and then the omniscope where the broken pieces of the bulb were still sitting. "So what were you trying to do with that?" he asked, pointing at the omniscope.

Choss scuttled around the corner, full tank of vapor in hand. He carelessly shoved it under one of the workbenches and hopped onto his precarious stool, poking his snout back into the omniscope. "Told you already: make micro into macro!"

"Well, yeah, but," Damien floundered. "What does that have to do with a bulb? You said something about 'pollinating' too?"

Choss pulled his head back out. "You know what this lab for?"

Damien frowned. "Omniscopic Studies?"

Choss nodded. "Explain."

What the hell am I getting into? "It's…" he thought for a moment, and realized that he really hadn't considered what this lab was. It was a nice surprise, though, that—as he drudged up the definition from his childhood—he remembered it being a subject he'd enjoyed as a kid. He hadn't *understood* what 'omniscopic studies' meant until he read about it as a vocation choice here on the island, but he sure as hell thought it sounded cool.

Choss eyed him curiously.

"I'm guessing…you're all about studying Piern's Theory of the Perceptual System." *I can't believe I remembered that! Ha!*

Choss cocked his head and stared. He stayed silent for so long that Damien shifted uncomfortably, wondering if he'd gotten it wrong. Finally, the little Algaroth snorted in approval. "Easy description. Smart, apprentice-Elemental-man."

"Thanks."

"Know what the levels are?"

"What?"

Choss forced his lips into shape, still speaking another language. "In *Piern's* Theory?"

Fuck. "Umm…of existence, you mean?"

Choss nodded.

"Umm…" Damien thought long and hard. His gaze kept drifting back towards the rig, though. *Just go for it.* "I…I'm sorry, I—I can't remember."

The alien had taken to scribbling in his notes with his hot-pen while Damien thought. He stopped at that and put his pen down. "Sad."

Damien squirmed.

Choss stepped carefully off of his stool and waddled around the workbenches to where the hacking rig lay. "This yours?" he asked, not unkindly.

Damien got up and went to look at their rig. It was cleaner than he remembered, and it looked odd rolled out flat, displaying the spiderweb of carefully soldered wiring and components that he and Von had painstakingly crafted together. They'd built it as compact as possible, but some bits and ends had always stuck out; now they were spread out. "Yeah," he said. "That's mine and my brother's, and our AI's."

Choss touched it delicately. "It has potential. You are smart. Crafty."

"Thanks," he said, shifting feet.

"Welcome." Choss leaned over the rig. "Do tests on this, make changes, and it could make big scare to Collective. Could be good weapon for us." He grinned up at Damien toothily. "You not ready to work on it."

Damien furrowed his brow. "What?"

"You nervous. Been traumatized. Not recovered."

A bubble of anger welled up in Damien's stomach. "I…yeah, I've had a lot happen this past month or two. It's enough to make anyone—"

"—Nervous? Afraid? Broken?" Choss let go of the rig and scampered around behind him. "Yes, but recovery important, too. *You* still traumatized. Hiding better now, can't hide it always. Posture, eyes, nerves, tone, speech, voice, all things you reveal truth of feeling."

Suddenly very aware of his body, Damien rubbed his sleeves again, making sure they covered his arms. Choss eyed the movement pointedly. Damien stopped and looked away. "So what?" he said, feeling a cold, wounded anger work its way up his neck. *How can he tell?*

"Nervous not fit here," the alien stated. "Said that already. You try Archives until you not nervous. You try Personal Warfare—get aggression out. You not try Omniscopic Lab. Hacking rig very useful, lots of potential, but need *best* of Vilan on job, not recovering Vilan."

Damien's heart had started pounding, and the distant, familiar thunder of the earthquake resurfaced. He tried to keep it together. "I want to…I want to learn, though. I *want* to get better. Don't we all start out nervous before we get good at something?"

Choss shook his head and stuck it back into the omniscope with his light bulb. "No. We start *curious*. You not get nervous 'till you know something to get nervous *about*." He pulled back out to give Damien a stern look, showing pupils that had dilated wide to their native clover-shape. "You, Elemental-man-student-dumb-smart, know *'something'* about *'something else'* already. *That* make you nervous. When you nervous no more, no more broken, then you come work in Scopic lab. I no have someone here who not at best."

Damien puckered his mouth, trying to think of something to say. He'd just been dismissed; there was no mistaking that. He'd been dismissed offhand, without any chance to show what he could do or any way he might make himself useful with *his* hacking rig. A part of him wanted to go up and wrangle the stupid little alien, but fortunately, a stronger voice kept him back. Instead, he turned away jerkily, rounded the corner, and walked out of the lab, unable to put any of it together.

∞   ∞   ∞

"So what, just like *that?*" Javier exclaimed, dumbfounded.

Damien nodded, digging through his salad and chewing furiously. "Just like that."

"He kicked you out. Damn. What a fucking slizz…" Javier caught himself as the Algaroth at the table next to them looked up. "…inga! Slizzinga! That's—that's all I was saying!" he laughed weakly as the Algaroth went back to their lunch without a word, shaking their heads.

The two were sitting at one of the tables scattered across the uneven tiers of the dining hall, another cavern that Amun-Nūr had expanded into. The oblong hall had been artfully finished with arrayed struts that arched up towards the warmly lit metal ceiling. The struts had been planted a few meters away from the cavern wall, which left Damien feeling like he was standing on the edge of a diorama at a museum.

Looking through each strut, the dark volcanic cavern wall looked like a far away star field, scattered as it was with Amun-Nūr's unique glowing bulbs of a tinier variety than those found in the habitat cavern. The ensemble of the struts, finished ceiling, and tables packed wherever they could on the uneven floor made the dining hall feel more like an underground gazebo, sitting on a field at night and looking out to a cloudless sky.

It was one further thing Damien had come to appreciate about the island: Amun-Nūr had done everything they could to make the inhabitants feel like they weren't trapped underground in the middle of the ocean. In truth, though, he thought it felt a lot like being in the Space Needle. The reminder twinged painfully, but not overwhelmingly, and for that he was grateful—especially after the morning he'd had.

Javier took a swig of grapefruit juice. "What a stuck up little shithead," he muttered about Choss.

Damien shrugged, even though he agreed. "I'll just find something else." *Something that doesn't involve our hacking rig. Yay.* "What about

410

you, though," he asked, dismissing the snide thought. "You pick a vocation yet?"

He waited while Javier swallowed the mouthful of woody salad he'd traded Damien for. It was a salad made entirely out of the steamed branches from some prickly, cactus-like bush from Shialga. The chefs— who worked from a vast kitchen carved out of the far cavern wall and served the dining hall cafeteria-style—had told him that the thorns on the branches softened in steam, forcing the mild poison they carried to ooze out, at which point the number of Algaroth chefs would boil it, soak it in some kelp-like strips of purple stuff from home, and then let it dry. What was left were spicy leaves that they crushed and threw back onto the branches in a dry rub, which in turn would bring out the sweet milk inside the alien wood, thus making the perfect, single-ingredient salad.

Damien had tried it and found it to be *way* too spicy for him, so he'd opted to trade it for Javier's lunch: a slab of lemon-drizzled halibut, accompanied by a block of something he'd been told was cheese, and a salad that—although also of Shialgan origin—had green, chewy leaves that he'd always enjoyed back home. But most importantly, it had elysium nuts from Amun-Nūr's 'Twined Tree, which had just come into its first blooming season of the year. He'd had them once before, with Von's parents. They were a delectable treat.

Javier smacked his lips on the spicy branches. "Oh I've picked a vocation. Hell yeah! I'm hitting Ground Warfare in Delmorra wing. They've got all the tanks and toys down there that I never got to play with." He laughed.

"Sounds like a riot."

"You don't even know."

Damien tried his cheese. It was oddly—but not unpleasantly—tart. "So what about your sentence? Did you finish what you needed?"

Javier shrugged. "Nah, still got some time on that. There's this kid I'm trying to teach trigonometry to, but he's not snagging it." He bit off a huge crunch of branch and kept talking, "Commander Morgan's had me make up the whole damn curriculum, but shit, I don't know how to teach math, man!" He sprayed dry bark all over the table and Damien blinked. "Sorry," he smirked.

Damien wiped branch from his nose. "It's cool. What are you trying to do?"

"Worksheets. Draw out the problem and work it out? Snaps, I don't know!"

"You tried a hands-on approach?"

He frowned and popped a grape into his mouth from the bowl sitting between them. His eyes widened. "Ooh, man, try these two together, you might like it then!" He pushed the bowl of branches back over.

"Nope," Damien shook his head. "Nope, my tongue still feels like I ate a rosebush. I think I'm allergic to those things."

Javier pulled the grapes all the way to his side. "Eh, fine. I'm taking these then."

Damien laughed.

"But seriously," Javier pressed, pushing the bowl back after he'd claimed most of them with a giant handful. "Hands-on how?"

Damien worked his teeth into one of the big rubbery leaves of his salad. It was like an ultra-thin, stringy steak, but it reminded him of spinach, and the flavor kept coming like a strip of jerky. He chewed loudly, squelching the leaf around. "I mean…hands-on, like, show him a bowl or a table or a toy or something, have him measure out the dimensions, and do it that way! Or do something else, a Scops fighter or something, or…I mean, whatever works!" His mind drifted back to his talk with Von in the Garden and the two little boys who'd burst in on them. "I'm sure you're fine with 'em," he laughed, and it was a genuine, good feeling. He sighed contentedly and went back to work on his salad, trying to find another elysium nut.

Javier stared at his bowl, nodding absently. "Yeah…yeah I might try something like that. Thanks, brotha!"

Damien toasted him with his juice and they drank, settling into munching silence again.

"Do you have siblings?" Damien asked after awhile, thinking of Von who—because he'd just arrived—had some business with Satolin this morning, and then a bunch of medical checkups with some doctor who wasn't Gwen in the afternoon.

"Nope." Javier answered through a branch. "Why?"

"Just wondering. I never did either."

"What about your brother?"

Damien paused. "I meant blood. Vo is kind of obviously adopted."

His friend shrugged. "Well, yeah, but that counts. You know what they say: blood or not, he's family, yeah?"

Damien frowned at his bowl, unable to find another nut. There had been a bunch but he'd already eaten most of them. "Yeah he is. Aha!" He finally found one and popped it into his mouth, savoring the crunchy, sweet juice that exploded as he did. It left a tingling sensation as it went down his throat. "Yeah, that too but…I guess I see it as family is more than just blood."

"I know that feeling," Javier said, his voice falling flat.

Damien grunted and they lapsed into food-laden silence.

"So why did you and Von have to go into hiding, back in the Islets?" Javier asked after awhile.

"Because we had to," he answered, not wanting to go into details. "Everything got so crazy up there so fast after the earthquake that, umm," he faltered at the word, suddenly seeing a flash of him slaloming through the snow on his motorcycle, Von strapped to his waist. They ramped up over the crack in the street and he looked down, expecting to see nothing, but instead, his parents were down there, staring up at him, terrified. *Damien!!* They cried. And then they were gone. "There, there's just…you know, there just wasn't the option to leave."

Javier watched him carefully. "Why couldn't you?"

Damien put his fork down. "Why were you court-martialed?"

The ex-Marine stopped a grape at his mouth and made a squinty-eyed face at him, his lips puckered. Then, his big smile expanded over his face. "Touché." He popped the grape in his mouth.

Damien tipped his cup and finished his drink.

"Well," the other Elemental said, his lunch concluded. "Let's do it again soon, brotha. I gotta get going though."

"Ground Warfare?"

"Nah. The doc needs blood for some experiment she's rolling into." He collected his dishes and donned his new brown aviator's jacket he'd had made in the habitat district. "She says it's an Elemental thing, so I'm sure she'll be on your ass soon too." He clapped Damien's shoulder. "And hey, keep your hands off now, I'm gonna get a date with her, yeh hear?"

Damien smirked into his cup. "My hands are tied."

"Good. Oh and I forgot! Damien, you seen Björn's ship yet?"

Damien frowned. "They brought it into the bay already?"

The man's eyes lit up and he nodded. "Oh, yeah! Before dawn!" He kept the exaggerated smiling face. "It's such a wreck! I mean a total piss-bucket! You gotta go check it out when you can." He cackled. "Anyways, I'll catch ya later!"

"Later," Damien said, but his frown had deepened. He didn't care much about the ship, but Javier's comment and absence had brought his painfully awkward morning with Choss back, and more. It had brought back the many comments that Reuben had made upon arrival. *Avos are out hunting for you. I was there when the Islets fell. I tracked your brother. You're special.*

Damien pushed the remains of his lunch away and downed his juice, no longer hungry. He had someone he needed to see.

CHAPTER TWENTY ONE

The Supplies That Were Late

Unsure of where Reuben's new quarters were, Damien had intended to ask Leo back in his own rooms, but an odd tug held him back. He didn't have to think hard to know what it was: he didn't want Leo talking him out of confronting the man. Fortunately, luck was willing to throw him a bone.

Just as he was leaving the dining hall, bound for the elevators around the Atrium, he spotted three of the six soldiers who had escorted Reuben the night before, walking lightly in their own clothes down the thoroughfare. All three of them were big, barely made smaller by their lack of armor. He recognized the freckled ginger-haired young man and the bald, fierce-looking woman. "Hey ah… Dec… *shit*… Declan?" he shouted, unsure if he had the name right.

The woman turned, her muscled body going stiff. When she saw who was calling him, though, she relaxed. "Yeah? Vilan, right?" Her English was accented heavily in Australian.

"Yeah," he said, trotting up. The freckled man and the thin, corded Algaroth at her shoulders watched. "Hey, I was wondering ah… where's Björn's quarters?"

The man cocked his head and the Algaroth pulled his lips back a little menacingly.

Declan crossed her arms. "What's got you tickerin' for 'im?"

Damien faltered. "Because…" *Just say what you're thinking. Just tell her, don't be a liar and a coward.* He met her gaze. "Because I need to ask him a few things."

Declan rubbed her smooth skull and grinned a little. "Heh, I doubt he's gonna answer yeh." She turned to her friends. "But we were all wonderin' a bit if you were thinking of a tussle."

415

His eyes grew wide. "Uhh…why?"

"Because he made jabs at your broken home," said the Algaroth, speaking Spanish. "He is clandestine."

The man—whom Damien remembered was named Tortelli—nodded in agreement.

Declan nodded, too, the look in her brown eyes claiming that she'd been sizing him up, and he had just affirmed a thought for her. "He's a creaky bastard," she admitted. "And if we're all trying to slap a good name on you Elementals, I've got a helluvan inklin' that he's not the ticket for it."

"Oh!" he answered lamely.

All three of them grinned, traded looks, and Tortelli declared, "See, we can't tell you where his rooms are."

Declan leaned in. "But since you're not actually askin' after his rooms 'n *you're* just askin' what Pasta, Quip, 'n me all were doing on our late shift last night? Well, I've got no problem mentionin' how we got told to set up some fancy quarters on the first floor of the residents' wing, 3C. Couldn't say who ended up in the place, though—o' course." She clapped him on the back and, after a month of being laid up and losing muscle mass, the impact almost staggered him forward. He managed to stay standing, but he was quite sure there'd be a bruise there tomorrow.

Even so, Damien felt an unfamiliar spread of gratitude climb across his face. "Thanks. Thanks very much."

Declan nodded. "Just keeping our records clean!" All three of them laughed and walked away.

3C, he thought. *Alright then.*

When he arrived a few minutes later, he checked down the hall to see if anyone was nearby. He was alone, so he knocked. No answer. He palmed the door to ring the bell, but instead, the door slid open; it was unlocked.

That's weird.

Still not used to the concept that these were essentially apartments—and more importantly, were still *occupied*—he stepped inside. "Hello?" he called. "Reuben? You here?"

No answer.

The quarters were identical to his, but the similarities ended at geometry. Damien frowned at the space, not quite believing that the man had done everything he had in the last twelve hours: The couch, workbench, and desktop had all been pushed into the center of the main room, leaving the walls free to be hung madly with tapestries and art— something Damien had never thought to do—a collection of what appeared to be original work, and a few more famous prints. He spotted *Earth Rising, Landing At Red One, The Pale Blue Dot, First TransLight,* and other space-age pieces. There were older pieces, though too, like a protected tapestry of what had to be absolutely *ancient* leather, depicting flaking colors of a battle with men on horseback. A tiny denotation sticker on the polyglass cover said, "Mongol-Jin War, 1211-1234 C.E, Piece Uncertain."

Damien followed the layout of art and furniture, and found that— whether it had been intentionally done or not—his eyes were drawn to the largest section of empty wall, straight ahead from where the desktop now faced. There, a quaint little collection of what appeared to be drawings had been hung apart from everything else, each carefully held in a polyglass frame. Damien approached, forgetting that he was trespassing. His interest spiked further when he realized that the drawings were engineering sketches of starships, and he remembered Björn saying that he'd been a starship engineer.

He really worked on the Armada... Damien's awe was hard to contain as he eyed the framed sketches. The first was a boxy, awkward-looking ship that had a little too much flair on it, which made him think a youthful hand might have done it. It was faded and crinkled, but in the corner, he spotted the title. It read, "H.S.S. **Heart of Odin**, cruiser. Norwegian Descent."

"A First Fleet ship...before they figured out gravity plating," he whispered aloud, noting the centrifuge on the cruiser that had given artificial gravity in those days. "Wow."

Next to the *Odin* was the small, darting profile of the H.S.S. *Heimdallr's Gaze,* another Norwegian-built ship, and the Third Fleet's sleuth. Above that was the titanic, steamrolling profile of the H.S.S. *Nebulous*, the Fourth Fleet carrier built in the early days of the Earth Global Alliance. Next to that were the fearsome curves of the H.S.S. *Krasnaya Soyuz*, a Second Fleet capitol ship commissioned by the lands that became the Russian Protectorate in the Eurasian Union. Above and around those were others that Damien recognized, like the *Galveston*, the *Sir Wallace Faulkner,* the *Gagarin*, the *Antilon*, the *Stern der Menschen*, and the *Wehdah*. There were a couple that he couldn't place, too, but one particularly drew his attention.

The sketch above the *Heart of Odin* was done marginally larger than the rest, but it was at the center of the collection. He could see a few similarities in it to the profile of *Odin*, but this ship was a bit cleaner, more streamlined, and looked much more dangerous. The title line read, "H.S.S. **Ocular Corona**" with no other information to speak of. Damien had never heard of it.

The sound of a vent clicking to life somewhere brought Damien rushing out of his giddy history venture. He whipped around, thinking someone was there, but he was still alone. Taken out of his fugue though, his gaze traveled over the workbench. A cup was sitting on the edge, filled with drawing utensils and holographic modeling tools. There were pencils, pens, pastels, vertex tweezers, wireframe tongs, spatial pliers, and more, all the quality tools of a designer.

He continued looking over Reuben's things scattered over the workbench and desktop. It looked like he'd been living here for years. A couple of half-finished drawings were sitting over the Pip pad, along with a couple of other knick-knacks that Damien couldn't figure out. Finally his gaze settled on an odd necklace. It had a thick silver chain with a large pendant at the bottom. The pendant was made of some mix of a greenish and amber jewel. It looked rough and heavy, held in place by a silver cap over the stone. The cool color glinting off of it drew Damien's gaze, and it seemed to pulse from within. He reached out to pick it up.

There was a flash of pale light and a hissing, cracking sound.

"YEOW!!" he shrieked, yanking his hand back and cradling it. His fingers had flashed to numb and unresponsive, and he had a flash of memory of the Algaroth, Loss, and his frostbite. He shivered.

"The next one will snap your fingers off."

Reuben Björn was standing in the doorway to the bathroom, from where the sounds of that vent were coming. His black hair was wet and he had only a towel on. His skin was deathly pale and the bones in his chest looked like they were about to burst out of his skin.

Despite the moment, Damien had the absurd thought that the man— were he a little less malnourished—probably looked like some traveling food-enthusiast on vacation or something. He just had that casually assertive look about him. The idea almost made Damien want to crack out laughing.

"Did you hear me, Vilan?" he spat.

Damien clutched his cold hand. "Yeah! Yeah I heard you! You could've just told me not to touch it!"

"You should have knocked before barging in," he countered, switching from Norwegian to English.

"It was unlocked…" he trailed off, realizing how stupid that sounded.

Reuben snatched the necklace from the desk. "And that made it alright to snoop?" He huffed as he put the necklace on. The pendant hung to the middle of his hairless chest. "Christ, no wonder you're here."

Damien was taken aback. "What?"

Reuben's dark eyes flashed. "The fact that you have to ask that proves me right. You've got problems, kid. You wouldn't be here if you'd figured out that Seattle was a death trap, waiting for you to trigger a cascade that's brought me all the way out here, even if this *is* what I was looking for." He snatched his second towel from where he'd dropped it and walked back into the bathroom, rubbing his hair.

The words bit into Damien hard, but the man's utter dismissal deflated his fury from broiling over. "Hey! What? What do you mean? Who the fuck do you think you are, huh?" He pounded a fist on the door hard enough to jar his unfrozen hand. He gasped as pain shot through his wrist. *So much for being in control.*

Reuben didn't answer. The sounds of running water came through the door.

He waited, fuming. *What cascade? He was in Seattle. He's blaming me too? Why the hell didn't he get in touch?*

The water stopped and the door opened. The Ice Elemental was clothed in loose, dark brown pants and a flowing, open white shirt that revealed the necklace bouncing on his chest.

"You're still here?" He pushed past.

Damien's lip twitched. "Look, you said a bunch of shit last night that I want answers to!"

"I'm not in the mood."

Damien dug in, not willing to accept dismissal, not twice in a day. "What the hell do you know about me, huh? *Everything?*"

Reuben's mocking, haughty laugh was perhaps the most insulting thing Damien had ever heard. "Oh you jumped up, overgrown child. How long have you been here now? A month? Have you taken more than a second to enjoy the view outside this little paradise?"

Damien narrowed his eyes, set his jaw, and clenched his fists, which didn't occur to him how childish that looked.

Reuben saw it and laughed again. "I shouldn't even tell you if that's how you can respond," he sighed monumentally. "But I might as well. It's only all of our lives." He stalked over to the dresser drawers in the bed-closet and grabbed neatly folded clothes, brought them to the couch, unfolded them, and started refolding them. "The Over-Seer's had his eye on your broken city for years. About since he broke the San Andreas Fault, I'd imagine. I have to guess that something horrible happened to you because of that quake and you displayed your powers, didn't you? You probably lost someone, too, so it was a *special* outburst?"

His black eyes cut right through Damien's head, and Damien had no response.

"Hmm," Björn went on. "So he probably heard about you then. He couldn't find you though, Puget Command wasn't sure who you were, and no one in the Islets would come forward. So you just kept up your self-important game of booby-traps and charades and thought you were doing something." He stopped. "I have news for you, kid. There are a lot of parties who've wanted you for a long time. You should consider why."

Damien's anger was starting to mix with everything he thought he'd been working past since the Core. His fury was giving way to some toxic mixture that left his tongue glued to the roof of his mouth. His lips had gone dry too, so he swallowed loudly.

"I guess you can't," Reuben said in his mild way. "And here I am, answering the questions that you as an adult should be able to figure out for yourself."

"What—what the hell am I figuring out?" Damien tumbled out, his voice much smaller than he'd hoped it would sound.

Björn hissed through clenched teeth. He looked at Damien then with such loathing that he felt his anger crumble further. "Good people are dying all over the world right now because you got away from the Islets. Croll Tan's entire stock of Avos have been cut loose to hunt for you. The lives they end are on your head if you don't understand the *why* of this situation."

"…What situation?" Damien mumbled, his fists slowly uncurling. The cold snap in his left hand had faded, but it was still tingly. He felt an odd, dull throb starting to block his thoughts at the top of his spine. It was a thick, clotting feeling, like there was an immense pressure of something fighting to get through a very small tube. He had a feeling it was a raging outburst, and he wanted it, but couldn't figure out how to get it.

Reuben shook his head once. "Do I have to lead you to it? Like a dog?"

Damien took a deep breath. His jawbones were starting to hurt from clenching his teeth so hard. The throbbing in his head got worse.

"Apparently so." Reuben gave a mock bow. "Understood. Alright then: here's the deal, boy. I'm sure you've heard people talking about how Croll Tan would make a dangerous chess player?"

Damien breathed carefully. "…Yes."

"Oh good. Well then you know how to *play* chess, correct?"

"…Yes."

"Excellent. Good first steps." Reuben grabbed his refolded clothes and stuffed them back in their drawer. "Then tell me, Mr. Vilan: what do you need to do to win a game of chess?"

Is this really fucking happening? Hit him. Break his fucking nose! But his body wouldn't listen. "Wipe the other player out," he submitted.

"Or?"

Damien blew air carefully out of his nose. "Or take their king."

Reuben walked towards him. "And what's *our* king, Mr. Vilan?"

Damien had no idea, and he knew his eyes said so.

"The Nukes, boy. Our Nukes! Our 'Final Option' against the apocalypse. The end of the line, the only thing The Collective needs to remove in order to beat us the easy way without losing any more valuable pieces of their own, and harvest the whole planet to their happy hearts' content."

Damien frowned, causing Reuben to snort a laugh again.

"Are you really that thick?"

Still, he couldn't respond. He just couldn't, fucking, move.

Reuben took a deep breath and all at once, his cool conceit was back. "I'll spell it out for you then." He clasped his hands politely, just how he had the night before. "The Over-Seer needs a way around our Nukes. You can make black holes. He couldn't find you before. Now he knows who you are." He started advancing on Damien, one sentence at a time. "Croll Tan shored up his defenses in November. A Supply Fleet is coming. His army stayed close to Seattle. He's hunted Elementals before. Bombs explode out. Black holes collapse *in*. The Over-Seer could request *anything he wanted* from The Collective for the promise of Earth, and he would probably *get it*."

Damien backed into the wall and banged his head, but he didn't break eye contact.

"I've got more news for you, kid. You don't live in a world of easy decisions anymore. Being an Elemental is something that you don't get to choose, we've all already figured that one out, but if you can't understand that the power running in your blood is a valuable resource, and you decide to just coast along with the game and not actually *play?*" Reuben jerked a thumb at the door. "Then you should just keep doing what you're doing and see where it gets you, but I can't condone that, because I know where it will get us. Do you know where? *Dead.*"

The man looked away to catch his breath and keep his cool face in check. When he turned back, the beady pits of his black eyes probably betrayed nothing, but Damien imagined he could see a burning rage behind them, one that would absolutely overpower Damien's own were he to try and pit it against the man.

Damien flinched as Reuben leaned close to him, jabbing a finger in his chest with every word. "Make. The. Connection."

But Damien, at that moment, so dumbfounded by rage, drowning in guilt and memories, and feeling that horrible pressure of a vast headache in his brain, just couldn't do it.

Finally, Reuben pulled away. "You know what I think you need, Vilan? What you should probably get?"

"…What?" Damien asked meekly.

WHACK.

"A reality check."

Reuben's hand whipped over Damien's face so hard that stars exploded and he was thrown to the floor. The sound of the impact was crisp and explosive in the quiet room, and by the time he'd blinked the stars away, his face was on fire. He could already feel a handprint forming. He crouched on his knees, holding his face, uncomprehending. "Wha—"

"—Grow the fuck up, kid. *Everybody* has lost someone in this war. *Everyone* has lost a home or someone they loved. If you want to sink into that, fine, but then you better consider eating a bullet or taking brick shoes into the ocean if you don't have other plans, because I'll be damned if I see you walk into the arms of the enemy and ruin us all."

Damien refused to let the tears of pain fall from his eyes as he wrenched his jaw. His ragged, stunned, rage-filled heaving blew towards the ground.

"I even thought I saw something in you when I first got here," Reuben went on, his voice inerrably flat. "But you know how long that lasted?"

423

"H-how long…" Damien whispered out. His voice cracked. It was taking every fiber of control not to touch his face again.

"Until I stood on that cliff, looked at you, and said that you led me to this island. You responded by asking about *yourself*." He leaned in close and whispered, *"What about me?"*

Damien looked up as that sank in, but the Elemental was staring down at him with nothing but contempt. A long moment passed in which Björn looked like he had more to say, but finally, he just exhaled noisily and bent close to grab Damien by his shoulder. "Get out," he spat, and without another word, he kicked him out the door.

Damien impacted the far side of the hall and stood there, trembling. *What was he talking about? Black holes and the Nukes? What does me revealing myself have anything to do with the Supply Fleet? It…is it really my fault that the Islets fell? Is it all just this shit in my blood?*

"…Damien?"

Please no, he thought. He couldn't imagine a worse person to have just shown up. *Please no.*

"Damien, are you alright?" Gwen asked again.

He felt her hand on his shoulder and he flinched.

"What the godly hell just happened?" she asked, taking it away.

Still shaking, he turned his head.

She gasped at the handprint. *"Björn?"* Venom dripped from the word, and she was already turning to the door to his quarters.

"…Don't."

She stopped at his tiny, whimpered word.

"Please…just don't." He closed his eyes. "He's right."

Gwen looked utterly torn, standing between the door and Damien. Finally, she lowered her fist and came to his side. "Come on," she said, wrapping her arms around his shoulders. "Come on, let's get you to bed."

He went.

∞ ∞ ∞

Damien didn't get time to wallow in what had happened. He wanted to just stay in his room and let Reuben's truths sink into his brain. *Seattle was my fault. My parents were my fault. Croll Tan's Avos are loose, hunting for me and killing all the way, and it's my fault.* He winced at the sting on his face.

Gwen showed up early to find him regressed to his bed. She sighed. "Damien," she called from the living room. "I'm not indulging this today. Whatever Björn said last night can be dealt with later. We need your help."

Damien dragged his head around the partition. He'd impacted his pillow after she'd rubbed a light salve on his face the night before. The salve had ended up in his hair overnight and now his black tuft of bed head was stupendous. "Why," he grumbled, watching her dully.

She crossed her arms and shifted feet. "The Fleet's been sighted."

∞   ∞   ∞

Damien, Dr. Gwen, and Von arrived at the command wheel a short while later. It was packed with people.

Before they'd left, Gwen had asked if Damien wanted his face covered up. He'd said yes, so she'd applied a liberal amount of makeup. The smell and scratchy fluff of the powder on his face had almost made him gag, but he'd decided he didn't want to deal with everyone asking him what the hell happened just yet.

"Doctor," rumbled Satolin from next to the war table. "Damien, VoSilas, thank you for coming."

The three of them nodded and edged their way through the throng of islanders. Damien and Von stopped near Javier, while Gwen went on to Satolin's side.

Throughout the command wedge, humans and Algaroth stood expectantly, eyeing a large icon spinning over the war table. The icon was a picture of Earth set within a downward triangle. At each point of the triangle, a dot sat in a circle.

"You okay, brotha?" Javier whispered. "You look kinda flushed."

Damien resisted the urge to rub his face. "Just rushed getting over here."

"Right on," he turned away.

Damien looked away and started. Von was watching him suspiciously. "What?"

"You were flushed when you came out of your room," he whispered.

"It's nothing."

"Hrmm." Von turned back to the waiting leaders, unconvinced. Damien hadn't been willing to tell him either.

They waited a few anxious minutes while other stragglers came pelting into the wheel, adding to the general buzz of quiet, anxious voices. Satolin thanked each of the latecomers as they arrived, speaking calmly. "LiKoth, Dr. Charles, thank you for coming. Tosh, you as well. Sergeant Dugan, Sergeant Bilges, Captain DeMarko, welcome. Illya, Alexei, Nurse Donovan, Quarlet, you as well. Camden, Choss, Vellus, are there more? It's alright. No, there wasn't much warning. You'll see shortly, Diathla. Corporal Elliot, I'm glad you're on your feet. How's your knee? Good," and on it went.

Javier tapped Damien's shoulder. "Is this supposed to be so friendly? There's an all-lovin' *Supply Fleet* gunning for orbit!"

"He doesn't want to get us worried," Captain Romi cut in over their shoulder before Damien could answer. They both jumped.

"*What* the—"

"—Captain," said Damien, warmed to see the man.

"Damien," Captain Romi smiled and his jaw tattoo stretched. His dark eyes glowed warm. They shook. "How are you?"

Damien shrugged. *Björn's an asshole.* "A little nervous."

Romi nodded. "We'll be alright."

He nodded and turned to see Romi's copilot and his *vishi*. "Diesal Kel," he said.

Kel's implant whizzed and he grunted.

"Diesal Nisha."

Nisha bowed her head politely, flashing the white tattoos behind her eyes.

"Vilan," Kel growled. "Estrada."

Javier received no hello from Romi, but Kel's acknowledgment surprised him. He smiled awkwardly while Damien looked across the wheel as the last few people trickled in. He spied a cluster of Amun-Nūr's soldiers occupying much of the space near the wedge's tech stations. Declan, Tortelli, their Algaroth friend Loss, and Commander Morgan were among them.

Finally, the last few stragglers came through, and among them was Björn, who was wearing simple black pants and a thin grey turtleneck jacket, buttoned to his jugular. Damien's face twitched and his skin prickled. As if sensing the gaze, Reuben looked right through the crowd and locked eyes with Damien. The man shook his head almost imperceptibly and moved away.

"What the shit was *that?*" Javier whispered.

"Nothing," Damien assured him. But he felt both Javi's and Von's stares. "Fine, I'll tell you later okay?"

The two of them turned away as the Prohka began to speak. "I wish this were under better circumstances," the enormous Algaroth boomed. "The arrival of not one but *three* Elementals in the last month is cause for Amun-Nūr to see hope, and the newly arrived Reuben Björn—whom I know some of you remember—has brought us promising leads that could lead to yet another."

Murmurs of assent drifted through the crowd.

Satolin looked over at the slowly whirling icon on the war table. "However, that search will need to be postponed." He took a deep breath. "Shialga has sent an oddly timed Supply Fleet, and while we were led to understand that that fleet would not be arriving for over a week," he spared a flicker towards Reuben, who seemed not to notice. "It seems we miscalculated. That fleet is entering orbit in less than an hour."

Damien took a careful breath as a veritable storm of static and tension swept through the wheel. He could feel Von tense next to him, flattening his shoulder blades as a current charged through his body. "Breath, Vo," he whispered. Von nodded stiffly.

Satolin looked at the war table. "Leo, are we accessing the Triad?"

The war table came to life and Leo's full-sized avatar appeared, dominating the crowd as the lights dimmed. "I'm initiating handshake protocols now," he said, abnormally serious and calm. "It's gonna take a minute, though."

"Very good," the Prohka responded, half in shadow. He turned to Morgan. "Commander?"

Morgan stepped up a landing from his soldiers so that he could see over the crowd. He was wearing a decorated black dress uniform with green accents on his cuffs, under his arms, as trim along his collar, and at the base of his jacket. His left breast was covered in medals. "To those of you new to Amun-Nūr—and there are many of you today—the event you are about to witness is as secret as it gets." He removed his peaked cap and tucked it under his arm, revealing his salt-and-pepper buzz cut. "We value openness at our island, but it's easy to forget that Amun-Nūr does not officially exist."

A few snorts of laughter sounded, but Morgan remained serious.

"So," he went on. "When I tell you that the contents of this event *never happened*, you better feel the gravity of that statement." His eyes darted around the wedge, making sure they did. "Good. Then lets move forward. Leo?"

Leo bent towards the icon, dramatically posing. "Wait for it…" He jabbed the icon, sending it into a coin-like spin. "We're connecting!"

"Alright," said Morgan, parting the sea of humans and Algaroth so he could approach the war table. "Bring up the globe."

"Answering Commander, bringing up globe," Leo hawked, spreading his arms wide like a sorcerer conjuring an apparition.

The Earth-in-triangle icon chimed and went still. Leo snatched it out of the air and threw it at his feet, where it stopped flat with a *ping*. Immediately, the flat icon began to rise off the table, swelling in size as it did. The Earth quickly outgrew the triangle, swelled, and shifted from a flat image to a fully three-dimensional projection resting gently on a tripod stand, which had remained quite small.

"During The Conquering," Morgan asserted. "We lost our entire orbital mapping network. You all know this. It's been a consistently bloody thorn in our side for the duration of this war."

Damien remembered seeing the patchy globe in Admiral Baroda's office, and he remembered how surprisingly high quality it was, even with enormous swaths of land and sea missing. *This is garbage compared to that*, he thought, eyeing the map on the table. The thought was a little more acerbic than he intended. *Have they just given up out here or something?*

Morgan continued. "What many of you don't know is that the Earth Global Alliance had a special initiative in place from well before First Contact. It was a mission to the Asteroid Belt that was never intended as a permanent mapping replacement, but it damn well turned into one."

On the table, a tiny pin had appeared in the middle of the South Pacific, marking Amun-Nūr. Another pin appeared deep within what was once the North American state of Alaska, now regionally recognized as the Inupiat Tundra. Both pins started blipping into empty projected space as the hodge-podge globe spun.

"What you're about to witness is Earth's *only* remaining secret tool. The Collective have never been able to figure this one out, because we never told them about it." Morgan swelled with pride. "We're currently asking to connect with something called the 'Sol Monitoring Triad'. It allows a privileged few to access the most detailed map ever conceived of this planet."

Damien felt a chill go through him, through Von, through Javier, and a reasonable number of others in the wedge. Everyone else looked on as if they'd seen it before, though there was anything but expectance in their eyes. Those in the command wedge who had seen whatever was about to happen all had looks full of gratitude. *They know what a good map is worth.*

"The Triad consists of three space stations hidden within the Asteroid Belt, each one sitting exactly 120° equidistant from each other. Using TransLight mapping, these stations have maintained a real-time, three-dimensional blueprint of our entire Solar System."

"The concept is one unique to Earth," Satolin interrupted. "One that neither Algaroth, nor any other Collective species has ever produced. The Triad in and of itself makes humankind stand out."

Morgan nodded. "In short, they're priceless assets. The men and women living on *Hawking, Einstein,* and *Piern* Stations deserve your utmost gratitude, to whichever deity you prefer. They've given a multi-generational sacrifice so that Earth can spin on. Keep that in mind if you ever feel the need to reveal their existence to the enemy. If you can't manage that, eat a bullet instead."

Respectful quiet fell over the command wheel as the names hung in the air. *I couldn't ever do that,* Damien thought. *Space? Hell yes. My whole life out there...* He lowered his eyes then as Reuben's handprint tingled. He remembered what the man had said last night. *I had faith in you until the first thing you asked about was yourself.* Shame crept up his neck and he looked at his feet, thinking of Seattle. *It's all my fault.*

Leo cut into the quiet. "Connection established with Triad relay station McKinley." His voice was solemn.

A line of text spelled itself out in the air near the globe. At the same time, Earth reoriented itself so that the Inupiat Tundra was now the North Pole, the pin in the landscape pulsing insistently. Leo made a spreading motion between his thumb and index finger, and the map hurled closer towards the pin, zooming in as if they were approaching the planet through the eyes of an asteroid. When it stopped, the map was highly pixilated and choppy, but there was no mistaking the blowing cold landscape of the recovering Arctic. A mountain dominated the scene.

Above, the lines of text had finished forming:

Trifectal Time Zone—2
Sol Coordinates: Zulu Grid-09-// 11, -17, 20 \\-
S.M.T. *Piern*
Handshake Protocol... accepted

Access:
Gs-5. M

McKinley Station
Earth Lat: 63°N, 4', 41.17"
Earth Long: 150°W, 58', 8.33"

"We're in!" Leo hooted.

'Gs-5. M? Damien frowned. *That's… that's the same text I saw in the Core. Is* that *how they projected me out to the Sound?* Von shifted next to him and another thought occurred. *I guess Sato didn't trade with Baroda for access to the Triad after all. So… what did he have to do to get Von back here?* He badly wanted to ask but wasn't sure if it was the best idea.

The large, wall-mounted display behind the war table flickered to life, revealing a man sitting in what looked like a cold dark room. His pale, scruffy features were illuminated only by the pale light cast by the bank of computers in front of him.

"*Amun Command,*" said the man, his voice coming through scratchy. "*Gs-5 here. We've received your command codes and priority access, stand by for uplink to the Triad.*"

"We appreciate that, McKinley," said Morgan. "We'll wait."

The man nodded and eyed another display. The sound of furious typing filtered through, and the whole command wheel scrutinized the scene while they waited. The background was almost fathomless in the low-quality camera, but there was a flicker of grey light coming from somewhere. It looked cold.

The typing continued, and Damien's gaze slid towards the operator. He had a graying beard and tired eyes with a thin, nearly invisible scar that ran across his left cheek, cutting through the scruff. In a blink, the man's light-brown eyes flashed towards the camera and back. Damien flinched. He could swear the man's had looked right at him, but that was crazy, right? Wasn't he just looking into a camera into a sea of faces? Damien couldn't quite shake the feeling that the glance had picked him right out of the crowd. *That's…a little unsettling.*

"*Uplink established, Amun,*" said the operator. "*Hope you can do more good about this than we can.*" He cut the transmission before they had a response.

The screen vanished and the sound of trickling particles filled the wedge. There was a short delay, and then Leo announced, "I've got the access, kiddies. McKinley is patching us through! Hang tight."

A few seconds passed while the wheel held its breath. Then, a chime sounded, and Damien watched on in fascination as a cascade of teal-colored droplets flitted into existence above the projected, scratchy terrain over the war table.

"Downloading the map now," Leo confirmed, and the AI clapped once, sending out a crisp, clear gunshot through the wheel that made everyone flinch.

At the sound, the cloud of droplets were let loose from whatever force had held them up, and they fell with pristine efficiency onto the holographic mountain. A sound familiar to a rain stick filled the wedge as the droplets coated the entire projection, leaving a film of perfect snow.

Damien was so entranced by the peaceful sound and the cascade that he didn't notice that it had stopped. He opened his eyes, jarred by the quiet, and he looked at the table and frowned. *That's not a map*, was his first thought. And then the reality settled in, and he realized that he was not in fact looking through a window or at a video. It *was* a map he was seeing, but it wasn't just any map.

It was THE map. *The* definitive map ever conceived, so real that in that first moment of seeing it, Damien was utterly convinced of the wind on his face as it blew snow off the peak of Mt. McKinley. His fingers felt frozen and wet from picking up a handful of snow without gloves. His lungs were suddenly convinced that there wasn't enough air to be had in the wedge, and he involuntarily took a long, heaving breath…and he wasn't the only one.

Audible moans of approval rippled through Amun-Nūr's gathered souls as they took in the utterly complete, real-time blow of a storm on the sunny mountain. It was followed by peals of laughter, as Leo vanished and reappeared around the far side of McKinley, miniaturized but still a giant to the mountain and garbed in heavy winter gear. "Can we do this ALL the time?!" he called up to them.

Satolin's lips pulled back into a smile as men, women, and aliens all enjoyed the sight of the AI as he played in the snow like a kid. "If only, Leo. The Triad is the last mapping array in the Sol System. For it to stay a secret from The Collective, it must be used sparingly, or we risk losing it for good with no hope of ever getting it back."

Leo scooped up some holographic snow and blew it into the wind. "But it's so REAL!"

More laughter, and Damien even let a small chuckle escape his muddled mood. Finally, Morgan hit a button on the table, and the mountain shrank as the view pulled back.

"Hey!" Leo protested as his snowy playground shrank away. He leapt out of the way as the curve of Earth appeared, still held in perfect clarity. "I was using that!"

"Sorry," said Morgan flatly.

In response, Leo's winter garb was replaced by his mad doctor outfit that Damien had seen him wear before: long white labcoat, oversized goggles on his head, rubbery black gloves and boots. More laughter came from around the wedge, but it felt more forced.

As the globe shrank far back into orbit, Leo took the moment to stare down at it with almost comical intensity, as if he were contemplating how best to kick it. But then the Moon came into view, perfectly rendered. Morgan halted the map, and Leo stepped back to let everyone see more clearly.

Earth and her lone satellite hung in the air over the black table. No lines divided landmasses, but recent injuries from The Collective were visible, even from so far away: a hint of reddish tracks crisscrossed Africa and Australia. A thick, sickly spooge of the color throbbed over western Eurasia, and much of the Central American Passage was dotted with the glow.

We can only see all of that, though, because the sky is so clear, Damien reminded himself. *Particulates that we took care of,* and he took the moment to eye the rest of the world, which looked sharper than he ever remembered seeing.

The slowly advancing polar caps looked wispy and faded, but they were back; there was no denying that. Lush jungle had reclaimed vast swaths of Africa that wasn't showing signs of hurt. The exposed continent under the Antarctic ice was fading away again too, and the inlet sea in South America—the Gulf of the Amazon—looked a little less full than Damien remembered. *We've figured so much out*, he thought, letting the entirety of the world shrink the plaguing guilt weighing on him, even for a moment.

His reflection ended though as the Prohka's commanding voice brought everyone in the wheel back.

"They're here."

Damien snapped his attention back to see Satolin's focus had shifted to the wall. He turned around…and felt his own worries come crashing back, utterly smashing the moment he'd held. On the wall was a display he hadn't noticed before. It sat amidst other screens and monitors, unassumingly glaring down at them. The sight of it triggered an unpleasant liquidating in his bowels; Damien found himself desperately wishing he hadn't seen it.

The display was an odd collection of eleven bars sandwiched between two long timer strings. The top timer was still, but the bottom was flashing red, silently declaring a countdown long since completed and acknowledged, but not reset.

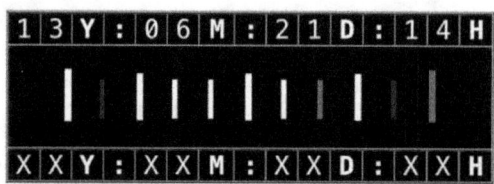

"Prohka," he asked loudly, his gaze glued to the top timer and the bars.

"Damien?"

"Is that…" his saliva had evaporated in his mouth, and his voice shook. "Is that the Conduit?"

Silence pervaded the wheel.

"It is."

"The countdown timer? For…for construction?"

"Yes."

Damien took in the eleven bars and closed his eyes, trying to still his beating heart. *So that's how long we have left.*

Eleven bars on the wall marked the jump rings of the dreaded Conduit, The Collective's TransLight super highway. Eleven bars glowed anywhere from brightly to not at all, telling whether each ring in question was completed, under construction, or not started yet. Eleven bars spelled the end of all things, for the day when the highway would be completed. Eleven bars under a clock, listing in the plainest numbers that Earth had thirteen years, six months, twenty-one days, and fourteen hours until The Collective would send the Harvest.

Damien opened his eyes to see Satolin looking at him. He'd attracted other gazes as well.

"We try not to think about it," said Daeduras.

The muscles in Damien's neck flexed as he forced his head up and down a couple of times, trying not to let his sudden sense of overwhelming insignificance take him. Oddly enough, a klaxon started to blare just then, shattering the moment of dread only to replace it with another fear, but one much more urgent. Damien looked up at the timers again to see the red X's had been replaced with zeros.

"Leo," Morgan snapped. "Have you picked them up?"

"Working!" Leo squawked. "Working! Hold on!"

"Jacque, Greufass, Clarkson, coordinate Stella," Satolin commanded, and the two humans and the Algaroth he'd addressed leapt to their stations.

People moved out of the way and the buzz of voices filled the wheel. Damien looked at his brother, who nodded to him solemnly. "It's happening."

"Looks like it."

"What's Stella?" Javier asked.

"Our high powered omniscope," Romi answered from behind. "It's hidden in the mountain's peak."

Shouts sounded across the wedge: confirmations that Stella was coming online.

"Leo. Coordinates!" shouted Morgan, leaning over a station nearby. "Where are they coming from?"

"The Triad's working the telemetry," Leo cried. "Give it a sec, bub!" Morgan growled.

"Oh gods…" Gwen whispered, and her voice triggered a tidal wave of recognition as they saw what she was looking at. Those closest to her wondered what she was talking about, and then they followed her gaze to the only place that made sense. Then the next person out would follow that first person's gaze, and so on. The realization spread through the command wedge like wildfire, and in a moment, even the shouting techs fell silent.

A tiny red circle had snapped to life over the table, just within the Moon's orbit. Telemetry spilled in lines off of it at an alarming rate. Damien thought he could just make out a few slivers of something inside the highlight. With each passing second, it slid closer to Earth.

Finally, Leo spoke up, sounding dry once more. "They're coming in westbound over Madagascar."

"Confirmed," one of the Stella techs called. "We're receiving the coordinates, Leo. Everyone hold."

"We see them," said another a moment later.

"Orienting Stella now," said the third.

"Jen," shouted the first tech to a youngish woman nearby. "Can you patch the feed from Stella to the wall?"

"I've got it!" Leo said, rolling over Jen's response. The display where they had just seen the view of McKinley Station flashed to life. Confusion rolled through the wedge, though, because the screen was clearly on, but it showed only black.

"Is it transmitting?" The first tech asked uncertainly.

"It sure is," said Leo. "What you're looking at is space. It's black like that."

Von snorted, eliciting looks.

"Thanks, Silas!" Leo smirked.

Von buried his head in his chest and Damien shook his head, hiding his grin.

"How long until they enter our sky?" asked the Prohka.

"Thirty-three seconds." Leo said. His suit had returned and he fidgeted with his tie, making it change patterns.

They waited.

Björn was the first to see them. "There they are," he said, a long half-minute later.

"Oh my." Leo added. "It looks like they're already launching dropships. That was quick."

It took a long second for Damien to see anything, but he kept an eye on the circle hanging on the table. It was slipping over the Atlantic, towards South America. Everything was abnormally silent. Then, the circle came over the horizon to where Amun-Nūr's pin still sat in the Pacific. As it did, a tiny mote of dust appeared on the black screen.

Here they come.

The seconds dragged out in silence. The tiny spot on the screen started as a speck of light on black, and it stayed that way for a long time, inching its way up the display on the wall. All eyes turned to it, watching. Eventually, the speck reached some critical marker on the horizon, and it started to expand. It grew larger, and the speck turned into a smear, and then a streak, and then a visible contrail curled out behind it. The comet of light continued across the sky, revealing nothing for even longer than before. Then, a black splotch appeared in the comet's center. After that, the splotch grew at an alarming rate, until at last, distinct shapes could finally be made out amidst the fire, and the splotch resolved into vessels.

"Snaps..." whispered Javi.

Damien felt his heart slow to an earthy drumbeat as the shapes took on a sharper tint. They were no longer blobs, but the vessels from which the pillar of fire came, spewing their raging wake across the sky. Once upon a time, Damien Vilan had wanted to see a Collective starship. Now, he wished they'd go away. *And those aren't starships*, he corrected himself. *Those are warships.*

There were four of them. Damien recognized the profiles of two as cargo carriers, and the other two as Collective dreadnoughts. The dreadnoughts had predatory builds; their vast, curving bulk as graceful as it was terrifying. Titanic boosters spewed fire from behind their splayed fins, marking their maneuverability as much as the bristling weapons that remained within the ships. Between the dreadnoughts were the cargo carriers, snub-nosed, and built like some skeletal creature's spine with long ribs cradling a mass of precious organs in its underbelly. Plates of heavy armor protected the gaps between ribs, but there was nowhere near the fluid danger of the dreadnoughts. Even so, the cargo carriers could be bringing any manner of horrors to Earth, while the dreadnoughts provided only an escort. They knew they could trigger a planet-wide cataclysm if they fired so much as a spit wad at the surface. Humanity had made that ultimatum to The Collective as Geneva was obliterated from orbit: Cease-fire, or we will use the Nukes.

Carrying the twenty-year status quo to the letter, The Collective's Supply Fleet descended on Earth with dooming grace. Their wake cut through the upper atmosphere, leaving split auroras of fire behind. Amun-Nūr—and all of humanity—looked up at the sky, and wondered just what the Over-Seer had brought.

Unable to tear his gaze away from the warships for the mere minutes it took them to cross the western horizon, Damien could see how the upper atmosphere had made the starships glow hotly from their descent. He thought it made them all look very, very angry.

"If anyone has any idea what's on those ships," Leo said. "We'd sure like to hear them."

CHAPTER TWENTY TWO

A Coward Without Fear

Damien remembered how it had been the last time a Supply Fleet arrived.

It had been three years ago, in July of 2142. He and Von had cracked into Leo's vault about two months before, and they'd been living in the bunker for about six months before that. They'd heard news from Bar and Shell that a few stargazing insurgents had spotted the fleet, and that everyone should lie low. Damien had argued how stupid that was because no Collective bombardment would fall to Earth, and the Over-Seer never pushed engagements or battles while his precious troops were being settled. Still, Croll Tan's army had been pushing hard up the west coast in recent months, and there were rumors that they were advancing on Portland. Not to mention there had been a surge in patrols spotted in Tacoma recently, and the Islets had seen some fierce fighting as more people left the quaked city every day. So, answering the order to hang tight and shut up like everyone else, Damien, Von, and Leo had laid low.

For nineteen days, the Supply Fleet had hung in the sky, ferrying its Shialgan cargo of fresh soldiers, workers, material goods, food, weapons of war, *new* weapons of war, and anything else The Collective required to the surface. Then, the constant swarm of dropships sped back along their spidery paths to their motherships, each one packed heavier than it had been when it descended with hundreds of kilotons of harvested Earth goods—the goods The Collective had based their entire war on taking. Flora, fauna, minerals, water, air, sand, stone, blood, tears, bones, cells, all of it. Everything was of value to them.

Over the years, The Collective had etched their merry way across the planet, dropping a web of small mining bases that fed into huge mining hubs that fed to orbital launch yards, all a part of the assembly line of stripping the planet. That's how it had been ever since First Contact, when they had taken what humanity allowed them to take. That went until The Conquering, when they decided those limits weren't enough and they took more. And up until this day, when they were taking more than ever, the tireless crews of Algaroth sped out into the wilderness and worked day and night, stripping everything from Earth's fertile crust for their empire, far across the stars.

So for nineteen days, the fleet had orbited the captured planet, and nineteen days had been the norm for the Supply Fleets since The Treaties of Longevity were first signed, marking peace between humanity and The Collective. It was a hard process, stealing so much from such a rich planet, after all.

And so, as Amun-Nūr slipped through day seven of this non-standard Supply Fleet in orbit, they knew it was going to be a long start to March.

Argyle Wing's omniscope, Stella, was programmed to follow the fleet every twenty-six minutes as it made a pass across the sky, where—for another seven minutes—the citizens of the island watched the feed on their screens, wondering if they were about to be exposed. Satolin and Commander Morgan had agreed to keep a tight lockdown on any signals leaving Amun-Nūr, and for good reason: It was common knowledge that the dreadnoughts above would do everything they could to help their Over-Seer; why wouldn't they? But after Reuben had literally brought it home to them how aggressively Croll Tan was hunting for the Elemental of Darkness, the islanders had undergone a transformation. Tensions ran high and worries were abundant, as every human and Algaroth who had given their life to being buried under the ocean, balked with every pass from above, unable to shake the feeling that the deadly craft were probing specifically for *them*.

Despite all this, life couldn't stop within the island, and Damien— who had already failed his first vocation—had to finally track down Gwen and chat with her about finding another. It was the afternoon of the Supply Fleet's eighth day in orbit, and he met her in one of the two cross labs in Delmorra Wing, which were used for communal testing across vocations.

Members of any department were invited to bring their work to the lab, check on each other's research, projects, or whatever they happened to be working on, and generally collaborate. The atmosphere in the island was generally abuzz with tension, and the lab felt only marginally less so, but that was likely due to it being mostly empty.

"Damien, hey!" Gwen called as he entered, wearing her usual lab coat with her hair up. She was holding a double-sized portfolio tablet in her lap. She waved him over.

He waved back and trudged across the concrete floor, hands in his pockets. "Hey," he mumbled, glancing around.

The cross lab was like an open warehouse, with marking lines painted on the floor to keep projects in their own space. Having spent so little time in Delmorra Wing but having heard so much about it from Javier, Damien was still surprised to see how much *room* the vocations on this side of the island had. He was also surprised to see how empty this lab was. Only three groups were scattered around: an armed quartet of Algaroth in a far corner, practicing what appeared to be an alien martial art or yoga; a mix of scientists were in the middle of the lab, all focused hard on some tube on its side that looked suspiciously like the control pedestal from the Core; and then there was the group that Gwen was sitting near, who were working at a long workbench, above which hung a projection of large, ring-shaped devices spread out like expanded circular ribs of some tunnel.

"Hey," Gwen smiled at him over her glasses. "How was your morning?" She eyed him closer. "And how's your face?"

Damien blinked away as he touched the fading marks from Reuben's hand. He shrugged. "It's fading. Had lunch with Vo."

She nodded. "How's he doing?" She patted the tabletop next to her.

He hopped up. *Perfect. He's adjusting perfectly.* "He's ah... he's doing okay! I think he misses home a little but he's making friends and settling in." He caught a subtle whiff of scent from the doctor. She smelled faintly of lavender and spring rain. It made his heart flutter.

She hummed. "I'm glad to hear it. Does he like working in the garden dome?"

441

"Yeah, I think so. I think he's missed tending to something living for awhile."

"Did he garden before the quake?"

"No, but he…I don't know. He just always had a thing for growing all kinds of, *stuff*, you know? I think we both just forgot all about doing that while we were living in the ah…in the bunker."

She patted his thigh, "You'll figure it out too." She smiled and adjusted her glasses. "So did you have a thought on where you might like to try for a new vocation?"

He looked over at the scientists arguing around the workbench. "I really haven't."

Gwen laughed lightly. "Oh so you just wanted to see me?"

He shrugged, cracking a half-smile. "You're comforting."

"That's one good thing accomplished for the day."

"How so?"

She waggled the end of her hot-pen towards the workbench and the bickering researchers. "They're trying to decipher why the fleet arrived off-schedule. Sato and I both agree that it's not a usual run from Shialga, and that's cause for concern, but it's valid to wonder if it *could* be here on schedule, and that's actually a bit worse."

"Why?"

"Because it could mean they have a very specific agenda for this fleet," she said. "Maybe to stop the World War Centennial, like Baroda thinks." She looked disconcerted at the idea.

Damien frowned. "Yeah, I remember he mentioned something like that when I met him, but…I guess I didn't realize that The Collective could be that specific with their fleets, could they? And does anyone even know *where* the Centennial's gonna be held?" he added. He'd spent some time in his solitude researching the globally significant ceremony, and the consensus was that no one knew where it was going to be, even though it wasn't even six months out.

She shook her head. "No, they don't know yet. No city is coming forward because they're terrified of painting a target on themselves." Then she frowned and cocked her head at him, a curious look on her face. "But…have you never heard about The Collective's supply schedule?"

He shook his head.

She wiggled into a more comfortable position on the counter. Both of their legs dangled, and her shoes were left forgotten on the floor. Damien—who was wearing his favorite combat boots and a pair of smoky grey jeans that Javi had been cool enough to track down from a seamstress in the habitat district—wasn't about to unlace his footwear. "The Supply Fleets run on a specific timeframe," said Gwen. "But their speed is based on how many Conduit rings they can use. We estimate that six of the Jump Rings are completed and operational, possibly a seventh, and at least two more are well under construction."

"So how does that affect the fleets?"

She opened her mouth to speak, but her eyes went vacant as an angry voice spoke up from the workbench. She smiled and nodded her head towards group. "Just listen."

Damien turned an ear.

"…No, no you're forgetting about the transit reduction!" a thirty-something, handsome tech was saying to his younger, thinner, acne-riddled companion. "Six Jump Rings active, and each reduces the independent transit time between the next jump by 64%! That's *cumulative*."

His thin companion's response was nasally and labored, like he was ready to start shouting but his voice just wasn't loud enough to merit an outburst. "I know that," he wheezed, pausing at odd intervals to breathe. "I'm merely stating that you're being inconclusive that this fleet could *possibly* have come along on their usual timetable. The Collective doesn't possess ships with enough acceleration to transcend this timeline without being aided by the Conduit."

"As far as we know," interjected a third researcher, a plump, middle-aged woman.

The handsome tech rolled his eyes. "*As far as we know*."

"You are voth refusing to recall that the fleets jum*f* vased on their slowest vessels," said the pale blue Algaroth. "Na*w*ely: the cargo carriers.

You are *w*issing that scout ships and war vessels are affected *w*uch *w*ore heavily *v*y the Conduit."

"Indeed. But you make a moot point Hora," wheezed the thin one. "All Supply Fleets have cargo carriers comprising their number; thus, they move only so fast as their slowest craft. We needn't calculate any jumps based on anything faster."

The fifth member of their team, a young female Algaroth who was perhaps half a head taller than Choss Chosska, tapped her tool-fingers on the workbench. "*V*ut what if it *was* faster?" The loud *TWINK* as she tapped hard got their attention.

"No, this fleet couldn't *v*e faster, we would have known already," said Hora.

The plump woman shook her head. "So we're back to gesticulating that this fleet has to be a special package? Lovely."

The handsome tech balked. "No! We're assuming this fleet was sent from Shialga *after* the absentee fleet last year."

"You're agreeing with me, dear."

"What?"

The woman shook her head.

"I agree with Evelyn," said the female Algaroth. "We should assu*w*e that our runs were always right, and last year's fleet si*w*fly did not a*ff*ear. We should also assu*w*e that the Conduit's construction has not changed in any way, and we should *v*uild our *f*latform from there."

"Thank you, Tisa," said Evelyn.

Tisa nodded.

"Terrible idea," muttered the handsome tech, his arms crossed.

"Do you, have a better one?" said Wheezy.

"I'm *working* on it!" he snapped.

"Should we step out then so you can…work in peace?"

"No, but Finch, I think you need to get worked into a few *pieces* right about now."

Finch—the wheezy one—shrugged, completely nonplussed. "I, practice Ey Dova," he labored. "I would like, you to try."

"What the hell's '*Ee Doo-va*'?"

Hora tapped the handsome tech's shoulder and pointed towards the back of the lab, where the quartet of martial arts-practicing Algaroth were currently putting each other in intense headlocks…using only one leg. "*Ay Doe-Vah*," he corrected.

The handsome man scoffed but the color faded from his cheeks as he glanced at Finch's long legs. "I still think it's just a late fleet," he muttered.

"You *just* said you thought it was a *s*f*e*cial delivery for the Over-Seer!" snapped Tisa.

"I changed my mind!"

"You have no proof, dear."

"Neither do you!"

"We're working on it!"

"Well you're not listening to what I'm saying!"

"You're not saying anything!"

And it devolved from there. Damien and Gwen looked on as they started pushing for access to the workbench control panel, each swatting the next away as they tried to make adjustments to the Jump Rings, now just calling each other outright names. Damien shook his head. *Babies.* His gaze drifted over them to the display of the Conduit rings.

Each ring was a joint in the TransLight superhighway that would connect Shialga to Earth. He didn't know how fast it would make traveling between the two planets when it was completed, but he knew that it would be quicker than the current speed of about a three-year journey through deep space, and he knew that whatever The Collective had on the other side, it undoubtedly would spell humanity's end.

Hanging amidst the other data hovering around the rings, Damien spied a log of all previous Supply Fleets. His eyes were drawn to the bottom, where he noticed that the one currently in orbit had already been labeled, "Supply Fleet 13 (14?)."

"Has it really only been thirteen?"

"Supply Fleets?" Gwen asked, shaking her head at the group.

"Yeah."

The doctor sighed. "It seems like more doesn't it? Most people just forget that the supply runs aren't the only fleets that came from Shialga. The Conquering fleet came from there. The First Contact one did too. The Collective have sent us so many that weren't related to material transport."

Damien glanced at the logs and thought they were probably about into the seven-minute window where the fleet would be overhead. He felt his gut clench a little. "So what does Sato think is so bad about this one? What does he think they're bringing down?"

She clucked her tongue and looked at him, very still. "He doesn't know, but he has theories."

"Do you think it's a game-changer? Or a doomsday device?"

She answered slowly. "I…think the latter is more likely *via* the former."

"Meaning?"

"Meaning Croll Tan has held his chair for the longest of any Over-Seer on Earth, and he's done so for a reason." She held the moment. "Because he's patient, and learned." She nodded, as if affirming her own observation.

"You aren't saying what it *is* though, your theory?"

"Well," she started, setting her portfolio tablet down. "The more popular opinion around the world suggests that it could be some sort of superweapon." She scoffed.

"You don't think that's it?"

She shook her head. "No. That's just wishful thinking by people who have an odd hope that The Collective will build something so enormous, so utterly destructive, that in its *enormous* complexity, one fatal flaw would be enough to blow it up, and we'd somehow get lucky."

"What, like, if someone left a vent or exhaust port uncovered on a planet-blaster gun or something and we managed to torpedo it?"

She chuckled. "Oh, something like that."

He grinned morbidly. *Who would be so stupid? The Collective Empire wouldn't, that's for sure.* "Well what's Amun-Nūr's theory then?" he eyed the bickering scientists, thinking it a bit odd how the islanders seemed to see themselves not as a part of the world. He didn't really know how to feel about that yet.

She granted him a soft, sad smile. "One theory offered here by Sato, myself, and a few others, goes as simple as this: We've thought for awhile that it would only be a matter of time before Croll Tan decided to try a virus on humanity."

Damien frowned. "A virus? Why?"

"Because viruses can be targeted." Her tone grew serious. "If Croll Tan *has* found a viral strain that can be distributed to humans and *only* humans, then he'll have found a way to end our resistance without ever losing one of his own. He could just sit back and watch as we struggled to contain a microscopic danger that we couldn't counter, and if he delivered it quietly enough, we would never be sure if it was him or not, thus, no one would agree to use the Final Option."

"The Nukes."

"Yes."

He frowned. "That doesn't make sense."

"Why?"

"Because…" *Because Reuben said the Avos are hunting me, not the bombs.* "Because…they're still hunting for the Nukes right? Trying to find where we buried all of them?"

"Every day."

"Why would they do that if they were planning to wipe us out without ever having to touch 'em?"

She hummed thoughtfully. "That's…an interesting idea, but one that I think Commander Morgan could explain away as *tactics*. The Over-Seer is keeping up appearances."

"Oh." He wrestled for a minute with telling her what Reuben had said, but he quickly lost his reasoning not to when he realized he didn't *have* a reason to keep it from her. "I still don't think that makes sense."

"Why not?"

"Because…everyone made a fuss that Tan wants *me* and…I don't know. Reuben said something about my blood and how I can make black holes and how that could affect the Nukes…" he trailed off, feeling conspicuously self-important.

Gwen squinted at him behind her glasses. "You didn't mention that before."

He hung his head. "I'm sorry. I think I just…I didn't want to believe that could be real."

She looked away. "Unfortunately, Damien, I think Björn is right."

Damien's chest constricted, but somehow it made him feel better. It made him feel more validated somehow. "So… you think that's what this Supply Fleet brought? Something to do with me?"

"It's what the Prohka thinks."

"But what about *you*?" he pressed.

Her head drooped. "I…I'd rather not believe its something so unstoppable."

"You think I'm unstoppable?"

Her brilliant green eyes met his navy gaze. "I think you could be."

Damien's jaw fell slack, but he was saved from answering by another rising ruckus at the workbench: the argument seemed to be going nowhere.

"Seems to be my queue for an intervention," she said with a sad wink. "We can talk more later, alright? Think about a vocation though." She squeezed his hand and walked away to clear up the argument, leaving Damien to his own devices.

∞　　　　　∞　　　　　∞

Damien left the cross lab, wondering just what Gwen had meant and thinking he should probably hunker down and pick a new vocation, when he bumped into Javier on his way up from the habitat district.

"Yo, Damien! Brotha! I've been looking for you man, where you been?"

"Oh, just chatting with Dr. Gwen about a new vocation."

"You picked one yet?"

"No."

Javier shrugged. "Eh, maybe you should try something out in the neighborhood," he jerked his thumb over his shoulder towards the habitat cavern, where a cool breeze was drifting into the Atrium. "I know you haven't spent shit for time out there. You should check it out!"

Damien swallowed, not entirely unsure why he'd been so averse to exploring the thriving district. *Too many people. Still not used to that.* "Yeah, maybe."

Javier rolled his eyes. "Uh huh. Well listen, I've been trying for *weeks* now to have a, ah, a little get-together and I think I've finally traded enough favors to make that happen tonight. You doin' anything?"

"Get-together? Like what?"

The man clapped his shoulders and started walking away backwards. "That's what I like to *hear!* Alright Dame, I'll see you in the Garden around ten, yeah?"

"Wait, what?" *Did I just agree to go?*

"No excuses bro! I'll see you later!"

Damien gawked as the man turned and took off down the thoroughfare, laughing and whooping. *Dame? Seriously?*

∞   ∞   ∞

Despite reservations, Damien's curiosity won out that evening, so he showered, shaved, put some pants and shoes on, donned his old jacket over a plain grey shirt, and made the trek across the island to the Celestial Garden.

"Oi! Damien!" Javier's voice found him as the double doors slid open. "We're back here!"

Damien looked around to see that the steam vents were mostly quiet now, as was the Garden itself. Through the cavern mouth, the ocean glinted darkly under a partly clouded sky.

Moving to the edge of the entryway veranda, he called out. "Javi? Where are you?" His voice carried far.

"To your right!"

Damien looked up but saw no one.

"Further, fella! Up—no not that far! Keep going to your right, dumbass! Little more—*ahp!* Yeeees there ya go! *He*-llo!"

Finally, he spotted Javier hanging over the side of one of the highest and farthest terraces. It was tucked just next to a dark crack in the cavern wall where a trickle of water was pouring out that might lead to who knew where. Damien wound his way down the main staircase and off one of the branches at Javier's direction, listening to him hoot and shout down from his perch. Unable to see many of the paths between the curtains of ivy and shrubbery, Damien had to double back more than once. The moist air was packed with the smells of greenery in bloom, and under it was the whiff of fresh, salty air.

"Damn, you take forever!" Javier's voice called, and Damien thought he heard someone laugh.

"Shut up!" he called back, unable to see anyone.

"I can get you lost!" Javi retorted.

"You said there's a staircase over here!"

"No, not there! Keep going…yes…yes! That's the one! Aaaand okay, stop! Left there. Yep, that's it."

Damien slipped around the stone pillar and through the entryway hidden by ivy. Up a short winding staircase that took him against the cavern wall, he stopped short.

Around the pillar and up two more steps was a pergola-covered patio, hidden from all inside the high-up terrace. Comfortable benches, plush woven chairs, and stone or wrought metal tables ringed the circular space. The near side of the patio was against the cavern wall to Damien's right, where a smooth wall of stone gave the terrace a sort of backing. From around the back of that stone and trickling along the top of the far railing before it fell away from sight, was the water coming out of the crack in the wall. Seated around the patio—to Damien's wild and pleasant surprise— were friends.

Nurse Sarah Donovan, Gwen, Von, Kel, Nisha, a white man whom Damien didn't know, Captain Romi, Javier, and Leo all were lounging on the terrace. The AI was languishing on his side, in his suit, on an obnoxious red sofa within the confines of a small Pip pad inset on a disguised stone pedestal. Everyone looked comfortable and clean and trimmed in their non-work attire, and Damien was shocked to see that even Dr. Gwen Whalen of the ever-present lab coat had changed out for a lacy green shirt, multi-colored shawl, a matching green skirt, and flowery, cream-colored slippers. She had left her hair up. Damien started too when he noticed Von wearing a contoured wrap-shirt that left his upper torso exposed and loose brown pants over bare feet. He noticed because he had thought Von was Satolin for a moment.

"There you are!" Javier beamed, looking sharp in black slacks, shiny shoes, a collared white shirt left with two buttons open, and four-button vest. He hopped up, practically dragging Damien onto the patio. "About damn time!"

"What is this?" Damien asked, a smile already creeping up his face.

"It's what I call an unwinding," said Javi, all dashing charm.

"Unwinding how?"

He held up a finger and addressed everyone present. "Okay, now that this damn shick is here—"

"Hey!"

"—I can *r-r-reveal* the big surprise!" he finished, rolling his *r*'s with a flourish.

The whole group looked on expectantly.

Javier clasped his hands and supplicated towards Captain Romi. "Roman, I have you to thank for this fine evening, would you care to do the honors?"

Romi flashed the faintest hint of irritation at Javier, but he sighed. "The crate is behind that rock," he said, pointing.

"Oh, you sly bastard," said Javier, reaching behind the rock in question with both arms and producing a small polyplastic crate that had been hidden under ivy. He hunched over it, popped the top, and the ex-Marine's face became alight. "Oh my. Mr. Sartohay, you've outdone it this time!"

"Just tell us what it is!" Gwen exclaimed.

"Damien, my man, you asked what an unwinding is? Well, it's what happens when we come into possession of the finest whiskey I could get my hands on!" He produced a crystal bottle full of amber liquid. The golden label and wax seal read 'Judge O'Malley's 30 Gold'.

Surprise dawned on all faces, followed by rampantly enthusiastic clapping and cheers.

Romi brought out a battered metal case, inside which was a collection of very old glasses. Nine of them went on the stone table in the middle of the patio; the rest went away. "Finest tumblers for the finest drinking!" he pronounced to more claps and laughter.

Damien took a seat between Gwen and Sarah Donovan. "How the hell did you get this?"

Javier shrugged. "Called in favors and had a little help." He tipped his head in Romi's direction.

Romi nodded back. "Kel and I *may* or *may not* have brought back a case of these on our last trip." He gave a mischievous little shrug and a smile. "Estrada here had a contact and was kind enough to donate one of the bottles to *Lotus*'s hold for our trouble."

"We agreed on two," Kel growled from his bench. Nisha sniggered next to him, and it sounded like the least offensive hissing you've ever heard.

"Ha!" Javier laughed. "I'll be sneaking that back as soon as I find it!"

"Like hell you will," said the doctor sharply, leaning forward and silencing everyone.

Javier stared and tensed.

"I'll be smuggling those bottles *myself* before you get down there!" she snatched up a tumbler and they applauded, laughter breaking out of even the tightest chests.

Javier poured three fingers for everyone. Kel and Nisha took their tumblers and eyed the twinkling liquid inside with obvious familiarity. Von, however, was very careful picking his up, never having tried it before. Leo sat lazily on his sofa, sipping a milky-white drink with a pink umbrella in it and eating grapes like an emperor.

"Well, I mean this is great and all," said Damien. "But what's the occasion?"

Javi handed him and Sarah their drinks. "Do we need one?"

"Well…" he trailed off. A tiny, fearful voice whispered in his ear that yes, they did. There was a Supply Fleet in orbit. The Over-Seer had his Avos running amok looking for Damien. Damien's nightmares continued dragging him through restless sleep. He hadn't been able to settle anywhere on this island yet. There was a good chance that this Supply Fleet was bringing a very dangerous weapon to the surface. There were other Elementals to find. As he pondered all of this in the span of a second, while Javier and Romi poured the last of the bottle into their own glasses—and immediately brought another one out to more cheers of approval—he looked around, saw the smiling faces, and he couldn't think of a better occasion to enjoy thirty year-old whiskey, here, amongst these people who had accepted him as family, even after all he'd been through.

Damien smiled the widest and truest as he had in a long time, and he said, "No, I guess we don't." Javier clapped happily as he toasted them all. "To friends!" They all cheered, then drank.

"To family!" shouted Leo from his couch. They drank to that, too, and the night had officially begun.

Damien could count the number of times he'd been drunk on his digits, and the last time had been well over four years ago, since before the bunker. With that in mind, he coughed and choked his way through the first two fingers of his first glass of O'Malley's, and thought he might already be feeling pleasantly fuzzy. He couldn't be sure, though, so he asked Javi what he thought.

"Try more, then you'll know!"

Damien and the others all thought that sounded splendid, so he did. *We need to be sure it's working.* He smirked, remembering being a kid in Seattle when his parents had let him try a sip of wine or cheap fruity liquor. His dad, Ewan, would let him have some on special occasions, and he'd hated it, but he still wanted it. It'd been a confusing time in his life.

Damien looked towards his brother.

Von had trouble with the whiskey. "It burns."

Kel's implant whizzed and the alien chortled. "It's *suffosed* to."

Von looked crestfallen that he didn't like it.

"It's an acquired taste, even for us. Here." Kel produced a long, fresh stick of oak bark and tossed it to the other alien. "I have a stash of those. Enjoy." Von thanked him and went to work on the bark, mumbling his way into the background, happily stoned. Kel took Von's whiskey off his hands.

Settled with their firsts, seconds, and thirds already for some, everyone broke into a story to tell, an experience to share, or a debate to have. At first, Javier made a point to try and out-drink them all for a show, but was quickly outgunned by that deceptive heavyweight, Dr. Gwen Whalen. She claimed it was from her Irish heritage.

"You should've seen my Papa and my brothers going at the pints back home," she said, laughing, her cheeks twinged pink and her glasses forgotten on the table. "They would go *all* night long into the wee hours of the mornin'! Me and my sister would have to carry his big lug home sometimes even! Oh gods did 'e weigh a *ton!*"

They all laughed and poked fun as her accent came out more and more thickly, but she didn't care.

"Ohh don't you be sayin' a *word* about my acce—*hic!*" Her hiccup nearly sent her tumbling off the perch she'd adopted on the side of the terrace, but she recovered and cheered when she had realized not a single drop of whiskey had spilled. They all laughed and toasted, this time to "no spillage!" and drank more.

As the night progressed, Damien learned that Javier's unnamed friend, a Ground Warfare specialist named Todd Hanson, was an aspiring tattoo artist who had done Nisha's white lines behind her eyes. He learned that Sarah Donovan had two brothers with her father back in the Regent Dynasty and that she was very shy, even when drunk. He learned Captain Romi and Kel had flown together for six years. He learned that Nisha come to Earth from Shialga in the Third Supply Fleet, twenty-six years ago, and she had met Kel on *Argyle* Station a few years later. Von talked about being born on Shialga, then moving to Earth before he was an Algaroth year old, and what it was like growing up on the XenoCon campus. Damien talked about how much he missed his motorcycle, and he and Javier got into a long argument about it because—as it turned out—Javier had owned one too.

At one point even, Leo—who had run an endless stream of smug, hilarious snark through the evening—gave up the sofa, spun his avatar into a bodacious curve of a woman, and tried to convince Javier that he was both real, and interested. Romi even had Leo's back, egging him on and reaffirming to Javier that he wasn't talking to an AI any longer.

"Nooo," Javi slurred. "Noo 'ss just Leo bein' a—*hic*—a shaper-changer...er."

"Not so, Marine," Romi laughed out. "Leo just called this lovely lady. She's the real deal."

"And not so far away as you might think!" The woman-Leo said with a wink and a shimmy.

Javier took so long to blink that Leo lost interest and started schmoozing up to Gwen, who was smiling at the AI.

"So, you come here often? Darlin'?" Leo traced his finger over the rim of a gold goblet that appeared in his hand. He had traded the buxom body for his own but kept the skimpy nightie, and added a cropped beard, cowboy hat, and exploding chest hair. "Yeh might say I'm a...bit of a scientist myself," he drawled out.

Then there was a high-pitched squeal, and Javier toppled out of his chair as he realized he was about to plant a huge kiss on the AI's projected backside. Everyone howled, and Leo replaced the outfit with a shirt adorned with palm trees and bright colors, sandals, and his black tie over it all.

The night went on and Damien took it all in. His vision was a little fuzzy, and he couldn't think in straight lines anymore, but eyeing Leo and eyeing his brother, good memories started drifting up, like the time when...

He paused. The memory had been there, and then it had floated away, like catching smoke.

Well what about with Von when we...

He paused again, this time with a frown. Why couldn't he think of any good memories?

"Damien!" Javier splattered out, holding out his glass and forcing his eyes to stay open. "You look, mmm…really depressed over there! What the fuck's eatin' acha man?"

Damien waved him off. "Nothin'. Just thinking a bit."

"Well *stop* it! Ain' nobody gonna be think—*hic*—in the morning! Err-kay?"

Damien grinned wide and nodded. "You got it, Javi."

"Mmm! Okay good. Glad to hear it—*hic*."

They all fell silent, staring off into the distance or into their drinks or—in Von's case—at his hand. A shard of bark hung loosely between the Algaroth's teeth while the rest of it was gripped tightly in his lap. "Whoa…" said the alien, stretching his digits. "My hand…"

Damien snorted and sipped.

"I hate thinking," said Javier into the silence that followed.

"Why?" Romi asked. He had been feeling the grooves in his tumbler, absentmindedly watching the trickle of water.

Javier looked at the captain, and all at once, Damien saw the ex-Marine's façade crumble. It was replaced by a raging sadness in his eyes. He saw guilt, and he saw hurt, and he saw a man who hid his emotions *very* well, far better than he did.

"Because I'm a coward." Javier answered.

Crickets chirped somewhere in the garden, and the ocean waves crashed against the rocks in the distance and below.

Javier sighed. In slow, deliberate action, he finished his whiskey and poured another glass, spilling a few precious drops as he did so on account of a shaky hand. "You know I had—*hic*—already finished a year of the Marines when I enlisted? *Hic*." He spoke to no one in particular. "It's true. I was in an early recruitment program. Got in when I was *sixteen*, and—*hic*—ran the fast-track to Special Forces."

Even Von stopped staring wide-eyed at his hand to listen as Javier's story began.

The Elemental took a large gulp, grimaced, and continued, his voice small. "I've been an Elemental most…most of my life. My parents knew it, a couple of other people, but it's always been with me. I never really wanted it though, you know? I just wanted to…to *fit in*." He grasped at the air like he was choking something. "Didn't matter though," he went on. "I knew this shit would catch up with me some day…" He fell silent again, and stayed that way for so long that Damien thought he should maybe say something. When Estrada did start up though, he had lowered his head and was speaking directly into his drink. "You remember the Seven Month Raid right?"

Everyone nodded, Captain Romi shifted a fraction in his chair, and Leo piped up, "Eight years ago. 2137. February to August, right after the Ninth Supply Fleet took off. It was a little…crippling for us, if memory serves."

Damien thought of how Gwen had mentioned that it was after the Seven Month Raid that Project S.E.H.A. had joined Amun-Nūr, and how Reuben had mentioned that's when he started looking for the island. *Damn, that was kind of a pivotal few months. Those last months before Croll Tan showed up.*

Javier nodded at Leo. "Yeah, well, that's the big picture." He shook his head. "I was in Mérida at the time, on the Yucatán Peninsula? I was only a year into Basic. My first year actually *on base*, and…and I was training with my squad when the Stingships came in and…and started bombing. It was in August."

No one made a peep. Even the sound of trickling water faded into the background.

Then, the man catapulted like he'd wanted to tell this story forever. "We were out on trash duty, me and my…my squad. The four of us had pranked our sergeant the night before. Handcuffed him to his desk! Ahh, and it'd been totally worth it, but that motherfucker wanted to spank all of us so bad. Ha, he just yelled and screamed and went all purple, you know? Screaming all kinds of shit about how we were just a bunch of shit-fed greenies and grummings and dickwhips and all kinds of other fun names. He told us we were skipping meals the next day and we could eat whatever we found on perimeter duty, and we had to do it handcuffed together."

He took another swig of whiskey before continuing. "So there we were, out poking at the wrappers that got out of the recycler or somebody's condom or whatever the hell…and that's when we saw them. We saw the Stingships and the transports. And if you cats remember, that was the Supply Fleet that first brought in heavy weapons…when I first saw Iceberg Tanks and Vulture Gunships. Goddamn white metal monsters and dragons 'n shit, just spewing fire everywhere." He trailed off, taking a last swig of his tumbler almost as an afterthought.

"Anyways, it's me, Derrick, Mathers, and Cass, all fucking handcuffed in a line. We said 'fuck this' to trash duty and we took off back for the base and…we get there and people are already running everywhere, they're shouting and screaming, and it takes like five seconds after that for the bombs to start dropping. I'm not talking those little missile pissers that Stingships have either, I'm talking heavy blanket plasma shit. It's nuts. Those things'll ruin your day. But anyways…so the four of us are standing there, and…and we turn around and see a strafe coming in. Five Stingships, they've got us lined up right on the air strip, ships are taking off and getting shot to shit before they can move, it's getting all smoky in the air, all that. And we're lined up and…and…" Javi choked and he tried to take a swig but his glass was empty, so he clapped his fist around the bottle and poured himself another couple of sips. "Ah, better." He smacked his lips. "So we're ah…we're all lined up for these shots, and I'm not even thinking about bein' Elemental, man. Snaps, I'm just glad I didn't piss myself.

"So yeah, our sergeant's yelling something at us that we need to get on a transport or something, and I turned and umm…I yelled back that I wasn't into that and I wanted my damn cuffs off cus I wanted to live to fight another day, right?" He queried the question around the circle, but there were only focused nods of agreement; no one realized it was directed at them. He continued, "Well…as I'm saying that, the strafe starts and just…man. My sergeant's head exploded with like—no, fuck that, his *top* exploded. Like the wettest grapefruit you've ever crushed in your life. And I'm splattered and I can't move and so I…I turn around to see Derrick is gone too. He didn't get hit but the strafe cut a tail fin off an Eagle fighter we were under and umm…it landed on him.

"So then the ah, the Stingships are past us and me and Cass and Mathers are all covered in Derrick and Sergeant Ephron and we're still cuffed but we think we're good but we umm…we're not." He swallowed hard and—upon realizing that his glass was empty again—uncapped the bottle and drank it straight. When he finished his swig, he looked at how much was left and poured a hefty portion into his tumbler, right up to the rim. He slurped the top of it off the glass without spilling, sniggered, then shivered visibly as the mouthful went down. He gagged and looked ready to breathe fire before he took a shaky breath. "Yeah. So we ah…it wasn't cool. We weren't cool. The three of us turned around and—I mean everything's already going to shit, we had no response time, it's a motherfucking massacre—but umm… The Collective they, they had another round to hit us with. They had a flight of Vultures. You ever seen a Vulture?"

Only Romi and Kel nodded.

"Yeah, so, they're *big*, dirty, smack-talkin' gunships. And the three of us turn around to see ten of those goddamn things flying at us in this, this *perfect* fucking formation, about to tear us new assholes. And…that's when I remembered I had powers. I don't know what the fuck triggered it but it like, it just hit me, you know? And I…I…" He sniffed. "I used it. I used my power, man, but…not how I should've."

"What happened?" asked Sarah Donovan.

Javier looked up at her as if he had forgotten she was there. "I used it to…to save myself."

"How?"

Javier glugged another bit of whiskey, and the effort seemed to nearly kick him over the edge. He tottered in his chair, ready to collapse. Then he blinked, righted himself, hiccupped once, and was fine. "I knew we couldn't get away, so I…I just made the ground kinda…kinda swallow me into like this…solid mud bubble or something. I dunno how to describe it."

"It's alright," said Gwen.

At the mention of swallowing ground, though, Damien's thoughts kicked into high gear. He gripped his empty tumbler a little tighter and shifted legs. Von glanced his way, but he said nothing either.

"They saw me disappear, too, my squad," Javier said miserably, unable to stop the wetness in his eyes anymore. "I straight fell into the ground with these cuffs on while the Vultures were bearing down on our sorry asses and…and Mathers saw me first and he started crying out, you know: *'What the fuck are you doing? Help us man! You gotta help!'* It ah…it was Cass that got me though…" Javier trailed off, and slowly looked up at Captain Romi, meeting the man's stone-still face. "Cass, he…he was like a little brother to me. And he just…he was such a good fucking *DUDE!*" he shouted the last word, making people jump. "He totally got it though," he went on, his voice slowly getting higher and smaller and scratchier. "That's what gets me. He just…he saw me, and I just saw it in his eyes when, when I was going under… and his hand came…came with…"

"What did you see?" asked Romi quietly, not breaking Javi's gaze.

"He, he knew!" his voice cracked, and tears leaked out at last. "He just knew what I was and what I was doing and he, he didn't say anything, Roman. I swear. He didn't say anything but…he, I think he understood and he umm… Cass reached out to me and I reached back and, I think he just knew in the way that he always did that, that I'd have to live with that moment forever, and I think he was cool with it. I know that sounds nuts but, but I think it's *true!*" He implored up at Romi. "Please, man. Please believe me." The tears were flowing freely now, a thick carpet of wetness down the man's strained face. "They…they died and, and I lived and I did *nothing* like a real Marine would've done. A *real* Marine would've said 'my life for theirs? I'll take it. Even if it tells everyone I've been lying to them my whole life, because really I could've been so much more helpful, because I'm a fucking *Elemental*', and you know what?" He turned his gaze from Romi to the bottle in his hand. He shook a finger at it with the kind of hatred that Damien knew all too well. Self-hatred. "It was a shitty moment of shitty, selfish, fuck-all-ness. I came out of that damn mud and crawled off that burning base with just *these*," and he flashed his scarred wrists. "I got them when the mud shit closed and it sealed me in safe. I was reaching for Cass and just…the *heat*, man…" his voice took on an ethereal note of pain, and he touched his wrists, giving Damien chills. "This dry, bake-your-shit-in-the-Sun kind of heat just rolled over us. The hottest thing you've ever felt in your life, shockwave from some plasma bombs. And my hands they…shit I don't know how I didn't pop like a blister but, I don't know. The air stayed cool inside but the mud got really hot. It didn't burn my hands but it cooked the fucking cuffs right up and," he waggled his wrists. "This is…this is all I got hit with."

"That and a court martial," said Romi, but it didn't sound demeaning, just fact.

"Yeah but…that came later."

Everyone's attention drifted to Romi now, who sat still for a long time as Javier whimpered. At one point, Sarah put her glass down and went to the Marine's side to rub a comforting hand on his back.

Romi's eyes had glazed over, and eventually, he looked up at them all. "Cass was my nephew," he said. "My sister's son. Alex Roman Cassidy." Saying the name seemed to bring a sudden measure of peace to the captain. "You never told me this before, Estrada."

Javi couldn't meet his gaze. "You knew what had happened. You know the Corps didn't kick me out. They said it was a 'casualty of war' thing, and you know the rest of the story. They packed me out to finish Basic like it was nothing, and it was downhill from there and I just…I *just*," he made like he was going to whip his tumbler away, but in seeing a tiny drop of whiskey in it he drank instead, almost grudgingly.

"It's done though, nothing of that can change," said Nisha, her light voice a soothing surprise out of the evening.

Javier shook his head, "*Anything* different would've been better than losing the entire fucking city! Than losing Cass! *That* was my problem! Instead of choosing to help the people who needed it THEN, at THAT moment, I freaked out like some fucking coward, and I reasoned it out later going, 'oh sure, now I could do something later, yeah? I could hold back to help people at the end and be a hero at a *big fucking finale* when I have the means to do it 'cus I can't do it now'!" He shook his head in disgust. "Shit doesn't work like that, man. It was all just so, *so*…" he clenched his fist, and looked like he dearly wanted to wing the bottle again, but he just gritted his teeth and set it down with deliberate, controlled slowness. The liquid barely shifted as he pulled his hands away.

"Backwards," said Damien into the quiet.

He swallowed and gave a full-bodied nod. "*Yes. Backwards.* That's it! It was fucking backwards! *Thank* you." Finally, Javier noticed how empty the bottle was getting and he offered it around the circle. Romi took it from him.

"Estrada, look at me."

He did, fear etched into his every feature.

Romi spoke slowly. "I loved Cass, and you're the reason he's dead. I'll never forgive you for that."

Javier's head hung.

"Keep your damn eyes on me, Marine."

He looked back up.

"I can't forgive you for that, but…" the captain poured another finger for himself, and another for Estrada. "You keep turning your life around like you have been, sharing a vintage as good as this? Then you'll have found a friend in me… and you'll have my forgiveness for all the rest that you've gone through." Captain Roman Sartohay held his glass up to the ex-Yucatán Jungler Marine, who swallowed hard and replied in kind.

They both drank a silent toast.

"Mmm," Romi added, smacking his lips. "Damn good whiskey."

They lapsed into thoughtful silence again. If only it had remained so.

As if in defiance of the moment, of the story just told, the rumbling memories came bursting up from nowhere, and the words tumbled out of Damien's mouth before he could stop them. "I killed my parents," he said, regretting it instantly.

But no one attacked him. No one turned on him to say he was a sonofabitch for trailing Javier's story with his own. No one looked at him with hate or disdain. They did respond though. Von's hand dropped slowly into his lap, Gwen put her glasses back down, Javier looked up, and Todd Hanson stared awkwardly into his empty glass, nearly forgotten in the quiet.

"Damien…" his brother pleaded.

"*No.*" It was already out. "It's true," he said. "I did. I killed them during the earthquake that took Seattle apart."

"You were trying to save them," said Leo, his voice kind.

"I didn't know *what* I was doing!" His voice rose quicker than Javier's had.

"That's what you saw, isn't it?" Romi asked. "During your demonstration in the Core? You relived it."

He closed his eyes, recalling the day. "Yes. In...*detail*." He looked at Gwen for strength. "I had to relive what I did six years ago. It was in the middle of the earthquake and my parents and my...my girlfriend were on the far side of a crack and I tried to bring them across with my power."

"Snaps..." said Javi, looking unabashedly shocked.

Romi looked to the doctor. "The Core isn't supposed to be able to do that."

"I don't think it did," said Leo. Everyone turned. "The Core was doing *exactly* what it was supposed to do that day. I think it was Damien's power."

"What?!" Todd Hanson exclaimed. Everyone looked at him. "Sorry."

"It's fine," said Damien, and he saw Von leaning forward. All eyes were on him now. He took a deep breath. "I think Leo's right. I didn't *remember* the earthquake before that day. Von and I never talked about it, we just remembered waking up the next morning and...well, while I was in the Core, I ran my demonstration but I kept having these weird flashes." Something suddenly occurred to him. "Have all of you actually *used* the Core?"

Everyone but Sarah and Todd nodded.

Damien didn't know what he'd been expecting, and he was curious what *their* experiences had been like, but now wasn't the time. His shock was palpable though. "Oh, okay. Well... Yeah. I don't know what it was like for all of you, but for me, I kept seeing flashes of home while I was in there. I saw some really weird stuff, but ah, as I was using up all the Elemental juice in me, I started to umm, to remember these bits and pieces of the quake. I thought I was going nuts or it was trauma kicking in cus I'd just seen the Islets start to fall, but..." He wasn't sure how to go about saying it, and he didn't want to undermine Javier baring his soul with another deep story. He shook his head. "Short version is that as I pushed myself to the limit, these memories came popping back. I used up all my power, and it must have let go of a block in my memory—the same power I can use on someone else—and it just so happened to be when…when the earthquake hit."

The quiet after Damien's story was much more thoughtful. The atmosphere was sympathetic, too, but less traumatically so. For once, he was okay with that.

Leo spoke up again, setting his gold goblet down. "My dear Damien, I can't say I'm surprised that it took you a month to recover from all of that."

Damien felt a surge of gratitude for the AI. The feeling blossomed tenfold, though, as there were nods of agreement and understanding from around the group. His surprise continued to grow. "Wait," he fumbled with his tumbler, glad of how cool it still was. "You…none of you thought I was crazy?"

"Of course not," said Romi.

"Loss is *veing* of Amun-Nūr, Vilan," said Kel, lounging back with his arm around his *vishi*, who was resting her head on his shoulder. The Algaroth itched his implant. "To co*we* here at all, we lose *w*uch."

"Elementals are powerful, Damien," Gwen added. "We don't know our limits yet, hardly any of us," she inquired between Damien and Javier.

Javi shook his head. "Not a damn clue."

Gwen shifted and brushed the stray locks of flaming hair from her brow that had come out through the evening. "I think now is as good a time as any to finally tell you this. What you did in the Core?"

"What about it?"

"You gave us more than I could have ever hoped," she smiled. "It's been almost two months now and I *still* haven't finished even combing the data we collected off of you."

"Wait, really?"

"Fuck yeah!" Javier exclaimed, his eyes dry. "I thought a demonstration meant a little showy-shit, you know? Snaps! When the doc told me you almost killed yourself to get it all out? I was like, 'man, *that* guy's got the balls'!"

Damien frowned at Gwen, but she nodded. "His words." She grinned, "Almost verbatim."

Others chuckled.

Between everyone looking at him, though, Damien locked eyes with the one person that mattered who hadn't weighed in yet. "Vo?" he inquired.

Von looked up at him, and he took a deep breath. "You didn't kill them, Damien. The earthquake got them. You might have even eased their passing."

"I…"

"No." Von's voice was surprisingly commanding. Damien stopped. "I know what you're thinking. I know you've thought it for a long time."

"What do you mean?"

Von shrank into his chair. "They were your parents first. I was never their son, but they took me in when other humans would have killed me. *My* parents were *already dead*. It isn't fair that I've lost TWO sets of them." His voice dropped to a whisper. "And both times it was out of my control." He looked up, and his emerald-gold eyes had never looked so bright as a single, bluish tear squeezed its way out. "You would have died if you'd pushed harder for them. I couldn't lose you, too."

Damien's heart thudded a stampede in his chest, and he wasn't sure how he felt. Angry? Nauseous? Grateful? Scared? Guilty? Loved? Maybe it was a bit of everything, but Von was right. *They* were *my parents first*. He didn't want to admit it, but he *had* thought that for years. All those years when his parents were getting to know Silas Torn, Silas Nilyana, and Silas Von. Lucy and Ewan Vilan had been Xenocultural Conglomerates, and their lives had been focused on the Algaroth, not on humans. The faint jealousy had always been with Damien, but when Torn and Nilyana died in the xenophobic riots during the year before The Conquering, Von had become family. Damien had never questioned it, and his bond with Torn and Nilyana's son had only waxed over the years. The jealousy hadn't mattered.

But the night of the quake, when Von had yanked Damien away from his parents, it had changed something…or it would have. Following his delirious two weeks after the Core, Damien had pieced together his long stint of delirium, and he'd realized that he *had* been angry at Von for saving him. He *had* been furious and jealous that *he'd* felt like the outsider child. But as time went on, he'd realized something, something that was culminating in this moment:

Had Damien's power not blocked all memory of the earthquake, the seed of jealousy surrounding his parents and his brother would probably have spread into one of those resilient, parasitic ideas that you could never hope to kill entirely. Damien's power had saved him from that. And here, sitting on this terrace with his brother, Von had done what he had always known how to do. He'd excised the cancerous thought bubbles in Damien's head before they took deep root, and now they lay out on the table, squirming…and dying.

Damien sighed long and hard. "They loved you more," he said quietly.

Immediately, the air changed.

The admission cracked a sieve in Damien's toxic thoughts and, like a nugget of calcified anger, he felt the hard shell pierce and begin to liquefy. A buried, core feeling of what had hurt so bad all along began to bleed out into nothing, and Damien felt it physically. A constriction he'd held onto for years loosened in his chest. He felt knots all over his body release their pent up cramps, and he shivered all over. The thundering memories of the earthquake and of his parents' screams reached some critical juncture with that sentence, and somehow, Damien knew that he'd just crossed beyond rock bottom. An uphill climb lay ahead, but the worst was now past. He could begin to heal, all in the span of a moment.

And if that wasn't affirmation enough, Von's next words cemented it. "No, they didn't," said his brother. "They loved us both."

Damien choked out a sad laugh at the absurd simplicity of the answer to his pain, and he closed his eyes. *It's all so easy on the other side, isn't it?* He shook his head. "I'm sorry."

"For what? For the power that you couldn't control?" Von leaned forward. "Damien, whatever happened that night was in place for *six years*, across all manner of distance. It stayed in place while I was half a world away. You have something in your veins like no one else. It's never been a surprise to me how creative you could get in keeping us alive with what you can do."

"Hear hear!" Leo hollered, toasting and bringing a few smiles back.

Von's eyes flickered to Leo, staying uncommonly soft as they did. "It was the three of us," he concluded. "And now, it's this place," Von opened his arms to the group sitting out with them. "We take small steps together."

Damien looked up from his glass, and he nodded at his brother, aware of everyone's gazes on him. "I guess you're right."

"I know I am."

And as that moment played out, as it started to slip towards when someone would eventually say that it was time to leave for the night, Todd Hanson spoke up. "Estrada," he said. "Next time you invite me to something like this, let's try beer instead of whiskey. Whiskey gets too intense."

Everyone laughed, and it was a pure thing. It was a good thing. And they all needed it.

They needed it because, at that very moment, on the far side of the world, the master strategist and lord of The Collective on Earth, Fourth Over-Seer, and favored son of Shialga, Croll Tan of clan Ruthilon, was sitting in his citadel at the heart of Solaroth surrounded by his Korodors, his Avos, and the resting emissaries who had come with the Supply Fleet. The emissaries had delivered the gift for which Croll Tan had asked, and he had thanked them with a respite. The Algaroth Royal sat in his private antechamber, at a banquet table with a human chessboard in front of him, centerpiece to all, and he watched the vestiges of a sumptuous feast fade away. He had enjoyed the game of chess for as long as he'd been on Earth, and he was thus far undefeated since his very first game.

On the board, Croll Tan always played black and humans were white; he never played first. On the board, barely any pieces were taken, but nearly everything had moved. On the board, it was black's turn. And on that board, Croll Tan was about to make his first move towards his endgame. He was going to take the first white pawn with his black king's-side knight. White would have no choice but to take that knight with their remaining rook. Black would answer with their queen to end the black rook, and the pure white of humanity would feel good at claiming a queen-sized piece. The board would be set up so that white would *think* that the Over-Seer had just set a fatal position, but they would be wrong. In reality, white would have just lost the game, even if they couldn't yet see.

Croll Tan eyed the board. The Algaroth Royal picked up the carved marble pieces, and moved his king's-side knight to take the lonely pawn. Then he moved white's rook into position, and he stopped. His many confidantes and trusted allies surrounded him, and they watched the pieces move. He removed his hand from the board, and said nothing.

He didn't have to. They knew it was time.

MASON J. TORALL

I remember the first time I looked up at the crescent moon and realized that lights filled the void of the thumbnail. My dad told me the lights weren't stars. They were a city. Home Luna, the first city on another world. I was so amazed. Looking back, that was when I knew what I wanted to be when I grew up. I wanted to see the Moon.

They all pass so quickly, those moments. So fleeting and emotional, yet baffling in their infinite staying power.

My dad told me how hard it was to build a city on the Moon. He said the dust up there was so fine that it was like flour, and it got into everything worse than sand. He said Home Luna spread for kilometers in every direction, lighting the Earth nights so that I was never in the dark, but the city looked even bigger because the Moon is so small.

Now that I've lived here for so many years, I don't know how some people go their whole lives without ever coming up. Of course… I suppose that makes it a cruel twist of fate that I'll never leave.

This is my final entry. I will write no more in this journal.

Seven of us are still trapped under the ruins of Apollo. We found a window to the surface, and at first I didn't know what I saw. Outside was half grey and half black. As it turned out, it was one of our starship construction berths. The whole thing's been torn to pieces, but I remember this berth was for our destroyers: Gagarin, Hisar, and Elysium.

They're all gone now. Just like Home Luna. Just like Apollo. Just like me.

We're going to die up here; I don't think I'll ever get to see Earth again, and perhaps neither will our starships. I sent them away from home to uncertain friends, and made it certain that children no longer look to the Moon and see light in the crescent.

The greatness of all things can be measured by how far they fall, planet or person. A bird might crash with the same resonance as a civilization, but we all fall just the same.

I had hoped humanity wasn't ready to fall.

—Lunar Admiral Jacob Hawkins,
Final entry in his personal journal
Dated June 24, 2130
Eighteen months after The Conquering

CHAPTER TWENTY THREE

The Call to War

An alarm threw Damien from his chair in his quarters.

The Supply Fleet had been in orbit eleven days, and Damien was writing an email to Gwen saying he had decided to try Personal Warfare as a vocation. He had just hit send when one of the Pip screens exploded with noise, almost giving him a heart attack out of the serene midafternoon quiet in which he'd been working.

BrEHHH! BrEHHH! BrEHHH!

"*Yiiie!*" Damien shrieked, throwing himself away from the sound and onto the floor.

BrEHHH! BrEHHH! BrEHHH!

He groaned, holding his back where he'd hit it against couch.

BrEHHH! BrEHHH! BrEHHH!

"Cease alarm!" he shouted, scrambling to his feet.

BrEHHH! BrEHHH! BrEHHH!

"LEO!!"

BrEHH—"It's off!" The AI shrieked, his face appearing on the main Pip screen.

"What the hell's going on?!"

Leo looked frazzled. "Emergency alarm. Sato wants you in the command wheel, *now!*"

"What for?!"

"Tan's making his move."

"WHAT?! The fleet's still in orbit though!"

Leo shoved his hand through his hair, fussing it up. "Looks like he counted on us thinking that, he's outmaneuvered us. Put some pants on!"

"I *have* pants on," he shouted back, shoving his feet into his old combat boots.

"Brush your teeth then!"

"*Why?!*"

"I don't know just get down here!" Leo vanished, leaving Damien breathing hard and cursing as he tried to lace his boots.

Bolting out of his room a few minutes later, Damien made his way to the command wheel. On the way, he heard an overhead announcement shouting warnings. He thought he heard something about 'Italian Peninsula' and 'Cairo', but the Atrium was buzzing with so much noise that he couldn't catch it. As he reached the hallway to the command wheel, he saw Reuben and Satolin standing off to the side, arguing. A flood of humans and Algaroth were working their way towards the wheel.

"—just what he wants us to do," Björn snapped as Damien came up.

"Yes, but it *will* draw them out," the Prohka growled.

"At what cost?"

"Their lives if they don't have protection."

"They're untested."

"And therefore vulnerable," Satolin agreed.

Reuben sneered as he saw Damien walking briskly past. "Is it just a soft spot you have for broken souls, Daeduras?" said the man, loud enough for Damien to catch it.

Damien didn't hear Satolin's response as he crossed the threshold into the wheel.

The command wheel was packed, and Damien saw that the polyglass partitions had been de-polarized, revealing the other two wedges beyond. He was startled as he realized all three wedges of the command wheel were identical to each other. *Backup command centers?* he wondered.

There wasn't time to wonder about that. On this evening, humans and Algaroth filled all three pie slices of the wheel. Inside the main wedge, facing the entry corridor, Damien spotted Von near Javier, Joval Tosh, and Loss. They were by the banks of tech stations on one of the higher landings. He pushed through the throng towards them.

"Hey," he hissed as he came up and bumped fists with Javier. "What the hell's going on?"

Before the Marine or Von could answer, Leo's voice crackled in Damien's implant, making him twist his head. "Croll Tan just dumped his armies out of hiding this morning," the AI hissed. "He's making a *daring* assault on Eurasia."

Damien frowned at Javier, who looked at him curiously. "Nothing in North America?"

"Not a peep. Gotta go!"

"What was that?" asked Javier.

Damien relayed it.

"Damn, really?" Javier looked surprised.

Damien shrugged, feeling his nerves tingling.

Von shushed them. "I think we'll find out now," he said, pointing towards the entrance to the wheel where Reuben and Satolin had just come through. Satolin took a position underneath the Conduit clock, which today read, "13Y : 06M : 10D : 02H."

"Leo," boomed Daeduras. "Can the island hear me?"

There was a pause, during which any remaining whispers died away. "They can now," Leo's voice cooed from above. "You're on, Prohka."

Satolin cleared his throat. "Amun-Nūr, this is Prohka Satolin speaking."

Far away down the hallway, Damien could hear the great Algaroth's voice echoing.

"Our assumptions that The Collective would never begin a major offensive while a Supply Fleet is in orbit are incorrect. The Over-Seer is making a move." Shocked whispers zipped through the wheel like wildfire. Leo made displays around the wheel showing a global map. "As of this moment, three distinct offensive bodies have begun to mobilize. The first is spilling out from inside the walls of Solaroth as we speak. Their destination is not yet known, but our friends in the Eurasian Union are predicting that they're moving against the Italian Peninsula."

On the displays, the sketchy map of the huge boot that poked into the Mediterranean Sea was highlighted in gold. Damien could tell that Amun-

Nūr didn't have the Triad to help them right now from the fuzzy images of the terrain.

"The second," the Prohka went on. "Has already assembled against their target."

The maps updated to show a gargantuan horde of red Collective markers advancing east through Cairo in Africa. "They are moving to take the Throat of Israel."

Satolin began pacing. "The final body is an airborne invasion force, bound for the Regent Dynasty via Australia." The map updated to show three growing columns of red speeding north from the coasts of the captured continent, bound for the mostly untouched green borders of the Dynasty. "Unfortunately," Daeduras projected, "none of these armies are our concern right now. Commander?"

Commander Morgan broke through the throng amidst more confused whispering. He pressed up against the war table. "Whatever Croll Tan is doing right now, we think it's a ruse."

"That'd be one elaborate ruse, sir!" someone shouted.

"Damn right it would, Nelson," Morgan replied. "But that seems to be the Over-Seer's style, wouldn't you say?"

Nelson didn't answer.

"Operator Ophelia, would you mind presenting what you recorded last night?"

A tall woman wearing a brown-and-green technical worksuit came through the throng to stand near Morgan. Her skin was as dark as midnight and she looked nervous. Damien saw her lips move but he couldn't hear anything.

"Speak up!" someone called.

"—tracked an explosion in the Himalayas!" She spoke up in a language that rang a bell for Damien but he wasn't sure why.

"What kind of explosion?" asked an armored Algaroth whom Damien had never seen.

Operator Ophelia looked to Morgan. The commander nodded and pointed at the war table. Ophelia excused her way through the people to where the input console was and slid in a memory stick. A second later, a much cleaner map of the highest mountain range on Earth—the Himalayas—seen from probably ten kilometers in the air, appeared on the war table. At the southeastern-most edge of the projection, the most inland tip of the Bang Sea—which had formed by the rising oceans submerging the country of Bangladesh nearly a century ago—could be seen. The map started to spin slowly.

Now that's *gotten some help from the Triad,* Damien noted, nodding to himself. Then he thought he could hear Ophelia speaking again, but her mumbling was just too quiet. Someone shouted at her and Morgan's gaze flashed in the general direction, silencing the heckler. Ophelia hung her head and the commander hurried to her side. He put a hand on her shoulder and whispered something while the wedge waited. A moment later she nodded, her back to Damien, and Morgan stepped away.

"Alright," said the commander. "Ophelia already briefed me on what's going on, so she's going to keep this updated." He scanned the crowd. "Here's what we know: Since the Supply Fleet has been in orbit, we've been given access to the Triad at quarter-daily intervals. Ophelia was on duty early this morning when the connection was made, and she managed to record *this* event."

A timestamp appeared over the table, and what looked like a dim flash showed up: a still image nestled in a valley just above the dark foot of the Himalayan Mountains. The time stamp accelerated forward across an hour, halted, and reset. Morgan spoke as it showed what turned out to be the endings of some flash, a glittering corona of light afterwards, and then a blizzard bearing down on the area. The valley was obscured at the end of the hour. The timer reset and played it again silently.

"At estimated oh-one-hundred hours this morning, Amun-Nūr local time," Morgan explained, "Operator Ophelia recorded the end of a large explosion. Unfortunately, the blizzard you see prevented us from further analysis. At approximately fourteen-fifteen hours this afternoon, during the third quarterly connection to the Triad today, we saw that the blizzard had mostly dissipated, leaving us to ponder on *this.*" He nodded to Ophelia, who changed the scan. The view remained the same, but the timestamp matched this afternoon.

"Ophelia, take us closer."

She brought the scan in towards the valley. The command wedge filled with frowning faces and muttered confusion as they took in what was shown.

The landscape showed a broad valley deep in snow. A blanket of the purest white spanned between the mountains to the north, east, and west. Tucked almost against the northernmost mountain, though, Damien could make out tiny bumps in the frozen landscape surrounded by even smaller black dots; it was a small, rural village. In silence, Morgan bid Ophelia to hone in on the landmark. Confusion in the wedge turned to fear as she did. A few strangled cries escaped as the bumps resolved into ruined buildings, and the dots resolved into bodies half-buried in snow.

The village couldn't have been larger than a few hundred people, but it seemed that everyone must have found their way into the cold spaces between rough-hewn structures. They lay everywhere, with dark splotches around and beneath them, tainting the snow. It was a scene out of a nightmare, made only worse by the silent detachment with which Amun-Nūr was viewing it from afar. Damien noticed it silently while others mentioned seeing what appeared to be an odd line of tracks, leading away from the village to the west.

Morgan's voice grew serious. "Whatever happened here, it seems to be a strange and convenient coincidence that it happened just when Croll Tan mobilized so much hardware. Yes, this event would make for more people keeping an eye on their local topography, but it also means that most eyes would be turned towards these three armies, providing good cover for whatever's going on under those mountains. In short: It doesn't take a stretch to conclude that the Over-Seer is testing whatever dangerous new toy he got from the Supply Fleet. The fact that he's moving so quickly only gives us a couple of possible answers to that eventual course: One, he's nervous about something. Or two, whatever he received is so useful that he can't wait to unbox it before the folks upstairs take a hike." He jerked his finger towards the sky. "It could be a bomb, it could be a bioweapon, or it could be something else," he concluded. "Regardless: it's something that *we*, as the only assumed group with both the manpower and the resources to track this down, need to do. Any questions?"

"It's only one village," said a familiar voice.

Commander Morgan turned and a few people stepped away to reveal Reuben Björn from the crowd. Damien narrowed his eyes, and he wasn't the only one.

"For how long?" Morgan retorted. "If this is a new weapon, we need to stop it before Tan decides to use it somewhere else. You're not a strategist, Björn."

"Personal fallacies aside," said Björn. "This feels too good to be true. I smell a trap."

Morgan kept still, but his eyes drifted towards Daeduras, who stepped up.

"In that case," said the Prohka. "You wouldn't mind accompanying the team that's going there, would you?"

Reuben registered shock for just long enough that Damien got to see it, which meant others had too. Smirks were traded around the wedge.

"Bastard's really not making friends around here, eh?" Javier whispered smugly. Damien nodded, smirking back.

"Of course I wouldn't mind," Reuben answered, recovering quickly. "What are these teams, exactly?"

Morgan gave the floor to Satolin.

"We're sending out everything we have," announced the Prohka, producing a large tablet and sending the info to the enormous Pip display next to the Conduit clock behind him. "The first team is 'Kehzalla', a Dekka word with no easy translation to human language, but its meaning is similar to 'just deliverance', or 'retribution'."

Duty rosters and assignments began to appear on the wall, and the crowd scrutinized them. There were three ships assigned to each of the four groups, with each ship hosting crew, complement, armament, and mission. Among those in Kehzalla group was Javier Estrada. Damien's stomach clenched at the idea of not going to battle with his friend, but he held his tongue.

"Kehzalla is bound to aid the Regent Dynasty Navy in warding off the Australian advance," said the Prohka. "We've already contacted the local command and they have assured us no harm will come to the Algaroth members of the team."

Damien saw the alien soldiers of Kehzalla nod approvingly. *I wouldn't have thought of that.*

"The second group is 'Echo'." Satolin put up the roster info. "You are bound for the Throat of Israel, where the Middle Kingdom armies are preparing for a ground invasion from Cairo." The globes highlighted the narrow channel of water that separated Africa from what used to be the Middle East. It had been flooded for almost a century, officially disconnecting Africa from Eurasia. "You will connect with the friendly forces congregating between New Gaza, Petra, and Jerusalem, and follow their instructions. The enemy's forces in Africa aren't well-known due to jungle cover, but you'll be given the best we can offer."

Damien recognized only Staff Sergeant Declan on that list.

"Group three is 'Notte' group, bound for the Italian Peninsula. You'll be tasked with perhaps the most important defense of this engagement. Your mission will be to hold the line of anti-air towers in the Apennine Mountains. Those towers are the defense grid that has kept the Regent Dynasty from invasion since The Conquering."

Damien suddenly had a hunch where he'd be going. Satolin was interrupted though by Javier.

"Do you really think they'll make landfall in Italy, Prohka? I mean, that Cairo army would have to break the entire Middle Kingdom to get through to the Dynasty. And come on, the Dynasty's Navy is still the best in the world!" Approving hoots made the rounds, making Javier beam. "But breaking the Italian defense grid?" he made a raspberry. "Get real."

A few people laughed, but Satolin paused and shook his head sadly. "Leo?"

Leo appeared in six different places around the wedge, each avatar speaking in unison so everyone could hear. "Oh, they'll make landfall, Mr. Estrada. If perhaps we had more Elementals to aid us, or a larger attack force, we might be able to keep them at bay. As it is…" Leo and his copies turned back to the Prohka.

Satolin resumed his briefing. "As it is, Amun-Nūr has to make a hard decision as to where we can provide aid. If Italy goes down, there isn't enough Naval presence in that region to stop the Over-Seer from pushing into the Middle Kingdom, but the Himalayas are more important. Allied forces have the air brigades in Istanbul, and they are calling in the majority of their pilots to defend both the Throat and the Peninsula, but we don't know if that will be enough. Furthermore, Notte, we've plied the regional government and military about spreading out aid, but we've heard nothing back."

"Which means?" Damien whispered to Javier, who shrugged. Satolin answered.

"What that means is: the allied forces may not know you're coming. They might not like having strange ships drop in reinforcements of heavily armed Algaroth, so you will do what it takes to earn their trust." The Prohka paused. "I also feel obligated to inform you all that our Lunar Admiral Baroda has strictly forbidden Amun-Nūr from becoming involved in these engagements."

Damien's jaw dropped, and the sudden surge of riotous anger in the wheel was overwhelming.

"*He believes*," the huge Algaroth roared over the shouting, and they quieted. "He believes that the Elementals should be held back at this island as a reveal to the world *after* Croll Tan has shown his hand." Satolin looked to Commander Morgan, who nodded. "We believe differently. We believe that it's past time Amun-Nūr joined the war and showed the people of Earth that we're a force to be reckoned with. We intend to do so. If any of you have an objection in line with the Admiral, I invite you step forward now. I will respect your wishes if you do."

No one, not even Reuben stepped forward.

Satolin's arctic-gold eyes grew warm. "Very well, then we move forward."

The Prohka stuck the roster on the wall, and Damien—who had been expecting to see his name—frowned. He'd been sure that Sato would send him to Italy, but he was wrong. On the roster, he saw only the *Sanguine Lotus*, captained by Roman Sartohay and Diesal Kel, and Staff Sergeant Tortelli, commanding a mixed squad of six.

A pit of both fear and gratitude began to form in his stomach. *That means...*

"Finally," Satolin boomed. "Team four is 'Aurora'. You'll be visiting the site of the explosion in the Himalayas and determining what caused it, with orders to return home for a regroup before we verify what needs to be done."

The final roster went on the wall, and Damien's concern balanced out. On one end of the list of names was Damien Vilan. On the other was Reuben Björn. In between, he saw Koro Valagan Loss, Silas Von, and Doctor Gwen Whalen. The ship they were riding on was called the *Deep Core*, captained by one Bruce Fagin and copiloted by Xiu Su-jin.

"You've all got your work cut out for you," Morgan spoke up. "We have faith in you. Captains: mission telemetry is being uploaded by Leo as we speak."

That sounded like the end of the briefing, but Satolin reclaimed the stage before anyone moved. "I have two addendums for you," he said. "First, whatever the Over-Seer is planning, we can all safely predict that it surrounds the Nukes or the Elementals. Should it be related to either of those things, you have my directive to capture or destroy that weapon at all costs. Any fallout after this event will land on my shoulders." His arctic gaze swept the room. "I needn't remind you of the consequences if Earth loses the Final Option."

There was a universal nod.

"Second, a reminder to all of you assigned to these missions: Elementals have historically appeared in times of chaos. This offensive is without question, a qualifying event to where an Elemental may just appear." His words were imploring, but his gaze was hard. "If one is to show themselves, you are to *protect them* as if they were your own blood. Guard them, help them, and if possible? Bring them home with you."

Another nod.

The Prohka beamed. "Then man your ships, all of you. Today, Amun-Nūr gives up its anonymity for the fight we always should have been fighting. It's time that we give back to the people of Earth, who have sheltered us—knowingly or not—for many long years. Give Croll Tan a reason to be upset with us, because an Over-Seer angry is an Over-Seer who can be beaten."

"Dismissed!" Morgan concluded, and though not everyone in the command wheel was a soldier, you wouldn't have known it by the proud salutes given all around, the cheers that pealed in notes only obtainable through a pre-mission pep talk. The sound was deafening.

Damien swallowed, and he looked to his friend. "You be safe over there, yeah?"

Javier raised an eyebrow. "I'm worried about *you*, Dame. Watch your back with that icy fucker, okay?"

Damien looked over his shoulder to see Reuben standing alone, arms crossed, looking at the roster as everyone else marched out. "I will."

"Björn won't try anything," Von assured him.

"Good," said Javi. "Don't get buried, yeah?"

"We won't," and the three left the wheel for their assignments.

Below in the hangar, Damien and Von were introduced to Captain Fagin and Xiu Su-jin. Fagin turned out to be a North American bush pilot who hailed from an old family ranch in the cornfields of the Midwest. He'd lost his wife and son to a psychopath who had been trying to kill his Algaroth friend almost fifteen years ago, and had been one of the few at the peace summit in Montreal where Reuben had first heard of Amun-Nūr. "Yeh keep our ship clean, don't stink up the toilet, and keep your tawdry head cool in a firefight, and we'll get along jus' fine, I wager," he drawled, shaking hands with Damien and surprising Von with an Algaroth elbow-pull-chest-push greeting.

Xiu Su-jin hailed from the former nation of Korea in the Regent Dynasty. Her family was military, and she'd been proud to be asked to join Project S.E.H.A. for her research into mutative atomic sequencing—an obscure field perfectly tailored to the project. Sadly, she hadn't been able to contact her family since S.E.H.A. moved to the island, and she knew they believed her to be dead. She was in her late fifties, but you would never know it with her youthful charm and commanding presence. "Illya!" she barked over the walkway to the hangar floor, speaking Korean. "Stock those scanners and tie them with rope! They are all calibrated properly and that takes time! Don't jostle them!"

A pale-blond woman much larger than Su-jin bowed her head and scurried up the loading ramp into *Deep Core*, hefting a huge black polyplastic crate.

Deep Core was a modified Scops fighter just like the *Sanguine Lotus*, but something about it just wasn't the same as Romi's ship. No adorning paint marked the black veneer, nor were there any decorations in the cockpit. Before Damien and Von finished helping Aurora to load up their vessels, Damien took a long glance around the hangar bay.

Arrayed around the docking berths, he saw all twelve of Amun-Nūr's ships being loaded for war. Reuben's caution about this being a trap had left a bit of a sour taste in his mouth. *Some of us may not be coming back.* The thought was sobering, but a shout from Su-jin brought him back, and it was quickly forgotten as the team made final preparations.

It was a long hour before the launching process began, and another before all twelve ships had exited the island that afternoon, but as *Deep Core* came churning out of the underwater tunnel beneath Amun-Nūr, the floodlit sight of a dozen amphibious aircraft floating like secretive, shadowy guardians in the ocean made Damien's breath catch. He was reminded of how important this place had become to him, and how good these people were. He knew that this island was something special, and an iron weight fell from his shoulders as the *Deep Core* fell in line along with her two partners—the *Polar Diamond* and the *Earth Clad*—completing the Aurora team. He had been in the sanctuary for almost three long months, and the knowledge that he was leaving it behind, even for a short time, was a breath of relief.

Captain Fagin snapped on the ship-to-ship comm and keyed that they were present. A few minutes later, the last ship—none other than the *Sanguine Lotus*—came barreling out of the tunnel, glorious in her dragon-esque body. The comms clacked and popped, and Captain Romi's voice filtered through the speakers. *"Inferno strike force, this is Notte-1. All ships, sound off."*

A clatter of voices listed their way through the channel. Four groups and twelve ships, twelve captains, and twelve copilots, all loaded as Morgan had decried. One group to each target, three ships to each group. Damien was too distracted to hear them all.

Finally, the captain of Kehzalla-3 sounded off, and Captain Romi confirmed the targets with the other squadron leaders: Notte group to Italy (with Romi, Kel, and Tortelli onboard), Kehzalla group to the Regent Dynasty (with Javier onboard), Echo group to the Throat of Israel (no familiar names aside from Declan), and Aurora group to the Himalayas (sporting Damien, Von, Gwen, and Reuben). All ships would stay underwater for a set amount of time to keep the Supply Fleet still looming in orbit from getting suspicious about the island. Afterwards, they would turn northwest for Eurasia.

"Praise you all," said Romi into the comm. *"Good luck."* Then the group comms were cut as the twelve ships accelerated through the water, northbound through the Pacific for Amun-Nūr's first proper engagement with The Collective.

Damien closed his eyes, thinking of his friends. *Good luck to you too, Captain.*

And they were on their way.

∞   ∞   ∞

Nearly an hour later, the twelve ships from Amun-Nūr erupted from the open ocean and accelerated to the northwest, sunlit droplets dancing off their metal hulls. Damien's stomach tumbled end over end as the *Deep Core* leapt out of the water. With an eerie whine and a screech, her engines kicked to life while the Aqua Pods receded into her slick, arrowed body. Captain Fagin yee-hawed as they became airborne, but Damien couldn't help but cringe at the idea that the Supply Fleet could be floating overhead right now, and could have just seen a whole pack of engine thrust appear in the middle of the ocean for no reason. He knew Amun-Nūr had timed their departure specifically so the fleet was on the other side of the world at that moment, but the worry still lingered.

A short while later, the group comms opened as the squad leader of Kehzalla, a woman piloting a ship called the *Chalice Archon*, offered her best wishes to Echo, Notte, and Aurora. Damien thought her voice sounded vaguely familiar but he didn't catch her name.

"Thank ya, ma'am," answered Fagin before she cut out.

Damien thought of Javi, and he looked out the port window to see the three ships peel away over the water and descend in the afternoon air, bound for the former Chinese coast. *Be safe*, he thought, unwilling to voice the prayer. Instead he chose to ask, "Couldn't we help them? We'll be so close."

Fagin sucked on a mouthful of chewing tobacco. "Not unless yeh want to abandon the mission?"

Damien turned his gaze back to the glistening Pacific. "No. Of course not…" He trailed off, unsure if he wanted to say more.

Su-jin looked back at him. "You want to save lives, Elemental?"

"Yes."

"Then you have to come to the realization that war will only take you in forks. There are no straight routes, and there are no returns. The choices you make are the ones you must stand by. Otherwise you risk losing your way down both paths."

Her casual wisdom was like a splash of icy water. Damien quickly pulled himself out of his descending worry, took a breath, and sat up straight. "Right. I'm sorry."

"Don't apologize. You shouldn't be sorry for not knowing what it's like."

"Thanks."

Su-jin nodded and turned back to her console. "Fagin, we are all set."

"Well, alrighty! Let's see if we cain't get this bird a quarter 'round the world in three hours, yeh?"

Su-jin bowed her head. The two of them worked in tandem, *Deep Core*'s engines ramped up, and they led the remaining nine ships towards the Throat, the Italian Peninsula, and the Himalayas.

Less than an hour later, a familiar alarm began beeping insistently from the center hemispheric console. Damien remembered that noise: it was same sound used for an S.O.S. or for hostiles at the edge of the scanning range. Romi had kept slapping it off the day they fled Seattle. Damien winced at the memory.

"What'cha got?" Fagin asked.

"Many ships," Su-jin remarked, her hands flying over controls as fast as her partners'. "*Many* ships."

"How far?" Von asked from behind the copilot's chair, leaning forward.

"They haven't picked us up," said Fagin, ignoring him.

Damien leaned around the captain's chair just in time to see a solid line of red on the radar. It was directly ahead.

"It's the invasion force," Von said solemnly.

"From Australia?" Damien pressed.

"It is," Su-jin answered quietly. "It's bigger than we thought…" She reached up and folded down a whole set of switches on the console above. "I will call the others. We're diving. We don't have time to go around and we do not want them picking us up."

"Roger that," the captain answered. He worked switches of his own as Su-jin opened the comm, spoke briefly to Notte and Echo, and then hung up. "They agree. They are following."

"Hot dandy." Fagin angled the ship down.

The four in the cockpit held tightly to their seats as Romi directed the *Deep Core* towards the ocean. It was only the second time Damien had experienced the dive, but he vividly remembered the excitement and terror at watching the depths come rushing up to meet them. This time was no different. His knuckles were white on the undersides of his chair, and he saw Von bracing similarly.

With a deafening splash, *Deep Core* vanished beneath the surface, followed by the eight ships behind. Damien thought they must have looked like quite the sight from afar: Enormous, silvery arrows, spearing into the ocean on trails of fire.

The cockpit was silent and shadowy beneath the waves as they went; the humming of the Aqua Pods distantly filled the air again. Damien awed at the way the sunlight plunged as far as it could reach beneath the surface, but eventually, inevitably, was stopped. There was no sea life to be seen, but he hadn't really expected to see any. He remembered thinking last time how dangerous the *Lotus* must look in the water, and *Deep Core* had the same draconic profile.

A long thirty minutes passed in quiet. At one point, the alarm went off again. More Collective aircraft had been spotted, but Su-jin snapped off the sound and they were left with only the display of red, slowly approaching.

"Can they really not see us underwater?" Damien whispered as the line came just ahead of them. He imagined the convoy of alien ships, flying well over ten kilometers above them, oblivious to the passage of Amun-Nūr's strike force.

"If they looked hard enough they probably would," Von proffered.

"Oh now, us captains take better care of our girls than *that*," said Fagin with a grin, but his tone was serious.

Su-jin spoke up. "They could probably spot us if they really tried."

Fagin raised an eyebrow at her, sucking at his tobacco, but he said nothing. Su-jin smiled excessively wide.

They didn't say anything else as they passed beneath the enemy. Fagin—after a one-word conversation with Captain Romi that consisted of "Longer?" "Yes."—decided to take no chances once the invasion convoy was behind them: The point captains instructed all of their ships to remain beneath the waves until they were far, far out of range.

When they were finally able to ascend once more, Su-jin cursed at the lost time. Fagin agreed and they pushed the nine ships to their max. No one in *Deep Core*'s cockpit voiced that their complaints of efficiency were in regards to an invasion force on the move, bound for human lands where they would soon claim thousands of innocents.

As they made their last stint of westerly acceleration, Damien noticed an odd phenomenon: afternoon seemed to be *receding* from the western horizon, and that was clearly wrong. When he voiced his observation, Su-jin answered, "We are traveling faster than the Earth is orbiting," she explained. "It makes it seem that time is going backwards. Really, we are just outrunning the Sun. We will most likely arrive at our destination a few hours before dark."

"Oh." He'd never thought about that before.

"Ahh now that's a good thing, too," added Fagin.

"Why?" Von asked.

"Well 'cause it's bound to be bitter *cold* up there, wouldn't yeh wager?"

Damien and Von traded the tightest, most irritated looks either of them had offered in long time. *Cold. I forgot.* "What about air?" Damien asked, keeping his voice neutral.

"Oh, Miss Doctor Whalen was good enough to supply us with air tanks and some pharmacological cocktails to keep us from blowin' up or some other such thang that happens at such extreme altitudes. Quite the potent mixture, from what I hear." He nodded at Su-jin. "Now Miss Whalen, she's a fine woman, if I do say so myself," he added.

Damien felt a confusing twinge in his gut at that but he didn't know what to make of it, so he just said, "Oh," again.

Finally, Aurora came to where they were to split off from their comrades, somewhere over the South China Sea, near the spit of land that was still known as Malaysia. They bid their farewells to Captain Romi and Kel with Notte and the brave soldiers of Echo before they turned further northwest and peeled away from the rest of the strike force, leaving just Damien, Von, Gwen, and Reuben. Damien watched the remaining six ships go, feeling unsettled.

It was just then—while the three ships of Aurora traveled faster than the Earth orbited—that Damien watched the evening give way to afternoon, and he felt a rare shiver of vertigo. He suddenly became very nauseous and felt very small at seeing a concept so big as orbital mechanics at play. He turned away, fighting his flipping stomach. For a moment, it *did* seem as if they were speeding backwards in time, even as the sun slid higher with each passing second.

"Damien?" Von asked, leaning over. "Are you alright?"

"Fine," Damien gritted his teeth. "I'm fine."

His brother nodded suspiciously and pulled back.

Damien gazed back out the polyport as they crawled towards the Bang Sea. "How long until Echo and Notte get to where they're going?"

It took Su-jin a minute to respond while she checked. "It will be another two or three hours."

Damien took a deep breath. His heart had begun a slow march towards an anxious drumbeat.

Another few minutes passed and he watched the radar as they blipped along the last two thousand kilometers to the region still known as Nepal. Finally, Fagin hit the internal comm panel and announced, "This is yer captain speaking. We've begun our final descent towards the valley. Strap your gear on and be ready for anythin'. It's time."

"This is really it, isn't it?" Damien asked after Fagin had turned the comms off. He hadn't noticed that his fists had gone white on the armrests. "We're going to war?"

Fagin glanced across the cabin. "Well, yeh, this is it."

Damien just nodded.

"Are you ready?"

He took a steadying breath, "You think anyone is? I've never been to war." He waited for an answer as Fagin and Su-jin worked in tandem to bring the ship down towards the planet.

"Hell no," said the captain finally. "Like I said: just keep yer head cool. Don't be a damned hero, we've lost plenty o' them."

Su-jin nodded. "Trust your instincts. They give good advice."

Damien swallowed.

∞   ∞   ∞

With scathing cracks in the frozen air, *Deep Core*, *Polar Diamond*, and *Earth Clad* fell towards the foothills of the Himalayan Mountains. At the last second, all three scooped up, barely missing rocky hills as Captain Fagin and Xiu Su-jin led the charge to the valley. They'd flown along the western edge of the blizzard from the night before, which left them stuck between the stilling afternoon sun in the west and the clouds to the east.

"*Cold landing in two minutes*," said Fagin over the comm. "*Hope ya'll packed warm, it's winter gear today, people.*" Loud chuckles drifted up to the crew deck from the cargo bay.

Damien breathed deep as Gwen and a female Algaroth doctor, Elora Kiveen, injected him and everyone else with a mixture of drugs, red blood cells, and oxygen to keep them from collapsing. Gwen explained what the cocktail was but it didn't make sense, even with Damien's medic background. He knew Leo would know, though, and for a minute he dearly wished the AI were here. *Sato's got him busy at the island, though. He likes it there.* Still, Damien missed him.

Gwen and Kiveen moved onward to Von, and then to the rest of the crew, poking everyone in the neck. A minute later, the ship settled to the ground. Weapons were unholstered, coats were zipped up, and buzzing little instruments were whipped out of lab coats. Damien forced himself to focus beyond the fizzle of the insulating drug as it spread through his system.

"*Koro, we're keepin' this channel open if you need us,*" said Fagin into the team's earpieces.

"Understood," said the newly promoted Koro Valagan Loss from across the crew deck. Damien hadn't noticed until then that the alien spoke Portuguese, but come to think of it, he hadn't ever heard the alien talk at all. *Weird.* He did notice though that Loss looked rather uncomfortable standing so close to the Ice Elemental, who had frozen and unfrozen his hands at their first meeting.

"*Ahh!*" Damien wailed. "Fucking snow!!"

Those were his first words as, another minute later, he and the rest of *Deep Core*'s crew huddled up as the rear cargo bay door fell open and spearing cold air cut into them. A few members of the team echoed the sentiment.

Outside, the sky was mostly grey with just enough cloud cover to make the afternoon sun peek in and out at them near the mountains. Through the holes in the canopy, the sky was crisp navy blue and getting darker. Ahead, a snowy embankment rose between them and the village, and on either side of them, *Polar Diamond* and *Earth Clad* had settled on their landing struts.

Damien glanced at the corner of his goggles. It was five-thirty. In their haste to head west, the team had gained significant daylight. Damien couldn't deny being grossly unexcited about the prospect of spending the night in this valley, if it came to that. He gripped his pistol tightly, finding comfort in it. His other hand lay cradled against his body, tucked into his heavy winter parka, and the weight of a Plaster rifle on his back felt good. Every member of the team was armed.

All around, the team hacked and coughed in the icy air. Algaroth had a similar tolerance to temperatures as humans did—they preferred a narrow band of degrees to be considered in "perfect" comfort, but *no one* could handle a change from below sea level to over 7,000 meters elevation in a matter of hours, thus the drugs. *Deep Core* also had emergency air tanks, but Doctor Gwen had recommended they don't stay out here too long.

Damien jerked at a whistle from ahead. Koro Loss waved them forward with his Gyro rifle. Damien joined the column at the middle as they started trudging through heavy, unpacked snow, eyeing the teams on both sides as they unloaded their gear. Even the short jaunt down the ramp and up the embankment was enough to make his lungs screech and his body ache from being mostly sedentary for three months. He quickly fell to the back of the middle line.

As each team member crested the rump in the landscape, they stopped for a moment at the view before the presence of someone behind pushed them forwards. Damien ascended second-to-last with only Von hissing along behind him. At the top, he took a long moment to breath, trying and failing to calm his howling heart from the excursion.

"Here," Von handed up an insulated canteen as he came level with him. Damien took it gratefully and downed a swig of vitamin-infused tea.

"Th-thanks," he said, handing it back.

"You're wheezing," said his brother plainly.

"Y-yeah…I know…" he said, trying to stay neutral. He rubbed his shoulders as Von came up next to him and they fell into silence.

Von gazed towards the looming peaks beyond the valley. "They're whiter than I thought they'd be."

Damien's laugh escaped as more of a shivering rattle, "*Ha*, well, th-that's because you've only s-s-seen old pictures of them!"

Von looked down at him, confused.

Damien snorted. "You saw them like they were about a-a hundred years ago! They were m-m-mostly dirt then!" He looked up long enough to glimpse the slumbering sentinels of the world before the wind made him duck.

"They came back from that state."

"What state?"

"Dirt," Von said. "They were mountains, whole only when they were clad in snow and cold. But then they were stripped of that cold and left at their core. Dirt."

Damien swallowed, distracted long enough to stop shivering. He looked up to find the gold-and-green eyes looking hard at the distant peaks.

"People are like that sometimes," said Von. "Algaroth and human. We all get stripped down sometimes."

Damien looked towards the mountains too, unsure of what to say. The ruined Sherpa village sat at the far end of the valley, nestled at the foot of a cliff face, appearing benign but lonely out there. The low clusters of structures were just losing their sunlight, the roofs poking through the ocean of flawless white, like tiny black pimples in a giants' landscape. The rump the brothers stood on crested and bowled forward, steeper than Damien would have liked. The crest spanned the valley. Damien felt a chill as he noted the bowl-like shape, but it had nothing to do with the cold. He couldn't explain why, though.

"How did they become white again?" Von asked.

"Uhh," Damien was caught off guard. The wind whipped up and he hunched his shoulders against it. Von continued staring at the peaks. "They…I mean, they got their snow cover back when we finished the energysphere, stabilized the climate, and pulled the crap out of the air and the ocean and put it to good use. I guess that's the best way to put it?"

"So they had help?"

Damien frowned, still confused. "Yes?"

"Hmm."

He waited. In the silence, he noted a distant whine above what must be this perpetual little storm. He strained his ears and realized that it was the howl of wind over the mountains, flinging clouds of snow off the great peaks. The sound made him feel small. It was something born of the planet, immense, immovable, and extreme in its benevolence as it could be in its wrath.

Finally, Von turned to gaze at his smaller brother. "Family isn't just blood, you know."

Damien suddenly realized that Von was talking about their shared trauma, about the earthquake, about the drinks in the Garden the other night, and about Damien's refusal—which they'd never talked about—to, well, *talk* about anything that was wrong. He nodded stiffly. "I know."

Von looked away. "Sometimes it's easier to just not face family than it is to confront someone who's been stripped down. It's something to think about." He let out a dire hiss as the wind hit them again. The alien stomped and shivered, finally strapping on his faceguard and goggles. "I would keep going first, but you shouldn't be left in the back."

"Why?"

"Elemental, dear Damien."

Damien couldn't help but laugh. It hurt his lungs, but he did it anyway. "Yeah, okay. We should c-catch up."

His brother nodded. "We should climb those peaks one day."

"Which one?"

"The tallest."

Damien winced and smiled as he started into the snow bowl. "When all this is over," he called back. "Let's do it."

They descended the hill slowly, following the tracks of Aurora team, already far ahead. Their footsteps and Damien's labored breathing were the only sounds in the valley beneath the slumbering sighs of the mountains.

MASON J. TORALL

Chapter Twenty Four

Blood, Eviscerated

The team, consisting of over fifty of Amun-Nūr's best soldiers and scientists, had stopped just outside the village for everyone to catch up. "Everyone accounted for?" Koro Loss roared back as Damien and Von arrived, surprisingly not the last ones. Loss's voice sounded tinny in Damien's earpiece.

"We're here!" Von called.

"Vilan!" Gwen called. "Get up here!"

Mustering the warmth in his legs, Damien trudged to the head of the column.

"Are you doing okay?"

He suppressed a cough. "I'm fine! Stop asking so we can get out of here sooner!"

She looked like she wanted to argue, but more wind silenced her.

They started moving again, and Damien looked up to see the sun already descending towards the mountains again, close to leave them in the cold, and the dark. The change from chilly to frigid was sudden as the faint warmth of sunlight left the valley floor. Every step became a trudge of mind over body, every effort a dragging effort on lungs and muscles. Damien lost track of how long he pushed forward, near the head of the column and off to the side a bit, until he became suddenly aware of a shadow ahead. He stopped short, his heart pounding. It was the first building, rising out of a long drift ahead.

He stopped to take a long breath that never seemed quite full enough. He tried to steel himself for what lay ahead. *It's bodies*, he reasoned. *You've seen bodies before, and you've already seen these bodies*. Another voice in his head didn't sound so sure though. *There's something about these bodies, though. Something you need to see, something special.*

Damien shivered, trying and failing to pump enough air into his lungs, trying to contain the slow spread of nervous fear that had started to prickle up his neck. Suddenly, he had a horrible sense that he was being watched. He spun around, and saw only the deepening grey shadows that were the rest of Aurora coming up and around him, like distantly moaning phantoms at foggy twilight. Beyond their little group, the valley was slowly vanishing in the snowy whorls that came with such weather: dull, shrouding, grey.

In the distance, he could see how the perpetual flurry hung low over the valley inside the snow bowl. Above it, the mountains loomed to the east and west, with azure sky to the south. Even as he looked, shadows climbed the pinkish cap of the eastern mountain, bouncing fading light into the valley. There was no one to be seen, but the feeling of being watched remained. He turned to move forward…and his spiked boot caught something stiff. He tumbled face-first into the snow, shouting out one syllable before the snow was suffocating him. *Fuck!*

A surge of terror shot through him as the freshly fallen powder collapsed under his weight, his foot still caught on that thing. He couldn't move without collapsing more snow, and there was no telling how far it would go. His pulse quickened, and then it got worse as he thought of how the snow could just, *collapse*. It really could. He could just push and this carpet of snow—who knows how deep it was—could simply open like a chasm and swallow him, the resulting cascade obscuring his body upside down, and poof! He was gone forever. Memories of the earthquake bubbled up, and panic threatened to overwhelm him.

He tried to control his breathing. "Help!" he cried, unable to reason anything else away. He couldn't tell how far his voice went. "HELP!" he shouted again, louder this time. He thought he felt a rumble of movement beneath him, but that had to be his thundering heart.

"Damien?!" a voice called.

"Help! I'm, I'm *stuck!*"

"We're coming! Just breathe!"

He tried, and failed. His chest felt tight, and he thought he might be slipping further down. He didn't even notice the cold.

But then, just when he was starting to feel like this would go on forever, he felt a hand on his back, then two, then five. They yanked him up, and just like that, it was over. Someone brushed the cold drifts off his face and body, and he was upright again.

"What the hell happened?" the person asked. He rubbed his frozen goggles to find that it was a tech that he didn't know. Next to the tech was Gwen and Von.

"I-I-I stumbled," he stuttered, still unsure of what he'd stumbled *on*. He turned to look, though, and supremely wished that he'd taken his fall over anything, *anything* else.

It was a body.

Given what had just happened, he was oddly struck by how close he'd been standing without spotting it; maybe ten paces at most. That sensation of being watched came rushing back, and he felt nervous again. A thought started to form, one he was already conscious of but that he didn't want to acknowledge. He couldn't stop it, and it popped up too late, fully formed. *Someone could easily hide out here if they just lay down*, he thought. *Perfect place for an ambush.* He looked down at the corpse, and knelt, intending to turn it over.

"WAIT, DAMIEN, WAIT!" Gwen screamed. He stopped.

"Why? What's wrong?"

She knelt next to him over the corpse. "You have *no* idea what happened here! Don't just run forward and grab something! Remember what the commander said about the possibility of a bloody *bioweapon*?!"

Oops. "S-s-sorry!"

She shook her head and donned heavy gloves over her winter ones before turning the body over. She swallowed. "Oh gods…" she said, and her voice was taken by the wind.

"Doctor?" It was one of the soldiers, his voice muffled behind a heavy balaclava.

"Damien…" Gwen whispered. The only reason he heard her was because of the comm.

He looked down as she moved to the side, and felt a heavy queasiness come over him:

The mutilated face of a teenage girl wailed up at them, her body trapped in a perpetual death scream. She was neither shot nor cut with blades as far as he could see. Her cause of death appeared far more intimate—and personally familiar to Damien. Even with the frostbite icing her features and snow hiding the blood, he could plainly tell that her body had been thrown around like a rag-doll and had had every inch of it trawled over brutally, all in a pattern akin to that of a chipper or a cheese grater. It was a dark, vicious power.

It looked similar to fazing.

Damien struggled to his feet so that the other team members could examine the girl. He had to suppress the urge to vomit. He found Reuben staring at him behind mirrored glasses. The man wore light pants and only a long-sleeve shirt tucked into thin gloves. Clearly the cold didn't bother him at all. The man kept staring at him. At least, Damien assumed that's what he was doing; he was awfully still.

Turning, Damien limped towards the village, ignoring Gwen's call to wait. He felt Reuben follow close behind. The village was half-drifted in snow, but the wind had blown an alley between two hewn buildings. He knew what he was going to find around the corner, but he had to see it anyway.

He saw.

Bodies lay everywhere. Of every age, shape, and gender. They lay strewn about, all in similar poses of agony and abuse at the hands of a weapon from which they couldn't fight, run, or hide. A massacre filled the little center of the village.

On the nearer side, facing south towards Aurora's ships, walls and doors had been splintered or cracked, and people hung half from their homes, but around the tightly clustered circle of structures, towards the cliff face, the buildings had been shorn away and nothing remained but hints of walls, already buried in white. Every person had been hacked and diced and split to pieces, their blood sent reeling through the air. Odd patches of pinkish mist and stick coated the village center. Even at a glance, Damien could tell that whatever did this had eviscerated not just their bodies, but their very blood…something he had seen many times before.

It was his power.

How…how does he have it? Damien wanted to hyperventilate, but only a tiny scream in his head told him that if he fell to gasping he'd never be able to get his breath back up here, and he'd quickly pass out…which would probably kill him in this extreme environment.

"It seems the Over-Seer has merited you a personal touch," said Reuben over his shoulder.

"Shut the fuck up," Damien snapped without turning. He could almost see the man's shrug through the back of this head. "I'm gonna kill him," he said, his fury rising as he spied the remains of a woman shielding the genderless bodies of her children, too mutilated to distinguish. "That son-of-a-bitch needs to die."

"And you'll be the one to do it, is that it?"

Damien had no answer. He was thinking about home.

From that first horrible moment, the evening was a blur. Damien spent it in a stupor, but he still managed to find it in him to be useful. The team spread about the area, combing the village as the temperature plummeted. What became quickly apparent to all was that many of the bodies showed other signs of murder. Most showed the frightening, fazing, eviscerated look that only Damien's Orbs could cause, but other bodies— all of which were buried in deeper snow—looked like they'd been killed in other ways. One tech blurted that it looked like some serial killer's playground of carbon dating, which merited angry ridicule, but didn't seem far off. It didn't take long after that for people to start drawing conclusions.

This is a testing ground, they realized. *This village has probably been dead for a long time, and The Collective keep bringing poor captured souls out here to test a new weapon on.* Damien knew he'd be having nightmares about this place long before he left it.

To make matters worse, the feeling of being watch persisted in his mind, one that was slowly proliferated as others began to ask odd questions about sights or sounds or sensations. No one wanted to admit it, but Aurora felt like they were wandering through the graveyard of a repeatedly failed laboratory experiment. On top of that, Captain Fagin made the trek across the valley alongside the captain of *Earth Clad*, a man named Aziz Nejem, so that they didn't have to relay certain ominous news through potentially hacked comm channels. They informed Aurora that Kehzalla had reported first engagement with the Australian attack force, Echo was just descending on the Throat of Israel, and Notte was about to reach Italy. They also relayed that the village had sent up no distress calls to local authorities; in fact they had been broadcasting an 'all-clear' sign. More importantly, though: the dead village was *still* broadcasting 'all-clear'.

At the news, the team's collective nerves shot through the roof, and the stench of an ambush rose like decay from the frozen corpses. "We need to find that transmitter," Koro Loss growled, instructing the team to play a game of telephone with the orders, but to maintain radio contact as if they were still exploring.

"*I've got more bodies over here!*" a tech called into the comm.

"*Fried equipment here! Foruvin, got a light?*"

"That hut hasn't been checked, move in pairs," whispered one of the soldiers. Then, "*Looks like a helluva patch job to this building,*" he said airily into the comm. "*Anyone see grenade damage here?*" Then in person, "Move!" he hissed. The coordinated pairs meandered as casually as they could to the hut in question. Reuben had noted how odd it looked because the door was still intact. Inside, they found it filled with equipment that didn't fit the locale. The gear was a human emergency transceiver setup, and it had been rigged to repeat a no-emergency beacon.

"I suppose now we know why no ones' picked this up," said Captain Nejem. He and Dr. Gwen stepped back outside with Damien while the others swarmed, dismantling the device.

"So, what happened here?" she asked.

"I think they were held hostage," gurgled Loss, approaching. "Or approximately. Have you seen the cliff face?"

"No?"

"Illya said she found a large cave there. From what she said I think they were building something inside, or storing something."

"Has anyone found the tracks we saw on the map?" Damien asked.

Gwen shook her head in her parka. "No, but they're looking. They might have been covered in snow already."

"With that false beacon still up?" Captain Fagin questioned. "No one'll come lookin' in on the village. It leaves us open to stay overnight if we have to. I for one motion *against* such action, but the option's there."

The wind started to pick up again. "Are they taking the beacon down?" Gwen asked, raising her voice.

Just then, an Algaroth tech came out of the hut. "Koro Loss, we are taking the beacon down."

The Koro's head snapped up. "*Carefully*, Vanda! If the enemy set that as a warning they might come—"

Pop, sounded a tiny noise in Damien's earpiece.

"*Shit!*" A voice cursed over the comm.

The group outside the hut froze.

Loss pressed a hand to his earpiece. "Klick, what was that?!" he demanded.

"*It's alright!*" another voice said. "*We thought the signal skipped while trying to dismantle it!*"

"Well *did it?*"

"*We... we aren't sure, Koro. Unconfirmed.*"

Loss growled while Damien and the others turned as one, each scanning what little distance they could glean beyond the village. The cold in Damien's chest receded against a buzz of tension, and he found himself wishing the former would stay. A flurry was closing in.

Loss took a step back towards the hut, clawed and gloved hand still grasping the side of his head. "Repeat yourself, Mactaggart. *Did you just badly tamper with the Over-Seer's beacon?*"

A full second of silence, and then...

An Algaroth whooped from inside, and Mactaggart answered, "*Negative! Negative, Koro! Signal has been disabled. We've attached an error on the back end to make it look like hardware failure. Someone will still come running, but without an emergency S.O.S, it won't be for a good while."*

"And Collective forces?"

"They don't know we're here," Klick answered, sounding relieved.

Loss rasped a relieved sigh. "Well done."

Everyone's shoulders loosed a little, but as if in answer, Damien heard another tiny *pop* in his earpiece, and his gut remained clenched. The feeling of being under observation returned with a vengeance. He flicked his earpiece, chalking it up to the cold.

"Okay," said Gwen, bouncing on the balls of her feet. "Now what?"

"We have to figure out what was in that cave," Damien spoke up. "And find those tracks!"

"What about the weather?" Von asked, his voice rising to a shout over the wind.

Fagin looked to the sky. The evening was growing darker. "I don't know but I'll prep bedrolls in the cargo bay! You folks ain't sleepin' out here!"

"I agree!"

Fagin and Nejem called their ships and left the team alone.

The evening dragged on, the cold tightened its grip on the valley, and Damien stared at a man who had been flung into a stone pillar. The fazed wounds were numerous and he had hit the pillar spine-first. It had snapped him into an unnatural backwards curl. Damien had been staring at it for twenty eternal minutes, long since having stopped focusing on the details of the cold body. The wind tore at his exposed skin.

"*KORO!*" one of the soldiers roared into the comm, forgetting their policy. "*Koro Loss! Over here! Look!*" The soldier tossed up a marker on everyone's displays, and the majority of the team converged.

Damien made his stiff way to the back of the village, holding at the wall to catch his breath. He was so exhausted. Around the flattened building, closest to the cliff face, one of the team had found a charred hunk of metal that didn't belong.

"What is it?" he heaved on arrival.

One of the soldiers near him answered, "Pavlov tripped over it. There's something beneath it petrified in the ice. They're digging it out now." Just as he said that, the two Algaroth and the human around the spot broke out ice picks and began hacking away at it.

More of the team arrived, and finally one of the picks split the air with a *CLING*, and everyone froze. For a split second, the only sound was the wind over the mountain and the snow whipping everywhere. Damien was grateful that a *true* storm hadn't come over them yet, but their visibility had started to diminish ever more heavily. The far end of the valley had already vanished completely, prompting some of the team to set up floodlights, and the freezing temperature was dropping further now that they were all in the shade. The evening had turned to sundown.

The team dove forward and hacked harder, finally cracking enough of the ice to pull the thing back by hand. A sheet of ice as tall as a human came away and they threw it off what lay beneath. Reuben appeared behind Damien.

"What is it?" asked a tech.

"Rawlen, get me the scanner!"

"Back up! Back up!"

"Have you got a read?"

"Not yet—*wait*… Wait, hold on," the tech that held the scanner scrambled to his feet. Everyone quieted. "No this…this can't be right." The scanner beeped.

"What is it?" Reuben called.

The tech turned and eyed the gaunt man. "There's, there's trace amounts of…fissile materials…radioactive isotopes…C^3 compounds…" he swallowed. "It's a…it's the outer casing of a Nuke. Not dangerous to our health by any means but, that's what it is."

The team fell silent.

"I wondered," Reuben muttered, so low that only Damien heard.

While the majority of the team went into a frenzy trying to confirm the dark suspicion, Damien knew he would be useless, so he walked away and towards the cliff face, wanting to see if there really was a cave there.

"Are we safe so close?" asked a tech.

"Where did they get one?"

"Someone call the Koro!"

"Where's the doctor?"

"Illya! She's with the others, with the Koro!"

"Thanks!"

"Rawlen, *where's my scanner?!*"

In ten steps, the village was swallowed behind Damien along with most of the voices as a sudden ocean of fog descended on the village, sapping the light. The comm kept the team in his ear and the questions poured out thicker as Aurora announced the terrible find to everyone: it was definitely the remains of a Nuke, a piece of humanity's Final Option.

"Maybe I spoke too soon earlier," said a voice behind him.

Damien limped in a circle to find Reuben standing a few paces away. He heard Gwen and Koro Loss say they were on their way from where the rest of the team was looking for the odd tracks. He couldn't help feeling nervous about them being too far away. "About wh-what?"

Reuben nodded back towards the village where Damien could just see shadows and lights as the team finally succumbed to the deepening shroud of night. "It's possible we should be thanking *you* for this."

Damien still didn't understand.

Reuben had finally put on a coat with a hood and had replaced his sunglasses for tactical goggles much like Damien's; only his were shaded white. He pulled his goggles down to reveal those dark eyes and eyebrows flecked with frost. "The Over-Seer has wanted an Elemental with your power for a long time. If the Supply Fleet brought him the means to make that happen *without* you, then he would deploy it as soon as it was ready."

Damien didn't want to answer, but he did. "You...you think he's found a way to replicate what I can do?"

Reuben made a noncommittal nod. His voice carried the distance between them easily. "That, or he's very close."

Damien's fear of being watched intensified again, and he became suddenly aware of an odd sizzling sound, coming from somewhere nearby. Or was it in his head? He wasn't sure. "What are you saying?"

"I'm saying that whatever this place is, I don't believe that the explosion we saw was an accident."

The sounds of ice picks chipping out the Nuke casing rose to the foreground of Damien's attention. "You think this is a trap."

"I think that Croll Tan lost your scent and he knew when his special Supply Fleet would arrive. I think that whatever he's doing across Eurasia right now, its purpose was to provoke Amun-Nūr from hiding." Reuben sounded infuriatingly knowing. "If that's the goal, he's succeeded spectacularly. And even if it isn't, this push is a win-win scenario for him. Italy will fall, the Dynasty Navy never recovered from the last time they went up against this Over-Seer, and the Throat doesn't stand a chance." Reuben met Damien's gaze with his cool arrogance. "If this is a trap, it's meant for *you*."

Damien refused to let that thought get to him, and he was getting tired of the man's superior remarks. "Well," he said, turning back towards the mountain. "That doesn't explain what he needed a Nuke for. And it doesn't help us figure out what the weapon could...actually...do..." he trailed off, unsure of what he was seeing in the dark. He squinted.

"I'd imagine he got his hands on a Nuke to see if he could *beat* them. It's as simple as that. I tried to get you to make that connection, but you're too self-absorbed to listen. This is clearly a testing ground for the enemy to—"

"Shut up for a second."

Reuben's silence was colder than the air.

"Do you see that?" he pointed.

The man replaced his goggles and approached. "I do."

Damien tapped the man's chest. "Call the others."

"Excuse me?"

He glared. "Fucking *do it*, Reuben!"

Björn's lip twitched but he turned away to call the team while Damien approached the odd glow. "*Aurora*," came the Elemental's voice over the comm. "*Vilan might have found something by the cliff face.*"

More than twenty voices gave variations of "*On our way.*"

507

Damien kept moving towards the glow. Above and beyond it, the cliff face loomed, but he couldn't tell if there was a cave nearby. He came closer and saw that he was looking at a drift of snow in a flat field just before the mountain. A sourceless glow emanated from an odd drift poking above the field. As he came closer, Damien saw strange little zips and curls of silvery-gold threads in the air. They looked like tiny sparks of lightning, but lazier, and faint. The zips left long shimmering trails behind them, coursing over the drift. Damien took a long hard moment before he figured out what it was. When he did, he keyed his comm. *"Aurora, this is Vilan, I definitely found something."* He used his goggles to toss a beacon over his position and stared.

Icicles hung thick from a bent cradle of metal, and were it not in such an odd place, the mangled thing could have been easily mistaken for something else, but the unmistakably *made* thing resolved itself when Damien finally tilted his head to account for the cradle on its side. A hundred years of innovation, one of them in nearly every major city on the planet, renewable, 80% clean and 100% recyclable energy output, and a world war later, the unmistakable casing of a Magnetic "Mag Fury" Fusion Reactor was a profile few people could fail to recognize. Even though this was merely the blown out remnant of a Mag Fury, Damien still knew what it was. The threads and zips were the dying flickers of hybrid Tesla-fusion currents, so thin and insubstantial that it was no wonder no one had seen them until dark. But now, as the last vestiges of the sun vanished and cold night swept the valley, the broken glow of the reactor shone bright as a beacon.

A power source, he realized. The idea dropped a swath of puzzle-pieces into place. *Whatever weapon Croll Tan was testing here, it needs a power source, a big one.* And on the heels of that thought: *That Nuke can't have gone off, it would have leveled this whole valley. So what the hell happened?*

"You're not the only one that found something," Koro Loss said into the comm, forgoing the nerves about being overheard. *"I need the team to split into three groups! Those with good eyes come to me back near the*

tracks, those with scanning equipment, split between Vilan's and the Nuke casing's location!"

"*Damien*," said Gwen as others answered. "*Come over to Loss!*"

Mind reeling, Damien answered over the wind while he watched a team from Aurora approach through the fog and wind. "Gwen? What did you find?!"

"*I just heard from Fagin and Su-jin. They've been working on a detailed topography of the valley, and they've been in contact with home!*"

"And?" Damien clapped the approaching team member's shoulders and pointed at the glow. They nodded and went towards it.

"*That drift we landed behind? It's not a drift. It's a blast crater!*"

Damien found Reuben standing alone. He didn't look the least bit surprised at any of this.

"The nuke?!" he shouted. "Can't be!" Reuben fell in line next to him and they wound their way past the many corpses, back through the packed center of the village, and to the western edge.

"*Why not?*"

"Because we would have known if a Nuke was detonated here." Reuben answered flatly. Damien's neck prickled.

Gwen's reply was hesitant. "*So, what made the crater?*"

Reuben looked at Damien, practically oozing incredulity. Damien grimaced behind his balaclava. "It must have been an older test. That snow at the edge was well-packed."

"*Gods…*" she breathed.

"*Where are you?*" Loss called.

"Almost there!" Damien and Reuben approached the marker set on the valley floor a good distance away from the village outskirts. It was horribly exposed. The team was looking for the tracks. Great spotlights had been set parallel to the ground at intervals to better highlight details in the landscape. Just as he spotted Loss and Gwen out there, there was a shout from somewhere midway between them. Damien turned towards the marker, where it had come from.

"*Found them! We found the tracks!*"

Pop.

509

Damien stopped, unsure if he'd heard that noise again.

"*Good,*" said Loss. "*Record it! Where?*"

"*Damien, are you coming?*"

Pop pop.

It was the noise he'd heard when they took the transmitter down.

Pop pop pop.

It was getting faster. Damien tried to breathe. Something was wrong. He could feel that Reuben had stopped next to him. He could hear it too.

"*Someone get me more light!*"

"Aurora, this is Vilan," Damien said calmly. "Is that transmitter down?"

"*What?!*" someone called over the wind that had just picked up into a roar.

"The transmitter," he repeated. "Is it broadcasting?"

Someone else came on the line. "*Vilan, I'm in the transmitter room. Nothing's live in here. Why? What did you...oh...hold on.*"

Damien's stomach dropped. His hand slid towards his pistol. *Where's Von?*

"Boon? What is it?"

"*I don't know,*" Boon answered. "*But it looks like there was a...a kill switch embedded in the signal.*"

"Meaning, what," said Reuben.

"*I think...when we took it down it...it sent out a warning, cover-up or not.*"

"*A warning to who?*" demanded Loss. It didn't matter.

Pop-pop-pop-pop-pop-pop-pop-pop-pop-pop-pop.

No one had time to react as the ambush hit.

The popping sound overloaded their earpieces. Light blazed in the fog above. The roar of the wind turned into the roar of some monster. Plasma fire blazed down to earth like a sudden storm of comets. Voices screamed in the earpieces.

"*What's going on?!*"

"*Up! Look up!*"

"*Oh shit—*"

"WE'RE UNDER ATTACK!"
"TAKE COVER!"
"AMBUSH!"
"DROPSHIP!"
"GRENADE!"
"TANK! ICEBERG TANK!"

Damien's rifle was off his back in an instant. He didn't know what was happening, he couldn't see anything, and he thought he saw a stream of diamond-white figures blazing through the snow. He saw Loss dive to protect Gwen. He felt explosions through his feet, and all he could think of was his brother. "VON!" he howled. "VON, WHERE ARE YOU?!"

"DAMIEN!!" Von's voice was strained. Screams filled the valley, and still Damien couldn't see what was over them.

"Aurora, get into cover! We're going airborne!" called Captain Fagin's voice, bringing a modicum of sanity to whatever the hell was happening.

At his side, Reuben Björn had seen something above, and pale white light blazed from his hand. The whirling snow focused up through the air in a growing spear of ice. Damien watched it climb for an instant, and then vanish in the belly of something large. An explosion finally lit up the valley around them, and Damien could see a Collective dropship, emblazoned against the sky as Reuben's frozen spear punctured its belly. He took in the scene around him:

The transmitter had called The Collective down on them. A flight of Stingships came zipping in from the west, but they weren't firing yet. The dropship that Reuben had just taken out had already let over twenty armed Algaroth onto the valley floor, and they were unleashing their weapons just fine. Battle cries and shouts of fear came from Aurora, bodies fell on both sides, and a second dropship was putting something down in the distance, beyond the tracks where Loss, Gwen, and others were hiding. The dead village lit up with weapons fire and exploding grenades. Snow, rubble, frozen body parts, and newly severed body parts went careening through the air. To the south, Damien heard what sounded like another explosion, but he turned to see it was the rising silhouettes of Aurora's three ships, ascending on pillars of flame against the dark horizon. The Stingships responded to Amun-Nūr's aircraft, and the tracers of infantry Gyro and Plaster shots lighting up the valley became ants under the quarreling giants of an aerial battle. Shots the size of a man's torso blasted through the air barely off the valley floor, ringing out against the mountains, making Damien certain an avalanche was about to go off. Two Stingships exploded, raining fire down on the village, crushing Collective and islanders alike. *Polar Diamond* took hits across its bow and down its body, but it didn't crash. The remaining Stingships banked past Aurora, and the two tightly packed groups spun around for another pass at each other. Amun-Nūr's three Scops fighters brought out their four heavy chainguns and dual Plaster cannons. Streams of fire thundered through the sky.

All of this happened in the span of a few seconds, before the dropship Reuben had crashed. It fell with a slow, merciless grace, as if it was merely lying down for bed. When it hit, though, it smote the surrounding three buildings, and Damien's earpiece screeched with the cries of the dying, kicking him into life as he yanked on Reuben's collar. "COME ON!" he shouted, pelting through the snow towards the nearest building. A Collective Algaroth appeared around a corner, and he shot it in the hip with his rifle. The beast cried out, but before Damien had even begun to feel his power rise through his veins, the soldier gasped and keeled over: its neck had been sealed in a block of ice. Reuben was on his tail.

He didn't have time to think about it as he leapt over the body, landed squarely on one of the *frozen* corpses, tripped, and fell through a doorway to his left. Whatever small building he was in was dark, barely less cold than outside, and the air was heavy with a musty stench.

"*ICEBERG!*" someone hollered again. Roars of Collective soldiers filled the village outside.

Reuben sent another spear of ice into the air from his perch in the doorway, narrowly missing a Stingship as it flew by overhead.

"*DAMIEN!*" Von roared again.

"I'm okay! Björn, cover me!"

"*Aurora,*" announced Captain Nejem, "*Get to the east end of the village! We are setting down!*" Affirmations filled the air and the earpiece…until a deafening bass note shook the earth, so heavy that Damien felt his lungs seize under the pressure as it filled the air. He scrambled to his feet towards a beam of snowy light slicing between the shutters at the window. He threw them open, sending one shutter shattering into the wall, all so he could catch a heart-stopping glimpse of what had landed across the valley to the west.

Gwen, Loss, and the one other standing member of the team looking for the tracks were running as hard as they could towards the village. A line of fire filled the valley floor behind them from a burning Stingship, and through it, Damien could see what the other dropship had brought.

The prowling curves of an Iceberg tank edged its way through the flaming wreckage. The enormous artillery's main gun curved up and behind the angular body like a scorpion's tail, the tip glowed white hot; a stinging railgun that propelled Gyro plasma ready to blister away the village in a few impacts. Much like a Razer skiff, the Iceberg's undercarriage was heavily armored, protecting its hovering thrusters from being attacked.

"Aurora!" Damien called to their de-cohesive unit. "Aurora, there's an Iceberg to the west! Extraction is landing to the east! Do you copy?!"

A chorus of strained shouts, affirmations, and denials filled his ears.

He touched his ear to repeat his message, but a clatter behind, coupled with that bass-roar of the monster that was an Iceberg tank, left him stymied. He turned to see three Algaroth kicking down the front door to his little building, while Reuben struggled with something out back.

"Oh no you don't," he spat, and the power of Darkness flared to black life in his veins. Smoke erupted from his body, the air in his lungs became charged with energy. Every muscle in his body tingled.

One of the soldiers pointed at him, the three of them leveled the pronged tips of their Gyro rifles, and Damien shook his head.

"Back off."

How Gwen knew what was about to happen, he couldn't say, but her warning came too late. "*Damien, don't use your power! DON'T—*"

513

Three months of being cooped up in the island poured out of him in a raging instant, bringing a Wave to life that put the one he'd used to destroy the Razer to shame. The tsunami of Darkness exploded within the confined space of the low building, sending the walls, ceiling, and soldiers disintegrating out into the village square. No plasma shots made it through this time, and their dying howls brought everyone's attention to him.

"—*ship coming in!*" Gwen's warning concluded. "*NO! THERE'S ANOTHER SHIP!!*" she wailed. "*The Diamond is hit but flying, we have everyone we can! Earth Clad is landing nearby; so is Deep Core! Your brother is already on Core! Get out of there!! Get out of there now! RUN!!*"

Somehow, even with his tiny victory, Damien knew the wind had just changed. He felt a new rumbling in the air. He smelled a different smell, felt a different feeling. Everything told him to look back out through that window, so he did.

Far to the west, coming in through the narrow valley between mountains where the tracks had apparently gone away, he saw three ships. Two of them were the winged and dangerous hulks of Vulture Gunships: enormous, prickly, bristling with weapons, and well-documented anathema to even a Scops assault fighter. The third was something different. The third had the long look of a predatory stingray about it, dominant, sleek, and cunning. It sailed smoothly through the snowy night air towards them, growing from a speck into a shape in mere seconds.

"*DAMIEN!!*"

Before he could react, cold dread sank into his bones as the bass note of the Iceberg roared a final time, and the tank fired.

"OH FU—"

The village square exploded.

CHAPTER TWENTY FIVE

Blood, Invigorated

Damien heard yelling, could feel something on his face, saw flashes through his eyelids. It all sounded far away. Then there was a jolt, and his eyes snapped open. Everything hurt, especially his back. He was freezing.

Someone was dragging him through snow and ash. The sounds of gunfire were all around as Amun-Nūr's troops fled towards the Aurora ships. Damien heard the zings of plasma, and a haze of flaming ash fell like rain. He reached up to his face and his fingers came away sticky. Blood was dripping down his cheeks. He must have hit something.

"—me a hand here," someone was shouting. "Come on, Vilan! We've gotta move, help me out!" Their voice came through to him slow; everything was moving so slow.

Damien forced his eyelids shut, and then back open. Over him loomed an unfamiliar man. His armor looked brown and red, not brown-and-green. *Blood?* Plasma streaked by above his head, and return shots from Plaster rifles filled the chaos. Snow was falling everywhere.

"The others," he mumbled out. "Gwen... Von... Loss..."

"They're fine," said the slow voice. "They're already airborne, along with Ice! You're coming with me!"

He thought the man was shouting, but it didn't sound like it. Everything was ringing.

Next thing he knew, someone was at his other shoulder, hoisting him to his feet. His head lolled and he slumped between them. Time sped up. In the distance he could hear the whines of aircraft, alien and human, and there was a bass roar in the ground. He realized his goggles had slipped down around his neck. The right lens had cracked.

515

A voice popped right next to his ringing ear, but it came from the earpiece worn by the shoulder on his left. *"They're coming around the corner!! Get your asses up here NOW!!"*

Romi? No, it wasn't him.

"On our way!" the woman at his other shoulder answered.

Then the world was full-speed again, and everything zipped by in a blur. They dragged Damien out of the drift he'd landed in, the sounds of the ambush whipping by. He smelled burning, his nose felt singed. Frigid air covered him. Then all of a sudden, hard deckplates clacked beneath his boots, it felt warm, and the sounds and smells were less oppressive. He heard engines roaring, explosions behind, cries from nearby, booms above.

"Martin!" his left shoulder support shouted. "Martin! Get over here! Infirmary! Get him to the infirmary!"

Damien was handed off to someone. He felt like he had been thrown. His back spasmed and he cried out, blinked with leaden eyelids, trying to figure out where he was. "You lucky bastard," the man carrying him said. "You should be dead already."

He gurgled and gagged, *"Hrmph*—good…for me…"

The overhead comm sounded. *"Crew, we are in the air in thirty seconds. Strap yourselves in! We have incoming!"*

Damien recognized the voice now. Captain Nejem. He was on *Earth Clad*. Von, Gwen, and Reuben were on other ships.

A door hissed open and Damien saw a medical slab coming up to meet him. He was nearly in its embrace when the floor lurched. *Or was that me?* He couldn't tell as the slab pulled away and the deck met him instead. *"Ahh!"* He wretched as his face twinged. He tried to stay conscious.

"Shit. Come on! Get up here, man!" Martin called from a distance. *Earth Clad* accelerated and he tumbled onto the slab.

"Get to your stations, people! They're right on our tail!" the captain called again on the overhead. *"Mayday! Mayday! Allied forces, this is Aurora Strike Three; we are under attack! Kehzalla, do you read?! We are under attack!"* Damien could swear he heard the sounds of plasma cannon fire over the engines and the wind.

"Here, lift your head," Martin ordered, frantic. Damien did so and felt a cold, stinging slap on his neck as the medic patched him in a rush. "Give me your arm." He grabbed Damien's arm and there was more pain. Damien's ears were still ringing. "Alright, I'll be back."

Martin never made the door.

The overhead crackled and the captain was already screaming by the time the channel opened. *"—UNKNOWN SHIP FIRING! BRACE! BRACE FOR IMPACT! BRACE FOR—"*

An explosion rent the air. The ship howled. Damien's head burst with stars as he was hurtled across the infirmary. Martin screamed. Metal wrenched from somewhere behind and above, and another explosion threw Damien's limp body to the back of the bay. Heat flooded the room as he slammed into the wall; there were other screams from all around. Then Damien got a last look as the ceiling caved in, smothering him as he blacked out in silence.

∞　　　　　　∞　　　　　　∞

With a gasp, Damien came back to the world. He tried to stand, but couldn't move. He blinked in the smoky air and looked down, hissing at the pain in his head and coughing at the acrid smell of burning chemicals. He was trapped beneath what looked like a broken support strut that had fallen from the ceiling. His torso was numb, but squinting down at his chest he saw that his body was drenched in a supply of broken gel packs. He sincerely hoped the gel was a numbing agent and that's why he couldn't feel anything.

The cabin came slowly into focus, illuminated by alternating white and red alarm lights. It made the ruined space shift between conflicting images: The white flashed, and it was a ruined infirmary. Then it turned red, giving a hellish glow to the sputtering fires, scattered equipment, and—

Damien felt nausea sweep him.

—And Martin's body, broken and thrown over the medical slab. Sparks flew from a cracked conduit over the corpse, and it looked like he

517

was about to catch fire. The medic's jaw hung slack, but the unseeing eyes stared right at Damien. The torn face dripped blood to the wrinkled metal deck.

"Hrrrnn…" Damien groaned and tried to pull his left arm out, but it wouldn't move. It too was trapped under the strut. "Hel—" he fell into a fit of coughing from the smoke. "Hello?!" He tried looking anywhere but at the body. He felt queasy.

No answer.

He coughed again. "Anyone?! Help!" The ship was eerily silent save for the spitting of fires and the distant creak of stressed metal. If he strained hard enough he thought he could hear far-off explosions and wind, but it might have been his imagination.

His head cleared a bit and he blinked the last of the fog away from his vision. His right arm was free, and from his semi-propped position against the wall, he could see a sliver of the door at the far end of the infirmary in the interior wall. It was mostly blocked by armor plates that had blown through, leaving a gaping breach. He couldn't see through the tangle of exposed circuitry.

Trying to keep calm, he took it one problem at a time. Most pressing were the fires. All around the infirmary there were small blazes coming to life. Even as he watched, Martin's hair caught at last—courtesy of the dented exterior wall and broken conduit—and the smell of burning flesh mingled with the rest, further searing his nostrils.

Then he heard another loud *creak* and a hiss. In the corner above his head, greenish fluid had started trickling in through the ceiling and ignited. The burning liquid sizzled its way down the cabinets and towards the floor, closing on Damien's body too fast for comfort.

"Anyone?! HELLO?!" he cried again, trying vainly to lift the metal strut with one arm.

There was still no answer. He thought about trying to focus his power to push it off, but he was too exhausted. The pool felt drained and whimpering, and the sheer effort of squirming was leaving him increasingly frantic and weak.

"I'M STUCK!"

Finally, he heard a loud noise outside, and footsteps.

"HEY! HEY, I'M IN THE INFIRMARY! I'M PINNED!"

The footsteps stopped, and Damien heard muted voices. The sounds of people moving about and clearing debris drifted in through the interior breach. Then something slammed the infirmary door with a *BANG*. The stuck plates groaned. He heard some sort of pneumatic noise before the next impact. He imagined they had a handheld battering ram. *Good*, he thought. It banged again and Damien spotted the sliver of door shift.

"YOU'VE GOT IT! HURRY!" His heart thudded as he glanced towards the liquid fire. It had dribbled off the counter, leaking over the floor. He could already feel the intense heat as whatever chemical it was let off more toxic fumes.

The door wrenched open. Damien's excitement and fear was brewing wildly now. The wall plates clattered to the deck, sparks flashing as metal bounced.

"I'm back here!"

Out of the smoky entryway came a figure, bruting its way over debris. The alarm lights shifted from red to white and back, and on the return, all hope, excitement, and quivering energy drained from Damien's limbs.

It was an Algaroth, clad in tightly contoured onyx armor. The pneumatic noise sounded again. *Hiss thump.*

Oh no.

Hiss thump.

The hellish red light highlighted a fierce alien visage; closer than it had been the last time they met, stuck in stark memory of that night. He knew that face. Damien stared into the snarling, hateful visage of an Avo, but not just any Avo: it was the very Avo he had wounded so grievously as they had fled the XenoCon campus, the one who had disconnected his matchsticks.

The alien's jaw was repaired, but a thick white scar ran up and behind its left eye, where its eye ridge had been chipped, the ganglia seared away. Its left arm now sported a thick plate over the shoulder. The plate had two downward-bladed spikes that descended almost to the commando's elbow, and had been used recently. Red blood dripped from the end of the spikes. Hatred filled the creature's gaze as it locked eyes with Damien.

A guttural growl escaped the Avo's throat, while Damien made a tiny sound of panic. He had no gun, no energy to use his power, and no one nearby to help him. For the first time, Damien felt paralyzed. There was no escape from this.

The Avo didn't move. It just stared at him, taking in the flaming infirmary, Martin's body turning to cinders, and the liquid flames working their way towards Damien, trapped. A glint of amusement danced in its vicious gaze as it measured the distance of the flames from his body. Damien held his breath, waiting to be shot, but then something peculiar happened.

The commando turned and stalked out of the room without a word, kicking the last wall plate away from the door with a frog-leg. The plate snapped from the net of cords that had kept it hanging and clattered to the deck, making Damien flinch. He heard the commando growl outside of the door, saying simply, "He's here."

The words sent a spear of dread through Damien's numb chest.

With an ominous thud, Damien heard something much larger move outside. His heart resumed a traumatic marathon. There was another commanding footstep. Then another, each a resounding *thud* on the deck. Finally, the largest black claw he had ever seen grasped the top of the doorway, and the newcomer ducked into the infirmary.

Damien's confusion fell away, stunned into oblivion. If he could have felt his legs, they would have gone limp as well. He shrank back against the wall on instinct, the inferior combatant yielding to a victor.

The monstrous Algaroth that stepped inside dwarfed even Satolin. Throbbing, bulging muscles lined the cracks in the armored body; his helmet was ornate, mixing silver and black, crested back with two menacing spikes; huge boots left the alien's splayed toes exposed, allowing each clawed foot to crush the deck beneath each step; and the hypnotic mass of creature dimmed the fires in the infirmary, not with his bulk, but with his wings. Carefully folded wings, the tips dragging against the ceiling, were enough to block out the entire far wall, what wasn't already hidden behind his considerable body. Last, were his eyes…the Algaroth Royal's eyes were pure, shining gold, focused unblinking at Damien's broken form.

Sparks and hot chemicals fell on the crux of exposed skin at the alien's knee, blistering and burning his leg, but there was no hint of acknowledgment. The ruthless, calculating eyes bespoke a monstrous intelligence, commanding all and bowing to none. Those were the eyes of a leader. They were the wings of the only Algaroth Royal on Earth.

It was the profile of the Over-Seer.

Croll Tan.

Croll Tan glared at Damien beneath the metal, and the Elemental's fear trickled away at the odd sensation of hopelessness. He was going to die here.

"I wondered in what state we would find each other, Damien Vilan of the Seattle Isles. I was concerned this crash might kill you." Croll Tan's English was perfect, his voice practiced and fluent, and the silky delicacy with which he selected his words sent a chill up Damien's spine—despite the calm settling over him. "You have been unusually elusive to some of my very best trackers." Tan gave the slightest nod back towards the door. "You even disappointed my dearest hunter. You remember my Avo, Draigon Shellack."

The commando had returned to the doorway, his considerable stature reduced to nothing in the shadow of the Over-Seer. Shellack resumed staring at Damien.

Damien dared not speak.

Tan thudded past the medical slab and swatted his wing at the table. The slab broke with a *CRACK*, and Martin's fiery corpse fell out of view. Damien flinched at the wet impact.

"I was saddened to hear that you found your way from the Seattle Islets to Amun-Nūr. Would you like to share where the deserters cower? It will net you nothing of course, but I confess myself curious."

Damien said nothing.

Croll Tan stopped on the pile of debris at Damien's feet and loomed, blocking out the white alarm lights above, but not the red ones on the wall.

The shifting nightmare was too jarring not to be real. "The Elementals have at last shown themselves," said Tan. "And all it took was the threat of an entire supernation, poised to topple. I find that intriguing."

"Why?" Damien whispered. He couldn't stop himself.

Tan's shining gold gaze fell to the strut covering Damien's body. "Unlike Amun-Nūr, I would choose to fight every battle were it my want, not wait until a fulcrum engagement."

Admiral Baroda's words came to Damien's mind then, about Tan being a cunning strategist who had played the game of war against humanity for longer than any of his predecessors. Damien kept his silence as the alarm lights shifted to white, illuminating blue skin as rich as sapphires and teeth as sharp as knives. The silence pervaded until the lights flickered back to red, and the Over-Seer leaned in close. His breath was clean and smelled of fine red wine. It was liberating from the smoke, but somehow it only made Damien's resolve waver further.

"What do you want?" he finally breathed out, stronger than he'd thought his voice might be.

A thunderous chortle resonated barely a meter from Damien's face. The golden eyes shone with dark humor. "To pay homage, Damien. To the peak of a species."

Croll Tan hissed then, whipping around to stare at the flaming liquid, which had reached his clawed toes unnoticed. The burning chemicals boiled the blue skin with apparently more potency than the sparks. He kicked the cabinet—which had turned a sickly brown color under the flames—and it went cascading to the ground, sending splashes of the substance everywhere in the brief havoc. A single drop landed on Damien's free arm, and the poisonous burning made him cry out in agony.

What he didn't expect from that was the clarity the pain gave him. His body was still numb, but the raw sensation jumpstarted something else: he felt a weak surge of life to his depleted pool, and the Darkness inside him prickled. It was small, but it was something.

As Croll Tan spun back towards his prey, Damien lashed out with a tiny Wave. It erupted from his palm and right into the base of the Over-Seer's neck, small and focused, but not as strong as he'd hoped. The dark lord jerked back, but his only noise was a sharp intake of breath. Damien's single spark of hope faded as his pool hemorrhaged in exhaustion, and he knew that was all he had left.

The Wave had distorted and darkened Tan's thick neck-guard. From this close, Damien could clearly see the skin underneath: it had been rent open and dark blood had started to ooze out of a sickly collection of tears, reminding him of all the corpses buried in the snow. Tan didn't even flinch.

Croll Tan eyed the wound. "I appreciate your candor." Then the Over-Seer lashed out, and pinned Damien's free arm to the wall. Shellack appeared at his lord's shoulder, producing a short baton with a glowing tip. Tan turned it on with a *buzz*, and Damien struggled as the Over-Seer brought it down hard on his neck.

Paralyzing pain ignited in Damien's neck. His brain exploded in stars of agony, and his scream betrayed how intense it was.

"This didn't have to be done now, Damien," Tan said over the screams, not looking the least bit troubled at having to restrain the human. "We could have waited until returning to Solaroth; taken it from your arm."

"Ahhh—*AHHHH!!*" he howled. Tan pressed harder. The nub was burning hot, *searing* hot. Damien's vision started to go white.

"Life is balance, Elemental. You wound me, I repay the debt." Tan's eyes burned. "But in restoring balance, someone must be taught *not to repeat such a mistake.*"

At the last word, the buzzing stopped, and Damien was left twitching as the pain broke. His neck was on fire, and his wrist felt sprained from where Tan's hand had impacted. He blinked rapidly, gasping, as Tan handed the tool back to Shellack. The Avo was smiling a cruel smile. Tan looked down at the Elemental, eyeing whatever wound he had just inflicted. The Over-Seer's face flushed blue, and the dagger-filled mouth spread into a dominating grin. "Yes, that will do well."

"What—what are—what are you d-doing to me?" Damien panted. His neck felt as if it were bubbling away. He tried to kick or thrash, *something*, but nothing budged.

"I need your blood, Damien. I need your blood…*invigorated*."

"Wh-What?"

Shellack handed his lord another instrument. This one had a long vial on one end, a suction cup on the other.

"The blood of an Elemental," he hissed. "Essence of Darkness. Surely you can envision the value of such a thing?" The Over-Seer lashed out again. Harder this time, with his claw. The impact made a sickening crunch, and Damien gave a low moan as his wrist broke. Tan took no notice. "Or perhaps you take it for granted? You have a supply to last a lifetime, after all."

Shellack snorted over Tan's shoulder.

The Over-Seer lightly turned aside Damien's head with a claw, cutting his forehead. He then placed the suction cup over where he'd placed the hot buzzer. The skin was grossly tender and Damien flinched. "The Elemental who creates black holes," he said matter-of-factly, as if this were a conversation over lunch. "If the secrets to such power can be unlocked with your blood? Then I wager there are unfathomable uses for you and your kin. I confess to being saddened that I had to give up such a useful proving ground as that little village in order to draw you out. I had hoped we might spend some time there, together." He turned on the suction cup.

The buzzer had hurt like a hot poker, but this was pain at a different level of visceral. Neither exhausting himself in the Core nor being kicked back by the Iceberg's shockwave had ever felt anything like this. *Nothing* was physical pain like this. Damien felt like someone had attached a thousand fishhooks inside his torso and then started yanking them up and out through his neck, ravaging his insides. The device hummed pleasantly as Damien watched his blood fill the vial, unaware of how much noise he was making. His screams were far away, and he felt lightheaded. Eventually, he realized his cries had grown faint and weak as Tan traded Shellack for a second vial. It dimly registered that Shellack had just jerked his head around, his body going rigid as if he'd smelled something.

"You aren't going to die today, Elemental. This is just the beginning of a long relationship between you and I." Croll Tan's deep, crisp voice seemed further away. "I intend for you to be joined by your kin soon, after your *human* cousins are finished, but we can discuss that later. For now, as humans say: your blood is worth its weight in gold."

In his increasing delirium, Damien didn't know what to make of Shellack stalking towards the hole in the wall, teeth bared. *Hiss-thump* went the frog-legs.

"Earth is indeed a special planet," said Tan, removing the cup and tucking away the second vial. "I envy your guardianship—"

"My lord," Shellack growled from the wall. A distant whine filled the air.

"—But now you are charged as the steward to fell your people, and for that? I am sympathetic to your pain." Croll Tan grabbed the strut, intending to lift it and take Damien with him.

"*GON!*" Shellack roared at his Over-Seer, diving towards him, but he couldn't help his master. The whine grew louder and the next instant, an explosion blew out the outer wall of the infirmary. Draigon Shellack and Croll Tan vanished, thrown clean from the ship. It happened so fast that smoky floodlights filled the space before Damien knew what had happened. His ears rang again as he started slipping.

Voices and flashlights swept the infirmary. Someone ordered someone else to go look for the Over-Seer. Damien was fading, his eyes were heavy, and his neck throbbed louder than his heart.

"Well well," said a voice that rang familiar. "Looks like someone got himself into a clench-n-squeeze again with some slizzards he couldn't beat. That's gonna kill you someday, Package Boy."

Damien recognized her voice. It was the woman captaining the *Chalice Archon* with Kehzalla team, but now he remembered where he had heard it even before that: on the same night he had encountered Shellack, on a Blackwing, fleeing Seattle with Leo and Von.

It was Captain Deanna Huxley.

MASON J. TORALL

Chapter Twenty Six

Scars

Damien awoke coughing.

"Doctor!" someone shouted.

"I'm here, I'm here!" That was Gwen's voice.

Damien tasted the thick copper of blood as his cough subsided. His eyes fluttered.

"Damien? Can you hear me?"

"...Yes," his voice was weak. "I can hear just f-fine."

Gwen sighed in relief, "Don't you try to move. You've been under for...a while now. Can you focus?"

It was harder than he thought. The lights were dim and comfortable, but his eyelids struggled.

"It's okay. You take your time alright? Here, drink this."

Something thick, sweet, and disgusting poured down his throat and he gagged, trying not to spew it back up. He didn't realize he had until Gwen started dabbing his chin and chest with a warm towel. He coughed more and finally got his eyes open. Gwen's back was to him. He turned his head towards her—and was rewarded with a blazing pain.

"Don't!" she cried, spinning and grabbing his head as delicately as she could. "Don't turn your head that way! You're still tender."

Damien tried to hold back the pained tears and control his breathing. *I'm home.* The words drifted up into his mind with such certainty, that it took him a moment to remember where 'home' was. *Amun-Nūr. The Island of Amun-Nūr is home.* It was an unexpected thought that rang true, and he held onto it tightly. He glanced around, and saw he was in the recovery ward of the medical wing. "How long's it been?" he asked. He had an urge to touch his neck, but Gwen held him in place. Nurse Donovan was nearby, handing off tools. Another nurse was tending to a bed across from him. Damien's stomach tightened as he saw Doctor Kiveen on it, her blue body mostly covered in bandages. He trembled then as he caught Nurse Donovan handing Gwen something. At first he thought it was a baton, but it was only a swab.

Doctor Gwen swabbed his mouth, left and came back with a water sack and a straw. She set it on his chest. "Drink."

He managed only a mouthful before his stomach turned and he started coughing and dribbling again. She kindly wiped it away. "You're a lucky man, Elemental."

He took another hard breath. "How. Long."

She averted her gaze. "Four days."

His face stayed blank.

"I'm so sorry."

"What about the…the engagements? Italy?" he took a breath. "The Throat? Are you okay?"

She held up a hand to silence him. "I'm fine, but not now. You need to rest."

The way she said it only strengthened his resolve. "*Yes* now. What about Von? And Javi?"

She locked gazes with him, the twinkling green fire behind her glasses reflecting something sad. She sighed. "Both of them are here. They're safe, but… It's still going on. She clasped her hands. "The Throat is already taken. Italy is too—"

Romi.

"—And the Dynasty Navy is in retreat."

Damien tried to sit up but she held him down. "What—what about—"

"Roman and Kel are alright," she soothed. "*Lotus* collected as much information as they could, but they had to leave. They…they barely made it out and… Italy doesn't look good, especially in Rome."

Damien's heart sank. "What about everyone else? What about the…the village? Who made it back?" He closed his eyes as a new, horrible nightmare vision surfaced: the Iceberg tank, pounding its preparatory bass note into the ground and sending a shockwave that cracked open the earth to swallow his parents. With a titanic exertion of willpower, Damien pushed the thought away. He squirmed on the contoured foam of the hospital bed.

Gwen took his hand in hers. She looked away and swallowed hard. "The Over-Seer escaped and...*Earth Clad* is gone. No survivors. We...we lost a lot of others too." She sniffed and wiped her eyes, looking to where Elora Kiveen lay still. "Echo is still out there, but *Lotus* was the only ship from Notte to... to make it back. Everyone else, the squads, the ships, they..." she choked. "Roman and Kel managed to save a few, though. Harlan, Klick, a few others."

Damien's heart sank as he tried to remember who had been sent with Notte. The only name that came to mind was Staff Sergeant Tortelli. He asked, and Gwen shook her head.

"I'm sorry," she whispered, still holding his hand.

He closed his eyes. "I barely knew him."

"I know."

Fuck. Damien took a careful breath, thinking of the man's youthful freckly confidence, now shuttered. "What about the rest?"

"One of Kehzalla's ships is going to Istanbul to help the air brigades.

Kehzalla. They... Huxley showed up. Huxley! She saved me. He remembered then. Captain Huxley had saved his life. Again.

Nurse Donovan handed Gwen her double-portfolio tablet and whispered something in her ear. The doctor nodded. "Thank you, Sarah." She looked at Damien, her eyes wet. "You need to rest."

"But—"

"*No.*"

He relented. Mostly. "What about my face?"

Gwen sighed. She got up to retrieve a tablet and turned on the camera. She pulled back his soft bandages so he could see properly. The right side of his head made him go cold.

His face looked like half a corpse. Some impact in front of his ear had torn a chunk of his cheek clean off. Stretching his mouth hurt, but the icky, nauseating, *squelching* sound of his jaw working was too gross not to repeat over and over. He tilted the tablet, and could actually *see* the muscles inside his face. It was incredibly tender, and the wound was worsened by the flecks of cuts both large and small all over the rest of him. *You're lucky you didn't lose a damn eye.*

Or your head, he amended. Gwen winced as he stretched his jaw again, but she let him continue. *Squilch.*

He tilted the tablet again and realized his face was nothing compared to his brutalized neck. The skin was puckered, purple, and black. It looked like it had been boiled and then plucked at with pincers. The bruising spread outwards like a sunburst, turning gross yellow at the edges near his jaw and far down his collarbone.

"That's enough," said Gwen, and snatched away the camera. She went to replace the bandages he'd torn in his admiration.

Squilch. He had nothing to say.

When the soft, clean pads and covers were replaced on his face, the doctor squeezed his hand again, a controlled mask over her features. "Time to sleep, Damien. It'll be alright."

He did. He couldn't remember when he woke next, but he knew he had nightmares, even if he couldn't remember them. Over the next two days, news continued to roll in about the event which had been coined the Eurasian Inferno: The Italian defense grid had been broken, and The Collective were pushing hard onto the Peninsula, ravaging every city they could reach. Human forces continued pouring into the area from all over the world, turning many ancient cities into battlegrounds. Rome in particular was seeing massive skirmishes—but humanity was losing. The fresh forces from the Supply Fleet were apparently being put to punishing use.

At the Throat of Israel, Croll Tan's push to cross from Africa to Eurasia had proved a success, but less so than Italy. The staunch Middle Kingdom defenders had set up a thus-far unbreakable wall of artillery that had kept the enemy from reaching Petra, New Gaza, or Jerusalem. Even so, Tan's army had still managed to cross the Throat, and more troops were coming out of the African jungle every few hours.

In the Regent Dynasty, The Collective had made their first successful landfall ever. The Dynasty's Navy—which never had quite recovered from when they tried to take back Australia—had fought valiantly. But even aided by the three ships of Amun-Nūr's Kehzalla strike force, which included Captain Huxley's ship, the *Chalice Archon*, it wasn't enough. The steady stream of heavy aircraft coming out of Australia had forced the Navy to retreat, and now, The Collective were scurrying all over the Thai Spur (a peninsula that curves south into the mostly flooded former nation of Cambodia). The intel said that the enemy was already starting to build their first Dynasty mining hub.

Regarding Captain Huxley: Damien learned on his third day in recovery that his recommendation to Captain Romi about her had indeed been passed along. As it turned out, *Huxley* had been the bargaining chip that had brought Von from Peak Springs to the island. Admiral Baroda had become exhausted by the captain's tenacious tendencies, and in exchange for Silas Von's safe return to Damien's side, Prohka Satolin had agreed to take Deanna Huxley and her crew off Baroda's hands as well. She had arrived two days after the Supply Fleet was in orbit, taking the long and confined passage of a submarine to get to the island without alerting the warships above. She had promptly been given command of a Scops fighter called *Emerald Sunrise*...and had promptly renamed it the *Chalice Archon*. No one had argued.

Damien also learned that Huxley was the one who had not only been the first responder to Captain Nejem's mayday about the village, but she had returned Damien safely to Amun-Nūr, *and* had no sooner seen him personally to the medical wing than she had turned around and taken the *Archon* to Istanbul. Gwen informed Damien that Huxley had *also* been tasked by Commander Morgan to recruit some crack pilots out of the Middle Kingdom for Amun-Nūr. It went unsaid that the recruitment was needed to replace those who had been lost, like Aziz Nejem.

Amidst the barrage of global news, Prohka Satolin gave an island-wide announcement that, while there was yet to be a sign of Croll Tan's new weapon, the Supply Fleet had at last departed. The warships had left Earth laden with Earth cargo, leaving the planet once again to try their hand at breaking The Collective's hold before another fleet arrived. Gravely, though, the Prohka announced that Amun-Nūr had settled on a

531

prediction for the arrival of the next Supply Fleet. In the command wheel, the clock ceased flashing red zeros and reset to reflect the new ETA:

$$\boxed{0\,1\,\text{Y}\,:\,0\,2\,\text{M}\,:\,0\,2\,\text{D}\,:\,1\,4\,\text{H}}$$

By Damien's estimate, that would put the next Supply Fleet at Earth on August 22, 2146, not eighteen months from now. He shuddered at the news.

The bittersweet realization of more precious resources being taken away forever was normally cause for some celebration, but not this time. The storm of full-scale war, the likes of which Croll Tan hadn't pushed in years, had come to Earth. The cheer would have to wait.

∞   ∞   ∞

That same morning when the fleet finally departed, Damien had been left off of his knockout drugs so that Doctor Gwen could give him a coherent prognosis. It was a good thing too because the night before he had woken up shivering and crying out, thrashing at his neck and almost breaking his wrist again when he slammed it into his side table. Gwen had been there in a heartbeat, stopping him before he hurt himself further.

That morning, as his body ached and burned with the lack of heavy anesthetic, he found that he had to agree with her professional opinion that he should *absolutely* be dead. "You have minor injuries beyond what's worth the time to count," she said from the foot of his bed, displaying his body on a rolling display nearby. A female Algaroth nurse he'd never seen and a human male nurse who'd been tending to Doctor Kiveen until the end were present. "The shockwave from the Iceberg threw shrapnel all over your back, broke three ribs, and an unlucky piece bounced off of your spine—that's what hurts the most," she added as that very spot on his lower back flared over the low-dose of painkillers. "We still have to dislodge the metal."

He tried to control his breathing, "Is it—*fwhooo*—what's making everything—*fwhooo*—HURT so much? *Ahh!*" He seized as the spot sent a jolt of pain down his broken arm, where he swore he could *feel* where the nerve endings to his fingers had been crushed. His digits were numb. The Algaroth nurse had to press hard on his chest to keep him from flailing. He kept breathing in short, hyper-rasps.

Gwen repeated herself, ever patient. "Once we rebuild your wrist this afternoon we'll take care of the shrapnel. Then we'll finish cleaning up your face and neck."

"I want to see it again." The hole in his face made him look like a zombie, and it gave him morbid amusement. He wasn't sure why.

Her dry stare was all the answer he needed.

"Ok, fine but—*ehh*—what about my neck?"

Even her smile faltered. "Both will come tomorrow."

He hissed and nodded, resigned to being stuck. The Inferno was raging, and Satolin's bold claim that Amun-Nūr was a force to be reckoned with had so far fallen deeply short. It didn't help that he had yet to see the Prohka; his debrief about everything that had transpired in the valley had been done by Commander Morgan the day before yesterday—or, more accurately, as soon as Gwen had allowed it. He had relayed everything to the commander, from the corpses, to the corpses *beneath* the corpses, to the transmitter, the Nuke casing, the Mag Fury cradle, the tracks, the ambush, Croll Tan taking his blood, and everything he could remember about what the Over-Seer had said—which he realized wasn't much. Morgan had thanked him regardless, expressed his gratitude that Damien was alive, and assured him that they would keep him informed of whatever was coming.

That afternoon, night, and following morning were spent in surgery and in stupor-laden recovery. Croll Tan had pulverized his wrist and very nearly shorn his hand off with those black claws. Damien didn't need the doctor to tell him that his hand wouldn't be fully healed for a while, even with the bone plates they were installing. Nurse Donovan informed him that the damage to his neck would have to come last, but that Dr. Whalen could at least repair his face without any lasting scarring. The news had infuriated him more than made him happy, because it put him at eight days in the medical wing after the events in the valley, and every conscious moment left him positively *ticking* to be out of here, his neck be-damned. Gwen insisted, though, and she held reign over him for the time being.

Though the recovery, nightmares and waking bouts of terror assaulted him now as much as ever before…something was different now. He couldn't tell if it had something to do with the catharsis that night of drinks in the Garden, or if it was some other unseen change in him that had occurred, but Damien felt better somehow. *Stronger*. His bouts of terror would inevitably give way to rest now instead of plaguing him all night, and for the first time in his life, he felt like the thoughts he thought and the words he spoke were coming into alignment. Maybe it was simply getting distance from the trauma that spawned it all, but it was happening. He couldn't bring himself to believe that he was strong enough to simply *get over it*, and so he continued looking for the *thing* that had done it, but nothing came up. He was simply getting better.

Finally, on his ninth day in recovery, Damien received a slew of welcome visitors—most of whom he'd been told had tried to see him earlier, but he'd been too slagged to receive them properly.

First came Captain Romi, who beamed to see Damien sitting up in his bed, and Damien was similarly elated. Romi said that he didn't have much time but that Gwen had said he could come by this morning, so he had. Damien was sure to show his gratitude, but he could tell it only punched through the surface—the captain looked haggard and tired.

The two gave abridged stories about the valley and what had happened in Italy, but when Romi commented on how chipper Damien's general mood was, Damien frowned. "What do you mean?"

"I mean," the captain said simply, "that your list of supporters is growing. I've talked to more than one member of Aurora who said that you kept a cool head during the ambush."

"I don't remember—"

"*They* do. Loss even told me that he wished he'd made you his second-in-command, because he'd been occupied getting the doctor and those near him out while *you* looked at the big picture."

"But, the village...we lost our hard data," he said, under the assumption that the many scans, images, and data that Aurora had done on the village, the blast crater, the cave under the cliff (which the team had entered, even if Damien hadn't), the Nuke casing, the Mag Fury cradle, and the layers of murdered people had been lost in the ambush.

Romi gave a confused laugh. "What? No, it's all up in the wheel right now! Practically all of Argyle has been working 'round the clock to figure out what it is you found, putting together the pieces!" His forced cheerful air faltered. "They haven't figured out what Tan's weapon is yet, or what those tracks out of the valley were. Even Leo is stumped, but at least..." his smile trickled away altogether. "At least you made it worth it. We lost a lot of good people for this."

Damien shifted, feeling the irritating stick of an IV drip line taped into his hand. His voice dropped. "I know. I'm sorry about Tortelli and the others from Notte. It..." he struggled to find words.

Romi held up his hand. "Sorry isn't something you need to feel. It's the nature of war, and the only way to disgrace those who died fighting is to stop fighting." The captain looked away. "We all have that choice—to stop fighting—but I don't keep company with people who would, so," he grinned and looked back, "*You* at least must be doing something right, especially with finding the connection at the village."

Damien squirmed at that. "*I* didn't really find anything, and I didn't really *do* anything either."

The captain shrugged. "I stand by what I said: you have growing admiration from your peers, my friend. It might not be something discernible. It could be just a universal draw, but I think some people just have leadership in their blood."

Damien cringed at the thought of blood, but Romi seemed not to notice.

"We've lost a lot this past two weeks, but if there's anything I've learned through this war, it's that it's *people* that matter, not places.

You've helped a lot of people who would otherwise have died."

Something in Romi's pocket started buzzing. He tapped it. "I have to go, but I'm glad to see you're on the mend."

Damien nodded. "Thanks, I…I *feel* a little better. I'm glad you're safe too."

The man bowed, smiling. He offered to play a game of chess soon and Damien agreed—on the condition that it was after his cheek was healed. "I don't want to distract you into losing by looking like a corpse." Romi grinned and quipped that he *did* look terrifying with half of those skin-grafts in place, and then he bid the recovery ward a good day.

Von came next, but before he showed up, Damien had a question. "Gwen?" he asked from his bed.

She turned before entering her office. "Hmm?"

"I don't get it."

"Don't get what?"

He struggled to put it to words. "This Inferno, it's…we're getting ravaged but…

"But?"

He huffed. "I…I don't know."

She cocked her head. "Well maybe I'll dope you up and you'll remember then, eh?" She smiled. "I'll be in here if you need me."

He gave a limp snort and thanked her as she went away, leaving him to ponder his blankets. *I don't know why people are looking up to me.*

Von's arrival was glad but similarly short. He informed Damien that he'd been working extra hours outside of the garden dome to help techs in the command wedge. Exhaustion was running rampant as Amun-Nūr was indeed working in a frenzy, terrified that Croll Tan's weapon was about to be deployed, and they still had no idea what it was, where it might show up, and most importantly: *what it could do*. Regardless, the two had a good laugh about Von's luck with bullets apparently shifting to his brother. Damien said that if that were true, he would still need to get shot a second time, and he felt that being hit by an Iceberg tank's shockwave *more* than covered that.

They both laughed at that, which Damien instantly regretted because it strained his back, but the moment had been there anyway. More than ever, Von made him feel on the mend.

Just before lunch came Javier, whose mission with Kehzalla he had heard precious little about. After Damien told his tale of the valley, the proud and newly anointed Amun-Nūr Marine Private recounted, "Sounds like you did just as good a job as us, bro. Snaps. Shame you didn't beat their pants off."

"We were *ambushed!*" Damien exclaimed. "What the hell else were we supposed to do? I think we handled ourselves just damn *fine*, thank you very much."

Javier snorted. "Uh huh. Well, I'd have rather been that though then *our* shit." He rubbed his hands together. "That Australian advance, man… They pushed us hard."

"You gonna tell me what happened or what?"

"Yeah, yeah, just keep to your nasty puréed food while I talk." They sniggered at each other while Damien took a sip of the brownish sludge in his cup. It was actually very sweet, like a fruit smoothie. Gwen had refused to tell him what was in it though.

"So here's what happened…" Javi began, and he proceeded to give the long and detailed version of how Kehzalla had connected with the Dynasty Navy. There, they had been sent immediately to the coastal city of Phnom Angkor on the Thai Spur, where one of the Australian columns had broken through the defenses and were making landfall. "The ships just kept coming and coming," he spoke on. "It was fucking insanity. Snaps, you should've been there. Dunno if it would've helped though."

"Why?" Damien pressed, sinking back into his pillow; Gwen had just come by to give him his drugs for a midday nap. He'd argued but she'd stuck him anyway.

Javier fell into quivering silence, and Damien looked up to find the man looking at anything but him. "You've got something to say, Marine. Just say it."

Finally, his friend snickered. "You ah…has the news made it down here yet? Have ah, have you heard that it wasn't a total loss? For us I mean."

Damien felt the tug of sleep at him. "What news? No," he dribbled. "Tell me dammit."

"We had some help show up."

Damien turned to find Javier tense with excitement, giddy. "What kind?" His wrist twitched involuntarily and the IV in his knuckle scraped the bone. The blaze of pain pushed the drugs back for another minute or so. *Tomorrow*, he reminded himself. *She said you could move your fingers again tomorrow.*

"The family kind," Javier whispered. *"Elementals."*

Damien stopped itching and narrowed his eyes.

Javier gave him a knowing, smug nod. *"Ohh* yeah. And one of them came *back* with us! Ha! Be-*lieve* it, baby!"

Damien was too tired to be upset that he hadn't heard a hint about this before now. A few people had mentioned something about Elementals being spotted—just like Satolin had predicted they might do, and Croll Tan had planned for—but everyone had seemed rather evasive on the subject. "Explain," he demanded. "Less cryptic though, I'm exhausted, man. Give the details now and the flair later."

The reinstated Marine rolled his eyes, "Alright, fine." He leaned in close. "There were *two* of them at Angkor. Never seen anything like it. I think they knew each other or something cus they showed up together."

Damien waited.

"*Shit* you're boring when you're drugged up! I used to know a guy who would sleepwalk and *sing* when he went under! You're just so, so—"

"Javi," Damien said with as much bite as he could muster. "Shut up and tell me."

"Right. Fine, whatever," Javier's grin betrayed him. "Well, we were on the beach in this like…ceremonial dock district or something and the troops were air-dropping like bird shit. Our Kehzalla guys had hooked up with some local Army and Navy guys, but I'm not kidding, you couldn't see the fucking sky there was so many slizz—birds up there." Javier shook his head.

"So *then*," he went on. "Ha, well then *shit*. These two crazy bastards came out of nowhere and started blasting slizz—Algaroth—left and right. It was a shit-crazy-show. One of 'em I think is probably Wind or Air or something, cus he took out like ten of their dropships in some little tornado. Never heard of one like him. I don't know what ended up happening to him, but the other one…" Javier leaned in again, grasping Damien's shoulder to make sure he was listening. "The other one's the one that came back with us, and *maaaan* if you could've seen him work," Javier's voice was filled with awe. "He *buried* a platoon in one swoop."

Damien took a final, deep breath and refrained from hitting the call panel for Gwen's office. "You mean 'buried' like the expression or 'buried' like what *you* can do? What *was he*, Javi?"

Javier's dark eyes sparkled. "Fire."

Damien fell back into his pillow. "Where'd he come from?"

"Who knows? But my advice: if you catch him in a fight—or fuck, in the hallway," Javier smirked. "Or at dinner? Stay out of his way. That dude's a scary, *scary* man."

Damien was past his limit. He slid down the rest of the way into the blankets. "Mm well, guess I won't meet him until I'm out of here."

Javier shook his head and looked up as the nurse came in, ready to shoo him out. "Oh no, I think Sato's bringing him to meet you this afternoon."

Damien's eyes snapped open at Javier's retreating form. "What?"

"You heard me. Later!" The door to the ward closed and Damien heard Javier's barking laughter in the hall.

The recognition of what the Marine had just said never made it to the excitable center of Damien's brain. His waking thoughts slipped, and he was out like a light.

∞   ∞   ∞

539

He slept pretty well through his nap. When he awoke it was evening, and while what Javier had said earlier left him feeling curious and excited, it was eclipsed by Gwen's news that she'd be releasing him tomorrow morning. It put him in a downright pleasant disposition, and he even had solid breakfast for dinner before the Prohka arrived—oatmeal and a bowl of fruit, sliced into easily manageable pieces. He was proud of how little mess he was making.

"You puzzle me, Damien," said Satolin from the doorway to the ward.

Damien hadn't heard him come in. He twitched and nearly dropped his bowl, wincing. "What?" He blinked when he saw who it was. "Oh, Prohka! Hey! I uh… Why's that?" He turned his head with exaggerated slowness once he'd settled the fruit. The skin grafts on his face and neck were still bandaged and a little tender, and if he turned too hard his back would spasm.

"Because," Satolin answered, "you display such disconnect from those around you in a communal environment, but when you go to war, you throw yourself on any person unfortunate enough to be in peril. You have a guardian's instincts. It's an odd combination of standoffishness and martyrdom."

Damien didn't know what to say to that, but it triggered a thought at the idea of perspective. "Is that why everyone suddenly seems so…taken with me right now?"

Satolin shook his head. "Nothing of the sort has happened. Simply put: you made yourself family when you agreed to stay on the island—even if you spent a good amount of time trying to pull away from it. By now you should have figured out that the people here care as much about you as any true family, but trauma is taxing on all. You haven't applied yourself these past months as I'd hoped you would, and others have noticed."

Damien felt his mood begin to crumble and shame pinked his ears. "I…I never thought of it that way."

"Obviously not, and not for the want of telling you," the Prohka said curtly.

540

The words stung, and Damien was reminded of all the things that Reuben had said. He pursed his lips to keep his face steady. Shame flared hot all over, and suddenly his bandages were very itchy.

The Prohka took a deep breath before speaking again. When he did, his voice was softer. "That said, I'm grateful to see you on the mend…" he trailed off, looking troubled.

"Thanks, I—what's wrong?"

Satolin took a calculated breath. "This is…difficult, but it needs to be asked."

Damien clasped his hands and nodded for the Prohka to continue.

"When I heard of the ambush, I was afraid." Satolin's voice grew low. "I am not afraid to admit I was afraid. Yet, when I learned of your survival, all I could think was that you were lucky."

Damien furrowed his brow. "Lucky?" He looked pointedly at his own body in the bed.

Satolin shook his head. "No, not lucky in the sense of the damage done to you. Nor even lucky in how you survived." The Prohka's arctic-gold eyes glazed over and dilated, looking towards some far-off place. The look made Damien nervous. "I thought you were lucky because the Over-Seer made a mistake."

Damien was still confused. "Umm…you wish he'd taken me?"

"No, but his launching this Inferno while the fleet still orbited tells me that his tenure on Earth will be concluding soon."

"Why?"

"The resources he's committed to completing this board he's laid will leave him vulnerable to defeat, if his strategy fails. Tan would know this, and will have put careful safeguards in place for every contingency he can imagine—including his mistakes." Satolin ran a finger over his ganglia. "We don't know what those safeguards are but…I can imagine they'll involve his children."

A little prickle of nerves made Damien reach up to scratch his ear. "His, his what?"

Satolin nodded. "His children. Croll Tan never found a *vishi*, but before I came to Earth, I heard whispers that clan Ruthilon had conspired to forge an Over-Seer's bloodline."

The remains of Damien's dinner lay cold in his lap, mirroring the pit of nervousness forming in his stomach. "Isn't that...not at all how you told me your society works?"

"Correct. We have our house name and our Own name, but the clans we belong to privately maintain structure on Shialga." Satolin's predatory face looked hard, thoughtful, and worried. "I told you when you first arrived here that clan Ruthilon has managed to consolidate power for long decades, slowly coalescing at the peak of The Collective."

"Yeah."

Satolin finally looked at Damien. "If the whispers I heard ever had truth to them, then Croll Tan had not one but *two* successors...a nearly unheard of prospect in Algaroth birth within itself, but if you affix concerns that not only were they twins, they were of separate genders..."

The uninjured side of Damien's mouth fell open. *"A boy and a girl?* Croll Tan has two little Over-Seer *kids?!"*

"Not youths, Damien. They would be well of age already, held in plain sight within The Collective to garner unknowing support for clan Ruthilon." Satolin took a deep breath. "Some of us are well convinced that we learned who these secretive progenitors were some time ago."

"And?" Damien had a sudden flash that it was someone on the island, and he was utterly possessed by paranoia for a split second. The feeling departed as quickly as it had come.

"And nothing," the Prohka concluded. "We are uncertain, but if *either* of our guesses is correct, then the Algaroth in question are ones that merit Amun-Nūr's utmost caution, even across the stars."

Yeah, see? Can't be on the island. "So...what does this have to do with my recovery?"

"You escaped contact with the Fourth Over-Seer," Satolin lauded. "Did he reveal anything regarding successors?"

Damien thought on it. "No," he admitted. "He didn't *reveal* much of anything but...I still don't see why this is relevant?"

Satolin nodded to himself. "I understand." He focused back on Damien's bed. "I wanted to inform you with as much as we knew or suspected at present. There is no pressing danger, and I will be glad to clarify more of this subject later, but for now, I simply needed to hear from you directly regarding what Croll Tan might have said."

"He didn't say anything about kids."

"You needn't sound as if that is *your* failing, my fellow." The warmth returned to the Prohka's demeanor, and he stretched his broad shoulders as a nurse excused her way past him.

Damien sat still, unable to shake the nervous tingle. *Two kids. That bastard has two Over-Seer kids.*

Satolin stretched his jaw, flashing his omnivorous teeth. "Regarding both what I just asked and your earlier question on why many islanders seem so taken with you?"

"Yeah?"

"The world is too full of hurt to wallow in either for now. Put thoughts of other Over-Seers from your mind, there is nothing you can do for the moment." He halted until Damien nodded his assent. "So, specifically then to your question." He hummed for a moment, thinking. "In my experience, understanding the depths of another's pain is tricky and difficult. I consider it fortuitous that Algaroth and humans share so many behavioral tendencies, but we are still different, evolutionary barriers or no.

"One human may be so different from another that they may be unrecognizable, as is the case with any other life no matter how similar or dissimilar your biology. How bonds are formed is a mystery of the universe." The Prohka stepped further into the recovery ward. "On this island, we celebrate both alikes and differences as best we can, and to how you are being treated, well," Satolin tilted his head. "Offering the occasional shoulder for support is Amun-Nūr's way. *Taking* that shoulder is a choice, and it makes you none the weaker for doing so. It also means that you ought be there when others are in need. You have already passed through all of what I just described with those of us here, whom you've joined."

Damien stared at the juice soaking the bottom of the fruit bowl and nodded, unsure if he was being scolded or praised. For once though, he had the courage to say so. "I'm sorry," he said. "But I don't know what you're getting at."

Daeduras Satolin continued to surprise him. The alien's ganglia flicked pleasantly, and he smiled. "Then you're further along than many."

Damien blinked. "Umm… Thanks?"

"You're welcome." Satolin took a step. "Curiously, the purpose of my visitation was neither to incite questions regarding Tan's children, nor was it to explain others' perceptions of you *to* you," the great Algaroth chuckled. "Occasionally, though, you must say what's on your mind before it flees." His arctic-gold eyes were kind as he reached back to tap the door panel. "But since it came up and is now out of the way, there's someone with whom you need to be introduced."

The big alien stepped aside and—with the nonchalance of friends entering a restaurant for lunch—In from the hall…came an icon of a man. His quiet entry, lacking in fanfare, left Damien in immediate recognition that this was an extraordinary person. He stood apart from Satolin and barely came up to his chin—much like Damien—but upon his entry, the entire ward filled with his presence.

"Damien Vilan," said the Prohka. "Meet Caleb, an Elemental of Fire. Caleb, this is Damien Vilan, Elemental of Darkness." Satolin's eyes blazed full of excitement.

Caleb jerked his chin Damien's way, saying nothing. Damien didn't press him.

Even without being told, Damien could have spotted right away that the man was an Elemental; he absolutely *radiated* power. Caleb was the picture of a man too large for his body—which betrayed a lack of extreme features: He was tall, but not towering; built, but not buff; handsome but not dashing; and his clothes were layered but simple. His hair was of medium length, spiky, and a vibrant mix of warm hues. His eyes were hard, dark brown, and tumultuous in their gaze, but what made him appear so shocking—standing there in Amun-Nūr's medical wing—were the two enormous swords sheathed on his hips. Each sank from the man's waist to below his knees, and each was wrapped in scabbards to hold two distinctly unique weapons.

Damien met the man's gaze unblinking, despite the silence. He had never felt such intensity in a look before. He held it for only a second or two, but even that was enough to make him want to blink and turn away. Finally he did so, but the rage and power that practically leapt from Caleb's eyes was hard to forget, and he felt a tangible weight leave his shoulders as the Elemental finally looked elsewhere.

"You want me to wait for *this?*" Caleb snapped at Satolin, indicating the man in the bed.

The Prohka turned. "You are *going* to wait for him, if you want our help."

"Gabriel had to scuttle out of Angkor, and your *team* convinced me to come back here with the promise that we would go look for him. You're telling me the delay is for *him?*" He jabbed a finger in Damien's direction.

"If half of what you've told me about this Air Elemental is true, then he's a man who will do fine for now. He will understand, and we made it clear that there are other issues at present," said Satolin, his amiable attitude darkening. "We have a gestating lead on an Electric Elemental ourselves that had to be put aside for the Over-Seer's maneuvering."

Caleb said nothing. Damien looked on.

"You don't trust us," said the Prohka.

"No," the Fire Elemental crossed his arms. "I don't trust anyone who works with a Lunar Admiral."

Damien swore he saw Satolin give the faintest nod of agreement, but Caleb didn't see it. Instead, the Prohka turned to Damien. "Do you know when you'll be up and about?"

"Tomorrow morning," said Gwen, appearing from inside her walk-in medical preservator, pushing a broad cart laden with drugs, bandages, and tools. "Why?"

Satolin took in the three Elementals, and it occurred to Damien that that was in fact who was in the room. *Three of us in here, two more on the island, and two more for sure spotted out in the big world.* Damien grinned faintly to himself. *Quite the group we're pulling together.*

"Because," said Satolin. "Admiral Baroda will be here tomorrow evening for a...*reprimand*, regarding Amun-Nūr's involvement in this Inferno." The Algaroth's features clouded over.

Gwen stopped, looking nervous. "Damien won't be ready for that kind of strenuous activity. He's—"

"Uh, *yes* I will," Damien interrupted. "Get me the hell out of this bed!"

Satolin smirked, and Damien thought he saw a glimmer of dark humor in Caleb's eyes, but then he actually looked at the man's face, and knew he was crazy. That man wasn't the laughing type; it was just wishful thinking.

"You two may work out whatever is necessary, but the Admiral I'm sure would like Damien in attendance for this, and—"

"—But—"

"—No 'buts', Gwen. I want the Admiral here and off my island as fast as possible, and Damien deserves to have input on this."

Damien tried and failed to cut in. "Input on what?"

Gwen nodded. "If you insist."

"I do."

"Input on *what?*"

Satolin looked over, and suddenly the alien's strength seemed to leave him. "This visit by the good Admiral is likely his coming to inform Amun-Nūr that he can no longer support us, and our security is no longer his concern. He doesn't like when we don't follow orders."

"WHAT?!" Damien's shout made his throat rasp but he was glad he'd managed it.

"I'm sorry," Satolin shook his head. "I can't relay more at this time. We *will* get the opportunity to talk soon, that's my promise."

"...Alright," Damien allowed. His mind had started to race. "But what about the weapon? What about what we found?"

The Algaroth sighed. "Unless we can locate Croll Tan's device before the Admiral arrives, I'm afraid there's nothing we can do."

Damien went slack-jawed.

In response, the Algaroth bowed his head, resigned, and saw Caleb out without another word.

"Are you ready?" Gwen stood over him with a drip line.

"For what?"

Her eyes twinkled and she smiled. "Your last surgery."

"I thought we were done!" he moaned.

She laughed. "It's just the last touches to the grafts, that's all." Her look turned curious and she seemed to be wrestling with something.

"What?"

"Damien," she said slowly. "There is one other thing we could do while you're here…"

He frowned. "What thing?"

"Your arms," she said softly. "The scars. We…could clear up your arms if you like."

He was taken aback. "Oh." The thought had never occurred to him to wipe away the scars. "You can do that?"

"Of course. It'd take some extra time given how extensive they are, but it could be done, tonight even."

He thought on it. He'd had rough-skinned arms since he was nine years old. The blood he'd lost in the hollow had been his first mark as an Elemental. It had carried him through his whole life, kept him an outsider and afraid to ever wear a short-sleeved shirt or go to the beach. They had been a perpetual fear forever, but they'd been something he learned to live with as much as a bad mole or an unsightly deformity. The word 'hate' had never come to mind surrounding them, but maybe it had just always been something more vague.

Yet, even as he thought through what it would be like to live without them, to not always have to cover his arms, he knew he could never lose them. They *were* a mark of who he was, and that was never going to change. The scars on his arms told a story; just like every scar anywhere had a story attached to it. Whether it be a grisly drag across a man's face, a bear claw swiping a tree, or a broken rock in the ocean from some unknown impact. How things appeared reflected much of what they were without any need to dig, and Damien, after the journey he'd eased himself into, knew that wiping them out was wrong.

Finally he said, "Thanks but...I think I'll leave them."

She nodded. "I understand."

A few minutes later, as she removed the IV line and she watched Damien's eyes flutter shut, she whispered, "You're a brave, brave man," and then she wheeled him into surgery.

CHAPTER TWENTY SEVEN

On the Beach, Less the Strangers

Waves lapped at the shoreline, the sound of birds filled the air beyond the rustle of trees, the sand crunched soft and white under bare feet, and Damien smelled the cool April breeze. A thunderstorm was brewing on the western horizon, but the sun still shone above the far clouds over the treeline to the west. His wrist was repaired, his spine was wrapped in a support roll, and he was walking—stiffly, but walking nonetheless. "How did Amun-Nūr find this place?"

Gwen had forsaken her labcoat for only the second time since he'd known her. She wore a dark green tank top and tattered navy Capris. She had even left her glasses beneath the island and had let her hair down. It flowed down to her shoulders in brilliant red streams, blowing behind her in the wind. "One of the original members of Amun-Nūr found it," she answered. She walked beside him just between the dry sand and the incoming tide so that each wave washed over her bare lower calves and toes. She gave her girlish little giggle every time, and Damien couldn't help but find it adorable. "He found it doing a volcanic survey of Earth," she continued. "But he died long before anyone from Argyle and Delmorra made it here, so I never knew him." She hopped onto a rock and balanced there until a wave pushed her off.

Damien's body hurt, he was stiff, and he felt a little groggy from the drugs still fading from his system, but the endless cobalt sky and open air made him feel more alive than he had in a long, *long* time. He was glad Gwen had convinced both Morgan and Satolin that they needed to come out here to help him recover today, before Baroda arrived this evening. "What happened?"

Gwen's pace became a bit somber. "It was during the Incursion War. The Rauth got him."

The air threatened to chill around him, but Damien refused to let it. He hadn't heard the name of the *other* alien species humanity had fought for so long—a species not of The Collective—in years. "I'm surprised Sato wouldn't want to honor him somewhere," he pondered. "Like in the Atrium?"

She shrugged and her crimson curls bobbed. "Satolin has a portrait of them together somewhere, I think in his quarters, but it doesn't often come up. He was an artist and a friend." She glanced his way. "Why do you ask?"

"Just wondering."

They kept walking, and soon the waves lapped up at Damien's feet as the tide came in. He was ready to move up the beach a bit and out of the water as he waited for the next wave, but it didn't come. Limping along, he looked over to see Gwen's freckled, contented face keeping pace with his own. Her eyes were closed and her hand was outstretched towards the sea. The ocean water was kept at bay where her hand held, and the waves couldn't touch them. As he watched, her delicate hand drifted through the breeze, dancing and turning, and the water played along, following the Water Elemental's movements in a hypnotic spectacle.

He admired the water for some time, until his gaze wandered to her hand, up her pale arm, and then to her lovely form. Damien had never thought much on a 'type' for what kind of woman would attract him, but Gwen's slender frame, carefree hips, and delicate curves were more than enough to make his mouth go a little dry. His heart fluttered a bit, and he looked away as she started to hum sweetly to the open air. Damien didn't even notice the powered tingling coming off her soft, rosy skin.

"What's it like to be an Elemental?" he asked after awhile.

Gwen kept moving her hand, but the movement slowed. Her humming faded away into nothing, and her smile flickered. Finally, the languid rhythm of the waves was reclaimed by the Moon's tide.

"Gwen?"

She looked at him with those beautiful green eyes—because there was no doubt in him anywhere that they *were* beautiful—and her smile finally faded. "It's awful."

He frowned. "Why?"

She flicked her toes at the sand and watched the tufts of it fly ahead. "Because we're just like any other freak of nature."

They kept walking, Damien waited patiently, as she'd done countless times with him.

She sighed. "We're shunned and feared at first, and then loved when we prove ourselves to the world that we're *good* and not horrible people." Her hand went out and the water responded again. A spray of droplets came to hover over her fingers, coalescing and sparkling as the sun began its descent for the day. "Living as that kind of person is one thing, but *knowing* that the thing in your body that you can't explain, that *everyone* thinks is so extreme but they all *agree* is an article of change one way or another?" She took a breath. "I...I hate it."

Damien looked towards the stands of tropical foliage that marked the end of Amun-Nūr's sloping beach. He spotted sunlight beaming into the undergrowth amidst the occasional flicker of life, wondering what to say to that.

"I'm sorry," she said. "That's not the answer you wanted."

He looked back at her. "No, no it's okay. I just, I don't think we're like any other freak," he said.

Her face became cautiously curious.

He chewed on his answer. "I fell in love with it."

"How?"

His neck twinged and he stopped his hand a centimeter from it, remembering her warning about scratching. "Because...I'm not alone with it."

She brushed strands of her crimson hair behind her ears. "You've never told it to me like that."

He shrugged. "I've...never thought of it that way until now."

She nodded as if affirming something to herself, and they went on.

"I was thinking," he said. "The other day, when I asked about everyone suddenly being okay with me? I…well I thought more about it."

"And?"

"And I guess," he sighed. *Just say it.* "I don't know why they're looking up to me. I feel like I fucked up pretty bad these last few months."

Gwen sighed and stopped, crossing her arms. "People are hard to gauge, Damien. Know what I've seen though? Using you as an example?" He assented. She continued, "You spent the last few months having some pretty extensive bouts of being sullen and broken—and that's *okay*," she added at his face. "You could've been *much* worse, I'm sure!" She smiled. "We all need time to ourselves, but there's a point when we don't, and how you've applied yourself here? When you decided to go out and not think about everything that's happened to you, and just *DO?*" She ducked towards his plummeting chin and forced his gaze to follow her back upright. "You've been a hero, and I don't use that little word lightly."

Satolin talked to you, didn't he? "But—"

"No buts!" Even without her glasses, her eyes still sparked with authority. "Hero. *That's* what's made a difference. You have a streak of selflessness." She held his gaze for a moment that expanded outward, and Damien felt his tongue go dry again as he watched her brilliant eyes, so steady as they looked into his shifting ones. After a small eternity that he was close to being lost in, she looked away. "That's all the affirmation you're going to get from me today, Elemental." She laughed lightly. "Come on. We're out here for therapy." She took his hand long enough to get him moving, and he let her.

Soon the waters pushed them higher on the beach, Gwen played with the ocean spray, and the sun finally cast a shadow on them through the canopy of trees on their left. To the north and east was all water as they approached the northernmost tip of the island. Sunlight beckoned ahead.

"You know something," he said, thinking of a certain someone he'd met the day before. "I've always wanted a sword. I always thought that would be…special."

Her single peal of laughter was sweet and insulting at the same time. "Would you mean like a…'saber of dark' or something?"

He smirked. "I would *love* that, but I don't have a damn clue how to go about making one. I just remember reading about some weapons like that in pre-war stories, though I think they were sabers made of light or something…I can't really remember. I remember it was legendary stuff though of heroes and villains, good and evil, love and loss, all that."

She laughed, and it was such a lovely sound that Damien realized he wasn't sure if he'd ever really heard her do it before now.

"Oh don't look at me like that," she grinned. "Maybe we can figure something out for you sometime."

"Yeah, maybe." He picked a stone out of the sand between his toes and tried to toss it away. He stumbled and almost fell.

Gwen snickered behind her hand. "You're a fascinating creature, Mr. Vilan."

"Why?" he grumbled, recovering.

She stopped just beyond the border of the treeline on the north end of the island, and the sun lit her red hair like fire. She drank it in. "You just are. Now come into the light. I'll be happy to tell the Prohka that that's all you really needed. It's where you belong anyways, even if you *are* Darkness embodied." She held out her hand.

He let her bring him into the sunlight, and he reveled in the warmth of the world at the edge of land, at the end of the day. He let it all caress his healing body. They stood there a long time, not talking, watching the thunderstorm broil its way towards them, dark and omnipresent. Soon, distant booms of thunder rolled over them, the sunlight filtered behind clouds, and a cold wind kicked up, but even as the beach took on a stormy cast, there was nothing to mar the moment.

"Thank you, Gwen," he said, sitting next to her with his elbows propped on his knees and still looking at the overcast sky. "I…you've done so much for me since I got here. I—"

"Shh," she said, and cupped his face so she could kiss his cheek, rolling onto her hips to do it. "It's what I'm here for."

He blushed and mumbled. She just smiled at him.

While nothing could mar that afternoon they shared, many things could cut it short. As the two of them were lost in thought, standing on that beach together, they lost track of time. So much so that when a thunderclap lit the evening, startling them both to see the storm was practically on top of them, they decided it was time to bolt.

"Come on," she said loudly, scrambling to her feet. "The Admiral will be here soon, we need to get back inside!"

Damien agreed, and they ran. He moved as fast as he could, trying to maintain control of his breathing as his body shrieked that he shouldn't be doing this. They made it down the beach and around the boulders where a narrowly winding secret path took them to the cliff face that hid Amun-Nūr's surface shaft. Before they were halfway up though, they could see the dark curtain of rain closing fast, and they weren't far enough along to avoid it. They kept moving, and the curtain descended over them as smoothly as an encore at the theater. They were drenched in seconds but were near the top of the cliff, and they made it inside before the torrent took the island. The two of them made it into the elevator, shivering and wet, and Gwen started the old lift's descent into the ground.

They stood barely a pace from each other, shivering and laughing despite themselves but…neither moved to warm the other as they went down. In truth, Damien would spend many nights afterwards wondering how a rained out afternoon on the beach might have gone differently with her, if he should have done something, kissed her, *anything*, but the afternoon ended with a spark in his chest that hadn't been there before, and he didn't quite know what to do with it.

What he didn't know, was that Gwen would run a similar train of thought for a long time after just the same, wondering at the butterflies that filled her stomach whenever she thought of him.

∞   ∞   ∞

Far below the beach, Damien and Gwen entered the Long Atrium's top floor from the airlock to the surface, deep in discussion. Damien had remembered on the way down what Satolin had said about how they needed a way to find Croll Tan's weapon before Baroda arrived, and an idea had come to him like a bolt of lightning.

"Our hacking rig," he breathed as he waited for the airlock to close. "The rig! Holy shit, the *rig!*"

"What about it?" Gwen's flaming red hair hung wet and pasted to her brow and down her neck. There were puddles of water on the floor.

"Choss!" he exclaimed. "Choss Chosska's working on cracking it! We could use it! If he's done with whatever he's doing, Leo could use it to break into The Collective's network and figure out what the hell Croll Tan is up to! Do you know if he's made any progress?!" Excitement flooded him at the idea, never mind that it had taken so long to connect the dots.

"I-I'm not sure," she stuttered, but a wondering gleam had come to her eyes too.

They spent a few hurried minutes jabbering about if it were possible, weighing how long they had before Baroda arrived, and what they might need. Finally, the beginnings of a plan held between them, they bolted into the Atrium, drawing eyebrow-raising looks at how wet they were. Damien made a beeline to the elevators for Argyle Wing, and Gwen pelted to Satolin's personal office on the fifth floor.

A compounding painful sprint later, Damien practically fell through the door to the Omniscopic Studies lab, clutching his spine and gasping. "Cho—*Choss!*" he heaved. "Choss! Are you in here?" The lab was as dark as it had been when he first came, and looked almost unchanged. Rows of desks sprawled out in front of them, covered in chaotic experiments. To his left, the vats hiding the toxic substances gave off an almost imperceptibly luminescent glow.

"Damien-apprentice-man. You back," came Choss Chosska's voice from the second level.

Damien winced. He was pretty sure some of his bandages had come loose. "Yeah! Yeah, listen, I wanted to know if you'd made any progress on the hacking rig!"

"Rig? What for?"

Damien looked for the little alien, but he couldn't see him. "Because I think we can use it to figure out—*ah*—what Croll Tan's weapon is!" He found the nearest chair and collapsed into it, his breathing coming under control. *One of these days you need to start running or something.* He swatted the thought like a fly.

Choss didn't answer.

"Hello?"

"Why need my help?"

Damien frowned. "What do you mean?"

"I very busy. Lot's to do, research to run, work to accomplish. Why need my help?"

As Choss's strange language filtered through his aural implant, Damien finally figured out where he'd heard it before: it was the same language that Operator Ophelia spoke, but more importantly: it was Turk "Bar" Mburu's first language, and that's why both of them had sounded so familiar! It was Swahili. Damien became lost in thought as his heart finally slowed, remembering how nervous Ophelia had been delivering her report on the Himalayas. It made him think about why Choss had dismissed him last time, and it brought some of Bar's last words to mind:

"XenoCon," Von had said.

Bar had looked at us confused. "The campus? That is not so far away...but you have dangerous islets between here and there."

"We know," I said. "And tonight will be exceptionally so."

Bar had figured it out then. "You bring the gear to us because you think you will not return tonight. You think the Avos are after your box."

Shell had looked at us funny. "Why did you bring it all here?"

"For the good company," said Von.

Damien swallowed at the memory. *You think you will not return tonight.*

He hadn't been afraid to die that night because he'd just been *doing.* He, Von, and Leo, the three of them, they'd just been doing what needed to be done. No muss, no fuss, only the work. *And Choss let me go because he told me I was nervous about something. Was that just me?*

"You are thinking lots now." Choss interrupted his dialogue.

Damien looked up, and he saw two beady golden eyes bobbing in the air. The Algaroth was hanging upside down over the second-level walkway. Damien couldn't help but snort at the sight.

"Funny?"

The smile stayed. "Why are you hanging?"

"Gravity."

"What?"

"Gravity takes blood to brain. Sometimes good to think, sometimes good for nap."

"Oh," Damien itched his nose, recognizing what else needed to happen here. "Well I ah, I need your help but...I wanted to apologize for what happened last time, with the tablets?"

"Why?"

Damien frowned. "Why apologize? Because I made a mess? I cracked the vat with that hybrid virus stuff, from Jupiter?"

Choss cocked his head. "Apology's no good. Not care about that here."

Damien had forgotten how blunt the alien was. He blinked, maintaining his calm. "Maybe not for you, but it matters to me. I wanted to tell you that I was sorry."

Choss shut his eyes. "Okay."

They waited in silence. Damien assumed the alien was going to say more.

"Are you going to say?"

"What?"

"You here to say human-sorry? You not say 'sorry'. Not work if not said."

"Oh... I thought I did... But-but I am! I'm sorry. I *am* sorry. Truly."

His odd exercise complete, Choss curled up and over the railing and flipped to his feet in one fluid motion. "You offer, I prompt, *then* you say? No good. Apology come before asked to apologize."

Damien faltered. "But I need your help!"

Choss, barefoot as always, came *tink-tink-tinking* down the ladder. "You come to *help* first time. You made mess, then left."

Damien was silent as the little alien approached. He was about to apologize again when Choss stopped, blinking at him. "What?"

"You different."

"How so?"

Choss came closer, scrutinizing him. "You...fixed."

Damien couldn't help but pull back as the alien's inquisitive snout was thrust in his face. Choss's turquoise hide glistened, smelling like sour, milky alien sweat. "What does that mean?"

The dwarf took him in with a single sweeping look. "You not nervous anymore."

Damien froze. "How can you tell?"

"I tell. You better. You different. Nervous about other things still, not nervous here. That good. No nervous in Scopic lab."

"You think so?"

Choss pulled back to an appropriate distance. "Don't think it. *See* it. You stand taller. Eyes glow brighter, stronger. You got scars for being stupid. Scars teach things. You learned scars' lesson. Curious now. You curious now?"

Damien swallowed and nodded, perturbed by the alien's flawless observations. "Yes."

Choss turned and *tink-tink-tinked* his way around the pillar. "Okay. You say you work here *now*, not before."

So, just like that, Damien settled at his first vocation. *I guess I'll have to tell Gwen I can't go to Personal Warfare.* He grinned and started after Choss. "What about the rig?"

"Hacking rig? I retrieving; go sit. We work."

"We only have a few hours!" he shouted, coming around the corner to see the alien's research fort-ring still intact. A light strip came on beyond what he had originally thought was the wall of the lab, but was actually a door to a tall corridor stacked with large drawers on both sides, like deposit boxes. Choss was already halfway up a ladder to one drawer in particular. "Choss?"

"I hear you!" the alien snapped. "Only hours! Yes, know!" He skittered down the ladder with a small polyplastic crate in-hand. He handed it to Damien. Inside, held on a stand affixed to the bottom of the crate, was their hacking rig. Choss Chosska looked at him with his curious little golden eyes that, until then, Damien had failed to notice had lemon-yellow streaks in them, almost invisible in the gold. "Good?"

"Yeah," Damien marveled. "We're good." Setting the crate down on a workbench, he carefully pulled the rig out. *This is it; this is how we figure it out.*

"You say hours?" Choss plied. "How many?"

Damien shrugged. "I don't know. Two, maybe three?"

Choss grinned a devilish little lizard grin. "Oh, that plenty. We need not even one. Agreed?" but it wasn't Damien who he posed the question to.

One of the desktops around Choss's research fort flickered to life, and none other than Arthur Leonardo appeared in his finest suit and tie, straightening his cufflinks. "Not even one," he cooed, oozing debonair.

A broad smile broke Damien's face. "*Leo!* What're you doing here?"

Leo winked affably. "You might have *built* the rig, my dear Damien, but 'twas *I* who pr-r-r-ogrammed it!" he flourished, rolling his R's. He twirled his hands above his head and a pair of white satin conductor's gloves appeared over them. "This *jive* fellow Ka Chosska and I have been working out the wee kinks in it for some weeks now!"

Excitement blossomed in Damien's chest. "How?!"

Choss took the rig from Damien's arms. "Come. We show you. Confident-Damien-Elemental *built* it, after all."

Leo laughed.

With a wide grin and a burning determination, Damien followed.

∞   ∞   ∞

Not even one hour later, Damien shot out of the Omniscopic Studies lab, hacking rig in arm and brain buzzing. He'd called Gwen to tell Satolin to meet him at the command wheel urgently. Her excitement and relief had been palpable through the comm, and she promised they'd be there. But, Damien was halfway past the Argyle-Delmorra junction to the Long Atrium when someone called his name.

"Vilan!"

559

Screeching to a halt, he wrenched around too quick and his neck spasmed. He hissed as his body went rigid, the sudden halt staggering him against the wall. He didn't want to know how badly his bandages had become torn in the past few hours.

"Vilan!" they shouted again.

He looked around the corner of the huge Argyle-Delmorra-S.E.H.A. motif just in time to see her marching towards him from Delmorra Wing. His stomach dropped.

It was Huxley.

Oh. I—I—what do I do? What the hell do I do? He was rooted in place, wordless, cradling his hacking rig like he had cradled his backpack when he first met her. She was dressed in an Amun-Nūr captain's flight suit—green and brown—and she looked livid. There also seemed to be people following her wearing similar flight suits but theirs were uniform tan.

"*You,*" she snapped, pointing. "OOH I'm glad I caught you on your feet! You take a long fucking time to get patched up you know that? You little shit?"

Damien stuttered. With her hair pulled back in a ponytail that disappeared down her back, Huxley was just as striking as she'd looked when she ripped off her helmet onboard the Blackwing and displayed her dirt-flecked cheeks and icy blue eyes. "I—I'm sorry it…wasn't convenient? I've had a bit of a rough—"

"Shut up." And just like that, her lips were clasped to his. He couldn't move. She gave a fiery whimper as they locked while she held his face in an iron vice. For such a powerful woman, her embrace was soft and her teeth were delicate as they nibbled at his bottom lip. She pulled back with an audible *pop*. "*That's* for still being alive," she whispered.

"Ahh—okay! That's," he swallowed. "That's…I mean—"

WHAP.

Being someone who clearly held some distaste for an open hand, the impact of Huxley's second punch was harder than the first time. He stumbled into the wall again and his neck sparked with pain. *Thwunk*, went his skull. His skin grafts pulled and for a moment he thought they'd torn.

He didn't hear anyone screeching though so he assumed not, and he didn't taste blood this time, which was nice.

"*That* was for almost getting my ship shot the fuck down. TWICE."

With the wind knocked out of him, he barely managed half a word before she kissed him again, longer this time. "And *that*," she whispered, pulling him close. "Is for telling everyone how *good* I was at saving your ass. *Twice*." She bit his lip. "It seems to be a special number with you," and her eyes glittered, so close to his. She smelled faintly of coolant and leather.

He stayed there, reeling as she pulled away. People walked past with their heads resolutely downturned or openly staring. She slapped his cheek sweetly—thankfully on his uninjured side. "You didn't mention that you were so *interesting* before." She looked him up and down with a hand on her hip. "Elemental, huh? Wonder how that works…" Her finger traced its way along his jaw, and she wiggled her pinky at him as she pulled away.

Damien was then acutely aware of the four people standing a few paces away, watching the exchange with uncomfortable intensity. "Uhh…"

She followed his gaze and smirked. "Oh! Sorry, was I embarrassing you?" The smirk left her mouth to fill her eyes instead as she turned to include the group. "Don't be rude now," she chided, "*Introduce yourself.*"

Damien waved feebly, an oddly pained flutter in his chest with Gwen's face on it. "I'm Damien." *I've gotta get out of here.*

"Good. *These* are the finest pilots from the Istanbul air brigades. I stole them," she proclaimed proudly, daring him to contradict her. "Here we have Airman Emilio Silantos, Airmatron Mawaddah Osman, Technical Sergeant Aliana Lidiza, and Senior Airman Oman Khatib al-Kimyai." The four stood at attention, eyes straight ahead…except Damien saw the tough looking bearded one—Oman—and the blonde girl with the light skin—Aliana—steal a glance his way.

Huxley laughed at her own jokes and finally saw the rig in Damien's arms. "Still running packages, hmm?" She leaned in again. "You need something better for your time." Then, before he could say he needed to leave, she whistled at her pilots and walked away, head held high. "I'll see you soon, Dark boy!" She laughed high and full as she hummed her way away.

He watched her go, hand held to where she'd hit him. "Damn…" he muttered, and stumbled back to life, hoping he could get to the wheel before Baroda showed up and without any more distractions.

CHAPTER TWENTY EIGHT

A Rig to Remember

"We know how to find the weapon!" Damien blurted, "We know how to find the weapon!" Jogging the last meters into the command wedge, his face, wrist, spine, lungs, and pretty much everything else stung badly. As he came the last paces to the wheel though, he slowed, his words choked, and he stopped cold.

Arrayed around the command wedge was an impressive collection of people. Prohka Daeduras Satolin, Commander Jessop Morgan, Doctor Gwen Whalen, and Caleb were standing around the war table contemplating a patchy map of Eurasia. Javier, Von, Koro Loss, and Sergeant Declan were on the landing beneath the Conduit clock eyeing the leaders and new Elemental from above and behind. Reuben was standing off to the side alone. A full-sized Leo was wandering around a mannequin of himself on his plinth, armed with the tools of a fashionista, complete with sewing pins sticking out of his teeth; he was stretching an odd new suit over the mannequin. Joval Tosh, Captain Romi, Kel, Nisha, Captain Fagin, Xiu Su-jin, most of the surviving researchers and soldiers from Aurora, and a swath more whom Damien was slowly coming to know, were spread out amidst the working technicians in the wheel. Finally, the two gentlemen who had been—until Damien burst in—maintaining center-stage stopped to scrutinize him. Agent John Bunting of SIO stood tall, spidery, and pale, his eyes hidden behind his wraparound sunglasses. The other was Lunar Admiral Antonio Baroda, resplendent in his black-and-silver uniform and looking none too pleased.

As Damien came sweeping past the light traffic in and out of the wheel, nearly everyone's conversations died off to focus on him. He felt

563

his third cry of "I know how to find the weapon" die off in his throat, replaced by a mousy little squeak.

"Such has been the talk," said Admiral Baroda, turning resolutely neutral. "It's good to see you, son."

Flushed, Damien worked his mouth, trying to figure out the right thing to say. Thankfully, Satolin saved him from answering.

"Leo filled us in on your plan," the Prohka boomed. "Would you like to share the details?"

Leo popped his lips as he admired the suit on the mannequin. "*Ah! It's glorious, Prohka. Absolutely glorious.*"

Damien caught his breath, held his head high, and walked the last few paces into the wedge, presenting the hacking rig as he did. "This," he pronounced. "The hacking rig that Von, Leo, and I built." Curious and approving mutters drifted around the wedge.

"Yes," said Baroda. "The item that brought you into the Over-Seer's considerable sight."

"Uh, and eventually *here*," Javier added.

Baroda ignored him. "What of it?"

"Admiral, the three of us proved that this rig can hack The Collective's military network," Damien pleaded. "I have to guess that Croll Tan hasn't deployed his weapon yet, right?"

"Correct," Morgan affirmed.

Damien set the rig down on the war table. "Then this is the perfect opportunity to test it." He shared a glance with Von, who was beaming with pride. "On a large scale."

"And how might that be accomplished, Mr. Vilan?" Agent Bunting spoke up, his English accent forever giving him a credible tone.

While they'd been speaking, Leo had stuck two sewing pins into an invisible wall in the confines of his Pip plinth, lifted his mannequin, hung it on the pins, and proceeded to vanish and reappear on the war table sporting his favorite Sherlock Holmes outfit, magnifying glass and all. As Bunting finished his question and before Damien could answer, the AI spoke up. "It's jolly simple, chums!" He tossed his magnifying glass into the air where it defied physics and slowed to a hovering stop. Leo retrieved his calabash pipe from his belt and popped it in his mouth. "Yeh shee, all we really need ish to accshess the Triad!" He blew a perfect white smoke ring. "Mishter Chossh Chosshka and myshelf worked out a way to shync the rig up with McKinley Shtation, where they could ushe it to exshpand the back door I *bravely* inshtalled whilsh*t*," he enunciated the T, "Leo And Company were fleeing the XenoCon campush."

Admiral Baroda looked unconvinced. "That sounds like quite a device, son, but I'm not here today to discuss how best to solve the Over-Seer's threats. I'm here—"

"Why not?" Javier interjected again.

Baroda turned toward the Marine, slowly.

Javier was unfazed. "Since we're all present now, I'm just gonna toss this dumbass elephant out of the room, ya dig?" He jabbed a finger at Baroda. "*You're* here to make a fuss about *us* jumping into this whole Inferno business, right?"

Baroda's lips formed a thin line. "There are more factors involved than that, Estrada. Amun-Nūr disobeyed direct orders to remain uninvolved in this 'Inferno business', and now humanity is paying the price." He met Javier's gaze, and to the Elemental's credit, he looked proudly back, crisp in his new green dress uniform of Amun-Nūr's Marine Corps. "There are consequences to such disobediences that must be upheld." Baroda turned in a slow circle. "Court-martial."

Leo sent another smoke ring through the air. This one held in place in the middle of the war table. "Dear Admiral, must you *really* be reminded that Amun-Nūr is officially a non-military installation?"

Baroda turned to face the AI but to Damien's surprise, Gwen spoke up. "Admiral," she pleaded. "Things could have gone so much worse if we hadn't intervened, and no one would even *know* that the Over-Seer was planning something yet!"

"Doctor, what's happened thus far is—"

"—*Not* about to change," Satolin's voice was a thunderclap over the man. "We are well aware of our actions, but perhaps your points could be withheld for the moment. We nearly lost Damien, we *did* lose over one hundred others, and that says nothing of those across Eurasia, whose death tally continues to climb."

Baroda's thin lips drew thinner. "Prohka, had you not delayed my arrival for nearly two weeks, things might look slightly different." He glanced at Damien. "Vilan stands here in good health, as do the rest of yours who sustained injury. I am not above leniency for severe trauma, had I seen it sooner."

The cold glare that came into Daeduras Satolin's arctic-gold eyes was truly something to behold. "Wounds *were* sustained," he growled. "And I needn't remind you that, in cases of injury over action, medicine supersedes military." He took a long, deep breath, gnashing daggers at the Lunar Admiral. "And if you question my integrity again, you'll find your quarters more than adequate space in which you might peruse your intentions until you depart."

Leo blew another smoke ring into the quiet, this one a light cyan. It hung in the air inside the first.

Satolin moved to the hacking rig as a flush crept up out of Baroda's uniform. "If this device can tell us what Croll Tan is planning, not only would we be fools not to use it, but the aforementioned disobeyed orders should stand to reflect the man who *gave* them, not just those who carried them out."

Satolin couldn't have seen the flash of rage that slipped across the Admiral's face, but from how everyone was standing in the wedge, Damien had a feeling that he and Reuben were the only ones who caught it; no one else could have. He also saw a grim satisfaction cross the Prohka's features, too.

Baroda, neutrality renewed, looked towards the war table, where Leo had just finished his smoke ring sculpture. The pack of hovering shapes had formed a replica of the Monitoring Triad's icon: the upside-down triangle around Earth with the points detached from the shape. "Very well," the Admiral said stiffly. No one moved.

Leo raised an eyebrow at him. "*You* have access to the Triad, Admiral. Can you give it to me? Can I have it? Oh please?"

Baroda straightened his perfectly straight uniform. "Of course." He took prim steps to the table. "However," he stopped. "I would be neglectful if I didn't establish the stakes here."

Satolin looked like he had a retort, but Morgan—thankfully—had the diplomatic hand right now. "Understood, sir. What are they?"

"A rampant office is the *last* thing humanity needs right now. If this hacking rig doesn't work, I must follow through on the protocols and punishments for failing to obey orders. I must cease support of the sect and island of Amun-Nūr, and retract oversight of the security and resources I've allowed you. You understand the necessities for this decisive sort of action?"

"Eh," Caleb remarked dryly from his landing. "They might plead to be offered proper counseling and representation. I would."

Morgan overrode Baroda's response, sparing a hard look at Caleb as he did. "We understand, sir."

"Thank you, Commander."

Damien then held his breath as the Admiral turned to the table, but it was Leo's turn to interrupt.

"Actually," the AI said. Baroda flinched. "There's another stake that needs to be set."

"Which is?"

Leo lowered his pipe and turned his gaze first towards Damien, and then towards Von. Damien held himself steady, already having discussed what Leo was going to say, but Von didn't know yet. Leo looked sadly between the two of them before turning back to the majority of the wedge. "Doing this will break the rig," he admitted. "The little thing's too young to withstand this kind of mission on its own." A simulacra of their hacking rig appeared in the AI's arms and he ran his hands over it like one would a puppy. "If we had more time to play, we might be able to stabilize or duplicate the device, but it took a certain amount of, ah…" Leo balked like the next word was choking him. "*Luck*, to get it working in the first place."

Damien felt a surge of gratitude for his companion. It wasn't easy for an artificial construct to admit the existence of luck.

"The details are *far* too complicated for you, sir," Leo went on, eliciting a few muffled sniggers at the Admiral's expense. "But we just need to be clear—" he held out the projected rig and to everyone's great surprise, the thing suddenly came to life, wagged a cord that might have been a tail, and *barked*. Everyone jumped. "—we have to kill wittle Mr. Hackerbutts for this to work." To further the uncomfortableness, Leo tossed the false dog hacking rig into the air, where it yipped once, and then exploded in a shower of teal cubits. "Just needed to make sure everyone knows how *intense* this is gonna get," Leo sniffed and wiped a tear from his face with a handkerchief, which caught fire as he dropped it. "He was so beautiful."

Damien was the first to recover from the odd scene, and he just caught Admiral Baroda popping his jaw closed from dumbfounded gaping at the AI. He smirked privately. *Try arguing with THAT for four years and then maybe you can think about going into politics.*

Commander Morgan, who seemed to have taken on the role of mediator, also recovered quickly. "Are there any other stakes before we start this process?"

No objections were raised.

"Very good. Admiral, if you would?"

Baroda took an extra split-second to shake off Leo's display before leaning over the war table. A moment later, the Triad's *real* icon solidified inside Leo's smoky one, scattering the projected one into wisps.

While they waited, Satolin motioned to Koro Loss, and the Algaroth stepped forward.

"Alright, here is what we know and can guess regarding the Over-Seer's weapon," crowed the squad leader in Portuguese. Leo brought up displays and data collected from the village while Loss briefed the wedge. "The village in the Himalayas was most likely a testing ground for Collective weapons. We don't know how long ago they captured it, but it was the perfect cover once they set up that transmitter." Damien flinched as images of the frozen corpses appeared. He swallowed. "Aurora's theory," Loss went on, "is that it wasn't just any testing ground; it was for the Over-Seer's sensitive arsenal." More images showed up, depicting the fazed victims, as well as the many others who'd been mutilated with more creative methods. "These are the forensics Aurora recovered."

Images of the Nuke casing, the transmitter array, the Mag Fury cradle, more bodies, and the tracks all came up together, complete with wireframe reconstructions of the Fury and the Nuke—had they been intact. A low buzz filled the wedge as quips of discussion broke out. On the war table, the Triad icon spun faster. It was Damien's first time scrutinizing the odd tracks, so he was sure to look at them closely. They were wide, deep gouges in the snow, staggered in an interlocking pattern that could have been a giant on skis pushing poles through the powder, or an enormous predator rocketing low to the ground, churning the drifts out behind it as each foot came down.

"Those tracks are our key," Morgan spoke up. "We don't believe they were made by any new vehicle, so come on, people!" he clapped at them, "*What* made them?!"

"Couldn't Leo figure it out?" someone hollered from near the hub of the wheel.

Leo turned, stroking his smooth chin. "Why, yes! If anyone had been willing to take molds from the tracks of *every* set of alien hardware *ever to land* on our little globe, I then of *course* could find it!" He cocked his head. "But no *advanced intelligence* organic folk like your *fine* selves thought it would be important though, so no, I can't." Leo turned away, huffing melodramatically. "It's through no fault of my own!" He took another puff of his pipe.

"There aren't many vehicles they have that could make tracks that big," said Loss.

"What about an Iceberg?" someone offered.

"That already *is* a weapon!" someone countered.

"It could have been modified!" the first retorted, and the argument grew from there while they waited for the Triad.

As more voices started to join the chorus though, Damien noticed a few people actually *thinking* about what it could be, and he joined them. *The Nuke, the Fury, the tracks, the snow…* but something occurred to him. They were missing a critical component. *My blood.* "Oh shit," he breathed.

The whole thing had been an ambush, they had guessed that beforehand, but even being prepared hadn't been enough to save them from it. Why had they been ambushed though? Why had the Over-Seer *himself* been lying in wait?

Because he needed me.

Why did he need you? another voice came up.

Because of what I can do.

And what is that, exactly?

...I can make black holes, singularities.

Reuben's voice came to mind. *And why could Croll Tan have a use for that?*

Finally, it clicked. He didn't want to believe it, but it couldn't be anything else. The last piece fell into place. Comprehension dawned on Damien, and as if it were waiting for him or someone to make the connection, the Triad icon chimed loudly, silencing the wedge.

"I know what the weapon is," he uttered into the quiet, turning a couple of heads just as a feed appeared next to the Conduit clock. It was the grizzled operator in the cold gray room at McKinley Station. A picture-in-picture appeared, showing a copy-Leo sitting with a headset. Apparently, that was the feed that McKinley could currently view.

"This is Arthur Leonardo, resident AI comm officer for the island of Amun-Nūr, how may I direct your call?"

The tired operator frowned. *"McKinley Station here. We received Admiralty clearance for Triad access? You're the operator for Amun Command, I thought?"*

"Yes sir, you did," answered copy-Leo from the screen. *"We had some recent trouble in frozen paradise so we enlisted the help of one Lunar Admiral Baroda. We thought you might be able to help too!"* The copy-Leo vanished, revealing the full command wedge and Leo standing on the war table.

The operator looked surprised at seeing so many people. He looked at another monitor. *"Amun Command, is this...in regards to that hacking rig you had one of yours build?"*

Satolin stepped up. "McKinley, we can confirm about the rig, but the credit doesn't go to us."

"*Who should we thank, then?*"

The Prohka indicated Damien, Von, and Leo. "These three."

Damien's pulse was racing. *I know what the weapon is. I know what it is.*

The operator's tired eyes showed a flicker of curiosity as he looked between them. He scratched his thick, graying beard. "*Well, I don't know what put you three to cobbling that rig together, but I've spoken to your AI, and in fact...*" he rolled his chair off-screen, typed something, and rolled back, protocol reinstated. "*In fact, we just received telemetry from it. Amun Command, I am confirming uplink of the hacking rig, we're syncing it now.*"

"What?" Baroda exclaimed.

"Leo?" Morgan snapped, "Did you already—"

"Choss and I installed it," Damien interrupted, pointing at the rig, where the new component had just blipped to life. "Just now. It needed a long-range transmitter for McKinley to get access...and it's what will probably fry the rig." He perked up and glanced towards the operator, who was fixated on him. "But there's more..." he stumbled under the operator's surprisingly scrutinous gaze. "I, I know what the weapon is."

As all eyes turned to him, Damien felt a sudden spit of nerves. He wasn't sure if he could really do this. *Is it really what you think it is? Oh shit, what if it isn't? What if it isn't? He took your blood, if he sets that weapon off it'll be your fault! It'll be the quake all over again.*

"Damien?" said the Prohka, not unkindly. "What's the weapon?"

Time slowed as Damien looked up.

More than sixty people were watching him. He could feel their gazes searching this pale, dark-haired, bandaged man who had screwed up so many times in his life that he sometimes genuinely wondered if he was qualified to put pants on in the morning. He felt cold and sweaty, but for the first time, every person in the room was staring at him with something he'd never seen. They were staring at him with hope. Wonder, hope, and curiosity were etched into their eyes; from Gwen's glistening appraisal, to

Leo's admiring grin, to Loss's grateful nodding, all the way to the strange operator on the wall whose tired features continued to fixate on him. Even less friendly faces were turned his way, like the new Elemental, Caleb, who looked guarded but listening, and even Reuben Björn, whose disdain still filtered into his features, was locked on the Elemental of Darkness, looking for a flicker of light.

Damien swallowed into the silence, taking in their expectant wonderings, and he started talking. He wasn't really aware of it, because another feed of thought had come to life in the back of his mind. It was born of all that had happened these past months, fueled by his trauma, his recovery, and the family that was Amun-Nūr who had helped him through it. "I think the weapon is some sort of…suppression device."

When no one stopped him, the courage came at long last to drive on, and drive on he did.

"Whatever the weapon is," he began, "it needs power to function." He pointed at the projection of the overturned reactor cradle. "A Mag Fury is a good source of power."

"What about the Nuke?" Javier plied.

In that rear feed, Damien thought about how, for as long as he could remember, he had been an outsider. He had followed his parents as they pampered his brother growing up—which hadn't been Von's fault—while he had been awkward around other children. He had always found the company of adults preferable, but after the hollow he had been isolated by more than just introversion. Thinking of his recent acceptance of his scarred arms, he knew he'd made that his strength, but he hadn't really been given a choice. He and Von had lived for seven years on their own, and Damien knew that had they not been a keen and observant pair, they never would have survived.

He looked at Reuben, thinking of how the man had pushed for him to figure it out…and wondering why he hadn't just *told* him. "The Nuke is the goal," he said, noting an immediate reaction from the McKinley man, who showed recognition and went into a furious frenzy across the monitors they couldn't see. "The village wasn't some hostage location that they dropped a Nuke on, or some place where they were going up *against* one…they were testing Tan's weapon *on* a Nuke." The wedge was silent. "They were trying to contain it."

In the brief pause, Damien saw the hacking rig's lights flicker. *McKinley must be taking hold of it*, he thought, glancing at the operator. "I think Tan needed my blood to finish his weapon because…because I can make black holes. The *reason* he needed to do that is to get around the Nukes. After all, the only way The Collective can maneuver us into checkmate is by getting rid of the Final Option." His heart was thundering away. "If we don't have that, he never has to lose another soul. He could just pull everything back to Solaroth and wait for the next Fleet, and when they got here, they'd bomb us all away and leave the planet unscarred."

Recognition began sparking across the wheel. Gwen's jaw hung open. "So his weapon—"

"Is some kind of…prototype black hole generator," Damien finished. "I think."

Though no one looked away from him, the mood shifted quickly. Uncertain glances were traded all around, nervous breathing, tense shoulders—which were made tangibly felt through the wave of static coming off the Algaroth in the room—but no one had directed their fear at him. They were looking for him to say more in fact. They *wanted* him to say more.

"But what about the blast crater," asked one of the Aurora techs. *Rawlen, I think*. "The whole valley had that snow bowl. Was that a Nuke?"

Damien remembered asking the same question just before the ambush. "I don't think so." He pondered on it as he watched the McKinley operator work furiously over other screens that faced away from the camera. "If it had, and his weapon didn't work? It would've leveled everything. It would've leveled the Himalayas."

"So what was it?"

Damien shrugged, and the feed flickered through more thoughts. It occurred to him then that the last few months had been more than just some hiccup in his life, like the first time you wrecked your car or your first broken heart. Everything he had known, everything he'd been, everything he'd been *comfortable* with—even as it was awkward to admit to having *been* comfortable with the life he and his brother had shared in the bunker—had been uprooted. Four years was a long time to adjust to a certain way of living, and when Shellack and the other Avos had chased him from his home (for which he felt grim justice at the irony that Croll Tan's order for the Avos to capture him and then destroy Seattle had ultimately allowed for Damien's escape) everything had been thrown up in the air. He hadn't been able to settle since then, and as he continued explaining what he'd pieced together, he realized he had been nuts to think that a few days or even a few weeks could have possibly been enough for him to come back together. "I don't know what the blast was," he answered, "but I don't think it's what's important."

He took a step towards the war table and pointed at the projections. "I think the bodies were proof that Tan's been working on this for a long time. I think the transmitter was recent, because when he realized that he couldn't replicate what I could do, he needed to lure me—*us*—out, and that's why I think there was a Nuke casing in the valley: because he might have had a whole Nuke, or he might have had a piece, but regardless, the weapon wasn't doing what it was supposed to." He looked down at his hands, "And that was…why he took my blood."

"So, how would the weapon suppress the explosion?" asked a soldier from Aurora.

Damien took a deep breath, thinking on his healing body, thinking about what Tan had done, and unwittingly, something bubbled to the surface. Something came to mind then that he had never thought about before: He hadn't caused the earthquake that broke the Islets, nor had it been the planet shivering its crust along the mantle. It had been Croll Tan. When the Over-Seer was fighting to gain a foothold on the North American west coast, Tan had used a one-shot weapon that was later called a "fault ram" to shatter the San Andreas Fault, devastating the Americas. The earthquake had been a direct result of *that* incident, and so how could it have been *Damien's* fault that his parents died?

And so, as he chewed on his answer about Croll Tan's black hole weapon, a bolt of lightning shot through his brain; a jolt that couldn't possibly have come without such hindsight.

I didn't kill my parents.

A tentative chill crept through him. Was it possible? He wondered. *No. No,* he blinked hard. "I, I think the weapon…" he trailed off with all eyes on him.

"Damien?"

No. He knew the truth of what he'd done. He *had* killed his parents with his Elemental powers. *That's* what it had been, what else could have possibly happened that day?

It was hanging right there.

"Damien, are you alright?"

The earthquake was before him then, in his mind once more. Ewan and Lucy were screaming for their son, Von was dragging him away, and his power of Night swirled all around. Damien focused.

What if he hadn't cast his power that day? What if he hadn't been there when the Islets were rent apart? What if he hadn't been Elemental? He would have stood there and watched, helpless, as the earth shattered and roared, and still his parents would have tumbled into the darkness below. They would have died no matter what he did. His brother had saved him from his own needless death. And besides, when it was over, Damien had had family beside him with whom to mourn.

It wasn't my fault, he realized, stunning himself with the voracity of the answer. *If I did kill my parents, it was mercy. It was kindness. It was quick. That was the day they were going to die one way or another.* He had never thought much on fate, but this seemed like nothing else. *It's not my fault that they died.*

"Damien?"

Someone was trying to get his attention, but he didn't hear them. A great ringing filled his ears as he remembered. He remembered the guilt, the pain, the *agony,* the horrible things that had driven him for so long, that had made him push people away and made him question what he said as opposed to what he thought. He remembered all those years spent alone, filled with knots in his stomach so tight that he couldn't eat, and here, in this moment, at long last…

He let it go.

He let the guilt fall through the crack in the earth at his parents' murder, and be swallowed into nothing. Like Satolin had told him, and Von had told him, and Leo had told him, and Gwen had told him, and everyone else had told him for so many months—*and like I realized yesterday about my scars*, he thought—it was a part of who he was now. It was pain, it was agony, but it *hadn't killed him*. And he knew that what didn't kill him had made him stronger.

Amidst the discordant symphony of angry voices that had broken out in his silence, Damien realized that he was home.

"Vilan!" the person shouted. "Are you alright?" It was—to his great surprise—Joval Tosh, the Algaroth who operated the Core.

Damien came back, and looked up with a light in his eyes above a wide, glowing smile, feeling lighter than he had in years. "I think I'll be fine, yes. How are you?"

There were chortles of nervous laughter all around, and Damien blinked again. He knew on some level it was him they were laughing at, but for the first time ever he didn't care. The midnight blue Algaroth gave him a funny look. "Shiny. Are you here?"

"I'm on me feet, aren't I?"

Javier laughed.

"You were saying what the weapon is?"

Damien nodded, smiling to himself. "Yeah. I was."

"And?" Baroda pressed.

In the span of an instant, Damien's newfound resolve warmed his body, hardening into a sort of shell. A pure, unfiltered nugget of strength came alive inside him, and the last vestiges of worry fled his mind. He knew what he was doing. "I think Tan's generator suppresses the Nukes with black holes," he announced, his voice ringing out strong. "It swallows the explosion *before* the Nuke can do its job."

"It swallows the explosion," repeated Captain Fagin looking nervous. "Well I'll be."

"Yes."

Koro Loss's lip twitched. "So those tracks must have removed the weapon? It must have been stored in that cave in the cliff."

"Definitely was big enough," a tall woman chimed in near the center of the wheel.

"So now it's on the move," said Romi.

"And has been for days," added Leo.

"It could be going anywhere," said someone.

"It must be going for a specific target, something out of their usual reach," Reuben added, a refreshing and unusual sparkle of realization in his eyes. "They might be hiding it somewhere until they can get it safely to its target."

Gwen gazed towards the images of the bodies. "And we don't know where that is?"

"Nope," said Damien. He looked towards the McKinley operator again who—to his inward shock—flashed him a single approving nod. "McKinley, is the rig working?"

At that very moment, the grizzled old man glanced across his monitors as a chime tinned through the speakers. "*Yes, it looks to be.*" He turned back to them. "*Hold on, Amun Command. We might just have something.*"

They waited in tense silence, all eyes on the Triad.

You have to find it, Damien pleaded silently. *You have to.*

Then, at last, the man's voice called triumphant from off-camera, "*Amun! This is McKinley, pull up your globe, the rig is working! Repeat, your hacking rig is—*"

A tiny spark came out of the hacking rig.

"*No,*" Von gasped.

"*—We're plotting the course now. The backdoor you installed in the Islets did the trick! We've narrowed it down to—*"

Before anyone could respond, a visible shock zipped through the device, a flash of light popped, and the smell of burning circuitry filled the wedge.

"No!" Leo shrieked, running across the table. "No-no-no-no-no-no-no not yet! Baby oh no not yet, we're so close!!"

Damien's heart stopped as he beheld the ruins of Von's, his, and Leo's work. Blackened crisps and cords hung off the rig, and there was an audible sizzling from inside one of the cases they'd strapped together. The collective mood of the wedge shifted to one of a group in limbo, hanging on the edge of a knife. No one moved; no one made a sound. They just stared at the smoking rig. Damien, feeling like a dream had just turned into a walking nightmare, drifted towards the table, where Leo was wailing.

"You were s-so beautiful!!!" the AI cried, tears flying down his face.

"Damien…" Von whispered.

Damien looked up at the monitor. "McKinley?"

The screen looked frozen.

Please… no. "McKinley Station?"

They waited, and Damien locked eyes with his brother over their AI companion, feeling as if they'd just lost a friend. "McKinley?"

Nothing. The silence…dragged out.

Damien hung his head. *We're buried.*

Multiple faces in the wheel went slowly from hopeful, to cautious, and finally to crestfallen. The tiny sparks of a solution died as their heads fell, and crushed sighs escaped more than one mouth.

"*Amun Command?*"

Damien looked up.

The operator was sitting in his chair, frowning at the scene in the wedge. "*Where's your globe?*"

"We'll pull it up in a moment, McKinley," said Morgan into the quiet. "We just lost the rig."

"*What? No you didn't.*"

Heads jerked up, Leo stopped mewling. "What? What do you mean?"

The operator's light-brown eyes took on a heroic shine. "*We just uploaded the schematics and the programs your AI wrote,*" he said. "*Your rig was just immortalized in our system—*"

The riotous cheers drowned out his words. The knife's edge vanished, and Amun-Nūr tumbled onto the right side. Relief flooded Damien's chest and Leo sprang into the air with joy. Morgan and Satolin traded grateful pats, and Gwen clasped her hands in front of her face, breathing hard. *He saved it. He saved our rig!* The cheers died down.

"…*only be on a train*," the operator concluded. "*The tracks give us only two options for what's hauling that weapon*," the operator repeated. "*And only one of those is on Earth.*"

"What are they?" demanded Admiral Baroda, who had been remarkably silent this whole time.

The operator's gaze lingered on the Admiral. "*One is a fault ram, the other is a cargo train.*"

The thought of another fault ram cracking a tectonic plate somewhere was enough to make Damien stop in his tracks, but something about that didn't sound right.

"The tracks," murmured Loss. "A cargo train… they were hiding it in the cave near the village."

"That's it," agreed Morgan. "That makes sense."

A tingle of purpose came into the air, a direction for them to turn at last, a *mission*. They had something to do.

"McKinley," Satolin barked over the congratulatory air. "Can you track the train? Can you find it?"

The operator shrugged his head, uncertain. "*We already have, Prohka. But it's on the move already.*"

The excitement slowly faded.

"Can you lay it out for us?"

"*Bring up your globe—oh.*"

Leo had the globe up before he concluded his sentence. "On it!" he cheered.

"*Amun Command,*" said the operator. "*The Triad is washing all possible matches for you now… McKinley Station receiving… Forwarding the train's path… We have three matches… Now two… stand by.*"

They waited.

"*Stand by.*"

The globe spun, the perfectly rendered Earth a jewel to behold.

"*McKinley Station confirming,*" he announced. "*We have a match.*"

The globe zoomed in as Damien had seen it do before. All eyes were fixed on it as a yellow plot ran out from the Himalayas. It sped west along the base of the mountains, then took a hard turn south, out over the Bang

Sea and the Indian Ocean. It skirted the Indian coast, clearly over open water. Damien wasn't the first to notice that either.

"A cargo train? On water?" someone hollered. That can't be—"

"It's not a surface vehicle," Reuben cut them off. "It's one of their mining hover-trains, to transport cargo."

"Those things are fast," commented Caleb, looking anything but perturbed at the idea.

Captain Romi nodded. "Very fast."

"*We're tracking its path over the past two weeks*," added the operator. "*Coming up on current position now.*"

On the war table, everyone followed the path of the yellow line all the way across the Indian Ocean, to where it halted at Madagascar.

"What's it doing?" someone wondered.

"Taking a shit," someone else quipped, a few people laughed.

Damien however, wasn't so sure. *I didn't know they had a presence there.* He saw he wasn't the only one to note a Collective cargo train on the isolated jungle island off the southeast coast of Africa. *We might need to look into that.*

The path sat over Madagascar for so long that they thought it was perhaps where the train was now… but they weren't so lucky. The map pulled back, a timestamp appeared over the table, speeding through the last few days towards today. Then, as the timer crossed no sooner than last night, the train suddenly took action again and barreled north-northwest, straight through the heart of Africa. A tiny red pin appeared as the timestamp halted at the current hour, and in only a few seconds, it blipped significant kilometers forward.

Everyone was silent.

"So what's their target?" Damien asked.

"McKinley?" plied Morgan.

"*The rig let us plot that too,*" said the operator, full of wonder. "*Look.*"

The map jumped ahead of the red marker and traced a dotted line across the globe. It ran north, deep through the African desert, the jungle, the savannah, and then desert again, north through more jungle, and north further still, across the vast continent, avoiding all other red markers that showed Collective forces. Everyone watched it silently, wondering where it would end. Damien realized it first. He watched the dotted line approach the Mediterranean Sea, and fear began to shape the moment again. *The Eurasian Inferno...what places did Croll Tan hit?* He counted the spots off: the Thai Spur, the Himalayas, the Throat of Israel, and the Italian Peninsula. The train had come west from the Himalayas, away from the Spur, and it was too deep in the African jungle to merit turning towards the Throat, but Italy...

Damien watched on in horror as the boot-shaped peninsula grew larger, and still he hoped he was wrong. He thought of the reactor needed to power the weapon, and how during his recovery he'd heard that The Collective had taken more than one of Italy's Mag Fury's, and still he hoped he was wrong. But when the projected path finally stopped, a flashing marker appeared over a city that Amun-Nūr knew was ripe for annihilation. *Or a demonstration to force our surrender.*

The train was bound for the Vatican, in the heart of Rome, one of the cities where the Fury had indeed been lost, human defenses pushed back.

"*Target confirmed*," announced the operator. "*The Over-Seer's prototype generator is bound on a cargo train for Rome. Our best guess is that it's going for a demonstration of Tan's weapon.*"

Damien looked up at the screen, somehow unsurprised that the man had come to the same conclusion as he.

Commander Morgan stepped up. "Alright then. How do we hit it?"

"You don't," said a voice.

It was so decisive and jarring, that it took a moment for everyone to realize that it was Admiral Baroda who had spoken.

Commander Morgan frowned. "Sir?"

Everyone fell quiet. The McKinley feed popped a hint of static.

"I can't allow Amun-Nūr to be involved in this," Baroda proclaimed. "It's simply too dangerous, and it stands to be as disastrous as your involvement in the Inferno."

Silence.

Is he serious? Damien traded looks with Von and then with Javi, both of them looked floored.

From the war table, Leo—who had traded most of his Holmes garb for his suit—examined his pipe. "You know, the *Admiral* is decorated and fancy, but the *Admiral* doesn't technically have jurisdiction on Amun-Nūr, *does* the Admiral? I do believe that we should take Mr. Caleb No-Last-Name's advice and plead an Amendment and whatnot!" he finished with the flourish of a quill pen.

The pin of the train continued moving across Africa. Baroda held his chin up. "Technically, Leonardo, this island does not exist; therefore I don't find it productive to squabble over constituent semantics."

"I do, though," Javier added. "I think we deserve proper council if you're gonna go this bat-shit nuts on us. *I know* how you deal with people who drop out of being your favorites. Is this about to be like how you punished me? Because I got shot at a few more times than I expected when you were keeping me 'safe' before the court-martial."

That little revelation had words that Baroda clearly didn't like.

"You can't take our security," Javier finished.

Baroda tried to answer but Satolin spoke first, "As I've said before, *Admiral*, I offer my thanks for your support in the past. You brought us Project S.E.H.A., and you have given us great resources to ply our work, but your sovereignty does not extend this deep beneath the ocean." The Prohka uncrossed his arms and implored to the man. "Antonio, Amun-Nūr has the resources, the ships, and the *will* to help, *right now*. You have to see that this is bigger than you or I."

Baroda took a long slow breath that made his intentions plenty clear.

The great alien's peaceable tone vanished. "I see."

Suddenly, the Admiral turned on Damien. "Son, I know you, and I know your brother. I know that you recognize how disastrous this Inferno business has become. Surely you're smart enough to see how ill-advised this pursuit is. You were nearly taken by the Over-Seer after all! The very thing that we knew could be the end of us!"

All eyes were on Damien as he frowned, and—running on a sudden crazy urge to be ornery—said, "I'm sorry, Admiral. It's been a long few months, could you… refresh my memory about the conversation we had? Didn't you say something about the Elementals being the only pieces that Croll Tan doesn't understand, and that Earth needs people like us?"

In the newly freed recesses of Damien's thoughts, he felt an unusual flood of delight as the Admiral's eyes narrowed. "I didn't say that. Weren't you listening?"

"Just now or that day?"

Baroda huffed. "That…both."

"Oh. No, I'm sorry I tuned out for a minute there. Didn't you say something else about using Elementals to safeguard the Nukes instead of helping this war today and every day, like Satolin suggests?" He was surprising himself at his spunk, but looks of delighted curiosity were spreading around the wheel, focused intently on Damien Vilan standing his ground with a Lunar Admiral.

"You're twisting my words," Baroda answered in a clipped tone.

"He most certainly is not!" said Leo. "I have an audio log right here," he produced an ancient little square that Damien recognized as a pre-war memory device called a 'cassette tape'. "That could confirm it. See here, they are *your* words, honorable Admiral Antonio."

Before the Admiral could do anything, Leo had popped the cassette tape into a cassette player, and the sounds of Camp Cascade's evacuation flooded the command wheel. A ship took off in the distance, and Admiral Baroda's voice came through loud and clear, courtesy of Damien's aural implant (which he had never thought about Leo *recording* conversations through, and wasn't sure how he felt about it now). *"Damien, the Elementals are humanity's last fresh players. They're the only pieces on our chessboard that Croll Tan does not understand, and we need pieces like that. Tan is a strategist, yes; he's cunning, and he is hunting you. Given the opportunity to catch you, he will. If he can observe you, he'll understand you. And if he outmaneuvers you, he will destroy you—more than just you, in fact. Don't let those things happen."*

Leo pulled out the tape, waggled it for everyone to see, then crushed it in hand and sprinkled the flicker of pre-war plastic and celluloid into his pipe.

Everyone stared.

"What?" Leo cackled. "Oh, don't worry, I still have that file." He winked and blew more rings.

Baroda turned to Damien and said nothing. A vein was starting to throb in the man's neck.

Damien's blessedly clear thoughts returned to Croll Tan as he eyed the pin over Africa. *I would choose to fight every battle—were it my want—not wait until a fulcrum engagement.* Damien's stomach churned in anger and fear at the thought of the Over-Seer, but there was no denying what he'd said; he agreed. "I think every battle is worth fighting if we can, sir, and I think you're insane if you believe leaving this island to The Collective is a good idea." He saw Reuben shake his head, and saw Gwen give an upset little sigh, but otherwise everyone present—including his brother, the McKinley operator, Morgan, Satolin, and Caleb—gave him looks of approval.

The Admiral had had enough. "It doesn't matter," he said coolly, and turned to the Prohka. "I gave you this island, Daeduras, and I can reclaim it if I need to."

Prohka Satolin took a step out of the crowd, descended to the landing to where Baroda stood, and bent at the knees to look the man dead-on. "Oh?"

Baroda visibly recoiled. He looked for more support, but it was clear the tide in the command wheel was turning against him. Only Agent John Bunting—who had been nearly invisible in his continuing silence, even standing in plain view—remained looking resolutely ahead from behind his sunglasses...but he wasn't moving to aid Baroda, either. Finally, the Admiral whirled on Damien, the flush creeping well into his cheeks now as he replaced a thin, planted smile on his face. "After everything I did for you," he grated, barely getting the words out from behind his teeth. "Getting you out of that city, taking care of—"

"Actually, sir?" said a voice from behind Damien. He whirled to see that it was Huxley standing in the entryway, her arms folded. Her four recruits—Airman Silantos, Airmatron Osman, Sergeant Lidiza, and Senior Airman Khatib—were arrayed behind her. "*I* did that."

Baroda took one look at who spoke, his expression grew further irritated, and he waved her off as he bowled on back towards Damien. Huxley and her recruits moved up near Leo's dark plinth as the man came on. "After *everything* that you've put so many people through, you think you can—"

"Admiral," said the commanding Algaroth in the room, who was the last of clan Daeduras. Satolin's voice was a whispered warning.

Baroda finally stopped, straightened, and turned. Satolin held out a hand. "Amun-Nūr is going to stop this train. May I show you the hangar?"

Damien could almost *hear* the Prohka's satisfaction as Lunar Admiral Baroda's thin smile curdled. He finally saw that he'd lost. There was nothing he could do; he had no allies here. He refused to even look around the wedge again. Instead, back turned to Damien, the Admiral took a breath, pulled his uniform straight, and turned to leave, stiff as a board.

Damien couldn't stop his recklessly satisfied mouth from letting one more thing fly. "Sir?" he called.

The Admiral half-turned in the doorway. "What."

"About what you said, about this venture being a bad idea?"

He couldn't tell if the curiosity in Baroda's eyes was genuine, but he thought he saw it briefly.

He met the Admiral's gaze. "Bad ventures are kind of my thing, but I'm not great at them, *clearly*," he held up his still-bandaged hand. "So don't ever trust me around one of yours."

Baroda looked like he could have shot Damien then and there.

"Oh, and sir?" Damien met the man's gaze with unflinching resolve. "You don't know me."

"HA!"

Everyone jumped as the stupendous, one-note laugh burst forth from Caleb, who was looking at Damien with a full ounce less indifference.

Antonio Baroda glared at the lot of them for a second longer before storming away. Agent Bunting nodded once in the general direction of the war table, which encompassed the display showing McKinley, Damien, and a few others, so Damien couldn't tell for whom it was meant, but then the SIO agent departed. Damien looked to the Prohka, whose arctic-golden eyes shone with pride, as did those of everyone else in the wheel. *Thank you*, their eyes all said. *Thank you.*

Damien closed his eyes. At long last, he had found his center. Whatever came next would be what he made of it, and he knew that even in the pain of loss and the guilt of terrible acts, he had family here.

"So," Leo interjected. "The train, eh?"

With the Admiral gone and the pin moving ever further through Africa, the mood of the wheel spun wildly into focus, and the people of Amun-Nūr became charged with energy.

"How do we hit it," demanded Morgan, bringing them all full circle.

"That's easy," growled Joval Tosh in Russian. "Use the jungle."

"Why's that now?" drawled Captain Fagin.

"Because no human or Algaroth radar can get good readings through foliage that thick," Tosh answered. "Everything moves in there, everything is *alive*." The Core operator's onyx-flecked golden eyes glittered. "The train would not be able to pick a strike out of the air beneath the canopy."

"Surprise attack," said Huxley. "I like your style, Tosh."

Tosh nodded her way.

Morgan looked thoughtful. "That sounds solid, but what about emergency signals? If the Over-Seer gets word that we've invaded his precious weapon, he might just mortar the whole thing and take all of us with it."

"And *that* would be tragic," said Javier. People laughed as a positively *electric* vibe filled the air. Purpose can do that.

Diesal Kel spoke up. "The jungle should probably scramble those signals too."

"*Probably?*" Caleb glared. "Probably isn't good enough."

"It's good enough if we stay on station," countered Romi. He plied the other captains, who nodded. "If there's a stray signal, we'll block it."

The Fire Elemental shrugged away, unconvinced and unfazed.

And just like that, in a few short minutes, they had a plan of attack. The McKinley operator confirmed that he would keep the Triad access open as long as he could, but it would be up to them after that.

Damien nodded to himself as it all fell into place over a hurried few minutes of discussion, but as they wrapped up, he became keenly aware that there was something they weren't taking into account, and it was gnawing at him. Finally, as they neared agreement on the best plan they could throw together, he spoke up. "What about the Over-Seer?"

"What about him?" asked Morgan.

"Doesn't anyone think it's weird that this thing is sort of his baby, and he's not with it?"

Multiple voices spoke up at once, but Leo broke through the chatter. "Over-Seer's aren't field agents, you know that."

"But this is different," Damien insisted. "If that train is going to Rome for a demonstration…it could—"

"End the war?" Caleb offered. The man's words scratched like sandpaper.

"Yes. Force our surrender? Croll Tan's gone through a LOT of trouble to keep this a secret so he can get it to the Vatican without it being noticed—but why? It has to be a prototype, but that doesn't all add up."

"Prototypes are vulnerable," said Von. Many of the soldiers agreed, and some smirked.

Damien shifted feet. "Yeah but, *something* isn't right here. Think about it," he spun in place while he spoke. "He wanted to take a lot more than just two vials of my blood, he talked about us having a…long relationship together." He turned. "Reuben, you were right that the whole Inferno was a ruse to draw the Elementals out of hiding, okay, I can admit that. Plus, this thing is being sent without an *escort* through plenty of human-controlled territory across half a continent? Why didn't he just load the train up from Solaroth and send it that way? It would've been more direct."

"Well, 'cus that entire corridor is a battle zone," Captain Fagin remarked. "Coming up from the south is easier."

"But why that far? I just don't get what *we*," he pointed out the Elementals. "Had to do with all this aside from him wanting *me*."

"You're not making a lot of sense," someone noted.

Damien looked up. The whole wedge was looking at him again, and he didn't have a good answer. He didn't want to lose all the confidence they'd just placed in him by worrying about wild theories. "Alright," he said. "Alright, you're right. Let's, let's get going then. Let's go get 'em!"

"Alright!"

"Let's do this!"

A chorus of cheers rose through the command wheel, but Damien wasn't convinced. His gut told him he was right. His gut said that whatever Croll Tan had loaded on that train, that used his blood, it was only half the story, and if he'd learned anything in his time with Amun-Nūr, it was that he should trust his gut. There was more going on here, but it wasn't the problem of today, and so it would be saved for tomorrow.

Let's do this. And he was shocked into a smile as others echoed his thought out loud.

"Alright!"

"Let's do this!"

"Let's go storm a train!"

"You mean rob?"

"Sure!"

CHAPTER TWENTY NINE

The Great Train Robbery

"Captain, we're coming up on the train," said Leo.

"Understood," Romi answered. He hit the inter-ship comm. "Eclipse Two, Eclipse Three, this is Eclipse One, did you get that?"

"*Roger E-One,*" came Huxley's voice. "*We're off your port stern, in formation.*"

"*E-Two this is E-Three, your tail's draggin' Hux, mind straightening up like a professional?*"

"*Shut it, Bruce. At least one of us knows how to loosen up.*"

Damien snorted, as did others.

"Alright you two," said Romi. "Anyone see the train yet?"

Fagin responded fast with his twang. "*E-Three here, sightin' confirmed. No visual yet but the train is in the woods. All stages are set; target's path is confirmed. We even got a confirmation from McKinley. The mission is a go. Repeat we are green-lit. Godspeed to ya'll.*"

"I'd wonder if God was actually curious about any of this," Reuben said absently from the chair across from Damien.

Damien frowned at him but chose not to ask. Instead, he leaned around Kel's chair, "So McKinley was right? It's headed for the Vatican?"

Romi glanced back. "It looks that way, yes."

"Hmm."

"You two better get back there," the captain added after a minute.

Damien and Reuben left the cockpit, leaving the view of endless jungle zipping by.

"*Sanguine Lotus,*" Romi's voice popped on the intra-ship comm. "*We're making our final approach. Prep your gear, it's time.*"

On the crew deck, Damien found Gwen and Javier stuffing gear into pockets and checking weapons. "Gwen?" he asked when he noticed she didn't have a drop suit on. "Aren't you coming?"

She looked at him with those bright green eyes and smiled. "No. I changed my mind. I'm just going to guide you in."

"Why?"

She cupped his cheek. "Because, I'll only slow you down. I'm no soldier."

"But—"

"It's decided," she said with her authoritative look. "Get dressed."

Damien did as he was told while Reuben went below to check his gear.

"So this is it then," Javier said, yanking on his straps. "The end of the line."

Damien looked up at him from tying his boots. "You don't think we're gonna make it out?"

"We only have a landing zone, brotha! This plan has no exit strategy, and when there's no exit strategy, it's usually because there wasn't any reason to plan one."

Damien stared at his friend for a long moment and then returned to his boots. Javier was about to say something further when Damien said, "Don't Marines usually *make* an exit?" He looked back up and grabbed his ruddy old backpack, all patched up and newly sewn, packed with a few essentials.

Javier stopped. Then, a slow grin crossed his face as a spark danced in his eyes. "Yeah, I guess we usually do."

They nodded and finished strapping on their gear.

"Hey, Koro Von," said Javier. "How's your squad?"

"They're all loaded nicely," Von answered from *Deep Core*, sounding pleased with his impromptu title, courtesy of Commander Morgan and the six soldiers who had practically leapt to be under his command.

Damien closed his eyes, trying to force down the worry in his stomach about his brother. He opened a channel to the others. "What about the rest of you?"

"*We're set over here,*" Koro Loss answered from Huxley's ship.

"*Just fine,*" Reuben answered from belowdeck.

Caleb cut in from the *Core*, "*I'm set here. Just steer clear of me and you'll all be fine.*"

"Sort of defeats the idea of a team doesn't it?" Javier asked, raising his eyebrows at Damien.

"*It's for all of YOUR protection as much as mine. I don't like being careful about where I ignite things.*"

Damien grinned, "You'd be surprised how intimidating it can be to see a group of people walking out of a wall of flame, Caleb. You should stay close if you can."

The man harrumphed.

"*We're closing on the train. Three minutes,*" said Romi.

"I think you guys might want to see this." Leo said clearly into everyone's ears, "If you'll direct your attention forward, you'll soon see the Transport of Evil."

Damien and Javier raced back to the cockpit to get a better view.

"Almost there," Romi said as they came in, "Final words just came in from home and from McKinley: Rome's a mess. Troops are all over the place, but there's still plenty of fighting, and a huge civilian populace is there that didn't manage to evacuate. It'll be a bloodbath if we can't stop this thing."

Damien and Javier nodded, determined.

Infinite shades of green flashed by beneath *Sanguine Lotus*, *Chalice Archon*, and *Deep Core* as the ships skimmed the highest reaches of the jungle.

"Wait for it…" said Leo.

They watched in tense anticipation as the strike force approached a sloping valley that descended steadily for kilometers and then peaked sharply to the horizon, blocking the view of anything beyond.

"We're almost on top of it," Kel said, checking the hemisphere display.

"Where?" Javier asked, his eyes searching the foliage.

"Oh, just give it a sec," was Leo's mischievous reply.

The trio of ships came up the far side of the valley, and Damien leaned forward.

"*There*," Leo remarked as they crossed the peak.

Damien's eyes went wide as they burst over the lip of the valley. From horizon to horizon, all he could see was jungle and a thin river snaking from southeast to northwest.

Wait…

"Yep," said Leo, reading his thoughts, "That's it."

The river wasn't a river at all. It was a convoy.

Damien felt the breath leave his body as they took it all in before the squad dropped back to the safety of the treetops.

The convoy was kilometers in length—to say nothing of its breadth. Even from this far away, Damien could see the swath of jungle the thing had cut, easily half a kilometer wide. Tens of small vehicles, each only visible because their humped backs poked above the jungle, followed dutifully in the column. They were so numerous that you could almost hopscotch between them.

"Snaps…" breathed Javier.

Each alien vehicle went zipping over a blackened trail of bulldozed jungle. A trail, Damien realized, that wound its way long behind the convoy, but also ahead of it too. He followed the distant break in the trees to the horizon, and realized that this wasn't new. This was an *established route*. The Collective had probably been sneaking out stolen materials for years through here.

This better be the last time they get to use this, he thought.

As they came closer, Damien spotted color-coded cargo containers strapped to the open beds of the rearmost vehicles.

"Leo," he asked, "what's in the crates?"

Leo appeared on the center console with a clipboard and a hot-pen stuck behind his ear. "Mmm let's see…" he tapped the board and spun around to stare at the vehicles, so far oblivious to their presence. "I see *quite* the variety of goodies down there! Looks like the Over-Seer wants to appease his almighty masters back home."

"Meaning?"

Leo looked slyly over his shoulder. A flicker of something malicious appeared in his eyes. "It's a little bit of *everything*." On the last word, Leo became a red horned devil, juggling tens of tiny terrarium balls. Each one had something different inside, from trees and metals and sand, to animals, plants, and even one filled with crusty yellow powder.

Drugs?

"Oh *snaps*," Javier repeated, watching Leo's little display and interrupting Damien's thoughts.

Damien's breath fell out of his mouth, "They really do want it all don't they…"

Leo nodded knowingly, "Yep."

Damien just shook his head as they passed the rearmost vehicles.

"So which one is the actual *train*?" Damien asked, craning over Kel.

"Head of the column," said Romi, looking towards a distant strip of metal winking at them from over the trees.

Damien couldn't make it out at first, but as they cut across a curve that took the convoy winding away from them and back, he saw it. Only for a brief second, but he saw it.

His eyes narrowed and his heart beat faster. But then the thing vanished behind a jutting spur of enormous trees. Eclipse Team banked around the near side.

"Almost there," said Romi.

They passed the forested spur and the trees settled back into the ocean of green. They were almost on top of it now, and Damien's body exploded in goosebumps as they finally lay eyes on the monstrosity before them:

Croll Tan's armored cargo train shot through the jungle, powered by neither steam nor coal, a craft clearly not of Earth. It did not run on electricity, and it was not bound to the ground like most of its ancestors of the planet. No, the behemoth of a vehicle below was an engine of war, and a big one at that. Damien even saw Leo gaping openly at it. The hot-pen fell from the AI's ears and out of sight.

"Not quite what you expected, Leo?" Damien asked, forcing lightness into his voice.

Leo owled his head around, eyes wide while his mouth dropped horribly below his collarbone.

Damien flinched. "Me neither."

The train had four decks. Railed and bristling walkways jutted out here and there along the sleek frame, many of them peppered with Gyro turrets or guards. Suggestions of tinted polyport windows ran along the silvery grooves in its sides, but otherwise the train appeared as a fortress, a ten thousand kiloton, speeding hover-fortress.

As if that weren't enough, *Lotus* skewed to the side a bit and Damien's resolves grew spotty as he spied something else directly beneath them; this was all going to get very complicated *very* fast. "Where the hell did *that* one come from?" He wanted to point out the second train but knew how stupid that was.

"Uhh," Romi and Kel worked furiously. "We're not sure…"

"Fuck!" Javier threw his arms up.

A *second* train was rocketing along next to the first one.

"Son of a bitch!" Damien echoed.

The second train looked as though someone had taken a Dynasty Navy aircraft carrier and stripped most of the armor plating away, leaving a haunting, skeletal mess. The cargo train rushed along low next to its towering armored escort, looking raw and unfinished. It looked as if huge slices had been sheared cleanly out of the train, leaving the remaining halves to be sewn back together. That had been done repeatedly down its breadth, and now long bowed beams of metal ran the length of the thing like a steel cradle, holding it all together. Between the sheared chunks, canyons remained with no bottom, inside which open walkways and decks, mazes of pipes, support metal, and shadowed platforms crisscrossed back and forth beneath what would have been a complete flight deck, but wasn't.

To complete the ugly copycat of a human Navy ship, a command tower rose from the thickest chunk of train midway down the body, where a gigantic crane had been tucked parallel to their course. Most troubling though, Damien saw that across the entire cargo train, any flat surface that might be large enough to support a colored cargo container had one.

Containers of every shape and color that ranged from the size of fighter jets to no bigger than a potted plant were stacked everywhere, the spoils of harvested Earth. In short, the second train was an open, messy, dangerously armed metal slab of stolen cargo.

"What do we do?" Damien asked.

Romi gave a dry snort. "You're dropping anyways. That weapon has to be here. I'd guess it's on the bigger one."

"Great."

"You had both better get back there. We need to move before they see us."

Ahead, Damien imagined he could already see the Mediterranean Sea, calling the train to Rome. He was about to follow Javier out of the cockpit when Romi craned his neck back. "Damien?"

He stopped. "Yeah?"

Captain Romi's face was set, but his eyes glowed warmly. "I don't envy you, my friend. I really don't."

Damien laughed.

"But good luck. If anyone can pull this off, I would bet on you."

"Ha, I hope you already have."

Romi nodded. "Kel's about to take on a lot of extra duties when we get back."

Kel's wizened ganglia flicked and he nodded. "He wagers you only destroy the weapon. *I* wager you destroy the entire train."

Damien glowed with gratitude, boosted by their confidence in him. "Thank you," he said. "Both of you. For...*everything*." He gripped both of their shoulders before leaving.

"We'll always be close by!" Romi called.

The others were waiting just like they'd planned: cramped along the outer door of the hidden compartment that housed *Lotus*'s Aqua Pod turbines. Captain Romi was going to open the pod bay doors so that Damien (with Leo in his pack), Reuben, and Javier could leap down to the train.

"Everyone ready for this?" Damien said, squeezing between the Aqua Pod and the door, his backpack—form-fitting as it was—pressing against him.

"Oh, I'm with you, man," said Javier. Reuben said nothing.

"But I'm *really* with you," Leo whispered sweetly in his ear.

Damien clicked the comm one more time. "Alright everyone, this is it! Use those call signs from now on, and keep in touch! Good luck!"

The other Elementals, the squads of troops on all three ships, and the captains all vowed their success. Then the doors opened, hot air and the smell of damp jungle rushed into the bay, and Damien slid on his goggles. He, Reuben and Javier leaned forward—only to be met with a *zing* of plasma. They pulled back.

"What the hell was that?!" the Marine barked.

"Time's up team!" Romi yelled. *"They've spotted us! Get down there NOW!"*

Damien peeked forward and more plasma shot up. *"Yeek!"* he leapt back, trying to figure out how to jump safely when he realized something. "Gwen, you said you were going to *guide* us down?!"

"Yes!" she shouted from his side.

"How the hell are you gonna do that?!"

"Just JUMP!" she howled, shoving him forwards. He felt a wave of Elemental static build off of her.

What's she doing?!

There wasn't any more time. He let her push him forwards. He grabbed Javier and Reuben and as one, they leapt out of the ship, narrowly avoiding being shot with another bolt of plasma from below.

"OOOOHHHHHH SHIIIIIIIIIIIIIT!!!!" they wailed as they fell.

The cargo train rose to meet them. Damien was sure that they were about to splatter on the textured black flooring, when he felt something overtake them.

Gwen?!

It was a broad stream of water, screaming down just behind them.

We're not gonna make it!

But then the water enveloped the three of them, and not a moment too soon. The stream defied physics and absorbed the impact as they bounced over the edge of a huge maroon container, keeping them from death by hard surface. The three tumbled over a railing and onto a level deep in one of the bottomless canyons. The water splashed away and Damien rolled across the gritty, textured flooring, leaping to his feet as fast as he could.

"I really...can't believe you just survived that..." Leo squeaked. Damien pictured the AI covering his eyes.

"No kidding." He shook the water out of his ears and looked around for Javier and Reuben. They were both nearby, as soaked as he was, but unharmed. "So, where's—"

TWING!

A Gyro shot zipped past his head and into the edge of the container nearby, answering the unfinished question. It reflected off the surface with the odd noise, and Damien hit the deck.

"Up high!" Javier yelled.

Damien spun around, already drawing Darkness down his arm and into an Orb.

"LEFT!" Reuben roared, but he didn't need to. Damien's Orb went wide as he jerked back around. He caught sight of a pale flash and heard a hiss. Two Algaroth in diamond-white Collective armor tumbled over the outer railing, their arms frozen hunks of ice.

Plasma scorched the ground from the high shooter and Damien unslung his rifle—this guy was too far to hit with his powers. He took a deep breath and rose from cover.

CRACK.

His Plaster shot hooked the alien's chin and jerked its helmet off in a spray of dark blood.

"Nailed it!" Damien shouted.

But then shouts came from further down the corridor of containers, and he sobered the moment. "We need to get to the others!" he yelled over the wind.

"No!" Reuben called back, his usual chilly demeanor fading with the mission. "You need to find that weapon! Get to the other train!"

"What about you?" Javier asked.

"I'll join the others so we can *trash this convoy!*"

Damien and Javier exchanged glances at the older man's sudden zeal, but they nodded, turning back towards the menacing silver of the bio-train across the jungle floor.

"Vilan!" Reuben shouted. The yells of the patrols were getting louder. "Good luck!"

Damien nodded, "You too!" Then he and Javier moved as one across the platform, leaving Reuben to fend for himself.

"*Darkness! Dark, do you copy?*" It was Koro Loss, using Damien's new call sign.

"I've got you Loss! What's your position?" Damien had to duck back as more plasma burst towards them from a lower level. Javier returned a spray of bullets. The aliens scattered.

"*Forward-train and above you! Look up!*"

They did, just in time to see a skirmish break out a little ways across the canyon and a few decks up. Seven of Amun-Nūr's brown-and-green armored soldiers burst through a doorway to tango with three enemy soldiers with bearded helmets. Damien watched as Koro Loss charged the middle alien, shot him with a pistol, and kicked him in the chest. The body flew over the edge and landed hard in the center of a cleared space on Damien and Javier's level.

"Are you alright?" Damien asked.

"*Oh, we're LIVELY!*" Loss responded, saluting them. "*Omega Squad has you covered all the way to that clearing. Move, now!*"

They did as told, fighting their way past the five or so containers to the clearing.

On arrival, they pulled up short as two Algaroth appeared around the corner, charging them. They both had the red stripes of Collective Koros. There wasn't any time to dive out of the way or shoot. The plasma barely missed Damien, and the other shot clipped Javier's shoulder armor, singing it.

"YAAAA!" They all screamed as the four engaged in close combat. Damien tucked his rifle and jabbed it butt-first into his enemy's jaw, staggering it. His Koro recovered and swung at Damien's head with outstretched claws. He ducked and finally found a proper opening to use his powers.

With a surge, Damien somersaulted away and spun around. A perfect Orb whipped up and into the Koro's face, detonating with more force than he could've hoped. The shadows sliced through the air, disorienting all but him as his combatant fell, its head a mangled mess.

Back on his feet, Damien spun to help Javier, but instead had to skip away to avoid a dark brown cargo container the size of a gorilla as it fell squarely on top of the other soldier with a wet crunch. Javier grinned his way.

"What the hell was that?!" Damien shouted at him.

Javier laughed, fiercely enjoying himself. "It was full of dirt! Their mistake!"

Damien shook his head, shocked. Then the comm crackled again. "Ice?" Damien asked.

"*No, I'm here,*" Reuben answered.

"Vo?"

There was no answer. Damien's chest tightened in worry.

"You two should get to the higher level," said Leo. "I think a window for crossing the trains is about to open." He always left a bad taste in Damien's mouth with that tone.

The pair spun, looking for stairs to try and get out of this canyon and up to the surface level when Koro Loss bellowed, "*HEADS DOWN!!*"

They answered and hit the deck. Damien barely got below a container before an unbroken stream of plasma filled the air they had just occupied.

"Turrets!" Leo yelped.

"FUCKING SLIZZARDS!" Javier cursed.

Damien cautiously lifted his head, trying to peek out, but another stream made him duck.

"Omega," he barked. "Can you see it?!"

"*No,*" Loss replied. "*There are two of them. The other is cutting through our cover!*"

Damien looked to the upper level and indeed saw the stream from another turret searing away at a long low crate hiding the seven members of Omega. "Get out of there!" he yelled. The turret was about to cut through the metal and into two of their heads.

"*GO!*" shouted Loss.

Omega scattered. One even pulled some impressive acrobatics and launched herself over the railing, bounced off an X-shaped support strut across the gap, and hopped onto the level below, vanishing into the shadows. The turret was too slow to respond, and soon the plasma stream ceased as it looked for a new target.

"How the hell do we get across?!" Damien listened as the other turret continued firing near them, albeit with a less concentrated stream. He wanted to keep moving, but the random fall of bolts made that impossible.

"I've got an idea!" Leo said.

"Hit me!"

"Ooh, you aren't gonna like—"

"LEO!" Javier shouted.

"Right. Okay, you need to get back across that clearing and you'll see stairs to a walkway that leads straight to the command tower. It runs along the outer edge of the cargo train, but it's on the side facing the armored one. At the command tower you'll find a ladder. Take it to the top and patch me into that big crane arm."

The pair exchanged glances.

"You want us to *jump* across?!" the Marine's mouth was agape. "On a crane arm??"

"Unless you want to wait for a taxi?"

Damien rolled his eyes, "And what about the damn turret?!"

"*Covered,*" a distantly familiar baritone announced. "*Hit 'em fellas!*"

Suddenly, the sounds of gunfire in his earpiece grew much louder. The two Elementals poked their heads out just in time to catch the second squad join the fight from all the way up on the surface level. Shocked, Damien recognized one of the airmen by his build and his voice: it was one of Huxley's boys. Whiskey Squad.

Damien watched as the gangway that had been so happily peppering away at them lurched beneath a storm of Plaster fire. Dents and strains appeared in the armor of the train, but the turret crumbled under the hellfire and the attending guard dropped to the deck.

"*GO!*" Huxley's big squad leader commanded.

They were on the move again, leaping over the two Koro's corpses to where Leo had indicated.

"AHH!" Javier screamed, pain washing over his features.

Damien spun to see a lucky pair of soldiers across the way where Omega had just been. One of them had hit Javier in the back. "JAVI!"

Damien fired a quick staccato of rounds. The spray went wide, but it gave them enough time to dive around the corner and down the stairs to the walkway.

"You okay?!"

Javier winced but nodded, "Oh yeah," he gasped. "*Yeah*, I'm just aces!"

Damien winced back. His wrist and back still twinged a little, but he knew he'd put painkillers in his pack if he needed them. "Alright, come on."

Javier nodded just as another pair of troops appeared at on a shadowed walkway above them hidden mostly by weaving piping. Damien threw a Wave in their direction. "*Now!* We gotta go!"

They bolted. He thought he heard a scream, but there wasn't time to check as they tore down the stairs towards the walkway. They met no one on the way, luckily, and slammed into the railing with almost enough force to throw them over.

"Whoa-whoa-whoa-*whoa-whoa!*" Damien threw his arm across Javi's chest to stop him.

They were standing on a gangway that ran along one of the metal cradle beams for the cargo train. It went around the stairs behind them towards the prow of the train, and took off far into the distance towards the aft. The armored fortress train loomed directly ahead, keeping pace.

"Let's move," Damien said, and he pulled Javi along.

In the intense wind it was hard to hear straight, but the sounds of firefights had broken out all over the cargo train. At one point Damien heard Whiskey Squad get into an engagement—and promptly lose three of their twelve soldiers. He winced as the hard orders to leave the bodies filled the channel.

Where the hell is Von?? His brother had yet to check in with his Alpha Squad.

They moved as fast as they could aft, getting into one small skirmish after another. All the while, shadowed treetops wheeled overhead and the armored trains' mass stayed steady with them as the jungle flashed by.

"*Dark,*" Reuben called as they reached the base of the command tower. He sounded winded. Javier cursed as the Algaroth he had just ambushed tumbled over the side with his combat knife stuck in its neck.

"I'm here, Ice."

"*They've pinned your location down. You have a large squad converging on you.*"

"From where?!" Damien shouted, spinning too hard into Javier as they went back-to-back. The wounded man groaned. "*Sorry!*" he whispered. Javier waved him off.

"*From one level above, on both sides of the command tower, and from both directions of that cradle walkway you're on.*"

With a lurch in his stomach, Damien saw the first soldiers charge around the corner at the back of the ship, still a good distance away but closing fast. "Shit," he said, firing. "Suggestions?" He looked towards the prow and spotted a jet of ice spear through the air between the two trains. It coated one of the far railings, making more soldiers fall to their death.

Leo answered first, "I'd start climbing!!"

Damien shoved Javier to the ladder, which had been blessedly unguarded. "Go first!"

"You're such an ass," the Marine grumbled, but he started climbing. Damien heard him wince on every other rung.

Damien was right behind. He let loose a spray of bullets and then moved to sling his gun. Just as he released his grip though, a lucky shot struck it, and the rifle was torn from his hand.

"NO!" he belched, barely staying on the ladder. He recovered fast, but watched his weapon fall to the deck. Damien spotted movement in his peripheral. He looked up to see at least six guards pelting towards them at the bottom of the tower, now two stories down.

"Uhh... Ice? Little help!"

"*In a moment!*" The sounds of hissing cold mingled with plasma on the comm.

"*I'm closing on you. Watch out.*" Caleb's hard voice finally joined the others on the channel, and Damien stared in flawless awe as he witnessed the man's power at last:

With a whistling roar, a wash of crimson flames *exploded* up through the lowermost level, directly in front of the troops below. Damien almost knocked into Javier's feet as they both stopped to watch. Leo shrieked at them to keep moving.

The walkway shuddered up and away beneath the torrential golden flames. Before the grated floor had stopped falling, Damien caught the glint of something shiny flashing through the air. Two alien heads rolled off the train, followed swiftly by the body of a third.

"YEAH!!" Damien cried, moving again, almost to the second-to-top level.

The Fire Elemental was a blur far below them, attracting the attention of everyone in sight. Gyro shots rained onto the lower deck from the cargo and armored trains, but Caleb didn't stop. Jets of fire spurted out as the man inside the maelstrom absorbed it all. The troops who had been so close to the ladder either emptied everything they had at the destructive menace or turned tail and sprinted away howling.

"KEEP MOVING!" Leo bellowed again, making Damien wince. They kept climbing.

"*Darkness!*" It was the small one of Huxley's who had had so much to say on the flight from the Islets to Camp Cascade. "*What're you nutters doing?!*"

Damien caught a glimpse of a grenade explosion deep in one of the canyons. "We're climbing!" he shouted back. He spared a second glance towards the blunt prow of the cargo train, far in the distance, and spied a second explosion as it popped to life, but he couldn't tell who or what it was.

Earth and Darkness climbed up and past the crane arm, which was tucked parallel to the cargo train's body, and hung a few meters out in the air between them and the armored fortress. Finally, a few rungs later, they reached the top of the ladder—only to be greeted with two unsuspecting snipers and their spotter, all in half-helms. The narrow nest they were in was so small that two aliens would have looked cramped, but now with *five* individuals, it got ugly fast.

With a snarl, the nearest Algaroth tried to turn a deadly Gyro Lance rifle on them, but Javier kicked it away.

"Fuckers!"

The Elemental collected a thick cloud of dust and threw it at the first sniper. The alien hissed and scrubbed at its face, blinded. Damien helped it along by grasping the creature's neck guard and pulling. The soldier's warbling shriek faded—and was abruptly cut short with a resounding *CLONG* as the alien sniper's body bounced off the crane arm. Damien leapt over the Marine and grasped the other two's faces, letting a Shroud flood out of his fingertips.

"AHHHRRRGH!" he bellowed as he grasped over their snouts. They flailed for a split second—and one managed to rake his left arm as it did. He cried out, but it faded as the smothering power of his Shroud overwhelmed the light inside their skulls. He gave another shove and the lifeless corpses plummeted to the containers below. "Are we clear?!" he shouted into the wind.

"We're good!" said Leo. "Now hop over the far side and climb down!"

"Why?!" Javier snapped.

"Just do it!"

They did, descending the short ladder to a tiny platform that dangled high over the viewports that looked to be the control cabin of the train. Around the corner was a path back around the command tower, leading out and onto the narrow walkway against the crane arm…the walkway they were supposed to take across the gap.

Don't think about it. He remembered feeling vertigo when they were up on the XenoCon building, but he flushed it away.

"Now plug me in!" Leo snapped.

Damien whipped off his pack and pulled Leo's cube from inside, setting it inside the reader on the console in front of them. "You good?"

"*In a minute!!*" Leo snapped. He sounded much more frightened than was normal in a fight.

Damien took the remainder of their breather to examine the carnage below. He was surprised at how many bodies he could spot. Engagements flashed all over the place, mingled with the occasional blast of color that spoke to Caleb or Reuben nearby. Worry flooded him as he spotted more than one body clad in Amun-Nūr's brown-and-green, but it was offset by the far greater ratio of white-clad corpses, silhouetted in pools of dark blood. They were doing well so far. He searched the sky for signs of *Lotus*, but she was long gone with *Archon* and *Core*. The captains' comm channel lay silent. *They better be jamming any emergency calls.*

"Okay! The crane's moving!" Leo screamed.

"The what?! Oh…right," mumbled Javier, wincing. Damien helped him up from his resting spot against the ladder, and spotted a red stain on the rungs.

He's okay, Damien thought, reassuring himself. "We've got a way across!" he shouted into the comm. "Converge on the crane and let's get moving!"

The others confirmed in short order, and Damien saw a surge in the four separate skirmishes, showing Reuben, Caleb, Whiskey, and Omega. The only voices he still didn't hear were Von's or his squads'. At the realization, utter terror clogged his thoughts. He clasped his ear while he squinted around for signs of his brother and his team. "Has anyone seen Von?!"

"*They landed ahead of us, Dark,*" said a woman's voice. It sounded like Declan. "*I saw them going down near the nose of the other train.*"

Damien's blood ran cold. What if they'd missed the landing? Panic gripped him as Javier rapped on his shoulder. "C'mon! Our ride's here!"

Damien snatched Leo's cube up and spun around the side of the command tower. A deafening whine filled the air as the crane came to life and started to swing out over the jungle. "Can *someone* tell me where he is?! We need them!"

He and Javier climbed onto the crane arm's narrow walkway. It had already spun three-quarters of the way towards the armored train.

"Damien," Javier finally said when no one offered a useful answer. "*Look!*"

The crane creaked to a stop, wobbling far too much for comfort, but it was oriented right across the gap. Damien looked to where Javier was pointing, at the head of the other train. Relief flooded him as he caught sight of what the man was staring at: From over the distant edges of the speeding fortress, Damien spotted five armored Algaroth clamoring over the roof of the transport.

It was Von and his squad.

"*We're here, Dark,*" his brother's voice filled the comm as he came into view. "*Alpha Squad reporting in. Sorry we're late. We landed on a tiny platform on the far side.*" His voice grew cold, "*We lost two on the way.*"

"I'm sorry," Damien said, trying to stay neutral. "Glad the rest of you made it. Now are you gonna help us get inside?" He and Javier were already about halfway across and had somehow still managed to avoid detection, though none of the Collective soldiers could have missed the crane arm coming to life.

Von's reply was lost as a shout echoed up at them. Damien whipped around to see what it was, but instead he had his face slammed against the crisscrossing crane arm, courtesy of Javier. He saw stars as his forehead smacked the painted yellow metal.

"Keep going!" Javier yelled, giving his pack a shove.

Damien shook off the stars and looked down for the first time—but sincerely wished he hadn't. He had been so distracted with finding Von that he hadn't even thought to check what he was walking on. He gazed through the grated metal flooring and realized just how high up they were.

Ohh snaps… He had to reach out and steady himself. He tried to take a deep breath but it caught. *Much,* much *higher than at XenoCon. Ohh boy…*

"Whoa, Damien, *Damien!*"

Javier grabbed his pack to keep him steady—and shoved him forward just in time for a spray of weapons fire to fill the air. "GOD DAMMIT!" the Earth Elemental screamed while they ducked. "That's IT!" An Elemental's static filled the windy air, and Damien's spine tingled.

Gripping the walkway tight, Damien turned back to see what Javi was doing.

Giving a thunderous shudder, the crane wobbled beneath them as Javier uttered a primeval declaration to the heavens. The power of the man's scream washed over Damien, and he stared in awe as a vortex of mud, rocks, and dirt came orbiting up from the planet at them. Entire trees were stuck in the mud, and it all whirled up into the space between the crane and the shooters on the cargo train below. The earthen shield blocked the onslaught of plasma fire, but great sloshes of jungle mud splattered over the side of the cargo train's deck, and whole squads of Algaroth tumbled out of sight. The damage was immense.

"THAT'S RIGHT BABY! MAMMA EARTH'S GOT A PLACE FOR YA!!" Javier cheered, his howl wild and invigorating.

"*YEAH!*" came Declan's shout.

"*Whoa…*" blubbered another of their soldiers.

The Earth Elemental's face glowed even as veins throbbed in his neck, and Damien had never seen the man happier. But then he looked down again, the blur of dead wood came rushing up, and he had the terrible sensation of falling. He caught himself and took a breath, though Leo's shout didn't help either. "New trouble!"

A pointer appeared in Damien's goggle display. He looked up and—trying to stay focused on his footing and not on the fact that he could almost see *over* the tops of the highest trees from here—spotted the new problem.

His thudding heart stilled as he watched a hidden chamber in the side of the armored train vent steam and open. The groove curled down and

607

outward like a huge protective arm, revealing—*Oh... that's not good*—an enormous cannon emplacement, glowing hot and reminiscent of the one found on an Iceberg Tank.

"Ohh, you've gotta be kidding," he moaned.

"I can't hold this forever!" Javier shouted over the wind and the wet sounds of plasma impacting mud.

"Let's call you done then!" Damien answered, grabbing Earth by the neck of his suit. The vortex abruptly collapsed and Gyro shots skipped through the air around them.

They focused on the walkway and began moving. Damien shunted his vertigo away as the beastly cannon settled into place. Plasma zipped past them in earnest, but none of it connected; they were too far away.

"Anyone think they can take care of that?!" Damien screeched as he locked eyes across the space with the cannon's operator, boxed in a protective chair alongside the weapon.

"*We're working on it,*" Reuben answered calmly.

"Step it up!" he howled as they reached three-quarters of the way across, the cannon now aimed squarely at the crane arm.

"*Wait, dammit!*" Caleb snarled.

"Can't wait, *can't wait, CAN'T WAIT*!!" Javier shrieked. "WORK FASTER!!" They both broke into a reckless charge as a familiar, bass-heavy monster's growl filled the air.

"*On our way!*" Von shouted.

With the same ascending bellow as when he heard it in the valley, the cannon discharged an enormous lance of plasma into the crane. Damien howled, "JUMP!!!" as loud as he could.

They pushed off with all their might, flying through open air as the shattered crane tumbled away. They howled together, falling towards the empty balcony below. They weren't close enough; they weren't going to make it! Damien reacted on instinct. He threw all of his focus into a Wave, and hoped like hell that it would only faze the railing and not the platform itself.

"WHHOOOAAAA!!" they both cried as the Wave impacted. The railing bent and whirled away a ruined mess of metal tinged violet along with some of the grated walkway—but enough remained that they caught the railing on their stomachs. They had the wind knocked out of them, but they pulled up as fast as they could.

"*GO!!*" Caleb's voice roared into the comm.

As Damien and Javier spun around, their cheers froze in their throats as another sight met their eyes:

Two ramps of ice appeared off the cargo train—immediately splintering as the force of the wind hit them—but they held, carrying their occupants forward. Over both came an Elemental, each holding on for dear life onto their own sickly green cargo container. Whatever was inside was clearly flammable, and Caleb had ignited his and Reuben's at the base, propelling the two ramshackle rockets across the gap.

"*NOW*," Caleb ordered, and while Reuben leapt from his container, Whiskey and Omega Squads popped up all across the cargo train, turning their fire exclusively on the cannon. Just in time, too, because it was growling again, this time right at Damien and Javier.

They'll blow out the train just to kill us, Damien thought, strangely ratified to realize just how dangerous he and Javier were merited.

A split-second later, the two missiles impacted the side of the armored train one after another, and sparks exploded across the cannon's armored length.

"You're done," Caleb decried, and his swords whistled through the air as the operator lit up inside his little box, rag-dolling from overkill.

A whorl of flame hit the cannon, and the entire emplacement exploded. Damien shielded his eyes as the hardware fell into the swirling jungle below.

"YEAHH HOOO!! You guys alright?!" Javier and Damien cheered as Caleb landed almost as gracefully as a bird on the smoking amputated cannon arm about a hundred meters forward from them.

"*Fine*," Caleb said, sheathing one of his swords.

"*HRRGH*," said Reuben, sounding like he had hit something. "*Just fine.*"

"*We're climbing into the foreward hole*," said Von of the hole made from Reuben's missile.

"*I'll definitely remember that one,*" exhaled Huxley's squad leader.

"Koro Loss?" Damien requested. "What about your squads?"

Gunfire filled the channel, and he looked back to the cargo train with dread. "*Omega here,*" growled the Koro. "*We're pinned! We're holed up in an isolated cargo room lined in silver crates! We won't be joining you.*"

Huxley's boys answered immediately. "*Whiskey's on our way, Omega. Hang tight!*"

Damien's elation at their crossing faded a little and he shared a look with Javier.

"*Alpha Squad is entering the train,*" confirmed Von.

"*I see you on that walkway, Ice!*" Loss shouted amidst yells and roars. "*GO!*"

Reuben stayed quiet.

"*All of you GO! This is what we do! Te'Vierda!*"

"*Te'Vierda,*" Damien heard Reuben mutter.

"*We have a job to do,*" said another Omega, her voice somber. "*And not a lot of time.*"

"We'll be back," promised Javier before turning away.

"You have to get inside," Leo shouted. "You're running out of time!"

Damien blinked as a map appeared in the corner of his goggle display. They were *much* closer to Rome than he would have liked. "Thank you, Koro," he said, before turning inside.

"*Thank us by making a difference, as we always hoped to do.*"

The door shut behind him and the comm snapped off, leaving Omega and Whiskey alone on the cargo train while Damien, Leo, and Javier entered a dimly lit hallway.

CHAPTER THIRTY

To Wield & Control

"Leo, how long do we have?!" Damien shouted as a Gyro shot whizzed into the rib-like support strut he had tucked behind.

"Forty minutes. But that's only to the edge of the jungle. After that it's open water and detection."

"*Seriously?!*" yelled Javier, pulling behind cover as well.

"I—you want me to show you the equation I used to calculate it?" Leo fussed. "I can."

Damien would have responded, but Von's voice cut over the channel. "*Dark, Alpha and Ice are approaching the conductor's cabin.*"

"Gotcha!" Damien launched a large Orb down the corridor. The violet corona filled the ribbed hallway and exploded. Enraged howling filled the air in the aftermath, and he and Javier took the opportunity to bolt in the opposite direction, away from the door through which they had just entered the train. Damien tried to ignore his shaking hands.

"*What was that?*" Von asked.

"Nothing, don't worry about it!" His chest felt heavy, too, but he kept moving. Javier was breathing hard from another graze right beneath where he'd been hit earlier.

"Not that way," Leo chirped. They stopped.

"Why not?"

Just then, a *plink, plink* echoed down the hall, and Damien's gut wrenched, thinking of the stairwell at XenoCon. He knew that noise. "DOWN!" Fear forced his instinct over thoughts, and he launched a Wave both ways down the corridor, hoping to catch the Fireworks grenade before it detonated.

He succeeded.

With a sigh of relief he saw the tiniest flash of a detonation just ahead, right as the Wave passed over it. The explosion became trapped in the fragments of Damien's power. Then, by sheer dumb luck, a door opened and the explosion—finding an outlet—vanished inside. The moans of more wounded aliens reached their ears from ahead and behind.

Javier gave him an appraising look. "Did you know that was coming?"

"No!" Damien shook his head, pleased with himself.

Javier's raised an approving eyebrow. "I'm impressed."

Leo interrupted, "I swear, the next time you stick me in your backpack I'm coming in with a cattle prod! Keep moving!!"

Javier heaved and bent over. "Chill, Leo! We—*ehh*, damn…we need a breather!"

"Do you want a breather or do you want another patrol to catch up to you in twenty, nineteen, eighteen—"

The pair moaned and kept going; skipping past the room the grenade had rolled into. Leo had managed to wirelessly tap into the armored train's internal sensors using some sneaky tricks with his cube and their comm signals, but the enemy's firewalls were thick, and he hadn't been able to take control of anything, nor could he find the location of the generator, *or* see what was inside the conductor's cabin.

"Ice, Fire, what's your status?" Damien asked as they rounded a corner into another long, dimly lit corridor, all on Leo's instruction. The constant thrum of the train's thrusters kept their vibrating footfalls eerily muted in these corridors, the deafening firefights reduced to a modicum of sound. The halls of the armored train were haunting too in their emptiness; the oppressive, ribbed metal supports that repeated through the trapezoidal corridors made them feel like they were running through the insides of a snake. It was disorienting, and it made them feel very unwelcome. Damien reflected that they *were* unwelcome, but still.

"*I'll update you if there's something to update, Dark,*" Reuben snapped. "*I'm approaching Von's team now.*"

Damien grimaced at the man but held his tongue and focused instead on running. *So much for playing nice.* "Alright. We're heading to the lower deck and then moving aft. Leo says there's a cargo bay on the bottom level. We'll keep you post—WHAT, Leo?!"

Leo had been steadily saying his name louder and louder until it got his attention. ("Damien. Damien. Damien. Hey, Damien. *Damien. Hey, Damien! Damien!*") "Change of plans. Turn right up ahead. Over the bodies and down the stairs, to Fire's aid we go! Go two decks down."

"What? Why?" Javier posed, but they did as instructed and entered a stairwell, descending two steps at a time. When both of them hissed at their wounds, they slowed and took just one instead.

"Trust me," said Leo.

The lights in the hallway flickered out just as they reached the second deck, and the two were pitched into blackness. They halted. A hellish glow replaced the dark, and Damien and Javier sighted their weapons. They heard some kind of swirling howl from below, and they descended the last few steps.

"*I said, BACK!*" Caleb's voice burst half through the comms and half from down the hall. An Algaroth's keening wail pitched in their ears, and Damien's eyes went wide as a soldier literally *flew* past them, engulfed in flames. They poked their heads out to see the body land some meters to the right, flailing while he burned alive. Looking left, they saw why the lights had gone out.

Caleb was in the hallway junction, surrounded by Collective soldiers and fighting furiously. Flames licked around his body and his eyes glowed a brilliant, deathly orange. His two swords sailed through the air amidst cries and roars as the enemy tried to get even a single shot through. In the dark, it looked like a strobing dance of shadows, flashing blood, and bloodthirsty heat.

"What was that about help?" Javier snarked, lowering his weapon. "I think he's doing just fine."

"Other direction, smarty-pants," said Leo. "*See!* I warned you!"

They looked back past the burning soldier and Damien's stomach lurched.

hiss-Thump, hiss-Thump, hiss-Thump.

613

The sound Damien had dreaded hearing this entire undertaking finally manifested as four Avos came sprinting down the hall with their Prism camouflage armor disengaged, revealing their contoured onyx armor in all its dark glory. The rhythmic *hiss-Thump, hiss-Thump* of their frog-legs offered a synchronized death march. Two held wrist-mounted grenade launchers, one wielded a big, modified Gyro Lance that looked more akin to a handheld railgun, and the fourth had slipped out a reversible *avosas* knife. They hadn't seen the pair of Elementals and were on a beeline for Caleb.

As Damien took in the scene about to unfold, a chill tug sent him to the past, brought on by the frog-legs: a young woman, a little boy, and an old man whom he had tried to save and been unable to. Far from submerging him in guilt, the memory brought back the thought of the power he'd tried to use that night. It was the same power that had almost torn him apart the day of his demonstration in the Core, when Seattle fell. He knew in that microsecond before the spark turned from a thought into an idea, that there was only one way out of this. There was only one way to beat the approaching commandos and save Caleb's life.

His Cloak.

"Dark!" Javier cried.

Damien dropped his bag and had already submerged into his power— depleted as it was—to dive deeper than he did for any of his other abilities. He dove past the memories of home and his parents once more, and found that they did not scream at him any longer. His entire focus honed in on the shadows of the corridor, flickering in the golden light produced by Fire.

Scorching and torching was Caleb's domain. Mud, earth, rocks, and stone were Javier's. Shivering dry cold was Reuben's, and the liquid of life was Gwen's, but shadows and the absence of light were *his*.

Even in the first second of his focused time-out-of-time, Damien knew things were different now. In his mind's eye, he could see the fissure between body and shadow that he knew so well, and a side thought popped up that he figured it must look similar to the other Elementals when they used *their* powers, right? He pushed it away for another day and focused.

Damien felt the place that belonged to him and him alone, and he let it envelop him.

Rather than fighting to control his power, he submitted to it in a way he had only done once before, on that very first eve in the hollow. He realized now why he hadn't been able to use his Cloak in the Core or on that bridge: it was because he had tried to *control* Darkness, not wield it. He couldn't control the night or the shadows any more than he could control the Moon.

What he *could* do was channel it.

Damien's Elemental power wrapped itself around, over, *inside* his body, and he slid into the loving embrace gladly as the fissure sighed and relaxed. A violet corona shone around him, and black smoke curled around so tight that it hid him from view. It wrapped and curled, turning, changing, thickening, until he was hidden in the tangible shadows. He stepped through the metaphysical fissure.

YES!

The flickering shadows in the doorway claimed his body, and where Damien stood one second, the next he did not. His senses vibrated—or what he could only describe as "senses"—and in the time it took for a single frog-leg to pump out a pneumatic *hiss* on impact, Damien's fazed body slipped inside the shadows from the stairwell, across the hall, and right in front of the first commando. To the naked eye, it appeared that he had practically teleported from one spot to the other, but it was really the lack of light that did it. He moved, wreathed in the shadows and filled with focus, sliding along the surface of the corridor and inhabiting the space where light did not touch, his physical body turned as close to incorporeal as was possible.

The moment passed, the frog-leg went from *hiss* to *thump*, and the Elemental of Darkness erupted from the wall, interrupting the elite enforcers' charge. Whirling, forgetting his recent injuries and letting the power saturate his limbs, Damien kicked the first Avo's grenade launcher as it fired. Coming upright, he lashed out at the Lance-wielder, moving faster than the eye could follow. He uppercut the beast's jaw so hard that it snapped at the hinges. He let his momentum continue as that one toppled.

The first Avo's grenade flew in the opposite direction, far off course. Damien's focused state heightened his access to his pool, and he used that to drop the tiny singularity of an Orb in the off-balance grenadier's chest cavity.

Splick. It fazed the Avo with a wet detonation.

Two down.

Damien Vilan, swirling assailant in painful shades of violet and black, had taken them by surprise, but these were Avos, not the common soldier. The second grenadier recovered first, swinging his launch-arm, intending to grapple with his assailant long enough for a grenade to take them both to a messy end...but even an Avo was still too slow.

Damien watched the alien's hand twitch, ready to fire a grenade. He took advantage of that and sent a tightly focused Orb splitting through the air, where it connected squarely on the snub barrel of the Avo's wrist-mounted launcher. He whipped away from the unfortunate opponent as the Orb and the grenade detonated, taking the Algaroth's limb.

In that second, the commando's scream felt like his own as Damien spun to face the fourth and final opponent. The last Avo had refocused with enough sense to plunge its curved *avosas* towards Damien's exposed neck. It would have been a lucky, lethal stab, had there not been a double, *CRACK, CRACK*, and the blade missed.

The swirling ambush was over in five seconds flat. Just enough time for Javier to have sighted his rifle, train it on the knife-wielder, and shoot it in the head as the blade fell towards Damien. The second shot put the grenadier out of his misery, ending the engagement just in time to watch Caleb finish off his crowd as well.

A fireball took two Algaroth to the ground as Caleb sheathed his swords in a fluid twirl. Then, before Damien or Javier realized what he was doing, Fire held his hands out, focusing on the three whimpering aliens that remained from the once enormous group. The blue faces warmed to a glowing orange, their guns clattered to the floor, and Damien and Javier stared in shock as Caleb cooked the injured from the inside out. The brutality was stunning, and Damien noted the man's orange eyes glinted, deeply satisfied.

The agonized alien keens died away, and the only sounds were those of a few sizzling corpses and the distant howl of wind over the train's thrusters. Despite Damien's discomfort with the kind of excess violence he'd just witnessed, he didn't think he had a lot of ground given what he'd just done, and now wasn't the time to mention it. "You alright?" he asked of the other Elemental. Sweat poured off his body and his head was spinning as he released the last vestiges of the Cloak, and he lamented that he couldn't bask in the glory of what he'd just accomplished, but now wasn't the time for that either. He replaced his bag with Leo's cube still inside and approached the bloody junction, breathing hard.

"Busy," Caleb answered, wiping one of his swords on white armor. "You?" he added it almost as an afterthought.

Damien panted as Javier remarked, "Oh, you know…something similar."

Caleb snorted and turned down the corridor, tromping over the bodies.

"Whoa, whoa," Damien said, reaching out. "Where're you going?"

Fire didn't stop walking. "Cockpit. The others are about to breach it."

Damien nodded, "Got it. We're heading aft."

"I'll let them know," and then he was gone.

"Not even a damn *thank you*?" said Javier, crossing his arms.

Damien shrugged. "C'mon," he said, feeling even heavier now. His neck had started throbbing, and his spine twinged every few steps, as did the rake down his arm from the sniper. "We need to get to that cargo bay."

"Leo," Javier asked as they began moving, "how long until—"

"Twenty-six minutes. You better move fast."

The two exchanged looks, and their pace quickened.

∞   ∞   ∞

As Damien and Javier moved towards the back of the train on the lowermost deck, they encountered less and less resistance. It seemed the enemy was running out of soldiers.

"Leo, have you heard from Omega or Whiskey? How's the cargo train look?" Damien asked as they moved past yet another empty room. He didn't know what to make of so much space, so many corridors, and so little *stuff.*

Leo responded after a contemplative pause. "I haven't. There aren't many good eyes out there worth using. There *is* a sensor on the command tower that says there's been a lot of damage sustained to a specially controlled room with…precious cargo with silver boxes—and that there's *still* damage being sustained—but that's it. I'm sorry. They might be alive, but I can't say."

The two men traded worried looks.

"What about the conductor's cabin?"

"It's been breached but…oh dear."

"What?" said Javier.

Leo hesitated, "It…it sounds like Reuben took a shot of some acidic weapon in the chest. He's…unconscious."

"Is he alright?" Damien asked, stopping short.

"No, no: *keep going,*" Leo snapped. "There you go. I don't know. Hold on, Alpha turned the team-comms off while they breached the conductor's cabin, I'll get back in."

The comm crackled as the channel went live again.

"Ice? Ice, are you there?" Damien asked, unable to control the worry in his voice.

"*It's Von,*" came the reply. "*Ice is alive, but barely. He's unconscious.*"

"What happened?"

Von hesitated. "*The conductor's cabin was full of Avos. They ambushed us.*"

Damien's stomach dropped. "Are you alright?"

"*Fine, I'm fine. But we lost people and…there's something else.*"

"What is it?"

"*Their leader, the one in charge of the convoy? It was him; it was the one from home that you told me about.*"

Damien's gaze narrowed. "Shellack," he growled.

"*Yes,*" said Von, apologetic. "*Damien, he…got away. He took two of the conductors and escaped through a hidden hatch or scurry-hole. We assume they left the craft.*"

A broiling fury shot through Damien's chest and he slowed to a hard, pounding walk.

"*…Damien?*" Von asked when he didn't answer.

"*Here,*" he answered through gritted teeth.

"*I'm very sorry.*"

Damien took a breath, still walking, "Don't be. It wasn't your fault."

"*I still am.*"

Leo urged them around a corner.

"Is the cabin secure?" Damien asked, following directions.

"*Yes. Have you found the weapon?*"

"We're almost there," Javier answered quickly, covering Damien's exasperated sigh.

According to Leo, they were nearing the main cargo bay. The uncomfortable thought tugged at Damien that there was still a chance the weapon wasn't here at all—unlikely as that felt—but the consequences didn't bear thinking about.

"*Understood,*" said Von. "*We'll hold here. Fire is escorting the wounded to an escape hatch. Update us when you find it.*"

"We will," Javier assured him. The comm snapped off.

"It's just through that door," said Leo.

Damien throttled his pistol grip and grumbled his way forward.

"Hey," said his friend, stopping him. "That Avo? We'll get him, man. We will."

Damien clenched his teeth. "God damn right we will," and he marched down the hall to the cargo bay.

"Ready?" Javier asked a moment later as they flanked the floor-to-ceiling cargo bay doors.

Damien nodded, pistol drawn.

Leo keyed the lock and a crack appeared. The doors rumbled to life. They churned open, but had only slid about a meter when Damien heard an ominous *ching!*

Damn. There wasn't time to say anything, even as he and Javi locked eyes.

They threw themselves backwards, yelling, just before an explosion belched out of the bay. Damien landed on his bag just behind the edge of a ribbed metal support, avoiding the mangled cargo doors by a hair's breadth as they blew off their track.

"*AHHHHHHH!!!*" Javier cried, not so lucky.

"JAVI!!" Damien called as the explosion buckled the corridor. The heat blistered over his body suit, and he shivered and moaned as his skin burned. He could feel his nostrils sear at the acrid scorch.

Fire sheared metal, and the reinforced corridor warped outwards under the force of the blast. It held though, keeping the train from blowing another hole. The second the fire passed, Damien leapt to his feet, ignoring the blood trickling down the side of his face. He skidded across the opening.

"Earth! Earth! Javi talk to me!"

Javier rolled on the deck, holding his side and leg. Damien winced as he saw the burns.

"Oh no…" he leaned forward to inspect the wounds.

Javier twitched and gasped, his words stuttering out over the pain. "How b-b-bad? Ha—*Ahh!*" he moaned as Damien gently lifted his arm. From the middle of his ribcage down to his left boot, the flesh had been scorched to a crisp. His armor had been cooked away and the entire area had become an unremarkable mass of blackened skin and mesh.

"Umm…" Damien cursed when he couldn't come up with a witty remark.

"Oh-oh good," he stammered. "So I don't feel like a b-baby for crying about this sh-sh-shit!"

Damien winced, "No, no you're not a baby. But yeah, it's pretty bad."

A call from inside the cargo bay interrupted them: an alien order, probably to go check the hall. He hadn't seen anything through the black smoke billowing out, but Damien had a bad feeling that this was an Avo's trap, and he doubted these ones would forego their Prism camouflage.

"Damien," Leo prompted.

"Hold on, man," Damien soothed, ignoring the voice in his ear as he reached in his pack for anesthetic.

"*Damien*," Leo repeated.

"What?!"

"It isn't in there. We have to move."

"*What* isn't in there?!" Damien cursed the tiny can of spray. It would never cover such a huge area. He emptied it over the man's side nevertheless.

"The weapon."

He stopped. A tingle ran up his spine. "What."

"It's okay though!" Leo rushed. "There's another bay, at the back of the train! I just found it."

"How do you know?" He reached underneath his friend to pick him up when he heard a single impact from inside.

hiss-Thump.

He groaned. *I hate Avos.* "Javi, c'mon," he said, frantic. "We've gotta move. C'mon, we've gotta go. We've gotta go *now*."

"Hurry," Leo urged.

Javier moaned as Damien picked him up. He held their gear awkwardly while trying to be gentle on the Marine's wounded side. He roughly sighted his pistol in his free hand, aiming it into the cloud.

"How far?" Damien whispered, sidling past and waiting for plasma to come streaking out.

"Forty meters, then turn left. The door will be on your right, in the middle of the corridor."

Damien cursed. It might has well have been four *thousand* meters with Javier wounded and angry commandos on their tail. "Any idea how to make it go faster?" he snapped as more frog-legs resounded inside. The two made their way down the darkened, burning corridor, and Damien fought the urge to panic.

"Not until you get to the other bay," said Leo, sounding just as frightened. "I'll tell you when to shoot. Go, go NOW!"

Damien lowered the pistol and focused wholly on running while Javier moaned on his shoulder, hobbling along with him.

hiss-Thump, hiss-Thump.

"Turn in three...two...one... NOW!" Leo ordered.

Damien was already spinning, firing his entire pistol clip down the hall as he swung Javier around and stormed away backwards. The air shimmered as multiple invisible surfaces were hit, and roars followed behind them. Then the pistol made a loud *CLACK* as the magazine ran dry.

"Prime it!" Leo ordered.

Damien had really hoped their escape wouldn't involve tossing his favorite pistol, but he knew they had no choice. He rounded the corner just as a hailstorm of Gyro zinged towards them. The heated bolts took out chunks of metal with angry hisses. Javier gasped as Damien reached around his torso, pressing against the burns—he needed both hands to flip the pistol's power cartridge around and reinstall it, priming the grenade inside.

"Get to the door, they're *comiiiiing!!*" Leo howled.

"ONE THING AT A TIME!!" Damien barked, but he pulled Javier roughly forward, making them both wince as he slammed the butt of the gun into his thigh, clacking the upside-down cartridge into place to start the timer.

"Get inside, go, *go, GO!*"

He could hear the commandos hot on their heels, their boots impacting with terrific power *HISS-THUMP, HISS-THUMP, HISS-THUMP.*

"NOW!!" Leo screamed, and Damien whirled the pistol back down the hall as they fell through the door. It clattered away wildly and he was sure he'd missed. Then, just before the door slammed shut, he saw half of an Avo come leaping around the corner; the alien's Prism cloak had partially failed and only its bloody head and torso were visible, making for a confusing image, but it didn't matter. The pistol bounced off the commando's invisible knees and sailed clean around the corner.

"YES!!" He cheered as the explosion went off. The roar of dying aliens was cut short as Leo slammed the secret bay's doors shut, leaving them in the dark.

CHAPTER THIRTY ONE

Checkmate, Black or White

They sat panting there in the dark, secret room; the smell of Javier's wounds filling what must be a small space. Damien gasped, too exhausted to try to look around. "How're you doing?" He shrugged off his pack and felt the adhesive release the bag. It thunked to the deck and he felt the cold of sweat on his spine through his armor mesh.

"*Hrrnn...*" the Marine breathed. "Feel...like a pot roast."

Damien snorted, grateful for the blanketing dark that surrounded them, but even that moment was cut short.

"Boys, I'm hitting the lights," said Leo.

With a loud hum, the Collective's odd lighting cores came on in the bay, revealing a space just as dark and moody as the rest of the train. Damien sat facing the heavy door, which had been disguised to look like a bulkhead. He never would have found it without Leo's help. He spun on his haunches, uncertain of what he might find...and froze as he laid eyes on their target at last.

The black hole generator sat benign, tucked carefully against the side of the compact secret bay: Croll Tan's secret weapon, courtesy of the Supply Fleet.

Acutely aware of his breathing, of every movement, Damien stood slowly, tensing as if the thing would come alive and eat him, even though it didn't look like a weapon at all. He wasn't sure why he had expected a missile or a wired steel drum, but this certainly wasn't that.

The black hole generator sat on a large inverted U-base loaded with dormant displays. On one end of the machine, a collection of tubes, boxes, and sinister contraptions fed towards the center. On the far side of the center, a claw-shaped funnel came out, cradling three rings that opened upwards. Between these items sat the centerpiece itself: the tank. The already small bay shrank at the mass of the huge sideways incubation tank, and Damien tried not to focus on the crystalline residue dusting the inside. The residue was a sickly, rusty color, like caked blood.

Damien trembled as he approached the consoles. On the intake side, a small tray stuck out from a little machine that looked like it had been added recently—it looked newer and shinier than the rest of the huge device. The tray had a neatly imprinted port in the center, where one might place a tube of some kind... or perhaps a vial of blood.

He shuddered as he traced the little tube up and up, to a tiny hole punched through the top of the incubator tank. The hole looked so small to offer such a volatile mixture to whatever Croll Tan had created.

Goddammit. Unadulterated rage billowed up from inside him. *He modified it. This thing is using my blood.* Damien swallowed heavily. *You shouldn't have made this fucking personal, Tan. I'm gonna kill you.* "This thing is...big," he said, shaking. "Any idea how to tear it apart?" He had an urge to start pulling cords and smashing controls, but he had a feeling that wouldn't be enough. The weapon looked complicated, but also hearty. It wouldn't break just by flipping a switch; of that he was certain.

"Hold on." Leo said.

"What is it?"

The AI didn't answer right away. Damien promptly started to pace around the machine, looking for an easy fix, despite his misgivings. When Leo finally did come back, the AI's voice sounded diffident. "I'm uh... I'm gonna let you talk to Von," he said.

Damien nodded and moved back to check on Javier. "Vo?" he asked when he heard the comm pop.

"*Here.*" His brother's voice also sounded flat.

"What's going on? We found the generator but we need help destroying it. How much time do we have?"

"*Not enough.*"

Damien's stomach sank. "...Why?"

"*We reach the coast in twelve minutes. That isn't our trouble, though.*"

Damien looked up from the tube of salve he had just found buried in his pack. He squeezed it over Javier's side, letting the man rub it in himself. "What is, then?"

Von didn't answer.

"Vo?"

"The plan's changed," Leo picked up the silence. "We can't destroy the machine just yet."

Damien made a shocked squeak and looked at the tank. "Why not?"

"Because the Over-Seer is on his way to Rome. You were right."

A chill coursed over Damien's body. He stood, cupping his ear. "Say it again."

"Croll Tan is on his way to the Vatican to turn on the weapon himself, just like you thought he would. This weapon is *his baby."*

"Leo? Are you sure?"

"Positive."

Damien's thoughts started to race. Had Tan been warned? He thought it unlikely with three Amun-Nūr ships blocking the convoy's signals, but if they were approaching the coast he couldn't be sure, and then he remembered that Shellack had escaped. *I'm gonna gut that fucking slizzard.*

"They don't know we're here. *Yet,"* said Leo, obviously remembering that little detail. "But they will."

There was no way they couldn't know, even if the survivalist Avo *hadn't* gotten a warning out. The cargo train was smeared with bodies, and the armored train had two smoking holes from Caleb's crate-missiles. Croll Tan would know the train had been attacked the moment he tried to make contact.

"Do you think he'll smite the train?" he asked.

"Smite? Oh yes," Leo answered. "Even a *legion* of troops couldn't do the kind of damage you all have managed to pull off. He'll know it was you peeps."

Javier moaned on the floor.

"What do we do?" Von asked.

Damien thought about it, but not for long. It was really very simple, but they wouldn't like it. "Fire, where are you?" he said, standing.

Caleb answered first. *"About to climb out a hole and bring in help for Ice, why?"*

"Get down here. Vo, you too. *Quickly.*"

There was a brief pause. *"Why?"* Caleb repeated.

"Earth's hurt," Damien pressed. "He needs evac. Anyone heard from Whiskey or Omega?"

"I can't hear them!" shouted a jittery someone from Von's team. *"I'm just outside and no one's answering!"*

Damien felt a single tendril of despair claw at his resolve, but he swatted it away. "Keep trying—and actually, Vo? Get your squad out too. Don't come down here."

Von's silence told Damien that he had figured out what his brother was doing. *"Damien, no."*

"I've got Romi and Huxley on the line," Leo announced. "They're on their way. Fagin is staying on-station to keep scrambling the train's signals."

Damien yanked his emergency pain kit from his pack. Two white pills sat inside. He pushed one into Javier's hand and popped the other. "Fire, where are you?" The pills would numb the throbbing pain in his back, neck, and wrist long enough to do what needed to be done.

"On my way."

"Damien," Von repeated. *"NO."*

"Cale, hurry up."

"DAMIEN—"

"Don't argue with me, Vo," Damien snapped. "There isn't any time."

"Time for what?" the frantic soldier asked.

"He wants to be a hero." Caleb said. Damien couldn't tell if he sounded admiring or derisive.

"What? Darkness? NO!" shouted the younger man.

"We don't have a choice!" Damien shouted over them. "Since the train will *still* make it to Rome, Tan will hopefully want to check on his precious machine first, *maybe* even keep it, and that'll give me time to nail him to the wall when he does."

"And what if he decides his weapon is worth sacrificing to take out some Elementals?!" Von shot back.

"Then he's only gonna get one."

Von choked on his retort and fell silent.

Damien continued digging in his pack and his hand brushed something cylindrical. He pulled it out and swallowed, a sad smile crossing his face. It was his rook; the one that Admiral Baroda had recovered from Huxley's Blackwing, and his last piece of home. The little chess piece made him think of his conversation with Satolin, about how Tan's move with this Inferno was an endgame play…and a tiny flicker of fear came up as he remembered what the Prohka had said about the Over-Seer potentially having dangerous twin children. He laughed in the quiet.

"What's so funny?!" Von snapped.

Damien looked hard at the little white tower, all chipped and dirty. "Vo, Tan made this his and my game when he took the Islets apart, and these are the final moves. We're both set for checkmate, and both of us have enough pieces committed that it won't end in a tie." He couldn't help but ponder if he was the one playing the black pieces or the white.

"What? No, forget it!" Von roared, ignoring him. *"I'm not leaving you!"*

He was about to make a retort when Leo cut in, "Von, he's right. It's a good plan."

Just then, the doors slid open and Caleb—hoisting Reuben's limp form over his shoulder—came into the secret bay, accompanied by a skittish looking young man of Alpha Squad. His nametag said "EMERY." Reuben's chest was blackened and smelled like decay, but it was lined with icy crystals that had stopped the spread of whatever hit him. Emery helped Caleb set the wounded Elemental down before running to Javier.

The Fire Elemental stared unblinking at the machine. "You made quite a mess back there," he said. His dry voice betrayed neither approval nor admonition.

"*I'M NOT LEAVING YOU AGAIN!*" Von howled when no one responded to him.

Damien closed his eyes. "You aren't," he said calmly. "I'm ordering you to leave."

"*You can't give me orders, Damien Vilan.*" Von's guttural voice finally cracked.

"Yes I can." He watched Caleb hoist Javier into his arms while Emery took Reuben.

Von didn't answer.

"Three minutes!" Leo yelped, hastening their departure. "Am I going with them or what?!"

Damien rolled his eyes and snatched up Leo's little cube from his pack. "I thought you'd want to join me, buddy?"

"Ha! Not a chance, Elemental. *Someone* has to write a ballad when you're dead."

Damien grinned as the nearly limp Javier took the cube and cradled it, nodding off. Damien cupped his earpiece again. "Von, I'm sorry."

Von whined over the comm, and he recognized it as more of a growl of sorrow.

"Be safe," he said. "Please. Take care of that squad of yours, and try not to get shot somewhere worse than the leg?"

Caleb and Emery—carrying Javier and Reuben—grabbed the last of their things.

"*Can you forgive me,*" Von asked quietly. "*For dragging you away from them?*"

Damien swallowed the lump in his throat and he blinked away his uncertainty. "I was gonna ask you to forgive *me* for saying they loved you more." His voice cracked. "You were right. They loved us both. Family is more than just blood."

The skittish little Emery stared at him, a little sad and confused smile filling his youthful face. "Good luck, Damien!"

"You too. Be safe."

Caleb gave him a hard stare. "It's about time someone else killed an Over-Seer," and he walked away.

"Safe trip home," Damien said to their retreating backs. He didn't wait for their answer for fear of losing his resolve. He palmed the door controls and watched as they slid shut, locking him in with the weapon.

"*Bye Darkness*," said Emery just before Damien muted all but one comm.

"Leo?" he asked.

"*I'm still here.*" The AI's voice came in through the earpiece this time instead of his aural implant.

"Are Loss and the others okay? Huxley's boys?"

"*The Archon just arrived, she's picking them up now. We don't know how many made it.*"

Damien hated not knowing before they left, but it couldn't be helped. "What about everyone else?"

"*Romi's here too. Von is getting on now. He's the last one.*"

"Thank you, Leo."

"*Always, my friend. See you down the road.*" Then the channel fizzled and popped as *Sanguine Lotus* pulled away from the train and the heavy walls blocked his signal.

Damien walked past Javier's blood on the floor and stopped at the tray where his blood was supposed to go, facing the monstrous device. "I think I'll play white, Tan," he whispered. "Your move," and he set his white rook down with a tiny *plink*.

∞   ∞   ∞

The armored train sped out of the jungle and over the Mediterranean Sea, splitting off from the rest of the convoy, and Damien found himself on his way to Rome. He felt the change in terrain when the train's thrusters began pulsing and pitching as it wheeled over open water. Damien went along as the thing sped up, rocketing its way to their final destination.

When it began to slow, Damien slipped into the nook he'd chosen to hide in and closed his eyes. His breathing slowed to deep, rhythmic beats, helping him focus. When the train finally stopped a long while later, he slipped through the fissure of body and shadow and wrapped himself in his Cloak.

The doors he had noted before they arrived—huge, and on the far side of the bay from where he'd entered—fell open to smoky air. Set after set of heavily armed troops rushed inside, but no Over-Seer. The Collective soldiers marched in without a word, sweeping their pronged Gyro rifles for any sign of the enemy. Their lights went over Damien more than once without pausing.

The door to the inside of the train opened, but he heard the soldiers give only a cursory check to the hall outside. Before he knew it, most of them had gone and an enormous vehicle tug appeared in the doorway, but still no Over-Seer.

Shit. He had hoped he could ambush Tan then and there.

The tug rolled into the bay and gently slid the black hole generator into an embrace. He knew he had to get out of there.

The second no one was watching, Damien bolted from between the two struts he'd hid between, wreathed in shadow, and he slid over the edge of the bay ramp. He felt his way around, taking in a quick scan of a vast brick courtyard before he spotted a Razer skiff, unmanned and parked behind a few stacks of crates and a broken sandbag barricade.

Swiftly, silently, Damien raced across the courtyard in his shadowed form, not quite incorporeal, but not entirely *there* either, and slid behind cover. He moved not a moment too soon.

A single shout echoed from somewhere distant, and a split-second later the world turned white as something exploded. The shockwave was so intense it rattled Damien's focus down to his core. The dark pool shook in his limbs, and he felt his submission to Darkness break. He gasped—and clapped a hand over his mouth—as he opened his eyes, once more in his own body.

He blinked, knowing what he was seeing but not comprehending it.

The train had been blown apart. An unseen force (he guessed artillery) had drilled its way to the heart of the armored behemoth and expanded, sending flaming kilos of metal and slag everywhere and making the courtyard a mess because of it, at least the parts he could see anyways.

Guess we made the right choice bailing out. He breathed a tiny sigh of relief. *Someone managed to warn them we were on the train.*

Damien searched behind him to make sure no one was nearby before he looked between the crates. A chill ran down his spine, and he was forced to admit that he admired The Collective's resolve and precision for destroying their own weapons with an army standing so close by.

They were in Vatican City. This was St. Peter's Basilica, in the *Piazza di San Pietro*—St. Peter's Square. It was the courtyard of the Pope, and a Catholic religious icon. Damien had never had any real desire to see the place, but he had never denied the beauty of its history and significance. Even if he wasn't certain about a controlling deity, Damien had come to understand a bit about *belief.*

At the least, the Piazza was supposed to be a beautiful place. Anger and pain welled up inside him as he saw around the setting sun, shadowing the looming Basilica in the distance. Huge swaths of it were burning. Plasma fires sizzled all around the square, and Damien stared out at a grand courtyard where a horde of aliens stood in their diamond-white armor, smeared from battle. Ranks upon ranks of them stared solemnly at either the Basilica or the ruins of the train, but there was still no Over-Seer.

Where IS he?! Doubt threatened to overtake his resolve. If Tan hadn't come...

He crept around the crates and spotted the tug, carrying the weapon. It rolled towards his crates and Damien shrank back, afraid of being spotted. He felt a heavy *thud* and looked back up to find the device only a short distance away across the open courtyard. The consoles faced him, offering a skewed picturesque view of the Basilica: the army of blue soldiers in diamond-white, the sunset sparkling off the domes of St. Peter's, distant columns of smoke from Rome on fire, crackling plasma fires in the Piazza, the black hole generator, and the burning fortress train, split open like a beastly melon off to the side.

Collective technicians in thin purple body suits swarmed over the machine. He saw one of them grab his rook and examine it.

That's not for you, he thought behind gritted teeth.

The tech called another over, and they examined the rook together.

You idiot, he thought, suddenly realizing what the hell he'd done. *You tipped your hand to be funny!*

The techs continued chattering about Damien's chess piece while more of them approached. He winced, unsure if he should move or not, when another rumble came from behind him. He spun to see a second tug roll into the courtyard, and he suppressed a dismayed moan as he realized what the new vessel was carrying: A Magnetic Fusion Reactor, just like he'd predicted. *Well, I guess at least we seem to be on track with figuring this thing out.* Rome's Mag Fury rolled up in its enormous metal cradle, the stolen power source for the generator. There was still no sign of Tan. Damien looked back towards the weapon and saw—with sinking dread— that the technicians had waved to a superior officer: a beast of an Algaroth, whose white armor was dented and battered, and who bore *four* times as many lines as a Koro. Damien didn't even know what rank that was, but he guessed pretty damn high. *No-no-no-no-no-no no, don't go over there!*

The battle commander approached the techs around the blood tray. The decorated Algaroth had grasped the rook between his tool-fingers and lifted it into sunlight to better examine the piece, when a distant whine became audible over the hiss and crackle of plasma fires. Everyone in the courtyard looked up and after a moment spotted the source: A ship. It was the same ship Damien had seen in that instant before the Iceberg blew up the village, the same one that had born him so many injuries: an angular stingray, heavily armed and sleek.

Croll Tan's gunship.

Damien's blood started to boil, but he held it together long enough to creep around the crates to the messy sandbag barricade, where he found an unexpected friend. "Hello there," he whispered, pulling the Plaster rifle from the dead man's hands. "I'll put this to good use, I promise."

The Over-Seer's stingray ship landed at the center of the army on a makeshift pad, right in the middle of the Piazza, over the toppled obelisk that had stood there until recently. Damien waited a short sprint away from the generator. He waited as the ship settled and a ramp descended. Figures began emerging. Each was a decorated Algaroth, their helmets and armor striped time and again to denote their rank, the highlights of their cream-white armor trimmed in gold. They had to be the Over-Seer's royal guards.

They descended with crisp precision, lining out a path from the ship towards the weapon. Then, every soul in the Piazza stiffened when another figure emerged, towering over all.

Croll-Tan.

Hatred boiled in Damien's veins. It mixed with the adrenaline, firing up a cocktail as he let the black pool spread through his body. His muscles tensed in anticipation as the enormous Algaroth stepped down from his ship.

C'mon, you son of a bitch.

Tan said not a word as he descended the steps, garbed in his eloquent armor. His helmet adorned his regal snout and eye ridges, hiding his ganglia and making his pure gold eyes glint from beneath them. A wave of tension swept the small army as *his* gaze swept over them. Tan stopped between the weapon and his ship, and unfurled his wings. Finally, Damien realized just how enormous the Algaroth Royal was. They stretched three times as wide as the creature to which they were attached, imposing at any distance. Thick, leathery membranes stretched between each finger of the wing, making them look like those of a giant bat. Tan's presence commanded attention, and Damien watched as a hundred recorders came alive throughout the army, filming the dark lord.

The great alien nodded, shook one of his wings, and approached the black hole generator. Damien couldn't help but be entranced by the grace of the usurper.

At the base of the weapon, the battle commander had—to Damien's eternal gratitude—crumpled the rook in his hand as the technicians connected the stolen Mag Fury to the base of the weapon. The generator came to life, glowing and fiving off a slow, resolute drumbeat. *Whum-bum, bum... Whum-bum, bum...*

Closer, Damien thought, *closer*.

Then, Tan whirled on his soldiers, his wings *whooshing* through the air, and his voice echoed in clear Dekka. The words translated neatly into

Damien's ear, but they captured none of the power of the speech in the native language.

"A great victory has been struck today," the Over-Seer crooned, spreading his huge arms wide, needing no microphones to project his deep voice. "When the people turn against you and choose outcasts over peace, then you know the face of evil!"

The army cheered its approval. Damien's lip twitched. *Whum-bum, bum…*

"Earth's greatness eluded us all," Tan continued. "Left as it was to humankind and their devices! They forfeited this land long ago, yet still they cling to entrenched life when it is no longer theirs to have." He turned towards the burning train. "The Elementals would see us removed from this world," he turned to the generator, "and humans would see us destroyed. But their final fall begins…tonight."

The roaring approval continued, and—despite himself—Damien was frozen, listening to the orator.

"Humankind," the Over-Seer said switching to English as his voice quieted to a growl. "I speak now to you: You see where I stand, in the center of your Vatican City? You see the army around me, and how I claimed Rome for my own? You see the device behind me?" The growl sank further, into a hiss that carried far. "This, at last, is the instrument of your end."

Whum, bum, bum. The drumbeat was speeding up

Tan's great golden eyes sparkled in the evening light. "With this weapon, your Final Option is no longer that. After the next Supply Fleet arrives from my home, another will come bearing siege ships. If you have not surrendered long before then, The Collective will *ensure* that you all die. I have found a way around your Nukes, and I am here to demonstrate it to you."

The Over-Seer fell silent and a dark, painful quiet filled the courtyard. His wings drooped, and Damien inched forward until Tan spoke again and he froze. "Religion," the Over-Seer crowed, almost musingly. "Religion—I've oft found—does not survive contact with the void." He pointed to the sky, slowly creeping from gold and red to black and starry. "So I have chosen this *Basilica* to ease the passing of faith!

"By the hands of your fourth Over-Seer," he swelled. "By my city of Solaroth, rightful capitol of the Sol System, *by our mighty COLLECTIVE!!*" At the final word, Croll Tan's enormous wings unfurled again, this time as if in great ecstasy, and blue bolts of a static overload coursed through them.

Damien had never seen an Algaroth show so much raw emotion like that, and he had never known that the anxious charge the aliens built up could be unleashed into something quite so stunning. In a mere moment, the Over-Seer's bat-like appendages were alight in a starburst, and Croll Tan *glowed* blue.

In the cheer that resounded, Damien had no doubts that the evil thing in front of him had to die, but he couldn't help but appreciate the kind of creature, from a far-away planet, that could stand as Croll Tan did, with as much intelligence and cunning as any that had existed on Earth. The Algaroth were incredible feats of the cosmos.

But they aren't the only ones, a voice said in the back of Damien's mind, and Damien stopped. He knew that voice. *Everyone* knew that voice. It was the voice of a hero, a martyr, and probably the only man in the world whom The Collective had ever wanted more than Damien.

Hawkins, he thought with a chill. *Admiral Hawkins.* Damien had always turned to the man's speeches in his darkest moments—particularly in the last few months, in fact, in his long days in his quarters after Seattle's fall.

Lunar Admiral Jacob Hawkins had said that once; that humankind deserved a chance to leave their mark on the cosmos. That even if humans were not remembered in their individual stories, or that they may not know what was to become of us beyond our lifetime, that humankind had earned its place among the stars, to exist, to thrive, and to *grow*.

It was in those moments—before he leapt from the safety of the vehicle to storm the greatest tyrant in the history of the world—that Damien Vilan understood what such a cosmic mark meant, and he knew at last, that he wanted to see it done. *We won't be broken today*, he thought with increasing resolve. It hardened inside of him into an impenetrable shell, protecting a single, simple idea:

We deserve to exist.

Damien's focus snapped back then as Tan spoke his last words, static charging the air and his wings aglow as the sun sank behind the clouds at the horizon, destined to return only briefly through the columns lining the edges of the Piazza before night descended.

"Humanity and the Elementals," Tan roared in Dekka, "have chosen oblivion over annexation into our Collective. They will go the path of other races before them, and vanish into nothingness!" The golden eyes twinkled with conviction as Tan lifted his gaze to the first visible stars. "And we? *WE* WILL BREAK THEIR SPIRIT AND SEND THEM THERE!!" Another bolt shot through the bones of Tan's wings and the dark lord was almost blinding to look upon, brilliant in his display of light as the army cheered in the shadows of St. Peter's.

Light can't save you, Damien thought, and as that very glow faded from Croll Tan's wings and the cheers of the army rattled his bones, Damien, who was shadows incarnate, knew it was now or never. The hypnotizing words had stopped, and the Over-Seer had turned towards the generator consoles. The drumbeat quickened, and Damien saw the first hints of *something* as it was pumped into the incubation tank: a flickering red blob, thick and writhing.

The black hole generator's cycle had begun. The drumbeat quickened.

Whum, bum, bum. Thrum, bum, bum. Whum, bum, bum. Thrum, bum, bum.

Letting his power flow to his limbs—and just as the sun fell into that space between clouds and horizon, igniting the sky as if they were on fire—Damien stood from the protective cover of the barricade and sighted his rifle. He was silent as he ran forward, while Croll Tan took deliberate steps to the ignition button.

Twenty meters. He was past all cover. Tan approached the console.

Ten meters. Shouts were spreading through the ranks as they spotted Damien. Tan leaned over the controls.

Five meters. Damien was at a dead run, the rifle trained squarely at the Royal's back. Indignation and fury shot through the army's ranks; warnings were shouted to the dark lord and the battle commander. Tan was about to palm the flickering display.

Three. Close enough.

"TAN!!!" Damien roared, squeezing off the trigger as fast and hard as he could while he let a torrential Wave build.

The shots sang true. Croll Tan snarled as super-heated slugs impacted over his helmet, jerking his head forward. A wide shot or two clipped his wings, causing more hisses of pain. But it wasn't enough. The alien's enormous palm slammed the console, beginning the final spinup of the machine.

Whum-bum-bum, Thrum-bum-bum, Whum-bum-bum, Thrum-bum-bum

Damien uttered an all-consuming challenge of rage and fear as he unleashed the Wave right behind the shots, spinning the rifle in his arms like a club. The Algaroth Royal was too fast. Tan had heard the cries of his army and recovered from the shots with blinding speed. His wings seized, flapped, and sprayed blood, propelling the Over-Seer over the bricks and out of the way of Damien's destructive energy. The Wave impacted the machine, warping and tearing the console to pieces, but the thing didn't stop.

And, to his horror, Damien saw that Tan had slipped a single vial of his blood into the tray, and it had already traveled up to the pinprick hole before the Wave broke the contraption. He threw an Orb at the cord. "You don't get to use that anymore!!" but too late: his blood dripped into the tank, causing an immediate reaction. The drumbeat expanded.

Whum-bum-bum-bum Thrum-bum-bum-bum Whum-bum-bum-bum Thrum-bum-bum-bum

The fury in Tan's eyes blazed hot, and it gave Damien some small satisfaction. Small.

"*You can't be here,*" he snarled, unbelieving. "I JUST ENDED YOU." He pointed at the smoldering train.

Damien shrugged. "You missed."

The great creature's wings flapped and he lowered his head to charge. The Royal shot at Damien with more speed than he could have imagined, and they collided. The Over-Seer's shining black claws raked across Damien's back and arms, cleaving the armor he wore like tissue paper.

"*GaHHahhHHH*!!" Darkness screamed as more of his blood was spilt. They tumbled to the ground, locked in their deadly dance. Tan's heavy armor pounded into the bricks, popping them out of place. The drumbeat continued to quicken.

From there, Damien was inside Tan's embrace. He threw all of his strength into a violent, unfocused spurt of power, right into the ornate breastplate. Damien's rage was so vicious though that the blast smattered around the creature's torso, causing a thousand pins and needles in Tan's blue hide and making him roar in agony, but it was superficial.

Knowing another strike might sever his spine, Damien kicked hard and rolled away. Tan lurched back from the kick and swung. His claws missed Damien's ankle by a fingernail, piercing the brick. Damien rolled upright and caught a quick glimpse of the machine. Inside it, his blood had mixed with the black pitch, and a swirling vortex had formed where the substances met. The amalgamation became bulbous bits of coagulated blood; thickening tendrils of an oily mess. It looked like evil and decay, a twisted singularity.

Whum-bum-bum-bum Thrum-bum-bum-bum Whum-bum-bum-bum Thrum-bum-bum-bum

Tan spat dark-purplish blood over the bricks. "You are all so *small*," he heaved, straightening and reaching slowly behind him. "To think that you or your 'family' can last through the coming storm."

"We've made it through worse ones than THIS!" Damien threw a heavy Orb, but Tan twisted away and it disappeared over the anxiously watching crowd. It was clear that they itched to unleash fire on the Elemental, but they wouldn't dare while he was embroiled with their commander. "You gonna send your *kids* on us, huh?"

The sun continued its descent behind the mountains, and Croll Tan registered a hint of surprise…but then an ominous chuckle gurgled forth from him instead. "No storm," he growled, his golden eyes glittering, "could prepare you for *them*. You've seen nothing."

Then he roared again, and Damien hit the brick to avoid the long blades the Over-Seer whipped out as he flew towards him. The speed of his enemy was daunting, and in the second it took for him to bend backwards, Tan crossed the eight meters between them and nearly slit Damien's throat.

Bouncing back, Damien changed footing and rolled out of the way as Tan made another pass, missing again. He snarled in fury as Damien launched a precision Orb this time, connecting under the alien's right armpit.

"*KYYYEAHHH!!*" the Over-Seer's scream pierced the air. It hurt Damien's ears, but the sound threw the drumbeat back into focus, and he chanced a quick glance at the generator.

Whum-bum-bum-bum-Thrum-bum-bum-bum-Whum-bum-bum-bum-Thrum-bum-bum-bum

He couldn't see the far side of the tank anymore, so filled as it was with the sickening muck. In that brief moment, Damien watched as it changed from a rough mass into a dark swirling merger of blood and oil. Tiny crimson flashes had begun deep inside the mass, micro-explosions that lit the Piazza with each detonation, reminding Damien a little of Choss's super bacteria.

He stared for a split-second too long, and Tan's raging counterattack connected with Damien's chest via an enormous, clawed foot.

"*OOHF!*" Damien gasped. Tan's foot slammed him to the ground. He managed to spread out and avoid cracking his head on the brick, but as the crushing weight stomped down on him, he felt ribs crack, and he cried out in gargled pain.

"You served your purpose, *Darkness*," Tan growled, using Damien's call sign. Oily blood dripped onto his forehead. "Now, you are *annoying*." Tan pushed harder, quashing Damien's fragile organs beneath the exposed, clawed toes.

Damien knew he had maybe two seconds before he was crushed. The pain blinded him, but with a cry, he focused enough to fall through the space between body and shadow, and he melted into the Piazza beneath Tan's foot.

I have to stop the machine, that's all that matters, he thought frantically as he reappeared. He stood much closer to the tank. Tan's look of shock at his vanishing act was the only second he needed. Damien turned and ran towards the weapon. The drumbeat had reached a fever pitch. He had no idea how to destroy the thing directly, so he had to think of something else.

And then, he had an idea; a crazy, absolutely *mad* idea, but he hadn't expected to leave here anyway. *Just have to line it all up at the right time*, he thought. *And in time*, he amended as he saw the inside of the tank. The drumbeat was contracting now.

Whum-bum-bum-Thrum-bum-bum-Whum-bum-bum-Thrum-bum-bum

The roar from behind propelled him the last three meters to the console. His chest burned and he choked for air.

"STAY AWAY FROM THAT!!" Tan commanded. Damien heard the wings flap once, twice; he was coming.

Focusing everything he had, Damien turned inwards. He drained the pool completely, pushing the limit—but careful not to push beyond the tug. His cells vibrated a familiar dance and he recalled the Core, Seattle, and family.

Vo, he thought, *I'm sorry.*

Whumbuh-Thrumbuh-Whumbuh-Thrumbuh-Whumbuh-Thrumbuh

The Over-Seer came, shooting up behind him, swinging his blades through the air. The great wings glowed blue with static tension. Damien opened his eyes, and he saw them reflected back in the dying sunlight bouncing off the incubation tank. His eyes were glowing, but instead of a corona of light, or vengeful flames, only a few flecks of the deepest purple smattered his blue irises. They looked powerful, and brimming with the energy only someone like him understood.

Elemental.

"Beautiful," he whispered, staring at the pink-and-golden sky and the few stars he could see beyond. He felt sorry, because he knew he would probably never get to see them up close.

"ELEMENTAL!!"

Croll Tan's roar came right behind him. He could feel the blades scissoring out near his head, about to decapitate him. Everything moved slowly, and Damien knew it was time.

As the blades sliced outwards and the great wings shadowed them both, Damien let his liquid fury go. A blinding violet light shattered his senses as every droplet of power he had left coursed through the air and towards its intended target.

It connected.

Croll Tan's blades continued to glide out, but behind the dark lord the Mag Fury Reactor clouted with the violet power of Darkness; Damien had managed to line everything up, just like he'd hoped. The Over-Seer now stood between him and the source of the generator's power.

Damien had used his Cloak to leap out of the Over-Seer's reach, and Croll Tan couldn't understand why his blades hadn't connected with anything as he crashed into his own weapon.

"How...?" the Algaroth Royal croaked, and just before he hit the tank, Tan looked up to see Damien standing not a stride away, staring into the golden eyes with his own brilliant, blue-and-purple ones.

"I wield the shadows," Damien whispered, and he let the Cloak claim him once more, as sound itself was stripped from the world at the force of the explosion.

Damien vanished from sight as the Mag Fury's shockwave enveloped them, consuming the black hole generator and its creator in the process. The tank shattered into a million pieces and the heat from the blast cooked all traces of the weapon from the air.

From the shadows of the Piazza, *within* them, protected by his most dangerous power yet mastered, Damien heard a scream from above as the Fourth Over-Seer was incinerated—along with his weapons, his army, and the front half of the Basilica. Damien barely clung to consciousness as it passed, but when it had, he saw a glistening sparkle in the air, the aftermath.

The Cloak fell away, and Damien Vilan stood in the ruins of the Over-Seer's army, near comatose exhaustion creeping into his bones. He looked at the wrecked base of the incubator and spotted Croll Tan's helmet lying on the bricks. A breeze laced with spring gusted through St. Peter's. He breathed it in, and watched closely as Tan's helmet gave out, blowing into the wind as ash, and he looked towards the rising darkening sky. He thought of home. Memories of the people he had loved, lost, and fought with surfaced like leaves in a river after a hard rain, and he knew that if they could see him now they would be proud. They stood there with him in that moment, allowing him to breathe humanity's first taste of freedom in twenty years.

CHAPTER THIRTY TWO

Geneva

With the end of the Fourth Over-Seer, the headless Collective—though disoriented—was far from beaten. The Eurasian Inferno was ultimately settled in Rome, but much had been lost. Croll Tan's full-scale ground war ceased almost overnight, and the Algaroth armies slunk back to their strongholds to lick their wounds and regroup. Unfortunately, even with the radical confidence boost on the human side of things, Solaroth remained unreachable and The Collective's utter dominance over Australia hardened in the following months after Croll Tan's passing. The aliens' hold on the west coast of North America was pushed a little, but not removed. They still held the Olympic Isle cities, too, and were setting to lay down mining roots in the cooling ruins of Camp Cascade. The ever-strong borders of the Regent Dynasty had been compromised on the Thai Spur, and the Throat of Israel became a stalemate. Tracks of the alien's harvesting toils thickened across Africa, and many other places—like the Central American Passage—remained as resolutely taken as ever.

And yet...

As summer came through the northern hemisphere of Earth, Antarctica saw its coldest reclamation of the once-icy continent in more than sixty years. Meteorologists and climatologists the world over celebrated the planet's slow return to a stable biosphere thanks to the *human*-made energysphere, but in more than one case, the Earth Global Alliance reported strange weather patterns in strange places that had nothing to do with them. Too many occurred to cite here, but without fail, these freak storms were unfailingly invaluable in hindering The Collective's harvest. Some said it was almost as if the planet had decided to fight back. Others thought it was God, *a* god, or gods. Some said it was science, but many more had begun to whisper that it was the Elementals.

Thanks to Croll Tan broadcasting his demonstration of the prototype black hole generator through the Intersystem, the entire world saw Damien's duel with the dark lord. They saw him lose blood defending them, they saw him almost defeated, and in the days and weeks following the event, they heard that he had survived…and the Over-Seer did not.

For Damien, his days of anonymity were over.

Whether they were supporters or skeptics, humans—and Algaroth—the world over could no longer question the existence of the Earth-born enigmas. Oh, there were plenty who said, "Bah," as they swilled their beers. "You're telling me that *all four* Over-Seers were done in by one of these power-wielding suckers? Bah." And his friend would say, "That's the talk," and they would go back to their work.

But concerning what was true and what wasn't regarding the deaths of four of The Collective's most treasured hands, Damien and those on the Island of Amun-Nūr learned (with a little help from that grizzled operator at McKinley Station) this: a call had indeed gone out from Solaroth. The message was not intercepted, but Amun-Nūr could imagine what it said:

"We've lost another Over-Seer. One of these 'Elementals' did it, and they're growing stronger. We're sorry. Send good help.

Signed,
The Nervous Collective on Earth."

Or something to that effect.

With the message well on its way through deep space, concern amidst the islanders over Croll Ruthilon Tan's supposed twin children spiked sharply, but not presently. A TransLight message back to Shialga would still take three months just to *get* there, to say nothing of how long it would take the unknown masters of The Collective to coordinate a response. They would assuredly send a replacement Over-Seer through the Conduit, but whether it turned out to be Croll Tan's children or some other menace, no one could say. What they *could* say with some certainty was that, by Amun-Nūr's calculation of the dreaded Conduit's construction, it would—

at fastest—take a replacement Over-Seer about eighteen months to reach Earth. Amun-Nūr couldn't be certain of this, but knowing that they might have a full year without an Over-Seer *or* any Collective reinforcements was a tempting prospect indeed. A lot could happen in a year.

So, for now, amidst a sudden global clangor for Damien to show his face, Amun-Nūr turned to their headless foe. They were determined to work out how exactly to cripple the enemy amidst the rumored power vacuum that had sprung to life behind the walls of Solaroth. For better or worse, it seemed that the vacuum was going to take time to resolve, but it didn't appear to be something that would tear the enemy apart from within. Croll Tan's surviving cabinet trustees were far too put-together for that.

What Amun-Nūr came up with instead, was a stroke of genius, but they needed Lunar Admiral Baroda to pull it off. After long discussion and hastily sewn wounds, the man agreed to handle the reality that the rumored sect of Amun-Nūr was a rumor no longer. Damien privately suspected that only trouble would come from the accord struck between the Prohka and the Admiral, but as summer wound towards fall (at least by Damien's northern hemispheric perspective; it was actually winter winding towards spring at Amun-Nūr) he decided that the strike with Amun-Nūr was a far more important concern.

So, with promises for Damien and the other Elementals to make a public appearance if this went well, Amun-Nūr became a part of their first official joint venture with the Eurasian Union, to take back a very special city just in time for a very important day—one that could very well have been ruined, had Croll Tan's generator not been stopped.

In western Eurasia, nearly dead center of what was once Europe, the city of Geneva was a slagged and ashen graveyard—the only city to be orbitally bombed during The Conquering before humanity brandished the Final Option. Amun-Nūr had chosen it because of its utterly historic significance to all humankind, but also because it would flush out the only tendril of Collective-held territory in this region of the world. Their strike was tactically and strategically sound, and Admiral Baroda hadn't been able to resist the double down, monumental boost reclaiming the city would do to global morale while simultaneously providing a perfect locale to host the still-uncertain World War Centennial.

Though retaking Geneva was difficult and dangerous for the joint human-Algaroth strike force, the sheer willpower of those responsible for the city's liberation could almost have been to shatter the Collective forces there on its own. That said—willpower or not—the strike went very well; *flawless*, actually:. The *Chalice Archon*, the *Sanguine Lotus*, the *Deep Core*, the *Lunar Echo*, and two of Huxley's new pilots (Sergeant Aliana Lidiza and Airmatron Mawaddah Osman) in two of Amun-Nūr's newly acquired Heron bombers ran run after run over Geneva, flakking the Collective presence in the area, flushing them out, and wiping them away. Staff Sergeant Declan brought in a mop-up ground force behind the air raid, while Damien and Caleb both brought their Elemental powers out to devastating affect against the remaining Collective. All the while, squadrons from the legendary Istanbul air brigades played shield grid for Amun-Nūr's strike force, as they defended wave after wave of Collective Stingships and Vultures desperately trying to hold the lost ground.

When the dust cleared, a few new fires burned in the gritty smut of buildings—the residue left from orbital plasma bombs—but Geneva was free, with minimal casualties.

Baroda and many other figures, figureheads, and leaders gave their thanks to Amun-Nūr and the pilots who pulled it off—some more stiffly than others. They offered seats of honor for the islanders at the celebration ceremony for which Amun-Nūr had decided to reclaim the city in the first place:

The World War Centennial.

∞ ∞ ∞

And so, on the morning of September 30, 2145, Damien Vilan, the other Elementals, and a few choice members of Amun-Nūr found themselves sitting in those seats of honor at a memorial promise ceremony to remember and honor the fallen, and to celebrate the present and future.

No one sat between the Elementals and the speaker's podium, behind which a misty courtyard awaited christening.

Rows upon rows of benches stretched back behind Damien on a green lawn recently cleared of rubble. He took in the scars of the city in the distance, eyeing the few new wounds from Amun-Nūr's reclamation strike, and far older ones beneath, untouched for twenty years since The Conquering. Behind the podium, the newly laid courtyard sat pristine in the footprint of what was once the Palace of Nations. Damien had noted earlier that the silvery, paneled bricks of the inlay had been placed in a huge figure-eight. At first he'd thought it was the number "8," but then realized that the idea had been to view it sideways in the symbol for infinity—hence, its new name: the Infinity Courtyard.

Damien and the others had arrived the previous evening, and Damien had spent the predawn hours looking on, fascinated, while hundreds of people ran about to clear the last dust in preparation for the ceremony. But as the Elementals had been shown to their seats, he couldn't deny the perks of having an Admiral as a friend, just as Romi had said once: The front row was a choice spot to be, and with how few of them were there, the Elementals had quite a lot of elbow room, while everyone behind sat packed to bursting on benches.

Caleb squirmed next to him.

"Problem?"

"I don't like crowds." The man looked over his shoulder. "Or backless seats."

"You're not in a crowd, and no one's stupid enough to poke *you*," he said pointedly.

The man glared. "You'd be surprised."

Damien grinned and turned back to the podium. The morning chill had given way to moist sunlight, and he closed his eyes to feel it. He must have sat there awhile because the next he knew, a hush had fallen over the murmuring crowd. He opened his eyes to see a man standing at the podium, waiting patiently. He bore no nametag, but was immediately recognizable in his pristine, black-and-silver uniform of a Lunar Admiral, another of the six remaining.

The crowd waited, and Damien heard the buzz of Intersystem cameras coming to life all around, so the world could see.

"Ladies and gentleman," the Admiral began. "Thank you all for coming. Today is an historic occasion, and we all would like to begin by offering our thanks to the Eurasian Union's 9th Airborne Regiment, with the assistance of the island of... '*Ah-mun New-r*'," there was scattered chuckling and Damien grinned. "Yes. Amun-Nūr, for their esteemed valiance in retaking Geneva. I would also like to thank…"

"Do you hate speeches, too?" Damien whispered to Caleb while the Admiral went down his list.

"Yes."

Damien grinned, and was pleasantly surprised to find the list was not so long as he'd been worried about.

"…many more to whom there simply isn't enough time to offer our gratitude, but know that your service has been instrumental in me standing here today, nonetheless." Murmurs of approval and broken claps echoed in the silence behind Damien. He kept his eyes fixed ahead and stifled another grin at the awkward air that followed.

"On most occasions," the Admiral went on. "It would be proper to introduce myself upon inception of a ceremony, but as our orator this morning is a man of caliber far beyond my own, I will only introduce him." Timid laughter followed, and the man let it play out. When it fell silent again, he went on. "Ladies and gentleman, guests on this hallowed ground, and to all of humanity: allow me to present André Piern, who will be conducting this keynote address for the World War Centennial. Thank you."

Excited whispers shot through the crowd, and someone hissed Damien's name.

"*Psst!*"

Damien leaned forward to find Javier cringing his way over Gwen. The Marine's ribcage bulged, still wrapped in bandages for his burns. "*What?!*" he hissed back.

"Is he a legit Piern? Like, descended from *The* Piern?"

"Hell if I know!" And they both shot back to their seats when someone shushed them.

A moment later, a man with dashing blonde hair and a chiseled face approached the podium. He wore a dress uniform of pure white, but bore no insignia, rank, or pins that could speak to which branch of the military he belonged. Damien guessed him to be in his late thirties.

André Piern took a long moment standing at the podium. So long, in fact, that people began turning in their seats to see what far-off landmark he was staring at. Damien had looked over his shoulder plenty since arriving. Outside the thin corridor of cleaned and rebuilt landmarks, Geneva looked much as it had the day after it burned: carpets of ash and plasma smut turning everything gray under the lumpy rubble. The city was still and silent, but Damien well appreciated that, this very morning, distant echoes of movement could be heard over the slagged rubble, and life stirred in the skeletal buildings.

Finally, Piern produced a beaten and dirty journal. It was bound in red leather and was packed with crinkled or loose pages and foldouts that stuck out in odd places. It took only a glance for Damien to guess the thing was completely full, front to back.

"Two hundred years ago," Piern began. His voice floated over the silent crowd and Intersystem recorder drones whizzed faintly. "The world erupted in chaos. The Second World War pitted nation against nation, and ideals against people. It ended with the dawn of a long and prosperous era in our history, but a complicated one." He paused. It was a tactile move, letting the sound of the windswept ruins and echoes of the dead city filter into the courtyard. He held it for just enough time for everyone to hear.

Then he continued, driving out the ghosts. "The time from that war to this very day, one century ago, when the Third World War began, was nothing if not complicated. The development from the analog to the digital, from manual to the automatic, was messy, and often destructive in its learning curve. And, as someone once said—though, the original penman of the quote is no longer known—'those who do not listen to history are doomed to repeat it'. Compelling words."

Piern unwound the cord that bound the red journal shut and went on. "With those words in mind, I invite you all to look back on that time, through the lenses of your own lives, and *remember*. Remember why the world was torn apart. Take a moment, and remember *why* we stand here today, on the centennial anniversary of one war and the bicentennial of another, able to say that World War Three truly was the last human war." He closed his eyes and leaned back from the podium, taking everyone aback by his full intention to make them reflect.

If quiet echoes had described the courtyard before, no words could describe the pensive chorus of silence that filled it now. Damien didn't have to look to know that the people around—even Caleb—had closed their eyes. He did the same.

"If World War Two jumpstarted our way to enlightenment," Piern said when his moment concluded, "then the Third World War paved the way to unity." His blue eyes grew clouded, and he gazed to the same spot he'd been looking earlier. "The Collective War may have done more damage in its long years than any conflict in history, but it was the last human war that sticks to me. Why? Because once a people realizes how unjustifiable it is to make war on your own species, all future conflicts are made less full of pain. A person can always find a brother, a lover, a daughter, a friend, in the comfort of another person with the knowledge that we *all* have suffered at the hands of something larger than any of us. We take comfort in the knowledge of shared hardship, and we are stronger for it, but it behooves me to mark the difference that it took our unity to bring aliens. It did not take aliens to bring our unity, and I find that encouraging."

Damien couldn't tell if it was Piern's speech, or the morning, or the quiet calm in his heart, but his gaze drifted off the man in white and found its way to the center of the far loop in the courtyard.

"I have here today," said Piern, "a passage, written by a man whom you should all recognize." He flashed the red-leather journal as he opened it to a bookmarked page. "He was a man who dedicated his entire existence to bettering his fellows, he was a friend to my father, a personal hero of mine, and he was both an inspiration and a great martyr in his final days. I hope you take these words of his work to heart." Piern cleared his throat.

From the first words, Damien had a good hunch whose journal that was. He sat up a little straighter, listening intently.

"*The Moon*," Piern began, and silence pervaded the courtyard. "*In English, it always sounded so...plain. In Japanese, Moon is 'Tsuki', in German it's 'Mond', and in Arabic it's 'Kamar', but I've always been partial to Spanish. 'La Luna' just has a poetry to it that does more justice than the other choices in humanity's many languages...*"

Damien swallowed. It was the late Lunar Admiral Jacob Hawkins, he was sure of it. Unsettled in the best way possible, his gaze drifted back to the courtyard, to the clear patch of sky beyond it. He frowned when he spotted a distant pile of rubble. He couldn't have said what the building had been, but it shuddered as a gust of wind hit it, sending a whole layer of ash into the air, further eroding the pile.

The dust reminded him of St. Peter's. The crystal-clear memory of Croll Tan's helmet came to mind, the second before it broke into ash. He had looked up at the sky to see stars and a crescent Moon afterwards, twinkling in the night sky over Rome, and he'd thought about the kind of destruction he had wreaked already on the world, just for being an Elemental.

If only he knew how to show that Elementals could do more than just destroy...

And then, Damien stopped thinking. He'd had an idea. There it was; the answer. A shimmering thread of thought had appeared in the quiet of his mind, hanging like a tiny golden line, waiting to be unzipped into...what, exactly?

Something new.

He latched onto it in a daze, feeling the intensity of the idea send shivers through his body as Piern's voice washed over him. "*We have always been creative creatures in that regard, but truly, La Luna is more than just our lone satellite...*"

He was totally unsure of what he was doing, or why he was suddenly so compelled to do it before the eyes of the entire world. Whispers came at him from all over.

"Damien?"

"What are you doing?"

"Get *back* here!"

He stood, ignoring them.

It was genuine inspiration, the inception of a great thought. And as gasps spread through the courtyard like wildfire, he stretched his senses to the world ahead.

"That's Vilan! That's the Elemental!"

"What's he doing?"

"He's going for Piern!"

Damien felt the pulsing of the world beneath his feet, and Piern stopped speaking only as he concluded the passage. *"If humankind failed to shake the waves of time, then hopefully in the course of our few million years on this plane, our souls, our cosmic energy, or our divine ascendancy—call it whatever you like—could still exist and know, that it was always enough for us simply to have lived."* He closed the red journal and looked not the least bit surprised when he saw Damien approaching the podium.

The gasps had turned into calls, and Damien heard movement behind him. No one moved to stop him though, and Piern said nothing as Damien approached.

We can do more than just destroy, he thought.

Something like never before pushed to escape his body, and he let it. It whispered through him and into the world. It was more than just the Darkness inside of him, the power of the Elementals; in fact it wasn't born of shadows. It was something he could only describe as born of *him*. It flowed into the ground through his feet instead of from his hands, but it flooded forward along a conduit to the point of his focus: the center of the far loop in the courtyard.

The shouts and gasps ceased as the first tendrils rose from the ground. A tremor of fear whipped through the assemblage, and it seemed for a brief moment as if everything would fall into chaos. But it didn't. The curiosity and fascination at what he was doing riveted people more wholly than the desire to flee.

With a whispered tinkling like sand over glass, Damien's dark tendrils rose from the paneled brick of the courtyard. They curved and spun, gliding elegantly upwards, never breaking. Damien could feel all eyes on the growth as he urged it higher, feeling his body rejuvenating even as the energy left him. He came closer to it, unaware of his body any longer.

Go, he whispered to it. *Go*.

And it did.

Yelps escaped a few members of the audience while everyone leaned back. The climbing tendrils of violet-and-black power climbed high into the air, five, ten, twenty meters, until they towered above, sending twinkling light bouncing through the graveyard city.

GO, he urged.

Then the glimmering pillar settled, shrinking a little lower to the ground as the crystalline-liquid began to harden. It changed from inscrutable, shimmering gel to a perfect geometric shape. Finally it stopped, hardening with a crisp crystal chime, and the last traces of Damien's power dribbled away and into the ground. Moans of awe reached his ears, and he realized all eyes were split between staring at him, and at the beautiful monument before them.

It was an obelisk.

He blinked, looking around. He stood halfway up the steps to the podium, right next to Piern. Damien looked up at his creation. It was enormous. Almost twenty meters tall, and it glistened in the fragmented light of the sun, filtered through the morning clouds above.

Just beneath the surface, the obelisk was made of fractured obsidian. Cracks shone beneath the perfect veneer, and it reflected dark purples and greens, inviting light into a sea of glassy black. But as Damien looked closer, there was something else too.

From within the obelisk, an unfamiliar glow emanated beneath the cracked sea, a glow that felt more like it came from the area itself, rather than his creation. The color that came to Damien's mind was *amber*, though it could hardly be described as such a hue. The obelisk filled the Infinity Courtyard with the strange, warm light, and it beat dimly, like the first stirring of an unknowable heartbeat.

"What is it?"

Damien looked up to see Piern standing not two paces from him, very still. "I…" he tried to describe the experience he had just had. "*I don't know…*" The awe in his voice filtered through the crowd, and Piern finally blinked, standing nose-to-nose with the Elemental. Damien's gaze finally left the obelisk. "But I know it's for all of you."

The speaker's mouth twitched at a smile for a split-second, and then his gaze slipped over Damien's shoulder. He seemed to notice Damien's kin for the first time. "*Elementals…*" he whispered. The courtyard remained still. Piern gestured once at the front row, bidding they rise. Slowly, hesitantly, they each left the bench and joined Damien at the podium one at a time.

Water. Earth. Ice. Fire.

And standing in front of them, his body glowing with a waxy potency he had never felt before.

Darkness.

Together they stood in front of humankind. For the first time, they gazed out openly at the world with their glowing eyes and earthly powers.

Then, André Piern—sparing a single glance for the obelisk—stepped back from the podium and held his hand out as if in introduction.

"The Elementals."

They couldn't possibly have hoped for the cheers to be so sudden, nor as remotely warm.

∞   ∞   ∞

That evening, when the ceremony had concluded, Damien walked back to the Infinity Courtyard alone.

The clouds that had threatened the latter part of the Centennial had cleared, and since Geneva was still without a Mag Fury, the city was dark.

As a result, there was not a single light for a long, long ways to filter the billions of dots of the night sky.

As Damien looked towards his creation, his gaze continued skywards, to the bright light above. It was a full Moon, hanging above his obelisk, and for once the scars of Home Luna did not look so deep. *One day*, he thought. *Maybe one day, I can visit the surface.*

"He may be gone, but this war is far from over," said a voice.

Damien hadn't heard him approach, but he was too at peace at the moment to worry about being attacked. "Who?"

Not one but two sets of feet stopped, and André Piern came to Damien's side. The man gazed up at the obelisk. "Admiral Hawkins."

Damien half snorted. "I thought you meant Croll Tan."

"Either. Or both." Piern looked at Damien, who only had eyes for the orb above. "The Collective will send Tan's children, you know that right? Or maybe they'll send the Volüul this time instead of more Algaroth."

Damien held his face tight to keep from showing surprise. "I know." *How does he know about them?*

"And you know how long we have until the Conduit is finished?"

Damien knew.

"So what's the Elementals part to play in all of this, Darkness?"

The night warmed around him, and Damien laughed out loud when he tried to come up with an answer. He looked at Piern. "I'm not sure yet."

Piern nodded. "In that case, perhaps I have someone here who can help you with your answer."

Damien turned to see who else was standing there, and his frown went slack.

The other person was a teenager. Or more: a young man who was scarcely not a kid anymore.

"Hi," Damien said.

"Hi," the kid answered. His dirty-blonde hair fell low over his hazel eyes and freckles. He looked a little ragged, and a little twitchy. He was short and skinny in a faded white band's t-shirt and torn jeans, generally pretty scrawny.

Piern looked like he was about to say something, but Damien didn't need him to. He already knew.

"You're an Elemental," he said.

The kid looked up, suddenly nervous. His flitting eyes jumped to Piern, bordering on accusatory.

Piern nodded, eyes closed, a small smile on his face.

He looked back at Damien. "Y-yeah? I am. I'm Milo. Who are you?"

After the events of today and the last few months, people had given Damien a sort of stand-alone honorific from the other Elementals. That title was about to dribble out of his mouth, when he realized how stupidly arrogant he'd sound introducing *himself* as that. He looked away from Milo, a laugh escaping him.

"What's so funny?"

Damien looked back. "Nothing. I'm an Elemental, too, though. My name's Damien."

"Oh," said Milo. "Nice to meet you."

"You too."

And that was how he met a Floral Elemental.

A short chat later, Piern, Damien, and Milo left the courtyard together, but not before Damien took a lingering look at his obelisk, wondering just what it meant. In truth, he didn't know. But, despite not feeling comfortable with the title his friends had given him, there *did* seem to be something to it. He couldn't say why he felt that way, or what he would do next, but he knew that whatever The Collective sent next, whomever they sent to Earth, Damien would be taking the reins of his life, and that thought alone cemented something for him. He had finally come to terms with one immovable certainty:

Damien is, was, and always would be,

The Dark Element.

It Was Bound
In Red

High in the northernmost mountains of North America, a hidden facility had been tucked into the side of Mt. McKinley. Inside, six souls had been tucked away from the world. They slept soundly in the cold and in the dark, used to their isolation together, but they were not all asleep.

While André Piern introduced Damien to Milo Gianni, one of those six souls was restless, waiting, sitting at his desk, doing what little he could to prepare for what he knew was coming.

The grizzled operator wrote in something, illuminated only by a single lighting strip on the wall next to his bunk, the scratch of his hot-pen the only sound over the storm outside. His beard was thick, his hair was growing grey, his light-brown eyes were bloodshot, and he was tired.

The tablet next to him chimed.

He stopped writing and opened the encoded message.

"*I know… you must… have heard,*" he whispered aloud, scratching it out unscrambled on a new page, "*but Solaroth… sent another plea… for help. It… wasn't bound… for the Conduit. I agree that… Tan's children… will be coming… but something else will… be here first… You… were… right. We have to assume… it'll be… the Cha'Ka.*" He paused, considering the chill that name left in air. "*I thought you should know, too… that… the Conduit's construction… is on-schedule. There's… still no word from… Cole… the Rauth… or the Armada… We… will… need… you… soon… signed… J.B.*"

He read it back, and then glanced towards the chalked markings on the wall. Eleven bars of different thickness and height were drawn there. Six of them were filled in, three had question marks etched over them; his best guess to how far along the Conduit was.

He read the note again, and sat in the dark for a long time, thinking. Eventually, he retrieved his hot-pen and finished his entry. Then, he closed the crisp red leather journal—a replacement for the one he gave Piern—bound it with the cord, and stuck it in the narrow notch of his bunk. Finally, he wrapped himself in blankets, dimmed the lights, and tried to forget the past.

As the strip darkened, the last thing to see in the room was a dusty uniform hanging next to the journal. As the tiny room darkened, a battered, dirty nametag glinted, dangling from the frayed black-and-silver jacket.

The etched nametag read, "Hawkins."

—||A Special Thank You||—

Seventy-four individuals from around the world found my Kickstarter sometime between November 17, 2014 and December 17, 2014. You wouldn't be reading this without them. Through the long journey to publication, there were supporters and then there were supporters. These folks are the latter.

—||The Casuals

Danielle Coleman

Derek Mason

Olivia Lynn McCauley

Christian Meyer[BC]

—||The Raws

Lucas Beechinor

Brittany Dion

Daniel Giguere[BC]

Brian D. Lambert

Anthony Pino-Valle

SwordFire

—||The Digitals

Shane Ching[BC]

Michael Downey

Jason E.

Scott Early[BC]

Tiffany Rakes

Mark Stickley

Philda Todzaniso

Daphne Wheat

Lisa Hornyak   Ian Wright[BC]

—||The Tangibles

Aly Albert   Aaron Pendergast

Jay Barry   Zane Showalter-Castorena

Nissa Day   Debbie Sjulstad

Nick Fin   Mark Stevens

Liam Gibbs   Greg Tausch

Sara Hartung   Lily D. Tayles

Jennifer Hekkers   Sally Tichota

Maura Holtman   Becky Torres

Mike Martinkus   Christopher Turner

Pierre Mercado   David Weir

Tina Nguyen   Ryan Zacher

Sam Novosad   Manuel & Sabrina

—||The Artistics

Katie Kramer   Samantha Nord

David Landry   Colleen Oakes

Aya McCallie   Beverley Toro

Jess McCallie

—||The Extra Artistics

David Hall
Kendra McCallie

—||The Collectors

Chad Bowden[BC]

Frank Bright

Sam Casey

*Brad Dancer[BC]

Roxanne Fredrickson

Catie Hill

Peter McQuillan

Yankton Robins

*Jacob "Ryoku" Walker[BC]

*Worm Collectors (They know what it means)

—||The Prolific Collectors

Marla Cooley

—||Lunar Admirals||—

--\\: Scott Allen
--\\: Alice Boyer
--\\: Nicholas Cipriani
--\\: Olivia Nguyen
--\\: Laurie Toro

—||Elementals||—

--\\: Annie & Don Lopez /--
--\\: Jessica Paetow /--
--\\: Tyler Robinson /--

—||Eon||—

∞ Dallas Porter ∞

Thank you. Thank you all.

.^{BC} is for the BackerClub members who specially contributed

ABOUT THE AUTHOR

Originally, Mason intended to be a Hollywood director/writer, but chose to pursue his start as a novelist instead. His deep love of science and the stars came from his father—an aerospace engineer, and his passion for storytelling and stories came from his mother—a literacy teacher. *The Dark Element* is Mason's first novel. His other works include artwork that no one will see, and student films that no one's heard of—and he intends to keep it that way. When he isn't avoiding sleep, Mason dabbles in a bit of everything, from tasting craft beer to 3-D sculpting, to exotic food, to being a GM, or spending a sunset in good company. He lives in Denver, Colorado, where dawn brings purple mountains' majesty, and nearly every sunset bleeds orange.